TALES
OF
CINDER

TALES
OF
CINDER

M.J. HAAG

Shattered Glass
— PUBLISHING —

TALES OF CINDER

BOOKS 1 - 3

DEFIANT

Magic can have deadly consequences.

When the sudden and suspicious death of Eloise's mother points to forbidden magic, Eloise is determined to bring her mother's murderer to justice. She will stop at nothing to find the killer…even if the clues lead right to the palace gates and the prince's manservant, Kaven. He is irrational, volatile, and prone to knocking women off horses. Given his personality, it should be easy to find the proof she needs to place him in irons.

However, when dark magic is used, nothing is as simple as it seems, and Eloise is about to learn that nightmares often hide behind fairy tale lives.

DISDAIN

A single blow shattered my life of glass. They shouldn't have left me with the shards.

Eloise knows the name of her mother's murderer, but she cannot speak it. A curse keeps her silent and locked in the tattered remains of her once charming life. Though magic holds her tongue, it doesn't quell the smoldering spark of her anger or her need to learn the reason behind her mother's death.

However, games of magic have dire consequences. Desperate to keep those she loves safe from the repercussions of her actions, Eloise must make a bold gamble with her safety and virtue that could win her everything or destroy her forever.

Two lives hang in the balance. For, if Cinder fails, Snow will fall, too.

DAMNATION

Abused but not beaten, I will break the curse.

With the reason behind her mother's death revealed, it's a race for Eloise to exact her revenge and prevent her stepsisters from marrying the prince. However, amidst the glittering jewels and colorful ballgowns, the royal court holds secrets of its own that will devastate Eloise and strike a final blow to her plans. Betrayed by the one person she thought she could trust, Eloise questions how far she's willing to go for revenge.

After all, in the game of kingdoms, everyone is a pawn.

DEFIANT

CHAPTER 1

THE SUDDEN BAYING OF HOUNDS STARTLED THE CHICKENS AT MY FEET.

"Hugh?" I called, shaking the grain dust from my apron.

"Here, Miss Eloise." Our groomsman appeared from the stable, leading Sugar by her reins.

"Does that sound like hunting dogs?"

"It does." He nimbly leapt onto Sugar's back. "I'll go warn the hunters away."

As Hugh rode down the rutted path leading away from our small estate, I turned toward the two-storied house I called home. Smoke curled from all four chimneys, but with the hint of spring in the crisp air, I knew the fires wouldn't be necessary for long.

Letting myself into the kitchen, I inhaled the warm yeasty smell of the bread dough Judith was kneading.

"Were those hounds we heard?" she asked.

"Yes. Hugh went to warn the owners off." I shrugged out of my cloak and hung it and my apron by the door.

"It's been happening too frequently in recent years. The king should remind people that he cares about these lands by visiting them more often." Judith, who'd been with our family since I'd been born sixteen years ago, knew just how infrequently the king left his castle.

"I'm sure he has bigger concerns with Prince Granger's negotiations in the north," I said.

"What could we possibly need from the north?" Anne asked as she set a tray with a tea service for three.

"My guess is wool," Judith said. "In those colder temperatures, the herds probably have thicker coats."

While they spoke, I inspected the tray for something to eat.

"I was about to take this to the sitting room," Anne said, noting my interest. "Mrs. Cartwright requested you join her and your sister in there."

"You know Mother would be upset if she heard you calling her that," I said. "You're supposed to use her given name, Margaret."

"In her presence," Anne said with a small smile. "Elsewhere, I'll respectfully use her title."

I followed Anne from the kitchen, glad that Mother had selected her out of the many who had applied for the position. Already a widow, Anne was only two years older than me and didn't want anything other than security in life. Something Mother wanted for Kellen and myself. Something I had no interest in if it came in the form of a husband.

From the study, I heard the soft murmur of Kellen's voice as she read to Mother. She paused when Anne and I entered the room.

Mother reclined on a settee by the window. Although the sunlight gave her pale skin a healthier glow, the blankets that covered her body and pillows that propped her head bespoke the true state of her well-being. Yet, as much as Mother lived the life of an invalid, her gaze still alertly found mine.

"Hounds again?" she asked.

"So it seems," I answered, taking the seat near her.

Kellen shut her book and looked at me. My twin was my opposite in almost every way. Her straight ebony hair contrasted with my wavy golden tresses. The startling blue of her eyes, as well as her pale skin, held no warmth, whereas my golden tones were reflected in the warm hazel of my gaze. While I was quick to let the world know every emotion I felt, she held everything inside. I also towered over her petite frame by four inches, which I never used to my advantage. I never had to because Kellen and I didn't fight. Ever. Our differences did not make me love my sister less. No, I loved her more for each one.

I leaned forward and placed a kiss on my mother's soft cheek, surprising her.

"What's that for?"

"For giving me a sister instead of a brother. She would have been beastly as a boy."

"I would have been too small to be beastly," Kellen said evenly. "And tormented for my manly inadequacies. The only safe thing Mother could do for me was make me a girl."

Mother snorted, a smile ghosting her lips, our banter amusing her as I'd hoped it would.

"Speaking of manly attributes...did either of you notice any of interest when you went to market?" she asked. "I'd rather hoped there would be callers soon."

I gave Kellen a side glance. She kept her gaze focused on Mother.

"What?" Mother asked, catching the look. "What happened?"

"Nothing of importance, Mother," Kellen said. She looked at Anne, who'd been preparing our tea, and accepted the first cup for Mother. The milky brown liquid was laced with medicine.

"I won't drink that until you girls tell me what happened," Mother said. The surly note in her words made me smile.

"Well, we know it's not Father who gave me my temper," I said.

"You're right," Mother said, relaxing visibly. "It is better to nurture kindness in every thought and deed than to let even a cinder of anger smolder in your soul. For it only takes a cinder to start a fire." Then, she looked at me, love reflecting in her gaze.

"A fire can easily destroy what it took a lifetime to build."

"Or the face of a shopkeeper's son," Kellen added.

Mother made a pained expression.

"Oh, Eloise, what did you do?"

"I tested the sturdiness of the blacksmith's newest frying pan. I'm happy to report the smith was quite pleased with the results."

5

"You hit a boy with a frying pan?"

"Well, if you must put it so brashly…yes."

Anne made a small noise and quickly excused herself.

Mother stared at me for a moment before taking her tea from Kellen and drinking it down in several long swallows. She handed back the cup and closed her eyes.

"I'm ready for the full adventurous tale, my darlings."

Kellen and I shared a smile and launched into a recounting of our market visit from the day before. We embellished a few places for entertainment purposes, but never so much as to veer from the truth. The truth being that, years ago, Kellen and I had gradually gained a reputation of sorts with the boys in town. My quick to ignite temper had earned me the nickname of Cinder while Kellen's abidingly cool exterior had earned her the name Snow.

"When Carver lobbed a ball of muddy snow at Kellen, I grabbed the pan to block it; but my aim was off. While the ball splattered us, the pan hit Carver with a resounding gong that gained the attention of just about everyone on the street."

Mother snorted a laugh and held out both of her hands without opening her eyes. The tea always made her tired.

Kellen took one, and I took the other. Mother's thin fingers felt so frail in my own.

"I have been blessed with two beautiful, headstrong daughters who not only know how to care for themselves but for others, too. Your beauty is not in the texture of your skin or the shine of your hair. It's what's inside each of you, and it's how you influence the world around us. You are my sun, Eloise. And you, my moon, Kellen. Both lights shine brightly and fill my life with joy."

She gave our hands a gentle squeeze.

"You would fill my life with more joy if one of those thick-headed miscreants had caught your fancy, though."

She peeked at us from under the lashes of one eye before closing it again.

"I hardly believe a miscreant—"

"Or a band of them," Kellen added.

"—is what you had in mind for our future spouses," I said.

Mother sighed.

"Too right you are. A handsome man with a good heart and steadfast loyalty, like your father, is what I hope for both of you. Go now. I need to rest. Anne dosed my tea again. Tell her this concoction tasted like shite from the yard."

I choked on my laugh while Kellen shook her head.

While Mother rested, we took the tray to the kitchen.

"How is she today?" Judith asked.

"The same," Kellen said. "Dying."

"Aren't we all?" Judith said, not put out by Kellen's bluntness. "Some of us just take longer going about it and don't see it for what it is. The end comes for all of us, Kellen. It's what we do with the days we have that matters."

Kellen nodded and grabbed her cloak. I did the same. Side by side, we walked down the hill toward town. Just before the path met the larger road, we took a small walking trail to the right and started the trek up the rocky incline. Neither of us spoke until we reached the top. There, we stood near the edge and looked out over Towdown.

"Mother received a letter from Father yesterday. He's due to return soon," Kellen said.

Mother hated when Father had to leave. However, given his profession, he left often.

"I don't blame him," Kellen said when I didn't speak.

I turned to look at my sister.

"For staying away," she clarified even though I knew my sister well enough to guess most of her thoughts.

The world might see Kellen's steady, light blue gaze and bland expression as being unfeeling. But, I knew better. I saw her expression for what it was. A mask to hide the pain. It hurt her to see Mother like this...almost as much as it hurt Father.

Wrapping my arms around Kellen, I stared down at the rooftops and the lazy spirals of smoke hazing the air. The din from town didn't reach us, and the wind kept all but the barest hint of smoke from the air. Just beyond the rooftops, I could see the glimmer of white stone in the sun. The castle.

With a sigh, Kellen placed her head on my shoulder and wrapped her arms around my waist in return.

"Mother knows we all love her deeply. That's why she hired Anne," I said. "She hopes we will leave when the time is right."

"Since marriage appeals to you as little as it appeals to me, I doubt either of us is going anywhere," Kellen said. "Having Anne here hasn't changed that."

"Mother's hope will continue, regardless."

Kellen lifted her head and stepped away from me.

"What does the future hold for us?" she asked.

"Spinsterhood, most likely. Nothing too terrifying," I said.

The faint pounding of hooves drew our attention.

"We'd better get back," she said.

I followed her down the familiar trail. By the time we made it to the stable, Hugh had already unsaddled Sugar.

"Was there any trouble?" I asked.

"None. The hounds don't belong to hunters. They belong to the Crown. It seems the Royal Retreat is due for a visit."

Kellen and I shared a look. I could barely recall the last time the rambling estate, a bit further up the hill, had been used. It had been at least five years ago. Neither Kellen nor I had gotten a glimpse of the royal entourage during the king's week-long visit then. We'd been strictly forbidden from leaving our small estate.

"We must tell Mother," Kellen said.

Judith was absent from the kitchen, but a small roast spit over the fire said she would return soon. I inhaled deeply.

"Stop smelling dinner, and tie your shoes," Kellen said without rancor.

"This is why you're four inches shorter. You don't appreciate your food, so you don't grow."

She snorted, and I knew I'd amused her even if her face didn't show it.

Anne was sitting quietly in the corner, reading from a primer, when we entered the parlor. She left us to wait for Mother to wake. It didn't take long for her to open her eyes and smile at us.

"Did you watch me sleep long?" she asked.

"Ages," I answered. "One doesn't often see a sleeping princess."

Her smile widened.

"Speaking of royalty," Kellen said. "It seems the hounds belong to the king. He has finally decided to visit his Royal Retreat."

The Royal Retreat was more than just a massive stretch of land north of Towdown. It was also the name of the sprawling home the royal family used when they wanted some time away from the castle.

"This is not good news," Mother said, looking concerned. "It would be best if you stayed out of the woods while the king is in residence at the retreat."

Most mothers would be excited for a chance encounter with royalty, especially since we lived on royal land and were allowed to hunt it when others were not. Not our mother.

"I cannot imagine needing two homes," I said, trying to distract her from her worry. "It's not fun cleaning one."

"Do you honestly think His Highness cleans anything?" Kellen asked.

I grinned.

"Certainly his privy. It wouldn't be fair to ask someone else to do that."

Kellen nudged me with her elbow, and I realized what I'd said. Mother used nothing but a chamber pot that Anne, Kellen, or I cleaned every day.

"They would rob him blind," I added smoothly.

"How so?" Kellen asked.

"Come now. It's obvious." I paused for a moment and glanced between Mother and Kellen. "His shite is gold."

Mother burst out laughing, and Kellen shook her head.

"Eloise, I hope that you find your beau soon."

"Why is that, Mother?"

"Because you'll soon outswear him. A lady shouldn't speak so."

"Too right. But, any man worthy of my interest will need to take me as I am. Filthy mouth and all."

Anne knocked on the open door, calling our attention.

"There is a delivery boy," she said.

"Send him in," Mother said.

Anne disappeared, and a few moments later, a youth walked in. He was dressed in neat trousers and a coat that was just a tad too short for his wrists. A common sight for growing boys. His gaze swept over the three of us, and he removed the floppy red cap with a gold emblem on it from his shaggy dark head to give a precise, small bow.

"Can we help you?" Mother asked.

"Yes, ma'am. I have a delivery for Mrs. Cartwright." He lifted the small, brown paper-wrapped package he held.

"I am she," Mother said.

The boy came forward.

"A coin, Kellen," Mother said.

Kellen gave the boy a copper in exchange for the package. With a bob of his head, he returned to Anne, who I knew would see him out.

Mother smiled in excitement as Kellen handed her the package. The gifts that Father always sent made his absence less cruel. Each one let us know he was thinking of us.

"I should wait until he returns to open it," she said.

I grinned.

"At least, until yours arrive," she added. Her eyes never left the package.

"He sent yours ahead of his arrival for a reason," Kellen said. "Open it. We want to see what it is."

Mother didn't need any further encouragement. She tugged the string free and removed the paper to expose a small, cloth-covered box. We all gasped when she removed the lid to reveal a gold encased emerald pendant strung on a delicate gold chain.

"Your father's latest venture must have done very well," Mother said, breathlessly.

She lifted the chain and let the pendant dangle in the sunlight. It almost seemed to glow with a light of its own.

"It's beautiful," Kellen said.

"Help me put it on. I want your father to see me wearing it when he returns."

Kellen stood and helped Mother ease the chain over her hair then rearranged her braid prettily to lay over one shoulder.

"There," she said, moving back.

The sunlight, streaming in through the window, reflected against the stone; and an unnatural green light flashed in Mother's eyes briefly as she looked at me.

"What do you think?" she asked.

"You've never been more beautiful," Kellen said when I hesitated.

She smiled and blinked heavily.

"I believe this gift overexcited me. I need to rest for a bit."

She didn't rest, though. She exhaled loudly, her lids half closing.

"Mother?" I said, standing to touch her face. "Mother?"

She didn't respond.

"I don't think she's breathing, Eloise," Kellen said softly.

CHAPTER 2

"ANNE!" I SCREAMED AS KELLEN PUT HER HEAD ON MOTHER'S CHEST.

Anne came running into the room, her skirts lifted to her knees.

Kellen straightened, looking at the woman.

"I can't hear her heart beating."

A moment of silence gripped the room, and a heavy weight settled on my chest.

The expression on Anne's face shifted from fear to grief to a carefully composed mask. She went to Mother and set her head to chest for a moment before facing us.

"Your mother's gone," she said softly. "We all knew the tincture wouldn't work forever. Your mother, most of all. She asked me to give each of you a message when the time came."

She stepped close to Kellen and wrapped my sister in her arms.

"You are my moon. When you look at the stars, know that I'm watching you and love you always." Kellen didn't wrap her arms around Anne in return, but it didn't stop Anne from pressing a kiss to my sister's temple.

My throat ached when Anne released Kellen and looked at me.

I welcomed her hug, and her message from my mother.

"Take care of your sister," she whispered. "Your light will need to burn brightly for both of you in the days to come. Know that I love you. Always. Know that I am with you when the sun touches your skin, and hear me in every songbird's voice."

I hugged Anne in return.

"Thank you."

When she was done, she sent us from the room.

"Send Judith to me. We will care for Margaret."

Kellen and I didn't speak as we went to the kitchen. I didn't have the words necessary to break the numb state of disbelief that entombed my mind.

"Mother is gone," Kellen said calmly. "Anne will need your help bathing her."

Judith stared at us in shock for a moment before she went running.

Kellen went straight for the door, and I followed in her wake.

We found Hugh was in the stable, oiling the leather fastenings of the carriage.

"Mother is gone," Kellen said. "You will need to fetch a coffin. We will bury her the day after tomorrow."

Hugh removed his hat, his expression filled with sorrow.

"My condolences, Kellen. Eloise."

I nodded at him, took my sister's hand, and led her down the drive to the path we always took when we needed to escape, even just for a moment.

Neither Kellen nor I spoke until we reached the ridge.

"It wasn't time," Kellen said in a flat voice, her eyes dull.

I stared off in the direction of the castle, my mind still numbed with a reality it seemed unable to process. Mother was dead. Gone forever. She was the reason we both still lived at home. The reason we never entertained thoughts of marriage.

She'd been sick as long as I could remember. A weak constitution many a learned doctor had said. Yet, I'd thought she would live as long as any other because we cared for her so well. Kellen and I had both expected to care for her until our hair turned grey with age.

In a single moment, everything had changed.

"What will become of us now?" Kellen asked, almost as if reading my mind.

I wrapped my arm around her waist and held her as she set her head on my shoulder. I hurt more for the pain I knew she struggled to contain and thought of Anne's message from Mother. Kellen needed me to be strong.

THE FRONT DOOR SLAMMED. I jumped at the loud noise, and Kellen looked up in surprise from the needlepoint she was pretending to do.

Since we'd returned from the ridge the day before, a hush had stolen over the house. No sisterly banter. No echo of Mother's laughter. Nothing but sitting and waiting to lay Mother to rest. No one would call on us during the seven days the house was in deep mourning. We'd ensured our privacy to grieve by draping the front door with black, as was custom, to warn away callers. After seven days, the gossipmongers would start to arrive to offer their condolences and glean what information they could from our misery.

Feeling the spark of my temper ignite at the loud intrusion, I stood and went to the hall.

The sight of Father standing in the entry, shaking out his jacket stunned me. He turned to find me staring at him and smiled widely, his eyes lighting with joy.

"Eloise! There you are. Come see what I've brought you."

I stared at him in confusion at the very typical greeting. Surely he'd seen the black draping on the door.

"Father, did you not—"

Kellen's hand settled on my shoulder.

"Hello, Father," she said.

"Kellen, my heart. You look lovelier every time I return. I brought you something special. Just what you need."

He reached into his coat and withdrew two paper packages. Kellen's was a small square. Mine was long. At least the length of my forearm.

"Let's sit in the parlor so we can open them," he said.

Kellen's fingers twitched on my shoulder.

"Perhaps your study, Father," she said as he started toward us.

"Nonsense. The parlor is where you always open gifts."

I glanced at Kellen, unsure what to do.

"He's not ready," she said softly.

I stepped forward to intercept him.

"Father, there's something you should know about Mother."

He stopped to place a kiss on my cheek.

"She has died, Eloise. We have not. She would not like us to act like we did."

With a fatherly pat on my shoulder, he walked around me and entered the parlor.

On a higher level, I knew what he said was pure truth. Yet, his words fell like a hammer to my heart. A whisper of noise and twin intuition told me Kellen still stood just behind me.

"Remember, some are better at hiding what they truly feel."

I nodded and took her hand. We entered the parlor where Mother was laid out in her best gown. Father stood looking out the window, less than an arm's length from her. He didn't acknowledge her presence at all when he turned to look at us.

"Go on, then. Open them," he said, gesturing to the packages on our chairs.

I dutifully picked up the package and sat to wait for Kellen to open hers. I always made her go first.

She removed the string and opened the paper to reveal a silky, red ribbon.

"Thank you, Father. It's beautiful."

I opened my package to find a small, bareroot tree. There were no shoots coming from the single stem, but it did have a few nubs that promised branches in the future.

"A pear tree," Father said when I glanced up at him. "You had a sweet tooth when I was last home."

I smiled slightly, remembering how I'd tried to talk Judith into making sweet pastries.

"Thank you, Father. These gifts are lovely."

"As are the two of you."

He inhaled deeply and tucked his hands behind his back. It was a pose Kellen and I knew well. The pose he used to deliver news he knew we wouldn't like. Such as his departure.

"You are of an age now," he began. "Old enough to make your own decisions and to care for yourselves."

My stomach dropped to my toes as I feared that this wasn't a departure speech but a proposal discussion.

"I expect now that your mother has passed on, it won't be long before you're married and gone from this house," he continued, unaware how the callously delivered words twisted my stomach.

"That being the case, I see no reason to delay my next venture. I will leave tomorrow."

I couldn't decide if I was relieved he wasn't trying to marry us off or angry that he seemed barely affected by Mother's death. Until he'd mentioned it, I hadn't been sure he'd even noticed.

"We bury Mother tomorrow," Kellen said. "You cannot leave until after that."

"Of course. Of course. We should see her to her final resting place near dawn. She loved watching the sun come up." For a moment, something crept into his gaze. Something real and alive and in pain. With a flash, it was gone again.

"I will tell Hugh of our plans and see you at dinner." He strode from the room without a backward glance.

"If that is love," Kellen said, "I want no part in it. Ever."

I captured her hand in mine and waited for her to look at me. When she did, I saw her careful mask was slipping. Anger reflected in her gaze.

"We don't know what he's feeling right now. And what he felt for

Mother is but one kind of love. Mother showed us another. Never forget hers. Or mine, Kellen."

She nodded and pulled away. I let her go, knowing she needed her space.

While she went to her room to regain an iron-fisted control over her emotions, I went to the kitchen. Judith and Anne were making pastries.

"Those look fancy," I said, dipping a finger in the lemon curd and earning a swat on my hand.

"They were fancy before you marked them."

I snorted and licked my finger.

"I only marked the one. Since it offends you, I'll remove it." Judith lifted her spoon menacingly as I reached again, and I laughed. It felt good. But it only lasted a moment before the pain crept back in.

Holding my hands up in surrender, I backed away from the table.

"Did Father return with the lemons?" They weren't a common item this side of the Dark Forest, but he was quick-witted with his trading.

"No. I bought them at market." Judith's humor fled as she wiped her hands on her apron and looked away from me. "Mrs. Cartwright was known by many even if she didn't leave the house. People will come to pay their respects, and we will have refreshments that will give the gossips something to talk about."

I hated the idea of opening our home to any visitors. Gossipmongers, all of them.

"If we offer them nothing, maybe they won't stay," I said.

Anne clucked her tongue.

"You're smarter than that, Eloise. That will be the first bit of information they'll slaver over." She assumed a gossipy pose and changed her voice. "'Can you believe those girls. They didn't offer us one bit of refreshment.'" She lowered her pitch to a snide whisper. "'Not surprised. With their father gone and their mother ill, they likely ran about like heathens.'"

"Your mother wouldn't tolerate that," Judith said. "Neither will I.

She raised you well. Two fine young women who know how to be proper young ladies. Her one hope was that you'd both marry well. I won't let lack of refreshments dash her dreams."

No matter how much I wanted to deny it, I knew there was truth in her words. And, as greatly as I hated the idea of catering to the gossips, I couldn't allow them to say anything negative about Mother. Not now. Not ever.

"You're right. Can I help?"

"No. Go spend time with your father. You never know how much you'll have."

I nodded and left with my cloak. A sweep of the yard turned up no trace of Father or Hugh. I stood by the chickens, wondering where the pair might have gone when I heard a faint, muffled thump and scrape. Following the noise through the trees to the west, I spotted Hugh in a small clearing not far from the house.

Sweat glistened on his pale, white torso as he worked dirt and stone from the shallow pit forming in the ground. I'd never seen him that unclothed before. But then, he'd never had to dig a grave for us. I swallowed hard and quietly turned away to leave him to his task.

Back at the house, I continued my search for Father and found him once again in the parlor, standing beside Mother. With his back to me, he stared out the window, and I took a moment to commit this instant to memory. It would be the last time I would ever see them together.

His once golden hair had lost much of its yellow at the sides, and new lines creased the corners of his eyes. He also looked a bit leaner than the last time I saw him. He'd always been a trim and fit man, not gaining girth around the middle like so many others his age. When he was here, he would carry Mother to and fro as needed. When he was away, he said he often loaded and unloaded merchandise. Better that he complete the tasks than pay someone else. It was his work ethic that influenced Kellen and me and why we willingly labored alongside those we employed, unlike many of the pampered girls of our means.

"Father," I said softly so as not to startle him. "I saw Hugh in the clearing to the west. It's a lovely spot."

"Yes. Lovely."

His tone indicated he wasn't in the room with me. His distance didn't bother me. In fact, I was quite used to conversing with someone who didn't want to talk.

"The morning sun will shine through the trees in winter, and a blanket of flowers will cover the ground in spring and summer. It will be pretty."

I sat and looked at Mother.

"She was looking forward to your return," I said.

He said nothing.

"She loved the necklace you sent her."

"Eh?" He turned to look at me.

"The necklace," I said, pointing. "It's very beautiful. Where did you find it?"

His gaze drifted to Mother. Not a single emotion crossed his features until his gaze landed on the necklace. Something flickered in his gaze, a pain so deep it hurt to witness. But it disappeared before he turned back to the window.

"Remove it," he said after a moment. "The dead need no ornaments. It will only incite thieves to disturb her grave."

"Yes, Father," I said softly, not bothering to refute his logic. A thief wouldn't know which graves might contain jewels until after they checked.

The moment my fingers touched the cold green stone, a bolt of heat seared my fingers. I gasped and released the jewel. The color swirled as it settled back on Mother's skin. I stared in horror and understanding. The glint I'd witnessed when Kellen put the necklace on Mother hadn't been a play of light. It'd been magic.

A sickening feeling settled into my stomach as I removed the necklace, avoiding the stone. I went to Father, my heart breaking with the possibility that he'd been so desperate to ease her suffering that he'd actually killed the woman I knew he loved very deeply.

Stepping in front of him, I held up the necklace and struggled not to cry.

"Why did you send this, Father? Why now?"

His gaze held mine for a long moment before going back to the trees behind me.

"I did not send it to your mother. Judith said that the last gift overtaxed her and warned me to send no more. If you will excuse me, there is much for me to do and very little time. I will see you at dinner."

He turned and strode from the room, leaving me with more questions than answers. I lifted the fine chain in my hand and studied the stone. If Father hadn't sent the necklace, who had?

I left the room and headed for the stairs. Kellen needed to know what had happened. Together, we could figure out who—

I stopped on the steps and looked down at the necklace. I couldn't tell Kellen. Ever. I knew how her mind worked and what she would think the moment I told her my suspicion that the necklace had killed Mother. Kellen had been the one to place the necklace around our mother's neck. And if Kellen knew the stone had ended Mother's life prematurely, she would never forgive herself.

My grip tightened on the chain as helplessness sparked anger.

As quietly as I could, I went to Mother's room and placed the offending necklace in her box of jewelry. My mind raced as I stared blindly at her other baubles. Who would have cause enough to want her dead? The need to know consumed me. I needed to find that delivery boy. Or maybe not. Perhaps I could deduce who if I knew the why.

I left the room and wandered the house. Try as I might, I couldn't think of a single reason why anyone would want Mother dead. She was—had been—a kind person. In recent years, she no longer went to town because she wasn't able, so she'd never had the opportunity to offend anyone. And, those who chose to come see her had always been graciously welcomed and treated like a dear friend. There hadn't been many of those visits, either. Other than Judith and

Anne, Mother had no dear friends. No family beyond us girls, either.

When Judith called me for dinner, Father and Kellen were already seated in the dining room. Candles lit the table, and a fire crackled in the fireplace.

As soon as I took my seat, Father gestured that we should begin eating. Since Mother's death, nothing appealed to me. But, I picked up my fork and took a bite, determined not to give Kellen any reason to suspect something was wrong.

After several silent minutes, Father spoke.

"We cannot undo what's been done. Our only option is to carry on and make the best of the circumstances in which we find ourselves. That was something your mother once said to me long ago. And she was right. That is why, tomorrow, I leave for my new venture. I know this won't be an easy time for you, and I'm sorry for that. I've made arrangements for someone to stay with you until I return."

"And how long will that be?" Kellen asked, her tone formal and indifferent. I knew better. She was angry.

"I'm not certain," he said.

I wasn't sure how I felt. I loved Father, and he had always put our needs before his own, working tirelessly to ensure we wanted for nothing. Yet, now when we most needed him to stay, he was set on leaving. His departure would surely be seen by the gossips as the abandonment it was. His disregard for Mother and us sparked my temper fiercely. Yet, if someone killed Mother, I would not ask him to stay. Without knowing who wanted Mother dead, I couldn't be certain Father wasn't also at risk. It was best that he was leaving.

"Where will this venture take you?" I asked, thinking that perhaps he might take us with him this time. It could be an adventure.

"To the kingdom of Turre."

My mouth dropped open.

"Surely you jest," I said. "That would take you through—"

"The Dark Forest. I know." He calmly took a bite of his roast.

21

I stared at him in shock, my thoughts colliding. Nothing good lived in the aptly named Dark Forest that ran from mountain range to mountain range, separating the kingdom of Drisdall from the kingdom of Turre. Kellen and I had grown up hearing tales of travelers who entered the dark depths never to return, and we listened to the faint, mournful howls on still nights.

"If you go, you will die," Kellen said, setting down her fork. "Is losing one parent not enough? Must we lose both?"

"Don't go, Father," I added. The possibility of a threat to his life if he remained was far better than the certainty of what he would face in the Dark Forest.

He sighed heavily.

"There is no need for such dramatic theatrics. You both know travelers passed through the Dark Forest at one time. I mean to establish a route again. Think of the trade possibilities. The riches. I heard rumor that the forest isn't as inhospitable as it once was. If that's true, it's more important than ever that I leave immediately. He who controls the route controls the trade."

Kellen looked down at her food, her cheeks flushed.

"Do not leave us, Father," I said again.

"My mind is set. I leave tomorrow after sunrise."

CHAPTER 3

I held Kellen's hand as Hugh shoveled dirt over Mother's coffin. Father stood at the head of her grave where a wooden marker now stood. A weak orange light filtered in through the trees and painted the clear blue sky. It was a beautiful day. A beautiful, terrible, heartbreaking day.

When Hugh finished, he nodded to us and left quietly.

Father hadn't said anything when he'd joined us outside and said nothing still. He stared down at the fresh earthy mound, once again closed off.

Kellen gave my hand a light squeeze and walked away. I was grateful she'd left before Father. At some point during my restless night, I'd decided to tell him about the necklace. It was something I should have done in the first place. I'd been too shocked to think clearly the day before, though.

"Father, there's something you should know."

He looked up at me.

"I believe the necklace killed Mother. Her eyes glowed the moment it settled around her neck. I thought it was a trick of the light, but when I touched it yesterday, I felt something. Magic, I think."

Father stepped toward me and grabbed my arms, his grip bruising.

"Say nothing of your suspicions ever again. Do you understand? To do so will mean your death."

"But—"

My father, who doted on Mother, Kellen, and me, and never spoke a harsh word, shook me firmly. I stared up at him in shock until I noted fear in his eyes. Fear for me. Fear for what even a whispered word of something so forbidden could do.

"Yes, Father," I said softly.

He released me with an unsteady exhale.

"Very good. Will you walk with me to the house?"

We traversed the path in silence, and when we rounded the house, I saw a horse saddled and waiting. Kellen stood on the front step, her expression closed off to what she was feeling.

"You're leaving already?" I asked, noting Father's red merchant jacket waiting atop the saddle.

"As I said I would."

"But, I thought once I told you—"

He gave me a sharp look.

"You are smart and resourceful girls. Keep your wits. Take care of one another. Mind the rules. You'll both be fine."

He agilely swung himself up onto the horse's back and removed something resting at the front of his saddle.

He handed me the bare branch he'd given me as a gift the day before.

"Don't forget to plant this. Farewell, my daughters."

Without any words of comfort, he prodded the horse forward.

Kellen turned on her heel and went into the house. I couldn't go inside. My mind was too full of grief, anger, and excessive questions to which I had no answers.

Instead, I ran back to my mother's grave and fell to my knees. I wished I could bury my feelings like Kellen. To suppress the hurt. But I couldn't. It boiled out of me in a torrent of tears.

I didn't understand Father's refusal to stay. Did he truly grieve so deeply that he couldn't see how desperately Kellen and I needed him?

If it was truly magic that had killed Mother what were Kellen and I to do? No. What was I to do? For the first time in my life, I felt completely alone.

It took some time for the tears to slow. When they did, the sun was peeking over the trees, and the soft chitter of animals had come alive around me. Wiping my face dry, I looked at my mother's grave. Time would flatten the mound of dirt. Plants would grow and disguise that a grave had ever existed. Only the marker would stand tall. But for how long? Maybe twenty years before it needed to be replaced? I dug a hole in the soft soil over her casket and planted the pear shoot.

Sitting back on my heels, I looked at the tiny thing.

"It's not much now," I said softly. "But someday, in spring, dainty white petals will rain down on your head. Their fragrance will perfume the air, and songbirds will sit in the branches. Their sweet melody will keep you company even if I'm not here."

My words caught, and I started to cry again.

A rustle and grunt from the nearby trees sent me to my feet, ready to bolt. Wild boar were wickedly dangerous.

"You stupid beast, walk faster or I'll see you on a plate."

An old woman with bits of twigs sticking out of her tangled nest of white hair tumbled out of the thicket. The worn and patched brown cloak that hung from her shoulders had seen better days. So had her dress. In her fist, she held one end of a rope on which she tugged mightily. An enormous pig reluctantly waddled into the clearing behind her.

I'd never seen such a well-fed beast. He was easily twice the size of the woman, and he didn't waddle with disdain but with strain. I didn't see how his small legs could support his body.

By appearances, they must have come from an outlying farm.

When the woman noticed me, she stopped tugging on the pig and gave me a pleasant smile.

"Good morning," she said. "I thought I heard someone out here. Could you be so kind as to tell me where 'here' is?"

Her lightly accented words told me she was from much further north.

"You are near Towdown. It's just over the next rise." I pointed to the south.

"Towdown," the woman said with distaste. "Not a place I wanted to visit. I've heard that magic has been banned here. Is that true?"

"Yes," I said nervously. As Father had recently reminded me, no one should speak openly of magic.

"Where were you hoping to be?" I asked, changing the subject.

"Adele preferably."

"Adele? I've never heard of that town."

The old woman considered me for a moment.

"Town? Never heard of it? Strange child. Everyone has heard of the city of Adele and its white towers. It's the best market for fine silks and fresh citrus."

I shrugged apologetically.

"I'm sorry. I don't often venture from my home, and when I do, it's only to visit Towdown's market."

She waved away my apology.

"It's no matter. I know where I am now and that I need to head west."

"Head west? You don't want to do that. There's nothing to the west but the Dark Forest." My gaze flicked to the pig. "You'll never make it through that cursed place with such a tasty treat for the beasts."

She gave the pig a satisfied smile.

"Do you hear that, pig? We can go through the Dark Forest, and I can watch you be eaten. Seems a fitting end for you."

The pig made a squealing sound almost as if he understood her.

Her smile faded as she cocked her head and studied me for a long quiet moment.

"I'm not sure what to think of you."

"Think of me?" I asked, careful to keep any hint of judgement from my tone.

I looked down at my skirt and saw where the material was stained with dirt from kneeling. I brushed as much as I could away before looking up again. Her gaze flicked to the mounded dirt at my feet.

"Who was that?" she asked.

"My mother."

"Was she a good woman?"

The blunt question surprised me.

"She was a very good woman," I said. "Her name was Margaret Cartwright."

"You sure you want to plant that tree there?" she asked.

"Yes. The marker will weather and rot long before a pear tree will."

She made a non-committal noise.

"What is your name?" she asked.

"Eloise."

"Do you practice magic?"

This woman was dangerous in her ignorance.

"No," I said emphatically. "I think it best that I go now."

"I must beg a favor, Eloise," she said, stopping me from leaving. "I'm old and tired, and this pig moves slower than me. I have places I must be and have no time to wait for him. If I leave him in your care, will you eat him?"

I looked at the pig, who stared back at me. I wasn't opposed to caring for animals, but I wasn't so sure about this one. Something in his eyes seemed to plead with me, an almost human quality that made me want to shiver and politely refuse her. However, I couldn't. I'd witnessed her struggle with the beast.

"No, ma'am. I will not eat him."

The woman started forward, tugging the pig along.

"Then I will leave him in your care for a while. I have nothing to offer you for his keep, though."

"There is no need. I like animals and won't mind caring for another one. It will be a welcome distraction."

I glanced at my mother's grave, feeling the sharp stab of grief anew.

The old woman caught my hand in her own. Turning it over, she studied my palm then glanced at the grave. Was she checking if I was dirty? When she looked up, she captured my gaze with a shrewdness that contradicted her age.

"I wasn't expecting this," she said softly.

"I beg your pardon?"

"Never mind me." She shook her head slightly. "Distractions are good when grieving, but don't forget these rules. Feed him lightly but once a day. He has been overindulged his whole life. If he continues to be over indulged, he will certainly die a horrible death. Do not trust him. He is an animal who would sacrifice you to gain his freedom. Walk him through the forest twice a week. You never know what he will find for you. He knows how to earn his keep."

She pressed the rope into my hand.

"If you need me, you can ask for Rose at the Brazen Belle in Towdown."

"I thought you were headed to Adele."

"I am. But, I believe there is business here that I must address first." She started past me, her stride surprisingly agile for her age. "Take care, Eloise, and mind the pig."

As soon as she disappeared, the pig started nosing the base of my skirts.

"None of that, now," I said. "If you misbehave with me, Hugh will take over your care. And, Hugh does not care for pigs."

The pig grunted and followed me willingly enough as I started toward the house. I decided not to notice how he was more docile with me than he had been with the old woman. Or the way he kept glancing at me. Instead, I focused on the encounter with the old woman. Rose.

Why would she ask if I practiced magic? As my father had warned me, it was dangerous to even utter the words, ignorant or not. But more than that, why would she ask it of me only hours after burying my mother whom I suspected had been killed by magic?

After tucking the pig into the vacant pig pen, I fetched water from the well and quickly washed my hands and face before going inside. Neither Judith nor Anne were in the kitchen.

While I nibbled on a bit of roast I'd found set aside for me, I considered the circumstance in which Kellen and I found ourselves. The expectations we'd once held for our future, to care for our ailing parent, had drastically changed. We could no longer hide away at the estate like we had. We were of an age where most girls were either betrothed or already wed. Although Mother had wanted the same for us, I knew the next trip to the market wasn't going to undo the impressions that had already been made.

Thankfully, the need to follow society's expectations to find a suitor would need to wait. Propriety demanded seven days of full-mourning. After that, a minimum of thirty days of half-mourning.

Kellen and I had four more days of peace.

"That's all you get," I said when the pig looked up at me. "The old woman is right. You'll die if I continue to overfeed you. Remember, pigs who still need fattening avoid the butcher's block."

The rattle of a carriage drew me away from the pig's pen and his displeased grunts. Instead of passing by, the sound seemed to draw closer. I moved to the house and paused on the steps, waiting to see who it might be. Behind me, a swath of black material hung from the door, an obvious reminder that we were a house in full-mourning.

I hoped it wasn't an over-eager gossipmonger. Whatever shred of patience I'd possessed for snooping people no longer existed.

A carriage rolled up the drive. Nondescript, it certainly looked like the type easily rented from a smith in town. I watched the contraption slow to a stop as the driver nodded down to me. Before he could move from his perch, the door to the carriage flew open, and a woman garbed in black stepped down without assistance. The laced veil obscured her identity only a moment before she flipped it back.

Her black hair stunned me as much as her face. With her soft brown eyes, dark hair, and pale skin, she looked just like Mother.

"Eloise, my darling." She came toward me, a smile on her lips while tears gathered in her eyes. "I'm so sorry." She wrapped me in her arms and held me tightly to her bosom while her hand smoothed over my hair.

Comfort enveloped me, and I hadn't realized how desperately I'd needed it. I only wished it was from someone I knew.

"Thank you," I said, hesitantly returning the hug. When she pulled back and gave me another tearful smile, I couldn't stop myself from asking, "Who are you?"

"Of course, Margaret wouldn't have mentioned an estranged cousin from her mother's side. How silly of me not to introduce myself. Call me Maeve. Consider me your fairy godmother. I'm here to set the world to rights."

She hooked her arm through mine and led me toward the house.

"When I heard your father planned to leave immediately, I offered to stay with you and Kellen. The two of you shouldn't face what's to come alone."

"Father mentioned making arrangements for someone to stay with us."

She stopped walking and looked at me with concern.

"He didn't tell you who?"

"No, ma'am."

She waved a hand in the air, a dismissive gesture Mother had often used.

"None of this ma'am nonsense. Call me Maeve or Auntie Maeve, if you prefer. I cannot believe that father of yours." She clucked her tongue and carefully removed her veil. "That's men for you, though. They don't deal well with grief and can't think clearly."

I opened my mouth to ask...well, anything, but a scrape of noise from the stairs drew our attention. I looked up to see Kellen, paler than usual, standing on the first landing. She was staring at Maeve. Given Maeve's resemblance to Mother, I understood her shock.

"Kellen, this is Maeve. She's here to help as Father mentioned."

Kellen blinked then nodded to Maeve.

"Welcome, Lady Maeve."

"Please call me Maeve or Auntie Maeve. There's no need for me to be Lady Grimmoire here. At least, not yet." She exhaled heavily and glanced at me. "We still have a few days of solitude before chaos descends, do we not?"

"Yes. Three more days."

"Very good. It will give us time to plan and prepare. But, that can wait for now. Is there somewhere I might rest for a bit?" she asked, looking between us. "Traveling always tires me."

Kellen and I shared a look. On the second floor, there were four bedrooms. Kellen and I shared the largest. Father had the smallest one, and Mother had the room with the nursery attached. With Mother gone, Anne had started sleeping downstairs with Judith in the room just off the kitchen. While Father's room was now also empty, we couldn't ask Maeve to sleep there. It would be highly improper, especially with visitors expected within days.

"I'll show you the way," Kellen said to Maeve.

I followed behind the pair as Kellen led her to Mother's room, Kellen having come to the same conclusion as I.

Maeve took one look at the room and shook her head.

"I cannot stay here. Is there an open servant's room? Even a mat in your attic would be welcome."

I looked around the beautifully furnished room in confusion.

"I'm sorry," I said. "This is all we have at the moment. You don't like it?"

Maeve caught me up in another hug.

"Dear child, this is your mother's room. Of course it's perfect." She pulled back and looked me in the eyes. "But, I'm here to ease your transition into a new life. To be your confidante and friend until you no longer need one. I'm not here to replace your mother or your memories of her. And, the last thing I want is for you to feel any animosity toward me. That wouldn't help any of us do what needs to be done. I fear that staying in this room would hinder our goals, not help them."

"We insist," Kellen said. "If you'd prefer not to sleep in this bed, there's another in the nursery that Anne used."

"We don't mind if you stay in here," I said. "There really isn't anywhere else."

Maeve gave us both searching looks and went to check the nursery.

"This does look comfortable. Are you sure you don't mind if I stay in this part?"

"Not at all," Kellen said.

"Perhaps after I rest, we can talk more, and you can introduce me to Anne."

THE WIND RATTLED the window near my head as I lay in bed. It was the only sound, beyond Kellen's steady breathing, that I could hear in the now quiet house. I rolled to my side and studied my sister's pale face in the weak moonlight.

"What do you think of her?" I asked quietly, seeing Kellen didn't yet sleep.

"She seems nice."

"She does. And Judith and Anne like her."

After waking from a long nap, Maeve had eaten lunch with us and then insisted on meeting our staff. She was cordial and friendly. Not what one would expect from someone who held the title of Lady Grimmoire.

"I was a bit surprised she wanted to see the pig," I said.

Kellen smiled in the dark.

"She didn't get too close, though, did she?"

I laughed. "No, she didn't. But that's okay. I don't think Mother would have gotten close, either."

We both grew quiet. It was nice having Maeve with us. It distracted us from the change in our routine since now there was no one to read to. No one to play for. No rhythm to our days without Mother's presence.

"It's childish, I know, but I don't want to like her," I said. "I know how I feel about her won't change what happened. Mother's gone. Yet, it feels wrong to like Maeve so quickly."

"Perhaps it's best to maintain your distance. Maeve is here for a purpose, and once that purpose is fulfilled, she'll leave."

I knew what Kellen was thinking. Maeve would leave like Mother and Father.

"I won't leave you," I said.

"People always leave, Eloise. It's in our nature...how we're made. If not through abandonment, then by death."

"Well then, I will never abandon you. Ever."

Her eyes softened before she closed them.

"I believe you," she whispered.

CHAPTER 4

THE SOFT MURMUR OF VOICES DREW ME TO THE HALL WHERE MAEVE AND Kellen stood, looking into Father's room.

"Good morning," I said.

Maeve turned and smiled at me.

"Good morning, Eloise. I'm sorry if we disturbed you."

"Not at all." I glanced at Father's room then Kellen, who was usually never up this early. "Is everything all right?"

Maeve gave me a troubled look.

"Since your father anticipates his latest endeavor to take some time, I arranged for everything I hold dear to arrive within a fortnight. Kellen and I were discussing if there might be a way to accommodate what will arrive."

I joined them at Father's door. His room was very crowded and removing all but his bed would likely free much of the space. However, clearing his room would feel like we were giving up on his return.

"He never mentioned how long he planned to be gone," I said.

"That's odd. He told me at least four months."

The news felt like a slap.

Maeve's expression softened.

"The sun has barely risen. Far too early for this conversation. Let us eat first. After, we can discuss my place here."

Kellen and I followed Maeve to the dining room where she started to take a seat.

"We eat in the kitchen in the morning," Kellen said. "It makes—made things easier for Judith."

"Of course," Maeve said, immediately changing course.

She followed us into the kitchen and greeted Judith and Anne as we sat at the table. She accepted her soft-boiled egg and didn't say anything when the pair joined us. I was very grateful for that. Anne and Judith were a part of our family. Hugh, too, though he preferred to eat earlier than the rest of us. Kellen and I had just lost our parents, and I refused to bend to social etiquette and distance myself from any of them.

After we finished our soft-boiled eggs, it didn't surprise me when Maeve once again brought up the problem of where to store her possessions.

"Mother's room makes the most sense," Kellen said. "We live in a modest home and need to be practical with how we use the space we have. Moving Mother's possessions to the attic is reasonable as Father might come back to us while Mother never will."

Maeve studied Kellen for a moment then reached out to put her hand over my sister's. However, Kellen moved her hand from the table before Maeve could touch her.

"Would you be interested in going to the market with me today, Lady Grimmoire?" Anne asked, smoothly deflecting the moment. "Judith can help the girls move Mrs. Cartwright's things to the attic while we're gone."

"I hate the idea of leaving all the work to the three of them," Maeve said, a light of impending protest in her eyes.

"As you've said, we have only a few days until visitors start arriving. A trip to the market is necessary and one Eloise and I cannot perform during our mourning period," Kellen said. "It makes sense to divide our numbers to complete what must be done in a short period of time."

Maeve inclined her head. "You are very sensible, Kellen. That will help you greatly in the days ahead."

I breathed a silent sigh of relief that Maeve wasn't put out by Kellen's manner. While Anne went to tell Hugh to hitch the wagon, Maeve accompanied us upstairs.

"Do not strain yourselves moving anything heavy," she warned. "Hugh can assist with those things when we return."

"We will be careful," I promised as my gaze wandered over Mother's things.

After Maeve left, it didn't take Kellen, Judith, and me long to dismantle and move the bed upstairs. Carrying the smaller pieces of furniture to the attic was a bit more tedious and required many trips.

Having returned for the next piece, a chair near the window, I paused to stare at the plain wooden box that contained every item Father had ever brought home for Mother. The green necklace was no longer there. It had never belonged with her treasured items. Instead, I'd hidden it under a board in our room before Maeve arrived.

Despite Father's warning, I couldn't put thoughts of the necklace out of my mind. Something had happened when I'd touched the pendant just as certainly as something had happened to Mother when Kellen had put it on her.

Although I knew Father's admonition to keep silent had been to protect me, I couldn't help my resentment that he'd done nothing after hearing my suspicions. Surely, he couldn't be agreeable with someone killing his wife? Perhaps that was the reason behind his determination to leave so quickly. If he had stayed and brought to light that someone had used magic on the king's own land, what would have happened? I swallowed hard. Father's death. Perhaps ours, too.

I should follow his example and put what happened behind me. Yet words lingered in my mind, haunting me with their insistence. Who? Why? Would I never know the answers?

Kellen walked into the room and caught me looking at Mother's jewelry box.

"Perhaps we should move the jewelry box to our room instead of the attic," she said.

"No, I don't think I can wear any of her treasures just yet. And seeing the box would only bring pain right now."

She nodded and didn't question me when I carried it out of the room.

The attic, already full of so many castoffs, was now crowded with the addition of Mother's furniture. There was still room to walk between pieces and find a safe place for the box in a back corner, though.

By midday, Mother's room was cleared, and Anne and Maeve had returned. We ate a companionable lunch in the kitchen then moved to the sitting room while Hugh moved the last pieces of furniture into the attic.

"Anne was quite informative today," Maeve said.

"Informative?" I asked.

"Yes. About who might be visiting and with whom I needed to have the most care."

"I'm not sure I understand," I said.

"The gossips," Maeve said bluntly. "Those who will come to give condolences but are really only here to gain information to share with their friends over tea."

"That would be every woman who passes over our threshold tomorrow," Kellen said.

"Not the men?" Maeve asked.

"Father had many business contacts. The men who call will likely only be here as a show of respect and will not linger long."

"I see," Maeve said. She glanced at me, but I couldn't contradict Kellen's assessment.

"Well, that does make me question how much effort and funds to put into refreshments."

"Unfortunately, no matter how much we dislike those who attend, we cannot slight our responsibilities," Kellen said. "To do so would reflect poorly on our love for our mother."

"You are quite right," Maeve said. "Then, there is only one other matter to discuss. Do you want to be present? If so, both of you will need to acquire the appropriate attire."

I looked down at my hands, dreading what she meant. The black gowns of mourning. Everywhere we went, people would know our grief. We wouldn't be able to escape it. Not even for a moment.

"I would prefer to mourn in solitude," Kellen said, saving me from trying to come up with a diplomatic answer.

"I agree," I said.

"Very well. I will welcome and speak to every guest on your behalves. Is there anything you wish me to say to them?"

"'Go away' has a nice ring to it," I said.

Maeve chuckled. "If only it were that easy."

"Thank them for coming to share our grief and offering their support in our time of need," Kellen said.

My sister always seemed to have the right words to say. But, I knew what she was thinking on the inside as her thoughts often echoed my own.

THE PIG TUGGED ME ALONG, content to root about the forest for whatever he smelled. Thanks to his nose, I had two dark mushrooms in my pocket. Judith would know what to do with them.

"Come, Mr. Pig," I said. "It's time for us to return home."

He stopped his rooting and looked up at me. I disliked the way it sometimes seemed as if he was thinking. Pigs didn't think. They couldn't. If I ever let myself believe they did, I'd never be able to eat bacon again.

A thud echoed through the barren trees, quickly followed by another. Frowning, I started toward the noise, glad for a reason not to return home. While spring was still struggling to make its presence known with gusty, cool winds, here in the shelter of the estate's forest, the breeze was mild and the temperature almost pleasant. Walking amongst the trees was much preferable to being shut in the house for another day.

The pig, however, didn't seem to be of the same mind. Before I took more than a few steps, he balked, tugging the rope from my hand.

"Go then. I'm sure some hunter would enjoy spotting you alone in the woods."

He let out a loud squeal, and I quickly shushed him.

"We don't know who is ahead. You're not the only one who might be accosted by wayward hunters." I picked up the rope. "Your silence might earn you an extra handful of grain when we return."

When he remained silent, I started forward again, weaving my way through the trees to find the source of the continuous sound. When we reached the tall oak that marked the boundary of our small estate, I hesitated. I knew very well what lay ahead and who I might find. Well, not who exactly.

My curiosity getting the better of me, I continued north. It didn't take long before I spotted a man through the trees.

Like when Hugh labored with the earth, this man wore no shirt while laboring to cut wood. Unlike Hugh, this man's back wasn't pale. It was golden and rippled in a captivating fashion with each swing of his ax.

"Stay here," I said absently to the pig, needing to move closer.

I crept forward on silent feet, watching the man work. Steam rose off of his torso, and his skin glistened in the early morning light. Though I wasn't close enough to see any detail in his features, my pulse sped with appreciation of what I could see. He had a handsome form to be sure.

If this was an example of the king's men, I hoped the king was prepared to stay at the Royal Retreat a good long while.

The man stopped suddenly and grabbed his shirt from a nearby log, wiping the sweat from his face. I waited in anticipation for him to turn, but he did not. Instead, he threw his shirt aside and reached for a water skin. When he tipped his head back to drink, the sunlight caught on his brown hair, turning it bronze.

My fingers twitched against the bark of the tree that hid me. What would he do if I stepped out and introduced myself? Probably think me wanton. Better to wait for him to be fully clothed.

Smiling to myself, I carefully backed away and almost tripped on the pig. Only nimble reflexes saved me from a fall and an awkward explanation. Scowling at the pig, I picked up his rope and quietly made my way back to the estate border.

My thoughts lingered on the man and his muscled torso. The moment that he swung and sun dappled his back, highlighting every ridge, repeated over and over in my mind. My cheeks warmed. Never before had I been so affected by a man. I knew a pretty face could hide an unsuitable character. *But it wasn't his face that had your heart racing*, I thought, my wistful smile returning.

The pig grunted and bumped into me.

"What?" I didn't like the way he was knowingly looking at me. "Who I look at is none of your concern. Now, do you want your grain or not?"

I gave the rope a tug, and he meekly followed me back to the house where I fed him a small portion of grain in his pen.

"Eloise," Kellen said from just behind me, making me jump.

When I turned to scowl at her, I caught the lingering hint of amusement.

"Are you here to startle me, or do you have a purpose?"

"A purpose. The first guest of the day has arrived. Would you like to go for a walk?"

In the three days since Maeve had entered our lives, Kellen and I had settled into an awkward routine. The awkwardness was due to our struggle to contrive tasks to keep ourselves occupied. Reading aloud without Mother there to listen seemed pointless and sad. The same with playing the piano. So Kellen and I found small things to do. I took care of the animals, which required very little of my time. And, Kellen organized the attic. When those tasks grew wearisome, we visited Mother's grave.

"A walk sounds nice," I said, dusting my hands off on my apron.

We gave the house wide berth and slipped into the trees. My

thoughts went to the man in the woods, and I briefly considered sharing the story with Kellen. However, given the reason behind this second walk, I decided to save the tale for later.

"Who is the first visitor?" I asked instead.

"I'm not certain. I slipped out through the kitchen and avoided the introductions. Some Lady or someone from a House of something or other."

"Probably here for the lemon tarts," I said. Judith made the best sweets. My mouth watered just thinking of the pastries that waited in cold storage

"Judith was counting the pastries this morning."

I grinned. Kellen knew I'd snuck down there yesterday to snitch one.

"Did she say anything?"

"Only that you were going to get fat."

I laughed.

My humor faded, however, when we reached the clearing, and I saw Mother's grave. Since her death, there were moments where I'd forget that Kellen and I were alone in the world. Then, some jarring reminder would shatter that fragile peace. It felt like the grieving would never end.

Kellen and I sat on the wooden bench that Hugh had placed there for us.

As I stared at the mound of dirt, I wished Mother was still with us. That Father was away on a normal business trip. And that Maeve, no matter how kind she was, wasn't living with us. In essence, I wanted the safety and ignorance of my old life to return.

The birdsong in the trees grew louder, and I thought of Mother's message to me. I tried to remind myself she was still with us in spirit, but it was too hard to hold such an unproven belief.

"It seems like it grew two inches overnight," Kellen said, jarring me from my thoughts.

"What has?"

Even as I asked, my gaze went to the pear tree. It remained nothing more than a single twig jutting from the ground, but Kellen was right. It did appear taller. I got up to look at the sapling closer and noted the buds were bigger as well.

"I'm glad it seems to be growing. It's like a piece of Father is here to watch over her, don't you think?"

I turned in time to catch Kellen's angry expression before she closed herself off again.

"There's no purpose in holding your anger," I said. "He's gone, and so is she. We cannot change how things are; we can only choose to accept them and move on."

"Move on," she said. "For what? A marriage to a man who will leave us just as readily as Father did?"

I returned to Kellen and set my head on her shoulder.

"Who said anything about us marrying some soddy men? We can make our own futures, can we not? Perhaps we should travel? We can pose as spinsters and see what lies to the north."

Kellen snorted, amused by my daydream. She set her head against mine.

"Let me hold my anger for a little while," she said. "I do so on Mother's behalf for she was never angry with Father a day in her life. And she should have been. At least twice."

"Twice?"

"The day he missed our birth and the day he missed her death. It's warranted."

My chest tightened, and my throat closed for a moment as I struggled with my own pain. When I finally spoke, my voice was soft.

"It's a fair request. However, you've already carried your anger for seven days. I think that's sufficient. It's time to let it go."

She sighed.

"If I let it go, I have nothing left to do with myself. I miss her terribly."

"Me, too. Perhaps it's time we decided on new hobbies. Or we could always attend a gathering or two. Become renowned gossips. Think of all the cakes we could eat."

Kellen snorted again.

"Tomorrow I'll go to town and see what new books I can find."

The bookstore was a safe distance from the market, which meant it was a haven for Kellen.

"Books instead of cakes?" I said. "It's like I don't even know you, sister."

"You know me better than anyone. Would you like me to find a book for you, or will you come with me?"

"I'll be at your side, of course. Those boorish boys in the market aren't to be trusted, and my aim is far better than yours."

She chuckled then quieted. We sat like that for a long time, both lost in our own thoughts, before hunger drove us back to the house. Judith had a simple midday meal prepared for us when we arrived.

While we ate, Judith and Anne worked quietly. Their lack of conversation made it painfully obvious someone still remained in the sitting room with Maeve. I wondered if it was the same person who had arrived earlier but didn't ask. It didn't matter who was here, only why they were here.

After lunch, Kellen and I went upstairs. Kellen entered Father's room to look over his collection of books to see if there was anything that might interest her. She'd never intruded on his space before. That she did so now could only mean she thought he wasn't coming back.

Leaving her to her quiet, I lay on my bed and pondered her questions of what was next for us. For all of my silly play about traveling, I wasn't yet ready to leave Towdown. There were questions that needed answers. Questions I'd tried to ignore but knew I couldn't. I needed to find the person responsible for robbing us of our family. I needed to know who had sent the necklace.

But not yet. First, I needed Kellen to choose her path in life. I needed to know she would be safe from any repercussions. Then, I could choose my own way and damn the consequences.

Sitting up, I checked the hall then carefully closed the door before kneeling at the end of my bed. I folded back the rug and pried up the floor board. It was a space I'd discovered many years ago. It had never held anything of importance because everything I had, I willingly shared with Kellen and Mother.

However, it had been the perfect place to keep the necklace. A safe place so no one would touch it and suffer the same fate as Mother.

Carefully reaching in, I unfolded the soft leather in which I'd wrapped the pendant.

The necklace was gone.

CHAPTER 5

I KNELT THERE AND STARED AT THE HIDEY-HOLE IN CONFUSION. HOW could the necklace be missing?

Grabbing the empty piece of leather, I replaced the board and righted the rug. The necklace didn't disappear on its own. I left the room and found Kellen still in Father's bedroom, looking at his meager collection of fictional stories amidst his accounting books.

She looked up as I entered.

"Unless I'm interested in reading the history of our accumulated wealth, or lack thereof, I'm afraid there isn't much here for me."

I closed the door so no one would overhear us.

"Please tell me you're not wearing it," I said in a hushed tone.

She frowned at me, her confusion clear.

"Wearing what?"

"The necklace. The green one that arrived for Mother. I had it in the hiding spot in the floor, and it's gone." I held out the empty piece of leather as proof.

"I didn't take it." She glanced at the leather then met my gaze. "Why did you hide it away if you didn't want any of Mother's jewelry as a reminder?"

There was no censure. Only my sister trying to understand my motivations.

"I didn't want the reminder." I sighed. "It's hard to explain. It was the last thing she received. It just felt important and private."

I couldn't lie to my sister. I never could. That was why all of what I said was true; yet, none of it came close to the truth.

"I understand," Kellen said. "Let's ask Judith and Anne."

However, Judith and Anne hadn't seen the necklace while tidying our room.

"You know how things are here," Judith said. "You can hear mice scratching in the walls at night. If you put a trinket in your hidey-hole, there's a chance that a mouse might have taken off with it. They like shiny things. We need a cat."

I knew she was right. Not about the cat but about the mice. The necklace wasn't the first item to go missing because of the cute pests. But, it was by far the most important. I should have known not to tempt fate by putting the necklace in the floor.

Angry with my own foolishness, I left the house alone. The wind tugged at my cloak as I walked toward Mother's grave. Having already visited with her today, I didn't stop again. Instead, I carried on through the trees, wandering the familiar woods.

Animals skittered through the underbrush, making way for my passing. Some scolded me with their little, outraged chitters. Normally, I would have been amused and paused to talk back to them. But, I couldn't. Not today. I was too angry.

How could I have been so careless? That necklace had been my one piece of proof that my mother hadn't died of a natural cause. Without it, the person responsible would never be brought to justice. Proof, when dealing with magic, was the key. Even with proof, things might have ended badly for me. However, without proof, my quest to find answers was over before it ever began.

I kicked at a fallen branch.

No, I couldn't think like that. The necklace wasn't gone forever. Just misplaced. If there were vermin in the house, they had to have a nest somewhere. I only needed to find it.

I was so lost in thought that the sudden, loud voice just in front of me took me by surprise.

"Leave now, by order of the king."

Startled, I jumped back as I looked up. My heel slipped, and I tumbled backward. Time slowed as our gazes locked. Though I hadn't glimpsed his face earlier, I recognized the man.

The dark blue eyes of the nap-headed scoundrel held mine. He had the audacity to smirk as I landed with a soft splat on the spring-dampened ground. A cold moisture seeped through my skirts and chilled my backside.

Stunned, I stared up at the man as he leaned on his walking stick. Close to my age, he was far more handsome than he had a right to be. His broad shoulders were properly covered by a rough coat this time, but my pulse nevertheless skipped a beat as I recalled how he looked without it. However, since I wasn't sure if his humor was meant to be shared or at my expense, I refused to give my attraction to the man any due.

"Did you intend to send me flying into the mud?" I asked.

"I find that's where most of your kind belong."

My mouth dropped open, and my already frayed temper ignited. He was just like all the other pretty faces in town.

"You are a boorish ass," I said, setting my hands on the ground to hoist myself up. I ignored the squish of mud between my fingers and the surprised lift to his brows.

"Boorish ass?"

"Yes. Are you hard of hearing?"

I struggled to my feet, regretting that I hadn't noted the wet ground before my fall. His smirk widened with growing amusement each time I slipped and dirtied myself further. When I finally won my footing back with no offer of help from him, I was ready to throw a rock at his head. I could already imagine the hollow sound it would make when it connected.

"I do suppose braying ass would suit you better," I said with deceptive calm as I shook as much mud as I could from my skirts.

His humor fled, and he frowned at me.

"You have no right to call me anything," he said, once again sounding high-handed. "I am not the one trespassing."

How ridiculously presumptuous of him. This time, it was I who wore the smirk.

"Are you sure about that? This is the king's land. While I indeed have permission to be here, I doubt you do. It would be in your best interest to flee before I summon the king's guard."

He tilted his head to consider me. The vivid blue of his eyes held me for a moment, and I once again found myself slipping into the pleasantness of his visage...until disdain flooded his expression.

"You have permission?" Doubt laced his every word.

I averted my gaze and started looking at the ground for a rock. Surely, the spring thaw would be kind enough to grace me with one. It didn't need to be large. Just big enough to knock some sense into the nit.

As I searched, I answered him.

"Yes, I live here. I'm Eloise Cartwright."

"Ah. I see."

The flat tone devoid of any emotion demanded my attention. Lacking a rock, I decided to show this bore his place using the sharp edge of my tongue.

"You probably couldn't see something if it were on the tip of your nose," I said. "Now, who are you?"

"That's none of your concern."

I snorted.

"As I would expect a person guilty of trespassing to say. Go away, fiend. Leave the king's land while you still stand."

He barked out a laugh.

"Are you always this abrasive?" he asked.

"When covered in mud and dealing with an overbearing—"

"Do not call me an ass again."

"Wouldn't think of it. Pig."

His expression darkened.

"That's not to your liking, either? As you've given me no other name to call you by, Officious Grunting Pig it shall be." I smirked.

"You have a viper's tongue."

"And you have the slow wit of a cod fish. Lacking any decency, you've proven yourself to be beneath me."

"Beneath you?"

"Please do try to keep up with this conversation. Or must I speak slower?"

Pink invaded his cheeks, and I knew I'd won this battle.

"You are most fortunate I'm a decent man, or I would see you beaten."

I snorted.

"Any decent person would introduce himself. You started this by yelling in my face and tossing accusations about."

His nostrils flared in his anger, but then, to my surprise, he bowed low.

"The name's Kaven," he said.

I barely heard. My gaze was fixated on the crest adorning his cap. It was the same crest that the delivery boy had worn. All righteous pride at besting this man fled, replaced by the cold, convicted anger filling my chest.

"What is that?" I demanded.

He straightened to give me a quizzical look.

"The crest on your hat. What does it mean? Who is it for?"

The suspicion returned to his gaze.

"It's the king's crest. How can you claim to live on these lands and not know the king's crest?"

I didn't answer. My mind was racing. What did it mean that a king's messenger delivered the necklace that killed my mother? It made no sense. We were on the king's land by his decree. Why would the king favor us with land then kill one of us?

Kaven, reached out, gripping my arms.

"Answer me, woman."

That snapped me from my thoughts.

"I know nothing of the king's crest because my mother forbade us from walking the woods when the king was in residence. Now, unhand me."

His eyes narrowed.

"I don't believe you."

"I don't care what you believe. You truly are a beast. How many more of you are there at the lodge?" I asked.

His grip tightened.

"Why do you want to know?"

"So I know how many people the king has brought to push me into the mud and torment me," I lied, trying to pull myself free from his steel grasp.

He didn't budge.

I stomped on the arch of his foot.

"Release me," I demanded.

He did so immediately and scowled at me.

"Go home, Eloise Cartwright. Listen to your mother's wise words."

I hated him. I hated all who'd come with him. And I vowed to find the necklace, the boy who delivered it, and the person responsible for it all. Even if that person was the king himself.

"Do not speak of my mother. She died the day after you arrived," I said glaring.

His anger vanished from his face. Nothing replaced it. No sympathy or pity.

"How?" he asked.

I swallowed hard. I couldn't tell what I knew. Not with him wearing the king's crest. No one would believe me that the king sent the magic amulet. Even speaking of the amulet would get me killed.

"My mother's health has been failing for years," I said instead.

"I'm sorry for your loss." He didn't sound sorry. He sounded distrustful. His next words confirmed it.

"Where is she buried?"

"In the clearing behind our home. She liked the trees and sunlight on her face."

Something shifted in his eyes, but I couldn't tell what.

"Tell me, Kaven. For how long must I avoid the woods I've called home?"

"I do not know."

He turned and left me standing in the woods, mud drying to my skirts. The birds started singing after a moment, and the small animals in the underbrush chittered at me.

"Nothing good will come of this," I said, thinking of Kaven's crest. The king's crest.

Father's warning to let go of what I knew rang in my ears once more. I'd thought I could wait until Kellen and I grieved, and she chose the future she wanted before I pursued answers. However, I now understood that I couldn't. Mother deserved more. Father had already abandoned her. I would not.

The walk home was cold and wearying. Thankfully, there were no visitors to spot my disheveled state when I slipped into the kitchen.

Judith looked up from whatever she was stirring over the fire.

"Eloise, what happened, child?"

"The spring mud tested my agile step and showed me that I was lacking. I think a washing is in order."

Her gaze swept me from head to foot.

"The mud is in your hair, too. A simple washing will not do. A full bath is needed. Sit on the stool. Anne and I will start drawing water."

The pair had the tub before the fire and half-filled before the kitchen door opened again. Kellen walked in and stopped abruptly at the sight of me.

"Sister, did the pig drag you through the mud?"

I grinned.

"Why, yes. A pig did do this. Unfortunately, not our sweet pig. However, you've just given me a brilliant idea for a name for our dear pig."

"Oh?"

"What do you think of Kaven?"

She tilted her head and gave me a quizzical look.

"I sense a story. Would you like me to help wash your hair while you tell it?"

"Please."

Judith and Anne left the kitchen to give us privacy. Kellen helped me out of my muddy things and started removing clumps of mud from my hair as I slipped into the tub of warm water and washed my arms and face.

"Who is Kaven?" she asked.

"A dolt I met in the trees behind our house. He startled me so badly I slipped and fell. Then, the boor didn't even have the manners to help me up. Instead, he began accusing me of trespassing. He was completely rude."

"Sounds like the boys in the market."

"Very much so," I agreed. Only this one had made my heart race and may have had a hand in Mother's death. I pushed that thought from my mind as Kellen answered.

"Then, of course we will name the pig after him. I've removed as much of the mud as I can. Now, you need to go under."

I looked at the murky water and sighed.

"I wish it was warmer out. Bathing at the pond would be infinitely more enjoyable."

Kellen made a sound of agreement, which stopped abruptly as I ducked under the water. Her fingers threaded in my hair, removing more mud as I held my breath. Being underwater was one of the things I liked about the pond. Nothing but fish could touch me. No sight or sound from the real world. It was an escape from troubling thoughts. One that Kellen and I enjoyed during the sweltering heat of summer.

When I reemerged, Kellen started soaping my hair.

"While you were out playing in mud, I was in the attic," she said. "I found something interesting in one of the trunks pushed into a dark corner."

"What's that?"

"Letters to Mother from an old friend. Do you recall Mother ever mentioning an Elspeth?"

I shook my head.

"Nor do I. Yet, from Elspeth's letters, it would seem they were

52

close. She apologized for leaving Mother so soon after our births and asked after us by name."

Kellen seemed intrigued by the idea that Mother had a friend. I could understand why. Although no one had said so, we'd grown up under the impression that Mother had no family. To discover Mother had an estranged cousin and, now, a friend from before our births felt odd. Why would Mother hide letters from us?

"How many letters are there?" I asked.

"A small trunk full."

"It would seem you found your hobby," I said, knowing the mystery of who Elspeth was would keep Kellen occupied for a time.

Kellen left me to sit impatiently on my own as I dried before the fire. With nothing to do but run my fingers through my hair, I dwelled on my meeting with Kaven.

I wished I hadn't met him as I had. That he hadn't been wearing that cap and crest. But that wish was purely selfish from the treacherous organ buried in my chest. My mind knew better. It was too coincidental that Mother died the day after Kaven had arrived and that he wore the king's emblem, the same as the boy who'd delivered the amulet. I needed to find the connection between Kaven and the boy; and the best way to do that was to go to the king's hunting retreat. What excuse could I give for my presence, though?

I thought of the pig and smiled. Tomorrow, the pig and I would go for a walk.

LOOKING TIRED, Maeve entered the dining room and joined us at the table. It felt odd taking meals there, but given the possibility of unexpected visitors, we had decided to follow formality for a while.

"How did everything go today?" Kellen asked Maeve as Judith served us bowls of stew.

"Well enough. We had twelve callers. Those whom Anne had

pointed out as the most vapid gossips were first. The questions they asked about Margaret's passing and her place at this estate bordered on unacceptable. They weren't even trying to hide where their interests lay. Unfortunately for them, the only juicy bit they received was the lemon tartlets. I anticipate we won't see many guests tomorrow because of it. How did you two occupy yourselves today?"

"I organized the attic," Kellen said. "There is more room now if any of your possessions do not fit in Mother's room."

"Thank you for your consideration." Maeve smiled warmly at Kellen before looking at me. "What about you, Eloise? Did you find a way to keep busy today?"

"I went for a walk and fell in some mud."

"A king's servant startled her," Kellen added.

I smiled at my sister. She hated when I said anything that made me sound clumsy or incompetent in any way.

"A king's servant?" Maeve asked. "Out here?"

"This estate sits on the king's land," Kellen said. "The Royal Retreat is further along the road through the trees. Several days before you arrived, we heard dogs and learned that the king would be in residence soon."

Maeve frowned.

"That doesn't bode well for us."

"What do you mean?" I asked, trying to suppress my excitement that I might have an ally in my suspicions against the Crown.

"If the king will be in residence, it gives the gossips more reason to return during the mourning period. They will use the excuse of condolences to try to gain information about the king." She looked at me. "The fact that you're walking in the woods and running into servants is troubling, too. I wouldn't dare suggest you refrain from your walks. I believe the fresh air is good for you. However, we will need to see both of you appropriately attired in mourning gowns. We don't want to start tongues wagging. We shall go tomorrow. Judith and Anne can turn away any visitors on our behalves."

The idea of going to town did not appeal to me. The trip would mean a regrettable delay in my walk to the king's estate. Based on the look on Kellen's face, she was likewise put out by the news. Though, the likely reason for that was due to the band of bullies who'd enjoyed tormenting us.

Maeve didn't seem to notice either of our subdued agreements.

"Judith mentioned that you lost a necklace because of vermin. Perhaps while we are in town, we should look for a house cat as well," she said.

CHAPTER 6

"Some airing will remove the musty smell in no time," Maeve said, holding a handkerchief to her nose.

I nodded and glanced at Kellen, who sat beside me in our small, seldom used family carriage. She watched out the window as I'd been doing. However, one wouldn't be able to tell if it was due to the need for fresh air or her interest in the passing countryside. At times, I envied her composure. At other times, I worried for her. She kept so much inside.

Reaching over, I clasped her hand. Her fingers curled around mine, the only acknowledgement she gave the gesture. That she continued to hold my hand was enough to know what she was truly feeling. My other hand clenched into a fist, and I almost hoped that the boys would be at the market again. My anger from my encounter with Kaven remained intact, and if I couldn't use him as a target, I'd find a substitute. There was no shortage of boorish swine in Towdown.

"I'm at a disadvantage," Maeve said interrupting my thoughts. "I'm unsure which shops are suitable for producing quality mourning attire."

"We usually see Madame Thread," Kellen said. "She's affordable and adequate."

Maeve blinked at her.

"Adequate is hardly an endorsement. I shouldn't imagine she's very respected with a name like Madame Thread."

I coughed lightly in the handkerchief I held in my free hand. However, my attempt to hide my humor wasn't lost on Maeve.

"I sound pretentious, don't I?" she said ruefully. "I don't mean to be. I only understand the importance of presentation. While you both are lovely, those who've visited us would still judge the cut and quality of the cloth covering you and try to find ways in which it is lacking. Unfortunately, with the King soon to be in residence, I fear we are not yet free of unwanted attention. To protect both of you from the ridicule of wagging tongues, I would like to see you attired by a seamstress of note."

"We understand," I said. Maeve's concern for us was touching. And, I appreciated that she wasn't attempting to shelter us from our harsh reality.

"Madame Todd's is well known and frequented by many of the gentry," Kellen said. "However, I'm not sure we brought enough coin for that."

Maeve waved away Kellen's concern.

"Your father's arrangement with me means you have no need to concern yourself with expenses."

Kellen smiled in acceptance, a mask to hide what she truly felt, and I struggled to do the same. What had Father been thinking to not only put the burden of two grieving girls on Maeve but also to expect her to cover our expenses while he was gone?

The carriage rolled through town, the wheels grating against the cobblestone that lined the streets of the more affluent districts. I watched the people, and a thought wormed its way into my mind. Would my family still be whole if we'd lived in town like everyone else?

Kellen's hold in my hand loosened, and I realized the carriage was slowing. I looked out at Madame Todd's and saw the swathes of prettily colored fabrics in the window.

"What if she doesn't make mourning garb?" I asked.

Maeve smiled at me. "No one refuses Lady Grimmoire, my darling."

The door opened, and Hugh offered his hand to Maeve. She nodded regally to him then stepped to the ground to wait for us, so we could enter the store together.

A floral scent, much like spring's first blooms, wrapped around us. It was a scent I rather enjoyed.

One of the girls welcomed us and asked how she could be of assistance.

"We're in need of two mourning wardrobes. At least three gowns each. Two suitable for daily wear, which includes accepting visitors. One for larger gatherings."

The girl hesitated.

"Will this be a problem?" Maeve asked.

"Not at all. May I have your names, please?"

"I am Lady Grimmoire, guardian to Eloise and Kellen Cartwright." She gestured to me then Kellen as she made the introductions.

"If you would care to have a seat, you may browse the sketches while I ask Madame Todd to join us."

Maeve smiled as the girl hurried off, leaving us to find our own way to the chairs placed at the left of the door.

"And that is how it is done," she said softly. "Note that there is no black fabric on display. Customers don't want to be reminded of mourning when shopping for pretty things. I'm also certain they do not keep enough fabric on hand for six gowns."

"Three each does seem a bit much," Kellen said.

"I promise I am not leading you astray from our goals," Maeve said. "Presentation and respecting your mother's memory are foremost."

She picked up a sketchbook and handed it to us.

"Look through this and find two gown styles you find suitable. I'll pick the third."

"Are we really going to a larger gathering while in mourning?" I asked.

"I'm not yet certain. However, it is prudent to be prepared."

Kellen and I looked through the book. There weren't many options that were as plain as we were used to. We selected our two dress styles and had just handed the book to Maeve when the girl returned with an older woman.

"Welcome to my shop. Paulette has told me you would like six mourning gowns. Have you any particular styles in mind?"

Maeve encouraged Kellen and me to show the gowns we'd selected, then she took the book and opened to the last page. The dress there had a full, flowing skirt that belled out in an elegant display with lace embellishments. The heartline bodice and trim sleeves looked exquisite and far too formal for anything we could possibly attend while in mourning.

Kellen and I shared a look.

"Are you certain you want this in black and not a soft grey?" the Madame asked.

"Yes, black. My wards are determined to be in mourning for the three months they are allowed. Their dear mother made them swear not to mourn a day beyond that. She was such a selfless woman, our Margaret. She knows these dears are of an age to marry and didn't want her passing to prevent her children from finding their happiness."

Madame Todd smiled and gave us an affectionate look.

"You are both lovely. I can see why your mother made you vow not to grieve too long. Black it is, then." She looked at Maeve. "How soon would you like these completed?"

"The first gown is needed tomorrow. All of the gowns within seven days. You will be appropriately compensated for the rush and awarded more if you can have them done sooner."

Madame bowed her head in a gracious acknowledgement.

"Come. Let us start with the measurements."

While Madame spoke in quiet tones with Maeve, two of the seamstresses led Kellen and me to the back of the shop where we stripped down to our underthings and were thoroughly measured.

When we finished, Maeve was waiting alone near the front of the store.

"Just a few more stops, my darlings," she said as we left Madame Todd's.

Hugh helped us into the carriage and closed the door. The conveyance bounced as he settled his weight into the driver's seat. A moment later, he called to the horses, and we started forward.

"Why do we need a dress tomorrow?" Kellen asked.

"And why did you say we'd promised not to mourn more than three months?" I added.

"The answer to both questions is simple. Presentation and appearance. The gossips will now know there is a timeframe for your grieving and will not judge you harshly if there is a slip because it's your mother's wish that you not grieve too long. The supposed vow paints your mother in a very gracious and irreproachable light. The request for an immediate gown shows just how deeply you're both grieving."

"While I understand the reasons for it, I disagree with lying," Kellen said.

Maeve quietly considered us before speaking.

"Although your mother did not ask you to make such a vow, do you think she would have if she'd known her time was near?"

"Yes," I said. "She wouldn't want us to grieve long."

The carriage started to slow. When I glanced out the window, I saw we were off the cobbled path on a dirt side street.

"I would like you both to wait here," Maeve said. "This shop is not suitable for unwed girls."

"What is it?" I asked.

"An herbalist. I find I need tinctures during my monthly cycle to help control the pain and bleeding. Did your mother speak to you of such things?"

Kellen and I both shook our heads.

"Should your monthly cycles ever cause you issue, please do feel you can come speak to me. I wouldn't want either of you to suffer when there are remedies."

The carriage stopped, and the door opened. In the silence that followed Maeve's departure, Kellen reached for my hand.

"I am not speaking to her about my monthly cycles."

I giggled.

Kellen and I started bleeding the same time years ago. Our cycles had never caused us much pain. Other than having to deal with extra clothing, it wasn't something I'd given much thought. But Kellen was right. Speaking with Maeve about monthly cycles wasn't something I was about to do, either.

It didn't take long for Maeve to return to us.

"Next stop is the cobbler."

"I would prefer to return home," Kellen said.

Maeve frowned.

"Are you feeling unwell?"

I knew that Kellen was feeling fine. However, the best cobbler, which is where Maeve would probably insist we go, was near the market district.

"Kellen is fine," I said, giving my sister's hand a reassuring squeeze. "It's only that our shoes are still in very good condition. It's unnecessary to purchase another pair."

Maeve smiled.

"Presentation and appearance, my darlings. Now, who is the best cobbler?"

Kellen answered, her voice carefully neutral.

When the carriage stopped, she and I both glanced out the windows while Maeve waited for the door. Kellen's fingers twitched in mine, and I followed her gaze. The boys who'd tormented us during our last excursion were leaning against a building not far away. All eyes were on our carriage. As soon as we stepped down, they would see us.

I couldn't stop the slow grin that parted my lips.

"Please don't cause trouble," Kellen said as Maeve stepped out.

"I won't start it," I said, moving to the door.

"I wasn't talking to you," she answered, making my grin widen.

"No smiling, Eloise," Maeve said softly. "Please appear suitably aggrieved."

My humor immediately fled. She was right. Now wasn't the time, no matter how badly I wished to strike out, to relieve myself of this impotent anger festering inside of me.

Maeve opened the shop door for us and let me step inside first. The cobbler immediately looked up from his work.

"Eloise Cartwright," he said. His brow lifted in surprise. "Kellen too. I didn't expect to see you so soon. Is there a problem with the fit of your boots?"

"No, sir," I answered. "We're here for a new pair."

Maeve stepped forward.

"My girls need something more refined to go with their mourning gowns."

"I see. You've come to the right place, miss…"

"Lady Grimmoire," Maeve said with a small smile. "How long will it take to complete a new pair?"

"I have a few orders to finish but could have them ready by the end of the week."

"That would be lovely. Do you need measurements?"

He shook his head.

"I took them a few weeks back."

"Splendid. Would you have time to look at my shoes? I'm afraid the heel has come loose."

"Of course."

"Girls, if you would like to look around the market for a set of black ribbons, we can leave as soon as we're done."

Kellen nodded and started toward the door before I could come up with a suitable excuse for us to remain with Maeve. Outside, the light blinded me for a moment.

"Where are you two off to?" Hugh asked from the top of the carriage.

"Hair ribbons," Kellen said.

"Try to stay out of trouble." The slight shake of his head that accompanied his words said just how much he believed we could.

Side by side, we walked away from the cobbler and headed toward the busy market. The boys watched us pass, their expressions laced with boredom.

"Is there any chance that they will ignore us?" Kellen asked.

"Doubtful."

"Fighting with them will reflect poorly on Mother's memory."

"I'm sure Mother would understand."

Kellen agreed.

I knew the exact moment the boys left their position against the building and started following us. A tingle ran down my back like a sixth sense. They drew closer but did nothing more than follow us.

Pretending not to notice them, Kellen and I stopped at a booth that displayed pretty ribbons.

"Do you have any in black?" Kellen asked.

"We do, miss." The woman turned her back to us and looked through a small chest she had on another table.

"Didn't expect to see you two so soon," a familiar voice said from behind us.

"We had rather hoped to never see you again," I said, without turning.

The woman searching through the ribbons glanced our way. I gave her a small smile.

"How many ribbons are you looking for?" she asked.

"Four please," Kellen said.

The woman handed us our ribbons, and Kellen gave her a copper. When we turned, the boys were no longer behind us but, instead, were looking at another stall's wares a fair distance away. They were obviously in a mood to torment us. A pot to the head apparently hadn't made them any smarter.

"Hugh would probably like a biscuit," Kellen said softly.

I smiled at my sister's cunning. The stall that sold the best biscuits belonged to a nice, old man tending a booth off the beaten track, away from prying eyes that might witness any scuffle between two mourning girls and a bunch of bullying boys.

"Hugh rarely gets a biscuit. You're very kind to think of him," I said.

We continued down the main thoroughfare, past our group of tormentors. It didn't take long for the boys to start following us again. Kellen and I wove our way through the crowds around the vendor stalls and took a left down one of the side streets.

The scent of butter and baking bread tickled my nose. The best biscuit vendor didn't charge much, which enabled everyone to enjoy his creations. Unfortunately, catering to the lesser folk meant others refused to patronize him.

When the man saw us approaching, he smiled and readied six biscuits. Enough for everyone in our household. He knew us well.

"Good morning, Ladies," he said, already holding up the bundle.

"Good morning." Kellen handed over the necessary coin with, perhaps, a little extra.

A scrape of noise from the alley's entrance briefly drew the man's gaze, and I knew a conflict would be unavoidable before returning to Maeve. Kellen understood the same.

"Would you happen to have any day-old biscuits?" she asked. "I do enjoy feeding the songbirds."

"My biscuits never last that long," he said. "However, I do have a few that are too hard to sell. My grandson is trying to help with the baking, but he doesn't have the eye yet to know when to remove them from the oven." He showed us a dozen dark brown biscuits.

"We'll take all of them," Kellen said.

The baker handed over the bundle, which I accepted while Kellen gave another coin.

"Thank you!" I called as we moved away.

Happy that we'd helped the baker as much as he'd helped us, Kellen and I moved down the alley at a brisk pace, not toward the main thoroughfare but deeper into the quiet areas that would bring us back around to the cobbler.

I knew the boys were following and hoped the baker wouldn't pay them any attention. It didn't take long after we rounded a corner for the boys to start heckling.

"Which do you think will speak to us today?" Alfie asked.

"It will be Cinder for certain," Carver answered. "Snow never speaks. Frozen lips, that one."

"At least for us."

"Maybe today that will change. What do you say, Snow? How about we try a kiss to thaw that heart of ice?"

Laughter echoed behind us, and I untied my bag of biscuits.

"The birds would have liked them," Kellen said.

"I'll save what I can," I said.

Gripping a biscuit, I turned and threw in one fluid motion, immediately reaching for another.

The first brown projectile hit Carver square between the eyes and exploded in a cloud of caramel colored crumbs. He cried out and clutched his forehead.

The second biscuit was already flying through the air and hit Alfie in the temple because he had turned to look at Carver. Alfie grunted and clutched his head.

Grinning, I looked at Samuel. He knew what was happening and batted away the biscuit I'd aimed at his head before it could connect.

"I didn't think you were stupid enough to try taunting us again after the pot," I said. "But, perhaps it only addled your wits enough to think you can win this."

A slow grin spread on Carver's face, and a tingle of awareness alerted me that we were no longer alone.

I pivoted on my heel and saw Maeve striding toward us. Her gaze swept over Kellen and me before focusing on the boys.

"What is the meaning of this?" she demanded.

All three boys shrugged, their expressions innocent.

"We don't know why they started throwing biscuits at us," Alfie said.

"Neither one is stable," Carver said.

"Mental, they are," Samuel added.

"I know very well they are quite stable despite the recent passing of their mother," Maeve said. "I'm curious why you thought to torment two grieving girls. Perhaps you are the ones without wit, and it would be best that I do speak with your parents. I would like your names, please."

Panicked expressions blossomed on their faces before they turned heel and ran.

Maeve looked at both of us.

"Are you two all right?" she asked.

I felt a little guilty that she was concerned about us when we were the ones who had enabled this trouble.

"Yes," Kellen said. "We're well. Those boys said nothing they haven't said before."

"You think they would be smarter and stay away, given your sister's accurate aim," Maeve said with a small smile at me.

I grinned in return.

"Now, I think it's about time we did something so these boys no longer bother you. Do you know their names?"

Kellen and I both gave hesitant nods.

"If you would be kind enough to direct me to the first home, I will indeed speak with their parents."

At each home, we stood behind Maeve as she recapped what she had seen and explained how the boys had been following us during multiple visits to town. When she suggested that the boys were teasing us because "the dear lads" didn't know the proper way to court a young woman who held their interests, I wanted to hide in my room for a good year. That she then offered to teach the boys the proper practice of courtship and suggested that the boys could renew their attempts at courting once they understood the rules only made my mortification worse. Thankfully, she reiterated such a courtship could not be before our mourning periods were up.

We left stunned parents in our wake. I heard one woman say to her husband that he better get the lash out and find their boy. If I hadn't been so horrified about the talk of courting, I would have laughed.

Back in the carriage, Kellen and I quietly stared at Maeve.

"You don't really want them to court us, do you?" I asked.

Maeve laughed.

"As a well-dressed woman of means, if I'd gone into those homes accusing the boys of bad behavior, I doubt they would have been punished. There's a line between those with wealth and those without. However, because I went in there as a woman of means and treated those parents as if we were equal, they listened. They will see a ruined chance at a good match—because distaste was clearly on your faces—and those boys will not be able to sit without pain for a week."

I leaned back into my seat, grinning.

"That is truly brilliant."

"Thank you," she said.

It was good to know that Kellen and I would be able to return to town for the dresses without needing to worry about the usual harassment. If only Maeve could so easily deal with the other issues in my life. That thought robbed me of any remaining humor, and I looked out the window.

I desperately wanted to confide in her. She'd handled the situation with our tormentors with a cleverness I admired. But more importantly, she hadn't thought for a moment that Kellen and I were the problem. Yet, it was that strength of conviction that stayed my tongue. Would she be a strong ally and as passionate as I was about uncovering Mother's murderer? Or would she be like my father and ardently insist on my silence?

Unable to risk the latter, I made up my mind. I alone would continue to bear the burden of knowledge that someone had had a hand in Mother's death. And, I alone would risk myself to expose that person.

Tonight, I would go to the king's estate. My mother's murderer would be named before I slept.

CHAPTER 7

"THANK YOU FOR ANOTHER LOVELY MEAL," I SAID TO JUDITH AS SHE took my plate.

I nudged Kellen under the table with my foot. As usual, she didn't acknowledge it.

"I think I'll go for a walk," I said standing.

Maeve frowned and glanced at the fading light through the window.

"Are you certain you want to walk now? It will be dark soon."

"It's the best time of day to walk. I'll be fine."

"Perhaps you should take Hugh with you," she suggested as Judith picked up Kellen's plate.

I didn't miss the poke that Kellen gave Judith and suppressed my grin.

"There's no need to worry, Maeve," Judith said. "Eloise has walked these woods in the dark plenty of times. There's nothing for her to fear."

"Go on then," Maeve said kindly, "and enjoy your walk. Don't stay out too long, though, or I will worry."

It felt odd hearing those words. My mother hadn't ever worried about my excursions.

Giving Maeve a small smile to show I appreciated her concern, I followed Judith from the room.

"What are you two up to now?" Judith asked when the door closed behind us.

"Up to? I only wanted a walk alone and, given the time of day and Maeve's good sense about appearances, didn't think she'd approve."

Judith snorted as I grabbed my cloak.

"So you thought to pull me in?"

"You're a solid voice of reason, Judith. That's why we always pull you in." I grinned and waved goodbye before letting myself out.

The cool night air wrapped around me as my humor faded. I set out for the king's estate, forgoing the pig and using the path to Mother's grave. The moon's full light guided me easily to the mound of dirt and the small pear tree that was thriving. I paused for a moment to speak to Mother.

"Lady Grimmoire was a sight to see, today," I said softly. "It's nice to have someone champion us. But it should be Father here. I try not to be angry with him. You know I do. But how can I not?"

The wind shook the sapling, and I noted the tiny branches protruding from its wisp-thin trunk. "Don't worry about Kellen or me. We're fine. And I'll keep my promises. I love you."

With that, I continued on my way, following the same route as before. I knew most of these woods as well as I knew the corners of my own home.

Weaving through the trees, I slowly made my way toward the king's estate. The low murmur of voices, the soft baying of dogs, and the occasional snort from a horse reached my ears before I saw the torch lights through the branches.

I stepped behind a thick tree trunk and pulled the dark hood over my head before peeking out to watch the people move about. Many of them wore caps with the king's crest. None looked as small as the boy who'd delivered the necklace, however. That didn't mean he wasn't here, only that I needed patience or perhaps courage to steal into their ranks.

The men moving about the yard were taking pieces of furniture and trunks off the back of several wagons and carrying them into the large retreat.

Kellen and I had always wanted to explore inside but had never been brave enough to break a lock. I couldn't say if it had been due to fear of the Crown's wrath or Mother's.

Amidst all of the workers, I spotted Kaven. The cap was missing from his head this time. So was his jacket. My stomach tightened at the sight of the light cloth straining against his arms as he carried an oilcloth covered painting toward the retreat. He really needed a better tailor…the ass.

"What are we looking at?" Kellen asked suddenly.

I jumped and turned to smack her arm. She grinned at me.

"Pull up your hood and stand behind a tree. We're going to get caught if you're not careful," I said softly.

She moved to the other side of me, still smiling.

"Quite the din they are making. Not conducive for the mending of a broken heart. What do you see when you stare out there?" she asked.

Kellen's appearance changed my plans for the evening. I couldn't very well lurk closer and search for the boy without her demanding to know why. So, I moved away from the tree and tugged her arm to indicate I was ready to leave.

"Nothing that interests me."

We didn't speak again until we put considerable distance between us and the retreat.

"Why did you follow me?" I asked.

"I was curious what warranted a kick to my shin at dinner."

"The scare you gave me while feeding the pig warranted the shin."

She chuckled.

"When I ran into Kaven, he was hedgy about how many men were with him. I want to know why."

"And did you learn why?"

I shook my head.

"Perhaps it's just me, but something feels wrong about the king's sudden use of the retreat. Why now?"

"You mean, why right when Mother dies?" Kellen added softly.

"Yes."

She exhaled slowly.

"You're angry, Eloise, and you want someone to blame. Please believe that I understand. But, finding blame will not change what's done." She reached out and took my hand in hers, stopping our progress.

"Don't let your anger goad you into something you will regret. I can't lose you, too."

I wrapped my arms around her and hugged her fiercely.

"Never, Kellen. You will never lose me. I swear I will never act so rashly as to cause you pain."

She hugged me in return.

"I believe you."

I TURNED this way and that before the mirror. Black wasn't my color. My golden hair and naturally sun-kissed skin robbed the look of its intended severity.

"You look lovely, miss," one of the girls kneeling at my feet said.

"Thank you," I replied automatically. I didn't care how I looked. I hated the dress and what it meant. But, I would endure.

Beside me, Kellen scarcely moved as her skirt was likewise hemmed. Unlike me, the dark color suited her. Pale and regally elegant, my sister would cause many a head to turn while wearing that dress. Not something she would enjoy. Thankfully, our time in these frocks would be short, and there would be more to our day than fittings.

As Maeve had predicted, the arrival of condoling visitors wasn't yet finished. So, she'd sent us to town to fetch our mourning garb without her. Neither Kellen nor I minded the chance to escape. In fact, I was quite looking forward to a stroll through the market.

"We're finished, miss. Would you like us to wrap your other dress?"

"Please," Kellen said, answering for me.

I realized, then, that our walk through the market would be done in our mourning dresses. It killed some of my anticipation.

I glanced at Kellen in the mirror and met her gaze. I knew she understood and felt the same.

When we left the shop, we returned to the wagon with our dresses.

"Where did Judith go?" I asked Hugh, who was charged with watching over any purchases Judith brought to the wagon.

"There's some cook she knows in one of them fancy houses. She went to ask for a pastry recipe to impress Lady Grimmoire."

"We're going to walk to the market," Kellen said.

He nodded and remained quiet as we left him.

One of the best things about Hugh was that he didn't judge us or try to dissuade us from our actions. When I'd asked him why, he told me that was what parents were for. After that, Kellen and I started bringing Hugh treats. He knew a bribe when he saw one and happily ate what we brought and kept quiet about any antics he might overhear or see.

Kellen and I had barely reached the edge of the market when we spotted Carver. He stood in his usual place. As I watched, a woman walked past, and the boy bowed formally. When he straightened, I saw his bruised cheek. He looked across the way at an older man who sat on a short stool. The man's scowl never left his face as he nodded at the boy.

I thought of Maeve's explanation the day before and guilt slowed my steps.

"He was not beaten because of us but because of his own actions. The bruise is his consequence, not yours," Kellen said.

She looped her arm through mine and propelled me forward.

When we came abreast with our tormentor, she stopped and faced him.

He bowed low.

"Miss Kellen. Miss Eloise. Please forgive my coarse behavior these past months. I hope when I come to call, you will be able to look at me with favor."

"Do not come to call, and I will find much favor in your lack of presence," Kellen said.

If it was possible, the boy's expression deadened further; and I felt a wealth of pity for him despite Kellen's warning not to.

"You can call on me," I said. "Do not expect to find favor after only one courtly bow and a few kind words, though. The deeds define the man, not the pretty words that fall from his lips."

Nudging Kellen, I started us on our way again.

"You were too kind to him."

"Perhaps kindness is what he needed. In all the trouble we have caused, never once did Mother or Father raise a hand to us. How differently would we have behaved if they had?" I asked then shrugged. "Does violence beget violence? If so, does kindness then beget kindness? I believe Mother thought so."

Kellen was quiet for several long moments.

"You're very like her," she said finally.

"How so? I've never seen Mother throw biscuits at anyone."

A smile briefly tugged Kellen's lips.

"Your temper might get the best of you, but you do think of others and how they feel. Mother did that."

"You do, too."

She didn't answer.

After doing a loop of the market, we returned to the wagon and found Judith waiting with Hugh.

"We're sorry we took so long," Kellen said.

"Nonsense," Judith said. "It's good for both of you to be seen. Maeve will be pleased you walked the market with your new dresses."

I looked down at my skirt and realized I'd forgotten what I wore.

How would I ever survive three months of nothing but black? The constant reminder of what was now missing in my life would eat holes through me.

"We're ready to leave if you are," Kellen said, releasing me so she could climb aboard the wagon.

I joined her, more than ready to return home so I could escape into the woods once more. Side by side, we silently endured the jostling return to the estate. Kellen excused herself to further organize the attic, which I knew meant she was still reading Mother's letters.

"I think I'll go for a walk and visit Mother," I said.

Judith absently nodded and went inside.

My feet carried me down the familiar path through the trees, and I stopped at the sight of Mother's grave. The sapling, which had been the length of my forearm when I planted it, now stretched to the height of my hips. No longer was it a single shoot but an actual small tree with several branches that jutted several inches from the thin trunk.

I moved closer, knowing there was only one explanation for the tree's rapid growth. Yet, there was no tingle or unnatural spark when I gently touched a branch. Staring at the tree, I hoped it wasn't born from the unnatural magic that had claimed my mother's life but rather from the love that had once nurtured us.

"Be at peace, Mother. Know that we are well and continue to love you, too," I said softly before continuing on.

Unlike the prior evening, the king's estate lay quiet. There was no wagon in the yard or restless horses. The lack of movement and noise made the entire thing feel sinister.

I debated sneaking inside but didn't trust the unexpected silence. Rubbing my arms, I leaned against the tree and huddled further into the warmth of my cloak. I stayed like that until my fingers and nose grew cold then gave up and started home.

It wasn't the building that interested me but the people within. There was no point lingering if there were no people to observe. My thoughts went to Kaven instead of the delivery boy, and I hurried away.

CREEPING DOWN THE STAIRS, I listened to the soft murmur of voices as I carefully edged my way along the wall. Kellen wasn't even out of bed yet. I couldn't imagine Maeve was too pleased with whomever thought to call at this hour.

Successfully reaching the dining room without detection, I slipped inside and went to the kitchen. The warmth of the room enveloped me.

"It's a bit early for a visitor, isn't it?" I asked, looking for my breakfast.

Anne moved about the kitchen in a bit of a frenzy.

"It is. Judith and I aren't yet ready."

"Can I help?"

"Please."

She set me to work while she started something for breakfast. I didn't mind rolling out pastry dough and cutting the required shapes under Anne's instruction, but it wasn't something Judith typically entrusted to anyone.

"Where is Judith?" I asked after I stacked the first set of thin dough disks. Layered with berries, it looked like it would become a delicate, towering treat once baked.

"I'm not sure. She wasn't here when I woke. I think she might have gone to town again to check with the cook about this recipe. There's nothing noted to sweeten it. I know Judith wanted it to be just right to impress Maeve, but I can't wait. We need something to serve the guests."

"What if we sprinkle a bit of sugar on the top?" I asked. "I've seen Judith glaze dough with the whites of an egg to get mint leaves to stick. We could do that to get the sugar to stick."

Anne paused her sorting of berries to consider it.

"We'll do half that way," she said. "On the chance it doesn't work well."

I nodded and started glazing and sugaring. In no time, the treats were baking in the oven, and I was at the table eating my egg.

Kellen strolled into the kitchen just after I cracked my shell. She had dark circles under her eyes and yawned as she walked.

"It's a bit early for visitors, isn't it?" she said, echoing my earlier question.

I grinned as Anne snorted.

"Sometimes, I swear the pair of you speak to each other with your minds."

"That would be a helpful trick," I said.

"Unfortunately, such a trait would likely see us sent to the forest," Kellen said, smothering another yawn. "Is there an extra egg?"

I took pity on her and fetched an egg.

"You were in bed before I was," I said. "How can you be so tired?"

Kellen shrugged and started eating. I considered her for a moment and knew I couldn't allow her to stay in the house another day. She wasn't doing well, and it had nothing to do with Mother's letters. I'd noticed it yesterday, too, in the way she'd been more subdued than usual.

"Since there's a visitor," I said. "Would you like to walk to town with me? We can visit the bookseller and find something to ease our boredom."

"That's a fair distance to walk while carrying books," she said.

"Judith likely took the wagon. We can meet her and gain a ride home."

"Then, a visit to the bookseller sounds like the thing." Kellen took a bite of her egg and nodded as if agreeing with herself.

As soon as we finished and helped Anne take the pretty pastries out of the oven, we left. The sun was out and the breeze absent for a nice change. I breathed deeply and tipped my head back.

"This is perfect."

"It is," Kellen agreed.

We'd barely made it past the shed when Hugh called out.

"Where are you two off to?"

"To town for books," I said.

"Do you want me to hitch the wagon?"

I stopped and frowned.

"The wagon is here?"

"Where else would it be?" he asked.

I glanced at Kellen.

"Judith wouldn't have walked to town with guests arriving at any time," she said.

"I agree. If she's not in town, then where is she?"

Kellen and I split up with Hugh. We checked the privy, the animal pens, Mother's grave, and everywhere else we could think of. Finally, we went inside to speak with Anne.

Her expression turned troubled when we related what we'd learned, and she glanced at the door.

"Should we tell Maeve?"

I understood her hesitation. Although Judith had been with us as long as Kellen and I could remember, would Maeve see Judith as hired help who abandoned her post or like a missing member of our family? Yet, with guests still arriving every day, we would be hard pressed to keep Judith's absence hidden for long.

"Maeve has followed our lead in everything to do with this household," Kellen said. "We have no reason to doubt she will continue to do so."

Anne nodded and left the room. Several minutes later, she returned with Maeve who gave us all a concerned look.

"I sent our visitor off with some pastries for her boys. Where have you all looked for Judith and where haven't we yet checked?" she asked.

We listed off where we'd already been and struggled to think of where else to look.

"While you think, I'm going to send Hugh to town with the wagon on the slim chance Judith did indeed walk. I'm sure our dear cook is well," she said, setting her hand on my arm and giving it a quick squeeze before leaving.

"What about the berry patch?" Kellen asked, pointing at the almost empty clay bowl. "Perhaps she went for more berries."

There was only one type of berry that was ripe this time of year. The tiny, dark fruits matured in the early spring within their thorny bramble. They weren't easy to find or easy to pick, but we were lucky enough to have a single patch on the king's land. It wasn't too far from the house.

"She should be back by now," I said, already moving toward the door.

The yard was quiet as Kellen and I left. My sister's steps matched mine as we hurried through the trees.

The patch came into sight along with a splash of white on the ground. I lifted my skirts and ran forward.

Judith's apron lay in the decaying mess of last year's leaves. Tiny berries rested on the material.

Lifting my gaze, I looked around the patch.

"She's gone," Kellen said flatly.

"But where?"

CHAPTER 8

I BENT AND PICKED UP THE APRON, FEELING THE CHILL IN THE MATERIAL.

"Anne said that Judith was gone when she woke," I said. "That meant Judith had to have come out here at first light."

Even if she had come out in the middle of the night, there wasn't anything in these woods that would bother her. Wild pigs were too hunted to be much of a nuisance. Any deer would be more likely to run than to attack. And wolves hadn't been seen in years. I'd heard rumors that after a sickness had hit Drisdall, they'd been hunted to the point that they'd all fled to the Dark Forest. Nothing here would have harmed her. Certainly nothing would have removed her apron and—

The sudden baying of hounds jerked my attention from the apron in my hands.

"Kellen, go home and tell the others what we found. I'm going to walk further and see if anyone at the king's estate has seen her."

Kellen caught my arm before I could walk off.

"Just observe from a distance," she said. "We can send Hugh to ask after her."

I nodded.

The brisk walk to the king's retreat didn't cool my temper or ease my fear. Where else could Judith have gone, if not there?

Stepping with care, I made my way to the same tree as the night before. Through the bramble and barren branches, I watched Kaven walk the well-trampled yard as he fed the hounds. He was speaking, but the hounds were making too much noise to distinguish his words.

Tree by tree, I moved closer, needing to hear. With the wind in my favor, the hounds ignored me and continued their harassment of Kaven for their meal.

"Down, you greedy mutts. There's enough for all of you. Fresh too. Just this morning."

My eyes widened, and I looked at the meat in his hand again, my stomach rolling.

He stopped throwing meat from the bucket to pat the head of one of the dogs.

"I know how you like it," he said with a chuckle. "Juicy and dripping and still warm."

I gagged.

"You best appreciate the effort I went through. This stag wasn't easy to bring down. But, it had a rack as big as any I've seen."

I breathed out a sigh of relief and let my gaze sweep over the yard. Nothing seemed out of place from the last time I'd watched the retreat. While I still firmly placed the fault of my mother's death on the Crown, I wasn't yet certain I could place Judith's disappearance there, too.

When Kaven turned away, I left my hiding place and returned home.

Maeve was waiting by the kitchen door when I entered the yard. Her worried expression changed to one of relief when she saw me.

"Oh, Eloise. I know I have no right, but I was so worried when Kellen said what you'd found then left you in the woods alone."

She embraced me firmly, and I could feel a tremble running through her. Guilt had me hugging her in return.

"I'm sorry, Maeve. I needed to know if Judith perhaps had a run-in with the king's hounds."

She pulled back to look me in the eye.

"Please tell me you did not accuse the king of taking our housemaid."

I smiled a little, knowing such a thought probably sent her into a panic, given her stance on appearances.

"No. I swear there were no accusations. I didn't even go to the door, just watched from the trees and saw a servant feeding the hounds. They seemed tame and unlikely to attack a person."

"Good. Please don't fret over Judith. I sent Hugh to town to look for her. Perhaps the apron was forgotten from yesterday."

I nodded although I didn't agree. Judith wasn't one to forget an apron in the woods.

Maeve's expression of worry softened as she looked at me. She reached out and patted my cheek.

"I can see you don't believe that's the case. You've suffered so much already. I would spare you any further troubling news if I could."

I believed her and wished again that I could confide in her. That I wouldn't need to carry the weight of my suspicions on my own.

"What is it?" she said with a small frown. "Your expression changed just now."

"It's nothing," I said, easing toward the kitchen door. She didn't stop me.

Inside, Anne was busy cutting more disks.

"Can I help?" I asked as I took off my cloak and hung it on a peg.

"Thank you, but no. This task is to keep me from worrying," Anne said.

"Where's Kellen?"

"Resting," Maeve said as she came in the door behind me. "I insisted. She looked as if she'd barely slept last night."

I nodded and with nothing else to do, drifted from the kitchen and found myself standing in the sitting room near the lounge that Mother favored.

"Was that her spot?" Maeve asked softly behind me.

"Yes. She loved the sun on her face and watching the wind in the trees."

81

Maeve moved to stand beside me, and together we stared out the window for several long moments.

"I know I am not your mother. Or your sister. And that you have no reason to confide in me. But I am here to listen if you have a need."

The offer proved too much of a temptation when I needed it most.

"The day my mother died, we heard hounds in the woods. Thinking it might be poachers, Hugh went to warn them off of the king's land. He returned to say it wasn't poachers, but the king's contingent here to prepare the retreat for the arrival of the king."

I turned from the window and sat in the chair I favored. The one that faced Mother's lounge. Maeve sat beside me in Kellen's usual chair. She didn't speak, just waited for me to continue.

"It wasn't long after that a messenger boy appeared with a wrapped box. We thought it a gift from Father. However, the necklace inside wasn't a gift, and it wasn't from father. The moment the pendant touched Mother's skin, an unnatural light lit her eyes, and she died."

Maeve's expression filled with shock and sorrow. I continued before she could interrupt.

"When I ran into the king's servant, he was wearing the same insignia on his cap as the messenger who'd delivered the necklace. It's the king's insignia." I gripped my hands in my lap, trying not to blurt out the blatant accusation that waited on the tip of my tongue. "I don't believe we will find Judith anywhere in town."

"I see," Maeve said. She looked out the window for a moment before clasping my hand.

"While the evidence surely leads one to believe there is only one conclusion, I cannot help but wonder what purpose the Crown would have for killing your mother. It makes no sense. There is no benefit. I am not disagreeing with you, dear one. I'm only stating that you need to consider carefully what would motivate the single most important person in this kingdom to care enough about your mother to kill her."

"I don't know." I sighed and studied the light pattern on Mother's lounge. Maeve patted my hands and left me to my thoughts.

She was right. There was no logical motivation for the king to concern himself over Mother's fate. Yet, we lived in a home on the king's land for a reason. Why?

I wasn't sure how long I sat there before I heard the faint rumble of a wagon in the yard. Hurrying through the house, I went to the kitchen, the first place Hugh would go if it were him and the last place a guest would go if we were so unfortunate.

The door opened, and Anne stopped her pastry cutting to look up at Hugh.

None of his usual humor lit his eyes. In fact, they looked quite dull.

"There wasn't any sign of her. I asked at all the usual haunts." He paused for a moment then turned around and left without another word.

Anne and I shared a look. Neither of us spoke. She picked up her knife and went back to cutting her pastries.

Angry at fate, I departed the kitchen and found my way upstairs. Kellen was sleeping soundly on top of her covers. The dark circles, that were under her eyes earlier, were missing. Taking care not to wake her, I joined her on the bed. It wasn't something I'd done in a long time. But I needed the comfort of my twin.

The gentle touch of a finger on my eyelid woke me some time later.

I opened my eyes and stared at Kellen.

"You snore," she said softly. "It scared the mice away."

"I do not snore. You do," I said, repeating the same thing we always said to each other when she found me in her bed.

She studied me for a moment.

"Something has been troubling you for a long time. Why haven't you confided in me?"

"Because you're hurt, and I'm older. I'm supposed to protect you."

"Older by a breath and a push doesn't count," she said. "Talk to me, Eloise. I don't like not sharing your thoughts."

"And I don't like you closing yourself off." I gently pulled my sister into a hug. "It's okay to cry, Kellen."

She hugged me in return.

"I couldn't imagine my life without you, Eloise. You are indeed the Cinder to my Snow."

I groaned and pulled back to look at her.

"I shouldn't have forgiven Carver. Those words hurt you too deeply."

She smiled.

"You forgave him because that's who you are. And the words only hurt because they are true. But I like being the way I am. I like pushing the pain aside. I don't like hurting. I don't like feeling alone or knowing that someday, eventually, everyone will leave me. Because that is just how life is meant to be lived. Leave me the protection of my cold heart, my Cinder. Don't burn it away with your love."

I could see the pain in my sister's eyes and her desperation to hold herself together. Nodding, I kissed her cheek.

"Now, tell me what upsets you so much that you think two full grown women can comfortably sleep on this narrow bed."

"I never thought it would be comfortable," I said with a small grin.

She stared at me, and I gave in with a sigh.

"I think the necklace killed Mother."

Kellen closed her eyes.

"I do too."

I should have known she'd noticed. We were far too similar in how we thought.

"The boy who delivered it was wearing the king's insignia, the same as Kaven. Now, with Judith missing…"

My sister opened her eyes and looked at me. In that moment, I saw my mother in her expression.

"Do not let your temper blind you from seeing all of the truth, not just part of it."

"What does that mean?"

She exhaled softly.

"Mother had secrets. I'm not sure what they were. But, they had something to do with our births. Haven't you ever wondered why we live here on the king's land?"

"Someone needs to watch for poachers and keep an eye on the retreat."

"Father is a businessman. A merchant. He isn't a groundskeeper. And he pays Hugh to keep these grounds, not the king's."

"What are you saying?"

"That there might be more happening than we understand, and acting rashly out of some misguided attempt at retribution could see us torn apart."

Now, I understood. She'd known all along that Mother's death had been unnatural and had kept quiet because quiet was safe. It kept us safe.

Her fingers threaded through mine.

"You promised," she said softly. "Forever."

With Judith's absence looming in my mind, I nodded slowly, fearing my promise would be our undoing.

"I will search no more."

"Thank you."

I took my time reading the spines of the books, looking for a title that sounded interesting. When I found an intriguing one, I plucked it from the shelf and opened to the first page.

"There needs to be a better way to determine what a book is about," Kellen said, snapping hers closed.

"Ask Mr. Bentwell," I said with a smirk. "He knows every book in here so well. He will tell you about them for hours if you asked."

"You're a horrible sister," Kellen said without any rancor.

My grin widened.

"Is there anything I can help you ladies find?" Mr. Bentwell called from his desk in the corner.

"No, thank you, Mr. Bentwell," Kellen said with a gracious smile. "We do so enjoy browsing the selection on our own. One never knows what will inspire the mind."

I had to turn my back to hide my mirth. She'd used his own quote against him. The scholar loved his books. He lent them out for a coin or two to those who had earned his trust. Mother first introduced us to Mr. Bentwell years ago when Kellen and I were still missing our front teeth and just learning our letters. Back when Mother still left the house occasionally.

My humor faded, and I closed the book.

"Actually, Mr. Bentwell," I said turning, "I could use your guidance. Grief eats at me, and I wish to escape to another place. Somewhere happier. Lighter. Can you recommend such a book?"

He looked at me with an understanding light in his eyes.

"I have just such a book about a maid who frees a man from a curse. It's not commonly borrowed, which is a shame. It's a lovely book with pretty drawings."

He stood from his desk and shuffled toward the shelves just to his right where he kept his favorite volumes. Neither Kellen nor I usually browse there for fear of a lengthy conversation. Today, a distraction was just what I needed, though.

Judith had never returned yesterday. Or this morning. Seeing Mother die had been a blow I never wished to repeat. Yet, the ignorance of Judith's fate continued to wear at me, unraveling my thoughts and creating a deeper grief that restlessly prodded my imagination to conjure every possible demise she might have met.

Mr. Bentwell suddenly plucked a tome from the shelves, jarring me from the darkening spiral of my thoughts.

"Here you are," he said. "I was terribly aggrieved to hear of your mother's passing. Please accept my sympathies." He plucked another volume from his shelf and handed it to me. "Give this one to your sister. I hope I'll see both of you again soon."

And with that, we were summarily dismissed from his shop.

Kellen hooked her arm through mine and tugged me away, likely before Mr. Bentwell could change his mind and start talking.

"He's sweet," I said when the door closed behind us.

"He is," she agreed.

We walked for a time toward the market.

"I hate town," Kellen said. "But I find I have no desire to return home, either. I'm a person without a proper place."

I briefly set my head on her shoulder, not an easy task given her four-inch height deficiency.

"I feel the same. These books will help. I do think we should also look at the paints. We have too much idle time on our hands. Our minds need distraction," I said, quoting our mother.

"Painting is a far more sensible suggestion than gatherings and cakes," she said, patting my head before lightly pushing me away.

I grinned just as Alfie stepped from the shadows. He froze when he saw us. We did the same.

For a moment, his eyes narrowed, and I wondered how I would ever explain a damaged book's spine to Mr. Bentwell when Alfie's expression cleared.

"I have no intention of courting either of you," he said with barely concealed anger. "My actions weren't some concealed attraction. I don't like you. It's that simple."

"Look, Kellen. Asses truly can speak. I can't say it's an improvement over the braying, though."

"I quite agree," Kellen said.

Instead of bristling, Alfie gave us a shallow bow.

"I shall do my best to avoid you shrews and would appreciate the same courtesy."

"With pleasure," I said.

He turned on his heel and stomped away.

"Why is it he doesn't like us?" I asked.

"It was probably that time you—"

"Don't say it," I said, remembering.

"—spit the ale in his face in front of his friends."

I shook my head. Kellen and I had snuck away from Mother during one of our jaunts into town and wandered too close to Alfie's family alehouse. I'd just picked up a discarded tankard curious to taste what everyone was drinking when Kellen had whispered in my ear, "What if it's cat piss?"

My sister's pranks, while entertaining, often saw me in trouble. However, that time, the prank had doomed both of us. Those words and Alfie's unfortunate timing had apparently sealed a lifelong hatred.

"I couldn't have timed that better if I had tried," she said.

"I'm still of a mind that you had tried."

She grinned, showing a rare glimpse of humor, and we made our way back to the wagon where Hugh waited.

"Finished?" he asked, his gaze missing its usual humor.

"Yes," Kellen said, settling onto the seat beside him.

The ride home was swift and quiet under grey skies. I'd hoped to read outside to avoid whichever guest Maeve entertained in the sitting room; however, rain started to fall just as the wagon rolled into the yard. Kellen and I held the books to our chests and ran for the kitchen door.

Anne looked up from her place by the fire. She'd been sitting quietly, staring into the flames.

"I've been thinking," she said. "What if Judith went to her family?"

Kellen and I shared a glance. Judith would have said something, not just up and left. However, Anne, like the rest of us, was struggling to understand what had happened to Judith. We all needed answers.

"Perhaps," Kellen said. "It's a few hours ride, correct?"

Anne nodded.

"We can send Hugh to check," I said, setting my book on the table.

I left the kitchen, pulling up my hood to run through the light rain to the shed where Hugh stayed. Barely inside the doors, I heard something. It was like a thump of flesh against something. I frowned and slowed my steps, wondering if I should retreat or announce my presence. I did neither.

Creeping forward, I peered through the cracks between the boards separating Hugh's quarters from the carriage house. I saw Hugh hitting a post repeatedly. He stopped suddenly and hung his head.

"I need you. End my torment and return to me."

I covered my mouth in surprise. Judith had been close to my mother's age. Close to Maeve's age. Hugh was several years younger, nearer Kellen and me than Judith. I'd never considered that they might have had feelings for one another.

Retreating to the door, I called out for Hugh.

"Just a moment," he called back.

When he appeared, his anguish was well-hidden.

"Anne suggested that we check with Judith's family. Would you be willing to ride there today, despite the rain?"

"Have you spoken to Maeve about this?" he asked.

I shook my head.

"We still have a visitor. Please Hugh. Judith means so much to us all."

He ran a hand through his hair, and I saw his raw knuckles but didn't comment.

"The rain is likely to get heavier. As much as I want to go, it would be foolish to risk the horse if she truly is there. I will leave as soon as the weather clears. Please let Maeve know of our plans."

He turned and closed himself back inside his room. With a heavy heart, I ran to the house to share the news with the others. Hugh's love for Judith, I kept to myself.

CHAPTER 9

"Don't be greedy," I said, scolding the fattest hen in the yard.

I threw more grain to the others and she ran to the new pile.

A sound from the shed drew my attention, and I watched as Hugh led out one of our horses. After two days of rain, I'd woken to peer out the window at a clear sky. Although dawn had barely been on the horizon, I'd rushed to dress and do my chores so I would be in the yard for Hugh's departure.

"Are you leaving, then?" I asked.

He nodded.

Shaking out my apron, I went to him as he mounted. The horse nuzzled into my palm, likely hoping for a treat, when I reached out to pet her nose.

"A safe journey to both of you," I said.

Hugh looked at the house for a moment before meeting my gaze.

"I will return before dinner." With that, he clucked to the horse, and the pair left the yard at a steady trot.

Chores finished, I returned to the house and crept back upstairs where Kellen still slept. We'd both stayed up far too late, reading by candlelight. She'd finished her book by the time the candle went out. I had a few more pages to mine and settled in to read. However, the story ended far too quickly, and I said farewell to the distraction. It had been a welcome one during the rain.

Closing the book, I watched my sister sleep and wondered what we would do today to keep ourselves occupied.

With Hugh gone, a ride into town for a new book wouldn't be feasible. Although there was another horse and Kellen and I both knew how to ride, I didn't think riding double while in our mourning garb would portray an image of which Maeve would approve.

"What are you thinking?" Kellen asked without opening her eyes.

"That I don't like when you do that."

She grinned lightly and looked at me.

"Did you finish your book?"

"Yes. I saw Hugh off this morning."

"Ah."

She rose for the day, and I accompanied her to the kitchen where we ate a quiet breakfast.

"I was thinking I would take the pig for a walk to hunt for more truffles," Anne said. "After all that rain, we should find a good amount. The mushrooms would go well in a stew with some of the venison in the cold storage."

"Are you sure?" I asked. "I can do it."

Anne shook her head.

"It would do me some good to leave the quiet of the kitchen."

We watched her take her cloak and walk out. The door had barely closed when the one leading to the dining room opened.

"Good morning, girls," Maeve said. She went straight to the board and took the egg Anne had waiting for her. "Did you sleep well? I thought I saw light from your room just before I fell asleep."

"We stayed up late reading," Kellen said. "The story was too intriguing to put aside."

Maeve smiled as she joined us.

"I do love a good story. Do you plan to return to town today for another?"

"Hugh left this morning," I said.

"I see. Tomorrow, then," she said with a kind smile. "Where is Anne this morning?"

"She took the pig for a walk. She's looking for truffles."

Maeve frowned.

"Alone?"

I felt my stomach dip and glanced at Kellen. Why hadn't we thought of that?

"The pig is quite large and much slower than Anne. If something is out there looking for a feast, I'm sure it will be the pig and not Anne who suffers," Kellen said, taking my hand and giving it an encouraging squeeze.

"I'm sure you're right," Maeve said. "Forget I said anything."

Outside, we heard the sound of a carriage. Maeve sighed and pushed aside her half-eaten egg.

"I will see you two at dinner. If you need me, you know where I'll be."

I nodded and watched her go.

"Do you think we should help her today?" I asked.

"Help her to do what? She's more skilled at social niceties than we are. If we went in there, we'd likely say something that would give the gossips exactly what they want."

I knew Kellen was right but still felt bad that Maeve had to speak with every unwelcomed busybody who lived in the kingdom of Drisdall.

"I think I'm going to retreat to the attic today," Kellen said, throwing her egg shell into the fire. "What are you going to do?"

I shrugged.

"I'll find something."

As soon as the door closed behind her, I grabbed my cloak and rushed outside. The tracks from the pig were easy to follow from the yard. Because of the rain, my portly friend left deep pits in the earth with each step.

I caught up with Anne on the other side of Mother's grave. The pig was rooting around on his tether, and Anne was looking up at the sky. The peace on her face begged for solitude. So, I kept my distance and did not intrude.

The distant baying of hounds interrupted the silence of the woods several times before she had a healthy pile of mushrooms in her little basket.

"Come, pig," she said. "Let's return you to your pen."

I followed her through the trees but stopped at Mother's grave, letting Anne continue home on her own.

With the plentiful rain, the pear tree had grown again. Far too much to be natural, though. It reached the height of my head and had branches the length of my arms. When I sat on the bench to study it, a small, darkly colored bird landed on one of the thin branches.

"What do you think of the tree?" I asked it. The bird chirped back at me, singing a pretty song. I listened for a while and thought of Mother.

When the song finished, I thanked the bird.

"Will you sing for her again tomorrow even if I'm not here?"

It took flight, roosting in a larger tree not far away.

"I hope that's a yes." I sighed and looked at the dirt covering Mother's grave. The rain and time had reduced the height of the mound. It looked barely more than a small bump now. Little shoots of green were sprouting from the ground, nothing growing as vigorously as the pear tree.

I stood and touched one of the branches.

"Watch over her. Keep what's left of her safe."

When I returned to the kitchen, the truffles were on the board, and the kitchen was empty. Voices echoed from the sitting room. With nothing else to do, I went in search of Kellen and found her in the attic, reading a letter.

"Haven't you read them all yet?"

"Twice actually."

"Then let's walk to town. Maeve is with a visitor, and there's nothing else to do."

"We'll take something to carry more than one book home this time," she said, standing.

The pair of us slipped past the sitting room and paused in the kitchen.

"We should leave a note so no one worries," Kellen said. It wasn't easy finding a slip of parchment for an idle note. It required more sneaking past the sitting room door to get to Father's study.

"How much can one woman need to say?" I said softly to Kellen. "First, it was her daughter's marriage, and now it's her husband's business ventures."

"Talking about one's success makes one feel more important," Kellen said when the kitchen door closed behind us.

"Bragging isn't becoming."

"Based on her lack of comment, I'm certain Maeve hears it for what it is."

We scrawled a quick note and left it on the block by the truffles.

The day was warming and the walk to town pleasant.

"Have you given our lives as liberated women of travel any further thought?" I asked Kellen when we reached the outskirts.

"Not really."

"Why not? I'm entirely serious."

"Which is why I don't need to give it thought. You have a way of making things happen, Eloise. If you want us to travel the world, we will. Thought on my part isn't necessary."

I huffed a breath.

"Of course it is. I need to know where you want to travel."

A small smile tugged at her lips at the sign of my exasperation. She enjoyed my flare for emotion even as she kept hers in check.

"I would love to see the snow in the north. I heard it can become so deep a woman can't walk in it with skirts. Pants are necessary."

I paused to look at her.

"Women wearing pants?"

She nodded, her smile growing.

"I can't tell if you're being serious now or not."

She laughed which made me think the latter.

"Fine. We shall travel to the north, and I will see for myself if there are indeed women wearing pants in order to walk through the snow."

We reached Mr. Bentwell's shop and let ourselves in. This time, instead of quietly browsing in hopes of avoiding a conversation, I tugged Kellen right up to his desk.

"Eloise and Kellen Cartwright," he said with a welcoming smile. "I didn't think I would see you again so soon."

"We devoured these books," I said, removing the books in question from the bag. "Would you have any others like them? Perhaps by the same authors?"

He chuckled.

"I do have several others that I think you'll like if those struck your fancy."

He stood and shuffled toward his prized shelves, sliding the books back into place before selecting new ones.

"Could we perhaps borrow two each this time?" Kellen asked.

"You've been bitten by the book bug, I see," he said. Without hesitation, he took two more from the shelves. "These will suit you, Kellen." He handed her two thick tomes. "And these will suit you, Eloise."

In no time, we were walking toward the market for a bite to eat.

"I should have read your book before returning it," I said. "This time, we should trade."

"If you wish."

We both inhaled deeply, catching the same scent. Following our noses, we ordered two fresh meat pies and started home.

"What comes after we see the north?" I asked.

"I don't know. What do you want to see?"

I thought about it for a moment.

"Turre. Or maybe somewhere even further south. Somewhere magic isn't banned."

Kellen gave me a curious look.

"Why?"

"Have you seen the pear tree?" I asked.

"I have."

"That's not natural. I'm certain it's growing like that because of magic. Is it residual magic because of Mother's death or is it something else? So many of our questions would already be answered if we had even a basic understanding of magic, I think."

"I see."

"Not that I'm pursuing anything, just idly dreaming about how it would be nice to have an explanation of how these things happened."

She gave me a small smile.

"I wouldn't mind knowing more, either. North then south it is. Perhaps we then go west before we return home to the east."

We idled away the distance with speculation over what we might see and learn and do in each area of our travels. When we reached the lane to our house, I noted fresh tracks and pointed them out to Kellen.

"One muddy rut looks like the other," she said with a shrug. "Do not get your hopes up that we will have a quiet house."

We passed the trees protecting the drive, and I groaned when I saw a second carriage had joined the first.

"It looks like you were right," Kellen said. "Those tracks were fresh."

We entered through the kitchen and set our books on the table.

"The note's still here," Kellen said, looking at the block.

The truffles hadn't moved either.

Before I had time to worry, the murmur of voices reached our ears. I moved to the dining room door and pushed it ajar enough to hear Maeve thank our guests and wish them a speedy journey.

I motioned to Kellen, and she stepped into the hall the moment the door closed.

"Have you seen Anne?" Maeve asked. "She didn't bring in tea or answer the door. I'm worried she didn't return from her walk."

"She returned," Kellen said. "There are truffles on the block."

Maeve's gaze grew more concerned.

"Has Hugh arrived?"

"I'm not certain," I said. "We just returned from town. We went for more books."

"Let us not worry just yet," Maeve said, gently herding us toward the kitchen. "I'll fix us some tea, and we'll wait for Anne. If she doesn't return by the time Hugh does, we will go look for her."

In the kitchen, Kellen found us something to eat while I made tea and Maeve paced. She checked the window constantly until I heard a soft, "about time." Opening the door, Maeve strode out.

Kellen and I followed and saw Hugh riding into the yard. Maeve hurried to his side.

"Anne's missing," she said. "You must find her. Check the woods."

He stared at Maeve for a long moment before nodding and sliding off the horse.

"We should split up," I said. "While there's still daylight."

Maeve shook her head.

"No. Hugh will look, and we will stay in the house."

"Four sets of eyes will cover more ground than one," I insisted.

Maeve came to me and took my hand in hers.

"Two people have already gone missing. I will not lose either of you."

While I understood her concern, I couldn't let fear of my own well-being stop me from helping someone I cared about. I glanced at Hugh, who was taking the saddle from the horse, and saw my chance.

"I understand," I said to Maeve. "Hugh, can I unsaddle Sugar for you? There's too little light left to waste."

Maeve released me as he nodded and started for the trees.

"Kellen, Anne will likely be chilled and hungry when she returns. Can you make something for dinner?" I asked.

"Of course," she said, already turning to the door.

Without looking at Maeve, I went to the horse.

"I'll brush you down, sweet thing," I crooned taking the reins. "You must be hot and tired from the long journey." I led her to the trough where she drank her fill. When she was done, I looked at the yard and saw it empty.

"Sorry, girl," I said softly, leading her into the stall. "A brushing will need to wait. Anne needs to be found before dark, and one man alone will not be enough."

I left her in the barn and snuck around the back to the woods. A familiar, low distant whistle echoed in the trees. The tune was one I'd often overheard when Hugh worked alone. I paused for a moment, trying to determine where he was and decided he was searching the area closest to the house.

Walking softly, I started down the path toward Mother's grave and listened carefully. The sound grew more distant, confirming my guess about Hugh's location. Nothing else moved once the whistle faded. The sound of my own passing and my gentle breathing kept me company as I watched the ground.

I saw my footprints and Anne's coming and going. Nothing else. My gaze swept the trees, my skin prickling. I felt watched. Halting, I turned a slow circle and saw nothing but the fading light of day.

Shaking off the feeling, I continued forward until I reached the clearing.

A bit of white against the new green robbed me of my hope. Woodenly, I walked forward and picked up Anne's cap. It hadn't been here this morning. That meant she'd returned to this spot after I'd watched her go to the house. Like Judith, Anne had disappeared.

"It's an odd tree, isn't it?" a voice said behind me.

I whirled to face Kaven. He was standing not far from me, facing my mother's grave and the pear tree.

"Where did you come from?" I demanded. "Why are you here?"

"Interesting questions coming from the girl who likes to lean against trees and watch other people."

He'd seen me but never acknowledged my presence? Why? Pulse racing, I stared at him, unsure and waiting for what he would do next.

"Nothing to say?" he asked, glancing at me before resuming his study of the tree. "It's growing much too quickly. Almost as if by magic."

He turned to face me and glanced at the cap in my hands.

"That doesn't belong to you."

My insides started to quake with rage. He knew and was baiting me. All of it. Mother's death by magic...the disappearances of our housemaids. After the delivery boy, Kaven had been in the woods. The same woods where people now disappeared. And, he'd been wearing the same hat as the boy.

Words piled in my mouth, choking me as I held my tongue. This man wasn't the King, only a representative. Yet, I couldn't accuse him. Not without proof when anything he said would likely hold more weight to the King than anything I could say.

"Last time we met, you had plenty to say," he said, stalking closer to me.

The deep blue of his gaze bore into mine. I raged at him. He'd taken so much. No more.

"Speak now, Eloise," he said when he towered over me. "Save yourself."

While meeting his gaze, I tugged back my long skirts and sharply lifted my knee. The connection to his groin was solid and true. With a grunt, his face reddened then paled as he cupped his testicles and slowly fell over.

I leaned over him, knowing I had several moments.

"I will see you hanged for what you've done," I said harshly. "I swear it on my mother's name, I will see you—"

Something caught my ankle, and I suddenly found myself on my back with a very angry man pinning me down. A vein throbbed in his forehead as his bloodshot gaze found mine.

"Pray, what have I done to deserve that?"

Each pain-laced word fell on my deaf ears. The thrumming of my heart and the certainty of my own demise robbed me of thought as my hand searched the ground for what I knew was nearby. My fingers closed over a rock, and I immediately brought it down on Kaven's head.

The man slumped on top of me.

Fear, and a frantic amount of wiggling, saw me free of his weight and running toward the house. It wasn't until I'd almost reached the door that I realized I'd dropped Anne's cap. I halted and looked back.

Kaven stood near a tree, leaning on it heavily, watching me. Our gazes locked across the distance. He held up the cap then turned and disappeared into the trees.

CHAPTER 10

KELLEN WAS IN THE KITCHEN WHEN I RETURNED SHAKEN AND MUDDY. I washed and said nothing about what had happened even though I saw the question in her gaze. When I was changed, I returned to the kitchen to help her with dinner.

Maeve joined us at the table. We'd just served ourselves when Hugh entered.

"I didn't find any sign of Anne," he said.

And still, I said nothing. What could I say without damning myself or Kellen in some way? I felt certain it was magic that killed Mother. That both Judith and Anne went missing less than a fortnight later couldn't be coincidence. Something was happening here. But what? It most certainly had to be tied to Kaven and the Crown. However, if I started crying magic, the king's men would descend, and it would be the remnants of my family who would suffer.

I looked at Kellen and found her watching me. I could almost hear her thoughts reminding me what I'd promised her. Bowing my head, I stared at the stew in my bowl.

"Thank you for looking, Hugh," Maeve said. "Join us."

Hugh usually never ate in the house, preferring to take his meals alone. However, this time he agreed. Kellen fetched him a bowl of stew and placed it on the opposite end of the table from Maeve.

Four people at the table. Just as it had been before Mother died. Yet, everything was different. I tried not to think about it and took a bite of the stew.

"I don't want you in the woods alone anymore," Maeve said after a moment of quiet eating. "I promised your father that I would keep you safe. I do not intend to break my word. It's too dangerous out there."

I nodded in quiet agreement. The woods were far too dangerous with Kaven lurking about.

After dinner, Kellen and I retreated to our room. She watched me close the door and sat on the edge of her bed. Of course she'd known I wouldn't brush the horse.

In a hushed voice, I told her what had transpired. The cap. Kaven's sudden appearance. My narrow escape.

"I want to ignore it," Kellen said. "To turn away and let someone else deal with this, but you're right. Mother, Judith, and now Anne. I don't believe this will stop."

"I agree. But what are we supposed to do? How are we supposed to stop this?"

"Perhaps we should speak with Maeve."

I shook my head.

"I did speak to her of my suspicions. Her opinion is the same as yours. That we cannot say anything for fear of being persecuted ourselves."

"Then, what do you suggest?"

"We now know that Kaven is involved. The messenger might have been unaware of the purpose for his delivery. The only part I'm uncertain about is the backing of the Crown. If the king knows of this, no amount of proof will save us."

"Then we run," Kellen said.

"How will we convince Maeve to—"

"No, Eloise. We run."

I nodded.

"All right. But, first, we try to find out if Kaven's actions are his own or that of the King's."

"Agreed."

As I lay in bed that night, my mind raced regarding how I could possibly determine the Crown's involvement. It wasn't until the sliver of the moon was high, its weak light shining through the window, that a fitful slumber claimed me.

When the sun rose, I was dressed and ready. This time, I was the one to poke my sister in the eye.

She groaned and rolled to her back before looking up at me.

"Why must you always wake so early?"

"I have a plan," I said quietly.

She sat up, her dark braid falling over her shoulder to her waist.

"Tell me."

I sat on the edge of her bed so we were close.

"We need to check the inside of the retreat for signs of magic. If we find some, we can anonymously—"

The soft knock on our door caused us both to jump. Kellen's gaze locked with mine for a moment. We would speak later. I went to answer the knock.

Maeve waited in the hall, already dressed for the day.

"Good morning. I'm glad you're already awake. Is Kellen? May I speak with you both?"

I opened the door wider and invited her in.

She smiled good morning to Kellen then began to pace the small confines of our room.

"We have a problem we can no longer keep to ourselves," she began. "We need to report the mysterious disappearances. Yet, I worry how such a thing will reflect on this household, and more importantly, the pair of you. In addition to reporting Judith and Anne missing, we will be challenged with finding replacements." She held up her hands as if to forestall any argument from us. "These replacements need not be permanent. If, no, when Judith and Anne return, of course they will be welcomed back. But, with the visitors and the rumors of the king's impending visit, we need help."

"I agree," Kellen said. "However, we need to be discreet in reporting the issue or it will make finding new help harder."

Maeve's expression turned grateful, and she exhaled hugely.

"I was so worried you would think ill of me for suggesting that we bring in others to work."

"Not at all," I said.

"It is the only practical course of action," Kellen agreed.

"Very good. Then, I'd like you both to dress and accompany Hugh and me to town. I cannot leave you home alone. Not with..." She shook her head.

"We'll be down in a few minutes," Kellen said.

I closed the door after Maeve left and shared a look with Kellen.

"It would be ideal to check the retreat while they're gone," I said.

Kellen shook her head and started to change.

"I disagree. If we find something and need assistance, we would be alone. Best to wait until we return. Besides, going to town can benefit us."

"In what way?"

"We might be able to learn what the king is up to and why the retreat is being prepared. All this trouble started with that, did it not?"

I agreed and willingly followed her down the stairs.

The trip to town didn't take long in the comfort of the carriage. And this time, we didn't need to cover our noses. Only a hint of dank and damp remained.

"I've asked Hugh to stop near the market so you can shop while we're here. I would prefer you not be present when I speak with the king's guard. The conversation will likely be upsetting, and I wouldn't put you through that. When I've finished, Hugh and I will return and find you."

Since Maeve's plan aligned with our goals, Kellen and I quickly agreed and found ourselves walking the market district with the early morning crowd.

"You know there's only one place to go for this kind of gossip," Kellen said.

"Try not to make me spit my ale this time."

We made our way to Alfie's family alehouse and found a table near the window. This close to the market district, Crumbs and Casks maintained a respectability most alehouses did not. A serving girl came to offer us a drink and some breakfast.

"Have you heard anything about the king retiring to his hunting retreat soon?" Kellen asked before the girl could leave.

"Not a thing. It wouldn't make sense for him to go there now, what with his son due back and all that."

"The prodigal prince is returning?" I asked in disbelief.

The girl nodded. "I heard that he found himself a wife during his time away. Some Lord's daughter from the far north. I'm excited to see what style of dresses the gentry will start wearing, trying to impress the girl."

"What if she wears pants?" Kellen asked. "I heard that the women wear pants that far north."

The serving girl looked intrigued before Alfie's father called her name and she hurried away.

"I wonder if Kaven is really there on behalf of the king, then," Kellen said softly.

"What we need is information from a source that is more likely to know the king's intentions."

"No one within the king's inner circle would ever consider sharing that information with the likes of us."

"The king's inner circle aren't the only ones privy to the comings and goings of the royal family."

"The king's guard? They would never speak to us about such matters, either."

She was right, but I still regretted not being with Maeve at the moment. Maybe Kellen and I would have overheard something.

Kellen's eyes lit up.

"You know who may know something?"

"Who?"

"The dressmaker. These guards have wives, don't they? Husbands confide in wives, and a good many wives love to gossip."

"Perfect. And we must stop in to check on our dresses," I said with a grin.

After we finished our meal, we left the alehouse and made our way to Madame Todd's. She wasn't surprised to see us and immediately showed us to the back rooms for a fitting.

"Your timing is impeccable," she said. "We just finished your gowns last night."

The dresses she produced were beautiful with the exception of all the black material. Kellen and I changed and stood in our positions for the hemming.

"Have you heard anything about the king retiring to his hunting retreat soon?" Kellen asked again.

"Not the king but the prince," one of the seamstresses said. "It would seem he's not yet ready to return to palace life and wants the solitude of the retreat."

"And his wife is okay with living in the woods?" Kellen asked.

"So it would seem," another said. "Not much is known about his wife."

"Other than she comes from the north, correct?" I said.

The girl nodded.

"I hear the women wear pants in the north," Kellen added. She was good at directing the conversation to keep the appearance of idle gossip.

They continued to share unimportant tidbits, such as the length of time the prince had been away, which we all knew; and the fact that the King was impatient for his son's return so the next generation might produce an heir. Again, more common knowledge.

"Perhaps that's the reason for the retreat," Kellen said, making my jaw drop. She laughed at me. "What? Mr. Bentwell's book collection includes some romantic pieces, too."

That set the girls giggling, and a few vowed to visit Mr. Bentwell.

When we were finished, they wrapped the gowns then led us out to the waiting room. Luck was on our side that we'd only just left with our heavy packages when we spotted Maeve walking toward us.

She smiled in greeting. "I'm so glad you remembered the gowns. It completely slipped my mind. Come, we had better return to the estate. With no one there to answer the door and turn visitors away, the gossips are sure to speculate on what is happening."

We followed her back the way she'd come.

"It's understandable you forgot," Kellen said. "You've been dealing with so much for us."

"The dresses are lovely," I added. "Thank you for selecting them."

Maeve smiled back at us.

"It was no trouble. I hope you didn't need to stand too long to get them fitted."

"Not too long," I said.

"The girls distracted us with conversation," Kellen added as we reached the carriage.

"Oh? Anything interesting?" Maeve asked, letting us enter first.

Kellen was dying to share the news just as much as I, but I was faster as we settled into the carriage for the journey home.

"It's not the king who's coming to the retreat but the prince and his new wife," I said.

Maeve gave us an indecipherable look before smiling kindly.

"Yes, I just heard the same at the guard house."

"Did they offer any help in finding Judith and Anne?" Kellen asked.

"Unfortunately, two housemaids do not warrant their attention. If someone of more note goes missing in the same manner, then perhaps the guard will be interested. Until then..." She lifted a shoulder and looked out the window, visibly upset.

The rest of the carriage ride was made in silence. When we stopped before our stable, we saw a carriage already waiting in the yard.

"Drat and bother," Maeve said under her breath.

"I'll fix some tea and bring it in to you," Kellen said.

"No. You can't be seen serving tea. But if you're willing to fix it and leave it in the dining room, I'll gladly fetch it from there."

Hugh helped Maeve down then took our packages into the kitchen while Maeve went directly to the visitors. We waited until everyone was inside before sneaking into the house through the kitchen door.

Hugh stood by the hearth, looking at the flames.

"Are you all right?" I asked softly.

"No. I feel so empty inside. Don't leave the house."

He turned and strode out. Both Kellen and I watched after him.

"He seems odd," Kellen said after a moment.

"I think he was in love with Judith."

Kellen looked at me, her brows high.

"Why do you think that?"

"I saw him hitting a post after he couldn't find her. And heard him say he felt empty without her."

"Poor Hugh," she said, her expression changing to one of pity before carefully clearing.

I knew how she felt. If she let pity in, she'd open herself to all the other emotions waiting to take control. Yet, closing herself off wasn't going to help her deal with the drastic changes that continued occurring in our lives.

"Is it ever going to get better for us?" I asked.

Kellen came and wrapped her arms around me.

"Don't give up hope. Not you, Eloise."

I hugged her in return.

"I'm trying not to. I just can't bear the thought that Judith and Anne might be lost to us for good."

"I know. But remember, we can't change what's already happened. We can only steer the course for our future."

I nodded and helped make the tea. When we were finished, we left the tray in the dining room before returning to the kitchen. Without speaking, we grabbed our cloaks and slipped out the door, ignoring Hugh's protective warning.

The walk through the woods was peaceful. Birds chirped, and small animals chittered at us from still barren branches.

"It's starting to smell like spring," Kellen said quietly.

I inhaled deeply, loving the smell.

A soft sound drew our attention. We paused and listened. I pointed to our right but motioned for Kellen to continue to follow me in the direction in which we'd been headed. Circling around, I spotted Kaven through the trees and stopped Kellen from going any further. He'd obviously noted my presence before, and I didn't want to risk him coming after me…us…again.

Bow gripped in his hand, he had his head tipped up to the sky. As I watched, he lifted the bow and rapidly fired two arrows with barely a glance before looking at the sky again.

Even from this distance, I could see the rage in his stance.

"Where are you?" he roared, scaring the birds and setting my heart hammering.

Motioning to Kellen, we backed away. But not toward home. Once he was out of sight, I lifted my skirts and hurried toward the retreat. Who knew how much time we had before he returned there?

Neither Kellen nor I spoke when the king's lodge came into view. She followed me to the back where I tried the door and found it locked. I looked at the stone work and started tying my skirts together.

"Are you sure?" Kellen whispered.

I nodded.

"Hide in the shrubs and call if he comes. I'll leave through the same window."

She moved back to stand watch as I used the stones to climb to a second story window. My fingers grew numb in moments from the damp and the cold on the rock, and my feet slipped twice. But I'd fallen that height before and knew it wouldn't hurt. Much.

Bracing my weight on my forearm, I used my other hand to push at the window and was rewarded when it swung inward without a sound. My muscles protested as I hauled myself over the ledge, but I made it.

Standing carefully, I looked around at the bedroom. Well-stuffed bed. Neat linens. Dust free baseboards. No cobwebs on the ceiling. A room meant for the royal family, then.

On light feet, I crept down the hall and peeked into each room. I wasn't sure what evidence of a murder or magic would look like, but I felt certain I would know it when I saw it.

In a room at the far end of the hall, I found a multitude of covered furniture and other items. Some of them looked familiar, and I realized they were the ones I saw unloaded from the wagons. I frowned as I studied the number. So many things to be unloaded then shoved away for storage. Why not air them in preparation? Unless, perhaps, the prince and his wife's arrival was delayed or unknown. That would be an explanation for Kaven's anger just now.

I lifted the cover from a few pieces and admired the pretty floral designs. After finding a box with lavish jewels, it became obvious that all of the items belonged to the princess. Tucking the box away, I moved to leave. A partially exposed painting behind the door caught my eye. It was a woman's bare shoulder.

Creeping closer, I pulled back the oil-cover and stared at a young woman who looked very similar to me. Her blue eyes seemed to lock with mine as I studied the blonde hair piled high on her head and threaded with ribbon to match the green of her dress. The painter had perfectly blushed her cheeks. Yet, she lacked life. She looked tired.

And I knew why.

A familiar green amulet lay nestled on her breast. A glint of light reflected on the stone, hinting at an unnatural life I knew it possessed.

Kellen's soft dove call reached my ears, and I hurried to cover the painting. Racing down the hall, I made it back to the bedroom when I heard the front door open.

Kellen was below, motioning for me to hurry. I didn't hesitate to throw my leg over the ledge and start my descent, not wasting time to close the window. I dropped the last few feet and took off at a run, trusting my sister to keep up with me.

We didn't stop until we reached the clearing where we collapsed in a heap on the bench beside Mother's grave.

"Did you find anything?" she asked, her breathing ragged but her voice soft.

"A picture of a woman wearing the same necklace as the one delivered to Mother."

"Was the King in the picture? Or the Prince?"

I shook my head. "Only her."

She sighed, and I understood why. A woman wearing the same necklace wasn't the evidence we needed, but clearly Mother's death was linked to the royal family. I wanted to rage and kick something. However, the sudden baying of hounds warned me I didn't have the time to lose my temper.

"We need to get inside," I said, grabbing Kellen's hand.

It wasn't until the kitchen door was firmly closed behind us that I breathed a little easier.

"What will prevent Kaven from coming here?" she asked.

"Nothing, but I don't think he will. Whatever he has planned, I believe he needs to remain hidden for a while longer. If he was ready to strike, we would be with Judith and Anne right now."

"You believe he's acting on his own then?"

"If he doesn't come pounding on our door, yes."

Kellen considered me for a moment and nodded.

"Let's start dinner."

Maeve found us in the kitchen an hour later.

"Mrs. Wineford just left," she said. "Thank you both for the tray and for preparing dinner. Tomorrow, we'll return to town to search for help."

"Perhaps, instead of all of us going, I can go with Hugh," I said. "That way, someone will be here to answer the door."

She considered me.

"Are you sure? Hiring kitchen help might not be easy."

"I'm sure. You're doing so much for us already while Kellen and I sit idle."

She waved away the comment and joined us at the table.

"Really, I'm doing very little but deflecting unwanted questions and listening to frivolous gossip for hours on end."

"I think we need to start setting aside certain hours for people to call," Kellen said. "Our new help can turn visitors away on our behalf and let them know the appropriate hours to call again. As you said, with royalty soon to be in residence at the retreat, the rush of visitors will only grow."

Maeve's expression lit up.

"That is a marvelous idea. It would free up my time so I can attend to other neglected matters. I have no idea what the expenses are for the estate or any repairs that might be needed. I should probably speak with Hugh after dinner."

"I can fix a plate for you to take to him."

"That's a lovely idea. We need him to keep his strength for us during these trying times."

CHAPTER 11

"Are you feeling well?" I asked Hugh.

His pallor seemed a little ashen in the morning light. Perhaps it was the jostle of the wagon on an empty stomach.

"I'm fine. Please stay close to me today. Maeve is worried you'll find trouble."

"Trouble? Me?" I grinned because he knew me well. He didn't grin back.

My humor died at the absence of his. I knew why he was so subdued. No matter how much I tried to tell myself that Judith was somewhere else, alive and well, I knew it was a lie. My heart wanted to break. Judith had been like a second mother to Kellen and me. Stern when we were trouble, loving when we needed comfort. But most importantly, always there.

"I miss her so much," I said.

"Don't talk like that," Hugh said gruffly.

I nodded and looked away so he wouldn't see the start of my tears, which I fought to blink back. He was right. I couldn't think like that. There had to be hope.

We traveled the rest of the way to town in silence, and Hugh parked the wagon not far from the market district.

"Where do you want to start?" he asked.

"I was thinking of ordering some breakfast at Crumbs and Casks and asking the serving girl if she knows of anyone who might be looking for kitchen work."

He grunted his acknowledgment and followed me down the street. When it came time to order, he left me at my own table and moved off to the bar. I didn't mind. It would be odd for an employee to be seated with me.

Along with a delicious meal, the serving girl gave me a few names and directions for finding the women. Hugh forestalled me from searching them out, though.

"First, I need to deliver a message to the Brazen Belle," he said. "The staff should be awake by now."

The name struck a familiar chord, and I didn't remember why until I saw a face I recognized. The old woman from the woods was sitting in the sunlight on the porch while shucking some peas. She didn't glance our way as we approached.

"Stay right here," Hugh said, stopping me from stepping onto the porch. "This is no place for a young miss."

I nodded and watched him go inside. The old woman winked at me and tossed me a pea.

"How's the pig?" she asked as I munched on the sweet green.

"Still big. But he seems happy enough."

The woman snorted.

"If he's happy enough, it means you're feeding him too much. Cut the portions. Are you walking him?"

"Yes, ma'am."

"Is he finding anything for you?"

"Truffles."

She cackled and slapped her knee.

"He would have a good nose that one. Tell him that's not good enough. He can do better."

I nodded just as Hugh returned.

He glanced suspiciously at the old woman.

"What were you telling her?"

"We were talking about the pig," I said to Hugh.

He came down the steps, grabbed my arm, and led me away.

"You aren't supposed to speak with the women there," he said.

"Was that a whorehouse?" I asked, my curiosity piqued. Behind us, the old woman laughed again, and Hugh lengthened his stride, his face reddening.

"I promise, Hugh. We were strictly discussing the pig. I wasn't educated in any way." I eased my arm from his grasp and patted his shoulder. "Besides, the woman is harmless and hardly a whore, given her age."

He gave a quick side-glance and seemed to relax a little.

"Before we visit the women the serving girl mentioned, I have a stop I'd like to make," I said.

Hugh followed me through the winding roads of Towdown toward the center of the city. The palace was just barely visible above the rooftops when I saw the home I needed.

"How much further are we going?" Hugh asked. "I think we've been gone too long. We don't want to worry Maeve."

"She won't be worried. She knows I'm with you," I said with a quick smiled. "Besides, the house we need is just there."

As I pointed, the door opened, and Anne's mother stepped out. I waved when she spotted us.

"We shouldn't be here," Hugh said.

"Nonsense. We need to ask after Anne."

He followed me, his growing nervousness clearly visible. I couldn't blame him. My stomach was in knots.

"Hello, Mrs. Tiller."

"Eloise, dear. I didn't expect to see you."

"I know. I apologize for coming unannounced, but I needed to know if you've seen Anne in the last few days?"

"No, but I know she'll visit when she has time. She loves your family. I was so sorry to hear about your mother, dear."

"Thank you, Mrs. Tiller." I swallowed hard, struggling with what I needed to say next. She noticed.

"What is it, dear?"

"I truly believe Anne loves us as much as we love her. That's why I'm here. She's missing."

"Missing?"

"I found her cap in the woods. Nothing else. Judith is missing, too."

Mrs. Tiller lifted her hand to her mouth. The color left her face, and her eyes started to water.

"We've searched the woods and notified the guard. I don't know where else to look. I'd hoped I would find her here," I finished sadly.

Mrs. Tiller remained quiet for a moment, her gaze unfocused. Then she shook her head, turned around, and went inside without another word.

"We shouldn't have come," Hugh said softly. "You've brought nothing but pain."

I wished Hugh was wrong. I'd desperately hoped that Mrs. Tiller had seen Anne.

"Come," Hugh said softly. "It's best if we leave searching for help for another day. We should return home."

Maeve had entrusted me with the task of returning with the help we desperately needed. Yet, while obligation urged me to disagree with Hugh's insistence we leave, I found myself nodding in agreement instead. After seeing Mrs. Tiller's devastated expression, I no longer had the resolve to bring more people into our home. Would we be heartlessly risking someone new without first determining the root of our problems? Lost in thought, I followed Hugh.

We'd only reached the market district when a commotion on one of the side streets caught my attention. A group of boys, some of them familiar to me, were surrounding another, smaller lad. I couldn't see what they were doing; but having been the center of such a circle before, I couldn't allow it to continue unchecked.

Without thought, I veered in that direction.

"Eloise," Hugh called.

"Just a moment," I said before calling to the boys. "You there! Stop pushing him."

The motley group broke a part and scattered in different directions. The little boy straightened, looked me in the eye, and placed what they'd been fighting over on his head.

My eyes widened at the sight of the cap with the king's insignia, and my gaze shifted to the lad's face. The delivery boy.

He turned and sprinted off in the opposite direction.

"Wait!" I lifted my skirts and bolted after him. I'd barely covered any distance when I was lifted off my feet and spun around.

I stared wide-eyed at Hugh's angry face.

"I told you to stay with me," he said.

"I know, but I need to—"

"Return home where you're safe. Will you listen, or must I carry you?"

I narrowed my eyes at him before catching myself. He didn't deserve to be a target for my temper. He was only worried about me, which I understood. Carefully masking my frustration, I promised to stay close, and Hugh released me.

My vexation still hadn't dissipated by the time we arrived at the wagon. It didn't ease during the ride home, either.

Maeve waited on the front step when we pulled into the yard. Her expression subtly changed to worry when she saw no one else accompanied us.

"Oh dear," she said, coming down the steps as I jumped from the wagon. "I feared it might not be an easy task. Has word already spread?" She looked to Hugh.

"It will now. Eloise spoke to Mrs. Tiller about Anne and Judith. Told her that she found Anne's cap in the woods." He looked down at the ground, his frustration and upset clear. I realized my slip, that only Kellen had known about the cap, and looked at Maeve.

She was visibly surprised.

"You should have told me, Eloise. Who is Mrs. Tiller?"

"Anne's mother," I said. "I rather hoped we'd find Anne there. That the cap I found in the woods meant nothing. Unfortunately, Mrs. Tiller said she hadn't seen Anne since well before her disappearance."

Pity clouded Maeve's features. There wasn't a hint of anger or admonishment that I hadn't confided in her.

"I never thought of Anne's mother," Maeve said. "I'm so sorry that you had to speak with her, Eloise. I should go see her immediately. What a mess." She looked truly upset.

"I'm sure Mrs. Tiller would like to hear from you, especially to know that we haven't given up hope. But probably not today. I let her know that we spoke with the king's guard, but she was very upset and went inside without a word."

"I understand." She exhaled slowly and looked away for a moment. "Were there no candidates then for help?"

"I did get a few names. We were going to check them, but Hugh insisted we'd been gone too long."

She glanced at Hugh with a frown.

"She tried running off."

I rolled my eyes.

"Really, Hugh, you make me sound like an errant child. I heard a lad being terrorized by his peers and stepped to the side to put a stop it."

"Of course you're not a child," Maeve said soothingly. She hooked my arm and guided me toward the house, leaning in close so her next words were just for me. "I believe Hugh feels guilt for Judith and Anne's disappearances. He probably feels an even greater need to protect the rest of us now. Try not to fault him for that."

"I vow I don't. I truly do understand."

She patted my hand.

"I knew you would."

We went inside and joined Kellen in the sitting room where she was reading one of Mr. Bentwell's books. She glanced at me, her expression changing as our gazes held.

"No guests?" I asked.

"No," Maeve said. "I let those who appeared know that we are now only accepting guests between ten and two so we can spend more time together in memory of your mother. I'm sure word is spreading quickly."

It felt good to know that Kellen and I wouldn't need to hide away the majority of the day anymore.

"Why don't you two read while I fix us something to eat?" Maeve suggested.

Kellen closed her book.

"We'll cook; you can look at the estate business. Eloise and I wouldn't know where to start with that."

Maeve smiled and moved off to the small writing desk where Mother and Judith used to go over household expenses. Kellen and I quietly left the room.

"What happened?" Kellen asked as soon as the kitchen door closed behind us.

"Your ability to read me is uncanny."

"You stared at me with an intensity equal to the pig's when you're about to feed him. It wasn't hard to deduce that you wanted to tell me something."

I laughed.

"You know me better than anyone."

"And no one will ever know me as well as you. Now tell me."

"I saw the boy who delivered the necklace."

She stopped slicing bread to stare at me. Her already pale skin paled further.

"You did?" she asked softly.

I nodded. "When I tried to chase him down, Hugh stopped me. But I know a few of the boys who were with him. Through them, I think I could find the boy. I just need to get to town without Hugh in tow."

Kellen considered me for a moment and exhaled heavily.

"You already have a plan, don't you?"

"Yes. I believe Hugh needs some tea with dinner," I said with a smile.

THE WORLD around me was full of night noises, the small sounds keeping me company on my ride into town. Kellen hadn't liked the idea of me going off on my own once everyone was abed. But I'd pointed out to her that both Judith and Anne disappeared during the day, and I also knew who to watch for.

However, she still wasn't fully convinced that Kaven was acting alone despite his frustration in the woods the day I'd snuck into the retreat and the fact that we'd not once run into anyone else. Neither of our beliefs could be proven without speaking to the lad who'd delivered the necklace, though. Thus, the necessity of my late-night ride.

While most of Towdown rested peacefully as I entered town, a few establishments still welcomed customers. It was their rowdy enjoyment of abundant libations that would keep me safely unnoticed. Hopefully.

I'd tied my hair back and tucked it into my hood to hide the golden sheen that might attract unwanted attention. I'd also borrowed one of Judith's dresses. I knew she wouldn't mind. Not when doing so was meant to help find both her and Anne. No one would question a woman of lower class going to an alehouse for a late meal.

Dismounting near the smith, I gave the boy there a coin to watch after the horse. Then, I walked the short distance to Crumbs and Casks. No one questioned the cloak I kept firmly in place and pulled low to cover my features.

It took some time before I spotted the boy, lurking in the shadows across the street. Not only was he a bully, he was also known for lifting coin from anyone too drunk to notice. Finishing my drink, I left the alehouse and walked down the street. When I was abreast with his shadow, I flicked a coin to him.

He caught it, his eyes wide with surprise.

"I have another one for you if you can answer a question for me."

"What's that?"

"Who was the boy with the cap today? The one with the king's insignia."

The boy snorted.

"Tommy Bell? That little shite is claiming he secretly works for the king. No one believes him. You shouldn't neither."

"Where can I find Tommy Bell?"

The boy gave me directions to a home on the outskirts of town. I tossed him another coin even though he deserved a beating for his part in today's disturbance. He nodded his thanks and watched me shrewdly as I walked away. I wasn't a drunkard though, so I was safe.

After collecting the horse, I tried finding Tommy Bell's home on my own, but it was impossible to spot any landmarks or signs in the dark. Twice, men called out to me, and only my wits and a quick mare kept me safe.

Knowing I was running out of time, I turned back and made my way home, relieved to leave the late-night debauchery behind and annoyed I hadn't located the boy. My mind dwelled on how I would find my way back to town in the daylight. Hugh would never allow me to chase down some random boy. And, given Maeve's worry and understanding of my suspicions, I doubted she'd allow it either.

I was so lost in thought, I did not immediately notice the silence in the trees. The mare did. She snorted and sidestepped a moment before something launched itself at me from the trees. The mass collided with me and knocked me sideways off the horse. We landed with bruising force that numbed my arm and robbed me of breath.

While I lay stunned, my attacker ripped back my hood.

"You?" Kaven said.

I opened my mouth, not to speak but struggling to inhale.

His angry expression turned to worry as he rolled off of me and helped me sit up.

"Breath out first then in," he said.

I managed to regain my air on the second try.

"Are you hurt?" he asked.

Turning to him with an incredulous gaze, I punched him square in the nose.

"Of course I'm hurt, you ass! You knocked me off my damn horse!"

He pinched the bridge of his nose, sniffed, and blinked at me.

"You have no idea how grateful I am that you do not hit as hard as you knee."

"Please, allow me to try once more."

He stood and offered me his hand, standing at an angle lest I attempt to maim his manhood again.

I reached for the hand and stopped, realizing what I'd been about to do. Instead, I slapped his hand away.

"Is this how you lured them? Kindness? A trick?"

Hands now at his sides, he tilted his head to study me.

"Lured who?"

"I will not fall for your games," I said. I glanced at my horse, wondering if I could make it to her and mount before he caught me.

"Why are you out here, Eloise?"

"That's none of you concern."

"I believe it is."

"Well, I believe it's not. If you're not here to accost me or drag me into the trees to kill me, then I must be on my way." I stood cautiously, focused on him.

"That's a strange thing to say."

"Is it?" I said, arching a brow at him. "Our first meeting you threatened me. Our second meeting you physically accosted me, warranting the defense of my person. Both encounters were hardly shining examples of chivalry."

"Only those who threaten the Crown need fear me."

"That's hardly a comfort since you would be the one to determine what warrants a threat. Did picking berries on your land threaten the Crown? Does my presence here threaten the Crown?"

"Did you enter the king's retreat two days past?"

My pulse leapt, but I kept my fear from my expression.

"Why would I enter the king's retreat? That would be death, wouldn't it?"

He tucked his hands in his pockets and considered me.

"A simple trespassing would be a slap on the wrist. Maybe a public flogging. Stealing from the king would cost you far more than that. Did you take something?"

I snorted.

"Did you not hear me? I'm too smart to do something so stupid."

"Or perhaps you left something for the prince to find." He took a menacing step toward me.

"Touch me and I'll—"

"That's enough of that," he said, grabbing me and tossing me over his shoulder.

I kicked hard, connecting with the front of his thigh. He grunted and swatted me on the butt hard enough to elicit a squeal.

"You beastly pig ass son of a—"

"I'll do it again," he warned.

A moment later, I was sitting sideways on my horse with Kaven's hands on my thighs to steady me.

Our gazes locked as he looked up at me, and my breath caught. What was it about Kaven that made my good sense flee and my heart beat so erratically?

"You are by far the prickliest woman I have ever met. Are you dangerous, Eloise?" he asked, reigniting my ability to reason.

"Ask your testicles," I said.

With a swift nudge of my heel, I sent the mare flying, knocking Kaven aside in my haste to get away. His low chuckle followed me up the road.

My pulse didn't begin to slow until I reached the path to our house. I glanced over my shoulder before dismounting and continuing on foot. The road was empty as I'd guessed it would be. Unsure what that meant, I snuck into the barn and quietly unsaddled the mare. There wasn't much of a risk that Hugh would hear me and wake. Not with the tea that Anne used to make for Mother in his belly. Hugh, though, was the least of my worries.

"That was close," I said to the horse. "No more night rides." She nickered softly as I wiped her down then returned her to her stall.

With a quick check to ensure everything was in place, I left the stable.

All was silent as I let myself into the kitchen and tiptoed toward the dining room. There, I had to pause to wipe my palms on my dress. In my mind, I imagined Maeve hearing me and her expression of disappointment. Hadn't I vowed I wasn't like a child? Yet, here I was sneaking around like one.

Taking a calming breath, I made my way up the stairs without a creak. The candle still burned in our room, not an unusual sight.

When I slipped into the bedroom, I found Kellen sitting up in bed, a book open in her lap, just as I'd left her. Her gaze met mine, and I smiled slightly. She sighed, closed the book, and blew out the candle. In the dark, I got ready for bed.

However, even as I lay safe and comfortable in my own home, sleep escaped me.

My mind dwelled on my meeting with Kaven. The encounter had been all wrong. He'd aggressively knocked me from the horse, and I had been certain I'd found my end. Especially since I had bashed his head with a rock the last time we'd met. Yet, he'd offered his hand to help me to my feet, and everything after that had been wary and—I frowned—courteous. No, that smack on my backside had not been courteous. However, it had been earned. I grinned in the dark, remembering the punch to his nose and the kick.

My humor faded as I struggled to come up with an explanation for his behavior. Was Kaven even more dangerous than I thought? Did he seek to lull me? To what purpose, though?

CHAPTER 12

"Must you be so loud?" I asked.

"Yes. It's not like you to sleep in. Wake up before it's noticed."

Sometimes, I hated Kellen's practical logic. I crawled out of bed and saw she'd already brushed out Judith's dress. Not a trace of dirt remained from my late-night encounter with Kaven.

"Thank you," I said.

She rolled her eyes at me and helped me with my hair as soon as my mourning dress was over my head. We'd just opened the door when Maeve stepped out of her room.

"Up late reading again?" she asked.

Kellen smiled.

"Mr. Bentwell's books are addicting. We will need another candle for our room, but I promise not to stay awake as long tonight."

Maeve waved away her concern.

"Reading is good for the mind."

Kellen's cheeks pinked as we made our way toward the stairs, and I blinked at my sister. There'd been only a handful of times I'd seen her flush.

She caught my look and shook her head slightly.

Keeping my question to myself, we followed Maeve to the entry where she stopped for her cloak.

"Promise that you'll stay inside while Hugh and I are gone," she said.

"I promise," Kellen and I said at the same time.

Maeve smiled.

"Good. Bar the doors until we return. Answer for no one." She hesitated. "I don't like leaving you like this."

"We will be fine," Kellen said. "If we hear something, we'll hide in the attic. No one will find us there."

Maeve nodded.

"We won't be long."

She opened the door and stepped out. The faint jangle of an approaching wagon stopped her from going further. She paused and looked back at us with a frown. I could see the indecision on her face.

"You've already turned away visitors and stated when we will receive guests. It won't look unusual for you to do the same today," Kellen said, moving to the door.

Maeve waved goodbye as Kellen closed it. She had her hand on the lock when she hesitated. She caught my look and shrugged.

"It would sound odd to our visitor if I slid the lock into place now."

I shook my head at her always considering mind.

"I'll go fix us breakfast. I'm hungry for hot oats this morning."

"That sounds lovely."

The door behind us opened before we reached the dining room. We both stopped and watched Maeve along with another woman enter.

"Fate saw fit to help us this morning," Maeve said, spotting us. "This is Sabine, Anne's cousin."

The young woman nodded to us.

"Anne's mother came to see me this morning. She said that Anne's taken a bit of leave and asked if I can step in for her to ensure she doesn't lose her position. I can cook and clean well, if you'll have me."

"We are very much in need of your assistance," Maeve said, "and we thank you for your kind offer."

"I'll fetch my bag from the wagon and tell my father that I'm staying."

Maeve waited until the girl left to look at us.

"I hope this is all right. I typically never hire without references."

"I'm sure this will be fine," Kellen said. "Better someone who knows Anne and won't be put out when she returns."

"Of course. And I'm so relieved I don't need to leave the two of you alone. I really must be off to speak with Mrs. Tiller. I feel terribly that she's already awake, thinking of her daughter," she waved at us again and hurried out the door, past Anne's cousin who was returning with her things.

Kellen discreetly bolted the door as soon as the woman was inside.

"Allow me to show you to your sleeping quarters and give you a tour of the kitchen," I said.

Less than an hour later, Kellen and I sat at the table eating the fruits of Sabine's labors.

"Is it all right?" she asked nervously.

"The best hot oats I've tasted," I assured her, taking another enthusiastic bite.

"I never knew toasting them could change the flavor so enjoyably," Kellen said.

The hot oats were truly good as was Sabine's company.

"I'm so grateful I could help. I was just released from the House of Cresstol." She sighed deeply. "My year was up. The mistress said she would give reference to any who asked, if Lady Grimmoire needs one."

"I think this is reference enough," I said, nodding toward my bowl.

"Do you think this position might be permanent once Anne returns?"

Kellen and I shared a subtle glance.

"It might be," Kellen said softly.

Sabine beamed.

"Mrs. Tiller had been vague about how long Anne would be gone, but I would happily fill in for Anne no matter the duration. Not that I'm hinting I want her position. I wouldn't do that to Anne."

"Of course not," Kellen agreed.

"Once you're finished, leave the dishes on the block. I'm going to go fetch some fresh linens for the beds."

She hurried from the room, already comfortable with our home's layout.

Kellen turned to me.

"Well? What happened last night? Do we know who's responsible?"

"I only know the boy's name. Tommy Bell. He lives on the southwest outskirts of town near a stable called the Whistling Steed."

"Sounds more like a name for an alehouse."

I flashed her a quick grin.

"I'd thought the same. Perhaps it would have been easier to find in the dark then. As it was, I had to give up and return home without speaking to our dear Tommy Bell. However, the boy who gave me his name said that Tommy claimed to be a secret messenger of the King but no one believed him."

"Not much of a secret if the boy is going around telling everyone."

"Very true. But that's not the oddest part of the evening," I said, carrying my bowl to the block.

"Oh?" she asked following me with hers.

"Kaven knocked me off my horse on my return home. I thought it would be the end of me."

"But it wasn't."

"No." I frowned and recalled our encounter. "After the initial fall, he seemed concerned, if still a little rude. He offered to help me up and called me prickly when I refused to believe he was actually kind. Then he plucked me off my feet and plopped me on my horse.

I believe he truly intended to send me home mostly unscathed with only a few bruises."

Kellen's expression grew contemplative and distant as it often did when she needed to work something out. While she thought through the events, I led the way to the sitting room.

From above, I could hear the sound of Sabine's soft humming as she changed the linens. I hadn't realized how much I'd missed that simple normality.

"It makes no sense," Kellen said sitting in her chair. "Why knock you off the horse and then help you up? Why take Anne and Judith and not you?"

"My thoughts exactly. I can only suppose I was not the intended target. But why Mother and not us?"

She made a noncommittal sound and stared out the window.

"Even if you were not the intended target last night, if you were to ever be an intended target, why treat you cordially?"

Why indeed? Unless I never was the intended target. Or, perhaps, he wasn't the one to blame for Mother, Judith, and Anne. My heart stumbled at the possibility of his innocence then beat rapidly in hope.

"When I found Anne's cap by Mother's grave, I'd been so certain it was him that I damaged his testicles. Quite severely, given the sounds he made. That encounter alone makes his restraint in retribution last night even more curious."

"His testicles?" she said, looking at me with wide, disbelieving eyes.

"Don't look at me like that. He gave me no choice. It was his testicles or my life."

"Of course, I'm only surprised you still have your life. Doubly so now."

"Exactly my thoughts."

She absently picked up her book from the side table and opened it.

"This whole situation is nonsensical," she said. "Why take two maids and not you? Although we find value in Anne and Judith, you and I both know the majority of the world does not find value in those of lesser status. Even you and I only have as much value as where we live and whatever remains of Father's estate."

"Perhaps that's why I was let go," I said. "Perhaps there was an assumed value to my existence. Or, perhaps," I said, giving voice to what Kellen had said all along, "Kaven is not responsible for what has transpired. But if not him, then who?"

"As you've pointed out repeatedly, no one else makes sense. All clues point back to Kaven. One kind act, which is out of character from all the other encounters, shouldn't so heavily sway us."

"You're right," I said. It was foolish to think his offered hand meant something more than a distraction.

"This will take some consideration," Kellen said.

"I agree. However, I hope it doesn't take us too long to determine his motivations. I worry for Sabine."

"The door is barred, and she's inside with us. For now, she's safe."

I sat in my chair and picked up my book as well. However, I struggled to read the words on the page. For, as much as I wanted to escape the reality of my circumstances, my mind continued to dwell on the problem of not only who killed my mother but how long it would be before someone else went missing?

THE SOUND of the entry door opening almost pulled my attention from the story. Although it had taken me a while to finally succumb to the melodic words of the author, I was now fully enraptured in the heroine's plight.

"Where are they?" I heard Maeve ask.

"In the sitting room, my lady."

The click of heels echoed in the hall, a note of agitation in the rhythm. It was that unusual sound that finally pulled me from the story and had me looking up. Kellen did the same.

Maeve entered looking weary and anxious.

"We had a bit of a delay leaving this morning. The horse had a stone lodged in its shoe. I must ask, did either of you take the horse last night?"

Kellen and I both wore twin expressions of surprise. Neither were faked.

"While I imagine that would be quite an adventure," Kellen said, "we both know it's not safe to venture out. Day or night. I much prefer my adventures to occur on the pages of my book. I fear my life is already too unpredictable for more."

"I quite agree," I said. "But it does bring to mind that I have been neglecting the animals. I haven't taken the pig for a walk in days." I closed my book. "I should probably correct that."

Maeve's gaze searched both of our faces. Her expression of upset faded to one of indulgence.

"You relieve me greatly," she said. "I don't know what I would do if one of you two disappeared in the middle of the night. If the pig needs a walk, it might be best to send Hugh."

I stood and walked to Maeve, taking her hand and giving it a light squeeze.

"It's not just the pig who needs a walk; I'm a bit restless with all of this time indoors. And, I don't mind walking him around the yard," I added quickly.

Any lingering doubt about us taking the horse last night seemed to vanish with my words.

"Of course. I'm sorry if I sounded accusing. Hugh swore he checked the mare before putting her up for the night."

I released her hand and hugged myself.

"He's not been himself with everything that's happening," I said, hating that I was diverting blame. "Perhaps he only overlooked it."

"I'm sure you're right. It's good that Sabine is here now. Is she settled in? I was so worried about the pair of you that I didn't ask."

"Yes, we gave her a tour of the house. However, I put off showing her the grounds. Now that you've returned, perhaps I could take her with me when I walk the pig."

"A splendid idea. While you do that, I think I might go lay down for a bit."

"Did it go poorly with Mrs. Tiller?" Kellen asked.

"The dear woman was quite surprised to see me this morning but very understanding when I explained what's been happening here and our request for her discretion. This whole ordeal is more taxing than I had imagined it would be."

Guilt nibbled at my conscience.

"We're sorry that we've burdened you," Kellen said.

"Nonsense. You're both a joy. It's everyone else who is the burden," she said with a conspiratorial smile. "I'll see you two at dinner."

She left the room, her steps slower than normal.

"I don't envy her that talk with Mrs. Tiller," I said softly.

"Neither do I. I'm guessing it didn't go as well as Maeve would like us to believe."

"I agree." I glanced at Kellen, who was vacantly gazing out the window once more. "Did you want to come outside with me?"

She shook her head. "My mind is busy. It's best I sit inside with my book."

I knew what she meant. She was still thinking over the problem of Kaven and his odd behavior. I knew that she, like me, was starting to doubt his guilt. But was it all just part of his ploy?

I went into the kitchen in search of Sabine and found her already preparing our evening meal.

"Would you like a tour of the yard?" I asked. "We have a few animals that I care for. The chickens are lovely for the fresh eggs. I usually put them there." I indicated the wooden bowl resting on the block. "We also have a pig that I'm caring for on behalf of someone else. He's not for eating."

Sabine smiled.

"That is a good thing because I don't know how to butcher a pig. However, I'm quite adept at pastries."

"I love pastries. There's a patch of—never mind. I can see you're busy." She wasn't that busy. However, I did not intend to tell her about the very berry patch where Judith disappeared.

Sabine wiped her hands on her apron.

"I'm never too busy to learn something new about the estate. I would love to accompany you. Let me just pull this off the fire so it doesn't scald."

She moved a simmering pot from the flames and grabbed her cloak.

Outside, I showed her the chickens first then the pig pen. The pig wasn't rooting about, which I found odd. And I realized I hadn't fed him yet that morning.

"Pig," I called, opening the gate. "It's time for a walk."

I heard a shuffling sound from the shelter at the back of the pen. Taking care where I stepped and lifting my skirts to avoid the muck, I approached his dwelling.

"Come now, pig. You know you must walk."

When I ducked down to peer in, an ear-splitting squeal rent the air at the same time the pig came flying at me. I just barely straightened in time to avoid being trampled. The large creature darted for the gate at full speed. I didn't know what he intended, since I'd closed it behind me. He seemed to notice it was closed at the last moment and came to a thunderous stop.

His sides heaved as he spun around looking for another avenue of escape.

"Miss Eloise, perhaps you should climb the fence," Sabine called.

I didn't move, keeping my attention on the pig. I'd never seen him act so crazed before.

"Are you hurt, Mr. Pig?" I asked softly. "Do you need tending?" I held out my hand. "You know I won't hurt you. Come now. Let's have a look at you."

The pig shook his ears and let out a series of squeals and grunts before trotting toward me. While I did my best to remain outwardly calm, I prepared myself to scramble over the fence if the pig decided it no longer wanted to be docile.

Slowing a few feet from me, the pig bumped his head against my hand.

"There now," I said softly, looking him over and seeing nothing amiss. "Did I startle you out of a nap?"

The pig seemed to calm, and I walked over to the sheltered rack where I kept his tether.

"Should we walk?" I asked.

The pig grunted and seemed his normal self once again.

"He normally doesn't act like that," I said, trying to assure Sabine who watched the pig with doubt. "He's quite tame and enjoys his walks. Usually I take him in the woods, but for today, we'll keep him to the yard."

"That's a sound idea. I think it would be best if I returned to the kitchen." I didn't try to stop her retreat. Pigs weren't for everyone.

My portly companion and I walked around the yard once then down the driveway. I would have turned there to come back, but the pig caught the scent of something and started up the road toward the retreat. He didn't go far before veering off the path to a thicket of bramble on the side.

"You have a knack for intruding," a voice said.

I jumped and the pig squealed, almost jarring my arm from its socket before he tore his tether out of my grasp. Thankfully the pig didn't go far, only just behind me as if using me as a shield. I looked from the pig to Kaven.

"It looks like you startled your brother," I said to the man.

Kaven snorted.

"Even the sounds you make are similar," I added.

"A bee's sting is much kinder than your sharp words," Kaven replied with a scowl.

I shrugged.

"If you don't like my reaction, perhaps you should stop jumping out at me."

"Fair enough. I was hoping I would see you today." There was something in his tone—Menace? Annoyance?—that had me retreating a step.

"I think I need to return," I said.

"Stay." The command was followed by a sudden hand around my arm.

I stared up at Kaven, wondering how he'd gotten so close so fast. With barely a thought, I fisted my hand to strike out. He caught my intended jab with ease, his fingers closing over my own.

"I have never met a woman as violent as you. Was your mother like this?"

"Do not speak of my mother," I hissed before trying to stomp on his foot.

He deftly moved out of my way.

"I'm learning your tricks," he said with a smirk. "What will you do now, my little wasp? You've nothing left but words."

"Pig," I said, "if ever you were to repay my care of you, now would be the time."

"Are you speaking to—"

Both of our eyes widened as the pig let out a crazed squeal and knocked into me. I flew into Kaven, sending us both to the ground. Kaven grunted at the double impact of his back hitting the ground and me landing on top of him.

I scrambled off of him with all haste, accidentally clipping his manhood this time.

"Sorry," I said even as I scooped up the pig's tether and sprinted for the house.

The pig kept up with me every step of the way. When we reached the pen, I scratched his ear.

"You're a very fine friend," I said. "Thank you."

The pig grunted as I closed the pen, and I pretended not to notice the way his too human gaze followed me.

Kellen was missing from the sitting room when I returned. Rather than seek her out, I went to the kitchen to check on Sabine. I spent the rest of the day listening to idle stories about Sabine's prior employers and the life of gentry in general. Hearing their common disregard for those they employed helped ease some of my guilt that Sabine was staying with us. Surely, with Kellen and I both watching her, she would be safe.

When dinner was ready, I went to wake Maeve. It felt odd to knock softly on her door and hear a voice other than Mother's.

"I'm sorry to wake you," I said through the panel. "Dinner is ready."

"I'll be right there," Maeve called. "Thank you for waking me."

Leaving her door, I checked our room for Kellen. Her book was lying open on her bed but Kellen was absent. Panic squeezed my chest. I whirled to tell Maeve and almost ran into my sister.

"Curse you, Kellen," I said irritably for the twofold scare she'd given me.

Her lips twitched.

"Were you looking for me?"

"You know I was. Dinner is ready."

"So I heard."

I moved toward the stairs, my annoyance clinging to me. Kellen reached out and clasped my hand.

"It wasn't intentional. This time," she said.

Her lingering humor and honest admission broke through my irritation.

"I hope someday you meet someone as in love with tricks as you are. Then you'll understand how unpleasant they can be."

"If they're so unpleasant, why do you always laugh?"

I grinned and shook my head. I never could stay mad at Kellen for long.

"Where were you?" I asked.

"In the attic."

"Did you finish your book already?" I asked as we reached the bottom step.

A scrape of noise above us had me turning to smile at Maeve.

"If you've finished, we can go to town tomorrow to fetch more," Maeve said.

"I haven't finished. It only reached a part that didn't sit well with me, so the book and I needed to part company for a while."

I chuckled.

In the dining room, Sabine had the table set and waiting. She lifted the cover from a bowl to reveal a light spring soup and removed a towel sheltering a basket of fluffy biscuits.

"These look delightful," I said, reaching for one.

Maeve complimented Sabine's skills after the first bite. I could tell the young woman desperately wanted to please us so she could secure a place for herself. While I liked her, I hoped her position wouldn't be as Judith or Anne's replacement. I wanted our friends safely returned. Yet, with each passing day, my hope of that happening was dwindling.

After dinner, Maeve and Sabine went to the sitting room to discuss supplies and expenses. Kellen grabbed me by the hand and dragged me upstairs. Instead of taking us to our bedroom as I expected, she led me to the attic.

When I'd last been up there, the space had been a disorganized mess of oil-cloth covered furniture. Since then, pieces had been moved and recovered, creating little pockets of space.

Kellen noticed my surprise at the change.

"Maeve had mentioned a delay in the arrival of her possessions, and I wanted to be sure there was enough storage space for anything that did not fit downstairs."

"How can you spend so much time up here?" I asked, suppressing a shiver and wishing for my cloak.

She just smiled as she guided me toward the back of the room. Finally, she stopped at a large stack of furniture and lifted one of the oil-cloths to reveal a small crawl space.

"After you," she said, motioning. "And keep quiet."

I crawled through a short tunnel and emerged into a cleared space within the cluster of furniture. A swath of oil-cloth created a ceiling for the nook. Moving further in, I sat on the floor and looked at the exposed items. There were books and an oil lamp and a chest.

Kellen came in behind me and noticed my shiver.

"It will warm well enough with both of us in here." She went to the chest and lifted the lid. "Mother saved strands of our hair, clothing, and other things in here," she said. "This is where I found the letters. They were at the very bottom. I thought they were nothing more than memories of the past, like the rest of the items. Then, I found this."

She reached toward the lid and pulled back a few inches of the fabric that lined the inside. Underneath, was a bit of parchment.

She removed and unfolded it. I leaned close to read it with her.

MARGARET,

ALTHOUGH MY HEART IS HEAVY, *I have not forgotten my promise. For the remainder of your life and that of your children, I grant you and your family use of the caretaker's cottage for the royal retreat north of Towdown.*

The retreat was Sevil's favorite place to visit, and I cannot see myself going there without her.

For all that you've done and sacrificed for the good of this kingdom and my family, I pledge my aid should you and your family ever have need.

Be well in life, Margaret. When we meet again, I hope it is in a safer time with far better circumstances.

AFTAN, *King of Drisdall*

I LOOKED UP AT KELLEN, stunned.

"I do not know what Mother did," she said, "but given the contents of this letter, I cannot believe her death is the result of the Crown."

My initial surprise gave way to a slow, burning anger.

"That means whoever killed her is acting against the Crown. And this letter gives us the audience we would need to present our case."

"Once we have proof," Kellen said.

"Yes. Once we have proof. I need to speak with Tommy Bell."

"I agree. However, there seems to be a second mystery surrounding this house," Kellen said, folding the letter.

"What do you mean?"

"There were three other letters with this one," she said. "Not from the King, but from Elspeth."

I frowned recalling what my sister had said about the letters she'd read thus far.

"Mother hid away three letters from her but not the rest?"

"Precisely why they intrigue me."

She handed over the letters.

I HOPE this letter finds you in good health, dear one. The ban on magic is making my search more difficult than I anticipated. However, I am certain I grow closer each day to discovering the identity of the one who killed the Queen. Keep the babes safely hidden until I can return.

E

I LOOKED UP AT KELLEN.

"Hidden?"

"Keep reading."

I'M RELIEVED to hear that the children are thriving despite the situation of their births. It is something that has weighed on my mind greatly since I left you. My search is not progressing as I had hoped. Every location spell I cast returns nothing. There is another spell I might try. However, we both know the cost of that which is cast in blood.

Keep the babes safely hidden until I can return.

E

I QUICKLY READ the last one.

TIME IS PASSING TOO QUICKLY. I fear I may need to give up this search or face too many questions when I finally settle somewhere. Kiss the babes for me and tell them that I will come to collect my charge from you soon.

E

I LOOKED UP AT KELLEN.

"Mother knew a caster," I said in awe.

"Very well, it would seem, if she had planned to give one of us over to the woman."

I frowned and read the last letter again but could not refute Kellen's suspicion.

"So it would seem. I wonder what happened."

"Perhaps whatever spell she thought to cast had a deadly result as she hinted it might."

"Or she was caught casting and sent to the forest," I said.

I placed the letters on the floor and studied them.

"You're right that there's a second mystery. What did Mother do for the kingdom that would warrant a letter of protection from the king? And why would she give one of us to a caster, the very type of person who was outlawed by the king?" I exhaled, trying not to let my frustration gain control of me. "Do you think Maeve would know anything about the events surrounding our births? The second letter alludes to something."

"Doubtful. Mother never mentioned her cousin. If Maeve was present at our births, I would think she would have been included in whatever events Mother had been involved in and would have remained in our lives. Despite that, I did consider approaching Maeve with this, but you saw her today. She's exhausted and has enough to worry over."

"Where does that leave us?"

"In the same ignorant position we were previously. That hasn't changed. The letter only proves the King thought of Mother in a kind light at one time. We know too little to assume more than that. You need to speak with Tommy Bell."

Hearing that statement, I knew she was officially releasing me from my promise to forget what was happening around us.

"You believe things will get worse, don't you?" I asked.

"I do."

Trying to dispel the chill her answer had given me, I looked around the space again.

"Was it like this when you found it?" I asked.

"It was." She returned the letters to their hiding place. "I think Mother used to come up here, too."

She'd come up here and hidden the letters she had received from Elspeth and the King. She'd also hidden the truth from us.

"Why didn't she tell us any of this?" I wondered.

"I don't know, but I doubt that knowing the tale behind those letters will change the course of events before us."

"I'll try again tonight," I said.

"Tonight? You were lucky last time. We should wait until tomorrow and find a reason to go to town."

"You know Maeve will not permit us out of Hugh's sight long enough to track down this boy. And, I'm less concerned about the dark than I am about letting these disappearances continue without hindrance. I will be safe tonight as I was last night."

Kellen gave me a doubtful look but didn't argue.

"Look at this," she said instead. She plucked one of the books from its position on the floor and handed it to me. I opened the cover and skimmed the hand-written scrawl that described the medicinal purposes of several plants.

"At first glance, these books seem like simple herbalist notes. However, I've been reading them and have come across other things. Potions."

I looked up from the book.

"These are books on magic?"

"I have a lot more reading to do before I can say that, but I believe so."

"Why would Mother keep books of magic?"

"I don't believe they were Mother's. Elspeth was a caster by her own admission. Based on her letters, she intended to return here."

"I'm glad she didn't." I couldn't imagine a life without Kellen beside me.

After crawling out of the hidden nook, Kellen showed me around the rest of the attic. There were many pieces that I could now see had never belonged to my parents. Having read the king's letter, I understood from where much of the furniture had come.

We returned to our room and settled in for an evening of reading while we waited for Maeve to retire. However, the candle burned low without a sound from below.

Kellen and I went to check on Maeve's whereabouts and found

her in the sitting room still at the desk. She seemed lost in thought until we entered. She looked up at us with clear eyes and a smile.

"Is everything all right, dears?"

"Yes," Kellen said. "We were worried since you hadn't come upstairs yet and wanted to check on you."

"You're so sweet. I seem to have an abundance of energy from my nap and much too much to think on. I cannot seem to find the deed for this house. It shouldn't pose any problems, but it is a curiosity given its proximity to the king's retreat. I don't suppose you know how your parents came to own such a property."

"Actually, I was rather hoping that would be a story you could share with us," I said. "Mother and Father never mentioned it, and we never thought to ask."

Maeve sighed.

"I thought as much. I'm sure we will find the deed somewhere. I'll check the papers in your father's room tomorrow. Meanwhile, I'll keep going over the books. Don't stay up too late tonight. Growing girls need their rest."

She looked at the papers, and I knew she was already distracted with whatever she had found there.

Kellen and I quietly withdrew, leaving Maeve to her thoughts. Back in our room with the door closed, Kellen tried to dissuade me from leaving that night.

"She has to sleep eventually," I said softly.

"Until she does, you had better change into your bedclothes. It would look suspicious if you're fully dressed if she comes to check on us."

Kellen's forethought saved us from being caught as Maeve did indeed check on us hours later.

"Still up reading?" she asked when she poked her head in. "I picked up one of your books, Kellen, and can understand what holds your attention so thoroughly."

Kellen blushed.

"They are quite difficult to put down," I agreed, wondering why my sister was acting so oddly.

"Can I fetch either of you something from the kitchen? I found some ledgers that detail your father's accounts, and fear I'll be up with them all night."

"We're fine, thank you," Kellen said.

I smiled and agreed.

As soon as Maeve closed the door, Kellen and I blew out the candle by silent agreement. There was no point in staying up that night.

We woke late the next morning to grey skies and a light rain, and I knew there would be no sneaking off that day either. The delay festered in my mind as an ominous sign. The need to do something crawled over my skin like an army of ants. It took every ounce of restraint to calmly lounge in the sitting room with a book in my lap all morning.

When a carriage rattled up the drive after our midday meal, Kellen and I hid in the kitchen with Sabine.

"Do you get visitors often?" she asked.

"Often enough," I said. "It seems that the Prince is returning and will be in residence at the retreat soon. It has many of the townspeople curious. They come here under the pretense of condolences and the false belief that we know more than they."

"I heard much the same news about the Prince while still at the House of Cresstol," Sabine said. "No one seems to know when he'll arrive, though. Everyone is waiting for banners to go up at the castle. A sure sign of an imminent welcome."

"Do you miss town life?" Kellen asked.

"No, miss. I quite like the quiet here. You two and Lady Grimmoire are gracious and kind. Not everyone in town can boast those traits."

She had shared enough stories that I believed her.

"Sometimes the quiet can be a bit dull," Kellen said.

I turned to give her a disbelieving look, and she kicked me under the table. With relief, I kicked her back, glad that she was up to something rather than calling our mother's death and the subsequent disappearances of our friends dull.

"I can imagine it might seem that way to two young girls. Maeve is sending me to town tomorrow with Hugh for some supplies. Would you like to accompany us?"

"That would be lovely," I said, appreciating my sister's wit.

"PLEASE STAY OUT OF TROUBLE," Maeve said before she waved then went inside.

"Do you two cause trouble often?" Sabine asked from her place on the seat beside Hugh.

"Rarely," Kellen said. "However, trouble does have a way of finding us."

I elbowed her.

"That was before Maeve spoke with the families of the boys who were causing us trouble. Since then, we've been trouble free."

"True," Kellen agreed.

We both glanced at Hugh, who had remained impassive through the whole conversation. He hit a particularly large divot in the road that lifted Kellen and me from our places in the back. She landed with a wince.

"I miss the carriage already," she said under her breath.

"Your backside has grown too soft," I said with a smirk, hiding my own wince. I would have preferred the carriage as well; however, the need for supplies necessitated the wagon.

The jostling ride had thoroughly bruised my backside by the time we reached town. Kellen watched me with a knowing grin as I eased from the wagon.

"Shall we meet here again in three hours?" Sabine asked.

"Meet?" Hugh said. "We should stay together."

Sabine laughed.

"I believe the last thing these two want is to stay with us while we're purchasing boring supplies."

"I did finish my book last night," Kellen said, lifting the bag at her side which did indeed hold a book. We'd come prepared with a reason to go off on our own. We hadn't anticipated Sabine proposing we do so.

"They'll be fine," Sabine said. "This isn't their first trip to town. If you two run into any trouble, I'm sure you'll find us easily enough in the market."

I nodded in agreement and hooked my arm through Kellen's.

"We might even read a book while we're there," she said. "I do like those slim volumes Mr. Bentwell has on the shelf by his desk."

As she spoke, I turned us toward the book shop, and we started on our way. When Hugh didn't stop us, I knew we'd won our way free of his company.

Turning the corner, Kellen and I stopped.

"Should we stay together, or should one of us go to Mr. Bentwell's?" she asked.

"I think it would look more suspicious if we split up."

"Together then."

It took us over an hour to walk to the outskirts of town and navigate the landmarks the boy had given me. Our dresses, even though mourning black, were too fine for the area. However, no one gave us more than a single curious glance as we passed.

I found the Bell home and knocked on the door. By luck, the young man in question answered.

"Are you Tommy Bell?" I asked politely.

He gave me a suspicious look, but there was no recognition in his eyes at the sight of Kellen or me.

"What if I were? What would you want with me?"

Kellen produced a copper to show him.

"We have a few harmless questions to ask you," she said.

He snatched the coin.

"What do ya want to know?"

"First, can you show me the king's cap you're said to have? It will prove that we are indeed speaking with Tommy Bell," I said.

"Just a moment," he said before he dashed off inside and returned with the cap in question sitting atop his head.

"You look quite dapper in that," Kellen said.

"What's dapper mean?"

"You look well-dressed and handsome," I clarified.

He grinned.

"Can you tell me how you came by such a hat?" Kellen asked.

"It's a king's hat. How do you think I came by it?"

"I'm afraid I have no idea how one comes to be in the service of the king, but I'm desperate to try to be a messenger myself," I said.

Kellen produced another coin.

"We promise not to accept any message from the king unless you've had a chance to take it first."

He studied us for a long moment.

"I wish I could help you. I truly do. I don't exactly recall how I came by this hat."

"What do you mean?" I asked.

"Well, I remember standing in the dark, watching for any abandoned dregs. My da likes when I can bring something home for him. A man came up to me and asked me a question. It was dark, and I couldn't see him clearly. Dark hair. Tall." He shrugged. "He gave me a package and told me to deliver it. Then he gave me the cap and a coin to see the job done."

"Where did this chap send you?"

"I don't know," he said.

As he answered, a flash of unnatural green light reflected in his eyes.

CHAPTER 14

I STARED AT YOUNG TOMMY BELL UNTIL THE LIGHT FADED. WITHOUT A doubt, it was the same light I'd seen in my mother's eyes before she died. However, Tommy remained whole and healthy, if increasingly more uncomfortable the longer I stared.

"Thank you, Tommy," Kellen said, taking my arm. "We'll try hanging around the alehouses and hope for the best. Have a pleasant day."

I nodded and managed a smile before Kellen led us away.

"You saw it too, didn't you?" I asked.

"I did."

"What do you think it means?" I asked.

"That we're even further from the truth than before. Why would a king, who put a ban on the use of magic, use magic to influence a young lad to deliver a package? Had it been from the King, his guard would have only needed to ask the boy, and young Tommy would have excitedly done it for the cap alone."

"Kaven is acting on his own."

"He has dark hair then? Kaven?"

I'd forgotten that Kellen had never had the displeasure of meeting him.

"In the light it's a warm brown. Darker than my hair, but far lighter than yours. At night..." I shrugged. "I suppose it could be dark if one weren't paying much attention."

She glanced knowingly at me. I'd been paying far too much attention to mistake his hair as dark.

"Then, I believe Kaven is acting without the king's knowledge. However, Kaven is the prince's servant. Perhaps this is a son's act against his father?"

I growled in frustration.

"I'm done with this game and want it over."

"And how do you propose ending it?"

"We know the king isn't involved, and we have the letter promising help. I say we confront Kaven to discover the truth and go to the king with whatever admission Kaven makes."

"And if there is no admission?"

I stopped walking and glared at Kellen.

"Are you being difficult for a reason?"

"Yes. To spare us both additional misery. If someone is willing to use magic and take people while daylight is shining, do you honestly believe they will openly admit their transgression? If Kaven is the culprit, you'll find yourself taken like Judith and Anne. And, I'll find myself without a sister. If Kaven isn't the culprit, you'll survive the encounter but likely cause a stir which is exactly what Maeve is working so hard to avoid."

Defeated by her logic, I started walking again.

"Then what would you have us do?"

"For now, I would have us arriving at Mr. Bentwell's post-haste."

Thanks to Kellen's ever-present cache of coins, we hired a small carriage to deliver us to the bookshop in mere minutes. We returned the read books and selected new ones at our leisure before returning to the market. We'd only just rounded the corner when we spotted Hugh and Sabine.

I waved and smiled.

"I hope you had enough time," Sabine said. "I hadn't anticipated Hugh's speed when I suggested three hours."

"It was plenty of time to select new books," Kellen said.

The ride home was quiet and much more comfortable, thanks to the bags of flour, sugar, and dried beans that Kellen and I used as seats.

When we arrived home, there was already a carriage in the drive.

"Bollocks, I'd best get inside. I'd hoped we'd left early enough that I would be back to answer the door for any guests."

"It's nothing to worry over," Kellen said. "Maeve doesn't mind answering it."

Sabine gave a grateful smile and hurried inside.

"Do you need any help carrying the supplies in?" I asked Hugh.

"No."

I hated that he was still hurting so.

"All right then. I think I'll take the pig for a walk before I go inside to read."

Kellen shot me a warning look.

"I know to stay on our property," I said. "I'm quite capable of listening, and Hugh will be in the yard if I need to call for help."

Neither tried to stop me as I went for the pig's tether. More than anything, I just needed time to think. I knew that Kellen had no idea what to do next. I didn't either. And that was entirely unacceptable.

Taking the pig, who was much more docile today, I started toward Mother's clearing.

"Stay close," Hugh warned.

I waved to acknowledge that I heard him and disappeared into the woods, not taking the path but veering to the left toward the ridge to make a slow circle of our property and avoid going anywhere near the retreat. The pig stopped occasionally to root in bracken and produced a few truffles.

Holding the black misshapen globes, I recalled the old woman at the Brazen Belle.

"Mr. Pig, these truffles are lovely, but the old woman who gave you to me said you can do better. She also said I should cut your portions even further."

The pig's head jerked up from where he'd been rooting, and he let out a concerned squeal.

I sighed.

"I wish my life was as simple as worrying over whether or not I would have enough to eat. What am I to do, Mr. Pig? Why are my friends disappearing? I would give anything to know where they are."

The pig grew agitated, pacing in a circle and grunting and squealing.

"Hush, my friend. I won't cut your portions. I intend to walk you more. I'll help you become the trim handsome pig I know you to be."

He stopped squealing and looked at me. Again, I was struck by how human some of his responses seemed. He probably just knew food and work-related words like "portion" and "walk."

"Come on," I said. "Let's keep walking."

He huffed a great breath then started trotting along the ridge, his nose to the ground. I didn't often walk him this way for fear that the land would give way under his weight and we would go tumbling to the trees below.

Near the pines tucked a fair distance from the back of the shed, the pig stopped abruptly. He grunted softly several times. However, he didn't otherwise move, his gaze fixated on the cluster of pines still a length away.

The absence of the birdsong, or any other noise beyond my breathing, created an unnatural hush as if the forest was waiting for what might happen next. It unnerved me as did the pig's odd behavior.

"What is it?" I asked the pig.

He walked around me and nudged me forward. I took two halting steps toward the evergreens, my skin prickling with trepidation.

"Perhaps we should—" The pig jostled me from behind, sending me into the dense green branches. He gave several squeals and grunts when I turned to look back at him. Human fear shown in his intelligent eyes, but he still moved toward me as if to continue nudging me along.

"I'm going," I said. "Don't hurry me."

He quieted and waited. Facing the trees, I took a step back to try to peer through the dense branches.

"Is anyone here?" I whispered.

Not a sound came from inside. Yet the tingle of awareness, of not being alone, continued. My hands shook as I pushed against the needled branches that caught in my hair and tugged at my clothes. Closing my eyes against the onslaught, I continued forward until I suddenly broke free.

My foot caught on something, and I went tumbling forward, a thick layer of needles cushioning my fall. Rolling to my side, I looked back at what had caused my fall.

Near the base of the trees lay two bodies. Skin wrinkled and shriveled like old grapes, they could have been there any number of years. Yet, the dresses and hair told me otherwise.

I'd found Anne and Judith.

My chest tightened, and my eyes watered as I stared at the remains of the two people I held dear. Their mouths were open and their hands partially raised as if to stave off an attack. What horrors had they faced before their deaths?

A questioning grunt drew me from my grief. I wiped my eyes and got to my feet, pushing my way through the branches once more. I fell to my knees before the pig.

"How did you know?" I asked, voice breaking.

He grunted and snuffled my hair. I let myself believe he was consoling me. I needed it.

"What am I to do?"

Although it was quite obvious the pair had died because of magic, I remained no closer to discovering who had killed them. The only clues I had were based on the conversation from young Tommy Bell. A man with dark hair.

However, Kellen was right that we couldn't assume it was Kaven, alone. Only one thing remained certain. We still had no idea who or what we were dealing with.

Getting to my feet, I started toward the house. I barely noticed the pig following me until it bumped my legs when we passed his pen. I opened the gate and watched the pig trot in. He went straight for his little shelter and hid away inside. I wished I could hide away somewhere, too.

With heavy steps, I went to the house. Poor Mr. and Mrs. Tiller. Anne was their only child. From Anne, I knew they had hopes she would remarry someday. Now, that would never happen.

Judith was, no, Judith had been Mother's age. Content with her spinster status, she'd happily worked for our family. Her own Mother and Father were being cared for by her siblings in a small village north of here. She hadn't gone home often, but I knew she'd still be missed by her loved ones. By us.

The kitchen door opened despite my numbed fingers. I hadn't even realized I'd gotten so cold.

"Eloise?" Kellen said, setting her book on the table and coming to me. "What's wrong?"

Sabine, who was at the cutting board, stopped her meal prep to come toward us. I looked at them both, feeling the tears gather again.

"I found Judith and Anne. Their bodies were left in a cluster of trees behind the shed."

Sabine covered her mouth with her hand, her eyes wide. Kellen took me by the arm and led me to the stool near the fire. As soon as I was seated, she moved away from me.

"Can you discreetly request Maeve's presence, Sabine?" she asked.

I looked at the pale woman and doubted any interruption would be subtle, given her state. Kellen seemed to think the same thing.

"Never mind. I'll fetch Maeve. Can you make some tea for Eloise?"

Sabine nodded, and Kellen left us in the kitchen. The silence grew deafening.

"I thought Anne was away visiting someone," she finally said.

"Anne disappeared in the middle of the day several days ago. Judith disappeared a few days before that. When Judith disappeared, we'd hoped she'd gone to visit her family. But, we checked, and they hadn't heard from her. When Anne disappeared, we reported the disappearances to the guard. They were unbothered by two housemaids gone missing."

Sabine joined me near the fire, slowly sitting on the other stool there.

"Could you tell what got them? Was it a wolf?" She shivered lightly. "I heard tales of a sickness and death years ago because of creatures from the Dark Forest."

"It was no creature from the forest," I said. "It was magic."

The door opened just as I spoke those last words. Maeve walked in with concern on her face.

"Eloise, we talked about you casting these accusations. Sabine, you mustn't listen to her."

"They're dead," I said. "Judith and Anne. I found their bodies between the ridge and the shed. It looks like the life was drawn from them, leaving behind nothing but dried husks. Without their clothes or their hair, they would have been unrecognizable."

Maeve stared at me as if weighing the truth of my words.

I stood.

"Come. I will show you."

"That's not necessary, Eloise. You're shaking. First, let's fix you some tea to calm your nerves."

I shook my head.

"The shaking will likely continue no matter what I drink. They're out there. Alone. Abandoned. Dead."

Sabine took my hand.

"Not abandoned," she said. "We will fetch them and bury them."

Maeve said nothing more as I led the way out the door. Hugh emerged from the shed when we neared.

"You had better come with us," Maeve said quietly. "We will need your strength."

No one spoke as I followed the path back to the trees and pushed my way into the hidden clearing. Sabine started crying when she saw what was left of her cousin. Kellen and Maeve paled but neither shed a tear. Maeve didn't know them well enough, and Kellen would never let herself feel that deeply. It didn't matter. I cried enough for both of them.

"There's room next to Mother," Kellen said. "Judith and Anne would like it there."

Sabine shook her head.

"It is a kind offer, but Anne belongs with her parents. And I'm sure Judith's kin would want her close as well."

"You're right," Maeve said. She took a calming breath. "Hugh and I will wrap the bodies and place them in the wagon. It's getting too late to travel to town tonight." I hadn't even noticed the darkening sky. "It would be safer to leave at first light."

Sabine looked at the bodies and quickly agreed.

"Back inside, girls. A calming tea will help you sleep tonight."

"Lady Grimmoire, thank you for the offer to care for the bodies, but such work is better left to me. I'll help Hugh then finish dinner."

"Don't worry about dinner," Kellen said. "Eloise and I will finish it."

"Very well," Maeve said. She stepped toward Sabine and hugged her. "I'm so sorry for the misfortune that has befallen your family."

Sabine hugged her in return. "Thank you, My Lady."

Kellen and I followed Maeve back to the house. While we cooked, Maeve paced in the kitchen.

"Do you still believe this to be the work of the King?" she asked, stopping abruptly.

"I'm not certain," I said. "There are many reasons to believe these deaths are related to the Royal Family. The arrival of the prince's servants the day of Mother's death. The King's insignia on the messenger's hat. And there is very little evidence to direct the blame elsewhere."

Maeve took my hands in her own.

"You must stop saying such things."

"What should we say?"

"Nothing."

I couldn't stop my look of disbelief.

"I understand your anguish and need for justice. But if you accuse the Crown of killing by use of magic with or without proof, you'll die, and your sister will truly be alone."

I glanced at Kellen who continued to cook as she listened to our exchange. Maeve's concern was very real and exactly Kellen's fear. Yet, it was the risk that something might happen to Kellen that spurred my insistence.

"And if the next victim is Kellen? What good will my silence have done?"

Maeve released my hands and considered me for a quiet moment.

"Kellen? Would you mind terribly if I spoke with Eloise privately?"

Kellen and I shared a look. We didn't keep secrets.

"Of course," Kellen said.

"Come with me, Eloise." Maeve turned and left the room. I quickly followed.

She led the way upstairs to her room. It was still empty save for the small bed in the side room and the large bag of clothes which she'd arrived with. She went to the bag and withdrew a folded piece of paper.

"I had hoped to never share this with you," she said. "You and Kellen have been through so much. But I need you to understand everything." She clasped my hand once more. "You and Kellen mean much to me. I want to keep you safe. To protect you from everything that is happening. It was what your father wished, too." She released my hand and looked down at the folded paper.

"Tell me honestly, Eloise…do you really think your father went to the Dark Forest to find a trade route?"

"Yes," I said firmly.

Maeve smiled sadly.

"I disagree. He loved your mother very much. Losing her hurt him in ways we will never understand."

I felt sick at what she was saying. Yes, my father had loved my mother very much, but so much that he had given up on life?

"I don't believe that."

"I know." She handed over the piece of paper.

I unfolded it and stared at the official document. A marriage license. Father's signature was on it along with Lady Grimmoire's.

"This is why I don't think he will return. The moment he heard of your mother's death, we wed. There is no love between us. He meant to leave you with someone who could protect you in full until you were ready to start your own lives."

The enormity of my situation hit me hard, and my hands started to tremble. Father wasn't coming back. Mother was gone. Judith and Anne were dead. All that remained in my world was Kellen.

"Why are you showing me this now?"

"You'd just lost your mother, and I didn't have the heart to tell you that you'd lost your father as well. I thought I could spare you. Discovering these deaths has changed that. Now, I worry that I won't be able to protect you. Especially if you choose to pursue the accusation of the Crown in the death of your mother, Judith, and Anne. I hope showing you this will help you understand why I'm urging you against it. Kellen needs you right now. She follows your lead while holding herself apart from all others. You are her strength. What would she do without you?"

"How will remaining idle keep us safe?" I asked.

"We won't remain idle. I will go to town and hire more help. More men like Hugh to protect the grounds. And you and Kellen will stay out of the woods."

I bowed my head and studied the document. How could everything have changed so much in that single moment of placing the necklace on Mother?

"I will not pursue my accusation of the Crown," I said looking up. "Unless there is no other choice. We will hide in the house, for now."

Maeve hugged me, her relief visible.

"Thank you, Eloise. And forgive me for telling you as I did." She pulled back to look at me. "I think it would be best not to tell Kellen of this. I fear for her wellbeing. She grieves so deeply already,

M.J. HAAG

keeping her pain to herself. Knowing that your father most likely will not return…"

I nodded and handed the license back.

Shortly after we returned to the kitchen, Sabine entered. Her silent, tear-streaked face reminded me that Kellen and I were not alone in our grief.

"I'm sorry for your loss," I said.

Sabine gave me a half-hearted smile as she sat on the stool by the fire and accepted a cup of the tea that Kellen had brewed.

"Thank you. And I am sorry for yours. I will leave with Anne and Judith at first light. There is no doubt now that magic was involved. We may not know who is to blame, but certainly the guard will have to give credence to the issue of their disappearance once they see the remains."

"I agree," said Maeve. "Judith and Anne serve as irrefutable proof that something is amiss in these woods."

158

CHAPTER 15

THE MOMENT THE COCK'S CROW SOUNDED, I FLEW OUT OF BED. I'D meant to wake before first light, but Kellen and I had stayed up late talking. Despite Maeve's warning to keep the news of her marriage to Father a secret, I had told Kellen. She had a right to know even if the information hurt her.

"Kellen, wake up." I hurried to slip into my dress as my sister sat up. "We're going to miss saying goodbye to Sabine."

That sparked some life into Kellen. She got out of bed and washed her face, the slight puffiness around her eyes barely noticeable. It hurt to know that she'd cried because of Father's abandonment of us. But it made me more determined to speak to Sabine again about bringing the bodies to the guard. If she was able to convince the guard that something was happening here on the king's lands, help would come quickly. And, perhaps we could then petition the king for help finding our father.

"What if they accuse her?" Kellen asked softly.

"Sabine wasn't hired on until after Mother, Judith, and Anne had already died. It would make no sense to accuse her."

"Very little in this world ever makes sense."

I gave her a quick hug.

"One look at those bodies, and the King's guards will know

magic is involved. They'll come help. The forest will be full of them, and they won't rest until they find the person responsible for all of the deaths."

Kellen nodded, and I helped her lace her dress then opened the door to rush downstairs, passing Maeve's already empty room.

When we entered the kitchen, we found Maeve by the fire watching three eggs boil.

"Good morning, my dears. Did you sleep well?"

"Yes, thank you. Where is Sabine?"

"She left before first light."

The news stunned me.

"Hugh is going to look for help while he's in town," Maeve continued. "I hope he'll return by lunch. Until then, the best I can do for breakfast is a boiled egg. I'm afraid my fondness of kitchen labors shows in my skill."

Maeve scooped an egg from the water with a wooden spoon. She only started to straighten when the egg rolled off and landed on the floor. The shell shattered and a scramble of semi-cooked egg whites and yolk spattered her skirt.

For a long moment, she looked down and did nothing. I knew that stance. It spoke of frustration and anger. The same emotions that often plagued me when circumstances were not favoring me. Much like now. Why had Sabine left so early? It was on the tip of my tongue to ask when Kellen nudged me.

"Eloise and I can make breakfast," she said.

"Thank you, Kellen." Maeve's words were barely a whisper.

She went to the table and began brushing off egg bits as Kellen and I set to work making something else for breakfast.

"I apologize," Maeve said suddenly. "I'm making a mess of things."

"One broken egg isn't a mess," Kellen said, pouring boiling water over oats.

I measured out the honey and nuts then covered the mixture.

"While that soaks, I think I'm going to go visit Mother," I said. "I'll eat when I return."

"Don't stray from the path," Maeve said.

Her lack of argument surprised me until I recalled I had never had the chance to tell her where I'd found Anne's cap. Too smart to bring it up and ruin my chance for freedom, I gave my word, grabbed my cloak, and fled the house.

Despite the deaths, the idea of walking the woods alone didn't frighten me. While some might say it was a lack of sense, I preferred to think of it as an extra bit of sense. The forest never frightened me because it didn't feel malevolent. People were wicked, not places—the Dark Forest excluded.

My feet carried me on a familiar path to Mother's grave. The sight of the pear tree, now twice my height and in full bloom, shocked me. A small bird sang in its branches. When I entered the clearing, the bird quieted but didn't fly away.

"Hello, little friend," I said. "Thank you for singing to Mother. She loved all your songs."

I sat on the bench and sighed, trying not to let the pain of missing my mother consume me.

"It feels as if a lifetime has passed since you left us, Mother. How has it only been weeks? So much has changed. You already know that Father is gone. We thought his absence would be extensive but temporary. However, Maeve showed me something that leads me to believe he never intended to return to us. He loved you so much, Mother. But, I wish he would have loved Kellen and me enough to have stayed. We could have used his guidance."

I took another deep breath and looked around the trees. It was quiet. Peacefully so. The scent of the pear blossoms washed over me, soothing me.

"Judith and Anne are gone. Taken by magic, like you. Kellen and Maeve don't want me to pursue whoever might be doing this for fear of the Crown's angry gaze landing on us. Yet, how can I sit idly by and watch those I love be taken from me one by one?" My throat tightened as I thought of Kellen. The only person I had left.

"I'm so angry, Mother. I'm trying to control it. I'm trying to think things through and not make any rash mistakes. However, I fear this idleness is, in itself, a rash mistake. I can only hope that Sabine has reached the guard and that they will take her seriously and not imprison her."

I sighed again, looking up at the bird who was watching me from a tree limb.

"Will you sing for us?" I asked.

To my surprise, it started warbling a pretty song. I closed my eyes, letting the sound wash away some of my pain and loneliness. When the song abruptly stopped, I opened my eyes and saw Kaven approaching in the distance.

He lifted his hands in surrender and peace. Warily, I watched him enter the clearing and halt on the other side of Mother's grave.

"You look so much like her, but you are nothing alike," he said.

"Who?"

"The princess," he said.

"Prince Graydon's princess-wife?" I frowned, confused by Kaven and his current intention.

"The very same," he said.

"You've seen her?"

"A man would need to be blind not to see such beauty."

My face began to warm at such a comparison.

"For her, it wasn't just on the outside."

My mouth dropped open.

"Are you saying I'm ugly on the inside?" I demanded.

"You have hit me in the face, bashed me with a rock, kicked me in the testicles, twice, and called me a pig. I can't exactly call any of that exemplary displays of inner beauty, now can I?"

The urge to hit him again had me fisting my hands in my lap. His gaze flicked to them, and he smirked knowingly.

"Truly, I cannot decide if your intent is to kill me or annoy me. Go away."

"Why would you think I would want to kill you?" he asked, his humor starting to fade.

"Considering you knocked me from my mount, how can I say otherwise?"

He grinned anew, a show of straight white teeth, which created a dimple in his right cheek. I blinked stupidly, once more noting how devastatingly handsome he was. Kaven was dangerous in too many ways.

"Go away," I repeated.

"I fear I cannot. I came to speak with you. When we first met, you mentioned your mother's passing. That day I came to pay my respects."

I snorted.

"You came to verify I spoke the truth."

He gave me a censoring look before continuing.

"Back then, this tree wasn't even to my knee. A single stem with no branches or leaves. Yet, look at it now."

His gaze pinned me.

"This tree has been touched by magic," he said lowly. "We must cut it down before it's noticed by others."

I stared at him. At the concern in his gaze, not for me but for the possibility that magic lingered nearby and that someone else might discover it. Could his worry be real?

"That tree was the last thing my father gave me before he left and likely the final memory I'll have of him. Keep that in mind when you do what you must." I stood to leave.

"Eloise, wait. I don't mean to take memories from you. I'm trying to keep you safe."

I made a scornful noise.

"Has there yet to be a meeting between us where I did not, at some point, land on the ground?" He opened his mouth, and I quickly cut him off. "Don't bother with excuses."

He considered me for a moment then inclined his head, and I felt satisfaction that I'd won that round.

"Before your mother died, did anyone new approach you? Were you given anything?"

My first thought went to the sound of hounds in the woods and news of the Crown's impending presence. Kaven had been the first new person here. After he'd arrived, so had the messenger boy and the necklace.

"Why do you ask?"

"I'm trying to determine how a single tree, in a forest full of them, is affected so."

"Perhaps my father bought it that way," I said. "Yes, it's touched by magic. How else can it be growing like it is? Yet, nothing malevolent has come from it. You heard the bird song. This place is still peaceful despite the magic. Have you ever considered that not all magic is bad?"

He held my gaze.

"Have you ever considered that not all magic is good?"

I thought of Mother, Judith, and Anne. Anger consumed me again. Without consideration of consequence, I crossed the clearing, standing toe to toe with Kaven.

"This is our land, by order of the king, to do with as we please. If you feel we've broken some sacred law, report us. Otherwise, leave this place and me in peace before I do something I most certainly will not regret."

He made a maddened sound.

"This meeting would have been much more enjoyable if you'd been on your back again."

My mouth fell open. Before I could respond, he pivoted on his heel and stalked away. I did the same, making sure to kick every fallen branch I crossed on the way to the house.

"Vexing, officious pig," I mumbled just before I reached the door.

I took a calming breath before I stepped inside. I needn't have worried, though. The kitchen was empty save for a covered bowl of hot oats for me. I ate slowly, repeating the conversation in my head. As much as Kaven provoked me, I struggled to continue my belief he was behind the attacks. I'd been isolated in the clearing. He could have taken me like the others. Why hadn't he?

"I HONESTLY DON'T MIND the work," Kellen said, checking the tea service.

Maeve was once again with a visitor, and with Sabine gone, Kellen was determined to fix a tray.

"Besides, Sabine isn't likely to return with Hugh. I'm certain she'll want to stay until Anne is buried."

"And to ensure the guard responds," I said.

Kellen nodded, and I watched her arrange some of the pastries that Sabine had made the day before.

"Did you finish your books already?" I asked.

She gave me a wry smile.

"Are you hinting that I should be cosseted away somewhere with my silly stories instead of helping?"

"Absolutely."

She rolled her eyes at me.

"Reading, while enjoyable, isn't enough to prevent this restlessness I feel."

She caught my surprised look.

"You're not the only one plagued by that condition."

"Would you like to go for a walk with me? I should take the pig out soon."

She shuddered.

"No, thank you." I knew the shudder wasn't for the pig but for what the pig had found the last time I'd taken him out, one of the many things we'd discussed the night before.

The sound of a wagon outside had us hurrying to deliver the tea tray to the dining room for Maeve. I planned to pepper Hugh with questions about Sabine's talk with the guard. However, it wasn't only Hugh who walked through the kitchen door a moment after we returned.

The first of a pair of questionably dressed women looked close to our age. Her brown gaze swept the room and locked on us. She smiled and performed a messy curtsey. The older women, behind her, bowed her head to us while also taking in the room.

I barely noticed Hugh enter because I couldn't stop looking at the generous display of bosom that the dresses of both women offered. The younger woman's flesh trembled with her excitement.

Kellen elbowed me. Hard.

I jerked my gaze up to find both women staring at us.

"Er...hello," I said.

"These are the new maids," Hugh said gruffly. With that, he turned and left.

The sound of the door closing seemed all the louder because of the subsequent silence.

Kellen nudged me again. Someday my sister would need to find her voice.

"I'm Eloise, and this is my sister, Kellen."

"I'm pleased to meet you," the younger woman said, smiling widely again. She didn't, however, offer her name.

"And you are?" I asked.

"Oh! I'm Catherine, and this is Heather. We're very grateful for this opportunity. We're hard workers and can listen well to direction."

Her earnestness and dress made me feel sorry for her. I'd been to town enough to know the sort of employment she'd had before this.

"Then this should work out well. We eat simple meals, but due to the passing of our mother are entertaining guests that expect more refined repast. Kellen and I can show you how to make a few of the pastries, if you'd like."

"We would like that very much," Catherine said.

Kellen and I gave them a tour of the kitchen. Each time I stepped close to either of the new women, my stomach gave a lurch at the strong smells of smoke and stale booze that clung to them.

"Maeve, our guardian, will be with our guest for a while yet. Would you like to freshen up before we begin? You'll have the kitchen to yourselves, and we have a few spare dresses you can change into, if you'd like." Certainly, Judith and Anne would approve.

"We tuck away the tub just here," Kellen said, pointing to a large cupboard to the left of the stove. "It's copper and heats nicely by the fire."

"Kellen and I can help you bring in water."

Heather gave a startled laugh.

"You want us to bathe in your tub?"

"Only if you want to," I said hesitantly.

The pair exchanged a glance, like Kellen and I often did, then nodded eagerly. However, they wouldn't hear of allowing us to haul the water. Once we showed them where the well was, they shooed us inside with a promise to have a stew ready for the midday meal within an hour.

Kellen and I snuck to our room.

"You know they're from a whorehouse," Kellen said.

"Yes."

"Don't you find that an odd occupational change?"

"Not at all. Which would you rather do? Lie on your back to service multiple men or cook for a respectable family."

Kellen glanced at her book and flushed.

"Sister, what are you reading that has you blushing?"

"A romantic book where the hero has manners and is devotedly loving to his bride. The loving is a bit detailed. She doesn't seem to mind being on her back rather than cooking."

At my wide-eyed look, she glanced at my book.

"Surely the same type of book Mr. Bentwell has been giving you."

I shook my head.

"Mine are fantastical tales of humorous adventure with happy endings for the heroine."

"Oh."

"Yes. Oh. Give me your book."

For the next hour, we read each other's books.

"This is so boring," Kellen said, closing my book.

"And this is far more than a bit detailed," I said, not taking my eyes from the page. "'He lovingly stroked her breast, toying with the rosy peak that begged for his hot, hungry mouth.' I repeat my earlier question," I said, closing her book. "What have you been reading? I can only imagine Mother's reaction to such a book."

Kellen's expression fell, and I knew I'd gone too far.

"She would have demanded to borrow it, and Anne would have scolded us for giving her something that would make her pulse race."

Kellen smiled slightly and stood.

"I'm not some delicate flower you need to protect constantly, Eloise. Although Mother was open about the joy she found in the marriage bed, I think you're right. She would probably question the wisdom of me reading about it. Likely she would think it would rob me of the joy to be found in the actual experience. However, I have no intention of ever participating in any of it. So none of that matters, does it?"

I shook my head, understanding Kellen probably better than she understood herself. She'd been hurt too much, too quickly, with the loss of those she loved. Instead of being angry at whoever took those lives from us, she pulled inward. She would rather never love again than risk the kind of pain she's endured.

Following her from the room, we quietly made our way back to the kitchen. A discreet knock on the door was answered with a cheery, "Enter."

The tub was drying before the fire, and Catherine and Heather were by the block, busily scooping a healthy serving of vegetable stew into two bowls.

"We'll bring this out to you in just a moment, miss and miss."

"We'd prefer to eat in the kitchen while there's company," I said. "And please call me Eloise. We don't stand on formality."

Catherine seemed pleased by the news, but I could see the doubt in Heather's expression. It only took a bit more coaxing for them to serve themselves and join us at the table.

"I swear to you, this is exactly what we did with our prior help," I said.

"Then, I can't understand why anyone would want to leave this position," Catherine said. "Good fortune for us they did, though."

Kellen and I exchanged a glance but didn't correct Catherine. Only time would tell if it was good fortune for them or not.

"When guests are here, Kellen and I usually take refuge here in the kitchen as well. We mostly read these days, and we promise to stay out of your way."

"As if you would ever be in our way," Heather said.

"What do you read?" Catherine asked.

Kellen immediately blushed and kicked me under the table. I grinned.

"Books about sex," I said, mischievously.

Catherine snorted. "I doubt those books are anything like the real act. Everything's probably all pretty words and long looks. That's not the real thing. A hard cock jammed up your twat before you even have time to think a happy thought is more like it. Every now and again, a real gentleman comes along and has the courtesy to wet the way with a bit of spittle."

Kellen and I wore twin expressions of shock.

Behind us, the door opened.

"Fetch Hugh," Maeve said, her face flushed and furious.

CHAPTER 16

CATHERINE POPPED UP FROM HER SPOT, PERFORMED HER MESSY CURTSEY, and rushed out the door.

"Send Hugh to the sitting room," she said. "Girls, go to your room."

She left without another word.

"Bollocks. I knew this was too good to be true," Heather said.

"What do you mean?"

"That there was gentry. Gentry doesn't tolerate the likes of us. Not unless it's one of the men wanting a quick fuck away from his wife's knowing gaze."

"I don't think it's that," Kellen said. "I think Maeve is upset about the topic of conversation she overheard."

"Exactly. We'll be in our own beds again before the sun sets."

The complete devastation on her face had me shaking my head.

"Not if you don't want to be," I said. "I'll go speak to Maeve. Your stew is delicious. You can cook, and I believe you're capable of cleaning and answering the door, too."

"We can do all of that," Heather said.

"Then there's no reason for you to leave."

Just as I left the kitchen, the main entry door opened, and Hugh's heavy steps echoed as he crossed the floor. He reached the sitting room before I could stop him. Unsure what to do, I hesitated in the hall.

"How could you?" Maeve's distressed tones easily reached my ears despite the partially closed door. "I cannot believe that is what you brought back. This household has a reputation to maintain."

"Forgive me, Maeve. Those were the only women I could find quickly. Maids with more experience are already employed."

"Then I hardly think you spent your time searching very wisely. I'm hard-pressed to believe there weren't two candidates more suitable for our needs in all of Towdown. You will search again tomorrow to find—

I knocked on the door.

"Come in," Maeve said, her tone still upset.

I opened the door, my gaze darting between Hugh and Maeve. Hugh looked dejected and as equally flushed as Maeve.

"I apologize for interrupting," I said. "I know the conversation in the kitchen just now seemed questionable—"

"Seemed questionable? No, Eloise. It was entirely inappropriate for someone of your age and position."

"I understand. But, they didn't know. They do now, and I'm sure it won't happen again. Kellen and I really like them. Catherine seems very eager to please, and Heather is determined to do what she must to make this work. Please give them another chance. Their stew is good, and with Sabine still in town, we're likely to be without help for a long while, especially once word gets out about what happened to Anne and Judith."

Maeve took a long calming breath.

"Leave us, Hugh."

He bobbed his head and left the room, shutting the door tightly behind us.

"You have a kind heart, Eloise. But, please try to see things from where I stand. How would our house ever endure if guests found out they were being served by whores?"

"Former whores," I corrected. "They want to be here. They don't want to go back to what they were doing. And I question why we should care what guests think of us. Kellen and I haven't met men who inspire any thoughts of a marital bond. What then does this estate's reputation even matter? And any guest who might see Catherine and Heather and recognize them wouldn't dare speak of how they knew them, would they? Please, Maeve. Everyone deserves a chance."

She sighed, her expression of irritation fading.

"You would think that's the case, but life often disagrees."

"Come speak with them. They're a little rough, but it's nothing a bit of guidance won't smooth."

"I'm not promising they will stay," Maeve said, following me from the room.

When I entered the kitchen, Kellen was at the table with her book and Catherine and Heather were washing the dishes. The sound of the door brought all motion to a halt.

Catherine and Heather turned to face us. I smiled encouragingly, but Heather's expression said she didn't expect anything more than an order to change and leave.

"To say that I'm displeased with your presence here is an understatement," Maeve said. "The conversation you were having with two unmarried girls of good breeding is reproachable."

I cringed a little on their behalves.

"We beg your pardon, Lady Grimmoire. It won't happen again. Kellen explained that we're not ever to speak of our experiences."

Maeve glanced at Kellen, who'd shut her book and watched the exchange.

"And do you think like your sister? Do you want to give these women a chance here, knowing what that might entail?"

Kellen looked at the table for a moment.

"I believe they would prefer to take their chances here than to return to where they were."

"She's got that right, ma'am. Please give us a chance. We'll do anything to stay. We don't mind emptying chamber pots or the like. The linens will always be fresh and your food served promptly." Catherine looked at Heather.

"You won't find more devoted help than us," Heather said, hope and desperation abloom in her gaze.

Maeve shook her head slightly.

"Don't get too comfortable. You're not suited to stay long in this house. I will put your word to the test in the days to come."

She turned toward me.

"Thank you, Maeve."

Her expression softened as she looked at me.

"Don't thank me yet. They may cause you nothing but grief in the future. It's your responsibility to teach them what they need to know. I expect no mistakes or coarse conversation after today. Now, my head aches fiercely. I must lie down."

She gave the women one last glance.

"Don't count on me for dinner."

With that, she left the room.

Catherine sagged with relief. "She's letting us stay."

"She is," Kellen said, standing. "I think we'd best show you how to make those pastries and explain any other duties you may have."

The four of us worked in the kitchen as the light outside slowly faded. Even while passing on the techniques that Judith had taught us, I listened for the sound of a carriage or horse to signal the King's Guard's arrival. However, all remained quiet outside.

When we finished with the pastries, Catherine sent us to the table to read while she and Heather fixed our dinner. I could see that Catherine was motivated and ambitious, not that Heather wasn't. She was just more subdued about it. Cautious.

Soon delectable, savory scents pulled me from my book and had me looking around the room in interest.

"Just a few more minutes," Catherine said.

The meat pies she set before us made my mouth water. The crust was golden and flakey.

"Let it cool or you'll scald your mouth," she said sitting beside me.

A moment of silence consumed the room.

"How did you become a whore?" Kellen asked.

Heather choked on her water, and Catherine patted her back.

"I don't think we should talk about that."

"Maeve's objection to the conversation was in the vivid detail," I said. "If you explain without referencing body parts, I think it will be fine."

Catherine looked doubtful, but I could see she didn't want to say no either.

"It just happened. There was a boy I liked. He talked me into doing things and gave me a coin after we finished. My family didn't have a lot of money, and my sister had married a goat farmer who lived more poorly than we did. I figured what I'd done hadn't been bad, and the coin was good."

Regret filled her gaze.

"It got worse, though, didn't it?" Kellen asked softly.

"It did."

"There are bad people in this world," Heather said. "People who like to hurt others for the sake of hurting them. You don't always have a choice in who you invite in."

My heart hurt for them.

"How old are you?" Kellen asked.

"I'll be eighteen this summer," Catherine said.

"I'll be twenty-three," Heather said.

I turned to my meat pie to hide my shock. Catherine looked closer to twenty-three and Heather near Judith's age. Their lives had aged them beyond their years.

Breaking open the crust, I inhaled the steam.

"This smells delightful, Catherine."

"Wait until you taste it," Heather said.

IN MY STOCKINGS, I paced the narrow confines of our room, pausing occasionally to glance out the window.

"If you don't stop, I'm going to smother you with your pillow," Kellen said without looking away from her book.

I quietly flopped on my bed.

"I'm going mad with the waiting."

"So I've noticed. The guard will appear when they appear."

"If they appear," I said, saying what we were both thinking.

Kellen sighed.

"If they didn't believe Maeve the first time, why did you suppose they would place more credence on the word of a housemaid?"

"Not her word. She had visible proof with her."

"If they even allowed her to show it. You were at that table with me while Catherine shared her story. The world isn't the kind and gentle place we would like it to be. Our parents kept us safe from the worst of it. But they aren't here now, and we need to come to terms with the reality of our lives."

I sat up and stared at my sister.

"Which is what exactly?"

She pulled her gaze from the pages to meet mine.

"The reality is that people will continue to leave our lives whether we want them to or not. Some partings will be agreeable and full of smiles. Some will be a blunt rending of our lives and filled with grief and tears like Mother's departure."

"And Judith and Anne's."

Kellen nodded and went back to her pages.

"I can accept the former but not the latter."

"Your lack of acceptance will only make the hurting worse."

Her comment and lack of emotion concerned me. Kellen was retreating too far into herself, and I worried what would happen if life continued to steal those we cared for. As kind as she'd been to Catherine and Heather, I'd noted how she'd also maintained a distance. I was the only one who remained close to Kellen. Not even Maeve had won her way in. And that troubled me greatly.

Moving to kneel beside Kellen, I plucked the book from her hands.

"And if I'm torn from your life, Kellen, what will you do?"

She shut her eyes.

"Blow out the candle, Eloise. I'm tired."

I poked her eyelid.

"No, you're not. You're avoiding the topic. Look at me, and speak your heart."

She looked at me, pain already in her gaze.

"If I lose you, there is nothing for me in this life."

It was just as I'd thought. She'd already given up and was only waiting for the end. I hugged her tightly, feeling her arms wrap around me just as fiercely.

"Our situation is not dire," I whispered. "You mustn't think so."

"Believe as you will, and I will do the same," she said.

"That's not good enough. I love you, sister. More than anyone. And because of that, we must make a promise."

Pulling back, I spoke my heart.

"If we're torn apart, the one who remains will find a way to live. Not a hollow existence but one filled with purpose and meaning that the other sister would approve of. Because we won't only be living for ourselves, we'll be living for both of us."

Tears pooled in Kellen's eyes, and I felt mine answer.

"Do you swear to do this?" I asked.

She remained silent for a very long time. It wasn't because she was overcome with emotions but rather she was considering the consequences of making such a promise. Because, I knew once she made it, she wouldn't break it. Just as she knew I wouldn't break mine.

"I swear," she said finally.

Releasing her, I smiled.

"Now continue reading your sex books."

She flushed fiercely.

"It's a wonder that Maeve allows you to read them when she so objected to the conversation in the kitchen," I added.

Kellen frowned at me.

"You're right. You don't think Maeve is bigoted toward Heather and Catherine because of their prior occupation, do you?"

"Given her strict adherence to appearance, perhaps she is."

I stood and blew out the candle.

"I was going to read more," Kellen said, objecting to the dark.

"You haven't been sleeping enough, and it's robbing you of your good sense. The book will be there tomorrow."

Kellen grumped, but I heard her crawl under her covers.

Too restless to sleep, I undressed then went to look out the window. The stars were bright in the night sky, and I thought of Father. Was he now staring up at the same stars but from Turre? Though Kellen and I both believe his survival would be an unlikely outcome to his adventure through the Dark Forest, especially now that we knew his intent, I could only hope for his continued existence even more.

Mother would want him to live. To find happiness again. It's what she'd want for all of us.

Glancing at Kellen's peaceful outline in the dark, I wondered how either of us would find happiness. The promise I'd pulled from her had been born of desperation. A way to ensure that, if something did happen to me, she wouldn't give up on living. Yet, I couldn't help but wonder what our futures would hold if the killer was found in time for us to emerge unharmed. We would be far from unscathed.

As I stared out into the darkness, something moved in the yard below. I looked down as a cloaked figure moved across the yard toward the shed.

"Kellen," I said softly.

There was no answer. Worried one of the new maids needed something, I left my room, keeping an eye on Maeve's closed door. It wouldn't do to alert her that something might be amiss.

I slipped through the kitchen and went out the back door, lightly running across the yard in my bare feet. A flicker of candlelight flashed between the boards, and I wanted to curse. Hugh, a light sleeper, was going to notice the light, and whichever one of the pair prowled the shed was going to get caught.

The light dimmed just before I reached the outer entrance.

From inside, I heard Hugh.

"You shouldn't have come."

I bit my lip, not sure what to do. Hugh might not mention the late-night prowling to Maeve. However, if I intervened, he would certainly mention my involvement to Maeve, given his increased protectiveness.

The sound of a slap rang through the air, and my eyes widened.

"I deserved that," Hugh said.

A moment later, he groaned. It wasn't a pained groan. Rather, the sound of it made my cheeks flush. The cold wrapped around my toes, quickly chilling me as I stood there in stunned silence.

Certainly, I had to be misunderstanding the situation.

Unsure, I slipped inside and moved closer to the boards separating Hugh's living quarters from the shed. The candle had been extinguished, leaving only the barely discernible glow from his stove.

Shadows moved within. Heavy breathing, escalating in pace, matched the rhythm of the movements. The sound of flesh against flesh made it quite clear what I was hearing. As did Hugh's words.

"You are pleasure made flesh. Let me taste you. Touch you."

The fire flared briefly. In that glimpse, I saw a woman sitting on top of Hugh. The way she moved, and the bare expanse of flesh from shoulder to hip brought to mind Catherine's words.

Frowning, I turned away from the view. A feeling of disquiet stole through me. It felt wrong what they were doing, and I couldn't place why. Perhaps it was the idea that she might think she needed to have sex with Hugh in order to stay here. I shook my head. Surely not. Maeve had been clear it was based on her opinion of them, not Hugh's.

I snuck back into the house and quickly wiped my feet on the rug before going upstairs.

"Kellen," I said as soon as the door was closed. She didn't answer so I poked her.

"I was sleeping. You told me to sleep."

"I know. But I just saw Hugh having sex with one of the maids."

She lifted her head.

"And?"

"What happens if Maeve finds out?"

"You heard Sabine. Affairs of the staff aren't important to the heads of household so long as they don't interfere with the work. I'm sure Maeve won't care."

I'd forgotten about that story from Sabine.

"What about Judith? How could Hugh recover from his grief so quickly as to love another?"

"Sex doesn't mean love," Kellen said. "And you shouldn't judge his actions. We all heal differently. Maybe what he's doing is to help him forget Judith."

I sat on my bed and stared into the dark, feeling Kellen's words hitting a tender spot in me. Is that what I'd been doing? Was I focusing on finding a murderer so I could avoid the pain quietly eating away at my insides? So I could forget Mother?

CHAPTER 17

I couldn't look at Hugh. Since I didn't know which of the maids had been with him last night, it was a little easier to speak to them. But only just. Thankfully, Maeve wasn't at the breakfast table to notice any oddity in my behavior. However, Kellen's awareness of the situation more than made up for Maeve's absence. Every time Kellen caught me studying any of the three, my shin suffered the toe on her slipper.

"Heather and I were wondering if there's a household schedule. What days are washing days? What days are supply days? And so forth."

"We go to town when we need supplies. The distance isn't far," I said.

"The linens are washed once every two weeks. When they're washed is entirely up to you," Kellen said. "The prior maid washed them only a few days ago."

"General tidying and meals are the only daily tasks," I said.

"We thought you might say that," Catherine said, sharing a glance with Heather.

"What is it?" I asked.

Heather got up and went to a cooling rack behind the block where a linen covered plate waited.

"Anyone can make a simple meal and clean a room. We knew in order to stay we would need to do something more," Catherine said. My stomach churned; and I quickly glanced at Kellen, which earned me another kick.

"We made these last night after you both retired for the evening," Heather said, carrying the plate to the table. "Would you try them and tell us what you think?"

With relief, I looked at the small multi-colored pastries daintily arranged on the plate that Heather set on the table. They were much like the lemon curd pastries that we'd shown them how to make, but with an additional dark red jam.

Taking one from the plate, I took a tentative bite. The familiar sweetness of the briarberry jam played off the tartness of the lemon curd.

"These are delicious," I said, watching Kellen take her first bite.

Hugh continued to work his way through his hot oats, purposefully ignoring us. I wondered if he'd already sampled a tart.

"Well done," Kellen said after a swallow.

"We're glad you like them," Catherine said. "We wanted to make something that might impress Lady Grimmoire. There's only these twelve, but if Heather or I could go to the market for more briarberries, we could make them for the guests."

Kellen and I looked at Hugh.

"You'll need to check with Maeve," he said without looking up.

I smiled at Catherine as Heather returned the plate.

"I'm sure she'll be fine with it." I finished my pastry and continued with the oats. Even the oats they'd made were good. I only wished Maeve had joined us so she could know that for herself.

As if my thoughts summoned her, she walked through the dining room door.

"Hugh," she said, stopping short at the sight of him. "Why are you eating in here?"

An uncomfortable silence fell as he flushed and glanced down at his bowl.

"Never mind that," she said. "I want you to go to town. The herbs I requested should be there."

He nodded and stood to leave while Maeve glanced at Kellen and me.

"Good morning, my dears."

"Good morning," we answered.

"Your timing is perfect, Maeve," I said, reaching for a pastry. "I want you to try this."

She took the small treat hesitantly.

"Why?"

"To see if it's fit to serve our guests. Kellen and I both tried it and found it enjoyable."

Maeve took a bite and looked at Catherine and Heather.

"You made this?"

They nodded.

"You've impressed me."

I grinned at Heather and Catherine.

"Since Hugh is going to town, perhaps one of them could accompany him and search the market for more briarberries."

Maeve's gaze met mine, and I was sure we were thinking the same thing. Why send one of them to town to pay coin for something we could pick from our own land?

Her expression softened.

"I think that's a lovely idea. Why don't you and Catherine go? She might need your help negotiating on behalf of this house."

I knew what she was really saying. Make sure Catherine didn't do anything to embarrass us and reveal her former occupation.

"Remember to stay together, though," Maeve added.

I glanced at Catherine, who nodded enthusiastically.

"You had better go catch Hugh before he leaves," Maeve said before leaving the room again.

As Catherine and I hurried to get our cloaks, I promised to find Kellen another book if there was time.

During the ride to town, I watched Catherine and Hugh closely. Since there were only the three of us, we all sat on the bench.

Catherine had insisted I take the middle because it was more secure. However, I questioned the validity of that reason.

"I'm a bit nervous," Catherine said softly.

"Why?"

"What if someone recognizes me at the market? I don't want to bring shame to anyone."

"You won't. And you look completely different in that dress and with your hair pulled back."

"Tell me if anyone recognizes you," Hugh said. "I'll take care of it."

Catherine blushed and nodded.

The evidence of who'd been with Hugh was right there, and I struggled with how I felt about it. In the end, I decided I was glad. Kellen held everything in and was slowly dying inside because of it. I didn't want that for Hugh. If being with Catherine gave him a moment's reprieve from the pain of losing Judith, then who was I to judge him harshly. As Kellen pointed out, everyone grieved and healed differently. And perhaps their dalliance would turn into something more.

Catherine's worry over being recognized proved unnecessary once we entered Towdown. No one gave us more than a curious look. And, as we walked the market, the vendors were too busy trying to sell their goods to care who handed over the coin. Likewise, those looking to purchase goods were too occupied negotiating a lower price to notice.

A stall selling hair ribbons caught my eye. Kellen and I had ribbons aplenty to match our dresses. However, both Catherine and Heather had used bits of twine to tie back their hair.

"I think I see briarberries ahead," Catherine said.

I looked at the stall in question and cringed at the crowd around it.

"I think I'm going to wait here by the ribbons."

"Are you sure? Hugh said we should stay together."

Hugh had left us the moment he parked the wagon to fetch the herbs from the herbalist that Maeve had previously visited.

"Hugh meant in sight of each other, not side by side. We will be fine. This is the market, after all."

"I'll try to hurry." She rushed off to the group, a determined expression on her face. I knew that her urgency would not have any influence on the speed of the sale and turned to study the ribbons.

I found two pale blue ribbons that would match the color of Heather and Catherine's dresses and gave a coin to the merchant for them.

Turning, I almost collided with a familiar figure.

"You," she said. "I wasn't expecting it to be you."

"Hello again, Rose," I said, looking at the old woman. "Who were you expecting?"

She smiled, showing a row of straight white teeth that contrasted with her weathered skin, and reached out to pat my hand. A tingle zipped along my flesh.

"Someone a bit older. What do you have there?" she asked, looking at my closed hands.

I turned my palm up.

"Ribbons for our maids. They didn't have any, and I thought they might like them."

"Aren't you a sweet child? Thinking of others. Kindness is virtuous, but it can bring trouble, too." She looked around the market. "Are you with someone?"

"My maid is just there," I said, gesturing toward the crush of people further down the way.

"Help me to that bench," Rose said. "We will watch and wait for her."

I looked at the occupied bench, ready to question her, when she hooked her hand through my arm, leaving me no other option but to help her. Not that she needed my assistance. Her steps were strong and sturdy.

When we reached the bench, she released me to glare at the two young men sitting on it.

"Remove yourselves and find something more useful to do with your time than chasing pretty skirts."

"Be gone, old woman," one man said irreverently.

The other looked at me and patted his lap.

"You can sit here, love."

Rose leaned toward the pair.

"If you act beastly, I will treat you beastly. Go!"

She said the last so loudly that the men jumped and slid off their seats, hurrying away.

Rose chuckled as she sat.

"They are so full of themselves." She looked at me. "A man can only hold what power we give them. If you never give them power, they will never have a hold over you."

She patted the seat beside her. Not wanting to appear rude, I sat. My gaze flicked to Catherine before returning to Rose, who was studying me with an uncomfortable intensity.

"Are you thirsty?" I asked. "I could fetch you something to drink."

The corner of her mouth lifted slightly as if I'd amused her.

"Would you see me killed by the King's guard?" the old woman asked suddenly. "Forced into the Dark Forest?"

"What?" I asked in surprise. "Certainly not."

She smiled again and grabbed my hand.

"Then tell me, Eloise Cartwright, why are you layered with magic?" She petted the back of my hand. "It coats your skin, clinging to you like water after a bath. What magic have you done or been near?"

I stared at her in shock. To speak so openly about magic begged for persecution of its use. Which explained her prior question. But how could she possibly know that I had been exposed to magic?

"I think magic killed my mother," I said absently, my mind racing.

If Rose could sense magic, did that then mean she could also use it? Kaven's words echoed in my mind. *Before your mother died, did anyone new approach you? Were you given anything?*

Rose's arrival wasn't before Mother's death but soon after. And she'd given me the pig.

My eyes widened as I stared at her.

"You?"

"Me? You think I killed your mother?" Rose cackled and slapped her knee. "Why would I do so? Random wickedness? No, I've had more reason to take a life and have never done so. The pig is proof. Now, why do you think I would want to kill your mother, child?"

I sighed and checked on Catherine's progress. She still wasn't any further into the crowd.

"Timing? Circumstance? I'm no longer certain. Very little makes sense to me of late."

Rose patted my hand.

"You will find that often in life. How is the pig? Did he find you anything useful?"

"Yes," I said, barely suppressing my shudder. "Though, I believe he tires of country life and would prefer to be with you."

She snorted.

"I doubt that very much."

I considered her for a moment.

"How do you know what's clinging to me?" I asked, too afraid to use the word magic.

"I think you already know the answer to that." Her gaze idly swept the crowd. "Like calls to like.

"When I sensed it in the clearing, I thought it was you using it. I wanted to see who would use magic in a place that isn't kind to those who do."

"What would you have done if it had been me?"

She considered me for a moment. For all appearances, she looked like an old woman passing time by watching the people around her, not an old woman discussing magic in the open.

"Nothing. There's no malevolence in you. However, there is malevolence here. I sense it from time to time, never long enough to find it, though. Except you. I'm curious who you would allow to use magic around you."

"Allow?" I asked.

Rose shrugged.

"Like a man, a caster can only use what power we allow them."

What she was saying didn't fully make sense to me. However, two things were clear. Rose knew about magic, and I had more questions regarding magic than I could count. Could I trust her to answer them honestly, though?

"How much do you know about magic?" I asked.

"Enough to know the magic clinging to you is too fresh to be from your mother's death. That magic still lingers at her grave."

I nodded and thought of the tree.

"Is there danger in visiting her?"

Rose glanced at me, her gaze filled with compassion.

"No, child. Speak to your mother as often as you like. There is nothing there to hurt you. Magic is neither good nor bad. Only the intent of the person wielding it."

"Can I ask you about something?"

"Haven't you already begun to?"

Taking my cue from her, I looked out over the crowd, watching the people hurry about their lives, not noticing those who might be observing them.

"Can objects kill a person?" I asked.

When Rose didn't answer, I glanced at her and found her studying me.

"What sort of object?"

"A necklace with a large stone."

"Perhaps. Do you still have it?"

I shook my head.

"It went missing."

Rose scowled at the ground for a moment.

"I met a woman from Towdown once. She told me of amulets made by a caster that protected the royal family against magic. Not long ago, I also heard of an amulet that killed."

"You did? What did it look like?"

"I do not know. I only know who the necklace killed."

"Who?"

"Prince Greydon's newly acquired wife barely a week after they'd wed."

"How long ago was that?"

"A few months."

Stunned, I looked out over the crowd and tried to find the connection. Who would want to kill a princess and my mother?

"I will be watching you, Eloise Cartwright. You have my word on that."

Rose stood with a quick pat to my knee and walked away. I stared after her, wondering if I should follow. It would do no good, though. My mind was still too overwhelmed with what I'd learned to form more questions.

"Who are you looking at?" Catherine asked, startling me.

"The old woman who shared the bench with me," I said. "Were you successful?"

Catherine held up a small bundle.

"I got the briarberries. I had to pay more than I would have liked, but I still think it's a fair deal. Is there anything else you wish to look at while we're here?"

"I think I've had enough of the market for one day. Let's go find Hugh," I said, standing.

"Do you know which herbalist he went to?" she asked.

I thought back, trying to remember the name of the shop.

"I don't think he ever said. I'm sure waiting for the briarberries took longer than the herbs, though. He's probably already by the wagon."

We'd only covered half the distance to the wagon when I heard my name called. I looked over my shoulder and saw Hugh. He looked annoyed.

"Where are you going?"

"Back to the wagon," Catherine said. "We found the briarberries Heather and I needed. Did you find what Lady Grimmoire required?"

"Did you speak to anyone?" he demanded, this time looking directly at me.

I frowned at him.

"What an odd thing to ask. Of course I did. What's gotten into you?"

A glint of green light flashed in his eyes just before he answered.

"Nothing. You ran off last time, and I don't want to be held responsible for any mistakes you make this time."

I stared at him in shock and growing fear. A plague had found its way into my home, and I had no idea how to stop it.

Hugh turned on his heel and would have stalked off had I not caught his arm and quickly stepped in front of him. He scowled down at me, his eyes clear of any unusual light.

"Are you all right, Hugh? Did something happen to you? Did you speak to someone?"

"We don't have time for your games. Come. Kellen and Maeve are waiting."

He shook off my hold and started toward the wagon. Catherine stepped up beside me as I stared after him.

"Did you see that?" I asked.

"He was a bit abrupt. Perhaps you should mention it to Lady Grimmoire."

"No, not that. That flash in his eyes."

"Men are prone to irritabilities. Tends to happen when their needs aren't being met. A quick dip of his wick, and he'll be right again."

Confused, I looked at her.

"Sorry, miss. Didn't mean to bring up that topic. Perhaps we should catch up, though."

She hadn't seen what I had. It only made me fear what was happening all the more.

CHAPTER 18

Kellen looked up from her book when I swept into the sitting room and closed the door. In silence, she watched me pace.

"Sister, why are you clutching blue hair ribbons?"

The random question halted my steps.

"What?"

"In your hand. Why are you holding ribbons like you want to rip them apart?"

I looked down at the forgotten items and tossed them onto a side table.

"Never mind the ribbons. I'm going mad. Nothing is making any sense, and I need your logic."

She closed her book.

"What is it?" she asked.

I sat in a chair across from her.

"Remember the old woman I told you about?"

"The one who gave you the pig?"

"Yes. She was in the market today. She grabbed my hand and started asking me questions. She said I had been touched by magic. But she didn't think it was from Mother's death. It was more recent. I was thinking it might be from Judith and Anne's deaths, but then I saw Hugh's eyes." I leaned toward Kellen. "They flashed green like the boy's. But Catherine didn't see it. How could she not see it?"

"Slow down, Eloise. Tell me everything you saw, said, and heard from the beginning. And keep your voice down. Maeve is resting with another headache."

Kellen listened intently for several minutes. When I finished, she looked out the window.

"Having logic is only useful when the situation is logical," she said. "What purpose would the Prince have to marry a woman and kill her with a magical necklace within weeks? And for her death to be kept quiet? It doesn't make sense. We must be missing something vital. Something we're not seeing. What could possibly connect Mother, Judith, and Anne to the prince's wife?"

"Judith and Anne? They didn't die like Mother."

"Didn't they? Perhaps not from the necklace, but certainly all three died by magic. They all came from different stations in life, with the exception of Judith and Anne. And the princess, while also dying because of the necklace, met her untimely end far from here."

"Kaven," I said slowly. At some point I'd started doubting his guilt enough that I'd stopped looking for it. Yet, there it was.

Kellen pinned me with a stare.

"You still believe it's the king's servant who is at the retreat?"

"He's the common thread. He admitted to seeing the princess, and he's here now."

"But why? What motive would he have to kill any of them? We could suppose the princess's death was an act against the Crown. Maybe because of resentment for having to serve his betters. But, that wouldn't make sense for Judith or Anne. Nor would the idea that he was a spurned lover. Mother was too old for him even if she had left the house in the last several years."

I sighed and leaned back in the chair.

"I'm frustrated to the point I want to throw caution to the wind and march over there to demand answers."

"Perhaps we could start a little closer to home and question Hugh."

I shook my head.

"He wasn't very receptive to any questions I asked during our ride home."

Kellen stood.

"Catherine was there. Perhaps what he had to say couldn't be said in front of her."

Anger beat at me at the amount of speculation surrounding the deaths and now Hugh.

"I will agree to this on one condition," I said.

"What's that?"

"If we learn nothing useful from Hugh, we go to the retreat yet today. I'm done waiting."

"I agree."

I grabbed the ribbons and followed Kellen to the kitchen.

Catherine stood by the oven, her face flushed from the heat, as she kept watch on whatever was inside.

"Are the pair of you hungry?" Heather asked. "The biscuits will be out of the oven in just a moment."

"No, thank you," Kellen said. "We're going to walk the pig around the yard."

"These are for you and Catherine," I said, setting the ribbons on the block by Heather. "I noticed you didn't have any."

"Thank you, miss."

With a smile, I grabbed my cloak and followed my sister out the door. We went straight to the shed.

"Hugh?" I called.

He didn't answer. Remembering what I'd seen through the boards the last time I'd peeked, I kept my gaze properly focused on the panel when I knocked on his door.

"Just look inside," Kellen said when we heard nothing.

I pulled the door open and quickly snuck a look inside his quarters before closing the door again.

"He's not there."

"Perhaps he's cleaning the pig's pen," Kellen said, uncertainty lacing her words.

However, he wasn't there either or raking the chicken yard or doing any of the other numerous tasks he would typically be doing this time of day. I stood in the middle of the drive and looked around.

A tingle shivered its way down my back, and I struggled not to let my temper take control.

"Not again," I said. "I won't. I refuse."

"He wasn't at the grave," Kellen said, joining me.

"We have to tell Maeve. We need to get the guards to look for him."

"Eloise, there's no sign Hugh was taken."

"He doesn't wear a cap or an apron to lose. What are you expecting to see? His pants on the ground?"

Kellen gave me a dry look.

"Well, that would certainly indicate something amiss, wouldn't it?"

"Kellen, I have an itch between my shoulder blades and something akin to a rock sitting in my stomach. I tell you, something is very wrong."

"Maeve went upstairs because she wasn't feeling well. I don't think we should disturb her because you have a bad feeling."

I saw it then. The fear in Kellen's eyes she was so desperately trying to hide. All my frustration left me. To acknowledge the fear trying to overtake her meant she would need to acknowledge the danger.

"You feel it too, don't you?"

She closed her eyes.

"Bad doesn't begin to capture what I feel. Like a knife in my breast, this growing feeling of foreboding is attempting to claim what I am." She opened her eyes and met my gaze. "Evil comes, sister. And I fear that we can no longer hide from it."

"What do you want to do, then?"

"Run," she said softly.

I pulled my sister to me and hugged her hard.

"Then that is what we'll do. Saddle the horse." Releasing her, I stepped back to pull the tack from the walls.

"Are we abandoning the rest?" Kellen asked.

I handed her the items and shook my head.

"I will collect a change of clothes for both of us and tell Maeve we're leaving. They can do as they choose."

She nodded and went to one of the stalls while I strode across the yard. It took all my control not to run. Whatever was taking the help had to be near. If it was near, it was watching. How else would all three disappear without the rest of us seeing something.

Fearful, I looked back at the shed. Was it wise to leave Kellen alone? Given that we'd just searched for Hugh separately and had both returned unharmed, I thought it was. Yet, I wouldn't chance Kellen's safety longer than necessary.

I entered the house quietly through the front door, not wanting to panic Heather and Catherine until I had a chance to speak with Maeve. Lifting my skirts, I rushed up the stairs.

I knocked lightly on Maeve's door. When there was no answer, I let myself in to wake her.

A familiar barrage of sounds, muffled grunts and groans along with slap of skin against skin, reached my ears. My steps slowed but did not stop. Drawn by the spectacle of my own foolishness, I approached the nursery door and soundlessly nudged it open an inch.

Maeve sat upon Hugh as she'd done the night before, her hands braced on his chest. Her breasts swung with each unseat and reseat of her hips over his. Hugh grunted and thrust upward to meet her, his face an expression of pleasure.

"Tell me who you serve," Maeve said.

"You. Always, you, Maeve."

"Tell me who you need."

"You. Don't leave me. I will do anything to keep you."

"Then, give me what I want."

The speed of her endeavors increased with her words. Hugh grabbed Maeve's hips and jerked into her. She grinned, a triumphant look, and her movements became frenzied. Hugh stiffened and threw his head back with a groan.

A thin stream of green light emerged from his mouth and merged with the glowing green amulet swinging between Maeve's breasts. Hugh's cheeks began to shrink in, giving him a familiar gaunt appearance.

Mother.

Judith.

Anne.

The answer to my question had been before me the whole time.

Maeve killed them all.

Silently, I backed away from the door and fled the room. How could I have been so blind? How could I have been such a fool?

At the bottom of the steps, I veered for the kitchen unable to leave Heather and Catherine to the same fate as Anne and Judith. Bursting into the kitchen, I startled the new help.

"Get out now," I whispered harshly.

Catherine's surprise turned to worry.

"What did we do, miss? Please. We'll do better."

"There's no time. You did nothing wrong. You need to leave now before she—"

The door opened behind me, and I whirled to face the threat.

Maeve walked in, pulling the sash of her dressing robe snug about her trim waist. My heart hammered in my chest, and I took a step back. The amulet hung exposed on her chest. It didn't glow now, but neither was it a dull, lifeless rock. That she wore what had killed my mother ignited something inside of me. Anger, laced with a deep pain, flayed me within.

Hugh entered behind her, bare except for the pants clinging to his hips. His eyes flashed green when he looked at me.

I retreated further.

"Are you trying to dismiss our help, Eloise?" Maeve asked. "While I agree their backgrounds are questionable, their work has been satisfactory."

"Thank you, Lady Grimmoire," Catherine said from behind me.

"Catherine and Heather, you both need to leave now," I said calmly.

Maeve made a sound of impatience.

"Eloise, your dramatics are beneath you. Yes, you found me having intercourse with the help. It's nothing to run from. Catherine, dear, can you fix some of the tea that Hugh brought in earlier? I think we all need to have a cup while we talk."

"You can't hide behind your lies anymore, Maeve. I saw the amulet and what it did to Hugh. You killed Judith and Anne. You killed my mother. I will see you punished."

I turned and ran for the door but didn't make it more than a few steps before I was pulled back by my hair.

"Your ignorance was your protection," Maeve said a moment before Hugh hit me.

Pain exploded in my face. My knees buckled, and I fell to the floor. Maeve's next words penetrated the buzzing in my ears.

"Hugh, go outside and fetch our lovely Kellen, would you?"

"No," I whimpered, my mind clouded. Mother's last message to me rang through my mind. I needed to protect Kellen.

The door opened, and I filled my lungs to scream one word.

"Run!"

Something collided with the back of my head, and I fell into darkness.

CHAPTER 19

PAIN PULLED ME FROM THE DEPTHS OF DARKNESS. IT RADIATED throughout my body, throbbing in time with my heart, only to return to my head threefold. I moved my hand to grip the offending fixture, but something rattled loudly. I winced at the sound and the unexpected weight straining my arm.

"Lie still, Eloise," Kellen said softly.

With effort, I opened my eyes and met my sister's worried gaze. Her usually pale skin was even more so. As she set a cool cloth on my brow, the momentary respite from the ache in my skull enabled me to note the fear that flickered in her gaze.

"What happened?" I asked, wincing at a new burst of pain. Why did speaking hurt my cheek? Why was I lying on the kitchen floor?

"What do you remember?" Kellen asked.

Snippets flashed in my mind. The messenger boy who delivered a cursed necklace. Mother dying and Father leaving. Judith and Anne going missing and finding the bodies, shriveled by magic. My suspicion of Kaven and the Crown. Seeing Hugh with Maeve while she wore the necklace. The same necklace that killed Mother.

A different kind of pain bloomed inside of me. A regret so deep that it bled. My mother's killer had crept into our house under the guise of comfort and support. How could I have been so blind?

"I remember enough," I said.

Closing myself off from the memories, I looked at my wrist and the metal encircling it. My gaze followed the links of heavy chain from the cuff to the source imbedded in the stone of the hearth.

"I don't recall how I became chained, though. Or why my head aches so dreadfully."

My sister turned the cloth over, replacing it on my forehead, and the coolness relieved some of the ache once again.

"I heard you yell for me to run," she said. "The horse was ready. I made it into the saddle before Hugh reached me." She swallowed hard and looked away.

I followed her gaze and saw Heather and Catherine sitting at the table, listening. Catherine's gaze met mine, and I saw her pity for me.

"For your safety, I cannot leave," Kellen said, reclaiming my attention. "Your current suffering serves as a warning to never disobey again."

Catherine stood.

"I will tell Maeve that Eloise is awake, now." She glanced at me. "I'm sorry, miss."

Heather stood, too.

"Come, Kellen. Remove the cloth and help me start the meal."

Kellen leaned down and pressed her lips to my forehead.

"I'm sorry, sister," she whispered before standing.

My mind was too fogged with my aches for me to understand why Kellen was sorry. Especially when I was the one who'd failed us.

While Kellen followed Heather, I gingerly tried moving. My thighs ached but my knees and ankles worked without pain. My hip hurt, and I hoped it was only from laying on the stone hearth. However, when I attempted to push myself upright, the agony in my side intensified. Since sitting up wasn't an option, I rolled to my back. The contact with the stone made me hiss, and I returned to my original position.

The door swung open, and Maeve strode in. She wore the same

kind expression she always had as her gaze flicked to Kellen before landing on me.

"How are you feeling, dear?" Maeve asked.

"Like I was beaten," I said, unable to keep the resentment from my tone.

"Oh, you poor thing." Concern and pity fill her gaze, sincere in every aspect of her expression and her tone.

For a moment, I was confused. She'd killed my mother and had me beaten. I couldn't breathe properly without it hurting. Was she truly apologetic?

My silent question was answered with the slow curve of her lips. The malevolent smile set my anger smoldering.

"I tried to warn you," she said. "Your inquisitive nature brought you to this. A beaten heap of human flesh before a fire." She walked toward me and squatted down, her skirts brushing my wrist.

"You could have lived a life of comfort had you only continued as you were," she said softly, her words only for me. "What you now know complicates things for you."

She lightly brushed away a strand of hair from my face, a gesture any observer might see as comforting. I now knew not to listen to my eyes.

"You're bruised and look as awful as you feel, I imagine."

She stood and primly clasped her hands in front of her.

"Life is all about appearance, Eloise. I'm afraid I cannot allow you to leave the kitchen until you once more look the part."

Maeve glanced at Heather.

"Has she said anything?"

"She asked why she was beaten and why her head hurts, My Lady."

"Nothing else?" Maeve pressed.

"No, ma'am."

"Please leave us."

Heather scurried from the room. At the block, Kellen continued to chop something.

"Look at me, Eloise," Maeve said, her voice commanding. As

soon as I met her gaze, the necklace glowed, and an uncomfortable warmth wrapped around me.

"The price of your knowledge is your silence. You will not be able to speak of what has happened here. Not a single incriminating word will leave your lips. You will protect me with every remark. You may know who killed your mother, but you will never utter the words to anyone. In this, my will is your will."

The glow stopped, and Maeve turned to Kellen.

"Do what you will for her. But remember, her continued recovery lies in your obedience."

With that, Maeve left the kitchen. Kellen set the knife aside and hurried to me.

"What was that?" I asked.

"We can no longer speak of what we know."

"That she—" My throat tightened painfully, and I winced.

I tried several more times to speak about magic, Mother's death, or anything that might implicate Maeve. However, as soon as I thought what to say, my throat closed before I could speak it.

Kellen nodded as I began to understand. Maeve had cursed us both.

I wanted to rage against what had happened, but I was too weak and sore to do anything but lay by the hearth and hate. Kellen knew me well and left my side only to return a short while later with cold water fresh from the well.

"You should run," I said after taking a long drink.

She shook her head. "She vowed—"

Kellen winced and rubbed her throat, and I could well imagine what Maeve vowed if Kellen couldn't speak it. I wouldn't leave my sister either if our roles were switched.

"We must do something," I said quietly.

"You must rest," Kellen said just as the door opened once more.

Heather and Catherine shuffled in, giving us both sympathetic looks.

"Can they speak of it?" I asked Kellen, remembering I'd accused Maeve in front of them.

Kellen shook her head.

"They are silenced like us."

Catherine looked up from whatever she'd been about to do at the block.

"Not like you," she said.

"You are correct. Not like us."

I sighed and rubbed my forehead.

"Does it ache?" Kellen asked.

"Dreadfully."

"I can make you some tea."

"No. I think it best I remain aware for a while." Kellen nodded and stood.

I watched in silence as she helped Heather and Catherine prepare a meal. Despite my efforts not to think of the past, memories slipped in. How we'd welcomed Maeve into our home. How we'd given her Mother's room. My fists clenched. How we'd listened to her advice and allowed her to meet with callers on our behalves. The way I'd confided my suspicions about the Crown.

Ignorant. Naïve. Stupid.

There wasn't an appropriate name for my level of self-loathing at that moment.

As I watched Kellen move around the kitchen, I wondered about our fates. Maeve had killed Mother, Judith, and Anne, not enslaved them. Why was Maeve keeping us? Why not kill us as she had the others? But more importantly, why was she doing any of this? There were far too many questions for my aching head and far too few answers to ease any of my anguish.

Catherine disappeared into the dining room with a tray while Kellen ladled out four more portions. I closed my eyes as Heather sat at the table with her portion.

"Are you well enough to sit up?" Kellen asked from nearby.

"What purpose does Maeve have for four maids?" I asked, meeting Kellen's gaze.

I saw the answer in her eyes. Maeve had no purpose other than that which she'd already revealed with the deaths of those before us.

Kellen's cool fingers stroked my cheek.

"I think we're different," Kellen said softly. "We have a part to play."

"If only we could see it."

"Perhaps it's better we do not."

I fisted my hands, wishing to hurt the woman who had injured me so grievously time and again.

Touching my throat, I raged against the curse that would prevent me from speaking her crimes and the chain binding me to the hearth. Unable to leave...unable to speak...Maeve likely thought I posed no threat to her. She didn't know me.

Exhaling slowly, I let the cinder of my hate grow. I, Eloise Cartwright, would find a way to stop the woman who killed my mother. And, the fire of my rage would destroy whatever Maeve sought to build with her lies and magic.

DISDAIN

CHAPTER 1

I LAY BEATEN AND CHAINED TO THE HEARTH, ANGER MY ONLY companion as the events that led me to this circumstance vividly replayed in my mind. I'd been so blind to who was responsible for the murder of my family, and that ignorance had cost me far too much. I would not allow Maeve to take any more from me.

A stab of agony shot through my face when I clenched my teeth at the thought of the woman who'd killed my mother. Maeve would pay. I'd find a way. Somehow.

The sound of the door opening stilled my tormented thoughts.

"You will need to prepare dinner tomorrow for a small group. Ten, perhaps. Something suitable to be served in a fine home."

"Yes, My Lady," Heather and Catherine said.

The sound of Maeve's voice enflamed my anger anew. Keeping my eyes closed, I forced myself to push the emotion aside so I could think logically.

Maeve was planning on serving dinner to guests. How could I use that to my advantage? Since I couldn't speak out against Maeve because of the spell or show myself to whoever might be due for dinner because of the damned chain around my wrist, there was little I could do.

A whisper of sound was the only hint of Maeve's approach.

"Stand, Eloise."

"I cannot. It hurts to move," I said.

"Stand, or I will call Hugh so your sister can feel what you feel."

Slowly, I turned my head and looked up at Maeve. One of my eyes no longer fully opened, but I could see her well enough. She watched me fight the pain that stabbed across my middle as I set my hand on the floor and began to lift myself. I let all the anger I felt show in my eyes as I leveraged myself onto all fours. It took another few moments to gain my feet and slowly straighten.

Behind Maeve, I saw that Kellen worked alongside Heather and Catherine. All three kept their gazes downcast. However, despite my recent beating and the agony ripping through me at being forced upright, I was far from submissive.

"Why?" I asked Maeve.

"Why what, Eloise?"

A small smile curved Maeve's lips when I opened my mouth and choked on my words.

"When you find your voice, I'll answer your questions. Until then, walk around and exercise your legs. I expect you and your sister present and in good form for dinner tomorrow." She stepped closer to me. "Appearances, Eloise. Don't forget. I should hate for Kellen to suffer for your ineptitude."

If Maeve was so concerned about appearances, why would she want me to attend a dinner with my face so obviously marred? It didn't benefit me to question her, though. I wanted others to see me as I was because, even if I couldn't condemn her for it, they would know it happened under her care.

She turned to the others.

"Have a list ready for Hugh first thing in the morning. He will fetch whatever is needed. I have accounts to look through. When dinner is ready, I'll take it in the sitting room."

She glanced at me once more then departed.

Kellen rushed to my side and wrapped a supportive arm around me. I grunted at the contact. I felt certain something was permanently damaged inside of me. It shouldn't have hurt so much to breathe.

"I need a chamber pot," I said, my words as broken as I felt.

Catherine fetched it for me, and Kellen lifted my skirts to help me use it. She gasped at the sight of my legs. I didn't look. I didn't want to know. When I tried to squat, I groaned in pain.

"How will you ever sit through a dinner?" Kellen asked softly.

Her question echoed my own thoughts. It would be hell, but I would endure it to spare Kellen the same fate I currently suffered.

After dinner, Catherine and Heather retreated to their room; and Maeve came to return Kellen to our room until morning.

"And Eloise?" Kellen asked.

"Eloise has yet to understand that there are worse fates than to be a pampered daughter of a merchant. She will sleep where she is tonight."

The stone hearth was hard, but the fire kept the chill at bay. Twice I woke to drink the tea that Kellen had left for me. All in hopes that rest would help the healing. However, when the sun rose, I felt each injury more deeply, not less so.

Catherine and Heather moved about quietly, neither speaking to me as I slowly rose to my feet. Breathing continued to hurt, as well as using the chamber pot. When I finished, Catherine set a washbasin on one of the stools near the fire and took away the pot.

I glanced down at the water. My cheek was colorfully swollen just below my eye, which was why opening it had been difficult. Between that and the dirt marring my face, I looked like I lived a very rough life. Given all that had happened, it felt an accurate portrayal.

Picking up the cloth that Catherine had left, I washed carefully.

The door to the kitchen opened, and Hugh walked in with his arms full of firewood. He didn't look at me as he filled the bin. When he finished stacking all of the pieces, he went to the table and sat. Catherine glanced at him then me. An unnamed emotion crossed her expression before it disappeared again.

"We're fixing hot oats," she said. "It will be a few more minutes."

While they cooked and he stared at the wall, I started walking in slow circles. My chain rattled occasionally and tugged at my wrist. The discomfort was nothing compared to everything else.

Kellen entered the kitchen just as Heather placed the bowls on the table. Maeve was a step behind my sister.

"We will sit together," Maeve said, taking her place at the head of the table. Catherine hastily handed me my oats and went to join the others.

"Do you have the supply list for Hugh?" Maeve asked. She blew on her oats and took a tentative first bite.

Catherine and Heather cast nervous glances at each other before Heather answered.

"Yes, ma'am. Will dove served with fall roots and a brandy-berry sauce suit you?"

"It sounds lovely. Make sure it tastes so."

Sitting on the stool by the fire, I ate my oats and stared at Maeve. I hated her and still wanted to demand answers for questions I was forbidden to speak. My inability to do so only made my rage fester.

"Kellen, once you're finished, you will return to your room." Maeve looked at me. "Eloise, I suggest you remove the loathing from your expression when you look at me, or I will take your eyes."

She said it so calmly and in such a gentle voice that I didn't doubt her promise. Exhaling slowly, I masked what I felt for her.

"Much better," she said. "I will not tolerate that look from you again. Am I clear, Eloise?"

"Yes."

"Now, there is much to do today; and the more you move before dinner, the better you will feel. Once Kellen is safely locked in her room, you will assist Heather and Catherine then bathe and dress for tonight's guests. If you do anything other than that, your sister will suffer."

As she said the word suffer, her necklace glowed, and Kellen hissed out a breath and dropped her spoon.

"Do you understand me, Eloise?" Maeve asked.

"Yes."

"Very good. Now finish your meal. You need your strength."

IN THE ENTRY, I stood beside Kellen. Maeve's gaze swept over us, lingering on our hair and fancy mourning dresses.

While the need to attire ourselves so formally worried me, I couldn't bring myself to hate what I wore. The snug lacings made it a bit easier to breath and move.

"Well done, girls," she said, her voice echoing with true praise, which I knew to be false.

She reached into her pocket and produced a small, dark vial which she held out to me.

"Drink it all. It will mask the unfortunate state of your face for several hours."

I took the vial and uncorked it. I could feel Kellen stiffen beside me. I knew it wasn't wise to drink anything from Maeve. However, it was less wise to disobey her. She'd proven that.

Tipping back my head, I drained the vial and shivered at the taste of the contents. A moment later, my face tingled.

"Much better," Maeve said.

I glanced at Kellen and noted a flicker of shock in her expression as she stared at my face. I touched my cheek, gingerly testing the puffy flesh. It still pained me greatly.

"You're no longer bruised," Kellen said.

Before I could question her, carriage wheels crunched against stone outside.

"Just in time," Maeve said. She gave us one last sweeping appraisal before meeting our gazes. "Do not be misled into believing the presence of guests will protect you from any transgressions. The punishments will only be that much worse for you and those who bear witness. Do you understand?"

Kellen and I both nodded. We understood very well what was at risk. Yet, I was free from the chain, and Kellen was free from her room. If a moment presented itself, we would run.

When Maeve turned her back to us, Kellen's hand slipped into mine, and she gave me a light squeeze. My sister would be ready this time. I knew it in my heart.

Maeve opened the door to a quartet of finely dressed gentlemen.

"Lady Grimmoire," the first one said with a dashing bow and a kiss to the back of her hand. "I was quite pleased when my wife returned from her visit with an invitation to sup with you in a week's time. Although, I must say I'm curious as to the reason why."

"All will be explained in good time," Maeve said. "Come. Let us retreat to the dining room. The fire will warm us as will the brandy." She turned to Kellen and me. "Please lead the way, Eloise. Kellen and I will wait for the remaining three guests to join us."

Kellen discreetly released my hand, and I led the way to the dining room. The men helped themselves to glasses of brandy then tried to enquire why they were invited without their wives.

"Is it a business proposition?" one asked.

"I'm sorry. I don't know."

"It must be business. Why else would we be here?" another asked.

Now that I knew what she'd done to my family, I could think of only one reason for her invitation. Yet, these were men of note. People who would be missed if they disappeared. Certainly, Maeve couldn't mean to kill them. Especially not when she'd invited them a week ago before our attempted escape and my beating. If not to kill them, why invite them at all? What purpose could they serve for her?

It wasn't long before Kellen and Maeve joined us with three other well-dressed men.

"Gentlemen, please have a seat," Maeve said. She looked at me then Kellen and motioned for us to sit to her right and left. I sat gingerly while the men took the remaining chairs.

"Thank you all for joining us this evening. Let us eat first and speak of business matters afterward," Maeve said.

The door to the kitchen opened, and Catherine and Heather emerged with covered platters. They began placing them before the men, making several trips to ensure everyone had a plate.

Maeve raised her glass.

"To new connections and power," she said. The men around the table brightened and returned her toast then lifted the lids from their platters.

Under the table, Kellen nudged me, and I hurried to unveil my meal. The little fowl sat prettily on a bed of sliced roots. The brandy-berry sauce glazed the crisp skin and had my mouth watering. I took my first bite, expecting delight only to embrace the pain of chewing. I kept my bland yet proper expression carefully in place and forced myself to keep going.

There was some light conversation around the table while we ate. It wasn't until I heard a familiar name that I fully paid any attention.

"Alliances aren't just for the Royal Houses," one man said.

"Agreed," another said. "Alliances for those of us in business are just as important. We must protect our interests in these dangerous times."

"Dangerous times?" Maeve asked.

"Yes. I suppose you don't hear much out here. But a Mrs. Tiller and her niece were found dead in their separate homes. Honest working women, the both of them."

Kellen briefly met my gaze then focused on her meal. I did the same, struggling to keep the anger and hate off my face.

"That's unfortunate," Maeve said. "Such deaths are unnecessary. But the topic of alliances does bring me to my purpose for inviting you here."

The men set down their forks and gave Maeve their full attention. From the corner of my eye, I caught movement in her amulet and kicked Kellen under the table. She glanced at me, and I closed my eyes, hoping she would do the same. I didn't know how Maeve's magic worked, but she'd asked me to look at her when she'd cursed me. I had no intention of being cursed again.

"I struggle to build my power with the paltry offerings in this secluded area," Maeve said, her chair scraping against the floor. "I'm inviting you to join me as I create an influence over this tired town. If you give your consent to help me in whatever small ways you can, I can offer you my support in return, along with limitless pleasure away from the censure of your wives."

One of the men at the table groaned his agreement. Then another. One by one they succumbed to whatever spell Maeve was casting.

"Girls, open your eyes," Maeve said.

I reluctantly did and saw the men had their gazes fixed on us. Panic bloomed in my chest as one reached under the table to stroke his groin.

"Catherine. Heather," Maeve called.

The door to the kitchen opened, and Heather and Catherine emerged fully nude. Shock and decency had my gaze locked on Catherine's face. She wore an expression of hopelessness.

"I believe Mr. Wineford would like his cock sucked," Maeve said, pointing to the man next to me.

Catherine came to his side, helping him loosen his trousers, and got to her knees. I quickly looked at Maeve, surely she didn't mean for—

The onset of wet slurps from Catherine and heated groans from the man made my face flush scarlet.

"Heather, choose one," Maeve said, gesturing to the remaining men.

Heather moved to another man and did the same as Catherine.

Two threads of green rose into the air and floated toward Maeve's necklace. A satisfied smile curled her lips as she looked at me.

"Tell me, Eloise. Do you wish to lead the life of a serving wench or that of a proper young lady?"

CHAPTER 2

"I WISH TO LEAD THE LIFE OF A PROPER YOUNG LADY," I SAID DEMURELY.

"I thought as much. Kellen, Eloise, come with me."

I quickly fled my seat, keeping my gaze fixed on the wall as I joined Maeve near the kitchen door. Despite my focus, I still glimpsed what was happening to poor Catherine and Heather.

The men were crowding around them, touching them. One man had lifted Catherine's hips so her backside was in the air. While she continued to service the first man with her mouth, the second man stood behind her with his pants around his ankles. He began to thrust into her vigorously.

My face heated further. Though I wished to save Heather and Catherine, I could do nothing unless I wanted to join them.

Kellen's fingers brushed against mine. Maeve's smile only grew at the gesture. She opened the door and waved for us to enter the kitchen. Another green thread joined the first two, and even as the door closed, it touched the amulet.

"Take off your dress," Maeve said, looking at me.

Panic took flight in my chest.

"Please, Maeve," Kellen begged softly. "Eloise won't—"

"I do not intend to send her to those men. Catherine and Heather will suit their needs well enough. Now remove the dress, Eloise. I will not repeat myself again."

With shaking fingers, I undid the row of buttons along the bodice then the ribbons underneath. The dress slid down my torso, and I carefully stepped out of the skirts. Standing in just my underthings, I clutched the mass of material to my chest.

Maeve held out her hand. Reluctantly, I surrendered the garment.

"Put the cuff around your wrist," Maeve said.

Relieved that I was only being chained to the fireplace, I did as she said. Once the metal clicked back into place, Maeve gave me a pleased smile.

"Very good, Eloise. You've done well today. I'm proud of the effort you've made. Perhaps in a few days we won't need the chains, and you'll be able to rest with your sister in the comfort of your own room. Wouldn't that be nice?"

I nodded, and Maeve looked at Kellen.

"Come, Kellen. Time to put you to bed. Perhaps tonight you won't mind the lock on your door."

"Thank you," Kellen said softly, giving me one last look before following Maeve from the room.

Though my body still ached, my mind was clear. I sat on the stool near the fire and stared into the flames, considering what I'd learned this evening while trying not to hear the sounds coming from the dining room. Pieces fell into place. The way the amulet glowed when Maeve used its power. The threads of green that came from the men. Whatever was happening in the dining room was a dangerous magic. I felt certain that Maeve was draining the men as a means to power her amulet. Why? And why now?

A week ago or more, Maeve had invited these men into our home. Was the outcome of this dinner her intent all along? Was that why she'd killed Judith and Anne? So she could bring two whores here to suit her purpose? I remembered Maeve's reaction to Heather and Catherine, though, and struggled with what was real and what had been pretense. She hadn't known I would overhear her slapping Hugh, had she? I felt certain her anger had been real. Would she have used any maid Hugh had found in such a manner? Or, the more chilling thought, would she have used Kellen and me if maids hadn't been found? Maeve wasn't above hurting us. My current state proved that. Yet, she hadn't let the men touch us tonight. Why? More importantly, why did she need more power?

I thought of the way the men's pleasure had fed the amulet. What was she planning to do with the power she collected? Nothing good. That much was obvious.

Rubbing my hand over my face, I tiredly reached for the cold tea still sitting by the stool and drained the contents. It was the same tea I'd used to send Hugh into a deeper sleep, and I hoped it would help me tonight. However, as I lay on the hearth waiting for sleep to claim me, I heard every grunt and masculine laugh from the adjoining room. My heart hurt for Heather and Catherine. They'd thought they'd escaped a life of whoring by coming here.

I wasn't sure how long I lay there drowsing before the sounds finally began to quiet.

The door separating the kitchen from the dining room opened, and I scrambled to my feet in a panic, almost passing out with the pain in my side. It wasn't any of the men entering the kitchen, though. Only Catherine and Heather, still nude and now flushed, both carrying stacks of plates.

Neither one would look at me.

"I'm so sorry," I said softly.

"Don't be," Catherine said. "You tried to warn us. It wasn't so bad."

She set her plates on the block and started back for the dining room.

"They weren't mean," Heather assured me. "It could have been much worse. Would it bother you if we bathed?"

"Not at all."

Outside, carriage wheels scraped against stone as our guests departed.

While Catherine collected the rest of the dishes, I moved the tub before the hearth, and Heather hauled water. They didn't even wait for it to warm before bathing. I sat on the stool and watched the flames, giving them what privacy I could.

Once they finished, they emptied the tub and started washing the dishes.

Tired and numb from the day and the pain of my still aching limbs, I lay down before the hearth once more. I was just dozing off when something brushed against me. I looked up at Catherine as she covered me with one of their blankets.

"Will you get in trouble for this?" I asked.

"I don't think so."

"I truly am sorry. I wish I could have done something."

Catherine shook her head.

"You made the right choice. I would have done the same."

She lightly brushed her fingers over my bruised cheek and left me.

I WAS SITTING on the stool by the fire when Kellen and Maeve joined us in the kitchen the next morning.

"Very well done last night, girls," Maeve said.

She sat at the table, and Catherine hurried to set a soft-boiled egg and a plate of fresh biscuits before her.

"Thank you, Catherine." Maeve used her spoon to crack into her egg. "I expect we will have more company of the female variety today. Please make sure to have a tea tray ready and some of those delightful pastries."

She finished her meal without a glance at me then left the room. As soon as she did, Kellen rushed to my side. Without a word, she hugged me tightly. It hurt my side and my face, but I didn't utter a sound. I couldn't. Not when she was shaking so badly.

"I thought she was going to make you go to them."

"Shh…" I said, stroking her hair. "I know. But, she didn't. It's all right."

"I'm so sorry, Eloise."

"There's nothing to be sorry for. None of this is your fault. You know that."

There was a scrape of noise behind us. I lifted my head and found Catherine cleaning up the table.

"I'm going to go walk the pig," Heather said.

"I'll go feed the chickens," Catherine said.

I studied their guilt-laced expressions as they left, slightly confused.

"They have ears," Kellen said, easing her embrace. "And mouths to repeat what they hear, whether they want to or not."

Then, I understood. They'd left so we could have a private word. I wouldn't waste the opportunity.

"You need to leave," I said. "Find a way to run."

"No. She promised she would—" Kellen winced and rubbed her throat.

"I don't think she will," I said, understanding what she couldn't say. "Maeve has had the opportunity and hasn't done anything. Instead, she's used my safety to control you. And yours to control me. Why, Kellen? Why would she want to control someone she intends—?" I winced when my throat clenched.

"She wouldn't." Kellen frowned. "Why does she need us controlled?"

The door behind her swung open, and Maeve looked at the pair of us on the floor.

"You need something to occupy your time, Kellen. Speaking to your sister of things you shouldn't will only cause you pain. It's time we start clearing your father's room. Come."

Kellen gave my hand a squeeze and rose to follow Maeve.

I stared after the pair, my mind racing. How had Maeve known of what we spoke? Perhaps she'd overheard us on her way in. Or perhaps there was something more to her knowing.

I studied the chain and touched the metal plate again, feeling the zing of magic. Magic Maeve had created. Could she be connected to it still?

Grabbing the chain, I gave a strong tug. The links clanked and scraped against the loop, but the plate didn't budge. I picked up the fire poker and tried prying at the plate to no avail.

I pretended to be tending the fire when the outside door opened and Catherine entered. She didn't comment on the poker I returned to the holder. While she started making a new batch of pastries, I struggled with what to do with myself. Tethered as I was, I couldn't offer my help. And given last night's events, any conversation filled with idle pleasantries would be inappropriate. I couldn't pretend it hadn't happened and didn't want her to either.

With nothing pleasant to discuss, I walked small circles, doing what I could to ease my aches. When I grew tired of that, I asked Catherine if she would make me some tea so I could rest. It helped me sleep well for a few hours, and I woke before lunch to listen as Catherine and Heather made small meat pies for each of us.

From my position on the floor, I stared at the flames and considered the plight of those within our home. I could do nothing to help any of us. And locked in her room at night or under Maeve's watchful eye during the day, Kellen was just as much of a prisoner as I.

While Heather and Catherine were free to come and go, they couldn't speak of Maeve's wrongdoings any more than Kellen or I could. Even if they could, though, I doubted they would speak out against Maeve. They feared her too much.

That meant, if Kellen and I were to be free again, we would need to free ourselves. However, even if one of us found a way to escape, how would we be able to rally help to save the other when we couldn't speak of what had happened?

I stuck my finger into the ash near the hearth and attempted to write "Maeve killed my mother" in the soot. As soon as I started the M, my throat squeezed uncomfortably. I ignored it and fought through the increasing discomfort to shape the second mountain of the M. Writing the letter "A" proved harder as breathing became difficult. Wheezing, I managed her full name before collapsing to the floor. The force strangling my airway didn't immediately ease, and I clawed at my throat.

Heather looked up from her pies, noticing my silent struggle.

"Eloise?" She rushed to my side and tried helping me to sit up. By the time I was upright, I could gasp in a breath. Then another. Slowly the pain eased.

"What happened?" she asked.

Behind her, Catherine stared at me with wide eyes. Moving my hand as if to better brace my weight, I wiped away the evidence of my attempt.

"Nothing more than my own stupidity," I rasped. "I'm sorry for startling you."

"Can I get you some more tea?" Catherine asked.

I shook my head.

"Some water would be better."

She nodded and quickly fetched some. I took a few tentative sips, wincing as I swallowed. My throat felt bruised. After watching me take several swallows, the pair went back to work preparing our midday meal.

I set aside the question of how we would rally help once one of us escaped and focused instead on thinking of a safe haven. Kellen and I had no other family or friends to turn to. Where could two women go?

"If you could travel anywhere, where would you go?" I asked Catherine and Heather.

Catherine frowned and gave it thought while Heather snorted.

"It does no good to dream of a better life," she said. "Best get used to the one you have because while your mind is wandering, your life could become much worse."

"There's no harm in dreaming. It helps pass time when things aren't pleasant," Catherine said, giving me an understanding smile. "I think I would like to see the south. I hear it's warm, even in the winter, and women wear gowns so thin you can see their skin through them. But they aren't considered whores for that display of flesh. Men treat them like sought after objects to be protected and revered."

Both Heather and I gave Catherine skeptical looks. The woman shrugged a shoulder.

"I'm not saying I believe it. Only that I'd like to travel there to see if it is true."

"I think the only truth to that story is that the south is warm."

"Where would you go, Eloise?" Catherine asked.

I turned to gaze at the fire.

"There's no point of dreaming of going anywhere when I'm chained," I said softly.

After that, they worked in silence until the kitchen door opened and Maeve walked in. She gave me a long hard look.

"What did Eloise do while I was gone?" she asked the pair.

"She moved around a bit then asked for tea to help her sleep. When she woke, she choked a bit but recovered," Catherine said.

"And she asked us where we would go if we could go anywhere," Heather added.

"Oh? And where would Eloise go?" Maeve asked, studying me.

"She said there was no point in her dreaming of going anywhere when she's chained," Catherine said.

Maeve's lips curled.

"Exactly why you wear the chains," she said softly. "I suggest you stop testing the limits of my spell. You might find yourself with Judith and Anne if you don't."

I nodded jerkily.

"Good. Let's eat," she said cheerfully. "Kellen and I have worked up an appetite."

Catherine and Heather served everyone before joining Kellen and Maeve at the table. Maeve had barely eaten more than a few bites when the sound of a carriage rattling up our drive filled the kitchen. She made a sound of annoyance and set her fork aside.

"Do not leave Kellen and Eloise unattended," she said to Catherine and Heather. Then, she pinned Kellen with a cold gaze. "If you try to run, your sister will suffer. Do you understand?"

Kellen nodded quickly.

Maeve swept out of the kitchen, and Kellen quickly stood with her plate and joined me by the fire.

"Are you all right?" she asked.

"As well as I can be. Why?" I looked down at the bruises visible on my arms and legs.

"I was with her when the—" She immediately stopped and touched her throat then her hand slid lower, resting just above her breast. She watched me steadily, and I knew she wanted me to understand something. It dawned on me when I looked at her chest again.

She'd seen Maeve's amulet glow when I tried writing Maeve's name in the soot. That meant Maeve was still connected to the spell. She would know any time either of us tried to speak against her or, in my case, write against her. That made the possibility of escaping to find help even more unlikely. Maeve would know any time we plotted.

I frowned and reconsidered. Perhaps not. The curse hadn't flared when I thought of running and finding help. It had only let Maeve know when I had tried to speak or write anything to implicate her of wrongdoing.

Catherine picked up the tea tray she'd hastily put together for the unexpected visitors and left the kitchen.

"She forgot the cream," Kellen said, standing. "I'll go get it."

While she descended into the cold storage, I continued eating. Heather started washing the dishes. A thought struck me, and I reached out once more to write in the soot.

You must run.

I wrote the message without a hint of pain. Relief swept through me, and I picked up my plate, slowly eating.

Kellen returned with the cream a few moments later and set the container on the table just as Catherine returned for it.

"Thank you," Catherine said before rushing out of the room once more.

Heather, with her back to us, didn't see me point to the fireplace as Kellen joined me. Nor did she see Kellen shake her head.

I wiped the message clean with my left hand and wrote a new one.

We need help.

I lifted my wrist, showing her the cuff binding me. She reached out and touched my bruised face then every additional bruise she could see. I understood what she was saying. Maeve would likely beat me again.

Wiping the message clean, I wrote the only thing I could think to convince her.

Without you, there is no control.

Kellen stared at my words for a long time.

"Are you two finished?" Heather said, glancing back at us.

"Almost," I said. "The crust on this meat pie is delicious. Is there more?"

Heather smiled slightly, obviously pleased with the compliment.

"I'm sorry, miss. We only made the six. When Catherine returns, she is going to take Hugh his portion."

"Let him eat oats," Kellen said, her eyes darkening. "He deserves nothing more."

Heather's expression showed her conflict.

"It's fine, Heather," I said. "Give Hugh his portion. I know where the blame for his actions truly lies."

Heather nodded and turned back to her wash water.

Kellen sighed.

"Fine. You will have your way."

To Heather it would sound like she was agreeing to let Hugh have his portion. But I knew better. She was agreeing to run.

Heart aching, I reached out and wiped away the soot. There had never been a time in my life when I'd been without my sister. Not like what I was proposing.

Kellen took my empty plate from me and sat on the stool. I leaned my head against her thigh, missing her already. Her fingers stroked through my hair, her gentle touch lulling me. We stayed like that for a long while. I shifted occasionally but remained close to her. This was our goodbye. Kellen had committed to finding us help, and she would discover a way to escape.

The sound of a carriage outside was the only warning we had before the door opened, and Maeve strode in.

"Kellen, I would like to continue clearing your father's room. Come," Maeve said. Kellen immediately stood and went to Maeve, who studied me closely.

"You're covered in soot, Eloise."

I glanced down at myself, only seeing the soot on my hand. Still, I wiped at my face with the unsoiled hand and tried to remove the soot from the dirty one by scrubbing it against the cleaner stones near the hearth. It only made the mess worse.

"Fetch the ash bucket for Eloise. She can clean the fireplace since she's covered in soot," Maeve said, looking at Heather before addressing me once more. "Perhaps next time you will find a way to stay cleaner."

I did my best to look suitably chastised as Maeve turned and left the room with Kellen in tow. On the inside, grief shredded me, and I wondered if I would ever see her again.

"Here are the buckets, miss," Heather said. "Put the cold ash in the empty one and use the other to wash away the soot."

I worked for hours cleaning the stone around the fire. Each time the water dirtied, one of the two maids would empty it and return with fresh water. When I finished, my arms ached from scrubbing, but the hearth looked as clean as I'd ever seen it. I, however, had never been filthier.

Without a word, Catherine hauled out the tub and started filling it with water.

CHAPTER 3

"HUGH!" MAEVE'S YELL ECHOED THROUGHOUT THE HOUSE.

I bolted upright from my place beside the hearth and looked at Heather and Catherine who were already quietly cooking the morning meal.

"What's happened?" I asked groggily.

"I don't know, miss," Catherine said, wiping her hands and rushing from the room.

While Catherine was unsure, I had no doubt what had caused Maeve's yell. Kellen had escaped. My heart pounded with excitement, hope, and fear.

After dinner last night, Kellen had helped me comb and braid my hair. With Maeve's permission, she'd also made me an extra strong batch of tea to help me sleep through the night. I'd known why Kellen had wanted me to sleep soundly and had thanked my sister. However, while Kellen hoped the tea would spare me, I knew the tea wouldn't stop what was to come.

"Are you hungry, miss?" Heather asked. "We have oats ready."

"Thank you, Heather. I think I'll use the chamber pot first."

I managed to empty my bladder and wash before Maeve entered the kitchen, Catherine in tow.

"Where is she?" Maeve asked.

I frowned and glanced at Catherine as if confused.

"Your sister," Catherine said.

Maeve reached out and slapped the woman.

"She knows very well of whom I speak. Keep your mouth closed unless I tell you to open it. Go fetch Hugh."

Catherine nodded and scurried for the outer door.

"I don't know where Kellen is," I said before Maeve could ask again.

Maeve stalked forward, anger lighting her gaze. I could feel the crackle of power that surrounded her.

"Do not lie to me, child. Every word you speak to me will be the truth."

The amulet at her neck glowed and an unnatural warmth wrapped around me, squeezing my skin before seeping inside.

"Now, where is your sister?" Maeve asked again.

The power wormed through me, nesting in my throat and coating my tongue.

"I don't know," I answered, relieved Kellen and I hadn't discussed where she would go.

Maeve's eyes narrowed.

"You knew she was going to run."

I remained silent.

"Tell me everything you told her yesterday."

"I told her I was all right."

"Omission is a lie," Maeve said, and her power surged again.

I was compelled to speak but still chose my own words.

"I told her to run. That you were using her to control me."

The kitchen door opened, and Hugh walked in, Catherine close at his heels. He didn't seem to notice. His gaze locked on Maeve and never wavered.

"I want you to hurt Eloise," she said. "And continue hurting her until she tells me everything."

Before I could say I had told her everything, Hugh pivoted and hit me. Pain exploded in my face, knocking me back. Robbed of breath from the first blow, I couldn't even make a sound when his foot connected with my already bruised thigh.

My mouth opened in silent agony. Hugh rained down blow after blow—arms, legs, ribs—showing me that I'd barely scraped the level of hell to which my life could descend with my first beating. However, unlike the first time, I remained conscious.

When he stopped, panting from his exertion, I lay limply on the floor. My pulse throbbed through my body, and I struggled to think beyond the agony I felt.

"Tell me everything," Maeve said softly. "What did you say?"

I coughed a laugh, too hurt to care that such a move might provoke her or that it sent another wave of pain through me.

"I said nothing. I wrote in the soot." It hurt to form those simple words with my bruised lips. "Told her to run. You control me through her." I shifted my gaze to look at Maeve, a slow smile curving my lips despite the pain. "Wise to chain me."

Rage filled Maeve's eyes. Her face flushed, and her hands fisted as she stared at me.

"Shall I hurt her more, Maeve?" Hugh asked.

Unconsciousness would be a blessing. Instead, she exhaled slowly and regained control.

"No. Our Eloise has nothing more to tell us. Go to town and find the best tracker you can. Bring him here quickly. Do not disappoint me, Hugh."

Hugh nodded and left.

"Look after Eloise," Maeve said. "If any ill fate claims her because of her punishment, the same will befall you."

As soon as she swept out of the room, Catherine and Heather both moved with speed. Heather ran outside, and Catherine grabbed the tub. I closed my eyes and drifted for a bit until strong arms gripped me.

"This will hurt, miss," Catherine said.

Suddenly I was lowered into a frigid bath. I groaned weakly and tried to lift myself out.

"Not yet, miss," Heather said. "Take a breath and go under. Let the water ease your pain."

I blinked at her, wondering if she was encouraging me to drown myself.

"Big breath," Catherine said.

I only had a moment to breathe shallowly before she pushed me under. The cold water soothed my throbbing face. Submerged, I realized most of my aches were benefiting from the treatment.

Hands tugged at me, and I emerged from the water gasping.

"Another big breath," Catherine said a moment before she eased me back under.

My vision swirled as I looked up from the water. Flames danced with shadows and faces above me. It was quiet and peaceful where I was, and I tiredly wished I could stay. The cold welcomed me, and the small inhale I'd taken escaped on a sigh.

They pulled me up quickly, and I feebly inhaled. Closing my eyes, I waited for whatever would come next, no longer caring.

"She can't rest on the stone," one of the pair said.

"I'll fetch my mattress," the other said.

Arms pulled me from the tub and back onto the floor. Each move sent more waves of pain through me, but I began to feel disconnected from it. Darkness bled through my vision, closing around me in a comforting embrace of nothingness. I welcomed it.

A pungent smell pierced my nose and jerked me back into awareness.

"You cannot sleep, Eloise," a voice said. "I know you're tired, but you must focus."

I blinked, unsure if I wanted to do what was asked of me. The beat of my heart echoed in my swollen face, aching arms, and bruised legs. Focusing meant acknowledging there wasn't a part of my body that didn't hurt.

"Think of your sister," another voice said softly. "She needs you."

The image of Kellen's face swam in my mind. My promise never to leave her had me trying to look around. The fire. The tub.

Catherine and Heather's worried expressions as they hovered over me. I remembered it all.

"Yes," I said. "Kellen."

"That's a good girl," Heather said. "We need to sit you up and fill you with some tea. It's something I made. It will keep you awake and help with the pain."

I gave the barest nod, wincing with the movement.

Heather slid her arm under my shoulders, leveraging me up as Catherine pressed a cup to my lips. I drank everything, each swallow more painful than the last. My stomach wanted to rebel, and I clasped Heather's arm when she would have lowered me. She moved behind me, letting me rest against her, and smoothed her hand over the top of my head.

"Fate can be fickle and cruel," she said softly. "But it's up to you whether to fight or accept what it hands you."

I thought of what it had handed me. Death. Brutality. Captivity. I refused to accept that would be the remainder of my life. Kellen had escaped. She would come for me and I needed to be ready.

"I'll fight," I said raggedly.

Catherine watched me from her place on the stool. I could see the fear in her eyes that I wouldn't have the strength to continue to live. Fear that she and Heather would be doomed to a fate similar to mine.

"Run," I said. "Like Kellen. Before you die."

Catherine looked at Heather. Heather's hand stilled on my head for only a moment before continuing.

"We've been in positions like this before, with clients who liked to hurt us. It will pass," Heather said softly.

I reached up and gripped her arm.

"It won't."

"It will. Kellen won't leave you here. She'll bring help," Catherine said. "We'll be fine until then."

I closed my eyes and sighed. My insides tingled oddly, and I realized some of the pain was fading. It made breathing easier.

"Feeling better?" Heather asked.

"Yes." The fire was warming my feet, but I shivered lightly in my wet shift. "Can I have dry clothes?"

"Not yet. You need to go back into the cold bath again. It will help the bruising and the pain. Ready to sit up?"

The bath was more shocking the second time. I shivered in the water and dunked down when told. When I reemerged, Heather had a towel waiting for me. I rubbed away what moisture I could and sat on the stool, wincing as the wood pressed against the bruised backs of my legs.

Catherine stood behind me, combing through my hair with gentle strokes.

Before my hair fully dried, the thunder of horse hooves rang out in the yard. Catherine and Heather, who had started fixing the midday meal, halted. It wasn't until that moment that I recalled Hugh had gone to town for a tracker. I thought of my sister and her inability to recognize an animal print in the dirt. Would she know to walk on firm ground? Would she know not to break branches? I frowned further, wondering if she would know to disguise herself while in town.

We listened to Hugh call out in the main entry.

"Continue cooking," I said to Heather and Catherine. "Whatever happens, Maeve will still expect a meal."

They started moving again but continued casting nervous glances at the door separating the kitchen from the dining room.

We didn't have to wait long before Maeve swept in with a man following her. He was large and well-muscled, his skin weathered from the outdoors. The dirty cap sat askew on his head with deep-brown unwashed hair poking out haphazardly.

His dark eyes swept over the room, barely hesitating on me or the manacle chaining me to the fireplace. The corners of his mouth turned down slightly though, and that gave me hope. Perhaps he would—

"This is Kellen's sister, Eloise," Maeve said. "When you find Kellen, be sure to describe in detail how Eloise appears now."

"Do you know where the girl might be headed?" the man asked, killing my hope.

Maeve glanced at me before shaking her head. Hugh, who'd entered behind the man, stepped forward.

"I suspect she will go to town. They know nothing else but this estate and Towdown."

Hugh's betrayal hurt even though I knew his willingness to help Maeve was due to a spell.

"We need Kellen found quickly and returned," Maeve said.

"There are many places to hide in Towdown," the tracker said.

"I have the means to help you find her." She withdrew a ribbon from her pocket. The vibrant red color was unmistakable. Kellen's ribbon.

"Heather, empty one of the spice boxes."

Heather turned to the shelves beyond the block and plucked a large spice box from the shelf. It held one of the more common herbs from our garden, which she dumped onto the block.

I watched Heather hand the small chest to Maeve and wondered what Maeve meant to do. The amulet around her neck began to glow as she opened the box and placed the ribbon inside.

"Treasure divided. Treasure made whole. Let what's lost be found. Let what's taken be returned."

A hum filled the air, and the wooden box began to pulse with a faint light. The glow from the necklace grew brighter with each word.

"If you should lose Kellen's trail, hold the box in your hands and command it to show you the way to Kellen. Its magic will guide you but at a cost. Each time you use it, you will age a year."

His gaze flicked to the box, but there was no fear, only curiosity.

"It shouldn't take me long then. I'll return with her soon."

"You will be rewarded if you do," she said. "But before returning, check the ribbon in the box. If the ribbon is whole, bring the girl to me alive."

"Unharmed?" he asked.

Maeve's gaze flicked to me.

"A few bruises will not concern me."

The man nodded his understanding.

"And if the ribbon does not stay whole?" he asked.

Maeve's lips curled into a smile that made my insides shiver.

"If the ribbon withers and fades into dust, cut the girl's heart out of her breast and place it in the box. Do you understand?"

"Yes, My Lady."

He bowed his head and left the room. Maeve looked at Hugh.

"Go back into town and extend an invitation to my partners. Let them know they can bring a friend if they so choose." Hugh nodded and quietly let himself out.

Maeve came to me, bending down so we were level. The pendant swung freely, now a dull green.

"I control whether the ribbon remains whole or turns to dust. If you cause trouble, the tracker will kill your sister. Do you understand, Eloise?"

I nodded, and the manacle around my wrist fell free.

"Help Heather and Catherine in the kitchen. If the meal is not ready on time, they will suffer the next beating. Do you understand, Eloise?" she repeated.

My loathing for the woman deepened.

"And do you know what will happen if you try to run?" she said softly.

"I will kill them all slowly, draining them of life as the blood leaves their bodies from a thousand small cuts. And when I find you again, you will bathe in it."

Unable to help myself, I shivered because I believed every word.

"I understand," I said, my voice rough.

"Good. And hope, for the sake of all the innocent people of Towdown, that Kellen hasn't done something to cause me ill fortune." She straightened and looked at the maids. "You can thank Kellen and Eloise for tonight's gathering and the power I need to replenish. Prepare the meal for fifteen guests," she said before sweeping out of the room.

I looked at Catherine and Heather in horror, understanding what

Kellen and I had condemned them to. They shared a look, and Catherine sighed.

"I'm so sorry," I rasped.

"Don't be. There are worse things than making fancy dinners and sucking on weathered old cocks."

"Really?" That sounded pretty horrible to me.

"Swallowing a bit of cum ain't so bad," Heather said. "Better than a busted rib."

I nodded and slowly stood, too afraid to ask what cum was.

"How can I help?" I took a step toward the block and almost collapsed. Although the pain was better, my strength had vanished.

"Sit on the mattress and rest," Catherine said.

Not arguing, I gingerly lowered myself to the soft bed. Exhaustion tugged at me, but my eyes refused to close. Instead of resting, I watched the pair move around the kitchen. Soon, the aroma of cooking meat filled the air. Heather brought me a bowl of mash which I slowly ate.

After that, I lounged on the mattress and thought of where Kellen might be and the magic box Maeve had given the tracker. With such a tool in his hands, the man was sure to find Kellen quickly. And, despite Maeve's words, I hoped that Kellen had already spoken to many people and found help. I didn't want anyone to die, but neither did I want to perish myself. Perhaps if enough people knew, Maeve would be forced to end her game—whatever it might be—before attaining her goal. I deeply feared what goal would drive a person to the depths of wickedness to which Maeve had descended.

The carriages started arriving just after dark.

Men's voices rose from the dining room, a jolly gathering, for they knew what awaited them this time. Heather and Catherine hurried to serve the dishes then returned to the kitchen to clean up what they could. When they finished, they stripped out of their gowns and waited near the door.

Anger tore at me. Self-loathing for being able to do nothing. Fury that Maeve was forcing Catherine and Heather to do what they'd come here to cease doing.

"I will find a way to stop her, I promise," I said softly.

"You mustn't speak like that," Catherine said quickly, looking upset.

"Especially not to us. Do you understand?"

I studied their worried expressions and nodded. Too well, I remembered the compulsion to tell Maeve everything.

"You're right. It's best to accept my place in life," I said. "I'll rest and heal so I can help you in the kitchen as best as I can."

Maeve called their names, and Catherine gave me a fleeting smile before they walked out the door. With the tea still numbing me from the pain and keeping me wide awake, I slowly moved around the kitchen. I couldn't do much. My strength eluded me, and I knew that running wouldn't be an option even if I wasn't concerned about Kellen, Catherine, and Heather.

In the dining room, the laughter became more subdued, replaced with the growing sound of groaning and panting. I returned to my bed and covered my ears, laying thusly for what seemed like half the night before things quieted.

When the kitchen door opened, Heather and Catherine shuffled in. They looked tired as they carried dishes to the wash bin. I sat up, feeling the aches and bruises more acutely now.

"Let me get the dishes while you wash," I said.

They nodded and moved toward the door.

"Do you want to dress first?" I asked, unsure if they were aware they would be walking out into the yard naked.

"No," Heather said wearily. "We would only dirty our clothes."

It was then that I noticed the odd sheen to their skin in certain places.

"A girl can only swallow so much cum," Catherine said. "If cum baths made a woman look young, I bet the wives of these men would never let them leave home."

The pair chuckled as they left. I didn't see what was so funny.

Limping my way to the dining room, I started gathering dishes. It took me a long while as I had to stop frequently to breathe and brace myself against the table. My legs started throbbing with increasing pain by the time I made it into the kitchen with the first stack of plates.

Heather and Catherine weren't yet back, so I returned to the dining room for more dishes.

Maeve walked in, the amulet around her neck once more a vibrant green. She paused at the sight of me.

"What are you doing?" she asked.

"Clearing the table while Heather and Catherine bathe."

She sighed as if exasperated with me.

"Eloise, this work is beneath you."

I frowned.

"But you told them to make sure I worked. I thought you wanted—"

"I want you to learn your place," she said. "Something you seem to have difficulty doing."

I said nothing. I didn't know if this was some new game or if there was something I truly wasn't understanding. More than anything, I wished Kellen was here. Not in pain or captivity with me, but to guide me. She was the smart one who could see things clearly. Not me.

Maeve continued to study me. The final stack of plates grew so heavy in my abused arms that I started to shake. Her lips curled slightly when she saw it.

"I think you might be learning, Eloise. Return those to the kitchen, then rest. Heather and Catherine will clean the rest of this."

She didn't need to ask if I understood, but I nodded automatically as if she had. Her smile widened further, and in that moment, I truly did understand. My place was under her thumb. Under her control. And, she was starting to believe she had me there.

She turned and left the room, and I stared after her, keeping my expression impassive. I'd let her think she was training me. My goal hadn't changed. I would find a way to stop her. Even if the tracker returned with my sister, I would find a way.

Maeve will suffer all that I suffer, I vowed silently.

CHAPTER 4

I SAT CAREFULLY ON THE BENCH BESIDE CATHERINE.

"You should be resting," Heather said, watching me.

"I will lose more strength if I lie about all day. I'm better if I move around."

"Trust us," Catherine said. "Rest heals faster than forcing yourself to move about."

The door swung open, and Maeve walked in with a large smile on her face. Catherine immediately rose to fetch Maeve's breakfast.

"Today is the day," she said, joining us at the table.

My heart stopped for a moment as fear clawed its way up my throat.

"Kellen?" I asked before I could stop myself.

Maeve's expression soured for a moment before it cleared and she continued to crack open her egg.

"Your ungrateful sister and the tracker remain unaccounted for. However, that will soon change. My things arrive today." Her gaze swept over me in scrutiny. "Take a proper bath and put on an appropriate dress. Be ready within the hour." She finished her egg and left the room.

"Come," Heather said. "We'll help you wash."

I was ready to crawl into bed by the time we were done but knew

I couldn't. With Heather's assistance, I dressed in one of my mourning gowns. The tight lacing made breathing less painful, and the tea Catherine once again made me drink alleviated most of the other aches. By the time I left the kitchen, I felt almost normal. However, like so many other things in my life, that was only an illusion.

The swelling in my cheek had increased overnight, making it difficult to fully open my eye. It served as a reminder that, although the pain was gone and I was once again dressed, I was far from the old Eloise.

Maeve paced the length of the foyer twice before noticing my presence. When she did, she stopped moving and studied me. A kind and caring smile lit her face.

"You look lovely, Eloise. A picture of refined beauty."

My stomach twisted at her words delivered with such sincerity. Did she truly think bruised and swollen was a picture of beauty? If so, I feared what Kellen's and my future would hold.

"I'm so nervous," she said. "It's been so long. Well over six months since I last saw them."

"Them?"

She ignored me and went to the door.

"It feels as if a piece of myself is finally returning. As if I'm about to be whole again."

That I could understand. Since Kellen left, it felt like a piece of myself was missing, too.

Maeve checked her reflection in the foyer mirror and met my gaze in the glass.

"So many things will change once the wagons get here. But your place won't. Do you understand, Eloise? You will remain important to me. Always."

I nodded. Like her previous statement, there was a scary truth lacing her words. How and why was I important to her? Was I only another sacrifice, or was I something more? I was about to give voice to my first question when the sound of several conveyances rumbling into the yard caught my attention.

Maeve's gaze swung to the door, and with giddy enthusiasm, she moved to open it. I trailed in her wake as she stepped outside.

A carriage pulled to a stop in front of the door. Behind it, three loaded wagons did the same. Before I could try to guess what all the oilcloth wrapped objects might be, the carriage door burst open, and a young woman dressed in a fine green gown emerged.

"Mama!" she shouted with joy as she ran at Maeve. Maeve caught her up in a tight hug. The girl's light brown hair swung slightly with the impact. Petite and slightly rounded, the girl didn't look much like her mother. It gave me hope.

"I've missed you, my darling Porcia," Maeve said softly.

She lifted her head and looked over her daughter's shoulders at the second young woman exiting the carriage. This one looked much more like Maeve with her tall, slender figure. However, where Maeve was dark, this one was golden, like me. She smiled at Maeve and gave her a more discreet hug.

"Hello, Mama," she said.

"Hello, my sweet Cecilia."

The three separated and turned to where I waited on the stairs.

"Girls, I would like to introduce you to one of your new stepsisters," Maeve said.

My breath caught, and I fought not to stare at Maeve in horror. How could I have forgotten? Father had married this monster, giving her more power over me than a set of chains.

"This is Eloise. Eloise, these are your new sisters, Porcia and Cecilia."

Cecilia smiled at me serenely as she came and gave me a firm hug. I involuntarily gasped at the pain that speared my rib cage. She loosened her hold. However, instead of asking if I was all right, she pulled back and placed a kiss on my swollen cheek. Had I been uninjured, it would have felt like a true welcome. However, since she chose to kiss me right where the swelling was the worst, I knew she was just like her mother.

She released me and stepped back for Porcia to embrace me. The younger girl's hold wasn't as tight as her sister's, but it still created an ache in my ribs despite the tea. When she kissed me, she chose the same spot as her sister, though.

"It warms my heart to see you girls welcome Eloise to our family." Maeve smiled at us then looked over the wagons.

"Is everything in order?" she asked.

"It is, Mama," Cecilia said. The girl motioned to the men who had been sitting in their seats staring straight ahead. At her signal, they climbed down from their perches and started untying the ropes securing the items in the wagon beds.

"Come inside, girls," Maeve said. "I'm sure you're ready for tea and a seat that doesn't jostle you."

Maeve left the door open behind us as we made our way into the house. The first man followed us inside, carrying in a small table which he set in the foyer before I entered the dining room.

"Catherine," Maeve called.

Catherine came straight away.

"Yes, Lady Grimmoire?"

"Tea please. And biscuits if you have them."

"Yes, ma'am." Her gaze never once flicked to me as she turned and disappeared into the kitchen once more.

"I have a room cleared for one of you," Maeve said. "The other still needs attention."

I'd never asked Kellen what they were doing in Father's room. But it made sense now, that Maeve would want it cleared so she could sleep there. I hated that any of them would be sleeping in mother's room. Even my new sisters.

"I'm sure the men outside will be happy to help us," Cecilia said.

"Very good. Now tell me about your journey. Was there any trouble?"

"None. We were very selective about our drivers. They've served us well along the way."

Maeve beamed at her daughters.

"It's so good to be together again. I hated leaving you behind."

"It was necessary," Porcia said. "We understood."

Catherine arrived with a tea tray and biscuits.

"Eloise, will you pour for us?" Maeve asked.

It was the task of a hostess to serve, one I didn't mind performing under normal circumstances. As it was, it hurt to stand, pour, then reach with cups extended. But I was sure Maeve knew that. They all accepted their tea with words of thanks and kind smiles. When I sat, I took a moment to catch my breath. They waited, watching me.

"Serve yourself, dear, so we can start," Maeve said gently.

No matter what tone she used, it was an order. My hand shook with exhaustion as I poured my cup and placed a biscuit on my plate.

"Well done, dear," she said. She sipped her tea and glanced out the door.

"Would you like me to tell the men to unload it straight away?" Cecilia asked.

"No. That's not necessary. It's only good to hear its call again. I didn't realize how much I missed it."

I kept my eyes fixed on my tea, taking a small sip while retaining the calm, relaxed expression I'd kept since the night before. It didn't surprise me that Maeve could hear something I couldn't. Whatever called to her was likely magical in nature, and likely just as deadly as her necklace.

They finished their tea in silence while I focused on the footfalls of the men as they came and went with pieces of furniture.

"Come, girls. It's time to show you your new home."

Maeve rose as did her daughters. Since I already knew this home, I remained seated. Maeve's gaze swung to me.

"You're one of my girls too, Eloise. Never doubt that. Come along."

I stood and followed on shaky legs. Perhaps when Maeve finally let me return to the kitchen, I would ask for another cold bath.

Maeve showed her daughters the sitting room, Father's small study which was rarely used, and the kitchen where Heather and Catherine were working to prepare the midday meal. After that, Maeve led us upstairs. There weren't that many steps, but each one brought a new level of agony. Twice, I had to stop to breathe. Maeve turned to watch me, waiting until I reached the top before continuing.

"This will be your room, Cecilia," Maeve said. "I know it will be snug, but you will fit in it better than your sister."

Cecilia's smile sharpened a little, and her gaze darted to Porcia who watched her toes.

"Do you see something interesting down there?" Maeve asked.

The girl's gaze immediately snapped up to her mother's.

"No, Mama."

"Good. Would you like to see where you will sleep?"

The girl nodded and smiled. We followed Maeve toward Mother's room. However, she didn't stop at that door. She continued to the room I shared with Kellen and opened the door.

"As I said, it still needs to be cleaned out. Perhaps you should start on that while Cecilia and I direct the men."

"Yes, Mama," Porcia said, looking a little pale.

"Very good. Come along Cecilia and Eloise." Maeve turned and walked away. I lingered a moment, staring longingly at my bed.

"She's waiting," Porcia said softly.

When I met her eyes, there was no pity or kindness there.

Turning, I limped toward the stairway where Maeve and Cecilia did indeed wait.

"I apologize for keeping you," I said.

"My," said Cecilia. "You do speak. I'm ever so grateful you're not a mute. I'm looking forward to having another sister with whom I can speak."

"As am I," I said serenely.

Cecilia's smile deepened.

"Come. I'm anxious to set our household to rights," Maeve said. She glided down the stairs and started looking at the pieces waiting to be carried upstairs.

Cecilia quirked a brow at me and executed the same graceful descent. When she reached the bottom, she turned. I smiled, ignoring the pain in my face, and smoothly moved down the steps. Slowly. Cecilia turned to her mother when I reached the bottom.

"I fear I packed it too well, and it may take them some time to unload it. Do you mind if I borrow one of the men to start setting up my room?"

"Not at all, dear. Keep an eye on your sister and ensure she's making progress in her room."

"Yes, Mother."

Cecilia nodded and walked out the door.

Despite the men moving in and out of the room, it felt as though I'd suddenly been left alone with Maeve. The long wooden rod from a wardrobe rested against the stair railing. My fingers itched to pick it up and bash the woman over her head. My uncertainty of successfully killing her stopped me from attempting it.

"What are you thinking, Eloise?" she asked.

I could feel the compulsion to answer and almost let my shock show. Catching myself just in time, I smiled serenely, already having learned it was what she expected.

"That I'm not strong enough in my current state. And I'm sorry for it."

She studied me for a moment then held out her hand. I accepted it, acting the part she wanted me to play.

"Sweet child, it pains me to see you unhappy. Let us agree never to argue again."

Did she truly believe that was what had happened? There'd been no arguing. Only her killing and subsequent commands to hurt me.

"Yes, Maeve," I said.

"Mama," she corrected.

I couldn't. I wouldn't. She would never be my mother.

She watched me intently, and I saw the moment an angry light started to grow in her eyes. She reached up to her necklace, stroking the stone with her free hand.

It's an act, I reminded myself. *Nothing this woman does or says has any true meaning.* To keep my sister safe, I would play her game.

"Yes, Mama," I said softly.

"It pleases me to hear you say that. Go now. Check on the

midday meal, and rest until it's ready." I wanted to ask her where she expected me to rest but caught the knowing look in her eyes.

"Yes, Mama." She released me, seemingly satisfied with my mock obedience.

I went to the kitchen and found Catherine and Heather sitting at the table, just waiting. They reminded me of the wagon drivers, and that worried me.

"Maeve—" Remembering their warning about what I said to them, I started again. "Mama asked that I come in here and check on the midday meal then rest."

Catherine and Heather exchanged a look.

"Mama?" Heather asked.

"She showed me a marriage certificate she and my father both signed before he left." I faced the fire quickly, hiding my face as the events before Maeve's arrival fell into place. Father's indifference regarding Mother's passing. His need to leave immediately. His choice to go to the Dark Forest. None of it had been him. Somehow, Maeve controlled him. She hadn't only killed one of my parents. She'd wanted to kill both. Why? Why kill both of them and not Kellen or me?

I shook with rage. Maeve had ripped apart my world, and I needed to learn why.

"Sit, miss," Heather said softly. "Try to rest as she wanted. Things will be better for you if you listen."

I nodded, knowing she was right and that she was only trying to protect me from an additional beating. Yet, I struggled to be calm enough to do as she suggested. I wanted to prowl the expanse of the kitchen and plot all the ways I could bring suffering to Maeve.

"It's here!" Maeve's voice rang out. "Cecilia, Porcia, Eloise."

Summoned, I had no choice but to answer.

I left the kitchen, my anger seething behind my carefully composed façade. In the main entry, Maeve stood before a wrapped object. As tall as she and twice as wide, the flat piece leaned against a wall.

Porcia and Cecilia made their way down the stairs and reached their mother before me. I watched Maeve reverently run her hand down the oilcloth.

"You've come so far," she said softly. "Faithful, true, and unbreakable. The one thing on which I can always depend."

I glanced at Porcia and Cecilia from under my lashes, but neither seemed bothered by their mother's affection for an inanimate object.

Maeve cut the thin ropes holding the oilcloth in place and slowly drew the covering off. Underneath, a clouded panel of glass reflected our murky images. Its thick wood frame bore evidence of extravagant workmanship. Carved decorative swirls merged with images of animals and plants. It should have been a thing of beauty. Yet, my stomach twisted while looking at it.

"There you are," Maeve said softly. "How I've longed for you."

She leaned forward and pressed her lips against the glass.

"We are pleased to reunite you, Mama," Cecilia said.

Maeve smiled lovingly at her daughter's reflection then ran her hands along the frame.

"Mirror, Mirror against the wall, I summon you now to answer my call. Show me Kellen."

The glass shimmered gold then green, our reflections fading as a new image developed. Through the dimly lit trees, my sister ran as if being chased. The cloak of her dark hood had fallen back, showing her pale skin and ebony braid.

"Show me the tracker," Maeve said. The image shifted to the man Maeve had sent after my sister. He sat upon a horse that trotted through trees.

"Good," Maeve said, glancing at me. "Our family will be together again soon."

"Yes, Mama," I said with a smile I truly felt. Not that I thought for a moment Kellen would be home soon. Wherever she had been wasn't where the tracker was. The lighting had been different along with the size of the trees. While I was relieved the tracker wasn't near her, I was also concerned. Why was Kellen running?

"Show me Prince Greydon," Maeve said.

I frowned slightly and watched the image of the tracker fade.

Nothing replaced the man's craggy face and worn mount, however. The glass darkened, showing nothing but a wall of black.

Maeve's smile faded. Cecilia reached out and pressed her sister back while retreating a step herself. I quickly did the same.

Maeve's scream of rage startled me, but not as much as when she whirled around, her eyes wildly searching. I swallowed hard, expecting to feel the hand of her wrath. Instead, she moved to grab the same wooden rod I had considered, then took to beating the mirror. The rod didn't shatter the surface. The glass and wood remained unmarked even after enduring several minutes of Maeve's anger.

Maeve stopped just as suddenly as she'd started, tossed the rod aside, and smoothed back her hair. Her gaze swept over the three of us.

"I apologize, my darlings. It would seem our prince still hides behind his charm." She took another calming breath. "I must ask for your patience a bit longer."

"And that is something we will unfailingly give, Mama," Cecilia said.

"We know everything you're doing is for us all," Porcia said.

Maeve nodded and looked at the mirror again.

"Mirror, show me who Kellen spoke to since leaving this house."

The image of Mr. Bentwell materialized on the glass. He sat at his desk, reading an old looking book, as he often did. The image shifted back to its original grey.

"Mirror, mirror against the wall, from my presence you may now withdraw."

Maeve turned to us and smiled serenely once more.

"I know you've only just arrived, my dears, but it would seem we have urgent business in town. Eloise, it would be best if you stay here for the time being. We will return with news."

Maeve started toward the door, and Cecilia and Porcia hurried to follow. The sound of the carriage moving outside only moments later bespoke Maeve's urgency.

Leaving the men to finish carrying things upstairs, I returned to the kitchen.

"Please tell Lady Grimmoire that the meal will be ready shortly," Heather said, already dishing portions of a light stew onto plates.

"There is no need," I said dully. "Mama just left."

"Left?" Catherine asked, straightening from her artfully stacked pastry plate. "To go where?"

I opened my mouth to speak, but the words "To kill Mr. Bentwell" stuck in my throat.

After all, one didn't speak out against Mama.

CHAPTER 5

I ate a quiet meal with Catherine and Heather. By the time I finished, all I could feel was the pulsing ache from my bruises.

"Is there anything that would help me heal faster than the tea?" I asked Catherine.

"Only rest and time, miss. The body will heal at its own pace."

I sighed and nodded. Her mattress still waited by the fire for me.

Surprisingly, the world drifted away easily when I closed my eyes. I didn't know how long I slept before Heather gently shook me awake.

"They've returned. Perhaps you should meet them at the door."

I nodded groggily and managed to stand without hurting myself too much. I'd just made it to the foyer when the door opened and the three women walked in speaking animatedly as women often did when returning from an outing. Most, however, didn't return covered in blood. However, the sight of their blood-spattered bodices and stained skirts didn't shock me as much as it should have.

"Eloise, my sweet," Maeve said. "I'm so glad you're here. We have a bit of a puzzle for you to solve."

"Yes, Mama," I said dutifully.

She held out her hand, and Porcia passed the book I hadn't noticed her carrying.

"It would seem Kellen, that sweet girl, only wanted to return a book and asked that Mr. Bentwell set aside a special one for you. She asked for it by title. Why would she want you to read this?" Maeve asked, handing the book to me.

I read the unfamiliar title then opened the book, leafing through the pages.

"I already thought to look for a message," Maeve said. "The book is unmarked with no notes hidden within its pages."

I looked up and let my confusion show.

"I don't know, Mama. I'm not familiar with this book and don't recall Kellen ever reading it, either."

"Read it. There's a reason she wanted you to. Solve the puzzle, Eloise."

"Yes, Mama," I said, hugging the book to my chest. "Are you hungry? Catherine and Heather have kept your plates warm."

"We ate while we were in town," Maeve said. Her lips curled in that way that made my blood run cold and my stomach twist as I saw the evidence of Mr. Bentwell's death with new eyes. Surely they didn't eat the man.

"Please tell the maids I would like a bath in my chambers," Cecilia said.

"Me, too," Porcia added.

"There's only the one tub. It's very large and doesn't easily fit in the rooms. We typically bathe in the kitchen."

Cecilia's eyes narrowed, and I glanced at Maeve, unsure what was expected of me.

"Everything is well, my loves. We knew when we came here we would live rustically for a time. A bath before a crackling fire is quite enjoyable."

"Of course, Mama," Cecilia said, her annoyance smoothing out.

"Yes, Mama," Porcia said just as serenely.

The pair moved off in the direction of the kitchen, and Maeve held out her hand.

"Come, child. Let's read together."

EXCEPT FOR MAEVE AND ME, the rest of the house had long since gone to bed. I rubbed my good eye, tired beyond compare, painfully shifted positions in my well-cushioned seat, and continued reading by the light of a candle.

Under Maeve's watchful gaze, I'd already read the majority of the book and still had no idea why my sister had requested it for me. Not that I was actually trying to understand why. If Kellen was being secretive about a message, then she didn't want Maeve to know. If I didn't know, then Maeve couldn't compel me to tell her.

Stifling yet another yawn, I turned the page and felt immediate relief that I was almost to the end. I didn't know how Kellen could stay up half the night purposely reading. While I most certainly enjoyed a good tale, I enjoyed sleep more.

When I finished the last words, I looked up at Maeve.

"If there is a hidden meaning in these pages, it escapes me," I said honestly. "It's a book of fables and fairy tales. Perhaps she thought it was something I might enjoy reading?"

Maeve stood and knelt before me.

"Your sister saw me beat you and knew that I would beat you again if she ran. Why would she risk your health to return a book and ask for another on your behalf? Do not pretend to be simple, Eloise." She gently smoothed back a bit of my hair. "It will not end well for you."

"I'm not simple, Mama," I said, holding her gaze, "but neither am I as smart as Kellen. Perhaps she thought I would understand, but she overestimated me."

Maeve considered me for a moment.

"Your sister knows you too well. If she thought you would understand, you will." She stood, taking the book from me. "Go rest. You'll read it again when you wake."

"Yes, Mama," I said, stiffly getting to my feet. She followed me to the kitchen and watched me gingerly lower myself, fully dressed, to the mattress beside the fire.

"This is no place for a well-bred girl to rest," she said. "Tomorrow, we will change your accommodations."

"Thank you, Mama," I said tiredly, not meaning a word of it.

"Good night, my sweet."

I fell into sleep's waiting arms before the door closed behind her.

The slight scuffle of sound as Catherine and Heather worked to prepare the morning meal didn't fully rouse me. Neither did Maeve or my dear stepsisters when they ate in the dining room. I dozed in that blissful space between awake and asleep until Catherine said my name.

"Do you think Eloise is all right? She's been sleeping a long time."

"She's healing, and Maeve kept her up late." The way Heather said Maeve's name was the first indication she'd ever given that she might hate the woman more than she feared her.

"I heard. I wonder what it is about that book."

"Don't wonder. Work. If we do as we're told, maybe we'll live long enough to go back to whoring."

"I hate whoring."

"Did you see the state of these dresses I'm washing? I think there are worse things than whoring."

They fell silent, and I lay there in guilt. A guilt that I knew I shouldn't feel but did regardless. If only they'd run when I told them. They could have been safely away. Then I realized that, even if they'd run, Maeve would have eventually gone after them for even knowing a hint of what she was doing. Just like Mrs. Tiller and Sabine. Just like Mr. Bentwell.

I shivered slightly and pulled the light blanket more closely around my shoulders.

"Miss, are you hungry?" Catherine asked.

Rolling over, I yawned and nodded. It took some time to sit up and then stand. Everything was stiff and sore. But slightly less so than the day before. And my eye could open more fully.

Catherine set a cloth-covered plate on the table.

"Would you like a warm salt bath?" Heather asked. "It will help with the remaining swelling and stiffness."

"That sounds lovely." I started to sit.

"Lady Grimmoire asked that we let her know once you're awake and fed," Catherine said.

I paused and looked at Heather then Catherine.

"I think I should perhaps bathe first?" They both nodded, and I smiled. They were trying to help me while still obeying Maeve. Although I appreciated their concern, I knew they were walking a fine line and hoped their kindness wouldn't get them in trouble.

Leaving the plate where it was, I moved to help Catherine and Heather.

"No, miss," Heather said. "Lady Grimmoire has made it clear to us you're not here as kitchen help. You're her daughter and should be treated as such." I didn't miss the way her gaze swept over my bruises or the doubt in her expression when she said the word daughter.

Choosing not to sit, I walked around the kitchen to work out what aches I could and watched Heather and Catherine fill the tub. They'd already had water boiling, so it didn't take long before I was floating in a warm salt water bath.

"This should help your recovery," Heather said, patting my shoulder after the final bucket of hot water was poured. With my hair piled up on the top of my head, I sunk deeper, letting the water lap at my chin. The heat seeped into my flesh, soothing me. It felt lovely and relaxing. I would have liked to stay in the water until it turned cold, but I knew lingering too long would bring Maeve's wrath down upon Heather and Catherine.

With reluctance, I pulled myself from the tub the moment the water lost its heated sting. Catherine was there with a towel for drying and a cream for the deeper bruises along my ribs.

"I'm not sure this will help," she said. "But it won't hurt."

"Thank you."

As soon as I was dressed, I grabbed my biscuit.

"I'll go to Mama with you."

I didn't want Catherine to face Maeve alone. Based on the angle of light coming through the kitchen window, I felt certain that Maeve and her daughters had eaten breakfast several hours ago.

Catherine gave me a grateful smile and led the way out of the kitchen. We found Maeve in the sitting room at the writing desk. She looked up as we walked in.

"Eloise, you are not a street urchin. You do not eat and walk but sit at a table like a refined person."

I quickly swallowed the bite of biscuit I had in my mouth and guiltily glanced down at the remains before meeting Maeve's gaze.

"I'm sorry, Mama. I slept longer than I should have and didn't want to keep you waiting any further," I said.

Her harsh expression softened.

"Sweet girl. You are so thoughtful. Next time, finish your breakfast and then come find me."

"Yes, Mama."

Maeve waved Catherine away, keeping her contemplative gaze on me.

"You look refreshed today," she commented.

"A benefit from the extra sleep I believe," I said. A part of me wondered if she would prevent me from sleeping so much in the future.

"Finish your biscuit, and then begin reading again," she said, pointing at the book that waited near the chair I'd used the day before.

"Yes, Mama."

Reading the stories a second time proved more entertaining. I lost myself to those worlds and let my imagination free instead of trying to analyze the stories for clues. By the time Catherine announced lunch, I was already halfway through them.

"Have you learned why your sister wanted you to read the book?" Maeve asked as the four of us sat at the table.

"I haven't yet, but perhaps I will before I reach the end again," I said, carefully choosing my words.

"Tell me about the stories," Maeve said.

"The first is about a boy who won't share his bread with a beggar. The beggar is secretly a caster who turns him into a toad for his greed then makes him into a soup and eats him."

Maeve's smile became genuine. Or as genuine as I'd yet to see.

"That tale sounds entertaining. And the next?"

"The next is about another boy, separate from the first and in another town. He steals a pie from the window of an old woman. Like the first story, she too possesses knowledge of magic and curses the boy, removing his ability to taste any food or drink. He dies slowly, starving himself because nothing pleases him."

Maeve considered me thoughtfully.

"I may need to read these tales. They sound lovely."

"I do like them," I said.

"Does the next one also mention someone who does magic?"

"Not someone but something. An enchanted well that grants wishes, but they all go horribly wrong."

She sighed.

"For the remainder of the day, I think it would be best if you work on straightening your room. You're not sleeping as well as you should where you are. And, sleeping before the hearth is not befitting for one of my daughters."

"Yes, Mama," I said. I glanced at Porcia, who met my gaze. Were we wondering the same thing? Would I be sharing my old room with her?

When we finished our meal, Maeve asked me to follow her. She led me to the attic door and unlocked it with a key. It had never been locked before.

We ascended the stairs, and I noted how Father's things had been shoved into the free space, once again cluttering what Kellen had tried to organize.

"It will take some time, but I'm sure you'll set this mess to rights," Maeve said.

I glanced at her, unsure of her meaning.

"Mama?"

"This is your room, my sweet. The largest in the house for the child I hold very dear. I'll call you for supper," she said before leaving me.

I listened to the door close and the lock slide into place. Turning, I looked around my new prison and felt a sense of relief. Locked in the attic wouldn't be so horrible. It was colder up here, but I also knew there were several comfortable beds, extra blankets, and even some of Mother's old clothes. I wouldn't freeze. At least, not until winter.

Before that gloomy thought could take hold, I set to work. I chose a spot in one corner of the attic near the chimney that came from Mother's old room. The heat from it would help warm my space, and I also had a small window for light.

Around my chosen area, I moved the bigger pieces of furniture into place, which took time and effort. On top of them, I began stacking smaller furniture I knew I wouldn't use. Eventually, I created two walls that reached the rafters. Using the oilcloths, I covered them both and looked around my cozy space. It was large enough for two beds, should Kellen be found.

Leaving my bedroom area, I surveyed the rest of the attic. So much furniture remained that I hadn't needed to touch the little cubby that Kellen discovered, or use Mother's or Father's furniture. I pulled the soft chair from Mother's room into a bit of clear space and sat for a few moments, tired and in pain.

As the light began to fade, I started to wonder if I would have the strength to set up my bed for the night.

A key turned in the lock below and the door opened.

"Miss?" Catherine called. "I brought you candles and a lamp."

Her footfalls echoed on the stairs as I struggled to rise from the chair. I saw her reach the top and look at the large, covered stack of furniture that made up one wall of my new room.

"What do you think?" I asked, coming to stand beside her.

"I think you've pushed yourself too far," she said. She looked me over. "You'll need a longer soak in the salt water bath tonight before you sleep."

I gave her a wry smile and followed her into the area I'd made.

"It likely won't do me any good. I've yet to set up my bed."

She put the candles and the lamp down.

"I'll do that. Just show me where the bed is."

She and I worked together to set up the two twin beds. She didn't comment on my insistence for a second one, and I didn't explain myself. It wasn't that I thought Kellen would be captured. I only wanted it to appear that I thought that way. It would likely appease Maeve. And I wanted to appease her. I wanted her to let her guard down. Not that I intended to run—I wasn't yet well enough to go farther than the drive or to willingly leave Catherine and Heather to their own fates. No, I wanted Maeve to believe I was falling in line with her plans so she would share them with me.

Catherine and I made up both beds with the blankets that we found in one of the trunks. They smelled a bit musty, but I didn't mind. I knew they would air out in the drafty attic space. We added a table and brought the chair inside the space as well. It was comfortably cozy, yet still had more space than my previous room.

"Nicely done," Maeve said from the opening to my space, startling both Catherine and me.

I looked up and watched her study the walls.

"You're more clever than you credit yourself." Maeve met my gaze. "It's time for dinner."

"Yes, Mama," I said, moving to join her. I didn't look at Catherine or thank her, feeling that it would be unwise to call attention to her.

I followed Maeve downstairs, wincing at each step. My legs hurt fiercely from climbing up on things. My arms and ribs hurt more from all of the lifting. I most certainly would benefit from a bath after dinner.

Joining Cecilia and Porcia, who already waited at the table, we ate a quiet meal. I stifled more yawns than I could count and could feel Maeve's gaze on me. She didn't comment, though.

When she finished, she sat back in her chair and studied me.

"Your concern for your sister hasn't escaped my notice," she said.

I kept my expression carefully blank.

"I want her home as badly as you do. Each time I check the mirror for her, however, I cannot tell where she is. I thought the book might help us, but perhaps you know the place." She leaned forward in her chair. "You will tell me if the place looks familiar, won't you?"

"Yes, Mama."

Her eyes narrowed ever so slightly, and I wondered what answer she'd wanted if not that one.

"The trees didn't look familiar to me. But all I know are the woods here and town," I said, repeating Hugh's assessment of my knowledge.

"I think, perhaps, it's time we look again."

Porcia and Cecilia rose with her. I hurried to do the same, wincing at the ache in my legs from sitting so long.

The mirror remained in the foyer, uncovered and now mounted to the wall.

Maeve stood before it, gave it a kiss, then repeated the words from the day before.

"Mirror, Mirror against the wall, I summon you now to answer my call. Show me Kellen."

The glass shimmered with magic again, and once the green faded along with our reflections, Kellen appeared. Her mourning dress was ripped in places, and she had scratches on her skin. However, the state of her dress concerned me less than the fact that she was fast asleep, which I found odd given the time of day. I studied the image, noting her long braid trailed out behind her, ending somewhere off the edge and that the blanket under her looked coarsely woven. Rough and slightly frayed.

"I don't recognize anything," I said, just as I caught the edge of her braid move ever so slightly. So focused on my sister and the relief she was safe and resting, I didn't recognize I was opening my mouth to speak until my words emerged without thought.

"I think someone is with her. Her braid just moved." I wanted to take my words back as soon as I said them.

Maeve stopped studying me and studied the mirror. The braid moved again. Her black hair in the dim lighting against the dark blanket made it hard to see, but it was there nonetheless.

Silently, I cursed the spell compelling me to speak the truth to Maeve.

"Show me who is with Kellen," Maeve commanded. The mirror went dark.

I frowned, and Cecilia and Porcia gasped.

"Surely, she's not—"

Maeve lifted her hand, silencing Porcia.

"I doubt she's with Prince Greydon. Likely she found herself a caster, thinking another will be able to help her." Based on the humor lacing Maeve's words, I knew Maeve believed the opposite.

She looked at me again.

"Does anything else catch your eye, Eloise?"

I studied my sister's peaceful face for a moment longer, memorizing her features as if this would be my last chance to see her.

"I'm sorry, Mama. Nothing is recognizable or familiar to me except my sister."

Maeve didn't get angry this time. She only nodded and asked to see the tracker. The man now sat near a fire. He looked older, and his eyes moved relentlessly as he watched the dark. Wherever he was, he gave the impression he wasn't safe.

"Do you recognize this place?" Maeve asked.

I shook my head slowly, gaze affixed to the mirror. Behind the man, something flickered. I stepped closer, involuntarily drawn. I barely noticed Maeve step away as I focused on the space beyond the man's shoulders.

The flicker came again as the flames before the image of the man flared then diminished.

"Eyes," I said softly, fighting to tamp down my joy.

The tracker might be hunting my sister, but something was hunting him as well.

CHAPTER 6

I LAY IN MY BED, READING THE BOOK FROM MY SISTER BY THE LIGHT OF A candle. The bath Maeve had allowed me, after I had pointed out that her hunter was being hunted, hadn't been a salt bath, but a hot bath filled with pungent herbs.

She'd washed my hair and spoke to me kindly as she worked. Every touch had been gentle and caring. That was my reward for being helpful. While I was grateful not to ache as I lay down to sleep, I wasn't foolish enough to want to continue to help Maeve, no matter what anguish it might save me.

I thought of my sister, laying so peacefully, and my heart ached. I missed her with every breath and hoped she was safe from whatever hunted the tracker. Yawning, I tried to focus on the next story but failed. Instead of wasting more of the candle, I blew it out and snuggled under the covers.

It felt as if I'd no sooner closed my eyes than I opened them again. However, the light coming through the window told me I'd slept a full night. I used the chamber pot then the washbasin Catherine had set up for me.

I'd only just laced up my dress when I heard the key turn in my door.

"Eloise, it's time for breakfast. Please bring the book."

I grabbed the book and moved quickly to the stairs.

"Did you sleep well?" Maeve asked as I descended.

"Yes, Mama. Thank you for the bath. It was lovely."

She smiled at me, her expression conveying a fondness for me that I doubted she had ever felt.

"I'm relieved to hear it helped. Is your room comfortable?" she asked, closing the door and leading the way to the stairs.

"Very. Thank you for considering our need for more space," I said. "Kellen will be pleased when she's home again."

Maeve turned sharply, studying me. Whatever she saw on my face seemed to content her because she continued to the dining room without further comment.

"I believe we've spent enough idle time here," Maeve said. "The visitors have stopped appearing of their own volition. Like us, I believe they tire of waiting to hear word of the prince's arrival. It's time to adapt."

Catherine and Heather entered the room and served our breakfast of hot oats. Maeve waited until they left again to continue.

"Cecilia, I believe you'll have more opportunity closer to the castle." Maeve reached into her pocket and withdrew a vial. "Porcia, I'd like you to go to the market." She handed each girl a vial.

"Where will you be, Mama?" Cecilia asked.

"I will start with the Houses. Many will have heard my name by now, thanks to my loyal followers."

The girls smiled and started eating their oats.

"What about me, Mama?" I asked.

Maeve paused with a spoon halfway to her mouth.

"How can I help?" I added.

She set her spoon down and clasped my hand across the table.

"Sweet child, you will have your chance to help soon."

I suppressed the shiver of dread that wanted to run through me at her words.

She released me and returned to her meal. I slowly did the same, the food curdling in my stomach. Before the tracker located my sister, I needed to know what Maeve planned for Kellen and me.

Why had Maeve spared us, and what was she doing here? Yet, pressing for information would not help me. It would only make Maeve suspicious. I would continue to recover and read the book to discover where Kellen might be so I could join her when the time was right.

I STOOD at the attic window, looking out at the trees and blue sky. It was a beautiful day, and more than anything, I wished I could walk out in the sun.

It had been more than a week since Kellen left and four days since I moved into the attic. Yet, there was no sign of help, which made me worry more for Kellen.

Sighing, I glanced at my chair where the book waited. Each day Maeve and her daughters went to town only to return each evening in a more foul mood. Maeve hadn't even asked me about the book last night, which both relieved and worried me. While Maeve's distraction meant I could focus on trying to discover why Kellen wanted me to read the book, I couldn't help but feel a sense of foreboding at what might have a greater priority to Maeve than finding Kellen.

Restless, I paced the path I'd created in the attic and focused on what I'd read. The only common theme within the stories was magic. In some way, each character was touched by it. But, I didn't understand where the message might be in that. Kellen and I had been touched by magic the moment the necklace arrived. The book was a bit late to serve as a warning for that. It either had to be a clue to where she went or a clue to something else she'd discovered.

I returned to my chair, determined to try again, and opened the book at random. The page was in the middle of the story of the enchanted well. One old woman had grown smart and started choosing her words with more care so that the well would grant her precisely what she wanted. I felt much like the old woman. Every time Maeve asked a question, the compulsion to answer honestly almost had me blurting my thoughts without the respectful wording or tone that Maeve expected. Also, like the old woman, I learned there are half-truths that could satisfy the spell.

However, I didn't think that was the warning Kellen meant. I shifted in my seat. While my bruising had mostly faded, and I breathed with ease once again, the chair wasn't comfortable. There was something in the back padding that continually dug into my spine. Frustrated, I twisted in my seat, prepared to poke at the backing when the book fell to the floor. I cringed and hoped I hadn't damaged the spine. Mr. Bentwell would never let me—

I swallowed hard as I remembered Mr. Bentwell's fate and that he would never see the book again.

Leaning to pick up the volume, I saw the spine had indeed pulled away from the pages. Tears of frustration mixed with sorrow gathered in my eyes. I hated that I was locked up here and that Kellen was out there. Somewhere. Mostly, I hated not doing anything.

As I picked up the book, a small slip of paper fell to the floor. Heart fluttering, I picked it up and read it.

This is but one book of many. Read them all for me. ~K

I stared at the note, dumbfounded. That was it? She wanted me to read more? I thought of poor Mr. Bentwell and wondered what, exactly, Kellen would have wanted me to read there. Her romance books? I scoffed at the idea even as my gaze swung to the back corner of the attic.

There was only one set of books that had interested Kellen after Maeve's arrival. The books of magic. Since being locked up, I'd been too nervous to venture into the hidden space that Kellen had found. Maeve tended to want me downstairs at the most unexpected times.

I chewed my lip and checked the window. No one was home now.

Decided, I quietly crossed the space and climbed into the small burrow. The books weren't where I last saw them. Instead of stacked neatly in the open, I found them wrapped and tucked away in Mother's trunk.

On a whim, I checked for the King's letter and found it missing. In its place, I found another note.

My throat tightened as I recognized my sister's neat writing.

IF YOU FIND THIS, *I'm likely gone. You were chained and beaten for our attempt to leave. Maeve locked me up here to store away Father's things. I took some time to read. Read what you can. There's knowledge in words. Perhaps you will find an answer where I did not. There must be a connection between our home and what's happened to us. I took the letter for safe keeping as I believe it's what Maeve was searching for as we went through Father's things. I'll find him and bring him home. He's the only one who can help us now.*

DREAD FILLED my heart as I understood where my sister had gone and why I'd glimpsed her running in terror. The tracker's fear now made more sense, too. Tales of the Dark Forest were told to children the moment they were born. No one entered the dark woods if they wanted to live. No one except my foolish, brave sister.

I folded the letter and tucked it back into place, tears blurring my vision. Without looking at the books or the letters from Elspeth, I left the burrow and returned to my chair.

The sun slowly sank as I sat there trying to sort through what I knew. Outside, the sound of hooves brought me out of my own thoughts. I rose and caught a glimpse of the rider before he rounded the house.

The tracker had returned, and he'd been alone. I paced back and forth, worrying my lip. Surely Maeve hadn't ordered for Kellen to be killed. Maeve had said Kellen and I were important to her and asked that Kellen be returned alive first, her safety a condition on my behavior. And I had behaved. I'd done everything Maeve had asked of me. My gaze fell on the book. Everything except for determining where my sister had gone. Was that why Maeve had stopped asking about the book? Because Kellen was dead?

Fear twisted my middle until I was sick with it, and no amount of pacing alleviated my anguish as I watched the window for my tormentor's return.

It took another hour before the carriage rolled into the yard. I hurried to the stairway, a bundle of nervous energy. The lock turned in the door almost immediately.

"Your mother would like you to join them in the sitting room," Catherine said when she saw me already descending.

"Any news?" I asked softly.

"The man didn't speak to us."

I hastened to the sitting room and found Maeve, Cecilia, and Porcia already comfortably seated. The tracker stood before them, a displeased scowl on his face. New lines marked the skin around his eyes and strands of white now intermingled with his dark hair.

"Here, Eloise," Maeve said, patting the chair to her left.

I quickly sat, watching Maeve.

"Thank you for waiting," she said to the man. "Tell us what you've learned and why you've returned without my daughter." Her words to the tracker and the underlying note of threat in them relieved me.

"She's in the Dark Forest," he said bluntly. He withdrew the box from his jacket pocket and handed it to Maeve. "The box led me straight to her, but something was hunting her. When it caught my scent, it started hunting me, too. The fire kept it at bay at night. Using that box kept it away during the day. It didn't like the magic."

"The girl," Maeve said lowly. "Where is she?"

"She found a cottage before I could get to her. There's a group of little men there guarding it. I couldn't get past them."

"Little men?" Maeve asked.

The man held out his hand at thigh height and raising it to about his waist.

"Somewhere in that range," he said.

"You couldn't defeat a group of short men?"

"Short, My Lady. Not weak."

From the corner of my eye, I watched Maeve's expression change from slightly annoyed to pleasant and charming.

"Is there anything else helpful you can tell us?"

"The cottage is in a sunny clearing."

"How is that helpful?" she asked.

"Your girl is stuck there until someone saves her. She'll never make it past the beast a second time, now that it knows she's there."

"Hmm," Maeve said, tapping her chin lightly. "I suppose that is helpful to know." She looked at me. "Are you content with the information he's provided?"

I looked at the tracker.

"Can you tell me more about these little men? Why were they defending her?"

"They weren't. They were defending their home. Not sure they even knew she was inside. With them at my front and the beast at my back, I didn't have much choice but to leave and return with this news while I could still tell it."

I looked at Maeve, trying to gauge if I'd heard everything or if something had been said before I'd arrived. What proof did I have that my sister was still alive?

"How do we know his words are true?" I asked.

Maeve smiled at me and lifted a hand to stroke my cheek at the area that still held a hint of fading bruise.

"You are a smart one, Eloise. Never doubt that."

She went to the man. Before I knew what was happening, blood showered my skirt, the carpet, and Maeve as the man clutched at his throat. The glint of light near Maeve's hand drew my eye to the blade she still held before I looked back at the tracker. I blinked at the red cascading through the man's fingers as he gasped and choked. Only Maeve's firm grip on his shoulder kept him standing.

"Let honest words spill from your lips as quickly as the blood spills from your throat. Does Kellen still live?"

"Yes," the man rasped.

"Can she escape the wood on her own?" she asked.

"No."

He gurgled and fell to the carpet, jerking as what remained of his vitality was inhaled by Maeve.

She gave a satisfied sigh and looked at Porcia.

"Please fetch Hugh."

Porcia left the room at a calm pace as if her pretty yellow skirt wasn't dotted with blood.

"Cecilia, can you let Heather and Catherine know we'll need to wash before dinner. Also, let them know they'll need to tidy in here as soon as possible."

Cecilia nodded and went to do as Maeve asked.

Stunned, I sat in my chair and stared at the dead man. Maeve noticed and returned to the chair beside me.

"Are you all right, my sweet?" she asked.

"Yes, Mama," I said though I was far from okay. While the death was gruesome and terrifying, that alone hadn't sent my heart racing. Kellen was still in the Dark Forest, protected only by a patch of sunlight and little men.

"Perhaps I'm not all right," I said.

"Tell me what troubles you."

"Kellen was alive when he last saw her, but how do we know she still is?"

Maeve patted my hand.

"You love your sister so. Let us check."

Maeve took my hand and led me from the room. I listened to her call upon her mirror and waited for the image of my sister. Once again, it showed her sleeping. It wasn't like her to sleep so early in the day. And it was most unlike her to sleep on the dirt.

I stared at her peaceful face, unsure what to do next. If what the tracker said was true, Kellen could no longer help me. Instead, she needed my help. But, how could I help her without endangering her further?

"What are you thinking?" Maeve asked.

"It's not like her to sleep so early," I said, choosing the safest thought to share. "Who has Kellen? Why can't we see them?"

Maeve tried again to get the mirror to show her the home where Kellen slept at night or the people who protected her. But, the first question only showed our home and the second showed me.

Maeve turned to me, an angry light in her eyes.

"Go to the dining room and wait for me there. This mirror vexes me."

I hurriedly left, and listened to the echo of the wooden rod smack against the mirror behind me.

In the dining room, I calmly took my seat at the table and checked my clothing. I'd never been so grateful to wear black. No visual reminder of the scene I just witnessed remained.

After the noise in the hall quieted, Maeve joined me, followed by Cecilia then Porcia. Catherine and Heather began serving a meal of roasted quail in brandied briarberry sauce on a bed of new spring greens. Catherine glanced at me as she set the plate before Porcia but quickly looked away. Did Heather and she think I was now under Maeve's thumb? Would they wonder if I had a part in what happened in the sitting room?

I daintily cut into the quail Heather had set before me and took my first bite.

"This is lovely," I said to no one in particular, keeping my focus on my food.

"You're quite right," Maeve said. "Thank you for preparing such a delicious meal, Heather and Catherine. Your hard work for this family is noticed and very appreciated."

"Thank you, My Lady," they both said quietly.

As they left the room, I hoped my praise had answered the question of whether or not I was involved.

"Girls, it would seem our first tracker failed us. I cannot, in good conscience, leave Kellen in danger in the Dark Forest. Tomorrow we must locate good, able-bodied men who will not run in fear at the sight of a beastie in the trees."

"Yes, Mama," both Cecilia and Porcia said between bites.

I could barely focus on my food as my mind raced. For certain, more than one question had been answered this evening. I now knew how Mr. Bentwell had died, and I also knew that Kellen wasn't yet out of danger from Maeve.

After dinner, I returned to my room where I once again read the book of fairy tales by the lamp's light. This time out of boredom rather than necessity. A whisper of noise pulled me from the story. I listened closely and heard it again.

Picking up the lamp, I left the bed and walked lightly across the floor. I followed the sound to the outside wall near the stairs. It seemed a voice was coming from under a stack of chairs. Moving them quietly, I found a vent in the floor.

Words drifted up to me, and I leaned closer to hear.

"…ruined my favorite dress," Cecilia said. "Blood never truly comes out. Now I have to draw from my store of power to remove it by other means. These are costly mistakes."

"Perhaps the mistake is using your power to clean a dress. It's better to purchase a new one," Porcia said.

Cecilia snorted.

"If we knew there was time, perhaps. But we don't know when he'll arrive, do we?"

Porcia sighed.

"No. We don't. I can't believe not a single person of worth knows where the prince is. He left before we did. He should be here by now. If we were in town, we would probably learn more."

Something creaked.

"Mama," Porcia said. "I didn't mean—"

"Quiet. You did mean. Cecilia, stop wasting your magic on cleaning silly gowns. Porcia is right in that. She's also right about no one of worth knowing anything. We've been overlooking the obvious. It's not someone of worth who would know the prince's whereabouts." A slap sounded in the room. "Even if we lived in town, we would know nothing more than we do now. This home is the gateway to the castle. Tomorrow, after we return from town, I will remove your doubt."

CHAPTER 7

Porcia had been exceptionally quiet at breakfast, and I couldn't help but wonder if she was fearing how her mother planned to remove her doubt once they returned from town. Most likely.

My stepsister's fear probably equaled my own, though for different reasons. Why were they trying to learn when the prince would arrive? How did they believe our home was a gateway to the castle? Because of proximity? I was tempted to tell Maeve that I'd never once seen any of the Royal family, despite living on the King's lands.

A lock slid in the door, and Catherine called out for me.

"I've brought your tray, miss."

I hurried to the top of the stairs and watched her ascend. Behind her, the door closed and locked as it had every day Maeve was gone and the midday meal could not be served in the dining room.

"I'm sorry you have to carry it up here," I said.

"There's no need to apologize." She met my gaze as she reached the top. "Heather and I know this is not your doing."

The way she said the words while holding my gaze brought tears of relief to my eyes. I quickly turned away and nodded, hating that I could not speak openly to her. Hating that she would be forced to repeat our conversation to Maeve, compelled by the same spell that bound me.

"I've brought you a nice stew and fresh biscuits," she said, moving around me to set the tray on a small table beside a chair I'd placed outside of my room. The chair was one from the pile I'd moved in order to better hear the conversation in Cecilia's room. I'd spent some time this morning uncovering all the vents under the guise of creating a sitting area for myself.

"It looks nice up here," Catherine said hesitantly as I took a seat.

"It's more spacious than I need," I said. "But it suits me well."

She lifted the lid from the soup bowl and uncovered the biscuits.

"Is there anything else you need before I take the chamber pot?" she asked.

I shook my head.

"Thank you, Catherine, to you and Heather both, for taking such good care of me."

"As your mother requested," Catherine said.

"Yes, as Mama requested."

She nodded, gave my shoulder a light squeeze, and went to my room for the chamber pot. I started to eat, my thoughts wandering back to what Maeve and her daughters were doing in town. I hoped they wouldn't find more trackers. Although the Dark Forest was dangerous, Kellen was safely out of Maeve's reach. That meant I could run when the time was right. But only if I could get Catherine and Heather to run with me.

"Have you given any thought where you would like to travel, if you could travel anywhere?" I asked.

Catherine gave me a knowing look.

"There's nowhere else I would rather be than here, miss. This place calls to me like no other. Don't let my lack of dreams influence yours," she said.

I wasn't certain, but it sounded like she was trying to tell me to run. While I watched, she began to roll back the sleeve of her gown. On the inside of her elbow, I saw a red mark that resembled the faint outline of a raven.

It was too perfect to be a birthmark, which could only mean that Maeve had done something to her.

"I think it's healthy for all young girls to dream a bit. Just so you keep your head where it's supposed to be."

And where, I wondered, was that? Unable to ask directly, I focused instead on her mark. "This soup is delicious. Leeks?"

Catherine nodded.

"Who goes to town for supplies?" I asked.

"Hugh," she said. "Heather and I provide a list of what we need so we can stay where we belong."

With that, I understood. Maeve had magically bound Heather and Catherine to the estate. Even if they wanted to run, they wouldn't be able to. And if I ran, they would suffer.

I set my spoon down and looked out the small window.

"The soup displeases you, miss?" Catherine asked quietly, and I knew we weren't speaking of the soup but her answer.

"Confined to this attic on a sunny day displeases me," I said bluntly. "I miss the sun and the wind and the sound of the trees. I miss visiting my mother's grave. I miss my sister."

She nodded, a sorrowful expression on her face, then left with the chamber pot.

I managed to finish the soup after it had long gone cold and clouds began to blot out the sun. I'd only just put the spoon aside again when I heard the rattle of an approaching carriage. I rose and checked the window.

Maeve had returned, but not alone. Several riders followed.

I hurriedly moved to the attic door to wait. Heather opened it several minutes later.

"Your mother is waiting for you in the sitting room."

I was already passing Heather and racing down the stairs. At the last moment, I slowed and entered the sitting room at a serene pace. Maeve stood in the center of the room with Cecilia and Porcia on each side of her but a step back. Before Maeve, with their backs to the windows, stood a group of five men. They all watched me enter.

"Good afternoon, Mama," I said, only looking at Maeve.

Maeve smiled and gestured to a chair against a wall. The simple unspoken command was clear. I was here to observe but not interfere.

I sat and watched Maeve face the men. She held her hand out to Cecilia, who placed five gold coins in her palm.

"By accepting a coin, you are binding yourself to my service," Maeve said. "Do you understand?"

The men nodded, and she handed each of them a coin. The moment they took them, a green light flashed in their eyes. I wondered if they were even aware they were now under her spell. I recalled Tommy Bell, and his reaction, and guessed that they did not.

"My daughter, Kellen, is missing," Maeve said. "She's in a cottage in the Dark Forest. I need you to go to her and await my command."

One of the men looked down at the coin.

"A gold piece to risk our lives in the Dark Forest? We all know the tales. There are creatures in those trees that will turn a man into a beast with a bite."

"If they don't eat you first," another man said.

"The gold coin is not payment but protection. So long as you have it on your person, no beast made of magic will be able to harm you."

"How do we know it will work?" the first man asked.

Cecilia picked up a lamp and began softly chanting words I couldn't quite hear. As I watched, the lamp blurred its appearance, changing like the mirror when it shifted images. It melted into the form of a small dog.

"Bite the man," Cecilia said.

The dog darted forward and jumped up to clamp down on the man's hand. The man lifted his arm and looked at the dog dangling from his fingers.

"Are you hurt?" Maeve asked.

"Not a bit," the man answered.

"Are you done questioning my authority and knowledge, or do you need further proof of the magic of which I'm capable?"

I saw the exact moment they all realized the precariousness of their situation.

"We need no proof, My Lady," the stockiest man said with a slight bow. "We are in your service and follow your command."

She smiled at the man.

"What is your name?"

"Grimm."

"A fine name," she said with a smile. "I believe fate led you to me, Grimm. You shall lead these men and report to me once you find my daughter. Kellen is a rare beauty, like her sister, with ebony hair and bright blue eyes. She's intelligent. Do not disregard her because of her gender."

She handed Grimm the box.

"To find her, have one of your men use this box." As with the previous tracker, she explained how the box worked, the cost of using it, and the purpose of the ribbon. Then Maeve held out her hand to Porcia. Her daughter handed over a blade, and I braced myself.

There was no throat slashing this time, though. Maeve took the man's hand and pricked his finger. His gaze never left her as she lifted it to her lips. A soft grunt escaped him the moment her mouth closed over the tip, and the front of his pants stirred as she began to suckle his finger. My cheeks heated as he moaned and closed his eyes.

When she released him, he looked at her, his eyes blazing green.

"We are bound now, Grimm," she said. "You can speak to me whenever you wish through any reflective surface. All you need to do is call my name. Maeve."

"I belong to you and only you," he said, the words reminiscent of Hugh's.

"I know," she said, releasing him. "And when you successfully complete your task and return to me, I will reward you in ways you cannot possibly imagine."

The man's gaze heated.

"Go," she said gently. "Fulfill my will. Find my daughter, and report to me. Do not return until I ask it of you."

He nodded, and the group left the room.

"Cecilia. Porcia. Please let Heather and Catherine know we're expecting guests tonight. Then go prepare yourselves. We'll take what little remains."

After they too left, Maeve crossed the room and sat beside me. She took my hand, her fingers squeezing me gently.

"Have no doubt they will find and retrieve your sister. I will not fail to reunite you again."

"Thank you, Mama."

"You asked what you could do to help, and I do have a task for you. Do you recall the prince's servant? The one you thought killed your mother?"

It took everything I had not to jerk from her touch at the mention of Kaven. It felt like a lifetime ago since I'd last laid eyes on the man that I'd mistakenly suspected of wrongdoing. So much had changed since then that I'd all but forgotten him.

"Yes," I said.

She tilted her head at me.

"Yes, Mama."

She smiled.

"I would like you to get to know him. I need you to gain his trust and confidence. Can you do that?"

My heart raced with excitement as my mind raced with the possibilities this opportunity might present. In order for me to gain Kaven's confidence, Maeve would need to let me out of the attic. I would be able to run. I briefly thought of Catherine and Heather then of Kellen. If I ran before the trackers reached her maybe—

"Do you think I ask too much?" Maeve asked.

I immediately regretted my silence.

"I'm not sure," I said honestly. "I wasn't very nice to him in the past. I'm afraid he might not be willing to spend time with me."

Maeve smiled widely.

"He's a man. I promise he will want to spend time with you if you approach him correctly."

Catherine entered the room.

"I beg your pardon, My Lady. How many guests should we prepare for tonight?"

"There will be twenty. Just a light meal. No need to waste good food on them. You can serve us a full meal afterward."

Confusion clouded Catherine's gaze, but she nodded and left the room. I was less confused. Whatever Maeve planned tonight, I doubted the men who arrived would see another sunrise after they entered our doors.

I STOOD before Maeve in the entry. Dressed in my finest mourning gown with my hair piled high, I endured her appraising gaze.

"You are quite lovely, Eloise," she said. "Dare I say…you might even be lovelier than my own daughters."

"Thank you, Mama," I said.

She made a non-committal noise.

"Catherine mentioned that you miss your walks outside. Why didn't you tell me?"

"I didn't want to appear ungrateful," I said. It was a very true statement. I feared what Maeve would do if I showed her anything but gratitude. Yet, saying what I had in front of Catherine had been a purposeful thing. I wanted Maeve to know I was chafing for a bit of freedom but not acting on those urges. I'd hoped it would help further win Maeve's trust.

"You should always speak freely with me," she said. "I want to know what you're thinking at all times."

Her amulet pulsed with life as she spoke the words. The familiar warmth wrapped around me. I raged against it, mentally pushing it away. I wouldn't tell her everything. What secrets I had were mine to keep. And, for the safety of Kellen, I could not tell Maeve everything. The warmth drifted away instead of seeping into my bones.

"Go on," Maeve said. "Tell me."

Nothing compelled me to speak. Shock rippled through me, and I masked it quickly with rash words.

"I want you to stop casting spells on me and treat me like a real daughter."

Maeve's eyes widened then she hugged me hard.

"My precious girl," she said against my ear. "I am treating you like my own daughter. Never doubt that."

I hugged her tightly in return and pitied Cecilia and Porcia if Maeve spoke the truth. When she released me, she stood by my side, holding my hand. Together, we waited to greet the first round of Maeve's victims.

"I hope Catherine and Heather make something sweet to follow dinner," I said randomly, knowing she would expect such things if the spell had worked.

Maeve's fingers twitched in mine, and she chuckled.

"You will make me proud, Eloise," Maeve said. "Of that, I am certain."

I doubted that very much. I'd seen the way she'd beaten the mirror in anger and knew pride wasn't what she would feel when I finally ran. I almost wished I could be there to see it.

The first carriage approached, distracting me from my pleasant thoughts. Maeve released me to greet the men and direct them to the dining room. When all twenty had arrived, we joined them.

Catherine and Heather immediately began to serve a cold soup, enduring a few grabs and fondles from the men as they did so.

"Thank you all for joining us tonight," Maeve said. "Especially on such short notice. I hope you've continued your discretion about our meetings."

A glimmer of green light flashed in the eyes of all but one man.

"William, who have you told?" Maeve asked.

"My son, My Lady. I wanted him to join us tonight. I said

nothing of what happens here, only that I was attending and wanted him to accompany me."

"You could not persuade him?" she asked.

"No. His wife just gave birth to their first babe. He chose to return home to her."

"You should have told him he'd get his cock sucked," one of the men said with a chuckle. "It would have convinced him."

Maeve smiled.

"I'm sure it would have. It's a pity he couldn't be here."

During the conversation, Catherine and Heather finished serving the men and took our bowls away.

"Why aren't you eating?" William asked, spoon partway to his mouth.

"We're waiting for the next course," Maeve said. "It's important not to overindulge and to preserve our figures. Don't you agree, Porcia?"

"Yes, Mama."

The men grunted their agreement and ate their soups. I studied Porcia's downturned gaze, realizing there was reproach in Maeve's words.

"Heather. Catherine," Maeve called abruptly before anyone finished their soup.

Already bare, the women entered the dining room.

"Show these men how a woman is meant to be loved," Maeve said.

My mouth dropped open in shock as Catherine turned to Heather and started kissing her. The men watched raptly, encouraging them to tweak each other's nipples and "slip a finger into her twattle." I turned away from what Heather and Catherine were doing and watched Maeve and her daughters.

As Heather and Catherine kissed passionately, the three women stood, each with a knife clutched in her hand. Maeve's amulet glowed brightly, and the men's eyes flashed bright green in response. They quieted but continued to watch the maids.

"Cecilia, you may have three," Maeve said. "Porcia, one should suffice. The rest are mine."

Cecilia and Porcia each positioned themselves behind a man as did Maeve. While I couldn't see what her daughters did, I could clearly watch Maeve.

With the knife, she pricked the back of the man's neck. He made a small sound, just enough to part his lips and allow the green light to escape. None of the men turned to look. The sounds that Heather and Catherine were making might have covered his gasp, but certainly the light was noticeable as it fed Maeve's amulet.

Twin lights came from the men Cecilia and Porcia had chosen, then disappeared into the chests of their gowns.

But, it was Maeve who had my attention. She went from man to man, doing the same to each until sixteen strands of green flowed toward her breast. The first man's features hollowed, echoing the look that I'd briefly glimpsed on Hugh. He thumped limply against the table, his gaze never leaving Catherine and Heather.

Maeve waved her hand, cutting off the thread. One by one she fed from them. Her skin began to glow with the power she gained.

"Return to your homes and make love to your wives. Remember nothing but the pleasure you received here," Maeve said.

Catherine and Heather broke apart as soon as the men stood and left the room.

"We're ready for our meal, now," Maeve said, returning to her seat.

I desperately wanted to offer to serve the meal in Catherine's and Heather's places but knew Maeve wouldn't approve. So I held my tongue and stared at the table.

"What are your thoughts, Eloise? You're very quiet."

I looked up to find Maeve studying me intently.

"I didn't realize you had used so much power on the trackers."

"I didn't. This harvest was for what I plan to do next."

The door opened, and Catherine and Heather entered with our covered plates.

"Perfect timing," Maeve said. "I'm famished."

CHAPTER 8

I'd barely eaten half my hot oats when a thunderous knocking at the main entry disturbed the silence. Surprised, I looked at Maeve. How hadn't we heard anything?

"Would you like me to answer the door, Mama?" Porcia asked, setting her spoon aside.

"Not this time. Heather," Maeve called.

Heather rushed from the kitchen.

"Yes, My Lady."

"Please answer the door."

Heather nodded and hurried to the main entry.

"Eat," Maeve said softly.

I brought my spoon to my mouth as I strained to hear Heather's softly spoken greeting. Approaching footfalls echoed against the floor. I glanced at Maeve, who calmly took a bite of her oats.

A moment later, a King's Guard entered the dining room ahead of Heather. The guard was finally here. After all this time. And to what good? I briefly considered what would happen if I attempted to tell the man anything of significance. I would choke on my words, for certain, and once they left, Kellen or I would certainly suffer for the attempt. I held my tongue and waited.

"Good morning, ladies," the guard said with a slight bow. "By the King's order, I have been asked to search your dwelling."

He withdrew a rolled piece of parchment from his jacket and offered it to Maeve as Heather scurried back to the kitchen. Her gaze briefly met mine, and I wondered if she'd thought the same thing about speaking.

Maeve glanced at the parchment then at the man as she set her spoon aside and wiped her mouth with her napkin.

"Your uniform and word are enough proof for me, Captain. Of course you may search as you've been ordered. Perhaps I can assist you in locating whatever it is you need."

"Your assistance is not required. Please remain seated and finish your morning meal. My sergeant-at-arms will remain with you in the event you have any questions while we complete the search."

He nodded to us as another man stepped into the room, then the captain left. The sergeant-at-arms' stoic expression didn't suggest he remained with us to answer questions but rather to contain us within the dining room.

I considered him for a long moment, trying desperately to think of a way to alert him of Maeve's actions. However, even that thought created a slight constriction in my throat.

"Eat, girls. I'm sure this is nothing more than a search for some errant servant who stole away with a crown jewel," Maeve said dismissively before taking a bite.

I struggled to do the same and not choke. Since I couldn't alert the guards, I decided to hope they would find something incriminating instead. However, if they did, I knew I might also be prosecuted since I was now officially Maeve's daughter as well. But I was willing to take the risk in order to free Catherine and Heather. Perhaps, if I was allowed to speak with the maids afterward, they could find help for Kellen.

"I bet it was the crown," Cecilia said, interrupting my thoughts. "Poor people always think the crown has more value than it really does."

"Of course it wasn't the crown," Porcia said. "It sits upon the King's head. What servant would be foolish enough to—"

"It wasn't the crown, miss. Nothing was stolen," the sergeant said.

Both Porcia and Cecilia turned to the man and blinked at him. I waited, watching to see if their guileless expressions would trick him into revealing more, but he remained silent.

"Girls, your oats are growing cold. Eat. I'm sure we will learn soon enough why we were interrupted at such an hour."

We ate in silence for several long minutes, listening to doors open and close and furniture being moved about. Finally, the banging stopped, and footsteps descended the stairs.

"I do hope no one touched my delicates," Cecilia said ever so softly to Porcia with a shiver. "I could never bring myself to wear them again."

The sergeant cleared his throat uncomfortably and stepped back as the captain returned.

"Thank you for your cooperation," the captain said.

"Did you find what you were looking for?" Maeve asked, standing.

"No, ma'am," he said.

"Are you certain you cannot tell me? I might be able to—"

"Unless you practice magic, I doubt you can assist."

Cecilia gasped.

"You cannot use magic to find what's missing. It's forbidden."

Her performance was exceptional. She truly was Maeve's daughter.

The man held up his hands.

"We are not looking to use magic. We are searching for signs that it's been used."

"But magic can only be used by a caster or enchanter?" Cecilia echoed. "Why would you search here?"

Before the man could be pulled into her inane banter that would most definitely lead nowhere, I asked a question of my own.

"What exactly would a sign of casting or enchanting look like?"

His gaze flicked to me.

"I can't say, miss."

"Because you've been sworn to secrecy or because you don't know?" I pressed.

"Eloise," Maeve said calmly, "that's quite enough."

I quickly looked down at the table.

"I'm sorry, Mama," I said quietly.

"It's quite acceptable for her to ask, Ma'am. My niece was curious about the same thing. The less you know, the safer you are," he said. "I must ask, who is sleeping in the attic space?"

My heart stalled then jack-rabbited into a speed that made my hands shake. How could I have forgotten about Mother's books?

"I do, sir," I said.

"Why?"

I looked up, confused.

"Why?" I echoed.

Maeve chuckled.

"As you can imagine, if you have a niece this age, the girls want their own spaces. My Eloise was willing to sacrifice a few conveniences to have the whole attic to herself. I thought she was quite clever with her walls and sitting area."

The man's gaze held mine as Maeve spoke.

"Do you believe yourself to be clever?" he asked.

I could feel Maeve's gaze bore into me.

"That's an unfair question, sir. If I answer that I do, I will sound vain. No young lady wants to sound vain."

He smiled slightly.

"Very true. What happened to your cheek?"

"As you can imagine, stacking that furniture so high is not without its dangers. I haven't been to the market in over a week because of my foolishness."

He nodded. "Do be careful in your future, clever endeavors."

I inclined my head and went back to eating, grateful he hadn't discovered the books.

The man said his farewell and left me to endure Maeve's scrutiny.

It was obvious she hadn't liked that I'd spoken at all. Unable to sit there in silence, I looked up and boldly met her gaze.

"I'm sorry, Mama. I didn't know what to say. I was afraid if I lied, he would know. I answered as truthfully as possible without implicating—" My throat closed, and I cringed.

She tilted her head at me.

"You were surprisingly adept at it."

Panic clawed at me as I realized what I'd done. I'd shown her how skilled I could be when answering her with the truth, but not the complete truth, as well. I said nothing, waiting for what she would do next.

"As the man said, you do have a clever mind, Eloise. It will be an asset to you if you use that cleverness appropriately."

"Yes, Mama," I said.

"What does it mean that they came here, Mama?" Porcia asked.

"That they know we're here," Cecilia said. "Why else would they be searching homes?"

"Perhaps it's just a precaution before our beloved prince arrives," Maeve said, looking at me.

"Do you think it wise to push the manservant for information so soon after the first search?" Porcia asked.

Maeve's cool gaze swung to her youngest.

"First?" I asked. It wasn't that I was trying to save Porcia from Maeve's wrath. Instead, I wanted to learn what I could. While I was unable to say anything before, perhaps I would find a time when I could speak. And when I did, I wanted to be able to say everything.

Maeve leaned back in her chair and tapped her fingers against the table, lost in thought for a moment. Then, she sighed and shook her head.

"Rather than speculate why or how often these searches will occur, girls, I want you to go to town and see what you can learn."

The girls immediately stood and left the room without finishing their breakfast. I took another bite of mine, not yet willing to give up my freedom for the day. Surprisingly, Maeve did the same. We ate in silence for several moments before Maeve pushed her bowl aside only half eaten.

"It's time," she said, standing. "Come Eloise, there is news."

Confused, I stood and followed her to the entry. She went straight to the mirror, kissed it, then spoke the words to wake it. Grimm's face slowly emerged from within the smoky expanse of glass without her asking to show him. Beyond him, I saw nothing but treetops. It appeared as if he was looking down at us. His expression brightened when he saw Maeve.

"My love, we've found the girl. As you said, she is in a cottage with seven small men. Miners by the looks of them. We're watching, waiting for them to leave. When they do, we will take the girl."

"Very good, Grimm. Thank you for your excellent work. Remember to watch the ribbon. Check it hourly."

Grimm's expression fell slightly.

"Forgive me, my heart. On our way here, I checked it constantly. During one check, the wind took the ribbon. I tried chasing it, but one of the beasts caught it, and I couldn't win it back."

Maeve glanced at me, her expression unreadable, before focusing on Grimm.

"Very well. Watch and continue to report to me."

She sent the mirror to sleep once more then turned to me. The silence grew as she studied me.

"The loss of the ribbon is unfortunate. However, don't mistake its absence as enticement to disobey me, or I will see Grimm beat Kellen far worse than the ones you've received. And, if you try to run and join your sister, I will have Grimm kill Kellen. Then, you will be returned to me by the very men who killed your sister."

I didn't doubt a word of her calmly delivered threat.

"You are mine. Do you understand?"

"Yes, Mama." I paused for a moment. "Does that mean you don't intend to bring Kellen home?"

"I'm sorry to ask for your patience a little longer, dear one. Grimm will ensure we reunite you with your sister."

Whether that reunion occurred when we were both alive remained to be the question.

"Now that we know Grimm is there, we will proceed as we discussed. Take the pig for a walk as you liked to do, and talk to Kaven. If you've not returned within the hour, I will use the mirror to tell Grimm you no longer wish to see your sister again. Do you understand?"

"Yes, Mama."

"Tell me what you really think, Eloise? Do you plan to run?"

"No, Mama. How did you know that Grimm was there with Kellen? And what would have happened if he had summoned you while the guard was here?" I asked, giving her one of my random thoughts to appease her.

"I can sense the mirror when it summons me. If I'm not here or unable to wake it, whoever summons me has to wait. The mirror will never reveal its nature unless I call upon it."

"Should I be worried about speaking with Kaven so soon after the search? Especially after how rude I've been to him?"

"Use that clever mind of yours, Eloise. Find out when the prince is due. You have an hour. Don't disappoint me."

I nodded and stood, eager to go outside no matter what the reason.

A few minutes later, dressed in a cloak and my sturdy shoes, I strode toward the woods, nearly dragging the pig along with me. He seemed oddly subdued, and I wondered if he had felt like a captive too, despite the walks Heather took with him.

"Please, Mr. Pig," I said softly. "Walk faster. I've been locked away in that house for too long, and she only gave me an hour."

The pig grunted and picked up speed. The oddity with which he seemed to understand me had faded in light of recent events. However, after my conversation with Rose and her obvious understanding about magic, I began to wonder what she might have done to the poor creature.

Elation filled me as another thought occurred. Rose had sensed the magic Maeve had been using near me. Perhaps the old woman would be able to help me find a way to free myself and the others without endangering Kellen. I only needed to find a way to get into town. And after that, a way to stop Maeve once I discovered what she intended to do with the prince.

Nothing a clever girl couldn't handle. I sighed and continued through the trees, letting the pig lead us off the trail as he snuffled and grunted with his nose to the ground.

But first, I needed to speak to Kaven and eat some crow. Not for Maeve's benefit but for my own peace of mind. I'd spoken so harshly to him because of my notions of his guilt. Granted, it hadn't helped that he had been surly and suspicious as well. However, I now realized how warranted his doubt of an unknown woman had been. I wished I had been more doubtful myself. Of Maeve. Of the messenger boy. Of everyone.

"The wasp has returned," a voice said from nearby.

Startled, I whirled around, dropping the pig's tether.

"No need to send your pig after me," Kaven said. He stood just behind a tree, his clear, deep blue eyes shifting between me and the pig.

"Is that fear I see in your eyes?" I said, unable to help myself.

He patted the tree and gave it a considering look.

"I wasn't sure I'd picked a tree large enough to stop the both of you."

I smiled, amused. He was likable now that I knew he wasn't evil. My humor faded as that thought reminded me of my purpose.

He noticed, and his answering smile faded.

"I thought you'd taken to avoiding the forest like you'd threatened to do the first time I met you."

"I've been unavoidably detained," I said.

"Does your detainment have anything to do with your bruised cheek?"

I lifted my hand to the cheek in question.

"After boasting of my intelligence, I would prefer not to talk about this."

He considered me for a moment then inclined his head.

"I will not mention it again."

"Thank you."

We stared at each other for a moment before I bent to fetch the pig's tether. The creature hadn't gone far, just a few steps away to snuffle the ground.

"You seem different," Kaven said, drawing my attention. "More subdued."

I gave a wry smile, thinking of all the things that were restraining me. A curse. Maeve's threat on Kellen's safety. The idea that Maeve might be watching me with her detestable mirror even now.

"That happens when one struggles with an overdue apology," I said smoothly.

His brows lifted.

"Apology?"

He looked right then left.

"I need to find somewhere to sit. I'm feeling faint."

I snorted and shook my head as he folded his arms and leaned against the tree, waiting expectantly.

"I'm sorry I hit you with the rock. It was unnecessarily forceful."

"And?"

"And I promise to use a branch next time."

He threw his head back and laughed, a dimple emerging on his cheek. I'd forgotten how handsome he was and didn't resent the way my middle did an odd flip at the sight of his humor. In fact, I embraced it and let myself desperately wish my life was currently on a different course. One that might involve him.

Gently tugging on the pig, I turned and resumed walking. Kaven quickly fell into step beside me.

"Is that what brought you out today?" he asked. "The need to apologize?"

"Don't flatter yourself. The pig was overdue for his walk. And I was eager for some sun on my face."

From the corner of my eye, I caught him studying me and glanced at him.

"What?"

"I'm still trying to understand you."

"Oh? I thought you were learning all my tricks," I said, remembering the last time we'd met and how he'd successfully deflected my blows.

"I believe I've barely begun to know you, Eloise Cartwright. But, I would like to."

His words sent a shiver of fear through me. This was exactly what Maeve wanted.

"That's a bit forward of you," I said primly.

He chuckled.

"You seem to appreciate forwardness."

"Sometimes." I stopped walking and faced him. "How long have you been with the prince?"

His humor fled, and mistrust crept into his gaze.

"Why do you ask?"

"I've lived here, on the King's land, my entire life. I want to know why."

The suspicion cleared.

"Your mother helped save the kingdom."

"My mother?" I shook my head and resumed walking. "My earliest memory of her is a day we went to the market. All the other women were walking briskly, buying what they needed. Mother did neither. She walked slowly, letting our maids haggle for better prices. She needed to sit and rest often and napped as soon as we returned home. How could a woman with no strength have saved the kingdom?"

"It's not strength that rights wrongs, Eloise, but determination."

I shrugged indifferently while storing that bit of information away. Determination I had in plenty. If what Kaven said was true about my mother, perhaps I was meant to follow in her footsteps and save the kingdom's Prince.

"Why are you out in the woods?" I asked. "Hasn't your errant Prince returned to ply you with work yet?"

"Are you trying to rid me of your pleasant company?"

"Hardly. My sharp words are good for you. As are menial tasks.

Surely there are some princely soiled underthings for you to scrub by now."

Kaven snorted.

"I've never met a woman open to discussing the washing of underthings."

"Such topics are acceptable when speaking of royalty, didn't you know? One simply must know everything about the lives of our betters."

He gave me an odd look, a cross between concern and disappointment.

"You sound as if you hate the Prince. Have you met him before to carry such animosity?"

"Animosity? I hold no such strong emotion for our errant Prince. The best I can conjure is disdainful indifference. His drawn-out impending appearance has disrupted my life," I said before I could stop myself.

"How so?"

"Visitors come under the guise of condolences to press for information about his Royal Highness's return as if we know more than the common populace in Towdown. I resent the intrusion as it's a constant reminder of what was taken from me."

"I'm sorry, Eloise."

"It is what it is. Lowly people such as ourselves have no influence on the decisions of our betters. We can only live with the consequences of them. But if you do have the Prince's ear, please tell him to get his royal backside home."

"I will inform him that a beautiful damsel impatiently awaits his return. Perhaps it will hasten his progress. Unless you plan to greet him with a rock."

I rolled my eyes.

"I've already sworn off rocks."

Kaven grinned.

"Do you truly have nothing better to do with your time than torment me?"

He gave an exaggerated sigh.

"There are a few things that do require my attention today. Will I find you walking tomorrow, Eloise?"

"Only if you continue to wander the woods like an idle miscreant."

"You wound me."

I could clearly see that I hadn't.

"When you speak with your Prince, you might want to mention your apparent boredom. I'm certain he will help you correct it."

CHAPTER 9

Maeve stopped pacing before the fire as soon as I opened the door to the otherwise empty kitchen. Turning, she watched me remove my cloak, her face an impartial mask that worried me more than her false kindness. The kindness was a ploy to hide who she really was while she strove to manipulate those around her. However, this was the calm before the storm where she let her real nature show.

When I looked up from removing my shoes, she stood before me. Her hand lashed out and connected with my cheek with a vicious crack. The strike stung, but I knew well that it could have been worse.

"I returned straight away after speaking with Kaven," I said nervously.

"Speaking with him, Eloise? You insulted him the entire time."

I'd known she would watch. Yet, hearing her admit it made the entire conversation with Kaven repeat in my head. Because Maeve was unfamiliar with my prior relationship with Kaven, I could understand why she thought I'd insulted him.

"I flirted with him."

"That was flirting?"

"Yes. He smiled and laughed and liked talking to me enough that he hopes to speak with me again tomorrow."

She considered me for a moment, some of the suppressed anger leaving her eyes.

"Have you kissed a boy, Eloise?"

The question startled me.

"No, Mama."

She sighed. "Then, the fault in this failure is mine."

"Failure? But he seemed to trust me and said he would speak with the prince."

"He was making light of your comments, my dear. It's clear the boy has interest in you. However, you lack the knowledge to foster it. But, I think I have just the way to educate you regarding how to correct your approach. Would you like to go for another outing tomorrow?"

I had seen her parties and feared how she meant to educate me. Yet, I knew there was only one right answer.

"Yes, Mama," I said.

She smiled at me, her expression filled with pride.

"Then you will go with Cecilia to the Brazen Belle to learn how real flirting is done."

My brows rose in surprise before I could stop myself. I knew very well what the Brazen Belle was.

"Don't fret so. No one will know it's you, and I promise you're only going to observe. You're too precious to me to be used like Catherine and Heather."

"Mama, please. He already noticed I was acting differently despite my efforts to the contrary. If I start acting out of character even more so, won't he become mistrustful?"

She tilted her head and looked at me.

"What do you suggest?"

"Kaven sees me as a young girl who has no experience with boys. Let me continue as such for a few days and see where it leads. I don't know your purpose in determining when the prince arrives or understand your urgency, but what are a few more days when so many have been spent already?"

Maeve said nothing as she stared at me for several long minutes. The throbbing in my cheek increased with each beat of my heart, and I began to fear that I'd pushed too far and would quickly suffer more abuse. Yet, despite her assurance that I would not be used like Heather and Catherine, I saw our fates intertwining if I went to a whorehouse to learn about flirting.

"You say you want to be a young lady of good breeding but are doing nothing to show me that is your true path. A young woman of good breeding is adept at learning information and sharing it, Eloise. What have you learned?"

I remained silent, knowing I'd learned nothing of use to her.

"We need to know when Prince Greydon will return," she continued. "You have three days to attempt to innocently gain the information. After that, you will learn to embrace the power of your beauty and clever wit. You will acquire the skills that women with less refinement have honed over the years to gain everything they desire. And, you will use everything you have to obtain what we need by the night of the fifth day. Do you understand, Eloise?"

"Yes, Mama."

"I don't think you do," she said with soft menace. "But after a visit to the Brazen Belle, you will. Now go to your room. The sight of your face is a sore reminder of your failure."

I hastened to leave her presence.

In the solace of the attic, I wet a cloth in the cool water of my washbasin and pressed it to my abused cheek. My life hovered on a precipice. A single misstep, and I would find myself in far worse circumstances than my current one. How would I ever convince Kaven to share the Prince's plans with me?

Sighing, I sat on my bed and looked across at its empty twin. I missed Kellen's calming presence. I missed Judith and Anne. And above all, I missed Mother. She would have been amused by each encounter I had with Kaven. Except, perhaps, the one where I bashed him with the rock. But even then, she would have warned me to curb my temper by using that patient voice of hers. She would have never slapped me.

I snorted, realizing the fruitlessness of comparing Maeve's actions to that of my mother's. My mother would have never murdered anyone much less seen either of her daughters physically punished for anything.

The need to free myself from Maeve's influence drove me to set aside the cloth and carefully dig out Mother's herbology books. Without the lock securing the door, I didn't spend any time absorbed in their pages, but rather spent my time familiarizing myself with their content in general.

Every book had notes about potions or spells. Most had sporadic entries that intertwined with the use of common enough tinctures. A few contained pages dedicated to certain potions. One that caught my eye was a potion to change one's appearance.

"Eloise," Maeve called from below.

I startled and looked around wide-eyed before collecting myself.

"Coming, Mama," I answered as I quietly hid the books.

Lightly running down the stairs, I found Maeve once again waiting for me in the entry. She stood near the mirror, the image of Heather and Catherine moving about our kitchen fading from view. Dread pooled in my stomach. Had Maeve witnessed me with the books? Would she ask what I'd been reading? Would she demand to see them?

"Your sisters are returning. It will be good for you to greet them and hear their success."

I said nothing, too relieved she hadn't called me down to question me. Though, I did wonder how she knew they were coming —perhaps she watched them with the mirror too—and what she would do if they hadn't been successful.

Outside, the rattle of an arriving carriage ceased, and I moved to wait a few steps behind Maeve. Cecilia threw open the door, a pleased smile on her face.

"I can see you have news. Let's move to the sitting room. I'll ring for tea."

"Please, no more tea. Another sip, and I'll float away."

Maeve smiled at her daughter, artfully took her arm, and led the girl into the sitting room. I glanced at Porcia, who lingered behind like me.

Her gaze flicked to my cheek.

"What happened?" she asked.

"I spoke with the manservant, but he wasn't forthcoming with the information Mama wanted."

Porcia's gaze slowly swept me from head to foot. Her scrutiny bore no hint of any malicious emotion. Yet, her next words contradicted her expression, as they often did.

"You'll learn to do as you're told."

She walked past me, entering the sitting room not far behind Maeve and Cecilia. Knowing Maeve wanted me present, I followed. Once again, she patted the seat beside her, bidding me to sit near. Cecilia, already seated across from her mother, watched me closely, a slight smirk curving her lips as I did as I was told.

"Tell us what you've learned," Maeve said.

"Searches are occurring in every home within Towdown, including those on the outskirts, like ours. They began after Mr. Fletcher's carriage was discovered idly wandering the streets last night. All four occupants were dead, and the driver was missing."

"Why are they searching homes for signs of magical use and not signs of the driver?" I asked. It would seem logical to me to suspect the driver if the man was missing.

Maeve glanced at me.

"You've seen the results of a magical death, and the result of completely draining a person's life energy."

Images of Anne and Judith filled my mind, and I quickly understood why the guards were searching homes. Maeve focused on Cecilia once more.

"I had hoped that Mr. Fletcher and his companions would make it home to their wives before the spell finished its work. Any news of the others?"

Cecilia looked at Porcia.

"All are still alive as far as the gossips know though a few have been struck by some mysterious illness that keeps them abed."

"That is perfect," Maeve said. "A mysterious malady is just what we need to help deflect suspicion. Porcia, I will leave it to you to foster that notion. Did either of you manage to entice new patrons to our nightly gatherings?"

"Yes, Mama," they both said.

"Lovely."

THE BIRDS CHIRPED EXCITEDLY though their pretty songs barely penetrated my notice as I wove through the trees. With no pig to slow me, I quickly made my way toward the Royal Retreat as my mind raced, trying to find a solution to all of the problems that plagued me.

Last evening, Maeve had once again used Heather and Catherine to entice another group of dinner companions into her service. I doubted even now that the men knew they were under Maeve's thrall or that she had fed from them. She had made me stay through the initial invitation, a reminder of Catherine and Heather's place in Maeve's household. And, my future place if I continued to fail her. She'd excused me only after a warning that I had three days to learn the Prince's whereabouts.

The sounds of the men's satisfied groans and the wet licking still haunted me. But as much as I wanted to save myself from such a fate, I feared what Maeve planned to do with the Prince and how many more would suffer if she gained the information she wanted.

I needed to find a way to warn Kaven. Yet, with the curse binding my words and Maeve watching my actions, I didn't see how I could stop anything. The idea of doing what I was told grated at me. But I needed to keep Kellen safe. The image of the mirror rose to my mind, and I cursed its existence yet again. What I wouldn't give to destroy it. Perhaps then I would have a chance.

I wished Mother hadn't died. Although I wouldn't have wanted to subject her to Maeve's cruelty, I would have felt less lost if she were still with me.

"Going somewhere?" Kaven asked in amusement.

I whirled and realized I'd walked right past him. A smile played about his lips, flashing the dimple I found so heartwarming, and his eyes twinkled with humor. He wore the same hat pulled down to his ears, his darker hair escaping the confines. Suddenly, I itched to touch it and know its texture.

Grinning wryly, I smoothed my hands over my skirts and looked away for a moment.

"I was coming to see you."

"And yet you walked by as if I did not exist."

Blushing slightly, I looked up at him.

"I know very well you exist."

"What were you thinking with such singular focus?"

"I was wondering if my mother would approve of what I'm doing."

"Meeting a lowly servant in the woods?"

I snorted, turned, and started walking more slowly this time, picking a direction at random. Kaven joined me.

"I can hardly consider you lowly when you think so highly of yourself," I said.

He gave me a quizzical look.

"You believe I think highly of myself?"

"Most certainly. You accused me of trespassing when we first met, and after you learned who I was, you still knocked me off my horse, spanked me—"

"There is no need to list my transgressions. I remember them well. And I sincerely apologize for all of them. It's not that I think highly of myself but rather that I have a need to protect those I serve."

"It's admirable that you do," I said, understanding his need to protect those close to him. Heather and Catherine weren't my family, yet I still wanted no ill to befall them.

"Do you believe the Prince needs such ardent protection as to accost a girl in the woods?" I asked the question sincerely, no playful teasing in my tone. He glanced at me and exhaled slowly.

"Yes. Although I no longer believe you're a threat, the next girl may be."

I tilted my head at him.

"How do you know I'm not a threat? Perhaps I'm the biggest threat of them all."

He stopped walking and studied me. The way his gaze swept over my face and lingered on my lips set my heart racing.

"I think it would be wisest if I say nothing further," he said softly. "Lest you refuse to meet me again tomorrow."

I forced a small smile, my heart heavy. For the sake of the kingdom, Kaven needed to see through me.

"I'm uncertain if it's wise," I said.

"Why?"

"I still don't understand your reason for wanting to speak with me after all I've done."

He shrugged slightly.

"You're the most real woman I've ever met."

I couldn't stop the disbelieving noise that escaped me.

"I shall tell my friends that all it takes is a knee to the testicles for a boy to take them seriously."

Kaven chuckled.

"That it does."

We walked in silence for several moments.

"Aren't you going to ask if I sent your message to the Prince?" he asked finally.

"Should I?"

"I have it on good authority that girls are very interested in everything royalty does."

I grinned.

"Most girls might be. I'm tired of the constant princely chatter. Why is his life so much more important than ours?"

Kaven's brows rose.

"You don't believe it is?"

"No. He's a person like any other. The only importance his life has is that which we give it. If the Prince and I were alone in the world, why should I grant him authority over me? His birthright doesn't make him better than I am, only more known. Thus, all lives should hold equal value to his."

"Such talk could be considered treasonous," he said gravely.

"And that way of thinking only proves my point."

"How so?"

"Rulers come into power two different ways," I said, holding his gaze, needing him to understand the deeper meaning of what I was telling him. "Some are lifted up from the people by the people, such as our current royal family. The power they have now was once given to them because the people trusted the judgment of the first king. Other rulers come into power by taking what they want through coercion or fear. But both, in the beginning, started out as a person just like you or me."

"I understand how you would think the Prince's life has equal value to the common man," he said. "But I don't understand how my remark about treason helped prove it."

"The idea that any who disagrees with the Royal family's edicts are guilty of treason is a fear tactic to ensure the King remains in power."

Kaven slowly shook his head at me.

"I'm unsure if I should be impressed with your logic or run in fear that you're preparing to start a revolution."

My heart started to pound as I said my final piece.

"A little of both might be in order if men ever took women seriously."

I held my breath as I studied his serious expression, daring to hope he would understand who his threat was.

"Can I tell you something?" he asked.

"Yes."

"The Prince isn't like that. He's not one to subjugate his people. He's kind and wants to bring about a true peace again."

My hope withered and died.

"Can I tell you something?" I asked.

He chuckled.

"You always do whether I want you to or not."

"I don't want to speak of the Prince again. His existence has brought me nothing but pain."

Kaven bowed slightly, and we continued walking. I liked Kaven as much as I disliked him. Why didn't he read deeper into my words and hear what I couldn't come out and say? Frustration robbed me of further conversation, not that it was needed. Without comment, we walked a circle that took us farther from the Retreat and closer to my home.

"Thank you for today," Kaven said. "It gets lonely out here."

"Have you ever thought of leaving?" I asked. "Packing a bag and journeying to places unknown?"

"Have you?" He studied me intently.

"Every day since my mother died," I said softly.

He took half a step closer.

"I'm sorry for the pain you suffer."

I shook my head and looked away.

"Suffering is part of life. It's a journey we all endure until it ends. Better to suffer than to never exist. For between the sufferings, there are moments of great joy," I said, thinking of the family I had known. "We only need to see those moments for what they are and hold onto their memories during the times of trial."

He shook his head slightly.

"You are still a puzzle to me, Eloise. I wish I would have known your mother. To raise a woman such as you, she had to be something special."

"She was."

"Will I see you tomorrow?"

"Perhaps."

I left him in the trees, already doubting I would return. If he were wise, his loyalty to the Royal family would stop him from saying anything no matter how much he might trust me. And that was just as it should be.

When I entered the kitchen, Maeve was once again waiting.

"Nothing of importance again," she said.

"I did not insult him today."

"No. Instead you lectured him. However, your assessment of rulers couldn't be truer. I'm very relieved you see the current king for what he is, a weak man clinging to the remnants of power that never should have belonged to him. It's time for a change, don't you agree?"

Heart pounding with realization, I uttered the necessary words.

"Yes, Mama."

Maeve smiled and swept from the room.

Stunned, I looked at Catherine and Heather who worked quietly at the cutting board. Both wore twin expressions of fear. Seeing them helped solidify the truth of what Maeve had just let slip.

She planned to overthrow the King. But how?

For the sake of the kingdom, I needed to find a way to free myself from Maeve's control.

CHAPTER 10

"Life rarely gives one what one wants," Maeve said, patting my cheek consolingly. "Better to come to terms with that now."

I nodded, trying to quell the fear churning in my middle.

"You will not cause Cecilia trouble, will you?"

I shook my head.

"Good. Enjoy your outing. Do not return until after midday. I have guests I plan to entertain."

Maeve wasn't yet dressed, her thin robe leaving very little to the imagination, and I could guess what type of entertaining she would do.

She turned to Cecilia and handed her two vials.

"Drink them as soon as you reach the edge of town," she said.

Cecilia nodded, and my worry only deepened. Over the last two days, Maeve's visits to town and my forced seclusion in the attic had allowed me time to read the books without fear of being watched. While I hadn't learned anything that would help me free myself, I now understood what those vials contained.

Maeve turned to me once more.

"When you return, you can take a nice walk before sunset to try your new skills. Learn well, Eloise."

I endured Maeve's hug then followed Cecilia outside and

climbed up into the wagon beside her. I wore an old dress Maeve had given me. Cecilia did the same.

"Are you ready for an adventure, dear sister?" Cecilia asked.

I didn't answer, and she chuckled as she clucked the horse into motion. It didn't take long to reach the edge of town. Cecilia slowed the horse and lifted her vial to her lips. I hesitantly did the same, swallowing the potion that would change my appearance so no one would recognize me. Part of me was relieved. I didn't want anyone to know my shame after today. Yet another part of me wished everyone would see what was happening to me so someone could help.

A tingle spread over my face, and I looked at Cecilia to see her features waver and change. Worried, I reached up to touch my nose and brow. Everything felt the same to me.

"It's not truly changing you," she said. "That would take far too much power."

She pocketed the vials and clucked to the horse. I watched the houses go by and tried not to think about what was to come. My time of innocence was at an end. The thought had barely formed when I realized that my innocence had ended long before this moment.

It didn't take long to arrive at the whorehouse. Cecilia pulled the wagon around back to a small stable and tossed a coin to the boy waiting there.

"Take care of the horse. We will be awhile," she said.

I followed her, fighting the urge to run. When Maeve had returned late last night and released me from the attic, she had shown me Grimm with Kellen in the background. Afterward, she had reminded me what fate awaited my sister if I disobeyed or tried to run today. The image of Kellen fast asleep in the sunny clearing steadied my resolve, and I entered the backroom of the Brazen Belle with determination that quickly faltered.

Although I'd seen Kellen naked before, and more recently, Heather and Catherine, I was unprepared for the general state of undress in the Brazen Belle's less public room. Women walked around with the tops of their dresses low enough to show their nipples, or worse, completely around their waist so their breasts were fully displayed. The men who lingered in the room watched with avid interest as the women moved from group to group, speaking to the men as if at a social gathering.

"Sit and watch," Cecilia said, leading me to a cushioned chair off to the side near a set of stairs. "Study how the women approach the men. They need to entice them to get them up to the private rooms with them. That is how they get paid. Do not move from this spot. I will return."

My eyes widened as I realized she planned to leave me. I reached for her, but she laughed and twisted out of the way.

"Don't be a child, Eloise. And do not look away or fail. If you return to Mama as ignorant in the ways of men as you were before, you know what will happen."

I wanted to claw Cecilia's laughing eyes out of her head as she walked away. Instead, I faced the room and did what I was told.

It didn't take long to see that the most successful women were the young ones who played coy...even if their breasts were bared. The pattern was simple enough. The woman smiled at a man and glanced away quickly to get his attention. Once he approached, she spoke softly as would a nervous maid. He would say something, and she would nod and take his hand. Occasionally, he would touch her breast as he spoke but not always. The older women were less sought after but did have some success with bolder tactics such as stepping in front of a man and placing his hand on her breast or under her skirt.

I was so engrossed in my study, I didn't notice someone sat beside me until a hand settled on my skirts just above the knee.

Heart hammering, I looked at the man and narrowed my eyes.

"I am not coy, and I am not for sale," I said plainly. "Be gone."

The man frowned but left to find more willing quarry. Feeling sick and afraid, I returned to my study.

"How's the pig?" a familiar voice asked.

I swiveled in my chair to look up at Rose. The old woman

watched me with a small smile. My eyes immediately began to water. The potion hadn't fooled her. She knew it was me.

Her expression changed to one of concern.

"You didn't eat him, did you?" she asked, sitting beside me. "If you did, I won't be angry. A bit ill, but not angry."

"No. Mr. Pig is well enough. It's you that brings tears to my eyes. I'm relieved you know me for who I am."

She tilted her head at me, a small frown creating even more wrinkles in her brow.

"Why hide who you are but feel relief when someone sees through the spell?"

I opened my mouth but nothing came out. I didn't try harder, too afraid Maeve would notice my attempt to speak freely.

Rose's eyes narrowed on me.

"Someone cast these spells on you, haven't they?"

I remained mute, giving no indication of truth in her words. Yet I felt unrestrained joy. Someone finally knew. She might not know it was Maeve who cast these spells, but at least she knew I was bespelled.

The old woman sighed and sat back in her chair, looking out over the room.

"Wipe the tears from your eyes, child. Whatever trouble you've gotten yourself into will likely only grow worse if you're found crying to me about it."

I quickly wiped my eyes and pretended to go back to studying the room.

"I know about spells to keep a person silent. I've used a few myself."

That admission worried me. She saw it in my expression and grinned.

"Don't worry. He deserved it. The beast had a tendency to lose his temper and yell at me. I'm not a woman who takes kindly to that sort of treatment."

One of the women on the floor walked up to us.

"Rose, you'll scare away the customers. You were told to stay in back."

"She's helping me," I said quickly. "I need to learn how to capture a man's—"

"I know why you're here," the woman said. "What good do you think an old woman's words will do you? Her twat dried up ages ago and hasn't seen a cock since then."

"Do you think cocks have evolved into something more mysterious than they were in my day?" Rose asked with a cackle. "Suck it or fuck it, it's the same result. A happy man willing to give up a little of his coin. There's no mystery in this business."

The girl glared at Rose and walked away. The old woman stared after her.

"Cocks might not have changed," she said softly. "But much in Towdown has." She glanced at me. "I find it odd that she knows your purpose here, and I do not."

"Why do you find that odd?"

She shrugged slightly.

"Like you, I'm unable to say much. Capturing a man's interest is easy. Are you sure you want to do that?"

I almost answered that I didn't. Then fear stayed my tongue instead of the curse. What if Maeve was watching? What would she do to Rose?

The old woman shook her head at me.

"Your fear is answer enough. You need help, but can't ask for it. And I can't help without understanding the full problem. We're in a bind, aren't we?"

I turned away from her, focusing my attention on the women once more.

"I wonder if they all know I'm watching," I said. "Do you think their behavior would change if they knew they were being observed?"

There was a long moment of silence beside me.

"Everyone's behavior changes when they know they're being watched," she said finally.

"Yes. It does."

"How is the pear tree by your mother's grave?" she asked.

I felt a pang and hoped the bird still sang to Mother in my absence.

"I'm not sure. I haven't been for a long while."

"You should go speak to the dead about what you cannot speak to the living. And stay true to yourself, Eloise. Many young women lose their way by not staying true to themselves." She glanced around the room, an indication of exactly what she meant, then patted my knee and left.

Her words stuck in my mind as I spent the next several hours in the chair. My backside had long since gone numb by the time Cecilia returned.

"We need to go now."

She didn't wait for me to stiffly get to my feet but hurried toward the door. I struggled to keep up and emerged to see the boy bringing the horse from the stable.

"Hurry and there's another coin in it for you," she said.

The boy quickly hitched the horse to the wagon, and Cecilia tossed him the promised coin as she clucked the beast into motion. We left the yard of the Brazen Belle just as my nose began to itch. I lifted my hand to scratch it, but she swatted my hand away.

"It's not real. Don't call attention to yourself."

I kept my hands clenched in my lap as she wove through the streets. The tingle stopped by the time we reached the outskirts and started on the path that led to our home and the Retreat.

"Do you think anyone noticed us change?" I asked.

Cecilia gave me a cutting look.

"If they did, we wouldn't still be in the wagon. We would be in a cell under the palace. I don't know why Mama continues to show you favor. You're unintelligent and not worth her consideration."

I sat quietly in the wagon for the rest of the journey home, my anger simmering. I didn't want Maeve's consideration or Cecilia's misguided jealous hate. I wanted them both gone.

Cecilia pulled the wagon to a stop before the shed in too little time and hopped down before Hugh even appeared. The main doors of the house opened, and Maeve stepped out, fully dressed.

"Welcome home, my darlings." Her gaze lingered on me as I climbed the steps. "Did everything go well?"

"Yes, Mama," Cecilia said, kissing her mother's cheek. "Eloise studied the entire time."

"How would you know?" I asked. "I didn't see you after you left me in the common room."

Maeve's gaze pinned her oldest daughter.

"You left her?"

Cecilia's smile faltered.

"I was never far, Mama."

"We will discuss this later. Leave me."

Cecilia cast a hateful glance my way before hurrying upstairs.

"What did you learn?" Maeve asked.

I repeated my assessment of what the younger whores did to see the most success and the bolder practices of the older whores.

"There's no need for the latter," Maeve said. "I think that may test the boy's trust in you."

"Yes, Mama."

She tilted her head at me.

"Why did you tell on your sister?"

"You said you wanted to know what I was thinking, and I disliked how she treated me on the way home."

"Oh? And how was that?"

"She said I wasn't intelligent enough to warrant your favor or consideration."

Maeve smiled slightly.

"You proved her wrong, didn't you?"

I couldn't help the smile that tugged my lips.

"I did."

"I hope it was worth making an enemy of your sister. Even Porcia hasn't been foolish enough for that. Now go upstairs and change into something more suitable. I believe you need to take a walk."

Maeve's warning about Cecilia didn't give me a moment's pause.

Cecilia could do no worse to me than Maeve herself. Hurrying upstairs, I quickly changed into one of my mourning gowns. When I returned to the foyer, Maeve nodded her approval.

"You will do well. Go. Gain the information I seek and truly win my favor."

With my nerves dancing in my stomach, I left the house.

I found myself on the path to my mother's grave without consciously intending to go there. It made sense though, given the anxiety plaguing me. Birds flitted between the trees, their songs beginning to soothe the rough edges of my emotions as I walked.

When I arrived in the clearing, I barely recognized the place. Moving to the bench Hugh had made for Kellen and me, I sat and looked up at the pear tree in awe. Its branches were thick with leaves that rustled in the early spring breeze. Blossoms still dappled the greenery, their sweet scent perfuming the air. I couldn't see any fruit yet but knew it was coming quickly, given the speed with which the tree had grown.

The bird who always sang for me while I sat by Mother's grave started singing, its little eyes watching me. A sense of peace settled over me, and I exhaled slowly. Remembering Rose's words, I whispered a quick plea.

"Please don't let Maeve hear me."

I watched a pear blossom fall slowly to the ground as I considered what to say.

"I'm sorry it's taken me so long to return. Life's been difficult since you left. I regret not seeing the necklace for what it was." My next words died in my throat, the curse preventing me from saying it was Maeve who killed her. Frustration welled within me that I couldn't even speak freely with no one around.

"You wanted so much more for our lives than what we have now," I said angrily. "I hate that our choices have been taken from us. But don't worry, Mother. I'm doing as you asked. I'm watching over Kellen and keeping her safe as best I can."

I tilted my head back, letting the sun warm my face.

"I'll do what I must, but I fear the consequences if I'm successful. I wish you were here to guide me."

The breeze drifted by, caressing my cheek as if my mother were indeed there and trying to comfort me.

Lost in thought about what I needed to do next—find Kaven—I remained where I was. For Kellen's sake, I couldn't refuse to do as Maeve asked. For the Prince's sake, I knew I should try to ruin my attempt. Yet, Maeve had made it clear that failure again wasn't an option. I silently wished there was a way to break her mirror. Without that and the ribbon, Kellen would be safe.

"Lost in thought again, I see," Kaven said.

He walked through the trees, approaching from the direction of the Retreat, and stepped into the clearing.

"At least this time, you aren't wandering the woods."

"How is it you always seem to find me?" I asked as he crossed the space to sit beside me.

"It's a question I often ask myself whenever I'm looking for you." He glanced at the pear tree where the little bird still sang. "The wildlife is louder around you."

I followed his gaze to the tree, ignoring his teasing smile.

"You didn't cut it down."

"I couldn't."

"Thank you."

I sat beside him for a moment, trying to work up the courage to give him a coy glance.

"You seem quieter today," he said. "Is something troubling you?"

"I'm struggling against a fate I cannot change," I said. "Each morning, I open my eyes and feel more frustration and anger than the day before. I can no longer see what is good in my life. Instead, I only see the bad."

I looked at him, meeting his troubled gaze.

"So much has been taken from me. When will it stop?"

His blue eyes held mine as he reached up and gently touched my cheek. I felt comforted and something else. Something more than I'd ever felt with a boy before. I licked my lips and tilted my head up. His gaze dipped to what I offered. His fingers gently tugged on a loose curl. I saw something shift in his eyes. A primal, deep emotion that set my heart racing. He leaned toward me, the fingers of his free hand touching mine. The simple contact warmed me better than any winter's fire.

My lips parted as anticipation and a heady mix of yearning shivered through me. At the last moment, he stopped.

"Eloise, I...I'm sorry. I cannot."

Embarrassment coursed through me, and heat flooded my face. I knew what I needed to do next. My palms grew sweaty at the thought of placing his hand on my breast.

I swallowed hard and pulled my hand from his.

"No, I'm sorry. Forgive me." I kissed his cheek lightly then bolted. He called my name, but I didn't stop running until I neared the house. Relief and fear warred inside of me. I'd done what I'd been told and failed. The kingdom might be safe, but I was not.

Steps slowing, I entered the kitchen. Maeve was there, waiting calmly at the table while sipping her tea. She set the cup aside when I entered.

"Where were you?" she asked.

"In the clearing," I said, confused. "With Kaven like you told me."

She studied me, giving nothing away.

"And? Did you discover when we can expect Prince Greydon?"

"No, Mama. I failed," I said, holding her gaze. "But, I don't understand how. I had his attention. He stared at my lips just as the men at the whorehouse had with the women they liked. But he didn't kiss me or whisper in my ear. Instead, he told me he couldn't."

"Couldn't what?" Maeve asked.

"I don't know."

Her eyes narrowed, and she tapped her fingers against the table. I waited for her to unleash her fury, hoping she would use me as a target and not Kellen.

"Innocence is a burden," Maeve said. "Tomorrow, someone with more knowledge will accompany you."

I PACED THE CLEARING, anxious to have my second attempt over and done. Cecilia stood near a tree, not far away, not that I could see her. The potion she'd used had changed her appearance to blend with her surroundings.

Despite her presence, the bird in the tree sang for me. Its song echoed among the trees. It didn't take long for Kaven to appear, and I was grateful for the tiny creature's help.

"I wasn't sure you'd return," he said, not approaching me.

"I'm still not sure I should have," I said.

"Eloise, I'm sorry if I hurt you."

I crossed the clearing so I stood toe to toe with him.

"You cannot hurt me," I said. "You can give me something much better."

I boldly grabbed his hand and lifted it to my cheek.

"Tell me you want nothing to do with me, and I will return home."

"I cannot," he said thickly.

"Then tell me what you do want from me."

His gaze dipped to my lips again, and Cecilia's presence faded from my mind as his free hand gently captured my arm. He tugged me closer to him. Close enough that I could smell the pine on his clothes from so much time outdoors.

"I want more than I can give in return," he said softly.

Taking his hand, I slowly slid it down my throat to my breast. My heart raced under his palm.

"I'm not asking for anything in return," I whispered.

He groaned, a tormented look crossing his face.

"Eloise, you tempt me to forget my purpose and forsake those depending on me to stay vigilant." His hand curled into a fist under mine, and he slowly withdrew.

"I beg you for your patience," he said. "When the Prince returns—"

"And when exactly will that be? It seems everything in my life now centers around the wayward Prince's return," I said hotly.

Kaven's expression turned more aggrieved.

"I cannot say when for I do not know. Forgive me."

Shaken, I whirled away from Kaven and struggled to guess what his lack of knowledge meant for me.

"I'm sorry, Eloise," he said again.

When I turned around to tell him to toss his apologies, he was already gone. Angry and afraid, I left the clearing. Cecilia fell in step beside me, the spell fading as we moved.

"He was delicious to look at, Eloise. For your sake, I do hope Mama gives you another chance at him. I imagine he would be remarkable between the sheets. I have half a mind to try for him myself." She made a humming sound. "I doubt it would do any good, though. He was interested in what you were offering. No doubt there. Yet, he refused. What a waste."

Her words, though vile, gave me hope that Maeve wouldn't be too upset about yet another failed attempt. However, as we drew closer to the house, I couldn't stop doubting that Maeve would allow me any more chances.

"How did it go?" Maeve asked, her gaze shifting between me and Cecilia when we entered the kitchen.

"He refused again," I said.

"Of course he did," Cecilia scoffed. "He clearly wasn't interested in what you were offering. Any fool could see that."

My mouth opened in shock, and I turned to Cecilia, anger clouding my eyes.

"How can you say that? You saw him."

"I did indeed. Can you deny that he fisted his hand after you brought it to your breast? Or that he left moments after you demanded to know when the Prince would return?"

Her lips curled in a small smirk, her gaze holding mine. "You can see by her silence it's true, Mama. So much time wasted."

I wanted to—something hit my back. The blow robbed me of breath and brought me to my knees. Before I could comprehend what had happened, another blow hit me, landing across my shoulders. I cried out and fell to my hands and knees.

"You've brought this upon yourself," Maeve said, her voice marked with anger.

I looked up just in time to see the wooden rod she used on the mirror fly toward my head. I lifted an arm, sparing myself from a direct hit. But my arm went immediately numb from the blow, and I collapsed to the floor. Strike after strike rained down on me. It seemed never ending, each one adding to the accumulating pain until I stopped feeling.

Maeve threw the rod aside.

"Leave her as she is. Do not help her. Do not comfort her. Cecilia, you and Porcia will go to town immediately. Starting today, we will entertain every night. See there is a group for each day of the week. I'm done waiting patiently. It's time we move forward."

I couldn't fear what was to come or pity the men. I could barely think beyond each painful inhale.

The door closed behind Maeve. A whisper of noise, the brush of cloth against stone, penetrated my awareness.

Gentle lips pressed against my cheek, and I imagined Mother kneeling over me, her gaze filled with worry and love.

"Tattling never goes unpunished," Cecilia whispered in my ear. Her hand came down on an exceptionally damaged spot as she pushed to her feet.

I hissed in agony.

"Never cross me again, my sweet sister."

Time floated by in a haze of semi-awareness. At some point, Heather told Catherine she was having pain in her knee and asked her to brew some of the tea that had helped me. When Catherine finished, she set the pot and cup on the hearth near my head. I knew what they were doing and worried they would find themselves in my place. Yet, I couldn't refuse the help.

I struggled to roll to my side then to lift the pot with my good arm. Much of the liquid slopped outside the cup. When I did manage to fill it, I shakily brought it to my lips and gulped the tepid contents. With no strength left, I collapsed to the floor and groaned at the contact of hard stone against my tender flesh.

The tea slowly began to work its magic, and I realized that this beating wasn't any worse than the previous ones. In a few ways, it was milder. My head wasn't fogged, and my face wasn't swollen. Most of the damage was to my back.

I briefly considered going to my room but rejected the idea. The tea was down here. As was food and water. So I remained where I was on the floor and slept while the tea kept me numb.

Raucous laughter woke me well after the sun had set. I lifted my head and groaned softly in pain. The kettle and pot were where I'd left them, and I helped myself to more tea. As the numbness settled over me like a warm blanket, awareness rose. Men were in the dining room. Based on the laughter and sounds of pleasure, so were Heather and Catherine.

I closed my eyes against my failures and drifted off again.

The next several days passed in the same manner. Tea, sleep, and dinner parties. Gradually, I weaned myself from the first two and plotted against the latter.

When I could move without pain, I bathed and returned to my room in the attic. My mourning dresses had been ripped to ribbons, which I didn't mind. However, all of my other dresses had been ruined as well. Angry, I stared at the one dress that remained, neatly laid out on my bed. It was a maid's dress.

With nothing else clean to wear, I put it on and bundled the soiled dress so it could be laundered. The next morning, I appeared for breakfast, determined to take my place at the table. I didn't want to be there. I needed to be. I needed to know what had happened during my time in the kitchen.

Only Maeve sat at the table, quietly eating a soft-boiled egg.

"Good morning, Mama," I said.

She turned in her seat to look at me, her welcoming smile fading.

"You've decided to stop trying to be the daughter I need, then?"

"No, Mama. My other dresses have been ruined. This was all that was left for me to wear."

A slow smile curled her lips, and she chuckled before gesturing to the chair beside her.

"I warned you not to cross your sister," she said. "You will need to find a way to earn her forgiveness. When I have time, I will have other dresses made for you."

"Yes, Mama," I answered as I sat. "I apologize I didn't discover what you wanted. The boy did finally reveal that he couldn't tell me because he didn't know."

"Ah." She reached out and smoothed back my hair. "However, knowing that does not make me regret your punishment. You failed me too many times. When I ask you to do something, it doesn't matter how it gets done, only that it does. Do you understand?"

"Yes, Mama."

"Good. Now, put the boy out of your mind."

"What would you like me to do next, Mama?"

Her gaze raked over me.

"Since you're dressed like a maid, you might as well act like one. Go help Heather and Catherine for the day." She waved her hand, dismissing me.

Heather and Catherine looked up when I entered the kitchen. Both had dark smudges under their eyes and gave me weary smiles.

"It's good to see you up," Heather said.

"It's good to be up. Cecilia destroyed all my dresses and left me this to wear," I said. "And since I look like a maid, Mama sent me in here to help you two. You look in need of rest. Tell me what to do and go nap."

Heather immediately shook her head.

"We cannot. We disappointed Lady Grimmoire last night, and she told us we cannot sleep until we redeem ourselves."

"How did you disappoint her?"

They shared a look.

"We refused something one of the men wanted."

I frowned, unable to imagine what they would have refused when they'd already done more than I'd known to do.

"Don't worry about us," Catherine said. "Come help us roll out this dough. We're hoping to make this a dinner she won't forget."

THE SOUND of many hooves racing into the yard interrupted our efforts less than an hour later. Heather quickly wiped her hands and headed for the door. She returned not long after with a vial.

"You're to take this," she said. "Lady Grimmoire wants you upstairs making beds when they search."

My heart lurched as I understood what was happening. The

King's Guard had returned. I uncorked the vial and drank the contents then hurried up the back staircase.

Footsteps echoed from the main stairs as I ducked into Cecilia's room, the closest to me. I didn't know what Maeve expected from this trickery but knew better than to hesitate to follow her instructions. I'd just started making Cecilia's bed when one of the guards entered the room. I looked up from my task and felt a jolt of surprise. It was the sergeant who'd endured Cecilia and Porcia's inane prattle during the first search.

"Step aside, miss," he said without a trace of recognition.

I moved away from the bed.

"Where are the young ladies of this house?"

"I don't know, sir. I'm sorry."

"Don't be. Please join your mistress in the dining room."

I glanced at the unmade bed, wondering what I should do.

"You can return to your task after we're done."

I nodded and left the room to join Maeve. She wasn't alone. The captain stood near the door, watching her while also watching his men move about the room. They looked in the sideboard, under the chairs, under the table, behind curtains...one even stood on a chair to check the candle holders in the overhead chandelier.

"This is utter nonsense," Maeve said from her place at the table. "You've already searched our home."

She glanced at me when I stepped farther into the room.

"Now what?"

"The guard sent me to you, My Lady," I said with a small curtsy. "He said I could finish my tasks once they were done."

"Sit," she said with a wave of her hand before returning her annoyed gaze to the captain. "Next, you'll be telling my kitchen staff to stop working."

"I truly apologize for the inconvenience. We are conducting our search as quickly and as thoroughly as possible."

"Yes. You are. I'm only struggling to understand why you did not do so the first time so you need not have returned."

"I assure you that we did do a thorough search. However, we've been ordered to do so again."

"I heard from my aunt's sister that bodies keep turning up dead," I said with false timidity. "She thinks it's a plague."

"Nonsense," Maeve said dismissively. "If it were a plague, the King wouldn't order our homes searched. You still believe it's someone using magic, don't you?"

"I cannot say, Mistress."

Maeve snorted.

"Mama?" a concerned voice called from the entry.

"In here my darlings," Maeve called.

Cecilia and Porcia entered, looking suitably concerned about the presence of the guards. Neither spared me more than a passing glance. However, I noted them well. Cecilia was wearing one of my dresses, and Porcia one of my hair ribbons. I hoped one of the guards pissed in my lovely stepsisters' beds.

"What's happening?" Cecilia asked.

"Another search," Maeve answered.

"I beg your pardon, Mistress, but where is your other daughter?"

"I sent her away. Given her curiosity regarding magic, I thought it best to distract her with other interests until everything is resolved. No mother should be separated from her child. I hope this situation resolves itself quickly."

"As do we all," he said.

One of his guards entered just then and said they'd searched the house and found nothing. I breathed a sigh of relief that I'd taken more care to hide my mother's books. Although at first glance they seemed innocent enough, I didn't want to risk anyone discovering them. Most of all Maeve.

"Thank you again for your time and patience."

Maeve nodded as the guards left. Once the door closed behind them, she looked at the girls.

"How many?"

"Sixteen so far," Cecilia said.

She tapped her fingers on the table.

"Good. Taking less from the new groups is preserving them."

"However, there's a rumor circulating that all the dead men were at the same gathering," Porcia said nervously.

Maeve's gaze flicked to Cecilia for confirmation.

"Just a few houses. The wives noted the men were absent on the same nights."

Maeve closed her eyes, taking a calming breath.

"We will need to cancel tonight's gathering and rearrange the others to reduce the chance of more clever wives noting the same thing."

"Yes, Mama," Cecilia said before turning toward me. "You look so different, dear sister. The potion suits you. Do you like my dress?"

"I'm surprised you would lower yourself to wear second-hand clothes. Perhaps if you stuff it a bit," I glanced pointedly at her chest, "it will fit you more attractively until Mama can have your own made for you."

Maeve laughed.

"Eloise, please tell Heather and Catherine there will be no need for a large dinner tonight."

Dismissed, I left the room.

AFTER SEVERAL DAYS avoiding the solace of the woods, I could no longer stand the pattern that had taken hold of my life. Waking, eating, pacing the confines of the attic, then finally going to the kitchen to offer my help to prepare the evening meal had taken its toll on me. As had the nightly parties.

I could no longer count the number of times I'd considered running. However, I was no closer to discovering Maeve's purpose or a way to break the mirror. With the mirror intact, Maeve would catch me before I found help and Kellen would bear the brunt of the punishment.

Restless, I descended from my self-imposed prison and went in search of Maeve.

"She and the girls went to town. She said she would be back before dinner," Heather said when I asked.

I itched to do something drastic. To make a run for it. To try to break the mirror. Anything. But fear and Heather's knowing gaze held me in place.

"Did she leave any instructions for me?"

"Only that if we allow anything to happen to you, it would cost us our lives," Catherine said quietly.

"But our lives are already forfeit," Heather added before turning away to resume her cooking.

At some point we'd all given up hope that Kellen would rouse an army to come rescue us. Not when she couldn't even manage to rouse herself. In every glimpse of her that I'd had through the mirror since she'd left, she always slept. And I worried for her.

"The sun and trees call to me. If Mama arrives, please let her know that I've taken the pig for a walk on the estate grounds. I'll return within an hour."

Catherine nodded acknowledgement, barely looking at me. I knew they doubted my words.

"I will not abandon you or my sister," I said before leaving.

Outside, the spring wind had warmed slightly and caressed my cheek in welcome. I inhaled deeply, letting myself feel a grain of hope in my unexpected, if temporary, freedom from Maeve's ever watchful gaze.

Mr. Pig greeted me at his gate.

"Ready for a walk?" I asked him. I quickly tethered him and led him away from the shed since I wasn't sure where Hugh was lurking. As soon as we were in the trees, I spoke softly to the pig.

"You helped me once before. I need your help again, now. Find me something I can use to break her mirror."

The pig let out a nervous squeal and sidestepped.

"Come now, Mr. Pig. If we don't stop her, who will? We both know what will happen if she continues. You saw the results of her efforts as well as I did. Now is our chance. We may not have another."

The pig grunted and put his nose to the ground. I walked behind him, watching and waiting for him to root up something astounding. An enchanted sword, preferably.

Instead of finding a miraculous weapon of some kind, he wandered into my mother's clearing and snorted at the pear tree. I looked at the heavily blossomed tree, fighting against the hopelessness weighing on me. Rose had hinted the pig was special. He'd found my friends when asked to find something more. Instead of asking him for help, maybe I should have asked Rose.

"I thought you were my friend," I said, removing his tether. "Go. See how well you fare in the world. The size you are, someone is sure to butcher you within a day."

In frustration, I threw the tether to the ground. The pig grunted then squealed and ran back toward the estate. I had a feeling I would find him cowering in his pen.

"You speak to him as if he can understand you."

The sound of Kaven's voice startled me, and I turned to glare at him.

"I speak to all animals as if they can understand me because I think they might. There are beasts in the Dark Forest that can speak, are there not? It would be foolish to assume only we are the intelligent ones."

He held up his hand in a placating manner.

"I meant no affront. It was only an observation." He cocked his head, studying me for a moment. "Why are you dressed as a maid?"

"Why are you here, Kaven? To ply me with more longing stares? Well, I'm not interested. Be gone. Leave me in peace."

"Eloise, I…"

I whirled around, looking for a rock or something else to throw at the knave. I found a branch and snatched it up. Before I could turn back to him, steely arms wrapped around my waist, locking me in place. The pressure of his chest against my back sent an enjoyable shiver through me. I railed at fate for its cruel reminders of the life I should have had. One where I was free to flirt and discover men at my leisure. Instead, I knew only their baser side.

"Release me or suffer," I hissed at him.

"I didn't mean to hurt you," he said against my ear.

My anger intensified.

"Accidental or intentional, pain is pain." I attempted to stomp on his foot, but he widened his stance.

He growled in my ear and released me. I spun around, ready to wield the branch. We glared at each other, neither moving.

"Fine," he said finally. "I'll leave you be. For now."

"Forever, you ass."

I swung the branch, but he twisted out of the way.

"Names won't change how you feel about me, Eloise. When you're calmer, you'll realize that."

He turned his back on me and stalked away.

"I look forward to our next meeting and your apology."

I screeched and threw the branch at his head. He ducked at the last minute. His laughter taunted me until he disappeared from sight.

As I stood there panting, body shaking with the need to chase him down and hurt him, I realized he wasn't the one I wanted to hurt. The latest beating I'd received was because of Cecilia's lies, not Kaven's cluelessness. But in the end, the blame for every pain I'd suffered fell to Maeve. And the anger I felt now was at my impotence to stop it from continuing.

"I hate," I whispered. "I hate so deeply it chokes the breath from me."

The breeze swept through the sunlit glade, washing over me with the light scent of pear blossoms. Rose's words not to lose myself suddenly echoed in my mind.

"Is there anything else to lose?"

I gave the pear tree and Mother's grave one last look then turned away. My steps were heavy on the way home, and my mind so occupied with dark thoughts that I didn't at first hear the impatient stomp of a horse's foot or the collective jangle of livery. When I did, I stopped just at the edge of the trees.

In the yard, another contingent of the King's Guards' horses waited. I bit my lip, understanding the house was being searched again and looked down at my dress. I couldn't go in there. Not without a potion to hide my face. Not with Maeve's lie about sending me away.

"Lies," I said softly to myself.

A rabbit bolted from its nearby warren and froze to look at me.

"Nothing good will come of this," I said to it. Then I turned to hurry away only to bounce off the chest of one of the guards.

"I think you're right, miss. Nothing good will come of this." He reached for me, and I ducked away, panicking. If he took me inside, the captain would see me and know. He would have questions I couldn't answer.

I tried to run but the guard caught me from behind.

"Do not struggle," he warned.

I didn't listen. I rarely did.

He hit me, his fist connecting with the side of my head. Dazed, I wondered how many blows one could suffer before one's intellect became affected. When I couldn't remember why I'd been hit, I decided I'd already suffered one blow too many.

The guard lifted me over his shoulder and carried me out of the woods.

"Tell the captain I found a maid in the woods who tried to run. I'm taking her to the castle."

My world spun again as I was tossed upon a horse, and a rider swung up behind me.

"I'll let him know."

"But I have to stay here," I said, my words slurred as a wave of dizziness pulled at me.

Something tickled the side of my face, and I absently lifted a hand to wipe away my hair. My fingers touched moisture, and I looked in curiosity at the red staining my hand. The man behind me clucked the horse into motion.

By the time we entered Towdown, my head throbbed fiercely. But my thinking had cleared enough to reconsider my circumstance. The guard had me. I couldn't say anything to incriminate Maeve. But I could tell the truth about who I was. Perhaps they would then question Maeve about her lie. Would it be enough to point suspicion at her for the deaths though? Probably not. Was it worth risking Kellen's safety to take the chance?

Ahead, the castle spires towered over the rooftops. I'd never been this close to the castle and would have preferred to keep it that way. As soon as the guard slowed from a gallop at the castle gates, I spoke in a rush.

"I'm Eloise Cartwright. I live at the estate. This is a mistake."

"Quiet," the guard said sharply, maneuvering the horse at a trot to veer toward the side stables, away from the grand front stairs.

"It's the truth," I said desperately. "Ask Lady Grimmoire. She will tell you."

"And do all young women who live at estates on royal land wear the clothes you do?"

I looked down at the plain, serviceable dress that most maids were known to wear. He dismounted and grabbed my waist as another guard jogged toward him.

"My other gowns were ruined." He plucked me from the saddle and gripped my arm, leading me toward the side door. "Ask Kaven about me. He's the manservant who is preparing the Royal Retreat for the Prince's arrival. He'll tell you."

He paused, sharing a look with the other guard.

"You seem to know a lot about what's happening at the Royal Retreat."

"Yes. You see? I live there."

"Or you've been watching it for a long while."

My growl of frustration was cut short with his next words.

"Take this one to the dungeons," the guard said. "We'll get the truth from her when the captain returns."

Fear consumed me.

CHAPTER 12

I STOOD IN THE DARK CELL, STARING AT THE SHADOWS THAT DANCED beyond the bars. The single torch in the passage didn't illuminate much inside the space in which I'd been thrown, and for that, I was grateful. Something scurried to my right, making me glad I was standing. I hadn't dared to sit for fear of the dank straw that littered the floor.

Time passed, measured only in the replacement of the guard. I shivered lightly and kept my hands away from the cut on my head, too afraid of contaminating it any further. I already worried what falling into the filth once had done.

Somewhere nearby, metal groaned against metal. Footsteps echoed, growing closer, but I did not approach the bars to look.

"Bring her," a firm voice said.

I trembled and clasped my hands before me. When the guard appeared, I did not move until he opened the door. He and another man stepped in.

"I will come with you willingly," I said, hoping to avoid more bruises.

"Good," the first guard said, grabbing me anyway. The second covered my head with a smelly sack, robbing me of what little vision

I'd had. Together, they tugged me forward. I stumbled, and their holds bit painfully into my flesh.

After several steps, they turned me. Light began to twinkle through the gaps in the coarsely woven material. I shifted my head, trying to see, and caught a glimpse of a man standing a few steps in front of several others.

The guards stopped me and forced me to my knees. I winced at the hard stone that dug into my shin.

"You were caught fleeing from royal lands. What were you doing there? Who are you?" a voice demanded.

"I swear to you, I am Eloise Cartwright. I live at the estate from which I was taken."

There was a low murmur of voices, then some of the light was extinguished.

"Remove her hood," the voice said.

The coarse material was lifted from my face. I blinked once against the dim torch light and focused on the man who stood before the rest. He wore the regalia of a prince from the fitted coat and ruffled cravat to the shiny black boots. His brown eyes swept over me before he glanced at the men behind him. Those closest were illuminated enough to see they were the wizened men who likely guided the Prince.

"Why did you run?" the guard asked.

"I was embarrassed to be caught wearing this dress."

"And why are you wearing it?"

"My other dresses were ruined."

The Prince made an impatient sound.

"Do not waste my time with the trivialities of a woman's wardrobe."

He nodded to a guard, and the man turned and slapped me. The crack echoed in my ears and stung my cheek. Some of the men, those hidden by the shadows, shifted as if uncomfortable with my treatment. Little did they know I'd suffered far worse.

I lifted my head, disdain in my eyes for the prince before me.

"If you don't want to hear about women's dresses, then don't ask about them."

There was a gasp and a chuckle. The Prince turned to glare at those behind him before focusing on me.

"You speak boldly for someone in my dungeon."

"I speak boldly because I know I've done nothing to warrant this treatment."

"How did your mother die, Eloise?"

I thought of the amulet, and my throat constricted.

"Why does anyone die? Because their bodies fail them in some way. My mother was weak for a very long time, and it only grew worse as the years passed. I believe your father knows something about that. You should ask him."

There was a collective gasp this time.

"Your mother's name is known by the Crown. Yours is not."

"Odd, considering I live on royal lands."

"Enough! You waste my time."

"And you waste mine," I said.

The guard slapped me again so forcefully my head turned. I swallowed hard and slowly straightened.

"You dare rebuke me?" the Prince asked.

"I dare," I agreed quietly. I lifted my head to look at him once more, my voice rising. "As the sovereign heir, it is your duty to protect the weak and the innocent. And by the rumored body count, I would say you're failing quite miserably. Open your eyes, Your Royal Magnificence, before you lose your kingdom."

"That sounds decidedly like a threat."

I couldn't disagree with him, but I didn't know what else to say to make him understand that the true threat was still waiting to be discovered.

There was another murmur behind the Prince, and one of his shadowy advisors stepped forward to whisper in his ear.

"What do you know of magic?" the prince asked.

"I know that it exists and that the King believes some of his people are dying because of it."

"Do you know why they are dying? Do you know the purpose behind these attacks?"

I snorted.

"I hope you have a better way to determine the guilty, Your Royal Benevolence, than questions that will only be answered with stout denials."

"Explain yourself," the old man said.

"If you believe me to be the person responsible, how do you honestly think I would answer? I would claim my innocence just as ardently as any innocent person would."

The Prince stared at me.

"My advisors are whispering behind me, debating your innocence for various reasons. Why should I spare you?"

My throat tightened around the words I raged to say. I lowered my head and took a few quietly wheezing breaths to calm myself. When I lifted my head again, I had the sense they were all watching me.

"Because I'm not afraid to show that I'm angry."

He gave an exasperated sigh and looked over his shoulder. The murmurs of frustrated old men rose.

"Explain," one voice said.

"I'm angry my mother died. I'm resentful that my father left, and my sister is gone. I hate the turn my life has taken. Look at me. I'm in the damn dungeon. But why would I hold the Crown responsible for what's happened to me? Except for this last part. To what purpose would I want to kill innocent people when I know the agony of loss myself? You will spare me because I have no reason to do whatever is being done."

There was silence as the Prince considered me.

"What if I told you your mother's death was the fault of the Crown?" he asked softly. "That she sacrificed her vitality to save the kingdom, and that was why she was so weak?"

"I would tell you that sounds like the woman I knew. Her body was weak, but her convictions never were. Not once did she show a hint of blame toward the Crown for the life she lived. Neither will I."

"Where are your father and sister? Why did they leave?"

"I wish I knew where they were," I said, truly pained. "I'd like to believe my father left to escape his grief. I've never seen a man love a woman so completely as he did my mother. It hurt him to see her failing strength over the years."

"And your sister?"

"She escaped to escape," I said with a helpless shrug.

"Release her," the Prince said with a negligent wave of his hand. "She's no more than a foolish girl in the wrong place at the wrong time."

I scowled at his back. Foolish girl? He wasn't more than a handful of years older than me.

"Pompous brat," I said under my breath.

The guard to my right cuffed me upside the head.

"Watch your tongue," he warned before hauling me to my feet. He held me in place as the Prince, the men in the back shadows, and the advisors left. Once the room cleared, the guard led me out a door and marched me to the side gate like some unwanted beggar.

With a shove, he forced me from the castle grounds just before dusk. Stumbling a few steps, I righted myself and glared back at the closed gate. That could have gone worse. However, it also could have gone much better. I recalled the conversation and came up with a thousand ways I could have answered differently. Regret clawed at me that what I'd said hadn't helped the Prince or his men see the threat to the kingdom was in my home.

Turning a slow circle, I got my bearings and started toward home. In the fresh air, a sharp odor slowly penetrated my nose. It took a moment to realize I was smelling whatever filth coated me. At the first well, I drew a bucket of water and tipped it over my head. Blood and grime ran down, staining my bodice. It took three more buckets to rinse away the worst of it enough to start the journey home.

Had I given the situation more than a passing thought, I would have endured the smell and waited to bathe when I reached home. As it was, walking home in a wet dress just before the sun set proved a very chilling experience. I shivered and rubbed my arms long before I reached the edge of town more than an hour later.

The cold and shivering didn't help the pain in my head, either. The steady ache increased to a pulsing throb. My anger grew with my pain. In the dark, I stumbled often on some hidden object as I made my way along the road leading to the Retreat. I clenched my teeth and found solace in imagining myself hitting the guard who took me from my home on a horse but failed to return me. Then I imagined hitting that ass of a prince.

I smiled slightly to myself at that image.

"Such a thing would only see me imprisoned again. But oh, what a lovely thought," I said to myself, staggering slightly on the road that seemed determined to never end. I could barely see my hand before my face and only knew I remained on the road because of the rut I followed. Then it suddenly ended. I turned a slow circle, trying to see where I might be.

A rumble came from overhead, and I looked up in annoyance.

"Could this get any worse?" I said to myself. Perhaps a flash of lightning would—

"That depends on your definition of worse," a familiar voice said.

The lightning I'd hoped for flashed just then, and I saw Kaven standing not far from me. Behind him towered the Royal Retreat.

"Bloody hell," I muttered as the light faded.

"Lost your way, my little wasp?"

"Obviously. It's darker than a—"

"No need to continue that thought," he said with a chuckle. "You look in need of assistance."

Another rumble sounded overhead.

"Not at all. I just need to wait for another bolt of lightning to show me the way." I tipped my head up to the sky, waiting, and gave a frustrated huff when nothing happened. Turning, I smacked my head against something, bruising my lip.

Kaven grunted. Lightning flashed, illuminating his chest inches from my face. I tipped my head back to glare at him.

"What are you doing?" I demanded, wincing at the taste of blood on my lip.

"I was going to help you inside."

"Inside the Retreat? Are you mad? That is the last place I would want to go. Prince Greydon is a royal ass. I can see why you like him."

Kaven snorted. Rain let loose just then, soaking my face.

"Come inside, Eloise," he said.

"Just turn me in the direction of home."

"Why is help so often rejected when it is needed the most? I saw the blood on your temple and watched you stagger your way up the drive. Let me help you."

I huffed in defeat.

"Fine. You may—" He scooped me up into his arms and started walking toward the house.

I stared up at him in astonishment. He caught the look and grinned in another flash of lightning.

"I'm feeling a bit of surprise, too. I'm not sure if it's you or the dress, but you're heavier than I expected."

I sputtered. "I am not heavy."

"If you'd like to remove the dress when we reach the Retreat, I'd be happy to try again."

I smacked the back of his head.

"Walk in silence, manservant."

He laughed and kicked open a side door that led us into a fire lit kitchen. I scowled at the drawn curtains. Had they been open, the light from the fire would have helped guide me on my own.

Annoyed, I turned my head to look up at him at the same time he bent to set me down. Our faces collided with surprising force. I gasped in pain against his mouth, my damaged lip protesting against the contact, and jerked back. He stared at me, his expression unreadable.

"I sincerely hope this doesn't count as my first kiss for I can only take it as an ill omen for any future romantic endeavors," I said.

He eased me to my feet, saying nothing as he moved to put more wood on the fire. I looked around the large kitchen in awe.

"What happened to you?" he asked.

I turned to look at him. His gaze swept up from the bottom of my soiled dress to my face. He frowned at whatever he saw.

"When I left you, you were angry but undamaged." He reached out and gently moved some of my hair away from my temple.

"This is the doing of your kind Prince. Doesn't every ruler who wants to bring about a true peace terrorize his people?"

"Eloise," he said in warning. "Tell me what happened."

"There was another search on the house. I panicked and ran."

"Why did you panic?"

"Look at me, Kaven. Am I dressed like a young lady of good breeding? No. And just as I suspected, when I tried to tell the guard who caught me who I was, he didn't believe me. Because I tried running, they automatically assumed that I'm some evil enchantress killing the magnanimous subjects of Towdown and threw me in the dungeon."

"That doesn't explain the cut on your head."

"The guard hit me to subdue me." I grinned slightly. "It seems it's not in my nature to go quietly."

"Eloise..." He surprised me by gently pulling me into his arms and hugging me. He was warm and smelled clean and good. More than that, his embrace emanated a level of comfort and concern I'd longed for since Kellen disappeared. Unable to help myself, I leaned into it, resting my forehead against his chest.

"Why must life be so difficult?" I whispered.

His hand ran over the back of my head, smoothing down my back. I shivered. Whether from his touch or the cold, I couldn't be sure.

"There is no way to say this without sounding coarse, but you must remove your dress. You'll never warm while wearing that sodden mess."

I slowly drew back and looked up at his face.

"There's no need for me to warm," I said. "I'm close to home. I'll rest a bit then find my way."

"You are infuriatingly stubborn," he said, sighing.

"It's my best quality."

He chuckled and released me. Taking my hand, he led me to a chair. I sat with a sigh and closed my eyes, letting the fire's warmth wash over my face.

"I'll return in a moment," he said freeing my fingers.

I shivered in the chair as the heat from the flames slowly penetrated my clothes. Steam rose from my bodice. I would be lucky not to fall ill after this.

A scrape of noise announced Kaven's return. I didn't turn to look at him, too tired to move. Something soft brushed against my face. I opened my eyes to look at him. His gaze remained focused on my hairline, which he washed with meticulous attention for several long minutes.

"It's a small cut," he said finally. "It bled a lot, though. If you're determined to return home, I'll hitch up a—"

"No," I said firmly, pushing his hand aside. The idea of him coming face to face with Maeve sent a lance of panic through me.

"I'm fine. I only needed to sit for a moment. I can make it home now."

"Eloise, it's raining. Please let me take you home."

"The last time I saw you, I asked you to leave me in peace. The time before that, you asked for the same."

"That's not what I—"

"Your precise words matter little. Your intent does. Focus on your obligations, Kaven, and I will do the same." I stood, my legs and head protesting.

Kaven's gaze narrowed on me.

"You can barely stand."

"What I can and cannot do is not your concern. I apologize for the unintended intrusion. The storm made it darker than I'd anticipated. I can find my way from here." With a brisk nod, I moved to the door, determination giving me strength.

Kaven followed me closely. I thought there would be another argument as I stepped out into the rain, but when I looked back, his steady gaze remained impassive as he watched me. I turned as regally as I could, lifted the sodden mass of my skirts, and started for home, grateful for the flicker of light from the open door.

The damned dress weighted my arms, making them burn with strain by the time I left the circle of light. I plodded along in the dark once more. If not for the occasional crack of lightning, I might have missed the gap in the trees that marked the path to my home.

Turning up the drive, I could think of nothing else but the warmth of the fire, and felt relief when I finally spotted dim light through the trees from the windows. My numb fingers trembled as I let myself into the kitchen. The fire crackled merrily in the hearth.

I shuffled in, dripping on the floor. A gasp brought my attention to Catherine and Heather. Their eyes were wide as they stared at me for a moment then rushed to me. Their hands made quick work of the dress, stockings and shoes. As soon as I stood in nothing but my transparent underthings, they moved me toward the stool by the fire.

"Sit," Catherine said. "I'll fetch a blanket."

She hurried from the room.

"You should have stayed away," Heather said softly. "You should have saved yourself."

I frowned up at her, the look in her eyes making my stomach twist with worry.

"The guard took me," I said through chattering teeth.

"I know." She smoothed a hand over my hair then went back to her cutting board.

The door opened, and Catherine hurried back in. No blanket weighted Catherine's arms, and fear filled her gaze. She joined Heather, neither working, only watching as Maeve entered the room followed by Hugh.

I hadn't seen him in too long. He looked gaunt now, sickly.

"I thought you were truly gone," she said softly.

My heart stopped.

"Kellen," I whispered.

Maeve smiled slowly. My anger boiled, and I clenched my fists.

"As I said, I thought you were truly gone."

As I held her gaze, thinking that I could now strike out at her, I realized it was a test of obedience. A test to see how far she cowed me. Maeve wasn't foolish enough to remove the one thing that kept me under her thumb. Regaining control over myself, I hid my ever-present anger under my mask of indifference.

Maeve's smile vanished.

"Please do tell me what happened, Mama," I said calmly. "I love Kellen too much not to know. Afterward, we should discuss what happened while I was in the King's dungeons."

She studied me for a moment.

"You test me?" she said softly.

"No, Mama. I remain your obedient daughter."

Her regard turned cold and calculating.

"Obedience can be broken with the right methods. Strip. I want to see what they did to you."

My gaze flicked to Hugh who watched me as well. Then Catherine and Heather.

"Is there a problem?" she asked.

"You once asked if I wanted to lead the life of a proper young lady. Should a proper young lady bare herself to a man not her husband?"

"Should a proper young lady question her mother?"

She nodded to Hugh, and he advanced on me.

"I'll do it," I said quickly.

"Too late," she said.

Hugh grabbed the front of my shift and ripped it from my body. However, before the material gave way under his force, it cut into my skin. I bit my abused lip to keep from making a sound and quickly covered my bare breasts.

"Hands down, Eloise. I want to see."

Swallowing hard and turning my head to stare at the flames, I held still as Hugh yanked my thin underclothes from my hips. His breath skimmed my belly as he bent forward, and I wanted to whimper against the offense.

"Step away, Hugh," Maeve said.

Her heels tapped on the ground as she circled me. Her finger trailed along my lower back, and I fought not to shudder at the contact.

"They barely touched you," she said. "It's hard to be sure if your unmarked state is because the spell held and you could say nothing or if you found a way to quickly implicate me to save yourself."

"I said nothing to implicate you," I said when she stood before me once more.

"I have to be sure," she whispered, stepping back with a smile.

Hugh stepped forward, his eyes glinting green.

CHAPTER 13

HATE, LIKE LOVE, HAD AN INFINITE CAPACITY. IT WAS A SIMPLE TRUTH that I discovered as I lay before the fire during the next several days, unable to move or see clearly. Catherine and Heather, forbidden from helping me, proved through small kindnesses that they weren't completely under Maeve's control unlike Hugh, who despite his wasted appearance, had used his unchanged strength to bring me low.

Yet no matter how many times he'd struck me as I related my tale of my time in the dungeon, I'd managed to withhold one tiny bit of information. I said nothing of the Prince. In my story, he was just another man among men who had questioned me.

A log fell in the fire, sending sparks drifting up the chimney. It reminded me of the stars, a sight I hadn't seen for far too long.

Standing shakily, I made my way to the door and walked out barefoot into the night. The cool air felt good on my bruised skin as I walked down the dirt lane to the path that led to the overlook. I sat near the edge, tucking my skirts around me since I wore nothing but the maid's dress.

The stars shone brightly over the castle. It was a beautiful sight, but it didn't touch me. Nothing could. The raw hate I felt for Maeve wrapped around me like a protective cloak. I clung to it desperately, for I knew what waited in the shadows of my mind. Utter despair and resignation. It whispered that jumping from the cliff would be a fine end to a pathetic life. That there was nothing in my power I could do to change the course of events except to choose the time and place of my own death.

A branch snapped behind me.

"What gave me away?" I asked softly.

"The owl. Did you not hear it?" Kaven asked.

I focused on the night sounds and did, indeed, hear the treacherous creature.

"It seems I'm offensive to man and beast alike," I said.

I could feel him coming closer.

"It was me in the house that day," I said. "I saw a picture of a beautiful woman with a green necklace. Was she the Princess?"

"She was."

"How did she die?" I asked, already knowing the answer.

"She fell ill shortly after marrying. At first, those closest to her thought it was nothing more than sickness from traveling. Then she grew worse. Healers were called. No one could determine the cause."

"But you know, don't you? That's why you asked if something or someone new appeared before my mother's death."

"Yes. I believe it was the necklace, which was given as a wedding gift to protect her and lost after her death."

A necklace that had been sent to my mother by Maeve. Why? And why kill the Princess with it?

"Why would someone want to hurt the Princess?"

Kaven sat beside me, looking out at the castle with me.

"It's rumored that years ago, long before the King married his late wife, Queen Sevil, there was another woman. She tried ensuring the King's love with spells and potions. She wanted to be queen. To become a power of reckoning. But she failed and fled. Not for long, though. Strange things started occurring several years after Aftan wed Sevil. Shortly after that, Queen Sevil died and King Afton decreed that, if he should ever marry again, the people should rise up against their new queen. Peace has held Drisdall since that day."

I let the story settle in my mind, trying to understand his point.

"I'm too tired to be clever," I said.

He chuckled.

"Then why are you out here?"

A hand brushed my cheek, and I winced.

"Look at me," he demanded.

I turned my head and stared at him in the moonlight. Enough days had passed so that the swelling was gone. But even the dark could not hide the discoloration below my eye.

"What good is looking at me? You cannot undo what's been done. Only time can do that."

"Eloise, I'm so sorry."

"Why? You didn't hit me."

"When I saw you that night, I didn't realize how bad it was. I should have never let you walk home unescorted."

Bitterly, I turned away once more and looked at the stars. Why could no one see what was happening within my home? For a brief moment, I considered pressing the issue. However, the memory of Anne and Judith's bodies dissuaded me. No, it was better that he thought the guard had done this to me. I would not give him any hint of my circumstance that might endanger him, too.

"Make it up to me by finishing your story," I said.

"It's not a story but history. And the Royal family believes it is repeating itself."

"They believe an evil caster is going to try to marry the King? Wouldn't the people still rise up against her?"

"Not the King, but Prince Greydon, heir to the Crown and currently unwed."

"Oh," I said as my mind raced.

While younger women frequently married older men, I didn't often hear of the opposite. Could Maeve's intention truly be to marry Prince Greydon? It made sense of her single-minded focus regarding Prince Greydon's arrival. But surely she couldn't think it would work when she was already known to the King and the King was protected from her influence by an amulet of his own. How did she think she would get the King to agree? The potions to change her appearance didn't last that long, and by her own mouth, a spell to change her appearance would be too costly.

No, she was far too clever to repeat her mistakes. If she failed once, she was going to try something else. But what?

"Why all these questions?" Kaven asked softly.

"So I understand why I'm suffering. So I can decide if protecting a prince is worth this price."

He gently wrapped an arm around me, likely intending to give me comfort; however, he only caused pain. I hissed out a breath and eased away from him.

"I'm deeply sorry for what they did to you. I'll speak to the Prince about the treatment of those they bring in for questioning."

"He's doing what he must. I should go," I said, getting to my feet.

He quickly stood and helped me up. His hand lingered on mine, warm and strong as he held my gaze. I wanted to lean into him. I wanted to beg him to help me. But most of all, I wanted to spare him from enduring Maeve's tormenting attention.

"How many have died now?" I asked.

His gaze darkened, and he glanced at the castle once more.

"Twenty-four."

"The deaths have slowed then."

"But not stopped."

"Stay safe, Kaven. Your life is worth as much as the Prince's in my eyes." I leaned up and gently brushed my lips to his cheek before slipping from his hold and walking the path home.

When I opened the door, Maeve was there. I said nothing to her as I poured myself a cup of water, which I drank before sitting by the fire.

"Where were you?" she asked.

"Looking at the stars, trying to remember why I cling so desperately to this life."

She stepped close and ran her hand over my hair.

"To protect your family," she said softly.

"Is that what I'm doing?"

Her hand stilled on my head. I didn't regret my words. To my very soul, I was tired of the games we played.

"If you've forgotten, perhaps I need to remind you."

"If that is what you wish." I stood and resumed my spot on the floor. "I'm ready."

She stood over me in silence for several long moments.

"Rest, my sweet Eloise. Tomorrow will be better for you."

She left the room, and I closed my eyes, tears finding their way down my cheeks. If Maeve said tomorrow would be better, I would surely suffer some new form of torture.

I SMOOTHED my hand over the soft skirt of the dress as the seamstress made small sounds of satisfaction. Behind me in the mirror, Maeve watched me closely.

"Does the dress suit you, Eloise?" she asked.

"Yes, Mama." The words fell flat. Not ungrateful or disrespectful, only wooden. I didn't trust the new dress or Maeve's benevolence.

"Poor darling. I can't imagine the terror you felt when the horse reared."

I nodded politely to the seamstress, keeping the pretense of the story Maeve had given to explain the fading bruises covering my body and my need for an immediate dress. It was a new seamstress, one who had no knowledge of my previous need for mourning gowns. One who was discreet and wouldn't spread the tale of my injuries.

"Can you have another one like this ready soon?" Maeve asked.

"Of course, My Lady."

"Very good. I'll have someone fetch it once it's complete. Come, Eloise."

I stepped down from the hemming stool and followed Maeve from the shop. Hugh waited nearby with the carriage.

"Take us home," Maeve said.

The idea of returning to that hell so soon fed the despair eating at me. Maeve noticed as I took my seat.

"Perhaps when we return, you would like to take the pig for a walk," she said.

"Yes, Mama." I turned to look out the window, pretending not to notice her frown.

"You're too spirited to be broken, Eloise. Kellen, yes. But not you. Dispel whatever plagues you, and act like a proper young lady should."

"I'm not sure I know that role anymore," I said softly. "Is it laying bloody and broken before a fire? Listening to the maids suck the cocks of our male dinner guests? Cleaning away soot and ash?" I turned my head and looked at her. "I haven't been a proper young lady in a very long time, and I truly don't believe that's what you want from me. It's only presentation and appearance that matter, after all."

She smiled slightly.

"There's my clever girl. When we return home, take the pig for a walk. Spend some time outdoors. I will require you at dinner again tonight."

I nodded and resumed my study of the passing homes, dreading what would happen once she stopped her act of loving stepmother.

When we pulled into the yard, I went straight to the pig's pen and let him out. I didn't bother with a tether.

"It's time for a walk, Mr. Pig."

He ambled along beside me as I made my way around the house to the trail that led to my mother's grave.

"Don't eat any of the flowers in the clearing," I said just before we reached it. "I don't think they're natural and don't want you to fall ill."

The pig grunted and veered slightly to root around between the trees. I stared after him, frowning. The old woman's words about casting a spell on a beast came back to me.

"Are you truly a pig?"

The pig's head jerked up and swiveled to look at me. He started squealing and grunting in earnest, and my stomach dipped.

"Were you once a man?"

His head bobbed, and I felt sick. Like me, he too had been cursed. Again, the conversation with Rose came to mind, and I thought of her promise that she'd only cursed those who deserved it. Is that how Maeve viewed my curse? That I'd deserved to be struck mute?

It was only then that I thought of Maeve and the mirror. I hoped she wasn't watching. For if she were, the poor man would surely soon be dead.

"Hush," I said softly. "We will both suffer if you make too much noise."

The pig fell silent and followed me to the bench. I sat on the wooden surface, and the pig lay down nearby. We were both quite stuck in our current circumstances.

Sitting in the sun, I felt the spring breeze caress my skin while the birds sang. The peace of the glade soothed the ragged edges of my frayed hope. However, when I left several hours later, I didn't feel more renewed but rather more bitter at the invisible shackles that prevented me from righting the wrongs that had been done to so many.

The pig followed me meekly back to his pen.

"I will try to find a way to speak to her," I said softly, thinking of Rose.

The pig squealed and ran to his shelter. I wondered if he feared Rose as much as I feared Maeve.

Leaving him, I let myself into the kitchen and found Heather and Catherine hard at work preparing another dinner feast.

"Can I help?" I asked.

"No, miss. Your mother gave strict orders that you're to do nothing to help prepare this meal."

I sighed and looked around the kitchen. It was on the tip of my tongue to apologize again, but I knew doing so would change nothing.

"Thank you for all the work that you do," I said instead then left the room.

Upstairs, I again started reading the book Mr. Bentwell had held for me per Kellen's request, wasting time until Maeve called me down for dinner.

I sat through the meal, detached from the conversation while still appearing every bit Maeve's attentive daughter. If Maeve noticed something amiss, she didn't comment. Once Catherine and Heather appeared for their true part of the feast, Maeve dismissed me.

Seeking the haven of my attic sanctuary felt wrong while Catherine and Heather endured so much to feed Maeve's ever increasing need for power. Yet, I retreated without protest. There was nothing I could do for them.

While I passed through the hall, my gaze landed on the mirror. It was the key to setting Kellen and me free. How did one break an unbreakable mirror, though? And even if I found a way, how would I survive Maeve's wrath because I knew I wouldn't leave Heather and Catherine to suffer in my place.

Once more in my room, I stared out at the stars through my tiny window, pondering the answers to those very questions.

The following days mimicked the first. The pig and I would go to the clearing and sit there in silence for hours. Near dinner, I would return to wash and prepare myself. I would eat, speak when spoken to, then retreat to the safety of my room and Kellen's book of tales.

Another dress appeared at some point, laid out on Kellen's bed. I changed when needed. Bathed when needed. Ate when needed. I became a hollow replica of my former self as the bruising faded completely.

"Eloise," Maeve said, setting her spoon aside at breakfast one morning. "You haven't been yourself for the last week. What is the matter with you, child? Are you ill?"

"Has it truly only been a week?" I asked absently. I took a small bite of oats, playing with my food more than eating it.

Maeve huffed.

"Honestly, Eloise, I think I might take you to a healer if you don't start acting yourself soon." Her tone, so filled with motherly worry, had me looking up at her. Her face was a complete mask of true concern. I stared at her, wondering if she was starting to believe her own lie.

"I'm fine, Mama," I said automatically.

She studied me, the look of worry never leaving her face.

"Would you like to go to town with Hugh to pick up supplies?"

"No, thank you. I upset Hugh when I'm with him."

Maeve frowned slightly.

"What do you mean? Has he hurt you?"

I almost howled with laughter at that.

"He scolds me to stay close when all I want to do is roam the market like I used to."

She considered me for a moment.

"Very well. Go to town with Hugh. Have your freedom for today. I think you've well learned the price of disobedience."

"Mama," Cecilia began, sounding annoyed.

"Quiet," Maeve said sharply. "I believe Eloise's melancholy is due to boredom and envy. The pair of you leave to visit with others daily while she's trapped here with nothing to entertain herself. Eloise knows what is at stake if she attempts anything. The spell is firmly in place, and Grimm awaits my call should the need arise. And I will be watching."

She studied me while she spoke, and I unflinchingly returned her gaze. I didn't allow myself to feel a shred of hope because I might be able to roam Towdown. There wasn't much I could do there anyway but pretend I was free. As she said, the spell held me even if my loyalty to my sister did not.

"Go," she said with a nod. "Fetch Hugh so the two of you can return before dark."

"Yes, Mama." I rose and left the room.

Hugh wasn't happy when he learned he was to take me to town

and set me free while he was there. Like Cecilia, he dared to voice protest. Also like Cecilia, he was put in his place.

"Need I remind you all that Eloise has already been on her own for a day? The day she was taken by the guard. Nothing has happened since. The spell is effective. Do not question my judgment again."

Duly reprimanded, Hugh drove me to town in silence. I roamed the market, looking at vendors' goods and buying nothing. A few people stopped me to offer their condolences. Many just nodded hello.

As I mingled with the people in the market, I felt a connection, not just to them but to all the people in Towdown and Drisdall. They knew nothing of the danger that lurked in their midst. Naïve, they went about their days as if they had an infinite amount of them. Yet, my heart hardened when I overheard how many had died in the same unusual manner as Judith and Anne. Well over forty now.

"Your mother wasn't…shriveled when she died, was she?" one woman asked in a hushed voice.

I knew it was fear and not the need for gossip that had prompted her to ask such a tactless question. Reaching out, I placed my hand over hers.

"My mother was sick for a very long time. She did not die in the same manner as the men and women who have died since then."

She nodded and gave my hand a squeeze.

"It relieves me that your house has been spared."

"Not entirely spared. There was a misunderstanding during one of the raids, and I was taken to the castle's dungeon for questioning."

She covered her heart as she stared at me in horror.

"Oh no. Whatever happened?" I explained about wearing a common dress and running in embarrassment.

She tsked in sympathy.

"Men don't understand such things. You poor dear. I've heard there've been many women taken for questioning. They are not treated well in the dungeon."

Even as she said that, a contingent of guards made their way through the market sending many of the people scattering.

"My husband is considering moving to the North," she said. "I hope he decides soon. I heard the guards are doubling their search efforts. They've been to our home twice already this week. Once in the middle of the night."

"What are they looking for?" I asked although I already knew the answer.

"Signs of magic. Why now, after all these years, I do not know."

I left her stall and returned to Hugh. The journey home was quiet, and Maeve waited by the door, a large smile on her face.

"I must send you to town more often," she said, descending to give me a large hug. I returned it, playing her game because I was too beaten down to fight it.

"You did well, speaking to so many and reminding them you are fit and content with life. It's useful to know how many have been discovered dead and that the searches are increasing in frequency."

She led me inside where a tea tray waited in the sitting room along with a new book.

"I thought perhaps you'd enjoy reading until dinner."

I picked up the book and found it was the type I liked. Maeve rarely seemed to miss any detail. It was a wonder she hadn't realized there was something amiss about the pig.

"Thank you, Mama," I said sitting.

She left me to read, calling me just before the first of her guests arrived. We'd just closed the door after greeting the last arrivals when a thunder of hooves rose outside. Maeve cursed softly and hurried me to the dining room.

"It would seem that the guard is here to ruin our merriment. Not a word about anything untoward that happens here." As soon as she spoke the command, the men's eyes flashed green.

"Heather," she called. "Please get the door."

Heather emerged with a nod and rushed to answer the knock at the main door. The Captain of the Guard followed her back into the room. He looked around in surprise.

"My Lady," he said with a bow. "I apologize for interrupting your gathering. We must search your home again."

"Do what you must. Warn your men to wipe their feet this time. Last time, they created extra work for my staff with their neglect."

"I will see to it." He looked over his shoulder and nodded to a man. The man disappeared from sight, and the captain returned his attention to us.

"This is an odd gathering," he said.

"How so?"

"All male guests for a household of females." His gaze landed on me. "When did you return?"

"She returned when the home she was at suffered the same searches as our own. There was no point in keeping her away any longer."

His gaze swept over the men.

"Why are you here, Mr. Steinman?"

The man scowled.

"The King pushes too far with these intrusions. I'm here on business, as is every man at this table."

"What kind of business?"

"Trade of course. We have the contacts but lack the funding to move any merchandise."

"And, I have the funding but lack the contacts. It would seem some men think women are only good for marriage and childbirth and do not care to work with a woman in a business sense. These men are more open minded."

The guard the captain had sent away returned with a woman. She was dressed like a maid but wore the King's insignia on her bodice.

"I ask that you step into the hall, one at a time."

"Why?" Maeve asked, her fingers twitching on the table.

"This search will be more thorough. We need to search your person."

CHAPTER 14

While Porcia and Cecilia made shocked noises, I stood.

"I'll go first," I said.

"You will not," Maeve said, grabbing for me.

While I had nothing to hide, I knew well that Maeve, Cecilia, and Porcia did. All three wore their amulets as they always did for these gatherings. Likely Maeve's mind was frantically working to find a way to object to a body search.

I lightly set my hand on top of hers and gave her a concerned look.

"Mama, do not let embarrassment rule your thoughts. I made that mistake and was taken to the dungeon and questioned."

Lifting my gaze to the captain who watched us steadily, I repeated my offer to go first. He motioned for me to proceed. Maeve released me with reluctance that I felt was quite true, and I walked into the hall with the King's woman.

The search was thorough as she patted my skirts and pockets. When she reached under my skirts and ran her hands up and down my legs and even cupped my intimate parts, I flushed scarlet.

"If it helps make this less embarrassing, I'm a midwife," the woman said softly. "This is nothing I haven't seen or touched before."

"Since you're not delivering my child at the moment, it does not help," I said, offering a small smile to take the sting from my words.

She chuckled and stood.

"I need to loosen your bodice and check there as well."

"Of course."

Having another woman swipe her hand between the valley of my breasts and under their curves did not bother me as much as when I'd been stripped in front of Hugh. His detached gaze as he'd hit me, without regard as to where, had been far more intolerable.

When the woman stepped away from me and looked at one of the two men who had stood watch over us, there wasn't a bit of me she hadn't touched.

"I found nothing," she said.

The second man went to the captain as the first man's gaze shifted to me.

"Please wait outside."

As I moved toward the door, Cecilia took my place. I knew it was her by her impertinent, "Remove your hands from my skirt."

Trying not to smirk, I let myself out and found a man with a torch waiting in the yard by the horses. Hugh stood near him, his arms crossed and a sullen look on his face.

"Were you searched, too?" I asked, joining him.

He cast me a dark look and didn't answer. I was no longer sure how much of the old Hugh still remained.

Slowly, every person from the dining room joined us, Maeve walking out the door last. Her gaze connected with Cecilia first, then me, before turning to the guard.

"Is there a reason we must stand in the cold now that we've been thoroughly violated?" she asked.

"The violation would have been more enjoyable if it had been the maid who'd done the searching," one of the men commented.

Maeve shot the man a scathing look.

"Is that how you truly feel?" she asked.

The man flushed and looked away just as the captain emerged from the kitchen door with the midwife in tow.

"You may return to your dinner," he said. "Again, I apologize for the inconvenience of this search, but I assure you we are making the Kingdom safer through our diligence."

"Are you, though?" I asked.

All eyes turned to me.

"I beg your pardon?" the captain asked.

"Are you making the Kingdom safer? If you're still searching, wouldn't that mean the problem still exists? Instead of making us feel safer, these searches are spreading fear. One woman in the market today said her family was leaving soon because of the way His Majesty is treating his subjects. If this continues, His Majesty will be a King of a kingdom without a people."

"Twit," Cecilia said under her breath from her place beside me.

"Cow," I said just as softly.

A man behind us snorted a laugh.

"Cecilia and Porcia, go inside," Maeve said before turning to her guests. "Gentleman, I think we should reschedule this meeting for another evening. I fear the meal my help made is now either cold or dry and inedible."

The men dispersed, and the guards moved to watch them climb into their shared carriages, leaving Maeve and me with the captain.

"I heard you were bold with your speech in the dungeon as well," he said, considering me.

"I've earned more than a few slaps in my life for speaking freely."

"I can imagine so," he agreed.

"However, you cannot refute my daughter's logic. The King's searches are not fixing whatever problems are plaguing him," Maeve said, wrapping her arm around me. "If you have no further questions for us, I think it's time I take Eloise inside before she upsets anyone other than her sister."

The captain's lips twitched at that, and he winked at me.

"You're not a twit. Don't let her goad you."

"Yes, sir," I said as if I truly admired him and his wisdom.

Maeve walked me to the house as the guards mounted their horses and rode off. Cecilia opened the door for us. Stepping inside, I heard the light clank of cutlery from the dining room as Catherine and Heather began cleaning the table. I was relieved they had a reprieve for tonight.

"What are we going to do, Mama?" Cecilia asked after a quick glare in my direction.

Maeve released me as she drew in a slow breath.

"It's time to do something to hasten the Prince's return. Cecilia, fetch what we need from the dining room. Porcia, fetch a knife and a bowl."

Maeve had only ever used magic. Why did she need a knife? My stomach twisted with fear as both her daughters hurried off. In the dining room, Cecilia lifted Maeve's chair cushion and removed an amulet.

"You've impressed me a great deal today," Maeve said drawing my attention. "If not for your quick thinking, it would have been me they had searched first."

The mask holding back my frustration and hate almost slipped.

"I'm glad I was of use."

"You're always of use, my precious girl," Maeve said. "Come with me." She took my hand and led me to the mirror.

"Mirror, mirror, against the wall. Answer now my humble call. The King still plagues me with his power and might. Show me those who are often in his sight."

The mirror's fog lifted and started showing image after image of royal servants, the King's advisors, and other people.

"Go back," Maeve said. "Yes, that one."

It was a man who stood very close to a void. When he spoke, his words sounded as if they were coming from a great distance, an echo that wasn't easy to distinguish or hear.

"Fear is spreading because of the searches, Your Majesty."

A sigh resonated through the mirror.

"Fear is better than more death," a voice said. "Continue with the searches. She must be found."

"Mama?" Porcia said, drawing Maeve's attention from the mirror.

I turned and saw Porcia offering Maeve a kitchen knife. Maeve took the knife, testing its edge before looking up at Cecilia, who was rejoining us along with Heather and Catherine. The pair cowered side by side, their steps reluctant as they trailed behind Cecilia.

When Cecilia stood before Maeve, she placed one of the amulets around her mother's neck then handed Porcia hers.

"Thank you," Maeve said. She looked at Heather and Catherine. "You have served us well. I would ask one more service before I set you free."

"Yes, My Lady," Heather said. Catherine looked too frightened to speak.

"I need a finger from each of you." As she spoke, Cecilia grabbed Catherine's hand and Porcia grabbed Heather's. Maeve sliced the smallest finger from both of them before I could blink. Time seemed to slow in the seconds that followed. The fingers fell. Both maids stared at the bloodless stumps on their hands. Catherine wailed first. Heather moaned and brought her hand to her chest. Blood started pouring from both of them.

"Porcia, you were supposed to catch them with the bowl," Maeve said, her voice laced with warning.

"S-sorry, Mama." Porcia's eyes looked wide in her pale face as she stared at the fingers on the floor.

Maeve lashed out and slapped Porcia hard.

"Say it correctly."

"I'm sorry, Mama," Porcia said, showing no indication she was even aware of the handprint now enflaming her cheek.

Porcia quickly bent to pick up the fingers and place them in the bowl, which she held out before both women. Cecilia pried Heather's hand away from her body and held it over the bowl, letting the blood drip over the fingers. Catherine quickly held her hand out, terror and pain accentuating the whites of her eyes.

"Blood and bone make my wish be known," Maeve said in a clear voice that rang in the hall.

Her amulet began to glow brightly, and she handed Cecilia her knife. With her hands free, Maeve lifted them toward Heather and Catherine, drawing from them the same green she'd drawn from the men.

"Let a sickness quietly grow and spread. Let those in contact fall gravely ill but not dead. To the proclamation bell I bind this curse. Only with the Prince's return will the sickness disperse."

Both women quieted, their eyes shifting to me. I moved to step forward, to intervene in some way, but Porcia gently laid her free hand on my arm. I didn't look at her, but at Cecilia's provoking smile. She wanted me to interrupt. My gaze shifted to Maeve as she moved her hands toward the mirror.

"Now, Porcia," she said.

Porcia gave my arm a quick squeeze then released me to throw the contents of the bowl at the mirror. Blood coated the glass, and I watched the fingers tumble along the surface to the ground. In the mirror, the man next to the void coughed lightly.

"It is done," Maeve said.

A wet gurgling noise erupted behind me at the same time something spattered my back. I whirled just in time to see Catherine fall to the floor and Cecilia's blade swipe across Heather's throat. The blood sprinkled my dress and Maeve's.

"No," I gasped, watching Heather clutch her throat. Her gaze held mine as she slowly crumpled.

The anger I'd been holding back for so long exploded within me. Disregarding the danger of the knife still gripped in Cecilia's hands, I flew at her. My fist landed a solid blow before I froze, suspended mid-movement.

"Girls, that's enough," Maeve said calmly. "When I release you, I expect proper behavior."

Cecilia's gaze danced with pure loathing as the magic freed us. I stepped back though I didn't want to. Cecilia's blade flicked out, and a small cut opened on my forearm.

"That's for calling me a cow."

"Cecilia, you can clean up the mess you made."

The victorious smile fell from her face as she looked at Maeve.

"But, Mama—"

"Now."

"Porcia, help Eloise bind that cut."

"Yes, Mama," Porcia said. She took my hand and tugged me from the room, making a wide circle around the bloody pool spreading beneath Catherine and Heather's bodies. Numbly, I followed, blood trailing down my arm and dripping to the floor as we made our way through the dining room to the kitchen.

Food waited on the cutting board, remnants of the meal Heather and Catherine had been clearing away that was a glaring reminder of what had just been lost. I blinked, trying to recall when everything went so terribly wrong. When the guards had arrived, I'd hoped it would mean our freedom. If I'd known Heather and Catherine would die if I'd stood first...

A tear fell from the corner of my eye.

"Don't," Porcia said in a forceful whisper. She gripped my shoulders and shook me until I focused on her. "Don't ever cry. Do you understand? The weak do not survive."

I blinked, forcing away the pain.

"Do the strong, though?" I asked.

"You're still here, aren't you?"

She released me and fetched some cloth strips that we used for our monthlies. I held out my arm as she washed and bound the wound.

"Why are you here?" I asked. "Why am I still alive?"

She looked up at me, our gazes holding for a long time.

"I'm here because I learned not to be weak. Just like you're learning."

In that moment, I saw a hint of past pain in her eyes.

"You don't want to be Cecilia's enemy," she said. "Find a way to make it right."

Her words, so close to Maeve's, made me frown.

"Perhaps it's Cecilia who doesn't want to make an enemy of me."

Porcia snorted and tied the ends of the bandage.

"Cecilia killed Catherine and Heather like she did because she knew it would hurt you. Would you have done the same to hurt her?"

HAUNTED BY THE DEATHS, I slept very little; so, with the first light, I rose and went outside to wash the blood from my dress. It took a long while to work the stains free, but I didn't mind. I thought of Catherine and Heather. Of the little ways they'd helped me. How, in the end, I'd been unable to do the same.

While Porcia's thinking would see the blame of their deaths on my shoulders, I knew where it belonged. I hated Cecilia almost as much as I hated Maeve, now. But my hatred and anger would need to remain hidden for a time yet.

When the dress was clean, I hung it out and went inside. The house was still quiet. I found some bread and cheese, which I sliced. I ate half and made up a plate with the rest. Leaving the kitchen with the plate in hand, I went up to Maeve's room and knocked softly on the door.

"Who is it?" she called softly.

"Eloise, Mama."

"Come in."

I opened the door, entering her room for the first time since I fled it weeks ago. Maeve was sitting up in bed, looking at me with curiosity.

"What's wrong?" she asked.

"Nothing. I brought this for you, thinking no one else would." I moved closer to the bed, sitting on the edge like I would have done for my own mother, and handed her the plate.

"Thank you," she said. "But you know this work is beneath you."

"You, as well."

She smiled and lifted a hand to smooth over my hair.

"Would it be all right with you if I went to the market early?" I asked. "This is the best time of day to watch and listen for news of the sickness."

She beamed at me.

"Very clever of you. Yes. You should wake Cecilia so she can go with you."

"Why does she hate me?" I asked boldly.

Maeve picked up a slice of cheese, studying it thoughtfully before looking at me.

"That's often the way between sisters. They compete for their mother's affection or the most handsome man in the kingdom."

"I'm not trying to steal affection or a man, though."

Maeve chuckled and patted my cheek.

"Go. Get your information. Tell Cecilia that she and Porcia should make the rounds, too. You might want to wake Porcia first."

She settled against her pillows, and I knew I was dismissed.

Leaving her room, I went to Porcia's room first, like Maeve had advised, and knocked on her door. She opened it, looking tired and decidedly annoyed.

"Mama wants us to go to town now for news," I said. "Cecilia is supposed to come with us, too."

"I do not envy you waking her," Porcia said. "I'll be ready shortly." She closed the door in my face.

Turning, I went to Cecilia's door, knocked loudly, and stepped back. When the door flew open, I was ready for her scowl.

"Mother wants us to leave for town immediately," I said.

Her eyes narrowed.

"Mother would never wake me this early."

I lifted my hand and gestured to Maeve's closed door down the hall.

"Go ask her if you must. I'll wake Hugh and be waiting for both you and Porcia outside."

I turned and was about to walk away when she grabbed my hair and pulled me back. I didn't cry out or struggle. Instead, I tilted my head as much as I was able and looked at her.

"I wanted to go alone. She insisted you go, too. I'm to walk the market and you're to make social calls with Porcia."

A smug smile curved her lips, and she released me with a shove. She didn't see my answering smile as I descended the stairs. As Porcia said, I was learning. I had no choice. I either played their game or died like Catherine and Heather. It was time to move beyond manipulation and subtle defiance. It was time to show them all how strong I could be. I would be risking everything, but I saw no other way.

Hugh grumbled about the hour but quickly readied the carriage when I said it was Maeve's wish we leave immediately. The ride to town was tense and quiet. Hugh dropped me off in the market district then took Cecilia and Porcia away.

I walked along the market, speaking with a person here and there, watching for signs of sickness. There weren't any, for which I was grateful. If there had been, I would have had no reason to leave the market.

Keeping a friendly smile on my face, I started on the route that would either lead to my salvation or demise.

I walked toward the Brazen Belle.

CHAPTER 15

A HUSH BLANKETED THE WHOREHOUSE THIS MORNING. A FEW PATRONS snored on the porch, likely the same place where they'd fallen asleep in a drunken stupor the night before.

Without hesitation, I walked boldly up the front steps and entered the establishment's large common room. It was less debasing than the back room I had been in previously. The women were covered, mostly, and there were tables and a bar for food and drink.

One of the serving women, sitting at a table, looked up at me, boredom in her gaze.

"Your nilly need a lick?" she asked. "I can do it for three coppers."

I had no idea what she meant by nilly but knew I didn't want her licking anything of mine.

"No, thank you. I'm here for Rose."

"She's in the kitchen. Sleeps by the fire." She waved me off and resumed her bored picking of loose stitches on her gaping bodice.

Leaving the common room for the direction she'd waved, I stepped into the kitchen. Rose lay on a mat near the dying fire. As I watched, she shivered lightly in her sleep. Despite knowing what she was, I went to place more wood on the fire for her.

"That's kind of you," she said softly without opening her eyes. "Kindness is not often freely given."

"I used to think it was," I said, sitting on the stool near her so we could continue to speak quietly.

She opened her eyes to look at me.

"I thought you might be back. Too bad talking to the tree didn't work."

"How did you know?"

"A little bird told me," she said with a wry smile.

"I need your help."

She chuckled.

"I knew that when you first tried to speak and couldn't. But I can't help you. That curse holding your tongue is layered and deep. Only the one who cast it can remove it before it's done."

"Done?"

"All curses have an end. Once the goal is met, the curse will break on its own."

I thought of the curse that Maeve cast last night. How the ill would become well again once the bells tolled to announce the Prince's return.

"I don't want you to remove it. I want something else. What I want will likely place you in grave danger, though. You might already be in danger, now, just for speaking with me. And, I have no means to compensate you for your help."

The old woman cackled softly.

"You have means of which you do not yet know." She motioned for me to help her up. Her grip was strong on my arm as she struggled to her feet.

"As for the danger," she said, straightening to her full height, which towered a few inches over me, "I've never been bothered by it before. Why should I start today? Tell me what it is you ask of me."

"Can you cast a spell on me to prevent any physical injury?"

She gazed at me thoughtfully.

"Is someone hurting you?"

"I can't answer that."

She studied me a moment then frowned.

"You already have a layer of protection."

"How do you explain the bruises?"

"This protection is something deeper. An awareness of others. A sense of danger."

I snorted.

"Well that failed me, too, when the—" I wanted to scream.

Rose gave me a pitying look. "I can give you something more. Something that will reflect any physical blow."

"Not reflect. Absorb."

"Are you certain you don't want to see the one hurting you hurt in return?"

I looked at the floor, trying to think of something to say to help her understand. "If you and I were in a field together, and I struck a bull with a sword then hid, would the bull look for me because I struck it or would it attack you because you were there at the time it was angered?"

"Ah. You're protecting someone else. Won't this person be hurt in your place?"

I thought of Kellen's peaceful face the last time I saw her and hoped not. Yet, I could no longer keep choosing her life over others. The memory of how it felt when the droplets of Catherine's blood hit my back would haunt me forever, and I didn't want more of such memories.

"Perhaps. But it's a risk I must take. And after you cast the spell, I'll need you to cast another."

Rose's brows rose.

"Another? You ask much."

"Once you're finished, I cannot be allowed to speak of what you've done for me. For your protection and for those I protect."

She studied me intently.

"That I can do."

"Will casting these spells hurt anyone?"

Her expression softened.

"No, child. No one will be harmed. Are you ready?"

She held out her hand to me. I glanced down at it, hesitating to put my trust in the woman before me.

"What did he do?" I asked, meeting her gaze.

"Pardon?"

"The pig. What did he do to cause you to curse him?"

She laughed slightly.

"You are a clever girl."

"I've been hearing that a lot lately."

She grinned and took my hand. A tingle of energy swept through me.

"The creature you care for wasn't always a pig. I only gave him his true form. Helped him, if you will."

The tingle grew stronger, burning its way under my skin to my very bones. I gasped then cried out. She placed her hand over my mouth to muffle the sound.

"Just a bit more," she said. "You're doing well."

The heat intensified until it felt like fire in my blood. Darkness swamped my peripheral; but before I welcomed its embrace, the heat vanished, replaced by a cooling numbness.

"There you are," she said, removing her hold. "By word and deed, you will not break or bleed. Nothing made of magic or by man will harm you. You will not speak of this or any past dealings with me, save in reference to the old woman whose pig you still tend. Both spells will break the moment you wed."

"Wed? Why then?"

"Because you won't need the protection of the spell when you have the protection of a husband."

"What if it's a prospective groom who is beating me?"

She patted my cheek.

"You're too clever to marry a brute. Trust me. You will not need it once you wed."

"How do you get your power if not by taking life?"

Rose's brows lifted.

"You are in a dangerous position, aren't you? How are you here?"

"Obedience won me some limited freedom. But I'm never truly free. What's been done here might already be known."

Rose cackled.

"That's very unlikely, child. This is my domain. What happens here is always private."

I stood, hoping she was right.

"Thank you for your help."

"You're welcome. As for your payment, I will call upon you in the future should I have a need of something. No more than two small favors. In addition to what I've already given you, I will tell you this. Magic is nothing more than the manipulation of the power in every living thing around us. To most it's an intangible energy. To a few gifted, it's the means to rule the world or to help those they love most."

I nodded, not entirely certain I understood what she meant. She seemed to sense that because she grinned at me and waved me off.

"Go. You'll want to set that clever mind of yours on a reason why you visited a whorehouse."

"I already have one. Has anyone gotten ill here?"

The humor left Rose's eyes.

"Two girls last night. Why?"

I shook my head and shrugged. "Do you know who they had entertained?"

"A guard from the castle, I believe."

I nodded.

"Thank you, Rose."

She didn't stop me from walking out. There were a few more patrons in the common room. One of the girls coughed lightly as she spoke to a man more interested in her breasts than her health. I hurried out the door.

The warmth of the day wrapped around me as I made my way back to the market. Vendors were set up now and fully shouting the superiority of their goods. I stopped at a stall to purchase something to eat and saw the vendor cough lightly. Moving on without ordering, I saw more signs of sickness already spreading in the market.

My stomach growled, and I wondered if Rose's spell would protect me from falling ill. Another thought struck me, and I couldn't help but smile at the thought of Cecilia being struck by this magical plague. Nothing would give me more pleasure than to see her suffer. Well, perhaps nothing other than Maeve's own suffering.

Not far from me, a woman coughed into her apron and the material came away bloody. The person she was speaking to saw the stain and backed away. A nearby vendor coughed, the sound wet and gurgling, and looked at his hand.

"Sickness," someone said.

A hush consumed the immediate area before everyone started yelling and moving. Some fled the market, likely for fear of becoming ill. Others remained, looking lost as they too began to cough.

"The King will help us, right Mama?" a child asked his sick mother.

"Yes, darling. He will."

Despite the recent searches that had scared so many, our ruler was still well loved. I wondered how long that would continue as the sickness Maeve had created slowly brought the Kingdom to its knees.

I left the market and waited near the spot where Hugh and the sisters had left me. It didn't take them long to return. Hugh coughed lightly into his hand after he pulled the carriage to a stop.

"I'll open the door for myself," I said quickly.

When I climbed in, Cecilia and Porcia were sitting opposite one another. I took the seat beside Porcia, and she gave an aggrieved sigh.

"You should have ridden on top with Hugh," Cecilia said, a knowing smile on her face.

"How many people have fallen ill?" I asked.

"Not many," Cecilia said with a shrug. "But it doesn't matter.

There is no doubt that mother's spell will work. It's only a matter of time before the King falls ill."

Her smugness ate at me. I wanted to strike out at her. Knowing that there would be no repercussions only made the urge harder to resist. Yet, I did resist it. If Maeve did not yet know what I'd done, I would prefer to keep it secret as long as possible, for I now had a plan.

MAEVE WAS PACING the steps when we pulled into the yard. Through the window of the carriage, our gazes locked. The rage there didn't bode well for me. But, I didn't regret my decision, and I hoped my feelings would remain unchanged no matter how she sought to punish me for what I'd done.

"Where were you?" she demanded when I stepped down. "You were in the market, and then you were gone. The mirror would show me nothing." Her gaze flicked from me to Hugh, and I lifted my hands, pleadingly as I sidestepped his meaty fist.

"I went to the Brazen Belle, Mama. Please."

She motioned for Hugh to stay.

"Explain yourself. Why did you leave the market?"

"The market was quiet, which I would expect at the hour, and I saw no one ill. Since the sickness started with a man in the castle, a man close to the King and to the guards, I went to the place the guards would most likely go during their free time to determine if the sickness was spreading. I didn't know the mirror wouldn't be able to find me. I swear. And, I did find sickness at the Brazen Belle. Two of the girls were already abed with it, and another coughed in the common room as she spoke to one of the men. When I returned to the market from there, I saw signs of it in the increased crowd. It's spreading quickly, and people are beginning to panic." I gestured to Hugh. "Hugh's coughing, too."

A slow smile curled Maeve's lips.

"Very well done, Eloise, my sweet. I apologize for getting so angry for nothing."

Cecilia made a small noise. When I glanced her way, she was glaring at me. Beside her, Porcia had gone pale and watched her sister with a hint of dread.

Maeve reclaimed my attention by wrapping her arm around my shoulder and hugging me to her side.

"What kind of reward would you like?" she asked.

"Reward?" The word struck fear in me. Maeve's rewards were often a calm before a new storm.

"I need no reward, Mama. Helping is enough."

"Come, now," she squeezed my arm harder. "I insist."

I glanced at Cecilia and Porcia. The hate in Cecilia's eyes only burned brighter now.

"I don't want any of us to fall ill," I said, looking up at Maeve. "Cecilia and Porcia are my sisters. I would spare them from what I saw. Coughing up blood cannot be pleasant. Hugh too, if it's possible."

"Consider it done."

I glanced at Cecilia, but her expression hadn't changed. If she tried hurting me again, my secret would be discovered far too quickly.

"You three go inside and fix us something to eat. I'll see if I can do something to make Hugh feel better."

The purr that had crawled into her voice made me sicken. I could well imagine what she intended to do with Hugh. I only hoped he would be cured of the plague in the process.

Following a healthy distance behind Porcia and Cecilia, we made our way to the kitchen door. As soon as it closed behind us, Cecilia whirled on me.

"You simple fool," she snarled. "You wasted a gift rarely given on an unnecessary request."

"I don't understand," I said. "I was trying to make amends."

"Amends?" She growled and paced the room. "We are her daughters. We are essential to Mama's plans. Of course she wouldn't allow us to fall ill. Not this close to the Prince's return. You could have had anything. You could have asked her to bring your sister home or to set her free, and Mama would have done it." Cecilia rounded on me. "She will never give you this opportunity again."

I didn't let her words distract me from the moment.

"I understand that you want to blame me, but know that my ignorance is not my fault. You both know Mama and her ways better than I. Either of you could have spoken to me. Could have helped me understand. As I said, I was trying to make amends. I want the anger between us gone."

Cecilia stared at me for a long moment.

"So long as she treats you like her favorite, that will never be."

I sighed.

"I don't seek her favor; you know that. Your anger is misguided."

"Are you suggesting I should be angry with Mama?"

"I suggest nothing. I'm only stating the truth."

She cast a glare at me then looked at Porcia.

"I have a headache. You can help Eloise make us something to eat. I'll be upstairs."

Porcia said nothing as Cecilia stormed from the room. But the look she gave me afterward was just as full of anger as Cecilia's.

"How have I angered you?" I asked, pretending to be exasperated.

"You are far from ignorant. Mother's proclaimed your cleverness time and again. Surely you knew she wouldn't allow us to fall ill. You purposely chose no reward."

"Untrue. Mama's," I said, stressing the word since she'd used the word mother, "lessons can be quite severe. I wasn't at all certain we wouldn't fall ill."

Some of the anger left Porcia's eyes.

"Go fix lunch," she said, sitting at the table.

Uncaring that she wasn't willing to help, I began fetching what I needed to make a light soup. However, the distant clanging of bells reached my ears before I managed to cut more than one slice of bread. I looked at Porcia. Her gaze flicked to me then the door.

"Her time has come again," she said softly. "She will finally realize her dream."

I saw the way Porcia's hand trembled.

"What is her dream?"

"To rule," she said simply.

The door banged open and Maeve strode in, her bodice loosely laced. She beamed at both of us.

"The bells have rung for the King's fall from health. The end has begun. Go get Cecilia."

Porcia hurriedly left the kitchen, and Maeve focused on me.

"There is much we need to do now that the time is here." She paced the length of the room, her mind racing. "Your sisters and I will need to gather more power but not here. It's too dangerous with the searches," she said absently. "We'll need to go to the homes. A little from each person as we exchange pleasantries. No more deaths to frighten the King into action. That phase is past us now." She looked at me and smiled again. "Our time is finally here."

"Yes, Mama," I said, smiling in return although I had no idea what she was talking about.

"Will you be all right here on your own? While we're in town, I will look for new maids. It wouldn't do to be without help for long."

"I'll be fine. And don't rush selecting the maids. Heather and Catherine were adequate, but if we're to entertain in the same sphere as the King, we'll need help that's more elevated."

Maeve paused her pacing to stare at me.

"Precisely. I had worried over what type of daughter you would be to me. Defiant? Bold? Meek? Loyal? What you are is so much more than a convenient key." She walked to me and hugged me.

"Thank you, Mama," I said, hugging her in return while imagining taking the bread knife and stabbing it into her back.

Cecilia and Porcia entered just then.

Maeve pulled away from me with a knowing smile on her lips and pressed a kiss to my cheek.

"We will return by dinner."

Cecilia glared at me before following her mother out the door. I waited there with the knife gripped tightly in my hand until I heard the carriage leave. As soon as the sound faded, I dropped the knife and checked the window. I was alone. Finally.

Picking up the poker, I went to the entry and gave the mirror a few experimental jabs and hits. Like Maeve's efforts with the rod, the poker did nothing. Scowling, I returned it to its place then went out to the shed. Every tool within the confines of that building failed to make even a mark on the mirror.

I looked around the kitchen but saw nothing useful. Why couldn't something bash the mirror as easily as I'd bashed Kaven's head? I grinned at the thought, not because it hurt him but because of his continued presence in my life despite all of the things I'd done to him. Kaven was much like the mirror.

Defeated for the moment, I left the house to put away all of the tools, then made my way to my mother's grave. I no longer needed a cloak for the walk as spring had finally obtained its hold over the land from winter's heavy hand. Breathing in the freshness, I wandered the trees until I spotted the clearing again. Birds sang out in welcome, their melodies echoing loudly in the branches. I watched the trees as I sat, waiting. It didn't take long for me to spot Kaven. When I did, I couldn't help my small smile or the heat that burst in my middle when he smiled in return.

"I was ready to knock on your door," he said. Although I knew his words were a tease, they struck fear in me.

"Never do that," I said. "Promise me."

"Are you ashamed of my lowly position?" he asked sincerely, no hurt in his tone.

"You're sitting. Hardly a low position. You could get much lower."

His eyes widened slightly, and his face flushed. I frowned, unsure how my teasing had offended him.

"I only meant—"

He placed a finger over my mouth.

"No, let me keep the image I have. It's a nice one."

My frown deepened, and he chuckled.

"You confuse me, too," he said. "An enticing combination of charm, innocence, and...something more."

"More?"

His gaze dipped to my lips, and I felt my face flush at his meaning.

"You aren't interested in that," I said.

"Untrue. I asked for your patience."

I snorted.

"It's irony that women have the reputation for not knowing their minds when you're the one being unclear."

He gave me a wry smile.

"I cannot argue your sentiment. But I want you to know I'm very interested in you as a woman, Eloise. However, I'm unable to act on it because of my current obligations."

I frowned at him, growing serious.

"What exactly are you asking me to be patient for? Your obligations to serve the Royal family to end? You've waited here alone for weeks now. Summer is nearly upon us. Are you saying that you're about to leave your service to the Crown after all that time? We both know you won't. If it were an option for you, you would have left long ago."

"Maybe there was something else keeping me here."

I looked away from him, studying the blossoms on the tree as reality set in. I could not encourage his interest. Yet, I couldn't do what was necessary to push him away. I liked Kaven, and I hoped that one day, when I clawed my way free of the tangled web of disaster that clung to my life, Kaven would still be there. Waiting for me.

"You have my patience if you give me yours," I said softly.

When I looked up, our gazes collided.

"You have enchanted me like no other."

My eyes widened.

"Don't say that. Never say that."

He nodded slowly in acknowledgement, his gaze never leaving mine. Slowly, he leaned forward.

"Forgive me, Eloise," he said.

I nodded slightly, barely breathing. He smiled, a soft knowing curve of his lips, just before his mouth settled over mine. The touch was light but sent my heart racing. He moved, imprinting upon me the texture of his skin. I inhaled his scent and lifted my hands to his chest.

He pulled away abruptly, placing distance between us and dislodging my touch but not leaving. We stared at one another.

"A first kiss for you, I believe," he said.

"Yes. Unless we count the one where you bloodied my lip."

He chuckled softly and touched my cheek gently.

"I'm relieved to see you recovered. I had truly worried. If not for…" He sighed. "Believe that I wanted to call on you."

"I believe you. But, please don't call on me. Not until I'm ready. There's so much in my life that I'm trying to survive."

I looked at my mother's grave again, astonished that I'd said so much without the spell choking me.

"I understand," he said. "You need time to grieve. I'll wait."

I said nothing to attempt to correct him. Instead, we sat in silence for several long minutes, and my mind drifted to my current dilemma. How did one break a magic mirror?

"What breaks iron?" I asked abruptly.

"Iron? What iron do you need to break?"

"None, actually. I was only curious."

"A strong blow might break it, depending on its thickness."

"What if one isn't strong? Is there a clever way to break it?"

He thought for a moment. "Changing from extreme heat to extreme cold could fracture it perhaps."

I grinned and stood.

"Why do I get the feeling you're off to break some iron?"

CHAPTER 16

I HEAVED AGAIN, SWEATING PROFUSELY FROM THE HEAT AND FROM MY effort to drag the mirror through the kitchen door. The memory of Kaven and Kellen, and what was at stake, spurred me to keep going. The door shut behind me and I paused, leaning the mirror against a support to wipe the sweat from my brow.

The fireplace here was the only one large enough for the mirror. Having stoked the fire as soon as I'd returned, the flames already licked their way up the chimney. I hoped Kaven's idea worked and imagined what I would do once the mirror was broken.

Kellen would be safely beyond Maeve's reach. As much as I wanted to race away and rescue my sister, she would need to wait. Too many lives were at risk to selfishly run from what was happening here. I needed to stay and learn what Maeve planned to do. She needed to be stopped. Thus, my need for Rose's spell of protection. Once I broke the mirror, Maeve's anger would be immeasurable.

Pulling the mirror once more, I worked it over to the fireplace and stood it on its end against the stone. The skin on my hands reddened being so close, and I wondered how I could manage to get the piece into the flames.

In the end, I positioned the stool before the hearth and set the mirror on it, pushing the cursed object close enough that one end was in the flames while the other end was on the stool. It would make it easier to accomplish what I next needed to achieve, which was removing the mirror.

Hurrying to the cold storage, I wrapped a chunk of last winter's ice in a heavy cloth. My arms strained to lift the huge block, and I briefly considered taking one of smaller size. But I needed the weight and the cold if this was to work.

Once it was in my arms, I held it to my chest and stumbled up the stairs, tripping several times on my skirts. Only a quick lean against the wall saved me from toppling down and likely killing myself.

I was panting heavily when I reached the kitchen. However, the mirror's glass was glowing an angry red, giving me hope. I set the ice on the block and unwrapped it. There was no bite of cold to pierce my hands. The block only felt hard and smooth when I touched it directly. However, when I removed my hand from it, I could feel its chill.

Leaving the ice, I went to the mirror. Instead of turning it like I'd planned, I reached my hand toward the flame. My skin warmed to the point of discomfort, and then I felt nothing. I touched a dancing flame. My flesh didn't burn or blacken. I remained unharmed.

Relieved at the proof of Rose's spell, I pulled the mirror directly from the flames and dropped it to the floor. Hurrying to the ice, I hefted it into my arms.

"Please work," I whispered just before I dropped the block on the glass.

The crash was deafening when the two met. The ice shattered into a thousand sharp shards that flew everywhere. Several hit me but didn't leave a mark. Beneath the crush of ice, the mirror's surface remained perfectly unblemished. I stared in horror for several long moments.

"No!"

I picked up the poker and beat the mirror with a rage comparable to Maeve's own.

That was when the door opened.

In my rage, I hadn't heard the carriage pull into the yard. But, I heard Maeve's angry shout a moment before I flew backward, hit by an invisible fist of air, and crashed into the table and bench. It didn't hurt, but it was disorienting. Lifting myself up slowly, I looked at Maeve, fear clawing at me.

Kellen.

"How dare you," Maeve said with a frightening cold calm. "I was ready to give you everything. You would have had a kingdom at your fingertips, and this is how you repay me? You try to take from me what is mine?"

"Only as you took from me, Mama," I said, standing, determined not to show what I felt.

Her lips pulled back in a silent snarl, and she bent to pick up the poker I'd dropped.

"I will take far more," she said advancing. She struck out, hitting me across the face. The blow moved me. But it didn't hurt.

I reached up to touch my cheek and check for blood as Maeve's gaze narrowed. She hit my hand, bending my fingers. Nothing gave way or broke.

"Who did this to you?" she demanded.

"I would tell you, Mama, but I've been cursed. I cannot speak of it."

She screeched and grabbed me by the arm, dragging me to the fire.

"You will speak."

She pushed me hard. I stumbled over the stool and fell into the hearth. Flames flared over my skirts, consuming the material. I felt nothing. I stood and shook out my skirt, trying to extinguish the blaze. My efforts only made the flames climb higher, devouring my clothes.

Ignoring it, I looked up at Maeve.

"I cannot speak, and I cannot be physically harmed."

Underneath Maeve's bodice, a light began to glow.

"Very well. As you are so keen on layering more spells upon your person, I will add another. Eloise Cartwright, you are bound to this estate by birth, by name, and by King's decree. And thus your freedom is bound to me."

I laughed, relieved.

"Do you truly believe I want to leave my home? You are mistaken. It's you who needs to leave. You have brought nothing but pain and misery to this home and this kingdom. But to what purpose? Is it truly for the Crown of Drisdall to sit upon your head? Why would you want a paltry command when you have such a formidable power already? Towdown was brought low with a single spell."

"You want to know why? Because I refuse to accept I have lost."

Disbelief robbed me of words. Had I been wrong? Was this about repeating an already failed attempt to wed into the Royal family?

She looked at Cecilia and Porcia.

"Your sister's dress is ruined. Perhaps you can help her."

Cecilia's hand closed over my arm in an unyielding grip.

"With pleasure, Mama." She viciously ripped what remained of the gown from my body, leaving me nude. I lifted my free arm to cover my breasts and attempted to jerk my other arm free.

"Do you think this makes me cower?" I asked, looking at Maeve. "Tremble with fear? This is nothing more than what's already been done to me."

"You're right."

"Porcia, fetch Hugh."

"He can't hurt me."

"Not physically, but there are so many more ways to be hurt, my child." She smiled and stepped closer, sweeping her hand over my cheek in a loving caress that reminded me far too much of Kaven.

"And I am far from done with hurting you."

She patted my cheek gently then looked at Cecilia. Something cold clamped around my wrist, and I looked down at the shackle in dismay.

"Help me with the mirror," Maeve said.

She and Cecilia righted it and leaned it against the butcher block. I saw myself smudged with soot and ash.

Maeve called to the mirror, asking to speak with Grimm. I hardened myself for what was to come. I'd known it was a risk to attempt to break the mirror and cursed myself for losing my temper and not hearing her return. I frowned, realizing Maeve's return had been too opportune.

"You knew," I said suddenly, recalling how she'd known the mirror was close before it had even arrived.

She glanced back at me, away from the emerging image of Grimm.

"Knew what?"

"That I was attempting to destroy it."

"Of course. From your first blow. However, it took time to finish our business and return home."

She smiled and faced Grimm.

"It's time to bring my daughter home by any means necessary, Grimm."

He nodded to her.

"But I prefer alive," she said.

My heart began to race as I imagined the threat coming for Kellen. I hoped the little men who had defended her previously would continue to do so even against a greater number.

The door to the kitchen opened, and Hugh stepped in, followed by Porcia.

"There you are," Maeve said with a purr. She moved to Hugh's side and slid her hand over the front of his trousers.

"Do you know why I spared him?" she asked, looking at me even as a bulge formed under her exploring hand.

"Not only is he young and virile, he is very well endowed. A delicious combination. It's been wrong of me to keep him to myself." She turned to Hugh. "There's no need to be gentle with her. She can't feel any pain. I wonder what she will feel as you hold her down and thrust into her in every way possible." She turned, a slow smile blooming on her face.

377

Terror engulfed me. I yanked at the chain, forgetting my worry over modesty as I desperately attempted to slip my hand free.

"Come, my darlings," she said. "This is unsuitable for the eyes of proper young ladies."

Cecilia cast a nasty grin at me. "Pain or not, your screams will echo in this pathetic excuse for a home, dear sister."

Porcia looked at me, her expression unreadable. "Try to learn this time."

Maeve smiled at her and gave her a motherly pat, which earned Porcia a scowl from Cecilia as they left through the dining room door. In the silence, I heard the rustle of cloth and looked at Hugh.

He tugged his shirt from his trousers, his gaze on my breasts. Covering them with my hands did nothing to snuff the single-minded intent reflected in his eyes.

"Don't do this," I said. "She has you under her spell. This isn't you. You would never hurt me."

He paused, and his gaze lifted to mine. A green light flickered in the depths of his eyes.

"Stop me," he whispered. In that brief moment, I heard the torment in Hugh's voice and saw it in his anguished expression. Then it vanished, and the sick pleasure returned as he reached down to rub himself.

"You'll like this," he said. He tugged his trousers open and moved closer to me. "Have you seen a cock before?"

I swallowed hard and backed up a step, the links of chain clanking with the movement.

"I would prefer never to see one," I said.

I sacrificed the arm covering my breasts to fumble behind me for anything that might help. Hugh reached forward, running a finger through the valley of my breasts. I shivered against the unwanted touch as my hand closed around something.

My eyes began to water when his palm covered one breast, and I eased my other hand from the apex of my legs.

"I've never had a virgin," he said softly.

My grip tightened on the metal, and I trembled with anguish as his fingers gently touched the hair between my legs.

"I'm begging you, Hugh. Don't make me do this."

This man had been with my family for more than half my life. As a child, I'd looked up to him, seeing him more as an older brother or young uncle than random hired help. He'd teased Kellen and me and watched over us. He'd nurtured our curiosity of the woods when Father was away and Mother too ill to leave the house. He taught me how to track the signs animals left behind.

Most importantly, he'd taught me to respect life.

Tears streaming down my cheeks, I shifted the poker in my hand.

"Forgive me," I whispered before thrusting it into his right eye. He screamed loudly and fumbled backward, grasping the iron rod. He pulled it out with another cry, and I gagged at the gore still stuck to the end.

"Bitch!" he roared, coming at me. He struck me in the face, knocking me aside. I fell near the hearth and grabbed a burning log.

Before I could swing it at him, he grabbed it from my hands with a pained grunt and tossed it aside.

"She gave me a task," he panted. He groped in his pants with his good hand and gripped my arm with the burnt one. His expression twisted with a blend of pleasure and pain. I kicked at him and he backhanded me. My chain rattled with our struggles. He lifted me in his arms then slammed me on the ground. Before I knew it, I was pinned under his weight. I could feel him trying to position himself as he held my free arm.

Everything slowed as I looked up at him. His face was bloody and angry. Underneath the mask, I still saw my friend. I saw him as I wrapped the chain around his neck. I saw him as I rolled and squirmed and beat at him. I saw him as his face reddened, and he gasped for air. And finally, at the end, he saw me.

"El…"

It was an apology, not just for the moment but for everything before what just occurred, too.

His weight slumped against me. Because it was wasted by

Maeve's magic, it didn't take me long to be free of his body. I sat beside him and silently cried. I cried for everyone I'd lost and everyone I had yet to lose.

I couldn't be sure how long I sat there before Maeve walked in.

"I told you there were more ways to be hurt. You will learn."

Anger blazed inside of me. Releasing his burned hand, I looked up at her.

"This is what you wanted?"

"Not at all. I wanted an obedient daughter. However, this is the bitter lesson that life must often teach us. We will always want what is just out of our reach."

"That's not a life lesson."

Her lips curved in a small smile.

"You are correct. That's our nature."

"Yours, not mine. I want nothing more than what I had before you came."

"That is because you had everything. Live with nothing for a few days and tell me you still need nothing."

She swept out of the room, leaving me as I was. A short time later, Cecilia and Porcia came and removed Hugh's body.

DIRTY, naked, and hungry, I lay on the cold stone before the unlit hearth. Had I been smart, I would have hidden away Hugh's shirt before he was taken to the woods.

Porcia entered the kitchen from the dining room.

"This is all your fault," she said angrily. "We had servants to do this."

"This" was the terribly menial task of slicing bread and salted meat for their morning meal. I turned my head to watch her, unable to help myself. Even day-old bread was better than no bread. Instead of seeing Porcia cutting bread, I saw the reflection of myself on the floor. I was hardly recognizable.

A ripple of something shimmered across the smoky surface. Had I not been staring at the mirror, I would have never noticed it. I glanced at Porcia who continued to grumble, unaware something had just happened. Not that it mattered because Maeve was very aware. She strode into the kitchen several long moments later.

There was a measured amount of impatience in her stride and expression. For two days, the mirror and the bells had remained silent, and Maeve's temperament had deteriorated by the hour. Porcia, well aware of her mother's mood, ducked her head and worked faster as Maeve approached the mirror.

"I am here. Show me who calls."

The mirror's surface clouded then cleared to reveal Grimm. The man looked delightfully terrible. His dirty, worn clothes hung torn and ragged from his body. Color darkened one eye, and his nose appeared swollen and crooked. Tufts of hair stuck out oddly near patches that seemed a bit thin.

"My Lady," he said with a deep bow and reverence.

"Where is she?" Maeve demanded.

"She remains with the small men. Magic protects them all. We could not get to her. I am all that remains. I wanted to gaze upon you one last time before I attempt to retrieve her again."

Maeve made a sound of impatience.

"Stay as you are and wait for my summons."

The mirror dimmed, and I saw Maeve's angry expression. Porcia, finished with her task of fixing them something to eat, set the knife aside and quietly carried the plate to the table. She said nothing, but Maeve watched her with a narrowed gaze.

"I'm surrounded by incompetent fools," she said softly before focusing on the mirror again. "How can one child elude so many?"

Her gaze met mine in the cloudy surface, and she slowly turned, a smile growing.

"What a sight you are," she said with a low chuckle. "I'm tempted to leave you just as you are. One of the fairest in the land reduced to the look of a starving street beggar. Prince Greydon certainly won't consider you now, will he?"

Cecilia swept into the room, her eyes dancing merrily.

"Of course, he wouldn't. Covered in soot and desperation, Eloise couldn't catch a man fresh from the docks."

Maeve's gaze locked on her daughter.

"Do you truly believe that?"

Some of Cecilia's humor faded as Maeve turned to the mirror.

"Show me the fairest in the land. Those with the beauty to tempt Prince Greydon's hand."

The surface shifted, growing dark for so long that I thought it was trying to indicate no woman would tempt Prince Greydon. Given his arrogant presence, I wouldn't have been surprised. Then the surface lightened, reflecting me even in my current state.

Cecilia gasped softly, and I fought not to laugh at her outrage. My image faded to be replaced by my sister. She once again slept, but far differently from before. She wore a light shift that left nothing to the imagination. Her hair lay in a dark halo around her pale face. Her slightly parted lips and the flush coloring of her cheeks made her seem more woman than young maid. I blinked at my twin in surprise before her image disappeared, and several others flashed on the surface before it finally showed Cecilia and Porcia.

"It will take more than dirt and questionable attire to hide your sister's beauty," Maeve said. There was no anger in her tone, only calculation. I wished I could hear her thoughts.

"Cecilia, go to the market for a piece of fruit. Select the most tempting one you find. Take a horse and make haste. Do not fail me."

"There is bread and meat, Mama," Porcia said softly.

Maeve turned on her youngest.

"The fruit is not for me, my sweet. It is for your sister, Kellen."

I fisted my hands and sat up, fighting the urge to shiver.

"What are you going to do?" I demanded.

"If you both refuse to see your value to me as proper young ladies, then it is my duty, as your mother, to help you learn." She turned to Porcia. "Come, my darling. I will need your help to trick your sister. She will return home on her own once I'm done with her."

CHAPTER 17

PORCIA ENTERED THE KITCHEN AND THREW A HOMESPUN, TAWNY CLOAK at me.

"Clean yourself with that, and I'll give you something to wear."

I quickly wiped my face, arms, and legs with the cloak. The yellow-brown color became more muted with my filth by the time I finished and tossed it back to her.

She hung the cloak on the corner of the mirror and left again, leaving me with my reflection. Though dirt no longer marred my face, I looked slovenly. Using my fingers, I combed my hair and created a rough braid in its length. It didn't help. How could the mirror possibly think a pompous ass like Prince Greydon would ever fall for me as I was?

I turned my back to the mirror and sat on the stool to wait for Porcia and my promised clothing. However, that wasn't who entered several minutes later. An old woman shuffled into the kitchen, her brown eyes sweeping the room and landing on the cloak.

Feeling an odd itch of awareness tingle its way up my back, I covered my chest.

She chuckled softly to herself, seeming not to notice me, and continued her slow pace across the room. The dress she wore hung from her thin frame and swished around her bare feet while the long, soft wisps of her light grey hair moved against her shoulders. When she reached the mirror, she tugged the cloak free and met my gaze in the glass.

"I've already seen all that you have, my darling. Covering yourself now is hardly worth the effort."

The words sent a chill through me as I stared into the brown eyes that struck a faint chord of familiarity. Other than a hint in the eyes, there was no resemblance between the woman before me and Maeve. However, the way she continued to study me as she settled the cloak around her shoulders left no doubt.

Porcia entered the room, a simple servant's dress in her arms.

Maeve nodded to Porcia, who handed me the dress. They both watched me step into the skirt then Maeve chuckled when I couldn't place my shackled arm into the sleeve. She waved her hand and the shackle fell away.

It felt good to be free of its weight, and I quickly slipped my arm into the dress.

"You may have clothing," Maeve said. "But you may not yet have your freedom."

The shackle immediately rose up and closed over my wrist again.

"Keep her chained unless there's a raid," Maeve said to Porcia.

"Yes, Mama."

Maeve's gaze drifted to the door a moment before we heard the horse's hooves pound into the yard. Cecilia arrived through the kitchen door a moment later. Her cheeks were rosy and her hair windswept. Her beauty was unmistakable.

She offered Maeve the small basket she carried.

"I picked the best and the worst," she said.

Maeve smiled at her daughter and patted her cheek. "Very clever of you."

I didn't miss the side glance that Cecilia gave me at Maeve's praise.

Maeve plucked an apple from the basket and held it up before the mirror. Its red perfection hinted at a juicy sweet treat.

"Such a rare bounty this time of year," Maeve said.

"It cost a small fortune," Cecilia said. "A boat laden with fruit had just docked."

A glow radiated from Maeve's chest as she gazed at the apple.

"With a bite of this fruit so juicy and sweet, a forbidden fate our Kellen will meet." Maeve's grin widened before she turned her back on me and continued the whispered spell.

Cecilia laughed and clasped her hands, her eyes dancing with delight as I strained to hear what Maeve said. I caught a few words. Sleep. Lover's touch. But nothing that would help me understand what curse she was weaving.

The reflection of green light died and Maeve tucked the apple into her basket before turning toward Cecilia.

"Remove the mirror from Eloise's sight while I'm gone. No need to tempt her. I'll return within three days. Hunt for news of the Prince. I expect glad tidings when I return."

Maeve shuffled to the door then paused before opening it.

"Oh, and see if you can break the protection spell."

With that, Maeve left and Cecilia turned to me with an evil smile.

THE GLOW from Cecilia's necklace faded with her final word. Porcia sat on the bench, watching from a safer distance. This wasn't Cecilia's first attempt to break the spell. I'd felt the unnatural tingle of her magic and hoped this endeavor would fail like the ones before.

Cecilia picked up the fire poker, her face twisting into an evil mask of anticipation. I prepared myself. She knew I wouldn't just stand there and take a blow and was counting on a fight. Which was why they'd shortened my chain for the time being, giving me only seven links. It was the chained arm she meant to hit and hoped to break.

She lifted the poker, and I fisted my hand. She struck fast, bringing the metal rod down on my arm as I kicked out at her. My foot grazed her thigh as the metal touched down on my arm. Light flared where the rod touched my skin, and I watched Cecilia fly across the room with an immense sense of satisfaction. Although I'd told Rose not to reflect back the damage meant for me, that seemed to have changed with Cecilia's last spell.

Porcia's eyes rounded as Cecilia crashed into the cutting block and crumpled to the floor.

"Foolish girl," Porcia said to me before rushing to her sister's side.

"Did it work?" Cecilia asked, her words slurred.

"No. The protection spell's hold seems to have tightened."

She helped Cecilia to her feet.

"Come, sister. Let us rest for a bit then go to town. We must have news before Mama returns."

Cecilia nodded, and I breathed a sigh of relief as the pair finally left me in peace. They had spent a day and a half attempting to break the spell protecting me. Cecilia had even gone so far as to wait until I slept and then attempted to beat me. Although I was unhurt, I was exhausted.

I sat on the stool and stared at the fire's dying embers. Now that I had clothes, there was no reason to withhold heat. Not that having either had greatly improved my situation. Though I was warm, I was still hungry and thirsty. Looking at the table set with bread, cheese, and a pitcher of wine, my stomach growled. Since Maeve left, Cecilia had made sure to leave both food and water visible but out of my reach.

Angry, I turned away from the sight and considered my circumstance and Kellen's. If the little men protecting her had beaten the trackers, perhaps they would see Maeve for what she was and continue to protect my sister. If Maeve failed, that meant she would return here and continue her plan, whatever that may be. And her greatest asset continued to be her damnable mirror and the amulet. Attached to Maeve as it was, the amulet would be as impossible to destroy as the mirror.

Something popped in the hearth, sending embers floating

upward. Idly turning the cuff circling my wrist, I tracked the path of one. Like me, it drifted on a course in which it had no control.

I sat there for a long while before I heard the sisters leave through the main door. Bitterly, I hoped Cecilia's ears would ring for a week.

My gaze once more returned to the table. Standing, I grabbed the stool and threw it at the broom propped against the wall. The rod fell sideways, just as far out of my reach as it had been before. Annoyed, I picked up the poker and once more attempted to stretch far enough to catch the longer object, not that the broom would do me much good if I managed to get it. The table was twice its distance from me. But I was tired of doing nothing.

The metal bit into my skin for only a moment before the discomfort vanished. I tugged, and I strained, my anger growing as the end of the poker came within an inch of the broom. I shouted and heaved with all of my might.

Suddenly, I fell forward.

I crashed against the floor in a heap and looked back at the hearth, confused. The chain hung from its anchor, and the manacle lay on the floor, still locked. I lifted my hand, looking at the undamaged skin with a growing smile.

I'd pulled myself free. I stood and rushed for the table only to stop short at the last second. If I ate the food, they would know I could free myself. I would have more freedom if they thought me still contained. Changing course, I went down to the cold storage and found some wilted carrots from last fall. I took three then returned to the kitchen and went to drink my fill from the well.

Breathing deeply, I debated what to do next. They had only just left, and the sun beckoned me to stay in its warmth as long as possible. Giving in to the urge, I walked around the house, following the path to Mother's grave. The birds sang loudly in greeting, and I smiled and twirled, lifting my arms to the sunlight.

Freedom had never felt so fine.

Smiling to myself, I entered the clearing. Instead of sitting on the bench, I walked among the flowers and inhaled their fresh scent until I stood near the tree. The little bird chirped at me in greeting.

"Hello, my little friend. Will you sing me a song?"

It warbled out a few happy notes, and I closed my eyes in contentment for a moment before resuming my circling walk in the flowers. It didn't take long for Kaven to appear. I stopped my wandering steps and watched his approach.

"You look tired," I said.

"So do you and many of the people of Towdown," he said.

I nodded sadly.

"I heard the bells and saw for myself the sickness spreading in the market two days ago."

He moved to the bench and sat, looking up at me.

"I was worried I would need to leave before I saw you again," he said.

"Leave?"

"Yes. With the King ill, the Prince will be expected to return to the castle now."

"Ah." I hadn't considered that and was as relieved that Kaven would be leaving as I was sad. He was the only friend I had left to me.

I sat beside him and leaned my head on his shoulder as I listened to the bird's song.

"I will come back," he said softly, his arm moving around my back.

"No," I said. "After the King is well again and when the Prince has less need of you, I will come to you. When I'm ready."

He held me close, his fingers tracing patterns on my side before he chuckled.

"Why is it you favor these dresses so?"

I turned my head to look up at him.

"Why ruin perfectly good dresses when I wander the woods?"

"You used to wear perfectly good dresses while climbing through windows."

I grinned.

"And I ruined them."

"Ah. So you're up to no good today?"

"Most definitely."

His laugh ended with a light cough. I jerked my head from his shoulder and looked at him.

"I'll be fine," he said softly.

"We both will," I said before closing the distance between us. At the last moment, he tried to pull back, but I threaded my fingers in his hair and tugged him forward.

Our lips met, and Kaven groaned. The hand at my side pressed into my ribs, pulling me closer and sending waves of warmth and desire through me. I lifted my free hand to his shoulder, exploring the feel of him under his rough coat. He was broad and strong and lifted me into his lap. I settled with a sigh, leaning into him.

His lips brushed mine once more before his tongue swiped my lower lip. I gasped at the sensation and the way it made my heart race. I opened my mouth to him, giving him entrance and trembling at the feel of his tongue stroking mine.

When he pulled back, I was panting for air.

"Eloise, I will come for you," he said firmly, hugging me close and breaking my heart for what could not be.

He didn't stay long after that but left with a resolved set to his shoulders. In the silence that followed, I looked at the bird.

"Why must I lose everyone I love?" I asked softly.

The bird chirped once, a sad note.

"It does not matter whether my motivation is a selfish desire for what I cannot have or the selfless need to save others. This needs to end. I only wish I had the means to break that damned mirror."

Something heavy and dark fell from the tree with a thump. Frowning, I stood and went to investigate. A black rock flecked with shining silver bits lay on the ground. It was no bigger than my hand. I looked up at the tree and watched several blossoms drift to the ground. The bird chirped at me from its branches as if encouraging me to take the rock.

I bent to retrieve it, the jagged edges biting into my palm as I picked it up. The pain did not fade, and I smiled in understanding.

"Thank you," I breathed before running from the clearing.

In the house, I searched everywhere for the mirror until only one place remained. Maeve's locked room. I grinned and ran to the attic, crawling into the hidey hole that Kellen had discovered. Rummaging through Mother's trunk, I found the second key to Mother's old room. I couldn't stop shaking as I rushed back downstairs and unlocked the door.

Hope fueled me, and resolve anchored me as I stepped into the room and found the mirror near the window.

I smiled at my reflection and lifted the rock. Then, I hesitated. If I did this, then what? I considered several outcomes. The mirror wouldn't break, and I would need to figure out how to slip back into the shackle. Although Maeve would know something had happened, being chained should protect me.

And if the mirror broke? My smile faded, and anger consumed me. I threw the rock. Time slowed. Sunlight glinted off the silver specks as it tumbled through the air. I held my breath, watching its reflection grow larger. The mirror sparked green a moment before the rock connected. Glass shattered outward along with the rock. The green light flared, and the large shards exploded into dust as the rock hit the floor and rolled to my feet.

I watched the black granules rain down on everything near the now empty wooden frame. The wood cracked and curled back in places. In the vacant space that once held the glass, the air shimmered, and the imprint of a face emerged, screaming in rage. It quickly disappeared.

Maeve knew her mirror was broken.

Smiling, I bent to pick up the stone. After locking the door and returning the key, I made my way to the kitchen where I held the stone for a moment, uncertain what to do with it. It seemed only right that, if it had come from Mother, I returned it to her.

Light played on its surface as I left the house and walked the path to the clearing. Digging a small hole in the earth above Mother's grave, I hid the one object that could hurt me through the protective spell.

"It worked," I said, patting the soil. "But I cannot yet leave, not until I know everything. I cannot allow more people to suffer as we have."

I returned to the house, drank my fill of water, then used some grease to slide my hand back into the shackle. Content, I put more wood on the fire and sat on the stool to wait.

The light faded from the sky before Porcia and Cecilia returned. I heard their laughter and animated conversation in the yard as they unsaddled the horse and approached the house.

"It won't be long now," Cecilia was saying as she opened the door.

Her gaze fell on me, and her smile widened.

"We have glorious news, sister. Mama will be so pleased when she returns."

I couldn't help the small smile that curved my lips.

Nothing would assuage Maeve's anger when she returned.

CHAPTER 18

CECILIA TIPPED HER HEAD TO LOOK AT ME.

"You don't believe me?"

"I do," I said smoothly. "And I hope that the news, whatever it may be, will please Mama enough that I might have a bit of food and something to drink."

Cecilia's smile grew beatific. She crossed the room, took a piece of bread from the plate, and threw it to me. I greedily grabbed it from the air and shoved it in my mouth. My stomach growled ravenously as I chewed.

"The news has pleased me enough that I will give you a bite to eat," Cecilia said.

I swallowed.

"What is the news?" I asked, already knowing what she would say.

"The Prince is returning soon," Porcia said with barely contained excitement, earning a glare from Cecilia.

"Why hasn't the bell tolled?" I asked.

"Because he's not yet here," Cecilia said. "But he will be based on the proclamations we saw all over town. In less than three days, there will be a ball. The first of many. For the next month, the kingdom will celebrate the Prince's return in grand style and welcome."

It made no sense to me. Why would they post about balls and celebration when so many were ill and suffering? Did the Royal family truly not care about their people?

Cecilia reached into her bodice and withdrew a square of parchment.

"They are playing right into our hands," she said, offering it to me.

I unfolded the proclamation and read the slanted script with care.

LET IT BE KNOWN,

To celebrate Prince Greydon's return in three days hence, the first in a month-long succession of grand balls will be held at sunset at the palace. Invitations will be delivered to all families in good standing with the Crown. Those who do not receive an invitation are invited to join the festivities outside of the palace gates. All are welcome to joyously greet our kingdom's most adored son.

I ALMOST ROLLED my eyes but managed to continue reading.

IN A MONTH HENCE, Prince Greydon will select his next bride or the Crown will fall to his successor. The bride must be of virtue and willingly submit to trials by magic to ensure there are no illusions to hide age or disadvantage. The Prince will wed a fair maid of his own age or forfeit his crown.

King Aftan

I READ the last paragraph twice more. Maeve had the power and skill to change her appearance to look of an age to the Prince. But it seemed that the King was anticipating that.

"How will this make Mama happy?" I asked, looking up. "She will be discovered during the trials, won't she?"

Cecilia laughed, nearly dancing back to the table to throw me another piece of bread. I willingly ate it and waited for her to explain. I knew she wouldn't pass an opportunity to show me how unclever I really was in her eyes.

"Do you really think Mama brought us here so she could marry the Prince?"

I nearly choked on my bread and looked at Porcia, who watched me with a small smile.

"Isn't it obvious to you yet?" Cecilia asked. "The King's health is questionable, and Prince Greydon is coming home to wed and produce an heir. The ball will be the event of the century. Every eligible maiden of good breeding will attend."

"In good standing with the Crown," I said, quoting the proclamation.

"And who is in better standing than the daughters of the woman who saved the kingdom? One both fair and dark as night. The other golden and kissed by the sun."

Cold understanding bloomed. Not only had my mother died so Maeve could position herself and her daughters close to the Royal Retreat, but so Maeve could use the identities of Margaret Cartwright's daughters to gain an invitation to a ball Maeve had ensured would happen. A ball where the Prince would select his future wife.

"Prince Greydon will take one look at me and fall madly in love," Cecilia said. "I hear his late wife and I share many similarities."

I recalled the words I had overheard long ago about this estate being the gateway to the Crown for them. They didn't mean to kill the Royal family, they meant to become part of it. What better way to overthrow the ruler? It would be subtle, and I had no doubt that the King and Prince would likely both mysteriously fall ill as soon as the new wife became pregnant.

"If you're meant to marry Prince Greydon, why am I still alive?"

Some of Cecilia's humor faded.

"Not only are you and Kellen the daughters of Margaret Cartwright, you're also the fairest in the land without need of spells or powders."

Maeve's question to the mirror about the fairest in the land made more sense. They'd known before ever coming here who might distract the Prince from Cecilia's beauty.

"The more reason to—" The words stopped, but there was no painful squeeze.

"Mama had hoped that she could bend to her will the fairest in the land, the true daughters of Margaret Cartwright. It would have made success that much sweeter knowing she'd bested the woman who'd bested her."

"Bested her? I don't understand."

"Don't you? It was Mama who tried to take the kingdom all those years ago. She'd gathered her strength after the King spurned her as his choice for wife and struck hard and fast. It would have worked if not for your mother's clever wit."

Cecilia took the paper from me.

"It was a proclamation much like this one that ruined Mama's chance to be a queen in her own right. But this will help rectify the mistakes of the past. I will wed Prince Greydon, and I will be Queen. Mama will have a kingdom at her fingertips through me."

Disbelief held my tongue. Maeve had been using pawns and appearances for a very long time to keep up her pretense of respectability. Once she was in the palace, I couldn't help but think she would tire of using Cecilia as her mouthpiece.

"And now that Mama doesn't need me anymore?" I asked. "Will I die when she returns?"

"If she wanted you dead, she would have killed you when she arrived. No, she'll want you to bear witness to her greatness and to know that your mother was nothing more than a temporary obstacle easily overcome and forgotten."

She smiled and swept from the room, Porcia following in her wake. As they moved away from the kitchen, they spoke of seamstresses and the gowns they would have made.

Turning toward the dying embers, I smiled and made a vow.

My mother risked her life to protect the kingdom, and I would do no less. Maeve and her daughters could not be allowed the throne. I let the cinder of my anger flame to life.

I knew the name of my mother's murderer, and now I knew why she'd died.

It was time to claim my revenge.

DAMNATION

CHAPTER 1

My stomach growled loudly, waking me. With a groan, I rolled to my back and winced as the chain holding me to the fireplace rattled loudly in the quiet of the kitchen.

As much as I dreaded Maeve's return, I hoped she would hurry.

I had no doubt she had sensed her mirror's destruction the moment it happened. And given that I'd attempted to break it once before, there was no question that I would be the one punished despite the manacle still securely wrapped around my wrist. However, while I knew Maeve would enter this home in a fury, I didn't fear her arrival. She couldn't hurt me, not truly.

No, I needed Maeve to return so I could hear what had become of Kellen. I thought of her, fast asleep somewhere, unable to prevent whatever Maeve had planned with her cursed apple. There was nothing I could do but fear for my sister's fate.

Sighing, I sat up and threw a log onto the embers. What would have happened if I hadn't witnessed Maeve with Hugh and her use of the amulet? Would Kellen and I still be together and safe, or would something more terrible have happened to us? Would all those innocent people still have died? I thought of Judith, Anne, and Mother and felt a bitter pang of longing.

Nothing could change the past. The choices I'd made were

irrevocable, and I would need to face the choices yet to come. And, it was those future choices that plagued my thoughts continuously. What should I do when Maeve returned? Should I acknowledge I'd broken her mirror or feign innocence? What would best serve my purpose to prevent one of my stepsisters from wedding the prince? Round and round went my thoughts.

The dining room door opened, and Porcia walked in.

"Good morning, Eloise," she said cordially. "Did you sleep well?"

"I haven't been fed more than a crust of bread since Mama left, and I've slept chained to the hearth. What answer do you think I can honestly give?"

"One that's dishonest," she said, meeting my gaze. "Have you learned nothing?"

There was no anger in the question. In fact, there was little emotion at all. In that moment, she reminded me of myself whenever I spoke to Maeve.

"I've always struggled at being an adept student," I said.

"Then your suffering has only just begun," she said.

Turning her back on me, she grabbed her cloak and went outside to collect eggs. A task I used to perform. One I desperately wanted to return to. I hated all of the time I'd been forced to spend indoors. If not for the uncertainty of the spell binding me to the estate, I might have tried to run instead of waiting here, chained like an animal. I gave my manacle an angry tug.

Cecilia took that moment to enter the dining room and let out a laugh.

"Do you honestly think you can free yourself? It's more than metal holding you in place. It's a curse. And no one's magic is stronger than Mama's."

Playing my role, I glared at her then turned to stare at the flames slowly licking their way up the log.

"Perhaps I made a mistake in feeding you yesterday," Cecilia said, sounding too much like Maeve. "Another day of hunger should make you more docile for Mama's return tomorrow."

I looked at Cecilia.

"Do you think that if I'm suitably starved beside the fire, Mama will praise you for your cleverness?" I asked. "Don't be daft. She's going to be upset. By your very own words, she wants me alive to witness her triumph."

Cecilia's eyes narrowed on me.

"I'm willing to risk her wrath to see you suffer."

Porcia entered the kitchen and removed her cloak.

"Good morning, sister. There are fresh eggs for breakfast as well as the stale bread you left on the table yesterday."

Cecilia's angry gaze swung to her sister, checking for any hint of reproach. Porcia remained focused on placing the eggs in a pot filled with water before carrying it to me.

"Place this on the fire, Eloise, and tell me when the water boils."

Without argument, I hung the pot over the flames because I knew doing so would annoy Cecilia.

"We should go to town as soon as we've eaten," Porcia said, joining her sister at the table. "With so many in Towdown now ill, we may not find a seamstress who can complete a dress for each of us in time for the ball. Finding one shop with two gowns already premade might be our only option."

"I agree. If we want the best selection—"

"Then you should have looked yesterday," I said. "The moment you saw the proclamation."

Cecilia glared at me, and I smiled. We both knew I was correct.

A noise rose, faint at first but growing louder.

"A rider," Cecilia said.

The thunder of hooves outside abruptly stopped. Porcia rose to see who it might be; but before she crossed half the room, the door flew open.

Maeve stormed into the kitchen, still disguised as the old crone. Her cloudy gaze swept the room, noting her daughters then me. I didn't miss the lingering look she gave the manacle circling my wrist. Just as I didn't miss the extra dirt that now clung to her clothes or the new rips to her garments. Whatever Maeve had done hadn't been easy.

"Mama," Porcia said in shock. "We weren't expecting you for another day."

Maeve lashed out, striking her daughter across the face.

"Do not speak," she said in her deep, grating voice.

Porcia lifted her hand to hold her cheek then thought better of it and clasped her hands in front of herself instead. Cecilia remained at the table, wisely not speaking as she warily watched her mother. Not that Maeve noticed.

She remained focused on me as a pulse of green light started at her chest. The glow grew larger and brighter with each beat until the emerald radiance enveloped her. The lines on her face smoothed, and her hair darkened as signs of her false age disappeared. Slowly, she straightened to her full height before the light faded away once more. But not from her eyes. The glow remained there as she studied me, her face flushed with anger.

I didn't consciously make my choice before words tumbled from my mouth in a rush.

"I didn't mean to kill Hugh, and I swear never to touch your mirror again. I vow I'll be a proper young lady. Please, Mama. I'll do as you ask if only you allow me to eat."

Her gaze narrowed on me, and my stomach took that moment to growl loudly. She looked at Porcia then Cecilia.

"Come with me," she said.

She strode from the room without another glance in my direction.

As soon as the door closed behind Porcia, I exhaled slowly and looked around me. Blame could still be cast in my direction if Maeve thought for a moment I'd escaped my bond. She would need proof that I hadn't. Pretending ignorance about any knowledge of the mirror's destruction wouldn't be enough.

Thinking quickly, I lay on the floor and stretched out to my full length, once again trying to reach for the broom. My breathing quiet in comparison to my pulse, I struggled to listen for sounds of their approach. The door swung open again just as my shoulder cracked from the strain of pulling against the manacle.

I sat up in a rush and guiltily met Maeve's scrutiny.

"What were you doing?" she asked.

Not needing to feign nervousness, my gaze flicked to Cecilia and Porcia. Cecilia's face was now as red as Porcia's.

Getting to my feet, I focused on Maeve.

"I was trying to get the broom. I thought I might be able to knock the bread from the table."

She tilted her head at me.

"When was the last time you fed your sister, Cecilia?"

"Last night."

"What did you feed her?" she asked without looking away from me.

"A crust of bread," Cecilia answered.

"Does Eloise look hungry to you?"

Cecilia glared at me.

"It had to be her, Mama. She's feigning her—"

Maeve pivoted so quickly that I heard the crack of her hand against Cecilia's cheek before noting her arm had moved.

"Can you make your stomach growl on command? You admitted to me that you spent time away from the estate. If she could free herself, would she not eat?" She pointed to the tray. "Was there any food missing?"

"We didn't check the cellar," Cecilia said defiantly.

"Check. And if everything is accounted for, you will pay for your incompetence with your blood."

"And Porcia?" Cecilia dared ask.

"Your sister never tried to claim competence greater than Eloise's, did she?"

With a nod, Cecilia went to the cellar. Maeve turned toward me.

"What happened while they were gone?" she asked.

I studied her for a quiet moment and saw that a hint of glow remained in her eyes.

"I tried to reach the broom. When that didn't work, I screamed long and loud. Then, I stared at the fire until I heard Porcia and Cecilia return."

"Did anyone come?"

I shook my head. "No, Mama."

"My mirror is destroyed, Eloise. What do you have to say?"

"Ah." I glanced at the fire for a moment before meeting her gaze. "How?"

"That seems to be the mystery, doesn't it? My bedroom door was locked, and you were chained in the kitchen. Despite that, Cecilia believes it was you who broke the mirror."

"As I've tried destroying it in the past, I can understand why. However, I tried breaking it because I feared you were going to use it to hurt Kellen. Why break it after you'd already left to…" I looked at the floor, truly unable to speak for several moments.

"Is she still alive?" I asked finally.

"She is," Maeve said.

Relief filled me only to leave just as quickly. Alive didn't mean safe.

"What did you do to her?" I asked, meeting her gaze.

Maeve's eyes hardened.

"I ensured she would be no threat to our plans to win the prince's affection."

My heart chilled at those words. *Yes,* I thought sadly. *Alive most assuredly did not mean safe.* Irrationally, I wished I hadn't destroyed the mirror so I could look upon my sister.

Footsteps heralded Cecilia's return. When she emerged from the cold storage, her face was pale.

"Everything is still there," she said.

"Go out to the shed. Find a lash. Don't stop until I come for you."

Cecilia nodded stiffly and started for the door.

"Mama," Porcia said hesitantly. "Perhaps Cecilia's punishment should wait until after we visit the dressmaker."

Maeve looked at her youngest daughter.

"Explain."

"A proclamation was made that there is to be a ball tomorrow evening to celebrate the Prince's return." She held her hand out to Cecilia.

Cecilia took the proclamation from her bodice and gave it to her sister. Porcia quickly handed it to Maeve.

"Cecilia and I were just about to leave for town to find gowns. We didn't want to wait too long or we might have difficulty obtaining the best."

Maeve unfolded the paper and read through it, a slow smile curving her lips.

"The mirror's loss will not go unpunished. However, your reason for staying that punishment is sound, my dear one. It wouldn't do to stir gossip immediately before the ball." She looked at Cecilia. "The evening we return from the ball, you will take the lashings for your incompetence in safeguarding the oldest and most trusted means we had to watch our quarry. Use this extra time wisely. Find proof that it was your sister."

Maeve glanced at me.

"Meanwhile, feed her. I will not have her die needlessly." She turned and started for the dining room. "I must change and clean up my room. We will leave for town immediately afterward."

In the silence following her departure, Cecilia took her sister's hand.

"Thank you," she said. "I will not forget your kindness when I am queen. Feed the bitch for me. I need to find proof of her guilt."

"Of course," Porcia said.

Cecilia swept from the room without a look at me.

"The eggs, Eloise," Porcia said.

I used my skirt to pull the pot from the fire and set it on the hearth. Porcia took it from there and removed the eggs with a spoon. She gave me two along with bread and water.

"Eat while you can. Cecilia will find something. Have no doubt."

Overhead, something banged loudly, followed by several more crashes.

I frowned and ate my food. The noise continued long after I

finished. When Maeve returned to the kitchen, she barely spared the ceiling a glance as she uncuffed me.

"Wash," she said.

Gratefully, I hurried outside to do as she commanded. I couldn't help but wish I had time for a full bath, though, instead of a quick swipe of a cloth at the trough outside.

Under Maeve's watchful eyes, I removed the soot from my skin and shook out my skirt.

"Don't bother," she said. "You'll change before we leave."

Her words caught my attention. Leave? Did that mean I was to go to town with them? I was so occupied with my thoughts that I didn't notice the silence inside.

"Mama!" Cecilia's shout rang out.

Looking up, I saw her leaning out an open window above, joy in her expression. In her hands, she held several papers and a familiar book. My heart froze, and my stomach wanted to expel my long-awaited breakfast.

"I found many items of interest in Eloise's room," she said before disappearing inside.

"Come, Eloise. Let us see if your sister has spared herself her lashings."

I followed Maeve inside, never more grateful for Rose's spell that kept me safe from physical harm.

"It's a spell book," Cecilia said, entering the kitchen moments after we did. "And letters from a caster named Elspeth." She held out the book and a pile of letters in one hand. In the other was a single folded piece of parchment.

"What is that?" Maeve asked.

"A letter from Kellen to Eloise. Proof that Eloise knew about the book and those letters." She gave the letters to Maeve. She read Kellen's letter first. Then, without looking up, she started reading the letters to Mother from Elspeth. Her face grew redder with each one, and the light started to pulse at her chest. When she finished, she gave the book the barest of glances.

"I knew your mother hadn't acted alone," Maeve said softly. She looked up, and her eyes glinted with a hard, green light.

"You knew of these letters, and you never told me?" She stood and slowly walked toward me. "Was it Elspeth who cast the spell of protection on you?"

I opened my mouth to deny it but choked on the words from the second spell Rose cast on me.

Maeve tilted her head to study me.

"What letter does your sister have?" she asked.

I swallowed hard and briefly thought of lying, but something in Maeve's eyes told me she already knew. As Kellen had said in her letter, Maeve had been searching for something.

"A letter from the King stating Margaret Cartwright had permission to live at the estate, and that should she or her children ever have need, they could call upon him."

Maeve halted before me, unmoving, gaze unfocused. I waited, ignoring the growing smile on Cecilia's face as she remained behind Maeve.

"Your sister is a disappointment to me, and I do not regret my decision to leave her where she is, out of our way." A secretive smile lifted Maeve's lips. "Eating the apple will ensure no Prince will touch her now. However, what am I to do with you?" She began to circle me and flicked my dirty hair. "Your deception cannot go unpunished. While you may not have broken the mirror, I cannot help but think you had a part in planning its destruction."

She stopped before me.

"I cannot hurt you, but I can hurt others while you watch."

I said nothing and kept my face perfectly blank.

"I know how losing Heather and Catherine pained you. I think perhaps it's time we found new help."

My chest tightened at the thought. How many more deaths would I have to witness?

"There's no need," I said. "I'm happy to cook and clean for you."

Maeve smiled knowingly.

"What a sweet, self-sacrificing offer. Would you still be so willing

409

if I were to host a dinner party tonight to celebrate the Prince's impending return?"

My stomach once again threatened to empty. I swallowed hard and remembered all of the things that Catherine and Heather had to do. Would I be able to endure such acts to spare others from having to endure them? My hands trembled.

Maeve's grin widened.

"I thought not. However, your suggestion has merit. For now, I will allow you to serve as a maid. If you perform your duties— washing, cooking, cleaning—then I will not need to bring any other maids here."

"Yes, Mama."

"However," she said, turning to look at Cecilia, "we will need more than a maid if we're to keep up appearances. Go to town and find a new man for us. Someone without family or ties to town. Someone like Hugh."

"Yes, Mama." Cecilia dipped her head and started toward the door.

"Cecilia," Maeve said, stopping her daughter just as she reached the door. "Don't mistake your paltry discovery as evidence to deflect blame for your failure. Whether broken by Eloise or some caster our dear Eloise has managed to find, it was your responsibility to protect the mirror. You will make amends."

"Yes, Mama."

Maeve smiled at Cecilia.

"I think the docks would be a suitable place to find the help we need. Remember, it must be someone passing through with no ties to the people in town. And, be sure to measure his 'worth' before returning. I will not settle for anything less than Hugh's measure." Maeve gave a sigh. "That man was magnificent in bed."

I shuddered slightly as Cecilia nodded once more and left.

Maeve's gaze pinned me.

"Prepare a bath. I'm sure whoever she finds will need a thorough washing before he's fit to serve us. And prepare something to eat. Impress me, Eloise, or I will bring others into this house who will."

CHAPTER 2

Naked and unashamed, the man stood before us in the kitchen. Although I kept my gaze firmly on his face, my cheeks felt as if I had sat too close to a roaring fire.

Maeve circled him like a wolf circled prey. This new man was much like Hugh in build and handsome enough to look upon once the salt was washed from his skin and hair. Maeve seemed to think so, too, as she ran a finger along his skin while the firelight glinted off the water still on his tall, lean frame. A small smile played about his mouth like he found her amusing.

I pitied him. Yet, there was little I could do to prevent what was to come. I'd already tried to warn him away when I'd brought him a rinse bucket.

"Are you sure you want to give up your life at sea to work on an estate run by a woman?"

"A life at sea can be very lonely, and your daughter was very persuasive that sinking my roots here would be worth my while."

Maeve chuckled.

"I do hope you are willing to sink your roots deeply, for I require absolute loyalty. Can you swear to give me that?"

He boldly lifted a hand and touched Maeve's cheek.

"You're a very fine woman." He glanced at the three of us. "You all are. I'd gladly service all of you."

Maeve captured his hand.

"Those are my daughters," she said, losing her humor. "You've met Cecilia. Beside her is Porcia. Behind them is Eloise. You will not touch any of them. It will be only me you serve."

"Aye, I can swear to give you my loyalty while you desire it."

"What is your name?"

"Seth, My Lady."

"I will take you into my service, Seth."

A green light flared and was absorbed into his soft brown eyes.

"Come," Maeve said. "Let us seal our pact in privacy."

His grin widened, and with a heavy heart, I watched them leave the room.

Cecilia turned to me.

"Eloise, drain the tub, and refill it for me with what remains of the potion. That man's seed is making me itch. He probably had the pox before Mama cleansed him."

She said it all with annoyance, not noting my shock. Everything Maeve had said about worth and measure suddenly made sense. Cecilia had lured the man here with her own body, and Maeve would ensure he stayed with the use of hers. I'd already witnessed the obsession that developed because of it.

I thought of poor Hugh, dead less than a week, and realized I no longer grieved him. I barely grieved Mother or Father anymore, either. Was I growing used to losing everyone? Even thoughts of Kellen, gone so long now, didn't cause me the same degree of anguish they once had. Was it perhaps because I'd finally realized how little control I had over my situation? Or, was my determination to stop Maeve hardening my heart against all of the people around me who were yet destined for damnation?

As I worked to empty the tub, I decided the reason didn't matter. I was grateful I no longer felt such deep sorrow. Detachment from the suffering of those around me would make it easier to do what I must.

Cecilia started stripping the moment I emptied the last clean bucket of water into the tub.

"Go straighten our rooms," she ordered as Porcia stepped forward to help her.

Leaving the kitchen, I went upstairs to tidy their rooms. The faint sound of low groans emanated from Maeve's chamber, and I hurried through my tasks so I could escape to my attic refuge.

However, what once had been a haven as much as a prison now lay in ruins. My walls were no more. Furniture rested in tumbled heaps across the large expanse. Smaller items, strewn about haphazardly, added to the disarray and made walking through the mess difficult. I picked up an old dress as I made my way toward where my sitting area had been. I wasn't sure if the gown was Mother's or something that was left here before we'd moved in.

Finding a chair, I righted it then sat and looked at the wreckage for a moment. Cecilia had vented her anger at me thoroughly. Not that it had saved her. I smiled a little at the thought of Maeve's words. Cecilia would be punished because I'd succeeded.

It didn't bother me that the attic lay in ruins. I'd made it a haven once and could easily do so again. Perhaps a bit more securely this time.

I'd only managed to clear a small path when I heard Maeve call me from below. I hurried down the stairs and found her waiting for me by the door.

"Seth is bringing the carriage around. It's time to go."

"Yes, Mama."

She held out her hand to me; and I moved toward her, eager to see how she would reverse her spell confining me to the estate. As soon as her hand closed around mine, I felt the tingle of her magic worm its way under my skin.

"Cross the boundaries of the estate at my side, and to me you will be tied."

She smiled at me and released my hand.

"Come let us see if that does the trick." She opened the door and ushered me outside. "Start walking to town."

Curious as to what she'd done, I started down the drive. I knew the moment I crossed the boundary of the estate. Something tugged at my middle, a nauseating twist that demanded I go back. My steps slowed.

"Keep going," Maeve called. I glanced back at her. She didn't stand by the carriage but several feet behind me.

I tried taking another step away from her and the nausea intensified.

"I'll help you," she said. Then she turned and walked back to the carriage. Each step brought an increased level of upset to my stomach.

Understanding her spell, I hurried after her. As soon as I crossed through the boundary, the feeling of sickness vanished.

Maeve said nothing as I climbed into the carriage and sat across from Porcia and Cecilia. Cecilia watched me with a knowing smile that quickly vanished when Maeve took the seat beside me.

"Won't it look odd for a servant to ride with us, Mama?" Cecilia asked.

"It will. But this is one exception to appearances I will allow. Despite her many flaws, Eloise is still my daughter. As are you. I will never give up on my children."

She turned to me.

"However, you will learn to obey."

"Yes, Mama."

The carriage lurched forward, and I watched out the window as we passed the spot where I'd stood. Nothing happened, and I exhaled slowly. If Maeve was with me, I would be able to leave the estate without repercussion. Yet, I would be bound to her side. Such a spell would certainly impede my efforts in finding a way to stop Maeve and my stepsisters from achieving their plans.

The ride through town was eerily quiet. Few people walked the streets. Even the market district was surprisingly barren with many of the vendor stalls empty.

"My prince had better hurry, or we won't have much of a kingdom left to rule," Cecilia said.

"They are ill, not dying," Maeve said. "Our subjects will be fine once the Prince returns."

The carriage pulled to a stop before the seamstress who had been used the last time dresses were required, but the sign before the door stated the shop was closed due to illness.

"Mama, we might have to cure the people we need," Porcia said.

Maeve turned her carefully composed face to her daughter.

"Sweetling, we have our distance from Towdown to explain our continued good health. However, if the people who help us are suddenly cured, do you not believe we will be questioned as the cause?"

Porcia flushed.

"I apologize for speaking without due consideration."

"Thank you," Maeve said. She looked out the window at Seth, who'd hopped down for direction from Maeve.

"Continue to drive around until you find a seamstress who is still amenable to work."

"Yes, My Lady."

Moments after he reclaimed his seat, the carriage rolled forward. Making an ever-widening circle around the market district, Seth searched as Maeve had asked. We passed many homes and businesses, most shuttered and dark. There were no children running through the streets or hiding in the shadows in any of the roads we traversed. At one common well, several women wore shawls over their mouths as they collected water. It was hard not to worry when faced with so much quiet despair.

Finally, the carriage slowed. Porcia leaned to look out the window with me.

"Madame Blye's Exquisite Trousseau and Accoutrement," Porcia said. "At least it's a well-known establishment. I was worried we'd end up at the docks looking for someone to sew."

"Nonsense," Maeve said. "I would never allow such a thing. Let's go in, my dears."

I waited, exiting the carriage last. Seth's hand closed around mine as he helped me down, and the warm way his fingers caressed my skin as he released me sent a coil of disgust straight to my stomach.

"Wait with the carriage," Maeve said. "We won't be long."

The bell above the door rang as Cecilia entered first. At the sound, a woman, dressed in a gown far too grand for a seamstress, straightened from her task of folding cloth samples.

"Good afternoon," she greeted us with a smile. "I'm Madame Blye. How may I help you?"

"We require gowns for the ball in two days' time," Maeve said. "Can you accommodate us?"

The woman's gaze swept over us. "Four gowns in two days?" She turned her head and lightly coughed into a white linen cloth she still held.

"Only two," Maeve said. "If you're too ill, I can—"

"Think nothing of my cough," the woman said. "I would be honored to create two exquisite gowns for you. Let's take some measurements and look at the cloth I have to offer, shall we? Then, we can discuss costs."

While Porcia and Cecilia stood for measurements, Maeve wandered the shop, looking at the various samples of cloth. I followed her, unable to endure more than ten feet between us before I felt the sickening pull to return to her side.

"What do you think of this color for Cecilia?" Maeve asked, holding up a lavender swatch. I considered it.

"It seems too subtle a color for Cecilia. What she wears should demand the attention she wants, should it not?"

Maeve sighed.

"You disappoint me."

My brows rose in surprise. "You truly want her to blend with all the other young women who will be there?"

"Not that." Maeve moved farther away from the seamstress as the woman discussed skirt sizes and embellishments with Cecilia and Porcia. Between the conversation and her coughing, I knew she wasn't listening to my discussion with Maeve.

"You are correct that the lavender will not do," Maeve said. "My disappointment is in your choice to spurn your gifts of beauty and intelligence when it should be you standing for a fitting."

While she acted like she wanted me to be fitted as one of her obedient daughters, I knew she hadn't absolved me of the mirror's destruction or my lies of omission. So I said nothing, knowing no answer I gave would be suitable. Instead, I focused on the colors before me.

"Red would be too bold and matronly," I said. "What about this subtle rose color?"

Maeve nodded her approval, and I looked at Porcia before returning to the colors.

"Porcia's fair skin and dark hair will make this a sound choice for her." I touched a cloth that was a deeper shade of purple than the lavender but not so bold as to make her look matronly.

"Very well done," Maeve said. She took the two choices and gave them to Madame Blye just as she finished the last measurements.

"I'll deliver the dresses to the estate, myself, the day after tomorrow to make final adjustments," she said.

"Very good." Maeve handed over a purse heavy with coin. "Ensure they are the best gowns to be seen at the ball, and we will return for more."

Based on the look on Madame Blye's face, the dresses would be as exquisite as her establishment's sign boasted.

"There's a cobbler, three doors down," she said. "If you stop there for measurements, I will ensure he has the material needed to make fine slippers to match."

Cecilia's eyes lit with delight, and Maeve nodded her agreement.

The cobbler greeted us as warmly as Madame Blye had and with the same cough. He promised to deliver the shoes to the seamstress so Cecilia and Porcia would have everything they needed to make a grand impression at the ball.

Giddy with excitement, the pair left the shop. I resented their behavior. This wasn't just an idle girl's fancy to go to the ball at the palace. This was so much more. It was a step in the right direction for them to achieve their goals. Despite Maeve's words that it should have been me preparing for the ball, I was relieved I was not. Free of the fittings and other obligations, I would have the time to plot and discover a way to put an end to Maeve's plans for good.

The desolation of the street outside the cobbler's cottage affirmed my need to do so quickly. Yes, the people of Towdown would recover when the bells chimed, but what about the next time Maeve sought to use them to force the King's hand? I'd witnessed the depths of her evil and feared for the kingdom's future if she succeeded.

In the carriage, I leaned against the seat, more than ready to return to the estate. However, the carriage did not head northwest as I expected.

"Where are we going?" I asked.

"To find the caster helping you, of course."

My stomach pitched violently, and I struggled to keep the fear from my eyes. Instead, I turned to look out the window. I watched the passing homes until I realized our direction. The Brazen Belle. How could she know? Had she witnessed it in the mirror?

As if reading my mind, Maeve began to speak.

"While traveling, I gave your problem great thought. The spell of protection woven into your being would have required a caster of great power and knowledge. It's an ability I would have sensed if it had been near me. While it is possible the caster could have come to the estate while I was away, there was another opportune moment that stood out to me. One instance where you were missing, and I was unable to locate you with the mirror."

She smiled and smoothed a hand over my hair.

"When I find your acquaintance at the Brazen Belle, we will put an end to the nasty spells keeping you from learning your lessons as a proper young lady should."

I couldn't speak. Fear closed my throat. I'd thought I'd been so clever with my excuse, but Maeve had still seen my absence for what it had been.

Through my ignorance and arrogance, I'd killed Rose.

The carriage came to a stop, and I looked out the window at the

Brazen Belle. Women stood on the porch. Their overflowing bosoms made their purpose clear. However, there were no merry calls this time, only coughing and idle stares at our carriage.

In the shade on the far side of the porch, Rose sat in her chair. She looked up and met my gaze briefly before returning to shelling her peas. She too coughed lightly, her cloth coming away bloody.

Maeve pulled me back from the window.

"It is best not to be seen here, my dear," she said, her eyes narrowing as she stared blankly in Porcia and Cecilia's direction.

"I sense no one of strength," Maeve said. "But if she's as strong as I believe, perhaps she's masking her presence as I've been masking mine." Maeve reached into her bodice and withdrew a vial which she handed to Cecilia.

"Go inside and speak with the others. Find out who has been casting and why. See if any recall Eloise's visit. And ask if there are any who are not ill."

Cecilia nodded, drank the vial, and left the carriage as a brunette marked with pox.

"Do you think anyone remembers dresses?" I asked, idly.

Maeve considered me for a moment.

"A very valid observation. I will tell Cecilia not to wear that dress in public again."

I cursed myself for saying anything.

We waited in the carriage for a long while before Cecilia returned.

"There are no new casters at the Brazen Belle. Those there still hold true to the oath they gave, verified by their blood."

"Freely given?" Maeve asked.

"Yes. All of them."

Maeve frowned, and her calculating gaze pinned me.

"Your choices are making things more difficult than they need to be."

She rapped on the carriage, and it started forward. Relief swam through my veins, and I resisted the urge to look out the window at Rose. Was she as powerful as Maeve suggested? I hoped so. For she might be the answer to stopping Maeve. Bound as I was to the estate, how would I ever get to her alone again, though?

Maeve interrupted my thoughts with thoughts of her own.

"We need to ensure this other caster will not interfere. We're too close now. There's no choice but to cast a location spell."

Cecilia and Porcia nodded, but I noticed the sudden sickly pallor in Porcia's face. Any relief I felt died. What did Maeve plan to do that had Porcia reacting so?

Maeve waited until the carriage was on the outskirts to knock on the top. As it slowed to a stop, she handed Porcia a purse heavy with coin.

"Be quick about it."

Cecilia nodded and grabbed her sister's hand. I watched out the window as they knocked on the door of a cottage. A thin woman answered. It was apparent she'd been ill long before Maeve's spell.

Maeve rapped on the roof again, and with a cluck from Seth, the carriage lurched forward.

"We aren't waiting for them?"

"No. People will note a carriage that lingers."

We drove a fair distance before Maeve stopped our progress once again. There, we waited. When Cecilia opened the door, her smile was wide.

"Fate was with us, Mama," she handed the coin purse back to Maeve. "The woman was amiable, and the child barely two."

"Well done."

Confused, I looked at Porcia. The girl's face was completely washed of any color.

"Are you well, Porcia?" I asked.

"Yes," she said woodenly. "Quite well, sister."

Maeve smiled.

"I know it wasn't easy on you, dear one. But remember, the younger the child…"

"The more powerful the magic," Porcia said, her hands tightly clasped in her lap. It was then I noticed the blood on them.

Maeve tapped on the roof to start the carriage moving.

"Let's hurry home before the heart cools. The magic is stronger when fresh," she said, examining the dark coin purse that glistened wetly.

Horror consumed me, and Cecilia chuckled softly, witnessing it.

"You said no one would die." My words grew rough with anger and sorrow.

"I said no maids would die," Maeve replied. "Did you honestly believe I would let your act of defiance go without consequence? I will find the person helping you and destroy her. No one will stand in my way."

CHAPTER 3

I sat on Judith's old bed and ran my hands over the sheets. The image of a small heart in a bowl filled with bloody water kept swimming before my eyes, no matter how hard I tried not to see it. The detachment I'd thought I'd gained was a lie. Shivering, I wrapped my arms around myself and let the tears fall.

Thoughts of the child whose life had been stolen consumed me and filled me with impotent rage. I wanted to scream and hurt everyone around me. I wanted to make them feel the pain I felt. Feel the pain of their victims.

These feelings had consumed me the moment I'd understood what was in the bag. So much so that I'd almost struck out at Maeve during the spell. The very knife she'd used to drain the tiny heart of its remaining blood had been right there on the butcher block.

It was only the thought of the consequences if I failed that had stayed my hand. I might hurt Maeve with a knife, but would I kill her? It wasn't a question of conviction—for I was more than willing to end her life—but a matter of strength and power. I overcame Hugh because he had wanted his end. But what of someone who didn't? In addition to her determination, Maeve had untold power. What if she had a spell protecting her as I had protecting me?

No, I couldn't let my temper rule me. I needed to think. To be detached. Yet, how could I after what I'd witnessed?

A scuff of noise came from the kitchen. I wiped away my tears, the only evidence of my momentary frailty, and stood just as Porcia appeared in the doorway.

Her face had regained a bit of her color since returning home.

"Mama is indisposed. There's no need to prepare a meal tonight."

I nodded, but she didn't leave. She stared at me for a moment then looked behind her before stepping into the room and closing the door.

"Things have been bad for you. But they can become much worse. Consider every consequence before you act. Please." She turned, reaching for the door. "For all our sakes."

She left, and I sat, thinking again of the heart in the bowl.

Much to Maeve's extreme displeasure, the spell hadn't worked. The child had died in vain, for the spell had shown nothing but mist when asked for the location of my co-conspirator. I doubted such a small victory could have felt emptier.

THE COCK'S crow woke me, and for a moment, my mind clung to the past. I rose from bed, thinking I would quietly sneak from the room so as to not wake Kellen on my way to feed the animals. But, the room wasn't my own. I looked down at Judith's bed and felt that tiny spark of joy I'd once felt rising at dawn fade into nothing.

Kellen was gone, hidden in the Dark Forest, afflicted by some unknown spell hidden in an apple. Father was missing, and Mother dead along with Anne and Judith and so many others. My will to carry on vanished. Why did one kingdom's fate matter so much? I thought of my playful talks with Kellen about leaving and traveling to see new lands. Why couldn't I do that? My chest squeezed as I recalled the spell trapping me here. There was no choice but to carry on.

Leaving the house, I fed the animals, promising the pig a walk soon before returning to the kitchen to start breakfast. I kept it to a simple meal of hot oats, toasted like Heather and Catherine had taught me.

When Maeve came down, I had the three bowls set on the table.

"You are missing a setting," she said. "Fetch your bowl."

I went back to the kitchen to serve myself a second portion, since I had already eaten. When I returned, Cecilia and Porcia were at the table. I sat to Maeve's right and waited for her to take the first bite.

"Very good," she said. "If only you were as useful a daughter as you are a maid."

I remained quiet and endured Cecilia's smirk as I ate.

From outside, a faint clanging reached my ears, and I paused with the spoon partway to my mouth. Maeve tilted her head, listening as well. A slow smile parted Maeve's lips at the distant sound of bells.

"Our divine prince has finally returned," she said. "I knew he wouldn't disappoint. Eloise, please tell Seth we will need him to go to market for us today. We're low on supplies." She looked at Porcia. "You can accompany him."

"Yes, Mama," Porcia and I said at almost the same time.

I ate quickly and went to the kitchen with my bowl. There, I hesitated. Maeve's command not to prepare a dinner the night before had meant the household went hungry. Unwilling to act heartlessly toward the man when he'd done nothing to deserve such treatment, I refilled my bowl for him and carried it outside.

I hadn't seen Seth since we'd returned from town but knew he'd made himself at home in Hugh's old room. I approached with a healthy amount of trepidation that had nothing to do with Seth and everything to do with the memories of the friend I'd lost.

Knocking on his door, I waited.

"Enter," Seth called.

I walked in and almost dropped the bowl. Completely naked and uncovered, Seth lay on his bed. He smiled at my shocked expression and reached down to grab himself.

"I'd rather hoped it would be you she sent to me."

"Mama said you will need to go to the market today for supplies." I set the bowl on his stove, not caring if it was hot or if it would ruin the dish. "Porcia will be going with you."

I turned and rushed out the door. He swore behind me, and I knew he would give chase. I picked up my skirts and ran with everything I had back to the house. When I flew into the kitchen, Porcia was there with the bowls from the dining room and looked up at me in astonishment.

"What is it?" she asked.

"Seth," I gasped.

She glanced behind me and frowned. I looked and saw an empty yard. Closing the door with shaky hands, I faced her.

"I believe he thought I was there to…"

"Fuck?"

I cringed at the use of the word but nodded.

"We must tell Mama. She was very clear to him."

She saw the apprehension in my eyes.

"It is better to tell her now than to be caught in a position where it might look like you're trying to steal her favorite toy."

She took my hand and led me to the dining room where Maeve still sat sipping tea.

"Mama," Porcia said. "Eloise had some trouble with Seth."

Her cool gaze shifted to me.

"Oh?"

"He was lying on the bed. Naked. Touching himself," I said.

She smiled slightly.

"I would have thought after your time in the Brazen Belle, something like that wouldn't be so shocking."

"He said he had hoped it was me you would send."

Her humor faded.

"I see. And did you hope I would send you to him?"

I shook my head vehemently.

"Good. I will not have you soiling yourself on someone such as him. You and your sister have more value if you are pure."

My gaze shifted to Porcia before I could stop myself.

"Speak," Maeve said.

"But didn't you tell Cecilia to measure Seth's worth before bringing him home?" I asked, using her own words.

Maeve waved away my concern.

"Cecilia lost her virginity long ago. You and Porcia are my pure ones." She rose and smiled at me. "That purity will be put to good use, have no doubt."

I waited until she left the room to look at Porcia.

"What does she mean?"

"After Cecilia passes the tests and weds the Prince, one of us will need to take her place to consummate the marriage. I'm glad you look more like Cecilia."

SWEAT AND DUST coated my skin as I dragged the heavy piece of furniture across the floor. Before Cecilia's destructive rage, I hadn't realized how much the dust covers were hiding. The amount of furniture in the attic was maddening. Unwilling to stack it again—any walls I made would likely fall based on Cecilia's whims—I tried to sensibly place what was there.

I had several sitting areas, four sleeping areas, and a line of washbasins in addition to trunks and armoires tucked into every corner possible. The space was cluttered but still passable.

"Eloise," Porcia called. "The seamstress is here. You're needed."

After telling me yesterday that I would be the virgin sacrifice on the Prince's wedding night, everyone had left me alone. Oh, I'd ensured the meals were made and waited table, but instead of joining them, I worked in my attic space, desperate for solitude so I could think. Unfortunately, nothing had sparked any inspiring ideas to free me and end Maeve's madness.

Wiping back the hair stuck to my forehead, I descended from my space. In the sitting room, I found the seamstress already unpacking a large trunk. Gone was her pallor and cough. Yesterday's bells had indeed broken the curse.

The seamstress saw me and waved me forward.

"Finish unpacking the second dress. Lay it out, and smooth away what wrinkles you can. After I finish with them, they'll need to be hung until tonight. I'll show you how to lace them up."

Cecilia, already standing on the hemming stool in the center of the open space, snickered. I glanced at Maeve, and she nodded.

Doing as Madame Blye dictated, I started pulling the dress from the trunk.

"Be careful," she said harshly. "The lace is delicate and will rip."

Taking more care, I worked in silence and wondered what new twist this was in Maeve's game. She said I was a daughter and that I should eat at the table. She valued appearances above all else. A thought struck me, and I frowned as I smoothed out any wrinkles I spotted in the overabundance of lace on Porcia's gown. If Maeve was allowing this lesser known seamstress to treat me like a servant, it meant my appearance as a respectable young woman no longer mattered. Once I performed my task as a sacrifice, I wouldn't be needed.

I took a fortifying breath and laid the gown over Mother's settee. Being aware of my definitive end wasn't a bad thing. I now knew how much time I had to stop Maeve. Right up until the wedding night...if I couldn't stop the wedding from happening in the first place.

"Girl," Madame Blye called. "Come here and hold this."

Accepting the pin cushion, I silently stood beside Cecilia as the seamstress knelt at her feet and praised my stepsister from her shiny hair to her beautifully long and narrow feet.

"You will adore the slippers the cobbler prepared for you. I managed to procure glass beads that will perfectly match the dress. When the toe of your slipper peeks from the hem, the glass will catch the light and sparkle beautifully."

The seamstress glanced at me.

"Get the shoes."

I didn't care for the woman. The way she fawned over Maeve, Cecilia, and Porcia then turned to me with a glint of disdain showed her true nature. Kindness was something that should be offered to all, not only those of wealth.

Turning to retrieve the shoes, I noted with a critical eye that the small band of beads sewn across the toe would hardly catch enough light to make them stand out. However, I kept the thought to myself as I offered the shoes to the woman.

"Help her put them on," she said, standing. She looked at Porcia. "Let's get you in your dress while they work."

I knelt at Cecilia's feet and held out one slipper.

"What do you think of my dress, Eloise?" Cecilia asked, lifting her foot.

I glanced up, taking measure of the seamstress's work. While the style was current and the color complementary, the embellishments were too numerous to let the color and design shine.

"You will stand out among the crowd and certainly draw the attention of the Royal family." I glanced at Porcia's gown, the skirt wider with its cascade of laced ruffles. "You both will."

Porcia smiled and looked to Maeve for approval.

"You're both lovely, my darlings."

Cecilia nudged me with the toe of her other foot, and I slid the second slipper on for her. When she stepped off of the stool, the skirt's back barely brushed the ground as she walked.

The seamstress made sounds of appreciation and helped Porcia onto the stool. We repeated the process for her, including the beaded slippers, then Madame Blye showed me how to lace and unlace the gowns as if I'd never worn such apparel myself. While mine hadn't ever been as grossly ornate, I had certainly worked lacings before.

I endured it all in silence and stood by as she packed up her stool into the small trunk.

"I hope you're pleased with the gowns," she said to Maeve.

"Indeed, I am."

"Would you like me to create two more for the next ball? I heard it is to occur this same day next week."

"Please. I would like final approval on color, however."

"Splendid. I will set aside some swatches for you." The seamstress turned to me. "Take the trunk to my wagon."

When I glanced at Maeve, she arched a brow at me. Not bothering to try to understand her purpose, I carried the trunk out. Once I was done loading it, I went to gather the pig for a walk. He squealed excitedly when he saw me.

After a jaunt in the trees between the cliff and Mother's clearing, I returned to the house and found the wagon gone.

"Eloise," Maeve called from the kitchen door. "Stop worrying about that pig. You need to heat bath water."

The pig squealed softly and ran for his enclosure as I quickly closed the gate.

"Hurry," she said as I crossed the yard. "We have much to do before dusk."

For the next several hours, I was in every sense of the word a lady's maid. I hauled water, helped my stepsisters wash their hair, brushed their hair until it shone beautifully, then helped them dress.

"Are you sure we should leave their hair down?" Maeve asked, studying her daughters with a critical eye.

"I only know how to braid hair," I said with an insincere apologetic shrug.

Maeve waved Cecilia forward and twisted her hair into a coil. Pinning that to Cecilia's head, Maeve let the end cascade down over Cecilia's shoulder.

"Porcia, yours will have to do. We're out of time."

I looked at the window and saw she was right. Dusk had fallen.

"Cecilia. Porcia. I will meet you in the carriage."

Cecilia smirked as she strode past me. Did she truly believe I cared that she was going to a ball and I wasn't?

"Eloise," Maeve said, drawing my attention. "There is laundry to be done and our rooms need to be straightened. If that's not enough to keep you occupied while we're gone, you can also clean out the pig's pen. There will be no more defiance. Do you understand?"

"Yes, Mama."

She nodded and hugged me as if her threat was an idle one, but we both knew differently. I watched her sweep from the room and slowly followed to listen for the sound of the carriage leaving. When it did, I raced upstairs to finish everything she said. I didn't care about impressing her; I wanted to finish quickly so I could go to the tree.

It took me over an hour before I had the wash hung outside and turned to the pig's pen. The task was certainly meant as a form of punishment, but I truly didn't mind it. However, by the time I finished, my back was sore, and I reeked fiercely.

"I wish I could bathe in the pond," I said to the pig as I closed the gate. He squealed and trotted toward me as if he thought it was a good idea.

"Like you, I'm stuck here. Swimming will have to wait." I threw him a wilted carrot, which I'd stuck in my pocket, and turned toward the path leading to Mother's clearing.

The night was quiet and the light breeze welcome as I sat under the stars. In the branches of the tree, the bird chirped to me softly before hushing once more.

"I've gotten myself in quite a tangle this time," I said softly. "If you're listening, I need help. Desperately. If there's a way to stop the Prince from marrying anyone at that ball tonight, please...tell me. Show me a sign. Give me something." I sighed and closed my eyes, tilting my head to the night sky.

The bird chirped. Once. Twice. Then it broke out into a merry song meant for the bright light of the rising sun. I opened my eyes, scanning the tree, and gasped at the twinkling bit of moonlit silver in the branches. As I watched, the bird pushed the object from the branch on which it rested and it fluttered to the ground. I rose, approaching cautiously.

The bird silenced as I reached the fallen mask. Picking it up, I marveled at the ornate work. Silver threads attached flakes of thin silver to the edge of the mask. Chips of clear stone inlaid in a cord of silk just inside that, then more silver embroidery imbedded the pale blue cloth that made up the mask. The silken ribbons teased my dirty fingers but did not become dirty. Truly, the mask was a gift made by magic. But to what purpose?

I looked up at the bird.

"I don't understand."

It chirped at me then tucked its beak under its wing.

Frowning, I tied the mask to my face. The world looked no different through it. But perhaps wearing a mask would trick Maeve's spell into thinking I could leave? I had no other guess why the bird would give me such a thing.

Hurrying through the woods, I entered the yard and strode down the driveway. As soon as I reached the same spot as the day before, I went flying backwards and landed hard on my backside.

"That wasn't supposed to happen," I mumbled, picking myself up slowly. Frustrated, I went to the well to wash then returned to my attic space where I hid the mask behind the chimney.

"What good is a mask when I can't leave the estate?" I grumbled. As much as I wanted to return to the tree and try again, I didn't dare. If Maeve felt me try to leave, she would undoubtedly return soon. It was better to let her find me sleeping.

Laying down, I closed my eyes.

It felt like only moments later that I was rudely pushed.

"Get up. This instant."

I registered the anger in Maeve's voice and quickly obeyed, getting to my feet before my eyes fully opened.

"Who was it?" she demanded.

"Huh?" I didn't mean to let my ineloquent confusion slip, but my mind was still slumbering peacefully.

"Who came to you?"

I blinked at her and frowned. She grabbed my throat, and I felt the warm tingle of a spell.

"Speak," she commanded.

"No one came here. I straightened the rooms, did the laundry, cleaned the pig's pen, and went to bed. My only company was the pig and a bird," I said.

She pushed me to my bed, and I winced at the contact. She noticed and narrowed her eyes at me.

"How are you hurt?"

"Not hurt. Sore from my labors."

Her anger melted away.

"Porcia, check the pig's pen. Tell me if it's properly cleaned." She glanced at Cecilia. "Check the laundry." Cecilia gave me an evil grin and left the attic.

"We both know she's going to dirty what I already washed and claim it wasn't done correctly."

Maeve smiled slightly.

"Then you had better get up from your bed if you want any sleep tonight. Henceforth, I expect you to be by the door, waiting for us when we arrive home."

Maeve turned to leave.

"And wash your dress. I won't tolerate that smell in my home."

CHAPTER 4

TIREDLY, I CLEANED THE BREAKFAST DISHES. AFTER REWASHING ALL OF the clothing that Cecilia had stomped into the dirt, I'd managed to return to my bed only an hour before dawn. However, I'd known I would need to rise with the cockcrow, regardless.

"We need to find out who that fat cow in the yellow dress was," Cecilia said. "She had the nerve to cut in front of me in line."

"I'm surprised you allowed it," Porcia said.

"If there had been a discreet way to remove her, I would have. The Prince would have noticed, though. Better to look kind than vengeful."

"Very true, sister."

While Maeve was still abed, Cecilia and Porcia were awake and at the kitchen table. I wished they would just leave. I'd fed them. Why stay?

"He was ever so handsome, don't you agree, Porcia?"

I rolled my eyes at Cecilia's obvious attempt to make me feel jealous.

"So very handsome," Porcia agreed. "I nearly fainted when he placed his hand on my waist. You're ever so lucky you managed a second dance."

"Luck had nothing to do with it. We spoke during our first dance.

Of nothing important really, but he seemed pleased with me enough to seek me out again."

Her fingers thrummed over the wood planks.

"Did you note the lump of his amulet hidden by his cravat?" Cecilia asked.

"No. How did you?"

Cecilia chuckled.

"A well-timed collision with another couple. He was ever so apologetic about it. The incident has me wondering if it might be possible to damage it during the next ball."

"Possibly," Porcia said. "Even the smallest fracture would weaken the amulet. If it were discovered, though, would that possibly jeopardize the next ball?"

"Perhaps. We will need to discuss this opportunity with Mama."

Behind me, the bench scraped against the floor, and I felt a small measure of relief that they were leaving. Once they did, I planned to go back to bed.

"You've been quiet this morning, dear sister," Cecilia said. "Staying here when we went to the ball must have been difficult. If you ask me nicely, I will speak on your behalf to Mama."

I glanced back at Cecilia.

"The only purpose for attending the ball is to win the Prince. Do you truly want me to compete against you, Cecilia?"

"Do you truly believe you could win?" she asked, her eyes narrowing at me. "The mirror might be able to see beyond your filth, but I doubt the prince will. He's led a life of privilege, and that has blinded better men than this kingdom's princeling. He will see you as nothing more than the worthless girl you are."

"Who are you trying to convince? Me or yourself?"

Cecilia pivoted and stormed from the room. Porcia let an exasperated sigh slip.

"You truly have no sense."

A clatter arose outside, and for a moment, I wondered what Cecilia was doing. Then, hounds started to bark. Porcia and I made for the door at the same time. When we stepped outside, the dust from wagons and horses passing on the road to the Retreat drifted on the air and made us cough.

A rider emerged, trotting up our drive. He wore the same attire as Kaven.

"Ho, Cartwright family," the man called cheerily.

Porcia and I shared a glance just before he pulled to a stop before us.

"The Prince has returned and is taking up residence at the Royal Retreat. He humbly asks that you stay on the land allotted to you as he plans to hunt the woods while here. If you have any questions or concerns, please send your man to the Retreat." He tipped his hat to us and wheeled his horse around to return to the caravan still proceeding to the Retreat.

"Mama will be so pleased," Porcia said neutrally. "I'd best tell her."

I turned to follow her into the house and wished the Prince was there so I might strangle him. How much had I lost, all in Maeve's pursuit of the Prince? And here he was, coming to live right next to them. I debated if the man was really worth saving. He'd been an ass when questioning me in the dungeon. Perhaps Cecilia was right, and a life of privilege had made him blind. However, a blind king was better than a vindictive, power-hungry queen.

Cecilia's squeal of delight rang through the house just as I stepped inside. I hoped this news would be enough to keep her from wrecking my room again.

GROANING, I sank deeper into the tub of hot water. The dining room door swung open, and Cecilia strode in.

"What do you think you're doing?" she demanded.

I dipped my head under the water, ignoring her, only to be yanked up by my hair a moment later. Her face was contorted with anger as she tugged harder.

"You do realize that doesn't hurt, don't you?"

She growled and shoved me under.

Instead of fighting her, I used my hands to douse her in as much water as I could. She released me and stepped back just as Maeve entered.

"What is the noise in here?" she asked.

"Cecilia was trying to drown me," I said before Cecilia could think of anything to explain her waterlogged state.

"I will not tolerate any more disturbances. Not while the Prince is in residence. Do you understand, Cecilia? Keep your jealousy to yourself, or it might be observed at the most inopportune time."

"Yes, Mama," she said between clenched teeth.

"Is there a reason you came in here?"

Cecilia remained mute. However, I knew the only reason was to torment me because she hadn't forgotten my remark from this morning.

"Go," Maeve said. "Leave Eloise alone. I will not warn you again."

"Yes, Mama."

Cecilia left me with Maeve. The woman considered me for a moment then sat on the stool near the tub.

"Thank you for bathing," she said. "I almost couldn't eat dinner."

After hearing the news of the Prince's arrival, Maeve had ordered the house cleaned from top to bottom. I'd spent hours doing as she'd bid. So many that I hadn't had to step foot in the kitchen, much to Porcia's dismay. So many that my body ached each time I moved.

Maeve continued to study me, making me wish the bathwater wasn't so clear.

"Did you need me to do something else?" I risked asking.

"Not tonight. You did well today. Dare I hope you've learned your lesson?" she asked.

I couldn't even recall why I was being punished anymore. Then I remembered the mirror.

"I shouldn't have tried to damage what was yours," I said. "I know that now."

She made a noncommittal noise.

"Come to me if your sister causes trouble," she said, rising. "The remainder of this day is yours to do with as you choose. So long as you stay on the estate."

She left the room, and I sagged against the edge of the tub. The only thing I wanted to do was sleep. However, the thump of furniture from above had me revising my plans for the evening. After washing away the lingering odor from cleaning the pig's pen from my hair, I dried, dressed, and slipped out the door.

Movement across the yard had me looking at the shed, where Seth leaned against its wall. His gaze swept over me, but he remained where he was. I debated going back inside then strode toward the path to Mother's clearing. I'd used a rock to bash one man upside the head and a chain to kill another. I wasn't helpless, and I refused to live in fear of Seth. There were far too many things I feared already.

In the fading light of the clearing, I sat on the bench with a sigh. For several minutes, I remained silent in an attempt to absorb the tranquility of the place. Too many thoughts crowded my mind to find peace, however.

I looked at the bird watching me from its perch, not joining the chorus of the other creatures around us.

"There's so much I want to tell you," I said. "I wish—"

A branch snapped, and I looked over to find Kaven on the other side of the clearing.

"Please don't stop. I didn't mean to intrude." He turned as if to leave. As much as I knew I should let him go, I was desperate for his company.

"It's okay. There's nothing I can say anyway."

He hesitated, studying me.

"Why not?"

I smiled slightly.

"Is this an attempt to persuade me to reveal my innermost secrets to you?"

He chuckled and crossed the clearing to sit beside me.

"I've missed you," he said.

As soon as he said the words, I realized how much I'd missed him, too. Knowing he'd been at the Retreat had been a comfort.

"And I you," I said softly. I studied him for a moment. "I was worried."

"You were? Why?"

"The last time I saw you, you were coughing like so many others."

Something flashed in his eyes before he looked away.

"What?" I asked.

He reached for my hand, lacing his fingers through mine. His warm touch sent a shiver through me. His eyes darkened, and his gaze dipped to my mouth briefly.

"I shouldn't have kissed you. It was a foolish, selfish thing to do." He caught my frown and smiled slightly. "Don't mistake me. I would kiss you again if you would allow me. But to kiss you when I was ill...I risked you."

I didn't know what to say because I'd never been at risk.

"The past cannot be undone," I said softly. "That is a truth with which I've come to terms. Don't let regret rob you of the here and now because I don't regret our kiss either."

He released my hand to gently run his fingers along my jaw.

"Eloise, I've grown far too fond of you," he said. "I can think of little else but your sharp tongue, mocking gaze, or sweet lips."

"That hardly sounds complimentary."

"Oh, it is. You've captured my interest like no other because you are like no other. I enjoy your wit and your charm when you choose to use them. Tell me there will be a day when you will be mine."

I frowned slightly.

"What exactly are you asking?"

He glanced down at my lips again and chuckled softly.

"Nothing I have the right to ask of you. Yet."

Before I could guess his intent, his fingers delved into my hair and his lips met mine. My heart gave a jolt before warmth spread like fire through my body. His tongue teased the seam of my mouth, and I gasped. With a groan, he swept inside. The first touch of his tongue to mine robbed me of all thought. I didn't know how long I lost myself to the feel of him before I heard a throat clearing.

Pushing away from him, I glanced at Kaven with wide eyes before looking at Cecilia, who stood on the path.

"My," she said fanning herself. "When Mama sent me to fetch you, I wasn't expecting to find this."

Panic rising, I stood.

"This isn't what it looks like," I said.

"I'm sure it's not," Cecilia said agreeably before looking at Kaven. "And who might you be?"

She knew very well who he was after witnessing my prior attempts to seduce him.

"This is Kaven," I said quickly. "He's here with the Prince."

"Ah. One of the Prince's servants."

Kaven gave her a deep bow.

"At your service, miss...?"

"Cecilia. I'm Eloise's sister."

"It's a pleasure to make your acquaintance. Please let your mother know I will call upon the Cartwright house tomorrow."

Cecilia's smile widened.

"I most certainly will. Come, Eloise. We had better return. Mama is expecting us."

I glanced at Kaven, wishing I could warn him in some way, but there was nothing I could say. Especially not in front of Cecilia.

Without a word, I turned from him and hurried toward the path, ignoring Cecilia's knowing smirk. She followed me, keeping pace until we reached the yard then she lifted her skirts to hurry to the house. Knowing her intent, I did not let her outpace me. She laughed all the way to the sitting room.

"Mama," she said breathlessly, "Eloise has something to tell you."

Maeve looked up from the book she was reading.

"What is it?" she asked as she looked at me.

"Kaven kissed me," I said bluntly.

"And it looked like you were kissing him back," Cecilia added snidely.

I shrugged helplessly at Maeve.

"What else was I to do?"

"Slap him," Maeve said firmly, closing her book.

"But I thought we wanted him to—"

"You were to flirt with him, not encourage him." She tapped her fingers on the arm of her chair.

I looked at Cecilia then Maeve and let my frustration show.

"How am I supposed to know the difference? You taught me how to flirt with him at a whorehouse. Everything that happened there was for encouragement. And certainly nothing showed me how to unflirt once I started."

Maeve stared at me for a moment then burst out laughing.

"Oh, Eloise. You are a treasure in your innocence. Even Porcia isn't so naïve."

I stood there, enduring her amusement. When she sobered, she stood and crossed the room to give my arm a reassuring squeeze.

"You made the best choice available to you. Don't worry about young Kaven. I will address the issue."

My stomach clenched with fear.

"You will have your chance tomorrow," Cecilia said. "He plans to call on us. See, sister? There's no need to worry."

I wanted to claw her eyes out.

THE KNOCK on the kitchen door paused my labor. I looked at Cecilia, who had been an annoyingly constant presence since the moment I woke. She rose from her spot at the table, took a pinch of flour to wipe on her cheek, and went to open the door.

"Good morning, Kaven," she said, pulling the door wider. "Do come in. Eloise and I were just baking bread."

My heart ached at the sight of him as he stepped into the kitchen.

As much as I feared for his safety and wished him away, I was also glad for his presence. His eyes swept the room, noting me before turning to Cecilia.

"You make your own bread?" he asked.

"It's much more cost effective than buying it at the market," she said, closing the door behind him.

He glanced at me, warmth lighting his eyes.

"It's not that. I thought ladies such as yourselves didn't need to bake."

"It's a skill that Mama insists every woman should master," Cecilia said. She gave Kaven a knowing smile. "I'm to fetch Mama. I'll be a few minutes."

He gave her a wide smile and a small bow.

"You have my gratitude."

As soon as the door closed he stepped toward me. My pulse raced with the understanding of his intent, and I held up both hands to stave him off.

"Don't," I warned.

He chuckled as if I played some cute game and caught me up in his arms. The press of his strong arms so firmly around my waist warmed my insides to a degree.

"But I've missed you," he said softly.

My heart gave an agreeable lurch at his sentiment. His blue gaze held mine expectantly, likely waiting for me to return his affection.

"Well, I haven't missed you," I lied. "Let me go before she returns."

I set my floured hands on his shoulders and pushed. He didn't budge. Instead, he dipped his head and nuzzled my neck, sending tingles of awareness into places I shouldn't acknowledge. They were so delicious, however, that I gasped and stilled.

He groaned and nibbled the tender skin just below my ear.

"She said we have a few minutes," he said softly.

Realizing I'd weakened, I pushed at him again.

"She was lying."

As soon as the words were out of my mouth, the door opened.

"Release my daughter at once," Maeve said sternly but without anger.

Kaven did as he was told and bowed deeply to Maeve.

"I beg for your forgiveness and a private word with you, mistress."

"You are not forgiven, and you can speak your piece here," she said, unmoved by Kaven's attempt at a charming smile.

"I've come to speak my intentions for Eloise," he said formally.

"Your intentions? I see." Maeve's tone and expression gave nothing away. She appeared neither upset nor startled by the news as she glanced at me.

"Eloise has captured my heart," he said. "I'm here to ask—"

"I'm afraid such a match would be unsuitable," Maeve said, not unkindly. "Despite her current mode of dress, I would see her settled comfortably in life. And I believe you could not hope to give that to her as she has no dowry. This home belongs to the Crown as do most of the items within it. You have nothing to give her, and she has nothing for you. I'm sorry, Kaven, but my answer is no. Firmly, no."

I glanced at Kaven, my heart breaking. He didn't look at me but bowed again to Maeve.

"Thank you for hearing me. While I will respect your answer, please know that I also hope to change your mind."

"An impossibility," Maeve said. "It's time you leave."

"I see. With your permission, I have a message to deliver."

She nodded.

"Your family is invited to the Retreat this evening for dinner. The Prince has heard of Eloise and the stories regarding her mother. He's also interested in meeting the woman who now holds the title of Mistress Cartwright."

"Please let His Highness know that he honors us with his interest and invitation, and we humbly accept."

CHAPTER 5

"This will have to do," Maeve said, holding up one of Cecilia's gowns to me.

That it was one she'd worn to the whorehouse didn't escape my notice. However, I doubted the Prince would know that.

"Porcia has more dresses than me, Mama. Perhaps we should try one of hers."

Maeve cut Cecilia a sharp look.

"You and Eloise share a similar shape, size, and coloring. She will wear one of your dresses, and you will say not a single word about it."

"Yes, Mama," she said softly.

"It's Eloise's interactions with that boy which have gained the attention of the Prince." Maeve focused on me, placing the dress in my arms. "Cecilia will accompany you on all your walks henceforth. Should you happen upon young Kaven, you will be chaperoned, and Cecilia will have an opportunity to impress him with her good nature as you have done."

"Yes, Mama," I said, cringing on the inside. I'd barely regained the small freedom of going outdoors, and now it was being taken from me yet again.

"Go dress. Make yourself presentable."

I turned to leave Cecilia's room, but Maeve stopped me with a question.

"Do you hold affection for the boy?" she asked.

"He is kind and handsome. I hold him in friendship, nothing more."

Maeve remained silent for a moment.

"Would you grieve his loss?"

Words escaped me as the pain of such an idea consumed me.

"I can see you would. Spare yourself such torment and behave accordingly tonight. Do you understand?"

"Yes, Mama." I cursed myself for showing even a hint of my affection for Kaven in front of her.

"Very good." She came to me and kissed my cheek. "Run along now. We will be waiting for you in the carriage."

I hurried upstairs to change. After a long day baking and cleaning, I would have preferred to crawl into my bed and sleep. However, I knew there would be no escaping the dinner to come. I resented the Prince's long overdue presence and hoped that tonight would proceed smoothly and spare Kaven any consequence of my folly.

Looking out at the moon shining through my small window, I thought of Kaven. My heart gave a lurch at the memory of his earnest offer for my hand. I let myself imagine a world where Maeve was stopped. A world where the King allowed Kaven and me to live here as man and wife. My skin flushed with the recollection of Kaven's kisses. Man and wife. For a moment, I let myself cling to that happy thought. I was tired of being so alone. And afraid. It was my fear that destroyed my dream. I couldn't allow my affection for Kaven to show. Until Maeve was stopped, I needed to keep him at a distance, no matter how much I wished to share the burden of my knowledge. I wouldn't condemn another to my hell.

As soon as I laced the dress and brushed out my hair, I went downstairs and found everyone already in the carriage. It seemed silly to have Seth drive us when the distance was so close, but Maeve was firm. Walking was for impoverished people who were beneath the Prince's notice.

I kept my thoughts of such ridiculousness to myself and watched out the window.

When we pulled into the yard, the door to the Retreat opened, and Kaven stepped out. I looked away quickly but not before I noted that he wore the same clothes from the morning. Or his welcoming smile at the sight of our carriage.

Seth opened the door for us, and Maeve descended first, followed by Cecilia, Porcia, and finally me.

"Welcome," Kaven said. "His Royal Highness is waiting for you in the parlor."

Kaven led the way to the room in question where the Prince struck a magnificent pose before the fire. His cropped dark brown hair was combed back in an overly perfect way that showcased his regal nose and cool blue-grey eyes. He breathed deeply as he watched us enter, the move expanding his chest and straining his jacket. It was a calculated move to impress his masculine presence upon us. I struggled not to snort and caught Kaven watching me. He winked, and I quickly looked away.

My gaze collided with the Prince's.

"Welcome to the Retreat," he said. "As we are neighbors, I thought it appropriate to make your acquaintance in person. Kaven spoke highly of you. Well, some of you."

I still hated the prick for my time in the dungeon and his condescending tone.

"Your Highness," Maeve said with a deep curtsy. "Allow me to introduce my daughters, Cecilia, Porcia, and Eloise."

While my sisters performed perfect curtsies, mine was half-hearted at best.

"Please rise," the Prince said. "Sit. Can I have my servant offer you anything to drink before we dine? I'm very interested to hear the story behind Mr. Cartwright's hasty marriage so soon after the infamous Mrs. Cartwright's demise."

My mouth dropped open. Could he be any ruder?

"Of course, Your Highness," Maeve said graciously. "Wine would benefit us all for such a tale."

He glanced at Kaven, who then left the room while Maeve sat near the Prince. Cecilia and Porcia hurried to take nearby seats as well. I kept my distance, choosing a chair as far as I could get from the Prince without making myself sick from the spell binding me to Maeve.

"What you must first know is that Atwell Cartwright loved Margaret without reservation, even in her slow deterioration. And, he saw their daughters as an extension of the remarkable woman he loved."

Maeve's words were making me ill, and it took everything in me not to let what I felt show in any way. One mistake a day was enough.

"He was as devoted to his children as I am to mine," she continued. "We both understood our children would be our future source of happiness. Thus, the day he received word of his wife's death, he came to me. As Margaret's cousin and a widow myself, he knew that I would be able to offer our children the protection they might need in his absence."

The Prince glanced at Cecilia and Porcia before his gaze landed on me. There was something in the depths of that look—a knowing, perhaps—that had me sitting straighter as he focused on Maeve again.

"And to where did Mr. Cartwright disappear? It seems odd he abandoned his children, you claim he loved well, so soon after losing his wife."

"Alas, his grief for his lost wife was greater than his love for the children they created."

Maeve's words echoed closely what I'd thought, myself. Yet, I hated her desperately for voicing such a lie, now, when we both knew it not to be true.

"He saw too much of Margaret in his children. I believe he sought to escape the reminder of what has now been lost to him."

"You do not seem upset by the news of your cousin's death," the Prince commented.

She shrugged slightly.

"I've suffered loss and know how the passing of time can dull the sharp edges of grief's pain. Atwell will learn that too, and if he is able, he will return."

"Why do you think he might not be able?"

"Before he left, he confided his plans to attempt to reestablish a trade route through the Dark Forest. Though I tried to dissuade him of the notion with a more suitable escape from pain, he was determined."

"Dare I ask what a more suitable escape would be?"

"Not in present company, Your Highness. While I'm a widow and well versed in what happens in a man's world, my daughters have been sheltered from such knowledge."

"Ah. I see."

His gaze once again swept over us before Kaven returned with flutes of wine.

"Thank you, Kaven."

"Of course, Your Highness. Dinner awaits your command."

Kaven served Maeve her drink first, leaving me for last. When he faced me, he smiled warmly and winked again. I tried to ignore him, but the wink made my heart race.

"Kaven has spoken highly of you, Eloise," the Prince said, calling my attention as Kaven left the room again. "I now feel the need to apologize to you for our first meeting."

Porcia choked on her drink and jerked her head toward me. Cecilia was subtler in her shock.

"First meeting, Your Highness?" Maeve asked.

Fear settled into the pit of my stomach.

"Eloise didn't tell you? I'm surprised. I would have thought she would have needed the comfort of a loved one after such a terrifying experience."

I could barely breathe. Though his concern and expression indicated genuine concern, the words were too provoking. It was almost as if he'd known I hadn't shared our meeting with Maeve. But, he couldn't possibly know the consequences of such a slip. Never had I been more grateful for the spell protecting me than at that moment. But what of Kaven?

Finding my voice, I grasped for the words that would salvage the situation.

"While I did indeed share my adventure in the dungeons with my family, I graciously omitted your involvement in hopes that you would make amends in person since we are neighbors. I didn't think an apology for dragging an innocent girl into your dungeon would take so long, though."

Silence reigned the room a moment before he laughed.

"I'm gladdened to see your time there did not dull the fire of your wit and sharp tongue." He strode toward me and offered his arm.

"Allow me to escort you to dinner to make up for my boorish behavior."

Having little choice, I stood and accepted. When he placed his hand over mine, I couldn't be sure whether it was due to him feeling my tremble of fear or just courtesy. We walked before the rest, leading the way to the dining room. I didn't note anything along the way. Instead, my fate when we returned home gripped my mind.

Kaven was there to pull out Maeve's chair as the Prince assisted me to mine. He was also the one who directed the rest of the staff to serve us.

The first course passed in relative silence. It gave me enough time to collect my thoughts and drive the conversation in a way that might just save Kaven from any harm.

"Did any maids catch your attention at the ball?" I asked bluntly.

"Eloise," Maeve said sharply.

The Prince chuckled.

"Do not let her direct nature concern you, mistress. My youth was filled with stories of her mother's similar directness. Therefore, I would expect no less from Eloise."

"You're too kind, Your Highness," Maeve said softly. I could hear the threat in her sweetness, though.

"What did you think of the ball?" he asked me.

"I prefer to keep my opinion of the balls to myself."

He laughed.

"It is far too late for you to withhold your thoughts now."

"Yes, Eloise," Maeve said. "Please, do entertain us with your thoughts."

"It seems silly to host balls where hundreds of women will vie for your attention when there are other means to get to know your prospective bride."

"Quite right," Cecilia said. "For example, intimate dinners such as this are much more conducive to conversation. Though I did so enjoy dancing with you at the first ball."

The Prince looked at Cecilia with a slightly puzzled frown.

"Perhaps Eloise is right about the balls being a fruitless endeavor. For my life, I cannot recall dancing with you. Although, I must admit my feet are still sore today from all the partners I twirled around the room."

Cecilia flushed slightly, her embarrassment, or perhaps anger, showing at his lack of recognition.

"You danced with me as well," Porcia said. "And I sympathize with your plight. There were a great many ladies in attendance but so few men. It might behoove you to encourage more males to attend the next one so the line of maids waiting for your attention isn't so long."

"Are you suggesting that the maids attending would rather not catch my attention?"

Porcia flushed scarlet.

"I believe my sister was only offering a suggestion that might alleviate your woefully overused feet," I said. "However, it is also wise for you to recognize that not every maid might desire to wed a Prince."

The Prince glanced at me.

"Wise indeed," he murmured. "Tell me more of yourself, Eloise. What is it you like to do with your free time?"

"I'm quite dull, Your Majesty, and prefer to spend my idle time lost in a book."

"Or walking amongst the trees while listening to birds sing?" the Prince asked.

I glanced at Kaven, who stood off to the side of the room, near Maeve. He flashed me a quick smile, and I scowled before I could stop myself. His loose lips were going to cost us both dearly.

"While I grieve for my mother, yes, I walk among the trees," I said. "Cecilia, what do you most enjoy doing with your idle time since coming to the estate? And what do you miss most about your old home?"

She artfully kept the conversation centered on her interests while the servants cleared our dishes for the next course. I inhaled the scent of perfectly cooked meat, and my mouth watered as my dish was set before me. A small, oblong loaf sat amidst a pool of gravy and roasted root vegetables.

"Cut into the bread," Kaven said, watching me.

Maeve glanced at me as well, a calculating look in her eye. Kaven needed to stop showing his interest in me.

"Kaven, why don't you help her?" the Prince suggested when I didn't move.

Kaven circled the table and leaned over me to cut my meat. I looked at the Prince with a smile.

"Thank you. It's a new dish for me. What is it called?"

"I haven't the faintest notion."

"Beef in a Blanket," Kaven said, close enough to my ear to send a shiver chasing down my spine. He placed my fork near my hand and stepped away.

"Kaven introduced me to this dish during our travels," the Prince said. "Not only is he usefully observant, he also has impeccable taste."

"That he does," Maeve said agreeably.

"How long has Kaven served you?" I asked.

The Prince glanced at Kaven, humor twinkling in his eyes.

"Since as long as I can remember. His father decided his fate at a young age, for which I'm very grateful. I couldn't imagine what would have become of me if not for Kaven's steadfast presence."

I looked at Kaven, too, and found him watching me, all humor absent from his gaze. Is that why he'd said he couldn't leave the Prince's service? Because Kaven was bound to the Prince for life? What good would my patience then do?

"It's very fortunate you have him, then," I said.

"Indeed. He has saved my life countless times. Poisoned food. Man-eating creatures set loose in my tent. There was even that time you—"

"Perhaps not an appropriate topic for the dining table," Kaven said softly.

"Too right," the Prince said with a smile before returning his attention to his food.

I took my first bite and tried to savor the food. However, I'd been with Maeve long enough to know the signs of her temper. Her quiet. Her rigid posture. Her very kind smile.

Through the remainder of the meal, Cecilia and Porcia both attempted to win the Prince's favor through conversation. Yet, it inevitably seemed to return to me.

"Would you walk with me, Eloise?" the Prince asked after we had finished eating.

I glanced at Maeve.

"I will allow it. With a chaperone, of course."

The Prince glanced at Porcia.

"You may follow us with Kaven's escort."

Porcia bowed her head and accepted Kaven's offered arm when he approached. I had no choice but to join the Prince. My hand rested lightly on his sleeve as he led me from the dining room.

"Did you enjoy yourself this evening?" he asked.

"Yes, Your Majesty."

He directed us toward a trophy room adjoining the dining room. My stomach knotted uncomfortably with each step I took further

M.J. HAAG

away from Maeve. It was fortunate that I didn't go flying backward, though. Explaining that away would have been impossible, and I would have likely found myself back in the dungeon this evening, regardless of Kaven's fondness for me.

Rather than focus on my discomfort, I studied the stuffed remains of one of many creatures crowded throughout the entire space.

"What I want to show you is further in," the Prince said.

I continued onward, fighting the pull in my middle and the sickening need to return to Maeve.

"Here," he said, stopping.

I looked at the giant creature, surprise distracting me for a moment. Frozen in time, with its lips curled in a vicious snarl, the beast stood on two legs but was stooped. Wickedly sharp claws tipped every digit. Its head reminded me of both wolf and bear.

"What is it?" I asked.

"It's what your mother helped to stop. A creature made of magic and sickness. A creature that was once human."

"Human?" I said, looking closer.

"Yes. We aren't sure how it started, but we know how it spread. With a bite, this creature would infect others. If not for your mother and her magic, the kingdom would have fallen."

I turned to the Prince. The hint of scornful patronization that had lingered in his tone since our first meeting was now absent, and I wasn't sure what that meant.

"You think my mother had magic?"

He smiled slightly.

"It would seem we were raised hearing different stories."

"I've heard none, actually. Not until after her passing."

"It saddened me to receive word that she had passed. I'm sorry for your loss. She did a great service for the kingdom." He took my hand and held it in his own as he looked at me.

I wasn't sure I cared for this new side of the Prince any more than I had the pompous side. I could no longer tell when a person was being true to their nature or hiding something more.

"You are one of the reasons I came to stay at the Retreat. I wanted to meet the Cartwright daughters. I'm curious where your sister is. Kellen, is it not?"

I eased my hand from his and stared at the beast once more.

"She left in the middle of the night to find our father," I said. "I can only hope that she's found him rather than beasts such as this when she entered the Dark Forest."

"She left? Alone? Why?"

"Why does anyone do anything rash?" I asked. "My stepmother sent men after her, but they haven't yet returned."

For a long moment, he said nothing.

"You've lost everyone you hold dear."

He had no idea how very much I had lost because of Maeve. A sudden pain knifed through my middle.

"Not everyone," I said with a smile I hardly felt. "I think we should perhaps return to the dining room."

He nodded and placed my hand on his arm. When his touch lingered, I moved my hand from under his.

"You don't care for me," he said.

"It's hard to care for someone I do not know."

"And equally hard to forgive mistreatment."

I looked up into his grey eyes.

"Very true, Your Majesty."

"I hope to sway your opinion of me."

We turned then, and I saw Porcia and Kaven only steps away. Porcia looked pale and flushed at the same time. Kaven looked annoyed. He looked pointedly at my hand on the Prince's arm. Really, what did Kaven expect me to do? Outright reject the Crowned Prince?

Ignoring him, I allowed the Prince to escort me back to the dining room.

"I look forward to seeing you soon," he said, releasing me. Then he honored me with a small bow.

"The Crown will forever be indebted to your family. As soon as we are able, we will send men to look for your father and sister."

"Thank you," I said with a bow of my head, wishing instead I could kick the man. Why had he waited until we were in front of Maeve to say such a thing?

"We look forward to our next meeting," Maeve said as she and Cecilia joined us. We all gave our curtsies then departed.

The carriage had barely started forward when Maeve rounded on me. She hit me hard enough that my head twisted to the side, and my bones cracked. Thankfully, there was no pain.

"You knew? How dare you not tell me."

"Would it have changed your course?" I asked, looking at her. "He still needed to be flushed into the open. The spell would have still needed to be cast."

Her eyes narrowed.

"What else have you been keeping from me?"

"Nothing that you haven't already discovered."

She tilted her head, studying me.

"This sudden boldness is unwelcome. If you believe the Prince's momentary interest will protect you, you are wrong." She turned to Porcia. "What was said while they were alone?"

"He showed her the creatures that attacked the kingdom and said it was her mother's magic that saved everyone. Then, he said that she was the reason he came to the Retreat. To meet her and Kellen. When he asked where Kellen was, Eloise said that she'd run off to find her father, and you had sent men after her but they hadn't yet returned. Nothing was said to implicate us. Instead, she inferred we were her family now."

Maeve considered me.

"Your lie of omission cannot go unpunished. It's a pity about the spell. A beating would have been easier for you."

"If anything happens to Kaven, the Prince will—.

"It's not Kaven who will suffer. Remember, your choices brought you to this fate."

Her amulet flashed brightly, and an abyss followed, swallowing me whole.

CHAPTER 6

THE OVERWHELMING NEED TO VOMIT JERKED ME UPRIGHT. TURNING MY head, I gagged once then emptied my stomach into the mud and straw. Despite that, the nausea didn't fade. Instead, my head thumped in time with my pulse as I gasped for breath.

I closed my eyes against the light of day, trying to find a moment's ease from the constant roiling of my stomach, but there was none. I continued to gag as I turned to my side and got to my knees. The ringing in my ears grew in volume as I tried to stand, only to stumble to my knees again.

Everything hurt as if I'd been beaten again. I blinked slowly, trying to clear my mind of the pain as I inspected my arms for injuries. However, I was too covered with filth to see. Gagging again, which had nothing to do with whatever was covering me, I tried to wipe my hands and arms clean. My efforts only made matters worse.

I struggled to my feet, panting, and noted that I was encumbered only by the shaking of my limbs. Confused, I glanced down at myself and stumbled at the sight of bare, dirty legs and torso. I touched my soot-covered stomach, trying to understand as I looked around.

The small dead-end alley in which I stood was stacked with

broken barrels and old straw. Nothing looked familiar. Frowning, I struggled to remember how I'd gotten here or why I was naked. I recalled the dinner with the Prince then—

A tug in my middle almost brought me to my knees again. My stomach heaved, and I coughed on bile. The burn in my throat was barely noticeable amidst all the other pain I suffered, and my vision swam dizzily. However, the urge to move, to start walking home, had me struggling to my feet once again.

"Ho! What do we have here, lads? This little bit seems to have lost her way."

I turned and found three men in the entrance to the alley. While the lead man leered at my filth-coated breasts with open fascination, the other two did not look tempted. Still, I used my hands in a feeble attempt to shield myself from their view.

"I ain't touching that," one said, sniffing. "She's covered in pig shite."

"A bit of water will clean her up."

My stomach heaved. Whether from the thought of these men touching me or whatever ailed me, I emptied my stomach again.

"Please," I gasped. "Help me."

One of them swore.

"She's sick."

Something hit my shoulder. I grunted as the impact knocked me off balance then lifted my head to see one of the men bending down for another rock. The rocks wouldn't hurt me, and even as wretched as I was, I knew I couldn't let them discover that. Such a mysterious ability would only bring much more unwanted attention to me.

I lurched toward the opening of the alley where they stood, needing to escape. They moved back as if being near me would cause them to fall ill, too. However, I knew better. The illness I felt was the magical pull to return home.

I rounded the corner, emerging onto the road. My eyes swept the area. I didn't know where I was. Looking up, I spotted the castle's turrets in the distance. I was in Towdown. How had I even left home?

Maeve's final words in the carriage came back to me. She'd done this.

Another pull knocked me forward. I put my hand on the nearest building to brace myself.

"Go on! Take your sickness from here. We don't want the likes of you in Towdown."

A rock hit me in the back as did something else firm and wet. I pitched forward, not to escape them but to make my way home to end my suffering.

People stopped to stare at me as I made slow progress through the streets. Mothers covered their children's eyes, a reminder that I wore nothing. Men stared, either laughing or making lewd comments. I kept my hands covering my front, only sacrificing what little modesty that gained to prevent myself from falling.

All the while, my tormentors stayed behind me, driving me forward with whatever they could find to throw at me. I didn't need to stop and look where I was. Though I had no idea, the pull kept me moving in the correct direction.

I turned a corner and found myself at the edge of the market district. The back alleys that I'd traversed so far had kept me from drawing a large crowd, something that would certainly happen if I went through the market. I turned around and attempted to take another route.

The men following me threw even more at me, trying to turn me back toward the market. But, I lifted my arms and ducked down, determined to find another way even as the pull caused me to gag and made my eyes water.

Winning my way to another side road, I continued on.

"Stop," someone yelled from ahead.

There wasn't a way I could stop even if I wanted to listen. My insides felt like they were on fire, now. I had to keep moving.

"Throw one more thing," the voice shouted, "and I'll find where you live and burn it to the ground."

I slowed and looked up, shocked by the vehemence in the words.

Ahead, I saw the backside of Crumbs and Casks with Alfie

standing by the rear door. He wasn't looking at me but at those that followed me.

"Go on! Leave the woman alone."

"She has a sickness," one of the men said.

"So did half the town not more than a week ago. No one used stones to cure it then, yet here we are, hale and hardy. Not everything is as it seems."

Grumbles came from behind me. Then silence.

I stumbled forward, grateful for even that small bit of a reprieve. Alfie rushed toward me, gripping my arms to help steady me as he guided me to a bench near the back door.

As soon as I sat, he pulled off his shirt.

"Put this on. I'll see if I can find a cloak or something, too."

I took the shirt with trembling hands and looked up at him. After all the years he and his friends had tormented Kellen and me, I never would have thought to receive any kindness from him.

His eyes widened as we stared at each other.

"No. This is enough," I said, standing. "Thank you."

"Wha—?"

Movement to my right caught my attention. I caught a glimpse of a familiar cloak before it disappeared. I continued to stare, waiting, and was rewarded when Porcia peeked around the corner at me. My stomach twisted.

"Should I call for a carriage?"

I leaned in and purposely threw up on him. He cried out in disgust but didn't move. Lifting my head, I looked him in the eye.

"Run," I whispered fiercely under the guise of wiping my mouth.

His eyes widened, and he ran back inside. I pivoted and stumbled in the direction of the estate as I tugged his shirt over my filthy body. Maeve meant this to be a punishment and wouldn't like that I now had a shirt. I smiled slightly, not caring.

The agony tearing at my insides did not ease with each step. Instead, the urgency to get home only grew more intense. My shuffling gait became a trundling jog.

When I reached the edge of town, Porcia called my name softly. I stopped and looked back at her. She waved me to a path between two houses. It was the opposite way I needed to go, but I followed her regardless. She was here for a reason. When we reached the backyard, several buckets of water waited along with a clean dress.

"Rinse what you can and dress. Mama doesn't want you returning to the estate like this."

I stripped from Alfie's shirt and dumped the buckets over my head in quick succession. They didn't clean me. Using the shirt, I dried myself, spreading the muck more than removing it from my skin, then tugged the dress over my head only to promptly throw up on myself. I looked down at the yellow stain, wondering how I still had anything in me.

"Mama will not be pleased," Porcia said. "You're no better than you were before."

"Her action is what brought this fate," I rasped, pivoting to start home.

Porcia walked with me in silence. I noted the way she wrung her hands as we walked the road home.

"Why you?" I asked.

"Because I ate everything I was served last night," she said.

I grunted, not understanding or truly caring what the reason was. As we neared the drive, I started to jog again. Porcia panted trying to keep up. The pain intensified until the last moment when I stepped over the estate's boundary. All the pain and sickness vanished. I stopped and took a deep, cleansing breath.

"Come, Mama is waiting."

"Let her wait," I said, moving toward the shed. At the horse trough, I stripped from the dress and sank into the water. Ducking under, I let it cover my head, cooling me and my rage. Naked, and covered in filth, I'd been driven through town by vicious men. Had the spell not protected me—

I screamed under the water and scrubbed at myself.

When I emerged, I felt no calmer.

A low chuckle reached my ears, and I looked up at Seth who leaned against the side of the shed near the end of the trough.

"Can't say I'll mind having to change out the water for the privilege of this view."

I glanced around and saw Porcia was missing.

"You'd better run, Seth," I said. "When Mama comes, she will not like what you're doing."

He smirked, glanced at the house, and paled.

I followed his gaze and saw Maeve standing in the now open door.

Seth nodded his head at her then went back into the depths of the shed.

While she crossed the yard, I exited the trough as gracefully as possible and looked down at myself. Although the water running down my skin wasn't clear, dirt no longer coated me.

"Have you no shame?" Maeve demanded angrily as she reached me. "A proper young lady does not bathe in the open."

"The buckets of water in town didn't clean me, and Porcia said you would be disappointed by my filth. Disappointing you so soon after my latest punishment didn't seem wise. And given that I just walked naked through town, I didn't think I was still a proper young lady. I apologize for misunderstanding." I kept my tone neutral, devoid of any emotion.

Maeve picked up my discarded dress and threw it at me. "Put it on."

I tugged the dress over my head and met her gaze. Anger rolled off of her, unmasked and unbridled. It paled in comparison to mine.

She took a deep breath and regained control.

"What if we'd had company, Eloise? What if the Prince was here to call upon us?"

I said nothing, and she sighed.

"You need to think before you act. While I appreciate your attempt to please me, it had the opposite effect."

"Sorry, Mama."

"Come," she said.

I followed her through the main doors of the house.

"Catherine! Heather!" Maeve yelled.

My eyes rounded, and I stared at Maeve in horror. What had she done? Were my friends alive? How? I saw them die with my own eyes.

Two women I didn't know hurried from the dining room and curtsied to Maeve.

"Yes, mistress?" the older one said.

"This is my daughter, Eloise. Eloise, this is Heather, and that is Catherine."

"The same names?" I said, unable to conceal my pain.

"I'm tired of learning new names. With the rate the maids leave this house, I thought it more expeditious to use the names we already know. At least until we know if this pair will last longer."

I heard the threat there. I wanted to kill her. Slowly. Painfully. The need burned a well inside of me. It was good and deep, hidden from my expression, but still there despite any word I might utter.

"You said no more maids."

"Honestly, Eloise. I don't know why you are so against help. Catherine and Heather are lovely women."

"We will do our best to see to your every need," Heather said.

"We truly want to stay," Catherine added.

I looked at them, closing myself off from the pain—past, present, and any that might find me in the future because of them.

"I'm so glad to hear that," Maeve said. "Because Eloise has had a bit of a mishap on the road and needs to bathe quite desperately. The tub is in the kitchen. Please see to it."

They both nodded and hurried off.

"Come, Eloise. There is more," Maeve said, heading toward the sitting room.

I followed her at a subdued paced.

Inside the room, I found Porcia and Cecilia already waiting.

"Sit," Maeve directed. She waited for me to comply then looked at Porcia. "Tell me everything."

Porcia recounted my experience in town, sparing no detail, right down to the rock that hit my tailbone and the clump of horse shit that someone had managed to lob at my head with dreadful accuracy.

"Perhaps the wash in the trough was a good decision," Maeve murmured with a glance at me.

Then Porcia shared the help I received.

"Did he recognize you?" Maeve asked.

"The entire time I walked, the spell worked its magic, making my ears ring and the world around me tip and tilt as I stumbled and vomited everywhere. Nothing made sense but finding my way home."

"Do not think to withhold information from me, again," she warned. "Did he recognize you?"

"If he did, I wouldn't have noticed. I vomited on him the moment he asked if he could call a carriage for me."

Maeve looked at Porcia.

"It's true. And he never called her by name, nor she by his."

Maeve remained quiet for a moment.

"The next time you defy me, I will have men hold you down and violate you in the most horrific ways so it haunts your dreams until your dying day. Yet, they will leave your precious virginity intact. Do you understand me?"

I swallowed hard and nodded, unable to speak past the lump in my throat.

"Good." She went to the desk and retrieved a bit of parchment that she held out to me. "While you were away, another invitation arrived. Written by the Prince himself."

The invitation formally requested the Cartwright family's presence at the next ball, which was to be masked, and promised the attendance of Drisdall's most suitable unmarried men in good standing with the Crown. The end of the note stated, "I am looking forward to Eloise's attendance." It was signed Prince Greydon, House of Drisdall, in an almost illegible scrawl.

"You want me to attend the ball?" I asked.

Cecilia snorted, and Maeve smiled.

"Of course not. You've proven yourself incapable of making

proper choices when left on your own. And you would be on your own at the ball, dancing with the Prince. No, as it's a masked ball and you and Cecilia are so similar in appearance, Cecilia will present herself as you if she must. You will stay here, where you belong until you are needed. After the ball, Cecilia will tell you everything so that you may discuss it as if you were there."

I glanced at Cecilia. She smiled at me. Was she even thinking Maeve's plan through?

"The Prince has spoken to me. Surely he will recognize a difference in our voices, regardless of the mask you wear. And if you are to be me, how will you win the Prince's affection as your own?"

"She doesn't need to speak," Maeve said, answering for her. "And she will win the Prince's affection outside of the ballroom. Starting today, you will walk with your sister. Twice a day. If you happen upon Kaven, you will speak well of your sister's many accomplishments. You will see to it that the Prince's curiosity is piqued enough that we receive another dinner invitation. This time because of Cecilia."

"Yes, Mama."

"Good. Now, go bathe. I cannot tolerate another moment of the smell emanating from you."

"Thank you for watching over me, Porcia," I said with a nod before leaving the room.

Instead of going to the kitchen, I went to my room. The water would take a while to heat and the tub even longer to fill. Rather than sit in the kitchen and risk learning more about the new maids, I sequestered myself in my attic space. I roamed the furniture placements and thought over the last two days.

The result of the dinner with the Prince could have been worse. Rather than exposing that we'd already met, he could have taken one look at Cecilia and fallen in love. As it was, he spent the majority of his time focused on me. His attention was another layer of safety for me.

Maeve believed the Prince's interest in me nothing more than a passing curiosity brought about because of Kaven's lofty esteem. I wasn't so sure. I'd noted the way Kaven frowned at the way the Prince touched me. Why frown if it was completely proper? Kaven must have sensed something I had not. He was, after all, very close to the Prince. Which also created a layer of protection for Kaven. His potential usefulness in swaying the Prince's opinion of Cecilia would keep Kaven reasonably safe for a time, no matter my behavior. And that explained why I'd walked the streets of Towdown naked instead of Kaven bearing the brunt of Maeve's wrath at my omission of the Prince's presence.

It was a dangerous game I played but no more dangerous than the one Maeve played.

The latest invitation to the ball worried me. The Prince was expecting me. I had no doubt that Cecilia and Maeve had a convincing plan for how Cecilia would portray me, or they wouldn't attempt such a thing. And by using the Prince's interest in me, it would put Cecilia that much closer to me.

A thought dawned, and I wanted to groan.

Cecilia would be close enough to crack the amulet. With it cracked, Cecilia wouldn't need to speak to win over the Prince's heart. It wouldn't matter who the Prince thought he was dancing with.

In agitation, I continued to pace around the room. How could I possibly stop them? If today had taught me anything, it was that I would never be able to leave the estate with Maeve's spell binding me to this place.

I found myself standing near the chimney and looked up at the spot where I'd hidden the mask the tree had given me. It had given me what I would need to attend the ball before I'd even known it would be a masked ball. If the tree could do that, surely it could also provide a cure to the spell holding me here. Why else give me the mask if not to attend?

"Miss Eloise," a voice called. "Your bath is ready."

"Coming."

CHAPTER 7

I TIPPED MY HEAD UP TO THE SUN AND LET THE LIGHT WARM MY FACE. Around me, the birds and other creatures were silent.

"I'm tired of sitting here," Cecilia said. "Let's walk toward the Retreat."

"You know I can't."

"What I know is that Mama gave you a task, and you're not doing it."

"I am doing it. Kaven finds me. I don't find him."

"That's the most ridiculous thing I've heard."

I shrugged my shoulders and looked out over Towdown. With Cecilia constantly in tow, I hadn't returned to the clearing and Mother's grave. At least, not for any extended period of time. Instead, I went everywhere else on the estate, even going so far as to walk the pig in the woods along the ridge. She hadn't liked that because of the pig and the distance from the Retreat. The memory of her annoyance then made it harder not to smile as she glared at me now.

"I'm returning to the house. The last four days have been a fruitless waste of my time." She stood and stormed off.

Our time together hadn't been entirely fruitless, though. Not for me, anyway. In the last few days, I'd enjoyed more time outside in the trees I loved than I had in previous weeks. And, I was entirely grateful that Kaven hadn't once happened upon us.

As the bird song slowly emerged and grew in volume, I stood and hurriedly shook out my skirts to follow after Cecilia. I knew the sound would draw Kaven to me, and I didn't want that to happen.

"Good afternoon, Miss Eloise," Catherine said with forced cheer as I entered the kitchen.

"Is it?" I answered coldly.

Cecilia narrowed her eyes at me from her place at the table as I removed my cloak and left the trio in the kitchen.

I hated that I treated the maids so coldly, but I believed my friendship and fondness for the true Catherine and Heather had been what led to their inevitable demise. After all, their deaths had been yet another means of punishing me. It was safer to act coldly toward the new maids than to form any bond. I wouldn't give Maeve more reason to hurt those who served us.

Heading for the stairs, I returned to my room as I did every afternoon, now. The day after my walk through town, I'd learned that Maeve had spun a lovely tale about me to the new help. One where I was an errant, misbehaved child, who cared little about how my actions might hurt myself or others. My cold behavior only gave more credence to her explanation and made Maeve's nightly routine of locking me in my room more befitting.

I minded neither the lock nor the lie. Both kept Catherine and Heather safer.

I roamed my room, walking amongst the memories of my past, as I waited for the knock on my door to signal that one of my sisters was bringing up a tray. Afterward, I would eat alone and listen for the carriage to leave. The nightly pilgrimage my unwanted family took to join the festivities of the lower class outside the castle was a routine they had been following for the last four days.

When the knock came, I was already sitting at my table.

"Good evening, sister," Cecilia said.

I rolled my eyes before I turned to face her.

"Good evening, sister. It's nice spending so much time with you and then having you wait on me like a commoner."

Her eyes narrowed on me, and she dropped the tray the few inches to the table, letting the juice from the beans splash on the wooden surface.

"Whatever is the matter, sister?" I asked with sugary sweetness.

"I will never be common."

"Oh? Tell me again how the common folk view you."

She leaned toward me.

"When I am queen, I will see you flayed and hung. Your body will rot at the end of a rope and no one will care because everyone you love is dead."

"But I love you, sister. And Porcia. And Mama. We're a family. Family doesn't hurt one another."

She bared her teeth at me.

"You know nothing about family."

I leaned back in my chair.

"Teasing aside, how are things progressing in Towdown? Do you think you're getting any closer to winning the Prince's favor since we're having no luck here?"

She studied me for a moment, likely trying to gauge my sincerity. It was a game I'd been playing with her since Maeve forbade her from striking out against me. I provoked her to the point she wanted to cause me physical harm, then I spoke nicely to her as if I cared.

"Of course, I'm closer. Despite your lack of help. It's not only the people who are taking note of me but the palace guards as well. I'm sure word is spreading."

I felt certain it was, too, and that worried me.

"Sit," I said, nudging out a chair with my foot. "I miss conversation while eating."

"I cannot. Mama is waiting below. We're to go to town again tonight."

I glanced at her dress, a deeply-hued frock.

"You should change into something lighter. Although it won't highlight your beauty, it will help you stand out more against the dull colors the commoners use."

"I want to blend with them, though."

I gave an indolent shrug.

"You've already worked to make them accept you as their own. Now, you need to stand out in the eyes of the Prince should he be walking the parapets. Which I believe he will tonight. Why else would Kaven be absent so long if not for an extended stay at the castle with the Prince."

Cecilia smoothed her hands over her dress.

"If you're wrong…"

"I'm not wrong about the people viewing you differently. If you've truly won their acceptance, the color or style of your dress won't matter so long as you continue to treat them as you have. However, I can make no promises about the Prince's appearance tonight. That is only speculation."

She reluctantly thanked me for my advice before leaving me alone. I smiled and quickly ate my food.

From the small window on the other side of the attic, I watched the wagon pull away from the house. Walking the length of the attic, I listened to Catherine and Heather move about below. When they finished turning down the beds for the night and returned to the first level, I retrieved the master key that Cecilia had been too blind to notice when she first ruined my attic sanctuary.

As soon as the house quieted, I carried my tray to the foot of the stairs, where I typically left it, and let myself out. Sneaking from the house wasn't hard. I'd wandered the rooms a few times the previous night just to test Catherine and Heather's awareness. The trick would be returning before Maeve and my stepsisters, for they would most certainly note me coming in through the front door.

Once outside, I breathed in deeply of the night air and made for the tree. I desperately needed Mother's help to understand how I was supposed to leave the estate to attend the ball with the mask it had given me. Cecilia was indeed winning over too many people with her efforts. Even Catherine and Heather liked her.

The weak moonlight guided my passage along the path. Even though I struggled to see, the creatures around me had no issue recognizing me. The moment I sat on the bench, they started making noise enough to wake the dead. I hoped Kaven was far from here and unlikely to hear—

"Eloise?"

My heart leapt, and I struggled to contain the joy I felt at his presence.

"You shouldn't be here."

"I couldn't stay away. It's been driving me mad that Cecilia has been a constant presence at your side for the last four days. I've wanted to speak with you."

"And she wanted to speak with you."

"Me? Why?" he asked, crossing the clearing.

"Because she has seen how you can influence the Prince's opinion. She wants to impress him."

"I see."

"I doubt you do. What were you thinking?" I asked as he sat beside me.

"At what point?"

"When you stated your interest in me to my stepmother. And, what are your intentions even? You haven't yet told me."

He chuckled softly and took one of my hands.

"I was thinking that I'm tired of trying to be patient. I want to marry you."

I snorted.

"You barely know me."

He laughed.

"That's a problem that marriage will quickly fix."

I opened my mouth to argue, but he took the opportunity to kiss me fiercely. I melted against the onslaught, able to do little else. My head swam, and my hands settled on his chest. When he pulled away, he grinned down at me.

"I've never felt, for anyone, what I feel for you. When we're together, I'm alive. You challenge me to be better than I am. And I want to be. Because of you. Yes, I want to marry you, Eloise. Yes, I'm willing to wait. But I don't want to. If you feel we don't know each other well enough, it only means we need to spend more time together. I will call on you again tomorrow."

His words penetrated the fog in my mind.

"No." I pushed against his chest, winning some space. "Your first attempt didn't progress very well. Why do you think the second would be any different?"

He frowned slightly, his frustration showing.

"Tell me what to do, then. How do I win your hand?"

"You don't," I said, pulling away from him. "I'm not supposed to be seeing you. I snuck from the house while my family is in town. If Mama finds out I spent time alone with you in the woods…"

His expression hardened.

"What? What will she do?"

"She will rush her plans for me. I do not want to be like the Prince, forced to marry a stranger within a month's time."

He considered me silently for a long moment.

"That is exactly why I need to persuade her that I am a good match for you."

"You can't."

"Why not?"

I looked up into his beautiful blue eyes and saw his determination and stubbornness. Both would get him killed. I knew then that I needed to let him go. But how?

His expression softened.

"Don't," he said softly.

"Don't what?"

"Find a reason to push me away."

My brows rose in surprise.

"I can read you better than you realize, Eloise. When you feel threatened, you don't run; you fight back. Why does marrying me scare you? I know my employ isn't it. You've made your stance on Drisdall's social system very clear. You see everyone as equals. If I am your equal, why do you want to run at the thought of marrying me? Is it my visage? Many a maid has told me I'm handsome."

I snorted again.

"Please. It is not your face or form. You know very well a flash of your dimple would send most females to their knees."

He grinned wickedly.

"You on your knees before me is an image that will keep me up for many nights to come."

I sighed.

"I cannot marry you, Kaven. It's as simple as that."

He studied me for a moment.

"Now or ever?"

I hesitated. It would be safer to say forever, but my heart wouldn't allow it.

"For now," I admitted softly. "I need you to stop pressing the matter for now."

"That I can do. But with great reluctance."

A small smile curved his lips before he kissed me once more.

"Tell me that I will see you the day after tomorrow," he said.

I blinked up at him, confused.

"You have no earnest need to see me tomorrow?" I asked.

"Oh, I do. But I especially want to see you at the ball. I want to hold you close and dance with you. I want the world to know you'll be mine. Eventually."

"You want me to attend a ball where the guest of honor is meant to select a bride from the women assembled? Don't you think that's a bit presumptuous? After all, Prince Greydon seems to have an interest in me."

"He does indeed," Kaven said in all seriousness.

"I think it best that I stay home. I wouldn't want to start a quarrel between the two of you."

A small smile tilted the corner of Kaven's mouth.

"He and I quarrel more often than I would like," he admitted.

"You quarrel with the Prince? Is that wise?"

"What happened to your thoughts of equality?"

"I believe in equality, but it's very apparent that the Prince does not."

"How so?"

"Only maids in good standing with the Crown may attend the ball. Those who are not in good standing are forced to watch from outside the palace gates. That is a definitive inequality if ever there was one."

"It's to protect the Prince. There is a threat to this kingdom, one that's already taken far too much life."

"I understand that well. The loss of his first wife truly necessitates care. But why do you think the threat is only possible from those in a lower class? What if I were the threat? You've never met me before. How do you know I wasn't the one responsible for the Prince's wife?"

"First, you're not old enough. Second, I believe the true threat would use a level of subtly of which you are not capable. After all, you hit me with a rock."

My mouth dropped open, and he leaned forward to kiss the tip of my nose.

"That was when I saw you for what you are."

"What am I?"

"An amazing woman worth knowing. One whose threat comes from her sharp wit and tongue, not magic. For if you had magic, you would have either used it against me then, or you would have never confronted me in the first place."

"I think the rock addled your mind."

He laughed, the deep sound making my stomach tighten. His humor faded as he looked at me and he leaned forward once more to capture my lips. It wasn't the kiss to show his affection and delight in me as it had been before. Nor was it one with the urgency of longing after an extended absence. Instead, his lips claimed mine with a barely restrained hunger that sent my pulse racing.

I grasped his shoulders, anchoring myself as my world spun. His arms slipped around me, holding me tightly, and the heat from the palms of his hands scorched my sides. He toyed with me, teasing me with his tongue as he pressed his chest to mine. The world tilted, and I found myself laying back on the bench. When he lifted his head for a moment, I panted for breath only to moan when his lips found the column of my throat.

"You call to me like no other," he whispered against my skin. "You are my shield and my light."

I barely heard him. He was kissing his way down to my neckline. My heart fluttered in my chest, anticipating what he would do next. There was a tug at my dress a moment before the night air cooled the heated skin of my breasts.

Kaven groaned and set his mouth on one peak. The heat of his tongue undid me. I gasped and arched underneath him.

"Eloise." He slowly kissed his way upward again, his lips once more claiming mine.

I lost myself. I would have done anything and everything he wanted at that moment, and I would have known nothing but joy. However, he abandoned me just as the kiss heated to a fevered state.

I blinked at the stars above, trying to breathe and form a coherent thought. When I realized he wasn't returning to me, I sat up and looked around. He paced the far side of the clearing.

"Kaven?"

"I'm tired of this game," he said harshly.

Hurt consumed me.

"I didn't know it was a game to you." I sat up and straightened my gown. Before I finished, he knelt in front of me and stopped my hands.

"You are not a game. What I feel for you is not a game. I'm frustrated with the waiting. With wanting you so much. Forgive me for speaking so bitterly. The vexation I feel has nothing to do with you and everything to do with anyone who is delaying the time when we can finally be together."

I frowned at him and smoothed my fingers along the light whiskers coating his jaw and cheeks. The same whiskers that had so nicely abraded my skin.

"Perhaps, it would be best if we did not see each other until such a time as we can truly be together."

His expression darkened, and I leaned forward to kiss him gently.

"You are not the only one to suffer when we meet like this," I added softly.

He sighed and rested his forehead against mine.

"As you wish."

CHAPTER 8

THE TIME I'D SPENT WITH KAVEN THE NIGHT BEFORE LAST CONSUMED ME, and I blindly stared at the small circle of light on the floor, dreading the conclusion to which I'd arrived. I needed to give myself to Kaven while attempting to win the heart of the Prince. It sounded like madness, but I knew it was the only way to ensure Maeve would not win.

I considered again Rose's words to me. *All curses have an end. Once the goal is met, the curse will break on its own.* By winning the Prince's heart, I felt certain the spell holding me silent would break. With the spell broken, I could condemn Maeve for her actions against the Crown. I only hoped that once the threat was removed, the Prince would understand my deception in marrying him as an impure woman and release me from our vows. If not, I would endure whatever punishment he saw fit, knowing that I'd kept the kingdom, and Kaven, safe.

If I couldn't win the Prince's heart, my impurity when taking Cecilia's place in the marriage bed would be noticed, and the whole deception would be exposed. It was a dangerous risk. Cecilia could lie and say I'd tricked my way into his bed, and I would be able to say nothing to implicate Maeve. That plan was, however, a last resort. I still hoped to end Maeve's attempt to gain access to the

Crown by exposing Cecilia and Porcia for what they really were. I wasn't quite sure how, though.

"Eloise, the seamstress is here for the final fittings," Maeve called to me from my doorway. "She's requested your assistance."

I sighed and descended the stairs.

"You've been unusually quiet," Maeve commented as she walked with me.

"Boredom and seclusion are dulling my conversation skills."

"Then it is a good thing you can assist today."

"It most certainly is, Mama."

Since keeping me locked in the attic, Maeve spent very little time with me. I'd thought, perhaps, that meant her focus had shifted to Cecilia...until she spoke.

"Your behavior is greatly improved, Eloise. I have a mind to request a dress be made for you for the final ball."

I looked up sharply to see if she was serious. If she meant for me to openly contend for the Prince's favor, it would make my effort to win him over that much harder because of Cecilia's inevitable interference.

"I will need to test your loyalty, of course."

My stomach tightened with fear.

"I would prefer to continue to support Cecilia in her endeavor to win the Prince's affection, Mama. She's worked so hard for this chance," I quickly said.

"Yet, she's continually failing where you succeeded with little effort. The mirror showed us that you would be his first choice. I think it's time to acknowledge that."

My mind raced, but I could say nothing in return as we entered the sitting room just then.

Cecilia stood upon the hemming stool. The angry light in her eyes made me wonder if she'd overheard Maeve's suggestion.

"Please repeat what you just told me," Cecilia said to Madame Blye, who kneeled at Cecilia's feet.

"The new proclamation announced at the festivities last night has set Towdown on its ear. I haven't slept since the night before last."

The dark circles under her eyes gave credence to her words.

"Get on with it," Cecilia said with cold impatience.

"Every maid—be she fair, in good standing with the Crown, or not—is invited to tonight's ball. It will be a crush." She waved at me. "Don't just stand there, girl. Help me with this hem. I have other dresses to alter yet this day."

I hurried forward and took the pin cushion from her. She had barely handed it off when she continued with her story.

"Every maid, and I mean each one, is preparing to make their way to the castle tonight. I can't imagine how the Royal family hopes to accommodate everyone. What with all the eligible men the Prince decreed would attend last week. Those who can't afford a new dress are handing over their coppers for pretty masks to match their best frocks."

She made quick work of the hemming while she spoke then stood to tug and smooth.

"Perfection," she announced. "Some of my best work. You'll even outshine my own gown tonight."

"You're going?" I couldn't hold back my surprise.

"I'm of an age and unmarried. Of course, I'm going."

"I meant no disrespect."

"Then perhaps you shouldn't speak."

Cecilia smirked at my reprimand, and Maeve said nothing.

Once Porcia's dress was fitted and the seamstress left, I spent the next several hours attending to Cecilia and Porcia. Scenting their baths after the maids hauled the water. Brushing out their hair before the fire. Helping tighten and tuck so they looked flawless in their gowns. Then, assisting Maeve with styling their hair.

"Look at these matching shoes," Cecilia said, preening in front of her mirror. "There are even more beads sewn to them than the last pair."

I dutifully looked at the shoes.

"They are lovely."

"Perhaps, once I'm queen," she said, "I'll give you this dress and these shoes."

"Thank you."

Maeve entered Cecilia's bedroom, her gaze pinning me.

"You prematurely thank your sister. She hasn't even managed to catch the Prince's notice yet."

Cecilia's smile vanished.

"I'm certain I will tonight."

"Tonight? When the room is sure to be crowded with five times as many maids as it was with the previous ball? You are neither simple nor a fool, so stop acting like one. I'm of a mind to have you strip from those clothes and give them to your sister."

I quickly stepped forward.

"No, Mama. Please."

Maeve looked at me, a pleased smile on her face.

"It is good of you to support your sister. Be sure you do not do so blindly."

"Yes, Mama."

She gave a stern look to Cecilia.

"Come along. It's time you prove yourself."

Maeve swept from the room. When I glanced at Cecilia, her face was flushed, and she stared at the vacant opening. If she'd wanted to flay and hang me for my rash words, I could only imagine what she wanted to do to her mother just then. I kept silent, too shrewd to draw attention to myself.

Without a glance my way, she left the room. I breathed a sigh of relief, and quietly followed. Maeve waited in the hall, the key in her hand.

"Goodnight, Mama," I said to her.

"Goodnight, my dear one. We will see the dressmaker tomorrow."

My chest tightened with worry, and I hurried upstairs. How did she believe she would control me if I—

"You cannot be serious," Cecilia's voice echoed through the far heat vent.

I moved closer on silent feet and caught the end of Maeve's response.

"—opportunity for what it is. The Prince is already fond of her. Let him think he's wedding her. However, it will be you speaking the vows."

"You still mean for me to be queen? Not Eloise?"

"Eloise will never be queen."

I waited for Cecilia to repeat her question about being queen, to demand the truth, but she remained quiet. Could she truly be that blind to her mother's true nature?

"We've delayed long enough. Come. We have a Prince to protect," Maeve said.

"How many maids from the mirror are still alive?" Cecilia asked.

"Three before you. Five after Porcia. But only two will attend."

"How do you know?"

"Six can no longer see."

The satisfaction in Maeve's words filled me with horror, and I covered my mouth with my hand.

"Thank you, Mama," Cecilia said happily.

I listened to their footsteps fade as I stood near the vent. She'd blinded girls just to prevent them from attending a ball? Who could be so cruel?

After the carriage left, I once again used the key to sneak from the house. This time, I had the mask tucked into my bodice. Although the creatures greeted me with their typical noise, I knew Kaven wouldn't be there to interrupt. Which was exactly why I'd waited until tonight when he too would be at the ball.

When I reached the clearing, I went to the tree and held up the mask.

"The mask alone will not help me win the Prince, for I cannot cross the estate's boundaries to attend the ball. Will you help me, please? I must win the Prince's affection. I must wed the Prince. There is no other way."

The white bird chirped from its perch, and the branches trembled, sending a shower of petals down around me. I looked up to see a shimmer of silvery blue light. It grew in shape and size, swirling and twirling in a sparkle of magnificent light until it solidified into cloth. The fabric fell in a tumble, but I recognized it for what it was. I caught the dress and held it up. The creation of magic and beauty glistened in the moonlight. Flower petals dotted the bodice and skirt. It was simple in its beauty and so much more.

I looked up at the tree.

"Will the dress help me leave?"

Again, the branches shook. This time, twin balls of light appeared. They glowed brighter than the dress had yet were much smaller. The bird sang a sweet song as the shape of two shoes gradually formed then fell to the ground with a thunk. I picked them up to see they were made of silver and glass. The slippers caught and reflected moonlight, no matter which way I turned them.

"These are beautiful, and I'm truly grateful. But, the mask didn't allow me to leave. Are you sure these will?"

The tree groaned, and a rending crack echoed through the clearing as more petals fell. Quickly, a split emerged down the middle of the beautiful tree. As I watched, each half bent further from the other. A shimmer began to grow in the space. Like Maeve's mirror, this shimmer started cloudy. But, unlike the mirror, the surface cleared into the image of a perfectly manicured garden.

A breeze swept over me, warm and scented with honeysuckle. I inhaled deeply and studied the image.

"It's not like the mirror at all, is it?" I said. "It's a means for me to leave the estate. The honeysuckle I smell is from that garden, isn't it?"

The bird stopped singing and tapped the wood several times before looking at me.

"I don't understand."

It tapped the wood again. Twelve times.

I still didn't understand but decided not to waste any more time. It was already well after eight.

Picking up the shoes, I slipped them onto my feet. Then, after a quick look around, I changed from my gown to the one given to me by the tree. Finally, I tied on my mask.

"How do I look?" I asked.

The bird sang loudly, and the song was echoed around me as dozens of birds flew from the trees. I wasn't afraid of them, but such a swarm flying straight at my head made me cringe and duck. However, they didn't do more than peck at my hair as they flew close for several moments then returned to their trees.

I reached up and touched my hair, feeling flower petals and ringlets held up by twigs and vines.

The bird tapped the wood again. Twelve times.

"You're right. There's no time to worry about hair. Thank you for your help. I love you, Mother."

I walked toward the shimmer and stepped between the split branches into a pool of water. Looking back, I saw the shimmer closing and felt a stab of worry. However, no pain or sickness affected me.

When the shimmer vanished, I saw nothing but the other side of the pond disappearing into the darkness. I looked around at the garden. Tall hedges blocked this part in. Music and the light of the castle beckoned ahead. I took a step forward and heard a splash. Lifting my skirts, I looked at light reflecting off my glass slippers as I walked on top of the water. Beneath me, I watched the fish swim.

"Remarkable," I said softly.

However, when I reached dry ground, trepidation filled my veins. The tree had given me what I needed to escape the estate without pain. But, could Maeve still sense me?

Knowing I didn't have time to ponder the consequences if she did, I hurried toward the castle, weaving my way out of the dark section of the garden to the light where several couples mingled. Steps led from the garden to the ballroom where strains of music floated on the air. Inside, I could see the swirling colors of numerous gowns.

"You are a vision," an unfamiliar voice said.

I turned to look at the masked man beside me. His jacket was clean but threadbare, and his mask a creation of common raven feathers. A group of gowned women stood in a cluster not far from where we stood and whispered while watching us.

"Please honor me with a dance," he said, earnestly. "I promised my mother I would dance at least once before returning home."

"Only once?"

He flushed slightly as the girls laughed, having heard my question, and I understood his dilemma.

"The honor is mine, good sir," I said with a curtsy. He bowed hastily and offered his arm. I spoke softly as we ascended the stairs.

"That should put them in their place," I said. "Ignore the ones who measure a man's value in the cut of his cloth. They will never make suitable wives. Instead, find one who will look you in the eye and measure your worth by your actions."

We stopped at the edge of the dance floor and faced each other.

"And how do you measure men?" he asked.

I smiled, knowing the answer he hoped for.

"I don't. Not yet. Perhaps I will when I'm looking for a husband."

His disappointment was brief as he offered me his hand then swept me onto the dance floor. After only a moment, he stepped on my foot and cringed. I laughed lightly.

"I assure you, my shoes are sturdy and you will cause me no harm."

"I'm sorry. I only learned the dance this week."

"Your mother?" I asked.

"Yes."

"She's a marvelous teacher if you're doing this well after so little time."

He chuckled.

"I've barely slept for all the dancing I've done. I'm not the only one. Most of my friends here are the same. Not all of them made the promise I did. Bast—beg your pardon—my friends are stuffing their faces at the table instead of dancing."

As I swept around the room, I noticed a few women watching us. Like my partner, they wore simpler clothes and masks.

"That might change when they see the success of your dancing."

"Do not call this a success too quickly. We should wait to see if you can walk after the song ends."

I laughed.

"So be it," I said.

When the song finished, I smiled at my partner and curtsied.

"I believe you will find another willing partner or two near the wall just to the side."

"Thank you, miss…"

"Since it's a masked ball, I'd prefer to keep my name to myself."

He chuckled, bowed, and left me just as the music started up again.

"You look in need of another partner," a familiar voice said.

Heart racing, I turned toward Kaven. But it wasn't the Kaven I knew. Gone were the cocky hat with the king's insignia and worn jacket. In their place, his light brown hair was combed neatly and glinted in the light of the candles almost as much as his golden jacket.

"May I have this dance?" he asked with a formal bow.

"You may," I answered with a curtsy.

A shiver stole through me the moment his hand closed over mine. He swept me up into a graceful dance that made my stomach swirl.

"You steal my breath with your beauty," he said softly.

"And you," I said, smoothing my hand over his shoulder. "A benefit of your occupation."

He grinned widely.

"It is indeed." His gaze swept over me again, lingering on my throat. "Where did you find such a dress? I don't think you'll escape a single man's notice in this."

"If I tell, then everyone will request the same dress. I'll keep the secret of its creation to myself."

He chuckled and pulled me a little closer. Still within propriety's bounds but close enough that I flushed. We danced in silence until the song ended.

"If you haven't yet presented yourself to the King, allow me to escort you." He offered his arm.

"I would rather not. I like the mystery of the mask as my family does not know I'm here. I've been strongly opposed to attending and would prefer to keep my presence a secret."

"Fear not. You are allowed to keep your mystery. It's a simple curtsy with no words exchanged."

I took his arm.

"Perhaps later. First, I need some refreshment."

As he led me from the floor, people parted way for him. I couldn't help but laugh lightly.

"What amuses you?" Kaven asked.

"The way people find value in the quality of your clothes. Do you think if they met you as I had, they would show the same deference?"

He studied those around us.

"Most assuredly not."

He glanced at me, his gaze warming.

"And that is precisely why I will not allow you to slip from my sight tonight."

"I don't understand."

"They do not only make way for me, princess."

My startled gaze swept the crowd again, and I saw he was correct. Many watched me just as closely as they watched Kaven. What a pair of imposters we were.

Leaving the ballroom, we found the adjoining room set with several long tables groaning under the weight of food the likes of which I'd never seen. People spoke in groups, sipping from flutes of wine or nibbling on tasty tidbits.

"What would you care to sample?" Kaven asked.

"That is an impossible decision. Everything looks delicious."

"Indeed."

The low rumble of his voice sent a wave of heat through me. When I looked up, I found his gaze on my lips.

"Focus," I said softly.

"I've never been more focused."

"On the food."

He sighed and looked at the offerings on the table before us. Without hesitation, he picked up a plate and placed a few options on it.

"Try these."

While I sampled the food, he led me around the room and pointed out the people he knew.

"That is Lord Greylin and his wife. Best to avoid her unless you want to spend the whole evening listening to the merits of their eldest daughter who is a year or two younger than you, I believe."

I chuckled as we moved throughout the room. He knew so much about the people of the court, and I tried to imagine what his life had been like in the shadow of the Prince. Had these people ever given Kaven the consideration he was due for being the intelligent man he was? Probably not. Like Maeve, they probably saw him as a tool. An instrument to be used to find a way into the Prince's inner circle. If the prince even had one.

When I finished my drink and food, Kaven surrendered the dishes to a passing servant and once again swept me onto the dance floor. While we danced, I watched for the Prince and Cecilia, determined to prevent her from cracking his amulet. But there wasn't any sign of either as Kaven and I remained for countless songs, reveling in each other's presence.

Though I enjoyed each moment I spent in his arms, I knew I could not stay there forever. Yet, the passage of time held no meaning until the large clock in the ballroom chimed the eleventh hour. The steady count of eleven rings reminded me of the bird's tapping.

"What has you frowning so?" Kaven asked.

"The hour. I didn't realize how late it had become."

He smiled slightly.

"I will take that as a compliment."

"Where is the Prince?" I asked. "The invitation we received said he was looking forward to seeing me. I should—"

"I'm sure he's occupied with some other maiden. There's no need for you to seek him out."

"You sound jealous."

"When have you ever sought me?" he asked, his gaze serious.

He *was* jealous. Yet, I could do nothing to assure him he had no need to feel so. The knowledge of what yet must be done broke my heart.

"To seek you out would only cause you anguish," I said.

"An anguish I would willingly endure for you."

CHAPTER 9

I WRENCHED AWAY FROM KAVEN'S HOLD, LEAVING HIM IN THE MIDDLE OF a dance. He had no idea of what he spoke, for when I sought him out to offer myself to him, I would just as quickly leave him to find the prince.

"Wait," Kaven called.

The crowd parted for me, making my escape from the dance easier. However, it also made it easier for Kaven to catch me by the arm. As he did so, I caught a familiar glimpse of dark hair. I quickly turned away from Porcia to face Kaven.

"Please do not make a scene," I said quietly.

"I wasn't the one to leave my partner in the middle of a dance."

He placed my hand on his arm and escorted me from the room.

"I'll take you to the Royal court where the King is receiving his guests. I'm sure you're likely to see the princely person you so desire there."

We walked in silence through the long, crowded halls. The abundance of people in attendance astounded me. As did the number of guards present. Many of the halls leading from the main one were blocked by the sword wielding men.

"Is this because of me?" I asked. "The additional men and the women?"

"Yes."

He still sounded annoyed.

"I'm sorry."

"Don't be. You were right. Excluding those of common background wasn't likely to keep the Royal family safer. Instead, it was building resentment. Opening the doors to all will garner goodwill."

"And the guards. Will they be able to keep the King and his son safe?"

"No one is safe when there is a caster using magic in secret to cause harm to the kingdom. We have all suffered in some way and will continue to do so until we have her in irons."

"Her?"

He flashed a smile at me.

"Though there have been male casters, the strongest have always been women. One caster, a woman, claimed it was because your gender is more closely tied to the moon and nature."

"Do you believe her?"

He shrugged.

"I've seen the way the woods come alive when you're walking. Who am I to deny there is a connection?"

"But I don't have magic."

"I would argue that you do."

"And that would likely see me hanged or in irons. Hold your infatuated tongue."

He laughed, drawing the attention of the nearby guests. Thankfully, he veered to lead us through two vast and ornately carved doors and out of their view. Concern regarding what might have been overheard faded as I saw what lay ahead.

At the other end of the grand room, a raised dais made it possible for all present to see the King in his splendor, and for our sovereign to view all who attended him. And there were many. The back half of the room was filled with people who watched the proceedings in the front half.

A row of guards stood at the base of the dais, facing the

gathering. Before them, a beautifully gowned maiden stepped forward from a short line of girls and curtsied to the King. He nodded, a man to his right welcomed the girl to the ball, and the girl moved to join another far longer line near a side door that was open to the night air.

There, the Prince danced with a pretty maid not dressed as finely as the others, but based on the glow tinting her cheeks, just as pleased to be in his presence. Not far away from the pair, a small set of musicians played a lovely melody.

While the maid looked entranced, the Prince looked bored.

"He looks less than pleased with his current partner," I said.

"He would rather not have to dance at all," Kaven said with a chuckle, guiding me to the line before the King. "I will meet you at the back of the room after your curtsy." He left my side then, and I felt a stab of guilt at his assumption I would forgo the dance with the Prince.

Glancing back at his retreating form, I caught sight of a woman watching me closely from within the depths of the crowd near the entrance. Her dark eyes swept over me, and I forced myself to calmly turn around and face the King. Although much of her face was hidden by an elaborate mask, I recognized Maeve's dress easily enough. If she was here, Cecilia couldn't be far away.

I surveyed the long line of maids waiting to dance with the Prince and saw Cecilia near the front. I would need to watch her closely. If she managed to crack the amulet, I would need to find a way to warn the Prince before she had a chance to cast a spell.

The line shuffled forward until there was no one else before me. I advanced toward the King and performed a curtsy that would have made my mother proud.

The King's voice rang out, creating a startled hush in the room.

"Rise and let me look at you."

I straightened, heart hammering in fear, and met the King's gaze. If he recognized me, all would be at risk. The urge to look at Cecilia almost overwhelmed me. However, one did not look away from the King. I withstood his scrutiny with as much courage as I possessed until his gaze swept the rest of the room, landing on the Prince approaching to my right.

His grey eyes lit with recognition behind his golden mask.

"Your beauty has silenced the room," he said with a deep bow. "Will you honor me with a dance?"

I looked to the King, who nodded before his gaze swept the room again. Facing the Prince, I accepted the hand he extended and let him sweep me into an extravagant dance that moved so quickly the skirts of my gown flared out. The purpose behind the dance was clear when he pulled me against his chest to steady me.

In my peripheral, I caught sight of Kaven moving through the crowd.

"You are bold," I said softly.

"I am allowed."

"Hardly."

With each turn he brought us closer to the guarded balcony until we danced on the terrace. The doors closed behind us, cutting off the music. He stopped abruptly and grinned at me.

"He will want my head for stealing you away. But can he blame me? I'm awestruck by what a decent dress can do for a maiden's appearance. You are a breathtaking sight," he said. "I can see why Kaven fancies you so."

I pulled myself from his arms and scowled.

"You are purposely provoking him?"

"Never. It is my duty to dance with every maid set before me."

"I wasn't set before you."

"Are you saying you didn't want to dance with me?"

The ass had me cornered. If I denied it, he would send me away and face Cecilia yet this eve. If I acknowledged my desire to dance with him, I would be painted a tease in both the Prince's and Kaven's eyes.

"As we've already danced, there is no point in answering that," I said.

He chuckled.

"Kaven warned me that you are prickly."

"Prickly?" I repeated, offended.

The Prince's grin widened, and I knew then that he was baiting me.

"Must you toy with everyone? You claim Kaven as a friend and disrespect his feelings. You claim to care about your kingdom's welfare but can't be bothered to bestow a kind smile to the maiden before me. Was the cut of her cloth not to your standards?" I demanded, flicking the golden cravat tied at his neck.

"You lecture me not to judge others based on their appearance, yet you do the same."

I opened my mouth to hotly deny his words, and he laughed.

"You truly do not see it? Here I stand, a man you've met thrice, a man you barely know. Based on what action do you believe me to be shallow enough to value a person on their dress?"

"Based on your own words. You just told me my dress made me more appealing."

His smile vanished.

"I've been taught from an early age to play a game. I was told it would keep me safe. My remark on your gown was nothing more than a compliment. My distance from my previous partner was nothing more than an attempt to protect her. There is an evil lurking in this kingdom, and it means to have the throne. Everything I do and say is to prevent that from happening, even bruising the feelings of my closest friend."

We stared at each other for a long moment, and I realized we were more alike than I could have ever imagined.

"Why did you bring me out here, then?"

"Curiosity. I wanted to know if you were the same type of woman as your mother. The type to give up her life to save a kingdom."

"And?"

"I rather hope you are not. I believe life would be dull without you in it." He gestured to the garden. "Would you care to walk?"

I nodded and set my hand on his arm to steady myself as we

descended to the well-kept grounds. The scent of honeysuckle teased my nose.

"The gardens are beautiful," I said. "Do you find time to enjoy them?"

"Rarely. Duty has kept me away far too long. And now that I'm here, duty consumes my time. Tell me about yourself."

"What would you like to know?"

"What brings you joy? Sorrow? Anger?"

I breathed deeply, considering his questions. The spell would prevent me from speaking the full truth, but I was determined to speak what truth I could.

"Very little has brought me joy since my mother's death."

"What brought you joy before her death?"

I thought back and smiled.

"Going to town with my sister and stirring up trouble. Reading. My father's returns because he always managed to bring the most marvelous gifts. Walking in the woods. However, losing those I love has brought a sorrow so deep it hurts to breathe at times. There are days it's difficult to remember what once brought me joy. Mostly, I feel anger."

He didn't ask why but walked beside me in silence through the maze of shrubs for a time.

"What brings you joy?" I asked.

"Being home. Seeing my father."

"And sorrow?"

He glanced at me.

"Those I've lost."

I recalled the wife who had looked so much like me and nodded in understanding.

"And anger?"

"The lies and games that are a part of my life every day." The words were laced with the emotion of which he spoke.

I stopped walking and put my hand upon his arm.

"I'm sorry for judging you so harshly. That day in the dungeon…"

"It was an unfortunate way to meet. I had no choice but to question you to the degree that I did. I had to ensure the kingdom's safety. After all, a pretty face does not mean innocence."

"No, it does not." I thought of the women in my home as I agreed with his assessment.

"Will you dine with me tomorrow evening?" he asked suddenly.

"You honor me with the invitation—"

"Speak freely," he said. "Tell me your true thoughts of dining with me."

"My stepmother will not permit it without her as a chaperone."

He smiled.

"That's to be expected. But what are your thoughts? Do you want to dine with me?"

I smiled, my heart aching.

"I do."

He exhaled slowly in return and looked at the castle.

"The hour grows late. I should return you to the court before the ball ends."

"When does it end?"

"At the stroke of midnight. Father insisted, saying that only in silence can he sleep."

Again I thought of the bird's twelve taps.

"I cannot return. Is there a side gate by which I can leave?" I asked, looking around.

"I assure you that Kaven will not be angry that you spent time with me. There is no need to run." His eyes twinkled with amusement.

"I do not seek to avoid Kaven but my family. I begged my stepmother to not force my attendance. She doesn't know I'm here."

His grey eyes studied me for a long moment through the mask.

"Do you think she would disapprove of the time you spent with me?"

"No. She would heartily approve, but she would want to know who I danced with before you."

"Ah. You do not want to admit you danced with Kaven."

"She's made her opposition to him clear," I said.

"I see." He veered to the left. "There is a gate just here. I will only allow you to slip away if you promise to attend the next ball."

"I cannot make such a promise. But I swear I will try to attend."

He smiled, kissed the back of my hand, and nodded to the guard to open the gate for me.

As soon as I was free from the garden, I lifted my skirts and ran. Thankfully, the streets were empty, the majority of Towdown's populace either abed or at the ball. I had made it a fair distance when the castle's clock sounded the first strike of the twelfth hour. My dress began to shimmer. I looked down in astonishment at the outline of my legs through the material.

"No," I groaned, understanding what was happening. The magic was fading.

I ran faster, weaving through streets in my desperation to reach the outskirts of town. I'd barely made it when the final bell rang and the last wisps of magic that made up my dress, shoes, and mask disappeared to leave me in my underclothes.

Whatever magic the tree had used to allow me to escape the estate seemed to hold though because I felt no illness.

Ducking into the woods, I continued on, grateful I hadn't stripped bare to wear the gown. As I moved, I plucked at my hair, removing the birds' work.

A warm tingle ran under my skin and faded the moment I crossed over the boundary of the estate's land, and I knew the spell allowing me to leave had been spent. I thought of the Prince's invitation and knew the tree's magic hadn't been wasted.

The house was quiet with a candle burning in the window near the door. Knowing I didn't have much time before Maeve returned, I circled the house, retrieved my clothes, then snuck inside.

I'd only just locked myself back in the attic when I heard the carriage roll into the yard. I hurried to wash my muddied feet then sat in the chair by the top of the stairs so I could hear what Cecilia and Porcia had to say as they undressed.

The horses nickered outside, and the carriage moved again.

However, the house remained quiet. Without warning, the door to the attic opened. Surprise drove me to my feet and gave Maeve pause.

"You're awake," she said. With a lit candle guiding her, she climbed the steps and looked around the open space suspiciously.

"Why are you still awake, Eloise?"

My mind raced, and I almost smiled as I found the perfect reason.

"I went to sleep during the last ball. You woke me and said you expected me awake and waiting after the next one."

"You remembered when I did not."

I faked my confusion.

"If you are not here for my attendance, why did you come? Not that I ever mind your attention."

"It's no longer important. As long as you're awake, come downstairs with me."

I followed her to the sitting room where Cecilia paced and Porcia sat, watching her sister warily.

"We must find out who she is," Cecilia said as soon as we entered.

"Calm yourself," Maeve said, blowing out the candle. It wasn't needed in the sitting room. Not only were the lamps lit, but the glow of the fire was strong enough to see the heavy makeup coating Maeve's face. She noticed my stare.

"A necessary measure," she said. "While I wash, Cecilia and Porcia will tell you what happened."

She left the room as I sat beside Porcia. She studied me closely then looked at Cecilia.

"I'm not sure who she is. But she danced with only two men in the main ballroom. First, some boy with a homespun coat and self-made mask, then with a man as devastatingly handsome as the Prince."

"Why are you concerned with this girl?" I asked.

"She captured the Prince's interest so thoroughly that he did not dance with another maiden." At my lack of reaction, she stomped her foot. "He did not dance with me, Eloise. I stood in that line for hours because he allowed the common trash in an hour before the ball was due to start. Hours wasted. When the King asked to look upon her, I wish she would have removed her mask so we might know her face."

Cecilia ripped her own mask from her face and crossed the room to throw it in the fire.

"The Prince and the King weren't the only ones infatuated with her," Porcia said softly. "Every man there watched her."

"Perhaps it was the mystery of her identity," I said.

Cecilia made a derisive sound.

"We were all wearing masks, Eloise. The rest of us didn't garner the same attention as she did."

"Describe her to me," I said. "Was she fair or dark? Did any features that you could see stand out to you?"

"Yes," she said brightening. "You know the people here."

"Not well," I said quickly. "Mother kept us to the estate unless escorted by—"

I couldn't say the names of those now dead.

"It matters not if you know the girl," Maeve said as she re-entered the room. "We will find her and remove her. There is time until the next ball. And since Cecilia never danced with the Prince, there's no need for you to pretend you were there." She sat beside me with a weary sigh. "It's a pity we no longer have my mirror. We would already know the face of our adversary."

"I'm so sorry, Mama," I said quickly.

She patted my hand.

"I do not hold you to blame."

Cecilia flinched and averted her gaze.

"We've all had a long night. It's time for us to retire." She turned to look at me. "Send Heather and Catherine to us. They can assist... with our dresses."

I stood and nodded, not fooled for a moment as to her true intentions.

CHAPTER 10

DRESSED FOR THE DAY, I WENT TO SIT AT MY TABLE BUT PAUSED AT THE sight of the open attic door. I listened, but the house was quiet. I cautiously descended, wondering what Maeve's new game might be. Did she simply expect me to prepare breakfast now that she no longer had servants to do so? Trying not to think of the fate of the maids, I made my way to the kitchen. When I entered the room, I froze in shock at the sight of Catherine and Heather preparing the morning meal.

Staring at the pair, I tried to see if Maeve had done something to them.

"Good morning, miss," Catherine said in a chipper voice.

"We'll have your breakfast ready in just a moment," Heather added. "If you would like to sit in the dining room, I'll bring your morning tea straight away."

I turned and left the kitchen without acknowledging them. I met Maeve as she was just entering the dining room.

"Good. I'm glad you're joining us again," she said.

"As am I. Why, though?"

"You said boredom and seclusion were robbing you of your social skills. That is not something I can allow. You're needed."

Cecilia entered just then.

"Needed for what, Mama?" she asked sharply.

Maeve turned her head slowly, cowing her daughter with a single, cold look.

"Do not mistake your place."

"I'm sorry, Mama." Cecilia sat quickly. Though she tried to appear contrite, the flush of anger stealing into her cheeks, along with her tight jaw, contradicted her effort.

Porcia entered the room last while tying off the end of her braid.

"Good morning, Mama," she said, taking the seat beside Cecilia.

The normalcy of the scene cut me deeply. How dim was the memory of the days when Kellen sat across from me at the table in the kitchen? Of her serious face as I caused some sort of mischief? I hadn't forgotten her, but neither had I thought of her in far too long.

The dining room door swung open, and Catherine entered with a tea set while Heather followed with a tray laden with bowls. They served us quickly and quietly but with good cheer.

"Thank you," Maeve said. "I will call if we need anything else." She waited until they withdrew before addressing us.

"We have one more chance. One more ball in which to impress the Prince. How do you plan to ensure he will choose you as his bride?" She pointedly looked at Cecilia.

"I will not wait for the ball. Each day, from now until the ball, I will invent reasons to go to the estate."

"That is bold and dangerous," Maeve said.

"And we are running out of time."

"The reasons need to be infallible."

"The patch of briarberries is on his land. I will take a basket today to collect anything that remains. When I'm done, I will go to his kitchen to offer them a portion, which is only right now that they are in residence and the bounty is from his land."

"Good." Maeve looked at Porcia next. "How do you plan to ensure he will choose you as his bride?"

Porcia's eyes widened in surprise, and she looked at Cecilia.

"The time for putting all our dreams on only one of you is past," Maeve said coldly. "Do not look at Cecilia to prevent our plans from falling to ruin. What do you plan to do to keep that from happening?"

"I will—"

The dining room door opened.

"Excuse me, mistress. A man just delivered this to me while I was outside."

She handed a letter to Maeve and quickly withdrew.

Maeve broke the King's seal. As she read the note, a smile spread.

"It would seem fortune agrees with Cecilia's plan to find reason to visit the Prince in his home. We've been invited to dinner again."

Porcia visibly sagged in relief.

NERVES TWISTED my stomach as the carriage bumped along the short expanse of road to the Royal Retreat. Surely the Prince would remember that my family knew nothing of my attendance at the ball and would stay silent about the matter. If not, I would have greater concerns than that of Maeve's desire to use me to lure the Prince if Cecilia failed tonight.

I stared out the window, my thoughts in a tangle along with my nerves. There was no escape for me. If Cecilia did succeed in gaining the Prince's interest tonight, I would still need to prevent the marriage from happening by forcing his attentions to me. There was a vast difference between throwing myself at the Prince of my own volition or under Maeve's command, though. Once Maeve committed to using me in full, I felt certain she would cast further spells to control me. My freedoms to thwart her were already far too limited, and I refused to become more of a puppet.

The carriage rolled to a stop, and the door opened. Kaven, backlit and larger than life, waited for us. My heart gave a painful beat at the sight of him.

"Good evening, ladies," he greeted. "His Majesty is waiting for you."

As I was the last to enter, he walked beside me. He didn't speak, but I felt his gaze on me. When I glanced up at him, there was no playful wink. Instead, a look filled with yearning stole my breath.

"I'm delighted you were able to join me tonight," the Prince said the moment we entered his sitting room. Once again, he struck a practiced pose by the fireplace. Though I liked him a little better after our conversation the night before, he still annoyed me.

We curtsied and waited for his invitation to sit in his presence. As soon as we did, Kaven left to fetch our drinks.

The Prince caught my gaze and grinned slightly. Panic laced its way up my throat, constricting my ability to breathe.

"I must say," he said, looking at Cecilia then Porcia, "I was very disappointed not to see any of you at last night's dance."

"We were there, Your Majesty." Cecilia graced him with a beatific smile. "I was standing in line to dance with you. Unfortunately, another swept you away for the rest of the evening. I can't say I recognized her. Who was she?"

"A maiden of mystery, it would seem," he said. "Hopefully, we can all learn more about her at the next ball."

"You wish to see her again?" I asked. "Why?"

"She intrigued me."

"In what way?"

He smiled slightly.

"Her need for mystery."

I wanted to kick him.

"That's no basis for true interest, only mild curiosity."

"Surely you didn't invite us here to speak of another woman," Cecilia said.

He turned toward her and gave an acknowledging bow.

"I assuredly did not. While the balls are my father's idea of a social gathering, I find they leave little room for conversation, which I crave."

After Kaven returned with our drinks, I sipped mine while listening to Cecilia deftly guide the conversation between her and the Prince. Whenever he politely tried to include Porcia or me, she answered on our behalves with a laugh. I glanced at Maeve, who watched it all with an impassivity I knew belied what she truly felt.

"Dinner awaits your command," Kaven said when Cecilia paused to breathe.

"Very good. Will you escort Mistress Cartwright while I escort Porcia?"

Kaven gave a bow and went to Maeve to offer his arm. If she didn't like it, she gave no hint. With a polite smile, she took his arm and let him lead her from the dining room, following Porcia and the Prince. Cecilia looked positively livid as she glared after her sister.

"Why her?" she hissed at me.

"He's being polite and rotating who he escorts," I said. "Or perhaps he noted the way you were cutting everyone else out of the conversation."

She turned her glare on me, and I shrugged.

"If you would rather I tell you idle puffery to the truth, I will gladly do so. You only need to state your preference."

She took a calming breath, smoothed her skirt, and gestured toward the dining room.

"Come, sister. Let us escort one another."

As I walked beside her, I noted her tight jaw and flushed neck. As with Maeve, I walked a fine line with Cecilia. If Maeve didn't decide to openly pit us against one another, I hoped that playing Cecilia's supporter would keep her from targeting me as her competition.

Kaven held out a chair for me beside Maeve's, and another servant helped Cecilia with hers. She seemed mollified by the seating arrangement which placed her to the Prince's right and Maeve to the Prince's left.

"Porcia mentioned there was quite a crush in the main ballroom last night," Cecilia said as the first course was served. "Barely enough room to move. Isn't that right, sister?"

Porcia quickly recovered from her surprise.

"That's right. The number in attendance was astounding. People were making use of your gardens to escape the crowd and provide more room for the dancers."

"Were you able to find suitable partners among the masked throng?" the Prince asked her, making me bristle.

"Yes, Your Majesty. A mask cannot hide one's wealth or standing with the Crown."

His gaze shifted to me, a hint of knowing amusement glinting in the depths of his eyes.

"And what did you think of the ball?" he asked.

My heart gave a violent lurch.

"I did not attend, Your Highness."

He frowned.

"Did you not receive my invitation specifically requesting your presence?"

"We did, Your Grace," Maeve said smoothly. "While we regret Eloise's absence last eve, we hope she will be able to attend the final ball."

He nodded to Maeve and set his soup aside only half eaten. Kaven quickly removed the dish. I wondered if the Prince's attitude frustrated Kaven as much as it did me.

"Will there be a theme for the final ball?" Cecilia asked, seizing the lull in conversation.

"I hadn't yet considered one. Do you have suggestions?"

"Something more intimate would give you an opportunity for conversation such as this," she said. "Perhaps a ball where attendees must offer a gold coin tribute to the Crown. The coins collected could then be used to improve the lives of those unable to attend."

I wondered if she could even hear herself. The servants cleared the rest of the first course and prepared for the next as the Prince answered.

"A kind gesture."

If he truly thought so, then I had never met two people more matched. If not for Cecilia's tendency to destroy, maim, and kill, I would leave the Prince to her greedy aspirations.

"While I appreciate the prospect of a smaller crowd, limiting our guest list, now, would only cause ill will among the people of Towdown and the Kingdom of Drisdall. I fear my need for quiet conversation will need to wait until I'm wed."

"Or until you invite us to dine with you again," Porcia said.

He chuckled.

"Indeed."

"Perhaps a color-themed ball, then. The ladies could dress in red and the men in royal blue."

"A fascinating idea. However, I did enjoy the mystery of the masks."

Cecilia's smile became a bit more brittle.

"And I wouldn't have this ball become a financial burden on anyone but my father," he said. "With so many already having masks, it seems the wisest choice. Plus, there is a certain level of equality when those with a less discerning eye cannot gauge the social standing of their partner."

For a moment, the conversation came to a halt.

"Eloise told us of your lovely trophy room, Your Majesty," Maeve said, breaking the uncomfortable silence. "Perhaps, when you're finished, you would be so kind as to show it to Cecilia."

He looked at Cecilia.

"Dead things interest you?"

I almost choked on my mouthful of tender meat.

"What interests you, interests me, Your Grace," Cecilia said skillfully.

"Then I would be delighted to escort you. But only if Eloise and Kaven follow us as chaperones."

Cecilia glanced at me, her smile never faltering. But, I could see the resentment because I was once again being included.

I nodded my agreement, only after Maeve gave her consent. When I glanced at Kaven, he watched me intently, not even trying to hide the attention he bestowed me. Shifting my gaze to my plate, I took another bite. I needed to remain focused on the Prince and Cecilia, not the memory of the time I'd spent dancing within Kaven's embrace. Yet, that was exactly where my mind dwelled. I recalled each touch and each look until my skin heated. Surely, he wouldn't say or do anything in Cecilia's presence that would give away our time together.

Too nervous to eat more, I set my fork aside, a signal that I was finished. As if the Prince had been waiting for me, he put his aside as well then stood.

"Shall we?" he asked, offering his arm to Cecilia.

Something brushed against my right arm, and I looked up to find Kaven standing beside me.

"Miss Cartwright?" he said formally.

I placed my hand in his and stood. His fingers caressed my skin as he set my hand on his arm. Steeling myself against Kaven, I looked at Maeve who watched us closely. This time, I was far too wise to show any preference for Kaven.

Giving her a small nod, I focused on Cecilia and the Prince as they left the room ahead of us. No matter the discomfort caused by the spell binding me to Maeve's proximity, I couldn't let the Prince and Cecilia out of my sight.

Whereas Kaven and I walked with a respectable distance between us, Cecilia leaned toward the Prince, letting his arm brush against her side.

"Do you plan to stay at the Retreat long?" Cecilia asked as they entered the adjoining room.

"Only until a bride is announced," he said. "My father will require us to live at the palace from then until the vows are spoken. After that, there is a tour of the kingdom to present the new princess."

"That sounds lovely," she said. "Will the King tour with the bride and groom?"

"That has not yet been decided." They slowed their pace to walk among the creatures. I was so focused on them that Kaven's abrupt halt made me stumble.

His eyes twinkled with amusement.

"There's no need to follow them further," he said. "We can watch from here."

Even as he said that, the pair disappeared behind the largest bear I'd ever seen. I was about to protest that we needed to follow when I heard Cecilia's next question.

"What is this?" A moment of silence followed. "Please tell me it is not a cameo of your late wife. I cannot hope to win your affection from a ghost."

Those words were spoken with sad acceptance, but I knew better.

Kaven's gaze turned serious, and he led me forward. We rounded the bear to find Cecilia touching the prince's chest, her fingers circling a spot near the end of his cravat.

"It is not a cameo," he said, taking her hand. "And my affections are not held by a ghost of the past."

"Such news relieves me," Cecilia said with a smile. "If not a cameo, what is it? It has an odd shape. Might you show me?"

He chuckled and began loosening his cravat. I didn't think. Instead, I purposely stumbled into Kaven hard enough to send him into the bear. The next few seconds slowed. The Prince glanced at the unstable bear and Kaven. Kaven reached out to prevent the creature's fall. Cecilia, her gaze fixed on the stone barely peeking from the Prince's loosened clothing, clasped a hunting mallet from a nearby display.

Without thought of consequence, I threw myself into the Prince, sending us both away from the rocking bear. He landed with a grunt, and my forehead connected with his chin as I toppled onto him.

"Forgive me, Your Majesty," I said, already scrambling off.

He blinked up at me with a widening grin as I offered him a hand.

"You continue to surprise me, Eloise. And no forgiveness is needed for such a selfless rescue." He rose to his feet without aid and righted his clothing. I breathed easier when the amulet was safely tucked away once more.

The Prince took my hand and bowed low over it. The feel of his lips on my skin sent a tingle of fear through me. What had I done?

"I will never forget this moment," he said.

He released me and looked over my right shoulder.

"Shall we continue our tour?"

I moved to the side, too afraid to look at Cecilia.

"Of course, Your Grace," she answered smoothly, stepping forward to take his arm once more. "Are you well? The fall didn't hurt you, did it?"

"No. I'm well. Your sister truly acted heroically."

As they moved on, I looked up at Kaven. He studied me carefully.

"What was that all about?" he asked softly.

"A clumsy attempt to right a possible wrong," I said. "My stumble sent you into the bear, and it looked like it might topple onto the Prince."

"And me. Or did you forget I was here."

The words cut deeply.

"I didn't forget. However, the King is less likely to imprison me if injury befalls you. I'm truly sorry, Kaven."

He didn't offer his arm again as he went to follow the Prince and Cecilia. Heart breaking, I followed in Kaven's wake until the couple completed their tour and returned to the dining room.

"Your daughters are lovely," the Prince said with a smile at Maeve. "Would you care for an after-dinner libation before you depart?"

"Please," Cecilia all but purred, not yet relinquishing his arm.

We moved to the sitting room where the Prince gracefully detached Cecilia and went to his favorite place before the fire.

"Mistress Cartwright, I would like the honor of walking Eloise home," he said without preamble.

Maeve's brows rose in shock. My stomach pitched, and I glanced at Cecilia. Cold hatred burned in her eyes. Porcia looked stunned.

"Chaperoned, of course," the Prince assured. "I will have one of my staff follow us."

I looked at Maeve, who watched the Prince closely. That she was pleased with the offer was evident in the ever so slight curving of her lips.

"While I would never deny the Crown Prince anything, as a Mother, I must also protect my daughter. A walk alone after dark is hardly suitable for an unmarried miss, even with a chaperone. I must ask what your intentions are."

"A show of gratitude, only. There was a mishap in the trophy room, and Eloise showed great care for my safety. I wish to repay that care with a few moments of my time. That is all."

"But of course, then," Maeve said. "I will hold you to your promise of a chaperone and trust you won't linger in the woods. It pains me to let my daughters out of my sight. This world can be a terrible place without the protection of a parent."

Understanding lit. Maeve would not free me from my curse for this walk. The moment she left me, I would feel the sickness of separation until I reached the estate's boundary.

Kaven arrived with the tray of drinks.

"Kaven, fetch Mrs. Wallace. I would like her to accompany me when I escort Eloise home."

"Here," Cecilia said standing. "Allow me to serve in your place as the hour grows late."

Kaven reluctantly handed her the tray and left the room. Cecilia served the Prince first, saving the last cup for herself.

"A toast to friendships," Cecilia said, raising her glass. "May ours continue to grow." She stared into the Prince's eyes as she took a sip.

"Indeed," he said, lifting the cup to his lips.

While Cecilia guided the conversation, I drank deeply of the sweet wine in hopes it would help dull the sickness to come. A pleasant numbness spread throughout my body before I emptied the glass.

An elderly woman entered the room. Her white hair was piled on top of her head in a long braid and a cloak was pulled over her shoulders. A pang of guilt struck me as her eyes swept the room. Walking through the woods was probably the last thing she wanted to do this evening.

"Ah, Mrs. Wallace," the Prince said. "Thank you for joining us."

"Of course, Your Majesty."

He drank the remainder of his wine and set the cup to the side.

"Come girls," Maeve said, standing. She curtsied to the Prince. "I will await my daughter at home."

He nodded and turned to me as Maeve and the others left the room.

"A few quiet moments at last," he said. He held out his hand to me then cringed. "If you will excuse me for a moment." He hurried from the room, leaving me alone with Mrs. Wallace.

"Hello," I said with a smile I didn't feel. My insides were already starting to twist violently. "I'm Eloise. It's nice to meet you, Mrs. Wallace."

"And you too, dear. The Prince seems quite taken with you."

"I'm nothing more than a curiosity to him."

"Oh? Why do you think that?"

"I'm told my mother once saved the kingdom."

"Indeed, she did. You look like her. Her hair was dark, though, and her skin paler."

"You knew her?"

"I'm old enough to know most people," she said with a smile.

Kaven strode into the room before I could ask her anything further.

"Mrs. Wallace, the Prince requests your presence."

Her brow rose.

"I know. That is why I'm here, silly boy."

Kaven grinned.

"It would seem the Prince's dinner isn't agreeing with him."

"I see." She looked at me. "Excuse me, Miss Eloise. It was a pleasure to meet you."

As soon as she left the room, my insides gave a violent pull.

"I must go," I said. "Please make my excuses."

I hurried to leave the room before I vomited on the floor, but Kaven grabbed my arm as I passed him.

"I can't allow you to walk home alone."

CHAPTER 11

"Is this the leisurely pace you would have set with the Prince?" Kaven asked.

His long legs had no trouble keeping up with me.

"You needn't sound so jealous," I said, too miserable to censor my words. "He is the one who wanted to walk me home. One does not deny the Prince what he wants."

"You're right. Most people wouldn't deny him. You are not most people. If you didn't want to walk with him, you would have refused."

He grabbed my arm again to stop me. My stomach heaved with the need to get to Maeve, and I kicked him in the shin. He yelped as he released me, and I picked up my skirts to run, no longer caring about appearances.

Surely Maeve had to know this would happen. What had she been thinking? The Prince would have been put out if I emptied my stomach in front of him.

Kaven caught up with me the moment I crossed over the estate's boundary and everything eased inside of me. This time, when he grabbed my arm, I stopped.

"Why did you kick me?" he demanded.

"Because you're being a grabby ass," I said, pulling my arm from his. "The Prince asked to walk me home, not lay me on the grass and have his way with me. Unlike you, who has taken uncountable liberties with me, the Prince's behavior has been above reproach. Now tell me truly, would he have done something to me on this walk home?"

"It's not what he might have done but what you might have allowed," Kaven said.

I slapped him hard, the crack ringing through the trees.

"I have never allowed any man what I've allowed you. And I regret—"

Eyes blazing, he gripped my shoulders and kissed me with a fury that left my lips bruised and body aching. After a moment, his hold softened. His hands smoothed down my arms, and I lost myself to the sweep of his tongue against mine.

Kaven was many things to me, but most of all, he was my anchor. The one bit of reality I could trust to be true to me with his feelings and his words. He was angry and hurt because he thought he might be losing me to the Prince. And he was right. I hated everything in that moment. Mostly myself. I didn't want to break Kaven or his dream of a future with me.

I poured the desperation and need I felt into the kiss, and when he finally pulled away, we were both gasping for air.

"I'm sorry," he whispered.

"Don't," I said, placing my finger over his lips. I needed him. Not just in that moment but in my life in any capacity. I stood on my toes to kiss his chin and jaw. Then, I reclaimed his lips for a bittersweet kiss.

"Will you wait here for me?" I asked softly. "I must return to the house so no one comes looking for me. But will you wait for me to return once everyone is abed?"

"Yes." The word was hoarse and full of need.

I kissed him once more then fled.

Inside the house, candles lit the entry, and the glow of the fire from the sitting room let me know that Maeve waited. However, she wasn't alone. Cecilia paced before the fireplace while Porcia sat nearby. All three looked at me the moment I entered.

"Traitor," Cecilia hissed.

"What were you thinking?" I countered, knowing I walked a dangerous line. "That he would just stand there as you clubbed his amulet? You risked us all with your rashness."

Her eyes widened, and she glanced at Maeve, who stilled.

"What happened?" Maeve asked with deadly calm.

"A small lapse in judgement, Mama," I said. "I'm sure it won't happen again."

Her gaze narrowed and pinned Cecilia.

"You were going to attempt to crack the amulet? While he was wearing it?"

"If it was cracked, we wouldn't need to worry about which of us held his interest," Cecilia said quickly. "I could cast a—"

Maeve stood and stalked toward her daughter. Porcia winced as her mother struck her sister hard. Cecilia didn't make a noise though I knew it had to hurt.

Maeve turned to me.

"Does he suspect?"

"No. I pushed him out of the way under the ruse that I was saving him."

Maeve exhaled slowly.

"And the walk home? Were you able to make any progress toward capturing his interest?"

"Even if he hadn't fallen ill and been unable to walk me, it would have been impossible to do more than run home because of the spell," I said.

Her gaze darkened again.

"Are you reproaching me?"

"No, Mama. I'm explaining the reason behind my failure. I cannot hope to compete with Cecilia or Porcia when it comes to the Prince."

She studied me thoughtfully.

"But only because of the restrictions. He's very drawn to you with little effort from yourself."

I said nothing.

"Tomorrow, you and I will go to town. We will see if you're worthy of my trust. Perhaps then, you will be a true contender."

Cecilia hid her fisted hands in her skirts as her mother turned to her.

"I find it odd that the Prince fell ill just after we left and was unable to escort your sister as he planned. Do you have anything to say on the matter?"

"I intend for him to wed me."

"I see. And the illness?"

"A simple powder in his drink to loosen his bowels. Nothing magic. Only an undetectable compound of herbs."

"As I said this morning, I care not which of you weds him—only that one of you does. Do not let your jealousy and ambitions prevent us from attaining our goal, Cecilia. When one of you succeeds, we will all be rewarded. There will be no more mistakes from you. You will not improvise. If you find yourself unable to follow my command precisely as it's given, I have no need of you. Do you understand?"

Cecilia's angry flush drained from her face, leaving only a ghostly paleness.

"Yes, Mama."

Maeve looked at the three of us.

"You've taxed me. I will speak with you all again in the morning."

She swept from the room; and Porcia, still seated, looked from Cecilia to me.

"Leave," Cecilia said, and Porcia quickly fled.

Cecilia closed the distance between us. Though I knew she couldn't hurt me physically, she and Maeve had taught me there were worse forms of punishment.

"I will share a bit of advice with you, dear sister. Daughters are easily replaced. Never forget that."

With those ominous words spoken, she left. I waited until her door closed to go to my room. There, I listened at the vents, waiting for the house to settle. My mind whirled with too many thoughts. What would Maeve's test of loyalty entail, and did I want to pass it? If I passed Maeve's test tomorrow, she would surely push me to win the Prince on her behalf. If I didn't pass it, she would still use me to bed the Prince. I was running out of time. Relief coursed through me that I'd asked Kaven to wait.

When I knew everyone slept, I snuck from the house with a quilt under my arm. Fear and nerves for what was to come made me jumpy until I reached the clearing and saw Kaven waiting there. He turned at my approach. Seeing him, his strength, his certainty, helped calm me.

With soft amusement, he watched me spread the quilt on the ground. That amusement faded as I sat and began loosening my gown.

"What are you doing?"

I paused, trying to read him. He'd made his interest and intent quite plain. He wanted me. Was he, like me, ignorant as to how specifically the deed should be done?

"Undressing. I thought it was required for sex. If my skirts don't get in the way, my underthings certainly will."

His gaze heated, following the movement of my fingers as I plucked at the cords for my bodice. He joined me on the quilt and caught my hands in his.

"I want you, Eloise. But not here. Not like this."

I looked at him, trying not to let my frustration show. Neither of us had the luxury of waiting for a ceremony that might never happen. If my fate was to sacrifice myself to the Prince, then who I gave my innocence to would be of my own choosing.

"I don't know my future. I don't know if I can give you what you want. But, this? This I can give. This is my choice. What's yours?"

Anger clouded his eyes.

"There is time. No one else will touch you until we are ready."

"How can you be sure?" I demanded. "You cannot possibly know my mind or anyone else's to foresee the future. How do you know I'm not already promised to another? Maeve alluded as much."

His expression darkened further.

"You are mine."

He gripped the back of my head and brought his lips to mine in a kiss filled with passion, anguish, and need. I held him just as tightly, feeling the same.

This time, it was his fingers tugging at the cords of my clothes as his heated kisses trailed from my mouth to my breasts. He plucked at one peak while he suckled the other. I shivered at the sensation and threaded my fingers through his hair, delighted in the feel of his tongue on my skin as he lowered me to the quilt. A heat began in my breast and spread to my middle. The warmth grew to an ache that pulsed with each suckle of his hot mouth.

His sudden abandonment of my flesh drew a soft mewl of denial from my lips, and I looked up at him.

"You rob me of all thought and blind me to consequence." His palm covered my exposed breast. "I am yours, Eloise. For all time. Tell me you are mine."

"I am yours tonight if you'll have me," I said.

He made an angry sound and dipped his head to claim the other breast. I gasped and arched into his mouth. The rub of his whiskers as he nuzzled me added to the tingle of pleasure, and I held him close, desperate for him to continue.

Something tugged at my skirt a moment before the fingers of his free hand glided up my legs. He suckled harder, distracting me so thoroughly, I didn't at first notice the tug on my underthings.

He lifted his head just as the material loosened.

"Tell me you'll wait for me. Wait for our vows," he said.

"She is set against our union," I said, speaking of Maeve. "My fate may not be my own to promise."

Anger clouded his expression.

"You would wed another after laying with me."

"I would give a piece of myself to you so you would always remember the love I bear for you, no matter what direction life takes me."

"You are the most stubborn—"

Lifting my mouth to his, I silenced his protest with a stroke of my tongue. A growl of frustration reverberated from him. The kiss shifted from my lead to his as he pushed my skirts higher. His fingers tugged harder at my underthings, exposing me to the night air. He broke away, panting. Instead of again questioning my choice, he met my gaze as his fingers brushed over my netherhair. I swallowed hard, trying not to let my fear of the unknown show.

He shifted his weight, nudging my legs open. I gasped and closed my eyes as his fingers feathered lower, parting my folds. A rush of heat swathed me as he gently explored until he found a spot that sent a rush of pleasure coursing through me. There, he stroked over my flesh for several moments.

I panted and spread my legs further to give him better access. He dipped his head to kiss my breast then nibbled his way up my throat. As he did so, his finger strokes dipped lower and lower until he teased my opening.

He brushed his lips over mine then lifted his head to look at me.

"I love you, Eloise," he said softly. Then his finger delved inside of me.

Any discomfort at the invasion quickly melted into pleasure as he slowly retreated and advanced. My legs moved of their own accord, twitching and straightening. A need built inside of me, growing in intensity.

His mouth closed over my breast once again. This time, I felt the scrape of his teeth on my flesh. A tingle jolted from my chest to between my legs, intensifying the pleasure of his fingers. Small sounds escaped me, and I gripped his shoulders.

He pulled away abruptly, leaving me exposed to the night air. I opened my eyes to see him loosening his pants. For one brief, horrible moment, I saw Hugh.

Clenching my eyes closed, I banished the thought. This was Kaven. He was safe. He would carefully take from me what I would entrust to no other.

"Eloise?" Kaven asked softly, his hand cupping my face. "Look at me."

When I opened my eyes again, Kaven was looking down at me with concern.

"It's not too late to change your mind."

"About what? Loving you? Never."

He smiled slightly and kissed me softly. His fingers returned to work their magic and reignited the needful flames that licked at me from inside. My mind emptied of thought as I allowed myself to feel every heated stroke. Every heated kiss. I began arching my hips in time with his touch. His mouth returned to my breast, and the sensation sent me into a spiral of pleasure I'd never thought possible. I cried out as it pulsed through me, clenching around Kaven's hand. He didn't stop moving his fingers until he'd wrung every last bit of wonder from me.

"That is just the beginning," he promised, settling his weight over me. His fingers were replaced with something thicker and warmer.

Dazed, I looked up into his eyes as he eased into me. His shaft stretched me with stinging discomfort.

"Wait," I gasped.

He set his glistening forehead against mine.

"Discomfort will give way to what you've just experienced. I swear to you."

I nodded, and he withdrew only to ease into me once more. It felt less invasive the second time. He didn't press further though I knew he wasn't fully seated. He stroked me, letting me feel the returning pleasure. I rocked up to meet him and a lance of pain pierced me. I cried out sharply, and he muted the sound with a hard kiss.

After a moment, the pain faded and his tongue distracted me. He broke away to kiss my jaw and my eyelids.

"I'm sorry for that," he breathed. "I wasn't expecting you to move."

"I wouldn't have if I'd known it would hurt."

"It won't again. Not like that."

As if to prove his words, he withdrew and slowly entered me once more. It felt odd, but not unpleasant. He reached between us, his fingers finding that spot that sent so much pleasure through me and rocked into me again. Before long, I was gasping and arching into each thrust. There was no room for his hand between us as his hips met mine again and again with a force that returned me to that moment of anticipation. This time, when the pleasure erupted, I knew what to expect and let myself tumble headlong into it.

Kaven's pace increased before he thrust deeply and stilled. His cock twitched within me, sending echoes of pleasure pulsing through my core. A low groan erupted from him a moment before his lips claimed mine. The kiss was sweet and tender and perfect.

Our breathing calmed, and I relished the feel of him on me even if he was still fully clothed. It was better that way. The image of his body wouldn't haunt me when I lay with the Prince.

"I swear I will not let you go," Kaven said as if hearing my thoughts. "You are mine, now and always."

I tilted my head back and looked up at him, my heart shattering.

"For now, you must," I said lightly. "I need to return before anyone discovers me missing."

He looked about to object. I placed a soft kiss upon his lips to prevent him from saying anything further. The time for words between us was finished. All that remained were actions. And, I knew that no words could amend those once done.

"Fine. I will release you for now. But know that I do not like doing so."

He rolled off of me and watched me stand, his gaze caressing my exposed breasts.

"I will never tire of looking at you," he said.

I tightened my bodice and hurried to leave before my despair showed.

It HURT TO SIT. I hadn't counted on that when joining Maeve and my stepsisters for breakfast. I hadn't counted on it aching every time I took a step, either. Had I not seen his manhood and known it to be a part of his flesh, I would have questioned what Kaven bludgeoned my insides with the night before.

Was that the way of life, then? No pleasure without pain? No happiness without misery?

A sigh escaped me.

"Is something amiss?" Maeve asked.

"No, Mama. Nothing amiss. Just a pinch of melancholy."

She patted my hand.

"Something easily remedied then. After you complete your task, we can visit the market and shop for whatever you'd like."

Cecilia's eyes stayed fixed on her bowl where she idly stirred her oats.

"Porcia, while we're out, I would like you to go berry picking and visit the Retreat as Cecilia proposed. Until the Prince chooses, you must all try to capture his attention."

"Yes, Mama," Porcia said.

"As soon as your sister is done playing with her food, we can leave," Maeve said, once again facing me. Cecilia immediately stopped what she was doing.

"I apologize, Mama. My appetite is absent this morning."

"Very well." Maeve stood. "Seth has everything prepared and the carriage waiting for us."

I dutifully followed, keeping any twinges of discomfort from showing on my face. A task that became more difficult during the jostling carriage ride to town. It wasn't until the carriage stopped that I saw we'd almost reached the docks.

Trepidation filled me as I looked out the window. We weren't far from where I'd woken the last time I'd been to town...when I'd walked the streets naked.

The carriage door opened, and Seth was there to offer Maeve a hand.

"Thank you," she said graciously, stepping down. "Remember, a woman in labor is the reason you will give. Nothing more. Keep everyone away."

The trepidation only grew stronger as Maeve led Cecilia and me to a rundown building and opened the door. There was nothing but darkness ahead when we stepped inside. The door shut behind us with a snick.

"Stay where you are."

A moment later, a spark ignited in the abyss, and flames slowly grew.

"Come along." She led us through a barren room that faintly smelled of musty old hay and dirt. A noise came from the doorway ahead.

My steps slowed, and Cecilia, who followed me, nudged me forward.

"Where is your courage, sister?" she asked softly.

"In the carriage. I should probably fetch it."

She snorted and prodded me forward toward Maeve, who stood just inside the room.

When I entered, I immediately saw the cause for the noise. A hooded man was bound to a chair, the only furniture in the room.

Fear coiled in my gut.

"Who is that?" I asked softly.

Maeve walked to him and yanked back the hood. Alfie blinked against the lamp's light.

"Why?" I asked.

"He did recognize you."

His gaze locked onto mine. I could see the terror there.

"He won't say anything," I said.

"I know." Maeve smoothed a hand over his hair. "I've already completed that spell, a mercy to repay him for the kindness he showed you. Much safer than cutting out his tongue."

He swallowed hard and paled. I felt like doing the same but knew better than to show what I felt. Instead, I met Maeve's gaze.

"Since he was so willing to help you once, I thought he would be the perfect candidate to help me test your loyalty."

"How?" I asked.

"Take his eyes."

CHAPTER 12

Horror should have filled me at her suggestion. That it didn't showed how much I'd already endured. Instead, I felt fear for Alfie. That fear fed the well of my anger.

"You can cut his eyes out with this," Maeve said, withdrawing a knife from her pocket and offering it to me. The lamp's light glinted off the lethal edge of the blade.

Cecilia pushed me toward her.

"Find your courage, sister. He's nothing to you. Do this and ensure your place."

Alfie paled.

"I can't."

Maeve's hand remained outstretched as she considered me.

"Can't means you're physically unable. I see nothing preventing you from doing as I asked. You have full use of your hands. You can hold yourself upright. You can see and move." She sighed. "You can, Eloise. I will tell you again. Cut out his eyes. Now, choose your response wisely."

"I refuse to intentionally harm another."

Maeve lowered the knife.

"I see. But, where was that refusal when you stabbed Hugh in the eye with the poker? I quite liked him. His death was a waste."

"It was. And though, through defense of my person, he was killed by my hand, I do not carry the weight of blame for his death."

She arched a brow at me.

"I see."

"Stupid," Cecilia said softly behind me.

Maeve's necklace began to glow.

"You will learn your place," she said a moment before I sank into the nothingness of oblivion.

I TURNED my head and vomited while still laying down. This time, I didn't wonder what was happening to me. I knew. Maeve had spelled me to sleep then left me. I spat and breathed through my nose, inhaling the same musty smell as before. She hadn't moved me this time.

Did she honestly think another naked walk through town would make me more compliant? There was nothing she could do to me that would ever force my hand enough to cut out—

"'Bout time you're awake," a rough voice said from nearby.

I jerked upright, the movement sending my stomach into another fit. The man laughed as I heaved.

"She said you would be sick and easy to handle."

Fear skittered its way up my spine as I remembered her last promise of punishment to have men hold me down and defile me in ways that would haunt my dreams until my death.

"Nothing I could catch, though," he continued. "She promised me that."

Fingers tangled into my hair and wrenched me upright.

"Let's have a look at you."

Anchored in place by my hair, I couldn't escape his other hand, which gripped my chin.

"You're a beauty. Ain't no dirt ever going to hide that."

Trying to focus, I blinked against the dim light of the lamp. The craggy face of an almost bald man swam into view. Yellow teeth gleamed as he grinned at me. His gaze swept over my face then lower. He made a satisfied sound.

"Ain't seen flesh so firm in far too many years."

He released my chin and covered one breast with his hand. Weakly, I smacked his touch away. He laughed.

"You're a mite thing. Barely any meat to you and no fight. Not worth my time, really."

My panic hitched higher. I struggled to push back the sickness enough to focus on protecting myself. Placing my hand in the middle of his stained shirt, I pushed with all my might.

He laughed again.

"You have more fight than I thought. Best we get this done then. She paid me well."

He released my hair, and I collapsed to the ground once more, my hand landing in my own upheaval. I gagged and tried to move away. The man's hand closed around my bare hip.

"None of that now."

I kicked out at him. His chuckle echoed in the room as he caught my ankle and pulled on my leg, dragging me.

"What a fine sight your cunny is. Are you pure? I ain't ever bedded one still with her maidenhead. In my youth, I didn't want the fumbling or crying. Just a good, wet fuck. Virgins never give you that. At least, that's what my pa told me."

All the while he spoke, he tugged me across the floor, bit by bit. I clawed at the dirt, trying to dig in and stop him. But I couldn't. I tried kicking and jerking my leg from his firm grip, but nothing worked.

"Here we are," he said. "I can't stand while I do this anymore. My knees can hold a fierce grudge. You hold still while I get ready."

He released me, and I rolled myself to my belly before hefting my weight up. The room swam dizzily. Nearby, I spotted a chair. One of the back rails was missing, and blood smeared the seat. Swallowing thickly, I turned my head away and saw the old man. He picked up something from a small table and turned toward me. The knife glinted in the light.

"No," I said, shuffling back.

"The time for fighting is past. Sit still and let me have my way with you."

He grabbed my hair and sat in the chair, yanking me toward his crotch. The odor of sweat and feces clogged my nose. I closed my eyes, sobbing silently, and struggled to pull away. He held firm. A weird noise almost escaped my notice in my efforts to free myself, but the feather soft tickle on my arm had me turning my head and opening my eyes.

"Be still," he said with another tug.

I blinked at the golden thread on my bicep, trying to understand its significance as that same odd noise repeated itself. My gut clenched, and the need to gag almost overwhelmed me as a hank of my hair drifted to the ground before my eyes. He sliced thrice more before I realized what he was doing. I began my struggles anew.

"I almost nicked you, twit. Stop moving, or you'll be as bloody as the boy that were here."

His words stilled me. I cared nothing about my own bleeding but that of Alfie.

"They killed him?" I slurred.

"Ain't my place to say."

With a vengeance, he went at my hair. Too grief-numb to fight, I stayed still between his legs.

"There now. You're done. Off you go. She told me to tell you she's waiting."

He grasped me under my arms and hefted me to my feet, taking the opportunity to paw at my breasts again. I swatted away from his hold and, ignoring his chuckle, stumbled toward the door.

The sunlight nearly blinded me when I stepped outside. The sound of water and the smell of salt cleansed the scent of the old man from my nose. I breathed in deeply, fighting the sickness trying to consume me. The pull to return to Maeve drove me to move.

"Who-who!" a man yelled. "A fine piece of ass if I've ever seen one. I'll give you four copper to suck my cock."

I didn't turn to look but shuffled forward.

"Don't be like that," the same voice yelled.

"I'll give you a half silver if you let me stick my cock anywhere I want," another voice called. Raucous laughter followed.

I stopped moving and turned toward the ships where men were lined up on the decks.

"I have the pox," I yelled, trying not to heave, "and a rash that burns fiercely each time my bowels let loose, which is far too often for my comfort. I have no coin to see a doctor, but if I suck all of your cocks, surely, I'll earn enough. When I'm cured, my cunny will be open for business again."

Several of the men made faces and turned away without a word. Those who still lingered no longer smiled.

"Come now," I cajoled. "My mouth is clean." My stomach chose that moment to revolt, and I heaved into the dirt.

"Get gone, wretch!" one of the men yelled.

I smiled and turned away from their accusatory gazes. How often men only praised external beauty when they thought they could benefit from it. Shallow creatures. No worse than women, though, I supposed. My sex judged just as harshly with their gossip.

A lump of cloth huddled near the next building slowed my steps. Something about it seemed familiar. Placing my hand on the wall for support, I blinked at the trousers. I'd seen them before. Hadn't I?

The soft sound of sobbing reached my ears.

"Are you all right?" I managed to ask.

The lump cringed then straightened, turning his head toward me. A bloody bandage covered his eyes, but I still recognized Alfie.

"Leave me, I beg you. Pay me no kindness."

My stomach heaved again, but there was nothing left in me. When I looked up, I caught sight of Cecilia standing at the end of the lane. She watched me with a twisted smile.

"I will show you no kindness today," I said softly. "But soon."

He started sobbing again and leaned his head against the wall.

Straightening away, I started forward once more. Once I was past the boy, Cecilia disappeared from sight. I followed the pull from the dock and through several narrow streets before it began to ease. At the next corner, I turned and the sickness vanished completely. The carriage waited only a few steps away, along with five buckets of water and Cecilia with a cloth and my dress.

"Hello, sister," she said with a twisted smile.

"Hello." I picked up a bucket and poured it over my head then rinsed my mouth from the second one before dumping that over me as well. When I reached for the cloth, she pulled it away.

"All of them. I pulled them from the well, just now, for you."

I emptied them in quick succession as she watched me.

"Your act of defiance changed nothing," she said. "The boy still lost his sight but by my hand. When will you learn and start listening to Mama."

Without answering, I took the cloth from her hand and rubbed it over my face and head.

"Your hair is quite lovely, sister."

"Thank you. I will be sure to refer you to the barber."

She shook her head, tossed my dress at me, and opened the carriage door.

I got in naked and tugged the dress on as Maeve watched.

"Based on your impertinent answers, I can see you have learned nothing."

"But I have, Mama."

"And what is that?" she asked.

"Cecilia is just like you."

LOCKED AWAY IN THE ATTIC, I cleaned myself as best as I could, using the washbasins Porcia had filled. I was grateful they were continuing to keep the staff safe from my vile influence. After today, I didn't think I could bear to witness anyone else's suffering. As it was, my anger had loosened my tongue far too much in front of Cecilia and Maeve.

I studied my reflection in the mirror and ran my hand over my coarsely cropped hair. Too short to lay flat, it stuck out in any direction it saw fit. Losing my hair angered me but not out of some misguided vanity. How would I now attend the ball without being recognized? And if I couldn't attend, how would I stop Maeve from getting everything she wanted?

Turning from the mirror, I dressed and went to the window. Birds flitted about in the branches, their merry songs barely reaching my ears. I wished to walk among the trees. To feel the sun on my face. To forget the bloody blindfold covering Alfie's eyes. Most of all, I wanted to cry. But, I refused to do it here where someone might witness my sorrow. Instead of doing any of that, I stared at the woods I loved and lost hours to memories of better times.

The door opened, pulling me from my reverie. When I turned, my knees ached, and I thought of the old man with a shudder. It could have been worse. He could have tried to use me. Never had I been more glad to have given myself to Kaven than the moment I heard the man compliment my firm flesh.

Footsteps echoed as someone ascended into my domain. Maeve looked me over when she reached the top of the stairs then set the tray she carried on the table.

I didn't immediately spit out the false thanks she expected, and her expression hardened.

"Where are my manners," I said with a smile. "They seem to have escaped me with all these wondrous thoughts floating in my head. Thank you for feeding me, Mama."

Too much sarcasm laced my words, and her resulting smile should have struck fear in me. I was too blindly angry, though.

"I see."

"I'm glad someone still does."

I turned toward the window.

"You test me?"

Glancing at her, I snorted.

"What will you do? Gouge out my eyes? Drain me of my essence? Walk me naked through the streets? Have men use me and touch me? Cut the hair from my head?" My voice rose with each question. "Do it all! I care not. You've already killed me; my body is only too stupid to die."

The anger immediately left her gaze.

"Then this tray was an unnecessary gesture. Enjoy your solitude."

She took the tray with her as she departed.

I cursed my temper. Though I wasn't the least bit hungry now, I would be tomorrow. And I doubted I would see another tray for some time.

Something crashed from below, and I smiled, hoping it was Maeve. It wasn't right that I should be the only one seething. My smile faded as I realized people tended to die when she was angry. I hurried toward the door, unsure what I could do or say to fix the mess I'd made.

The soft murmur of voices from the vents stopped me.

"…said to her."

I moved closer to Cecilia's vent.

"I don't know. But I've never seen her so angry."

"I didn't know she had the strength to overturn the table."

"You should never doubt Mama's capabilities in anything. Perhaps Eloise did something when Mama told her about the dinner."

I frowned and looked toward the attic door. Maeve had never brought me a tray before. It was always Cecilia or Porcia. How could I have so foolishly not recognized there might have been another reason for her visit?

"Do you think the Prince will turn us away if she's not with us?"

"Don't be silly. If he wanted to dine with Eloise alone, that's what he would have requested."

"I don't know…Kaven's expression was odd when Mama told him Eloise wasn't feeling well and might not be able to attend. I wouldn't be shocked if we receive another message cancelling the invitation before the night is over."

"Nonsense. I can feel tomorrow night will be my opportunity, Porcia. I will beguile the Prince with my womanly charm without Eloise there to distract him."

I quietly moved away from the vent and looked out the window at the fading light. Nothing moved out there. How long ago had Kaven called? I hoped that he didn't believe he'd somehow hurt me with last night's activities. Or worse, that I was avoiding him.

Tired from standing and thinking, I lay on my bed. I didn't bother to light a candle. Staring at the darkness above me, I listened to the bird song fade to be replaced with the occasional hoot of an owl. Below, the house quieted.

Though my day had been long and taxing, I couldn't sleep. In the silence, my mind kept returning to Alfie and dwelled on what I should have tried in order to prevent his fate. Deep down, I knew there was nothing. It had been a test of loyalty, and he had been the only one who knew me. Everyone else was already dead. Except Kellen. Maybe.

Rather than wait for the next tragedy to strike, I rose and padded across the floor in my bare feet. There was only one course of action that was open to me at this point. I needed to go to the tree. I hesitated and looked at the small patch of the outside world visible through the window. Although the hour was late, and this household was abed, would Kaven, too, be sleeping? Or was he wandering the woods in the hopes that I would meet him as I had the night before?

My hand lifted to touch my shorn hair. What excuse could I give for how I looked if he did happen upon me? Perhaps I should wait until tomorrow evening when—I shook my head. Waiting meant that Cecilia would have the Prince alone. He would be unprotected, and so would the kingdom.

Resolved, I snuck through the house and let myself outside. The cool ground anchored me to the moment. For now, I was free to do as I pleased. Free to feel the night wind on my face. Free to ask for help.

The bird in the clearing chirped a quiet greeting.

"Please stay silent for me," I said softly. "I cannot be discovered tonight."

The bird chirped again but did not sing.

I went to stand before the tree and looked up into the blossom laden branches.

"My life is changing faster than I think I can bear. Yet, I know I will. The suffering I've witnessed in Towdown cannot be allowed to continue. Help me to stop it. Please. Help me understand what I must do."

The little bird chirped twice, and the branches shook, raining down petals upon my head. Before me, a light flashed amidst the blossoms. As I watched, a bud rapidly grew on the branch nearest me until one by one the petals of the bloom opened to reveal a silver ring.

I took the ring and turned it in the moonlight. An inlaid golden crown stood out against the grey. My heart clenched, and I looked at the bird.

"I'm meant to marry him, aren't I?"

In response, the small creature took flight and landed on my finger. It sang a soft song filled with sorrow.

A lone tear trailed down my cheek.

"So be it," I whispered.

CHAPTER 13

WHEN THE ROOM BEGAN TO LIGHTEN, I SAT UP WITH A WEARY SIGH AND removed the chamber pot from under my bed. I hadn't lied the day before when I told Maeve she'd killed me. There was nothing left in me for her to hurt or take. My last hidden dream of a life with Kaven was gone, killed by the tree's gift of a groom's ring fit only for a prince.

The numbness and anger that consumed me at all that Maeve had taken or forced upon me left only a mere echo of the girl I used to be.

When I finished with the chamber pot, I went to the washbasin and froze at the sight of my hair in the mirror. Last night when I'd returned from my time with the tree, I'd hidden the ring behind the chimney and washed before changing into my nightgown. My hair had been the same jagged cropping as it had before. Since then, it had grown several inches, almost covering my ears.

I looked horrible, but I grinned. Maeve would be irate when she saw this. She would wonder who had helped me, again, and likely have a fit. I looked around the attic. There was nothing else to find here save the ring, and I'd hidden that higher than I could reach without the assistance of a chair.

Even the thought of waking again in town, naked and sick,

couldn't rob me of my humor as I dressed for the day and went to sit at the table. I didn't expect them to feed me this morning and wondered how much longer my hair would grow by the time they did.

Happiness, the true kind that cannot be contained, often made people do strange things. I was no exception. I threw open my window.

"Tis a fine morning, is it not?" I called softly to the birds. I grinned and started singing. It wasn't loud, just a happy song from my childhood. Something Kellen and I would sing while playing in the puddles after a rain. The birds joined me, creating a melody that shook the trees.

From the vents, I heard Cecilia yell for the birds to quiet. Suitably entertained for the morning, I took the book of fairytales and sat in a comfortable chair.

Porcia arrived with a tray near midday. I looked up from my story as she set it on the table.

"Thank you, sister. I'm quite famished."

Ignoring her wide-eyed stare, I pulled the tray close and scooped up a bite of oats.

"You had best fetch her quickly," I said. "She'll want to know." Putting the bite into my mouth, I groaned.

She pivoted and jogged down the stairs. The door closed but no key turned in the lock. I chuckled and began eating faster. It was probably foolish to fill my stomach, given Maeve's new favorite form of punishments, but I was too hungry to care. I'd barely finished my bowl when the door opened below. Pushing the tray aside, I waited. Maeve came alone, her gaze sweeping the room.

"No one came here," I said. "I went to bed shorn and woke like this. Well, not like this. I think it's grown more since waking." I touched the ends that were closer to my jawline than the bottom of my ear now.

She gazed at me thoughtfully.

"Yet, this is not the work of the protection spell as the hair was cut free from your head."

Her gaze swept the room again.

"How do you explain this then?"

"I cannot." For I couldn't. I didn't know how my hair was growing. However, I did have my suspicions. The tree. But I wasn't sure how.

"Very well. What has been undone can be done again."

She left the attic and returned a short while later with Seth and the shears Judith had kept in the kitchen. He approached with a mean look in his eyes.

"I won't struggle against this," I said looking at her. "He doesn't need to hold me."

"I believe he does."

He grabbed my arm and jerked me upright only to throw me toward a chair. I tumbled into it, falling to the floor. His weight landed on top of me.

"Where do you want me to hold her?" he asked.

"Anywhere you would like." She gripped my hair.

His weight shifted, and I felt his hand slide up my leg. The first snick of the shears echoed as I fought to free myself from Seth's hold.

"Foul retch, get off me!"

The speed with which Maeve wielded the shears was the only thing that stopped Seth from reaching my underthings.

"Release her," she said after the final snip.

He immediately obeyed, and I scrambled to my feet. Seth stood far too close, grinning smugly. I stomped on his foot then lifted a knee the moment he widened his stance. He fell to the floor with a grunt and looked up at Maeve as an unnatural flush slowly crept up his face.

I turned to her too, bracing myself for some form of retribution. Instead of directing any anger at me, Maeve arched a brow at Seth.

"I will not reprimand Eloise for that, and neither will you. Next time, take less joy in your task, and stand at a safer distance when finished. And never forget who holds your loyalty. You are mine to use as I see fit."

He nodded and slowly got to his feet. Seth wasn't as fully under her thrall as Hugh had been, for the look he gave me as he left was filled with promised retribution.

The door had hardly been closed for more than a few minutes after their departure when I heard Cecilia's screech of outrage from the vents.

"Cast a truth spell on her."

The sound of Maeve's voice was easily recognizable even if her words were not. I hurried toward the vent, light on my feet.

"I apologize, Mother. I certainly didn't mean for my suggestion to sound like an order. The idea of cancelling our appearance tonight has me distraught. Without her there, this could be my chance to lure the Prince."

"Without her there, this could be your chance to ruin everything as well. I wasn't blind to Kaven's reaction when I said she wouldn't be attending. Rather than provoke suspicion, it's wisest to send our regrets and state we're all feeling ill. It might also help pass any budding suspicion after your foolish sleight of hand with his wine."

I smiled and went back to my book.

MAEVE WAS RUNNING out of excuses, patience, and time, which made her dangerously unpredictable. I sat at the breakfast table, my gaze fixed on the stew before me as I listened to her fingers thrum over the wooden surface.

"We cannot postpone again, Mama," Porcia said softly.

"Do you think I don't know this?"

I could feel her gaze on me.

"I cannot decide if it's the Prince's fascination with you or the servant's that keeps him returning," she said.

My heart ached at the memory of Kaven's face as he'd looked upon me only moments ago. There'd been a desperate need in his eyes that hadn't escaped Maeve's notice. I couldn't begin to suppose what he might have been thinking of my avoidance of him since our time in the woods five nights ago.

"I suppose you think I should be grateful your hair has grown back," Maeve said. The edge to her words kept me silent.

Each morning, she cut my hair only for it to grow back to its old length even faster. This morning, it had only taken two hours.

"I know someone is helping you. These little games will do nothing to stop me from reclaiming what is rightfully mine." She pressed her hands flat against the table. "And when I have what I want, you will be truly punished for every moment of defiance you have shown me."

She hit the table hard.

"Look at me when I'm speaking to you."

I immediately met her gaze. From my peripheral, I could see Porcia's pale and terrified face and Cecilia's carefully blank one.

"I will flay the skin from you piece by piece, starting at your feet. Tell me who is helping you," she demanded.

I thought of Rose and opened my mouth. No sound emerged.

Maeve's face turned red, and I thought she would strike out at Cecilia, who was closest. Instead, she took a few calming breaths.

"Very well. We have a ball to prepare for. Cecilia, have the maids prepare the bath water. Porcia, send Seth to me. I will respond to the Prince that we will dine with him tomorrow. Eloise, back to your room. I will let you out tomorrow morning if one of your sisters is successful tonight. If not, I will ensure you succeed where they failed."

"Yes, Mama," all three of us said at the same time.

I fled quickly, escaping to my sanctuary. My shorn hair from this morning lay scattered near the table. Since that first morning, she hadn't used Seth to hold me down. And I hadn't fought her. There was no point when we both knew it would only grow back.

Going to my bed, I idled away the hours and listened to Cecilia and Porcia prepare for the ball.

There were no giggles and excited chatter this time. Only quiet whispers, which I couldn't even understand when standing directly above the vent.

I was impatient for them to leave so I could go to the tree to change. I needed to arrive at the ball first. My urgency, however, was torn between finding Kaven to apologize and approaching the Prince. How did one ask for a prince's hand in marriage? I wiped my suddenly sweaty palms on my gown and began pacing the floor.

When the hour arrived for my sisters to depart, my door opened once more, and Maeve ascended. In her hand, she held the shears. She looked at the hair I'd piled together from all of the shearings.

"You were restless today. I could hear you walking back and forth. To keep you busy, you will cut your hair tonight each time it grows back. I will check on the size of the pile when I return."

Her words didn't fool me. I knew the task had nothing to do with my restlessness and everything to do with her suspicion I was somehow gaining outside help.

With a racing pulse, I took the shears from her and said a weak, "Yes, Mama."

She nodded and left me, locking the door behind her.

I looked down at the shears and debated cutting away my hair now. If I did, it wouldn't regrow quickly enough to disguise me at the ball. If I didn't... I looked at the small mound of hair by the window. Given the hour and how quickly it had grown this morning, I wouldn't have a big enough pile by the time she returned. She would either believe I had disobeyed or that I had left to find help again. Both would lead to a worse fate if I failed to gain the Prince's affection tonight.

So, I couldn't fail.

Tossing the shears aside, I fetched the key and made my way downstairs. A soft noise from the dining room sent my heart racing. I looked around in panic and hurried to the wall near the dining room door.

"You want to go in the mistress's room or the older miss's?" one of the maids asked.

"Neither. Both make me feel as if I'm being watched."

"It's probably the one in the attic, peering through the floorboards."

They both left the dining room, focused on their conversation, and made their way to the stairs. I held my breath until they reached the landing and turned their backs to me. Heart racing, I slipped into the dining room and hurried for the kitchen door. Only when I reached the trees, could I draw a decent breath again.

Picking up my skirts, I ran along the path until I arrived in the clearing. The tree started to shiver as soon as I approached. I stood under its limbs as petals rained down on me and a light grew brightly in its branches.

When the dress fell, over half the branches were barren. After the shoes and mask fell, very little remained. With the dress bundled in my arms, I leaned my forehead against the trunk as it began to split.

"For all that you've already done and given me, I am forever grateful. Let us both hope tonight will be the end of this, and I will do what must be done."

The bird began to tap the wood impatiently, this time stopping at eleven.

I stepped back and began to strip from my gown.

"I will leave before the bells toll for the eleventh hour."

Standing in my shift, I shook out the dress and stared in awe at what the tree had created for me. The material seemed spun of silver and stitched with threads of gold. The colors glinted and played off one another in the moonlight. Hurrying, I dressed and marveled at the full skirt and elegant design that left much of my back exposed. The shoes, like the dress, were of both silver and gold. But, it was the mask that really drew my attention. Golden feathers swept out from the side, drawing one's attention to the diminutive golden beak that covered the top portion of my nose.

Silence filled the clearing, and I looked up to see the glimmer of the garden between its two halves. I quickly tied the mask in place and stepped through the shimmer. The soft strands of music greeted me on the other side.

Sparing no time to marvel at the beauty around me, I hastened from the water and across the lawn. People mingled just on the other side of the hedges and upon the steps. A few paused in the middle of whatever they were saying to stare at my sudden appearance. I didn't stop or offer any more than a hasty smile.

Couples were already dancing, but the ballroom didn't seem as crowded as it had been the time before. I'd almost made it across the space when an arm caught me around the waist.

"End my torment and dance with me," Kaven said in my ear.

I froze, heart beating hard as my chest tightened. I wanted nothing more than to idle away the hours in his arms. Closing my eyes against the pain, I shook my head.

"I cannot. I must see the Prince."

He turned me, and I forced myself to meet his gaze.

"Why?" he asked softly, taking my hand in his. Just the simple touch of his fingers against mine was enough to dampen some of my hurry.

"I'm supposed to present myself to the court first, not after I dance the night away."

"Hmm." He pulled me closer. "Are you sure? I don't recall a proclamation stating such."

I swallowed hard when he turned us into the dancers, joining their sweeping moves.

"Please, Kaven," I said softly. "Do not make this more difficult than it already is." The pain in my middle grew. "I cannot spend all my time with you."

"And why not? Am I not good enough for you?"

"For me, you are the sun and moon and stars. You bring light into my life where there is otherwise none."

His steps slowed.

"You need more time," he said.

"I need understanding," I said, for no amount of time would change what needed to be.

He sighed.

"I will take you, then."

We stopped spinning, and he offered his arm. I set my hand on it, hoping he wouldn't note the tremble. People watched us as we crossed the room.

I glanced at Kaven. Dressed in a white jacket trimmed with gold, he was a dashing figure.

"Is that a real gold mask?" I asked, noting the etchings on the otherwise unadorned surface.

"It is."

"Does it bother you to wear such riches frivolously when so many go hungry less than a catapult's throw from the castle?"

He glanced at me.

"Does it bother you to wear your frivolities?"

I looked down at the dress.

"Bother doesn't sufficiently describe how very much what I'm wearing disturbs me."

When I looked up at him, he was frowning.

"Why did you wear it then?"

"Because I must."

"As must I."

His words only served as a reminder of what I was about to do. He was a servant of the Prince. The very man I was about to openly proposition. It would break Kaven. But no more than it would break me.

Instead of going to the ornate doors of the court, he veered to one of the side halls. The guards who stood there nodded and let us pass.

"You're shaking," Kaven said, placing his hand over mine.

"We've just crossed into a part of the castle where guests are discouraged from going. By sword point. Of course I'm shaking."

He chuckled and led me toward a set of stairs protected by two more of the King's guard. They, too, nodded as we passed and began to ascend.

"There is nothing to worry about," he assured me. "You'll be welcomed."

He stopped in front of a plain door and knocked softly.

"Enter," a deep voice called.

Kaven opened the door and bade me to enter. Inside, the King stood by the fire, striking a pose so similar to the one I'd seen his son strike countless times before.

"Your Majesties, may I present to you Eloise Cartwright, Margaret Cartwright's daughter."

I gave a deep curtsy. The Prince, who had been sitting in a chair near his father, rose with a smile.

"Eloise," he said. "This is a welcome and pleasant surprise. You just saved me from a long lecture regarding my duties tonight."

The King harrumphed.

"Hardly a lecture. However, your presence is welcome, Miss Cartwright."

The King nodded at me and looked at Kaven.

"If Miss Cartwright can spare your presence," the King said, "we need to speak about tonight's plans."

"Of course, Sire," I said quickly.

Kaven waited for the King to precede him out the door, then left me alone with the Prince. The opportunity couldn't have been more perfect. When I turned, I gave a startled laugh at how closely the Prince now stood.

"I apologize," he said quickly. "I only wanted to thank you again for your timely intervention. You seem to have a knack for it."

"I am at your service. Always." I took a calming breath. "Which is why I insisted on speaking with you."

"Oh? How can I help you?"

He took my hand and set it on his arm to lead me to a seat.

"It's I who can help you," I said, as I turned toward him as he sat beside me. "For the sake of the kingdom, I will wed you if you would have me."

His brows rose, and he coughed out a laugh.

"I don't think Kaven would approve of your offer. Or my father."

"I don't see why not. Your father wants you to wed and produce an heir for the safety of the kingdom. Unless some maid has already ensnared your interest, I see no reason for your father to disapprove of our union. By your own words, my family is in good standing with the Crown, and I know I can pass all the tests required."

His humor faded in the face of my earnestness.

"Why would you do this?"

"For the sake of the kingdom and all those who fall under its rule. I've seen too much suffering to do nothing."

He glanced away, looking at the fire.

"Your offer is unexpected but not unwelcome. I will need some time to consider it."

"Of course. I will see myself to the main ballroom."

He nodded absently, and I left the room. A door down, the murmur of Kaven's voice drew my attention. I hesitated, wondering if I should wait for him to finish his discussion with the King or leave on my own. After my talk with the Prince, I wanted to leave without facing Kaven. But it would be cruel to let him hear of my proposal from the Prince instead of an explanation from my own lips.

I approached the door and heard more than I should.

"...send her away. You know what's at stake."

"Father, please. The longer we wait—"

"Greydon, enough," the King said sharply.

Unable to help myself, I moved forward until I could see around the partially closed door. I stared at the room's only two occupants in horror as pain sliced through my heart and robbed me of air. There was no mistake in whom the King addressed as Greydon or who Kaven had just addressed as Father.

CHAPTER 14

THE KING SIGHED WEARILY AND GRIPPED HIS SON'S SHOULDER, BOTH still unaware of my presence in the hall.

"I understand your concerns. The girl is lovely, no doubt, but she needs to leave. Immediately. The castle is the last place she should be seen."

Deceived. Used. Now, cast aside. Crushing the soft material in my fisted hands, I lifted my skirts and stepped away from the door.

The hallway suddenly felt too narrow, and I struggled to breathe as I hurried back the way I'd come.

"Eloise," the Prince said, emerging from his room just as I'd passed it.

Turning slowly, I looked at the imposter.

"What's happened?" he asked, moving toward me. "You're pale. Are you hurt?"

I flinched back when he reached for me.

"Do not touch me. Is it you I should call Kaven? Or is that name nothing more than a figment to fool simple maids?"

His hand dropped to his side.

"I see."

"I do not. What a jest my offer must have been for you. What new cruelty will I face on the morrow?"

"Eloise, it's not what you think."

"I believe it is." In my eyes, the King and his son were no different than Maeve and her daughters.

"I'm Garreth, second in line for the Crown, after my brother, Greydon. I stand in his place to protect him from those who are trying to cause him harm."

Behind him, Kaven—no, Greydon—stepped into the hall. He frowned when he saw me.

"She knows," the Prince said.

"Yes," I said softly. "She knows."

Fear lit in Kaven's eyes—I closed mine briefly, forcing myself to acknowledge there was no Kaven. Only Greydon.

When I opened them, Greydon was striding toward me. I shook my head, turned, and ran.

"Eloise, wait!"

His footfalls echoed behind me. So much anger gave me the will necessary to keep ahead of him. I sped the length of the hall and down the stairs, almost losing a shoe. The guards stepped toward me.

"Do not touch her," Greydon commanded. "Eloise, let me explain."

Every vile name I could think of bubbled up in my mind as I recalled the night we'd spent together. I'd thrown myself at him. What a fool I'd been. Prince Greydon had never been in danger. They'd been using Garreth to draw Maeve and her daughters out. Much like me, Garreth was the sacrifice.

"Stop this foolishness," he said as I reached the end.

Oh, I am, I thought silently.

The next set of guards didn't even hear me until I burst into the main hall filled with masked people, all gaily enjoying the commencement of the third ball. Those nearest the private hall hurriedly parted to make way for me. That commotion caused those between me and the exit to step aside.

I could hear Greydon behind me, but he didn't call my name or demand I be stopped. He didn't need to. He knew where I lived.

Reaching the outer doors, I panted for air and lifted my skirts higher to sprint down the steps. Below, I saw the familiar faces of Cecilia and Porcia. Faltering, I almost lost my balance. Instead, I lost a shoe.

Desperation saw me to the bottom, and I slipped from the castle grounds into the night.

NUMB, I listened to the snick of the shears and pulled another clump of hair forward. The golden strands fell victim to the sharp metal edges and floated to the floor with the rest.

I only did as Maeve had told me because I didn't know what else to do. I'd returned to the tree and cried at its roots. After removing my ballgown and tossing it into the branches, I'd redressed and returned to my room undetected. Emotionally raw at the betrayal of the Royal family and everyone else in my life, I struggled to form a single reasonable thought.

Why had Kaven kept everything from me? Why tell me I would be his forever when he had no right to make such promises? It didn't matter that I'd been of a mind not to accept his promise. I had pushed aside my own desire for happiness to help the people, offering him only one night together, nothing more. And, it didn't matter that I'd kept truths from him as well. It was only the spell and the need to protect him that kept me silent.

Out of hair, I lowered my hands and let my arms rest for a few minutes. My scalp tingled as the new hair rapidly grew. How many times had I cut every strand from my head? I looked down at the hair circling my chair. Many times from the looks of it.

The rattle of the carriage announced the return of those who had created all of my woes. Lifting my arms, I snicked away at my hair again. Silence continued in the house, but I wasn't lulled by it. And the sound of my door opening several moments later wasn't unexpected.

"Eloise, come down here."

"Yes, Mama," I said, immediately standing and setting the shears aside. My scalp tingled on the right half of my head, already regrowing what I'd clipped away.

Maeve stood at the bottom of the stairs, her eyes cold as she watched me descend. Her gaze flicked briefly to my hair. She said nothing about it as she turned and bade for me to follow.

Below, Porcia and Cecilia waited in the sitting room. Both seemed more subdued than usual.

"What happened?" I asked, trying to sound as if I cared. It was difficult to do when everything inside of me felt dead and heavy.

"The mystery maiden was there," Maeve said. "She ran from the ball, chased by the Prince's servant. Show me your feet."

I blinked in confusion and lifted my nightgown to peek at my own feet. They were clean despite running without a shoe.

"All of you," Maeve said impatiently. I looked at Porcia and Cecilia in confusion as they hurried to remove their stocking and shoes. "Line up with your sister. It's no wonder the Prince wasn't interested in the pair of you. You don't even have a full thought put together."

When the three of us stood in a row, Maeve studied our feet.

"Cecilia, yours might be a bit too long. You will need to cut away some of your heel. Porcia, yours are too wide. Likely all those years of overindulging your sweets. Cut away your little toe."

Porcia paled, and Maeve stepped before me.

"It always seems to come back to you, doesn't it, Eloise?" she said.

"I don't understand. Why do our feet matter?"

"Because the Prince has decreed he will have no other for his bride but the runaway maiden."

My stomach twisted. What was Greydon thinking?

"Since she is a mystery, a Royal procession will go from home to home with the slipper she lost tonight on the stairs. The maid who fits the slipper and can produce its match will be queen."

I now understood why she wanted Porcia and Cecilia to cut away bits of themselves. But why look at my feet?

"You think the shoe will fit me?" I asked, dread settling into my stomach.

"I was able to pick it up and study it for a moment before the Prince's servant took it in the name of the Crown. Yes, I believe it will fit you. But only if it does not fit my more obedient daughters first."

"How will you produce its match?"

"Don't worry about that. I always find a way. Go to your room and clean up the hair. Don't cut it again until the queen is chosen."

I nodded and hurried away.

In my room, I gathered up the hair in a spare bedsheet. Descending again, I found Maeve in the entry, staring at the place the mirror once resided. She turned at the sound of my approach.

She glanced at the bundle and pointed to the kitchen.

"Throw it in the fire. Hair burns quickly."

The sound of soft sobs coming from the direction of the kitchen made my stomach twist sickeningly as if I'd crossed the estate's boundaries. However, given Maeve's current mood, I didn't dare disobey.

With a quiet, "Yes, Mama," I left her in the entry and went to join my sisters in the kitchen.

"Stop crying," Cecilia said harshly as I opened the door.

Porcia looked up at me, her eyes red and her cheeks tear stained. At her feet, Cecilia knelt with a paring knife in her hand.

"What do you want?" she demanded.

"Mama told me to burn my hair." I quickly turned my back to them.

"It should be you who needs the knife," she said angrily. "Not us. We've always obeyed."

My skin crawled with disgust. It was their willingness to do whatever Maeve wanted and their perverse need for power that put them where they were. I held no pity for them.

"I'll slice along the side of the toe and cut it from the joint. It will leave more skin to sew it closed."

Not wanting to stay and witness what they were about to do, I threw the whole balled up sheet into the fire. It caught within moments, and the eye-watering stench of burning hair drove me from the room before Cecilia made the first cut.

I PACED THE FLOOR, watching the sky lighten. No one had come to lock my door last night, and I wasn't sure if that meant I was to go downstairs for breakfast or remain where I was. I would much prefer the latter. Solitude felt like a balm as I speculated the different outcomes for Greydon's newest deception.

It wasn't until I'd returned to my room the evening before that I gave the reason behind the proclamation any thought. He knew to whom the slipper belonged, so the proclamation was a trap for those who meant the Crown harm. Of course, many maids would fit the shoe. It was the maid who was not me, but able to produce the match, who would reveal herself as the caster. Would it be enough, though? Without a doubt, Maeve would see to it that Cecilia or Porcia would fit the shoe. But would her magic be able to recreate the missing shoe? And if so, would Greydon know it wasn't just the maid but the mother and sister as well? If not, I doubted I would be able to condemn them all with the spell still holding me mute. And, if Maeve wasn't condemned, she would still be free to find another way to get what she wanted.

I glanced at the chimney where the ring still remained hidden. The tree meant for me to wed Prince Greydon. Of that I was certain. I'd been willing to give myself over to the Prince because, arrogance aside, I'd thought him honest. But last night's revelation had me questioning everything, including how far I was willing to go to save a people who didn't even know me. I'd walked through

Towdown naked, and only one person had stepped forward to help me.

Why should I give so much for so very little in return? And I most certainly did not aspire to someday become a queen. While the position might offer some privilege, it offered far more obligation.

I thought back to when Kellen and I roamed as we would, free of responsibility and pain, and the desire to return to the days before Mother died overwhelmed me.

"There has to be another way," I whispered.

I didn't believe in fate. It was an excuse for those who didn't have the will to fight for what they wanted. I had will and then some. And I wanted the freedom to choose my own future.

Outside, early morning sunlight glinted through the treetops. I had time. No one, save the maids, ever rose so early. Decided, I hurried to escape my attic refuge. The house was quiet on the second floor, and I softly closed my door to tiptoe down the stairs. If I hurried, I could return from the clearing and be the first in the dining room.

The birds greeted me with a cheery song as I ran along the path. The cool morning air filled me with life and energy. I wished more than anything I could continue running through the trees. Run all the way to the Dark Forest and scream Kellen's name until she heard me.

Instead, I burst into Mother's clearing and fell to my knees at the base of the tree.

"There must be another way," I begged. "I cannot do what you want. Please."

The bird chirped from a branch, its song distressed.

"You don't understand. Everything has been a lie. Lies on top of lies. That isn't the life I want. I will not accept it."

The tree shivered and shook and above me a single bud appeared. It grew in size until its petals opened one by one. From inside, another ring fell into my hand.

With a sinking heart, I looked at the elegant ring. Smaller than the first, the band of silver was much thinner and more ornately carved. Instead of a gold crown, this one had a crown of diamond with sapphire chips at each peak. It was the female match to the male ring I already had. This one was meant for me.

I fisted my hand around the ring and drew back my arm to throw the unwanted jewelry into the woods. I would not do as it wanted.

A hand closed over mine.

Shocked, I looked up at Maeve as she pried my fingers apart. She took the ring and looked up at the tree.

"How is this possible? Who enchanted this tree?"

I scrambled to my feet, fear and anger loosening my tongue and spurring me to speak without first considering my words.

"Father gave me a pear tree shoot the day before we buried my mother. Once touched by—" My throat closed over the word.

"The magic from the amulet?" Maeve said, guessing what I meant to say.

I nodded.

"When I planted it here, I think what had touched her lingered and touched the tree."

"How does it work?"

In that moment, I knew I couldn't tell her. What would Maeve ask for? What would the tree give?

I stared at her defiantly, and she grabbed my arm.

"Do not think the Prince's affection for the manservant will stay my hand a second time. Tell me."

My mind raced. The manservant wasn't unprotected like she thought. Had I paid more attention during our night together, I felt certain I would have noted an amulet. However, even if she couldn't hurt him, she could still take her anger out on others. And, the tree never gave me what I wanted but what it thought I needed to stop her.

"I ask the tree for what I need, and it falls from the branches," I said, hoping I was right that the tree wouldn't help her.

Maeve released me and looked up at the budding leaves.

"I need a way to see those who seek to stop me from gaining the throne."

The little bird chirped in its nest and took flight. I watched it disappear into the forest, heading toward Towdown.

"Well?" Maeve said impatiently, still staring up in the branches.

"I don't think it's going to work. The bird flew away."

"You said it was the tree who granted you what you wanted."

I shook my head.

"It grants me what I need, not what I want. And the bird is always there. It's never flown away before."

Her cold gaze went to the ring in her hand before locking onto me.

"And what else has the tree given you?"

"A mask and a dress and shoes to match."

Her eyes widened in understanding, and she struck out, slapping me hard. My head jerked with the impact.

"You thought to use my power against me?" she demanded.

"Yes," I said simply, holding her gaze.

Her eyes narrowed on me.

"Where is the other shoe?"

"I gave it back to the tree when I returned."

She looked at the tree and put her hand to her chest.

"Let tinder burn to nothing but cinder. That made of gold, silver, or glass let the fire bypass."

With a flash of green light, the tree ignited. I grabbed Maeve's arm angrily.

"Without the tree, you have no hope of producing the matching shoe."

She struck me again, the impact sending me to the ground.

"Do not presume to admonish me," she yelled. "If the tree still holds the shoe, the flames will not touch it. If the tree does not, I have no use for it. And neither do you."

With tears filling my eyes, I watched my mother's tree, my father's last gift to me, burn to nothing in mere minutes. Maeve grabbed me and pushed me into the coal.

"Dig in the ashes. Find the shoe."

I shifted through the hot coals, my slippers burning away along with the base of my dress. The heat didn't touch my skin, though. I dug and dug but found no shoe. I did, however, find the remnants of the bird's little nest, filled with red hot coals. I swallowed hard, trying to tamp down the anger that shook my limbs.

Why was I listening to Maeve? To protect two maids I didn't even know? I was done trying to think rationally and keep my temper under control.

With an angry cry, I stood and threw a fistful of hot coals at Maeve. They scattered, hitting her face and bodice. Instead of crying out in pain, she laughed and brushed away the coals.

"I thought the spell of protection quite clever and decided I needed one for myself."

She stalked toward me and grabbed my arm.

"Is there anything else you would care to try?"

"Yes."

I punched her right in the mouth.

She laughed, and I tumbled headlong into oblivion.

CHAPTER 15

WAKING FROM MAEVE'S SPELL WASN'T LIKE WAKING FROM SLEEP. THERE was no hazy unclarity or pleasant restfulness. Rather, it was an instant awareness.

A clatter of noise rose outside.

Opening my eyes, the familiar sight of my attic space greeted me. However, the day's fading light cast shadows in the room.

I sat up and scanned myself, finding I still wore the charred remnants of my dress. That didn't make sense. I'd thrown coal at Maeve's face, and when that hadn't worked, I'd hit her. I wasn't foolish enough to believe either act would go unpunished. Yet, I was still clothed and comfortable on my bed instead of in a hovel in Towdown.

What did Maeve have planned now?

Hurrying from the bed, I moved to stand, and my eyes caught on the two dresses laying on the table I used for my solitary meals. Maid's dresses. And shoes. But the shoes were standing upright as if still—

A small pained sound escaped me as I recognized the shriveled twisted remains of the two maids. Throat tight and tears wetting my lashes, I went to them. How could I have been so foolish? I'd known what would happen and had acted rashly, regardless of the consequences.

A note waited on the chest of one. I picked it up and read the brief scrawl.

THEIR LIVES for your defiance and a shoe. Clean yourself and join us in the sitting room, or more will follow.

TEARS SPILLED over as the sounds in the yard continued.

"Poor Catherine and Heather," I said softly. "Killed twice over and for what? Her petty need for retribution."

I set my hand on the skirt of one. I wasn't even sure which it was.

"Rest peacefully, knowing that I am not yet finished. I will give my dying breath to see her fall. She will suffer for all that she's done."

Wiping my eyes, I noted the washbowl and gown that waited on the chair near the table. The dress wasn't one I recognized as belonging to Cecilia or Porcia. Holding it up to me, I found the length perfect, which meant Maeve had it made for me at some point. The knowledge that she still thought to use me grated at my raw nerves. I looked down at my ragged skirt and, for the briefest of moments, considered leaving it on. However, her note clearly stated what the outcome of such defiance would be.

"Eloise Cartwright," a male voice called from below. "We await your presence."

Stripping from the remnants of my gown, I quickly washed my face then changed. While I laced the dress, I struggled to piece together what Maeve might intend. She'd kept me under her spell for the majority of the day, only to wake me now when we had guests. Not a few but many from the sounds of the horses outside. And, the authority that clearly rang in the voice that just called to me could only mean one thing. The Prince and his contingent were here because of the proclamation.

My mind raced with my feet. When I reached the top of the main staircase, I stopped and stared at all of the men I glimpsed through the open entry door. A veritable army.

"Miss Cartwright?" a voice asked.

"Yes," I said, looking at the older man who waited at the bottom of the stairs. He wasn't dressed as a guard but wore a fine jacket to rival any I saw on the King.

"Your mother and sisters are waiting for you."

I slowly descended and took his arm, letting him escort me into the sitting room. Two guards stood sentinel just inside the door.

Standing before the fire, Prince Garreth's presence was as stately as ever. When he glanced at me, his gaze gave nothing away.

Maeve, sitting in a chair nearest to the door, smiled when I entered.

"There you are, darling. You've kept the Prince waiting."

I ignored her admonishment and looked at Cecilia and Porcia, who sat on a settee near the Prince. Porcia looked pale, her upper lip glistening. Cecilia looked unaffected by whatever she'd done to herself.

The final occupant in the room stood by the chair across from the pair. The chair to which I was being led. My heart started to race, and I refused to look at Greydon, who watched my approach. Instead, I focused on the firelight that glinted off the original slipper he held displayed prominently on a silken cushion.

In everything that had happened, I hadn't considered the impossibility of carrying out the proclamation. The slipper should have vanished at the eleventh hour like its partner. How was it still here? I thought of the ring in the attic and the one Maeve took, no longer sure what rules applied to the items given by the tree.

"Are there any other maidens in the house?" the older man asked after I sat.

"No, Lord Firth," Maeve said. "None."

"Very well. This day has been long as you can imagine. Now that all the maidens are present, we must ask if you have the match to this shoe."

There was a rustle of sound near my head, and Cecilia gasped.

"You recognize it, miss?" the older man asked.

"I do. Alas, I no longer have the match. It was broken in my race from the castle."

Doubt clouded the man's eyes.

"As we've heard many times today."

"And did the shoe fit those maids?"

"They did not," he said, reluctantly.

"Then allow me to prove to you that the shoe is mine."

Greydon stepped forward with the slipper, and my heart lurched at the sight of his broad shoulders as he passed the cushion to Lord Firth. The man knelt before Cecilia and removed her slipper. I watched in horror as my shoe easily slid into place over her foot.

She smiled brilliantly at Garreth.

"It fits," she said.

"So it does," he said calmly.

A bird flew into the room, startling us all.

"Check her heel while you kneel," it sang before flying from the room just as quickly as it had come.

Lord Firth glanced at Garreth, who nodded. Cecilia quickly removed her foot from his hold.

"Surely you're not going to believe an enchanted bird?" she said. "The creature itself is treachery."

"Remove the shoe and allow Lord Firth to inspect your foot without stocking."

"Sire," Maeve said, looking every inch the outraged mother. "Such a thing is highly improper."

"No more than choosing a bride solely based on her ability to wear a shoe. Don't you agree?" the Prince asked smoothly.

Maeve inclined her head, and I felt a burst of triumph as Lord Firth removed her shoe and stocking to find a good portion of her heel missing.

"I fell from our horse before the ball and hurt myself," Cecilia said quietly.

"Then you cannot be the one for surely you could not run in the shoe."

"But I can." She grabbed the shoe from Lord Firth and stuck her foot into it. "Watch."

She stood and, lifting her skirts, took her first running step. She made it three more before she began limping, and several more after that before the shoe became so slick with blood that it fell from her foot.

"Sit," Garreth commanded.

Ashen, Cecilia sat beside Porcia. I risked a glance at Maeve as Lord Firth removed the shoe and wiped it clean. Nothing showed in her expression, but I didn't miss the slight restlessness of her finger tapping at the arm of her chair.

"What of you, Porcia?" the Prince asked, drawing my attention to her. "Do you believe this to be your shoe?"

If possible, she paled further.

"Yes, Sire," she said quietly.

Lord Firth sighed and knelt by her feet. Her wince when he slid the shoe on was visible to all.

"It fits," Lord Firth said when she remained silent.

"What have you to say about that?" Garreth asked her.

Before she could answer, the bird swooped into the room again.

"Check her toe before you go."

Maeve's eyes tracked its progress as it flew out the door once more. Anger boiled just beneath the surface. She was failing, and she knew it. Her gaze shifted, and her eyes met mine. She visibly relaxed, and a small smile curled her lips.

Turning away from her, I watched as Lord Firth removed the shoe and Porcia's stocking. She offered no explanation for her missing small toe.

"It's been missing since birth and often gives her trouble," Maeve said. "I know the proclamation said no maid with disadvantage, but surely it only meant of face and figure, not foot."

"Will you persist and watch your daughter further injure herself when I insist she must prove she can run in the shoe?" Garreth asked, a note of annoyance creeping into his voice.

"No, your majesty," Maeve said meekly. "But I ask that you allow Eloise an opportunity to try the shoe before you leave."

I met Garreth's questioning gaze as Lord Firth gently removed the shoe from Porcia's now bleeding foot.

"Do you claim this shoe to be yours, Eloise?" His voice lacked any of the impatience it held when speaking to my step sisters.

"I cannot claim it as mine, for it is not."

Silence fell. I could feel Greydon's gaze on me but refused to look at him.

"What are you saying?" Garreth asked. "You do not wish to try the shoe?"

"Eloise didn't mean that, Your Majesty," Maeve said quickly, rising to stand beside my chair. With her hand resting lightly on my shoulder, she clarified, "She only meant she borrowed the shoe from her sisters. Isn't that right, Eloise?"

I looked at my hands and wondered what would happen to the people in the room if I said no. She couldn't kill Greydon and Garreth, but what of Lord Firth and the guards? She would care nothing for any of them.

Lifting my foot, I remained silent.

"There," Maeve said. "She's willing."

"Allow me," Greydon said, taking the shoe from Lord Firth.

Maeve's fingers twitched on my shoulder as Greydon knelt at my feet and lifted my skirt. He looked up at me, and I averted my gaze to look at Cecilia and Porcia. Porcia trembled in her seat. Cecilia appeared no more composed than her sister.

The shoe slipped easily onto my foot.

"It fits," Greydon said softly.

My heart stuttered for a moment. Clenching my fists in my lap, I set my foot on the ground and met Greydon's gaze.

"I will not wed Prince Greydon," I said.

Maeve laughed.

"She jests, Your Majesty."

I opened my mouth to damn us all with my further objection when the bird flew into the room again. Surprised, I watched it, wondering if it would accuse me of lies like it had Porcia and Cecilia. However, its words weren't about me as it circled the room.

"She comes! She comes!"

When it returned to the doorway, the guards were gone, and a figure with a familiar dirty cloak stood there.

"Have I come at a bad time to collect my pig?" Rose asked, glancing around the room.

"Not at all," I said quickly. I started to stand, ready for the escape she offered, when Maeve's hand closed over my shoulder.

"What pig?" Maeve asked.

"The pig in the yard. The one I left in Eloise's care the day her mother met the earth."

I saw the moment Maeve's eyes narrowed with suspicion, and I quickly shook my head at Rose. The old woman didn't seem to notice, though.

"Take your pig with my blessing and leave," Maeve said.

Rose shook her head as she smiled at Maeve.

"I couldn't do that without thanking Eloise for her tender care of such a wretched beast." Rose's bright blue gaze swept the room before landing on me. "He said you walked him when you could and never overfed him. More importantly, he said you protected him." She chuckled lowly, and Maeve released my arm.

"You are addled, old woman. Pigs do not speak. Remove yourself from my house."

Rose continued as if Maeve hadn't spoken.

"He asked that I apologize on his behalf for leading you to the bodies of your friends. I believe your grief truly moved him. He seems changed now. Oh, not enough for me to release him of his curse. He will need to do much more than show sympathy for others."

"Curse?" Greydon asked, stepping in front of Garreth.

"Call your guards, Your Majesty," Maeve said, also backing away from Rose. "The one who seeks to harm you has exposed herself."

"Indeed, she has," Rose said with a laugh.

"Guards!" Garreth called.

There was no answering rush of footsteps. Not even a rustle of noise.

"Caster," Maeve said harshly. "You will be hanged."

Rose laughed and held out her hand to me.

"Come here, child."

"No, Eloise," Greydon said. "Stay as you are."

Weary of all that I'd suffered and desperate for it to end no matter what the outcome, I stood.

"Eloise, don't!" Maeve said sharply. "You risk everything."

Ignoring her and Greydon, I went to Rose. The old woman's warm fingers closed around mine, and she smiled. A sense of peace settled over me.

"I'm sorry it took so long," she said. "Some evils hide themselves too well, and I had to be sure of the one with which I was dealing. I truly regret anything you may have suffered."

I gave a choked laugh that was closer to a sob, and Rose gave me a pitying look.

"I surmise it was much, then?"

I opened my mouth, but my words stuck in my throat, robbing me of air.

"Still held by her curse, I see."

Rose looked at Maeve.

"Release her," she said.

"I will not lose what is mine," Maeve replied with cold anger.

My gaze flew to her just as a green glow began to consume her bodice with blinding brilliance.

"Enough," Rose said sharply.

The light died, and Maeve's face turned to one of shock.

With a wave of Rose's hand, thin silver chains appeared at Maeve's feet and slowly wrapped their way up her torso. Maeve's eyes narrowed, and twice more, a light sparked from her amulet, only to sputter and die.

"Fetch her trinket, Eloise," Rose said. "I would get it myself, but young men with less than six inches of steel are worrisome. They always overcompensate with their zealousness."

I wasn't quite sure what she meant by that until I turned and saw both Greydon and Garreth brandishing small blades. Their gazes darted between me, Rose, and Maeve, who was precariously balanced on her feet.

Maeve glowered at me as I crossed the room and hooked my finger on her chain to pull the amulet from her cleavage.

Greydon swore.

Removing the ornament from around her neck, I turned to Rose.

"It's not for me to break," she said.

I looked down at the amulet that had caused me so much pain then crossed the room to Cecilia and Porcia. Both surrendered their amulets without protest. When I had all three, I set them on the floor, along with the shoe.

"Nor are they mine to break," I said, finally meeting Greydon's gaze.

"I believe they're yours, Prince Greydon. For all that was done to your family before it was done to mine."

"Eloise…" The apology in his gaze only hurt me further.

Turning from him, I went to Rose.

"No," Maeve said softly from behind me. "It cannot be."

It wasn't until that moment that I realized what I'd revealed.

"It is," Greydon said.

There was a sound of metal upon stone, and Maeve screamed. I glanced back and saw Greydon had broken her amulet with the fire poker. With defeated expressions, Cecilia and Porcia sat on the couch and watched him destroy theirs as well.

"Come, child," Rose said. "We should check on the guards."

"Caster, you are not going anywhere," Greydon said. "By the King's order—"

"I'm banished. I know."

"Not until the role you've played in this is clear."

Rose's gaze flicked to me, and I knew she wanted me to speak on her behalf. But I couldn't, not with her spell keeping me silent.

"Release me," I said.

She smiled, and a tingle started in my chest, spreading outward. I faced Greydon.

"Her role has been that of my protector when I could not protect myself."

"Protect you from what?"

I opened my mouth but no words emerged. The slight tightening in my throat warned me not to try too hard. Maeve's spell still held, despite the broken amulet Greydon now held.

He frowned at my continued silence.

"Who arrived first?" he asked. "The woman behind you or your stepmother?"

"Rose did."

"How then can you truly believe that your stepmother acted alone? They are both casters."

Rose stepped forward.

"And how do you propose I prove my innocence when I'm unaware of what you find me guilty of?"

I glanced at Rose.

"He thinks you killed his wife and my mother."

"And do you think that?" she asked me.

"No."

"I wonder why that is. Is it perhaps that you know who did kill his wife and your mother?"

"I cannot say."

"You do not know?"

"I did not say that."

"Ah." Her gaze flicked to Maeve. "Is that woman truly your stepmother?"

"She is. I saw the signed document myself."

"Do you care for her?"

I said nothing.

"Has she mistreated you?"

Rose knew well the answer to that, and she smiled at me when I remained mute.

"There is so much more to this story, Your Majesty," she said turning to Greydon, "and Eloise is the key. Not I. However, I've decided to remain until everything is revealed."

"Then, I must insist you accompany us to the castle. My father, King Aftan, will want to speak with you."

She inclined her head.

"I will meet you at the gates."

With that, the old woman disappeared. Moments later, guards rushed into the room.

Maeve, Porcia, and Cecilia were quickly taken outside, and I was jostled aside. I didn't care. The faster everyone left my home, the faster I could put the past several months behind me. The thought fractured me. How could I possibly move on?

Arms closed around my waist, and I found myself up in Greydon's arms before I knew his intent.

"Put me down."

"There is still the matter of the shoe," he said.

"The matter is settled for I have given my answer," I said. "If the kingdom is still in need of a queen, find another gullible maid."

I turned away from his pleading gaze as he stepped outside with me.

"I care not for what the kingdom's need for a queen might be, but my own," he said softly.

He brought me to a horse and helped me into the saddle. When he moved to join me, I planted my bare foot in his chest.

"Find another."

He scowled at me.

"I made you a promise," he said.

"To leave me alone forever?" I said sweetly.

"To be patient. To give you time. But, I also swore you were mine. Who I am changes nothing about how I feel for you."

"It changes everything for me."

I dug my heels into the steed, desperate to leave Greydon and put an end to the charade I'd been living.

CHAPTER 16

AFTER RACING FROM THE ESTATE'S BOUNDARIES AND ALMOST FALLING off the horse because of the resulting violent heaving, I returned to the yard, ignored Greydon's puzzled frown, and took a position just behind Maeve and her daughters. Maeve smirked knowingly but said nothing about my presence.

The ploddingly slow journey to the castle grated at me on many fronts. Maeve was caught and in chains—the magical links having slithered high enough up her gown to allow her to walk. Her amulet had been stripped from her. I should have been free, but I wasn't. Wouldn't that mean Maeve still had power? I opened my mouth to question the nearest guard but choked on my words. How could I be so close to freedom and still be every inch Maeve's prisoner?

Glaring, I watched Maeve walk proudly, her head high as if she weren't plodding along the dirt path after dark like some common woman. Beside her mother, Cecilia limped heavily. Her determination to keep pace was etched in every line of her cold, regal expression. It was Porcia who slowed the party with her staggering walk, causing the guards behind us to call a halt until she caught up with Maeve and Cecilia.

"Someone take the dark-haired girl upon his horse so we can reach the castle before midnight," Garreth called.

A guard rode up and plucked her from the ground.

"I would like the same courtesy," Cecilia said. However, when she looked hopefully at the guards around her, no one offered to take her up.

By the time we reached the castle, a good number of the town's people were following us, despite the hour. That Lord Firth lead our procession with the damnable shoe on display had much to do with their curiosity. As did the three bound women in our midst.

Rose waited at the castle gates, as promised, along with two guards, who kept glancing at her.

"That took much longer than I thought it should," she said. "Is it wise to keep a king waiting?"

"Hold your tongue, caster," Lord Firth said as he handed the cushioned shoe to a guard. "We are the King's emissary, and not to be rebuked by the likes of you."

Rose's gaze sharpened on the shoe.

"Why does the King's emissary need a woman's shoe? It hardly becomes your coloring or figure."

I couldn't help the smile that tugged at my lips as Lord Firth sputtered and dismounted.

"Now see here—"

"No, you need to see. I did not make that shoe for you." She looked at me and waved her hand in my direction.

"They were made for her."

The shoe disappeared from the pillow and reappeared on my foot. When I checked the other foot, I found the mate there as well, and my humor faded.

"I don't want the shoes," I said, looking up at her.

"What an ungrateful thing to say. Come along, the King is waiting, and I want to hear the story in full."

She turned and started through the castle gates.

"Stop her," Lord Firth ordered.

The guards who'd stood beside Rose shared a nervous glance.

"We've tried," one said. "But she keeps disappearing before we can touch her."

Rose's chuckle drifted behind her as she started up the castle stairs.

"No man may touch me without my permission," she called.

I was so engrossed in what was happening that I didn't notice Greydon at my side until his hands settled on my waist. He helped me from the horse but didn't immediately release me.

"The shoes look lovely on you," he said quietly.

As I looked up at his handsome, deceptive face, my heart lurched. I'd wanted this man when I'd thought him common and honest like me. He'd broken my trust and my heart by withholding who he was, yet the treacherous organ in my chest still pined for him. If he knew it, would he also seek to use that to his advantage to obtain what he wanted?

"Release me if you want your testicles to remain as they are," I said coolly.

He quickly released me and pivoted so his most prized possession was no longer an easy target.

"This level of aggression is uncalled for," he said, his own anger slipping. "I am not your enemy."

A harsh pull in my stomach and a sudden sickening had me stepping around him.

"That has yet to be determined," I said as I hurried toward Maeve.

The frustrated growl that followed me did nothing to soften my feelings toward him.

Inside the castle, Lord Firth and the guard led us directly to the King's court where numerous people already waited with the exception of Rose. I glanced around the room at those gathered to the right and left of the space, looking for the old woman, but could see her nowhere.

Greydon stepped up beside me and offered his arm. Ignoring it, I followed behind Maeve and my stepsisters, noting the hush that fell over the court as we proceeded forward, toward the King who sat upon his raised throne at the opposite end of the room. An older woman dressed in a plain gown stood on the lowest of the three steps to the King's platform.

"Stop there," she said when we'd crossed half the expanse.

The guard holding Maeve's chains jerked her to a stop. My stepmother studied the older woman as she studied us, her gaze sweeping dismissively over Maeve, Cecilia, and Porcia before finding me. Her expression changed slightly, a combination of joy and sorrow.

"You three stand accused of plotting against the Crown and for the use of magic. How do you plead?" the old woman asked.

"Not guilty, of course," Maeve said. "We've been brought here because one of my daughters has a cut on her heel and the other has a missing toe from birth. That's hardly plotting against the Crown."

The King leaned forward.

"Come now, Maverene," he said. "Admit your guilt. Do you think I don't recognize you? Did you think I would believe this a mere coincidence that you're here now when so much evil has befallen my people? We both know better. I've been long awaiting this moment."

Some of Maeve's mask of innocence dropped.

"As was I, Aftan. Though I imagined our roles reversed. Me on the throne and you in chains, begging for your life."

"Are you saying you plan to beg?"

She smiled serenely.

"I didn't then, and I won't now."

"I thought as much. Your petty acts have—"

"Petty? Petty! You arrogant prick of a man! My actions have never been petty. Unlike yours."

The King's face reddened.

"How you plea matters not. The court finds you guilty, regardless. Silence her and take her away!"

A guard grabbed for her, and I felt a moment of panic.

"Please, Your Majesty," I said, stepping forward. "Silence her if you must, but do not remove her."

Maeve started laughing like a mad woman.

"You see?" she cried. "My daughters are loyal to me."

A guard took a cravat from the nearest man and stuffed it in Maeve's mouth.

"Daughters?" the King said. "These women are not your daughters but your accomplices. You have no daughters."

Hate filled Maeve's gaze, and she screamed something at the King.

"Step forward, Eloise Cartwright," he said, turning his attention to me.

The mention of my name sent a low murmur through the room. I nervously stepped forward a few more feet. Neither he nor the older woman needed to tell me to stop. The slight tug in my stomach told me I'd gone far enough.

"I knew your mother," the king said. "She did a great many selfless acts in the service of this kingdom. Your defense of the vile creature behind you disappoints me. I expected you to be more like your mother."

My temper flared.

"I cannot be any more like her. My every action has been to—"

My throat tightened suddenly, choking the air from my lungs. Gasping, I still tried to force out the words that would convey all that I'd done and endured to attempt to stop Maeve. The spell gripped me harder, closing off my airway, which only increased my need to incriminate Maeve in every way possible. Strangled, pained sounds wheezed from my mouth until I could no longer breathe.

Defeated, I fell to my knees and stopped trying. The ability to breathe slowly returned, and I drew in one ragged breath then another.

A firm hand around my arm helped me stand again when I was ready. I looked up to thank whoever assisted me and met Greydon's tormented gaze.

"Eloise," he said softly. "I'm sorry. I didn't know."

I jerked away from his touch, angry at the whole damn Royal family.

"It is not pity, then, that moved you to speak," the King said.

"No, Sire."

"Perhaps, I can help determine what has transpired," Rose said, emerging from the crowd to the right.

"And you are?" the King asked.

"A simple old woman passing through Towdown on her way to Turre."

"Not simple," Greydon said, stepping toward his father. "Like Maverene, this woman made her presence known shortly after I arrived at the Retreat. That she also uses magic is too coincidental to be ignored."

"Elspeth," the King said, looking at the old woman near his dais. "Do you know her?"

My shocked gaze flew to Elspeth. That was the woman from my mother's letters? The muffled outrage from behind me said that Maeve had recognized the name as well.

Ignoring Maeve, Rose and Elspeth considered one another.

"I do not know her, Sire," Elspeth said.

"Nor do I know you," said Rose. "Should I?"

"No. What is your influence with magic? By blood or nature?"

"Never blood and preferably not nature, though I will when I must."

"What do you use then?" Elspeth asked, her confusion clear.

"Another, more infinitely powerful source that does not require any type of life sacrifice."

The crowd moved restlessly at that confession. I knew very little about the nature of magic with the exception of why all of it was so dangerous. Blood magic was dangerous in that it required a person's life essence, which was what Maeve had used time and again. Nature magic was the use of the endless energy found in nature. That this woman had found another form was worrisome.

"I require proof of your abilities," Elspeth said. "To assure you do not use blood."

Rose chuckled, and a tingle started in my fingertips, spreading rapidly over the length of my body. Looking down at myself, I watched my gown change from plain to luminescent. From wool to silk. I ran my hand over the ballgown I'd last worn then touched the mask now covering my face. With a good measure of annoyance, I tugged it free and looked at Rose.

"These walls clash with your gown, don't you agree, Eloise?" she said. With a snap of her fingers, the colors on the walls faded from red to a soft blue leafed with golden filigree.

A collective gasp echoed throughout the room.

"I hope you like the colors," Rose said. "As this is no illusion."

Elspeth looked at the King.

"If it were blood magic, we would have felt it."

"Does that sufficiently prove my innocence enough for you to accept my assistance?" Without waiting for anyone's approval, she continued. "Eloise is cursed. There are certain things of which she cannot speak without suffering a great deal of pain. It isn't a magic I can remove. However, I believe Maeve or Maverene, or whatever name she uses, could if she were so inclined."

Maeve made an insistent noise behind her gag.

"Let her speak," the King commanded.

The gag was removed, and she took a moment to wet her lips. Then with great show, she looked around the room before smiling at the King.

"Why should I show pity to the kingdom's apparent favored daughter when none will be shown to me?"

The King's face flushed anew.

"Once again, you are not thinking clearly," he said. "The kingdom may have decided your guilt, but we will not decide your fate. That, I will leave to Eloise. Do you believe she will show you pity when you've shown her none? Perhaps, freeing her now might spare you later."

A hot mixture of feeling flooded me at his words. I'd vowed Maeve would pay for all that I'd suffered, and now it would be within my power to see it done.

Maeve's gaze shifted to me. She smiled slightly and nodded her head at me in acknowledgement.

"Eloise is far too much like me, filled with anger and loathing, to show any pity now."

Her words struck me like a knife because I realized how true they were. I wanted to be nothing like Maeve.

"Then, you shall continue to enjoy the gag," the King said.

Maeve struggled but was gagged as ordered.

Once the room quieted, Rose circled me.

"Speak what you can," she said. "Maeve cursed you because she sought to keep you silent about something. Most likely her actions. Tell me what has happened to you and to the kingdom since she arrived."

She wasn't asking what Maeve had done or that I implicate Maeve in any way. She was asking me to relate events. I opened my mouth and tentatively spoke the first words.

"My sister left in the middle of the night." Admitting that truth, something that I'd already shared, was easy. The next was harder. "Our house maids died." My chest tightened as I recalled their shriveled forms. They were the first of many. But not all by Maeve's hand. Tears clogged my throat when I thought of Hugh.

"Our manservant died, too." The words began to spill from me. "As did many men in town. Many became ill. A small child died horribly. I walked the length of Towdown naked and covered in ash, vomiting. People threw rocks at me, among other things. One person showed pity. He was blinded. I was beaten. Almost raped. Starved. Chained."

"Stop." Greydon's broken plea pulled me from the memories.

Angry, I looked up at him.

"Why? Does your ignorance absolve you of any fault for what I've suffered? For what others have suffered while the Royal family stayed safely hidden away? Is it not your games for power and control that caused this?"

There was a rustle of noise from the front of the room, and when I looked, I saw the King descending the steps of his platform.

"Allow me to explain why the suffering was necessary," he said. "Years ago, when I was closer to Greydon's age, my father tasked me to find a suitable bride. He wanted me to choose a maiden from our kingdom rather than attempt to strike alliances with others. I toured the land, looking for a maiden who would not only capture my heart but make a suitable queen.

"I thought I found such a maiden in Maverene. She was fair to look upon and kind and just in her dealings with others. Or so I thought. It wasn't until she was faced with a test of fertility that her true nature was revealed. I released her, thinking her vehement cries for retribution no more than a woman's wounded pride."

Maeve made loud sounds from behind her gag, but the King ignored her.

"Then I found Sevil," he said. "She was everything Maverene was not and became a true queen, who ruled fairly and justly at my side. However, a few years after we'd wed, a plague befell our kingdom. It was unnatural in its form and swiftness."

I recalled the beast Garreth had shown me in the Royal Retreat's trophy room and shivered.

"Your mother helped stop the spread, and for a few months, we found peace once more. But Sevil and I knew it was nothing more than a trick. An attempt to lull us. And because of that, we kept a precious secret. That of Sevil's second pregnancy. However, such a thing is impossible to keep truly secret. During the final weeks of Sevil's seclusion, Maverene learned of it and began to attack the child while it still grew within Sevil. Only the amulet my wife wore kept the babe safe."

The King remained silent for a long moment.

"The man you know as Prince Greydon is actually Prince Garreth, my second son. He was taken away by a trusted friend the moment of his birth. To keep him safe, we let the kingdom believe he was dead while we searched for Maverene. Too often, Elspeth would draw close to finding Maverene only to have her disappear again."

"Meanwhile, my sons grew, and I aged. Time waits for no man, and I was forced to keep the secret of my second son's existence and send my first born to find a suitable bride. I had hoped Maverene had set aside her anger after so many years. However, when Prince

Greydon's wife died enroute to the castle, I knew the kingdom was not yet safe, and I needed to draw out the evil stalking us."

"The decisions made were never meant to retain power or control but to protect the kingdom from one who sought to hurt it. For, it was rarely the Royal family who suffered but our people."

The heavy weight that had formed inside of me the moment I learned Kaven's true identity remained firmly in place. Yet, some of the anger lifted. Maeve had never sought to hurt the people but the King, through his people. And, after living with her for so long, I knew that had the King given up his throne or taken her to be his wife, the same misery would have still befallen the kingdom. That was Maeve's nature. The King had made the best choice he had available to him. Hadn't I done the same? Hadn't those choices resulted in other people's misery? I thought of Mother, Judith, Anne, Hugh, the small child, and Alfie. If I didn't hold the blame for their treatment, was it fair to expect the King to hold the blame for mine.

"Thank you for telling me, Sire," I said.

The King nodded and squeezed my arm compassionately.

"The time for secrecy is at an end. I do not need you to speak against Maverene for me to know her guilt. You need only to speak her punishment."

An involuntary shiver ran through me as I was consumed by a severe chill followed by an uncomfortable heat. Inhaling sharply, I looked to Rose, who smiled slightly. Her words from when we sat in the kitchen of the Brazen Belle came back to me.

I smiled in return and turned to look at the gagged woman who had destroyed my life.

For the first time in months, I spoke freely.

"Maeve has killed men, women, and children. I would say let her suffer those travesties. Shave her head, blind her, beat her, strip her bare, and let her walk the streets so the people she has caused untold suffering can judge her as they will."

King Aftan nodded.

"A just ruling. So it shall be. Take Maverene away."

The guards began to drag her away, her cries of anger muted by the gag. The tug in my middle had me stumbling toward her.

"Wait," I called. "She cannot yet leave me. Nor I, her. If we're separated, I will suffer sickness unlike anything I've felt before."

"Was it cast after my spell of protection?"

I nodded, and Rose came to me, setting her hand on my heart and my head.

"Good. That means it won't have rooted as deeply as the first spell." She remained quiet for a moment then made a satisfied sound. "Just as I thought."

Another wave, hot and cold, spread throughout my body.

"Having them removed is much more pleasant that receiving them, isn't it?" Rose asked.

"It is. Thank you."

"You can remove Maverene," Rose said. "Eloise will be fine."

The guard looked at the King, who nodded his agreement, and I watched the men drag Maeve away, feeling true freedom.

"The hour grows late, and I have no knowledge of the two remaining women," the King said. "Let them share the same fate as the woman they chose to call mother."

"Wait," Cecilia cried. "Like Eloise, we were nothing more than pawns in Maverene's pursuit of power. Tell them, Eloise. Tell them we had no choice just like when you killed your lover, Hugh."

Anger blinded me. With a cry, I flew at her. She stepped behind her guard and, with an evil smile, knocked him forward as he drew his sword for her.

The honed edge of the blade flashed in the candle light as he stumbled toward me.

CHAPTER 17

STRONG ARMS CIRCLED MY WAIST AND SPUN ME ABOUT, SPARING ME FROM the blade but also keeping me from my target. I struggled against the firm hold as I was surrounded by guards. Instead of putting me in chains, they faced outward, shielding my struggle from the people gathered.

"He wasn't a lover but someone I loved," I yelled. "And the fault of his death lies on you and the evil bitch you call mother."

"Settle yourself," Greydon whispered in my ear. "Don't allow her to cause you further suffering. You're free from their will and better than they are in every way."

I inhaled deeply and calmed myself.

"Release me." He did so reluctantly, and the guards retreated, showing the two men who now held Cecilia tightly.

She watched me with a malicious glint in her eyes. Even caught and sentenced for treason, there was no remorse within her.

"At every turn, I watched your delight as others have suffered," I said.

"And you helped in that suffering," she replied. "You sat at the same table. You put your safety before the safety of others. How are we any different? Why should I be punished when you walk free?"

A murmur rose in the court.

"Because, however small my actions, they were always to fight against the outcome you and Maeve wanted. You wanted to be queen, Cecilia, for you, not for Maeve. And if you'd wed Garreth as you'd planned, everyone would have suffered."

"Lies," she hissed. "You have no proof."

"You wanted to break his charm of protection, and I pushed him out of the way."

"That was your attempt to break it," she said, lying.

"You poisoned his drink so he couldn't walk me home."

I looked at Porcia, who had remained subdued since entering the court.

"Do I speak the truth?"

"You do," she said softly. "Our actions brought unspeakable pain, suffering, and death to countless people here and across this kingdom. Any participation forced upon you was under great duress."

"Traitor," Cecilia said harshly.

"Your sentence, Eloise?" the King asked.

"Shave Cecilia's head, beat her, starve her, and brand her forehead so everyone knows her as a traitor to the Crown. But do not blind her. Let her witness every look of revulsion and know what it is to be alone in this world."

The guards dragged her away as she screeched words of revenge at me.

"And the other?" the King asked.

I looked at Porcia, who met my gaze steadily. The lack of hatred in her eyes gave me pause.

"How does a barren woman come to have two daughters?" I asked.

"She steals them. The ones who learn their lessons quickly live to learn more. The ones who don't...well, you saw what happens."

"She did to you and Cecilia what she did to me?"

"Not to Cecilia. Cecilia embraced all that Maeve was and all that she wanted, no matter what the cost."

"And you?"

"I could never forget my real mother's face," she said without malice. "Or what she would think of the monster I'd become."

"A monster you chose to become."

"Imagine not a few weeks of failed lessons but years. Cecilia and I weren't her only daughters. There were many who never learned their lessons. I learned from their mistakes and many of my own. I told you to learn quickly because I knew how it would progress. Magic can smooth away scars, so I bear no marks of what I endured. But, they were lessons I will never forget and would do anything never to repeat. I've suffered more than one person should and caused equal suffering in turn to spare myself."

I didn't like Porcia. However, I did understand what she was saying. She'd done what she must to survive. I hadn't had to endure years of Maeve's manipulations. If I had, would I have deaths on my conscious, too?

"I've done vile things, and I regret those actions more than you know," she continued. "I cannot change the past. Yet, I beg the court for mercy."

"You presume to ask for mercy after all the lives you've allowed Maeve to take?" the King said with outrage.

"Allowed? You had the support of an entire kingdom yet could not stop her, Your Majesty. I had no real power to stand against her and was spelled to prevent speaking against her until my actions had damned me just as certainly as they had her. It was never a question of allowing anything."

"It was survival," I said.

She nodded.

"All I request is a quick death. I'm tired and wish for this wretched excuse for a life to be over."

Had I not thought the same thing only weeks into my life with Maeve? Had I not sat on the cliff and considered jumping? I thought of all that I suffered since her arrival then tried to imagine years of it. I'd witnessed for myself how Maeve would lash out at the two. How Porcia had been her least favorite by far.

"A quick death would be a mercy," I agreed. "One I cannot justly give. Yet, having experienced Maeve's reeducation, I find I cannot fault you for self-preservation. It is what anyone would do."

"You did not," she said. "You continued to defy her."

"I defied her at great risk to Kellen's safety. My defiance cost others their lives. I once told someone that a king's life should hold no more value than a common man's life. I still believe that to be true. Thus, I cannot now say your life is less precious because of the circumstances you were forced into. Yet, you are not without guilt or cruelty.

"You will not be marked or mistreated. You will find menial employment in a bakery and work every day to serve the people who suffered because of your compliancy."

Porcia looked to the King, her expression showing neither relief nor fear. Only acceptance.

"Put her in the dungeon with the others," the King ordered. "She will watch their fates before seeking her own."

While the guard led Porcia away, the King turned to look at Rose.

"The use of magic in this kingdom is forbidden. For your service this night, I will suspend judgement against your crimes and suggest that you leave for Turre immediately."

"I understand, Sire. One can never be too watchful of the temerity of those with power."

She chuckled and disappeared. For a moment, the King just stared at the spot she'd been. Then, he turned to me and offered his arm.

"It's time for me to retire. Walk with me."

Setting my hand lightly on his sleeve, I left the whispering court and listened to several sets of footsteps echo behind us.

"Greydon has told me of his affection for you," the King said when we reached the private hallway that led to the rooms I'd seen the night of the last ball. "And his offer for your hand and of your recent rejection of that offer. I ask you to reconsider."

"My life has changed so rapidly, and there is too much yet unsaid to give a fair and honest answer. But, I can promise I no longer want to push either of your sons from the highest turret."

He chuckled.

"Your mother was an honest woman as well. We will speak of this again tomorrow. Until then, you'll be our guest."

The thought of spending the night here, so close to Greydon, upset me because I knew what would happen. He would seek me out. He would attempt to sway me with his words and touch. I wouldn't be forced to make a decision I was not yet ready to make.

"Forgive me, Sire, but I would prefer to go home. There's much I must set to rights."

"Oh?"

"The last two maids she brought to the house are in the attic. Dead. And Seth is still there. Though he is not guilty of murder, I do not trust him. There is little left of my mother and father, but I would like to keep what there is."

"I understand. However, I cannot let you go alone."

"I will take her home, Father," Greydon said from behind me.

"A guard or two will be fine," I said, quickly.

The King smiled.

"I think some time to discuss those unsaid things might be just what is needed before we speak again tomorrow. Don't you agree?" He didn't wait for my answer before looking beyond me. "Now that I've made known who you truly are, the kingdom will be watching. Take an escort and a chaperone."

"Yes, Father."

The King released my hand.

"Go. Garreth, you will attend me."

I stepped aside and allowed Garreth to pass me. Left alone with Greydon, I finally turned to look at him fully.

"Will you tell me everything?" he asked softly. "From the beginning?"

It was the last thing I'd expected him to say and the one thing that stalled my anger.

"It's not pleasant," I said.

"That's precisely why I need to hear it. I was so blinded by what my family was facing that I didn't know the full extent of what you were facing."

"You never suspected it was Maeve?"

He paused and offered me his arm, which I took.

"I began suspecting Maeve when I met Cecilia and she introduced herself as your sister. She said 'Mama' sent her to find you. I found it odd that after hearing you state your father's love for your mother, he would re-wed so quickly. However, as I asked questions during our encounters after that, you seemed ignorant of who Maeve might be. I never thought she was hurting you. You were her reason for maintaining a presence there. If all your family had gone missing, it would have been obvious."

Her need to keep me alive became so much clearer.

"Tell me what really happened," he said again.

As he led me to the stables, waited for our shared mount, and then started home, I related my sorrowful tale, beginning with the gift that I thought was from my father. The guards trailed in our wake, a discreet distance away.

I told Greydon how I'd suspected him because of the boy's cap. He said little as I spoke of Judith and Anne's deaths, Hugh's odd devotion to Maeve, or the first conversation I had with Rose about magic. I relived that moment of fear when I explained how I'd witnessed Maeve draining Hugh and how I'd tried to run.

Greydon's arms tightened around me as I continued through my beatings and the times spent chained to the hearth. It hurt to speak of Kellen and Maeve's use of the huntsman to keep me in line.

"I didn't know the depth of her depravity until her daughters arrived with her mirror," I said.

I told him of the dinners. Of how Maeve had used Heather and Catherine and drained the men. Of how she'd tried to use the mirror to find him, and used it to spy on Kellen and others in the court, instead.

Relaying the full tale took its toll on me. I relived every horrific moment. Every terrible death. When I needed to stop and grieve for a moment, he held me in silence. The quiet of the night and the gentle sway of the horse helped soothe me as well.

By the time we reached the road to the Royal Retreat, I'd told him everything. I felt lighter and freer for it.

"Forgive me, Eloise. In my self-centered need for revenge, I was blind to your suffering. I will never be able to forgive myself."

I twisted in his lap to look up at him.

"Don't be foolish. I purposely misled you so you wouldn't see the truth. It was only your ignorance and the Prince's favor that kept you safe. You wouldn't be here now if not for both. She threatened your safety many times to keep me in line."

"I am to just accept that you were beaten, chained, and taught how to act as a whore so I could remain safe?"

"No, you have a choice. You can dwell on what's happened and let your hate and anger destroy any chance of future happiness, or you can find a way to accept it and move forward to make a better, happier life for yourself."

He was silent as we started up the path to my home.

"I cannot tell you what to choose," I added. "But I will tell you what I choose. Tomorrow, I will watch Maeve suffer every torment she inflicted upon me, and I will pity her inability to let go of the past hate and anger that drove her to that point. Then, I will walk away and never think of her again."

He pressed a kiss to my temple and brought the horse to a halt in the yard.

"There should be enough room in the stable for the horses," I said. "If not, you can put them in with the pig. He won't bother them."

"With your permission, I'll dismiss your groomsman on your behalf, too," Greydon said, helping me down.

"Please do. When you're done, come inside. There are plenty of rooms and beds in the attic to accommodate everyone."

"I'll come in," Greydon said. "However, the guards will make use of the stables and keep watch out here."

I didn't comment about our lack of chaperone. After all, it was a moot point. My innocence was long since gone in many ways.

Instead, I nodded and let myself inside. The house echoed its silence around me as I crossed the entry, the dying fire from the sitting room barely casting any light. Upstairs, I went to the room that used to belong to Kellen and me and opened the door. Porcia had removed Kellen's bed but had kept much of the room the same, unlike Cecilia with Father's room.

Lighting a candle, I looked at the dress lying over the back of the chair beside the wardrobe. It was one of my old dresses. Cecilia had taken a knife to it, rending it down the middle from neckline to hem. There were other cuts in it too, making it irreparable. I wondered why Porcia had even kept it. Balling it up, I turned to leave the room, intending to gather all of their clothes to take into town with me the next day.

However, I froze at the sight of Seth in the doorway.

"I thought you might be the only one to return," he said.

"An obvious conclusion since the others were led away in chains."

"A pity for sure. I've never been so thoroughly fucked before coming here. Maeve rode me hard daily. I can still feel her on me, in me, calling to me." He looked at the window, in the direction of the castle. "I know right where she is. I can feel it." He smiled and looked at me.

"But the spell she kept trying to cast on me didn't quite take, I think, because I couldn't stop seeing you, bathed in moonlight as you washed in the horse trough."

He took a step toward me.

"I want to make you scream," he said. "I want to hear you moan my name as you ride me like she did."

I felt no fear as he approached me.

"Will you force me?" I asked.

He chuckled.

"I don't mind a bit of a struggle."

"I do," I said as he stopped before me. I could smell his sweat and the faint odor of horse.

"Do you know what happened to the last groomsman? The one you replaced? I killed him for trying to force himself on me."

Seth grinned.

"You're just building the anticipation, luv."

"Allow me to kill it," Greydon said from behind him.

Seth jerked and grunted, the smile fading from his lips. He pivoted slowly to face Greydon, and I saw the knife sticking out from Seth's back.

"Miss Cartwright planned to dismiss you," Greydon said. "After your compliancy with what has transpired here, I'm not quite so benevolent."

Seth slumped to his knees and looked up at me, coughing on his blood. I felt no pity for him.

"You should have left when you had the chance," I said.

As he fell to the floor, I looked at Greydon.

"Can you have the guards remove him as well as the maids upstairs? We can use the wagon to take them to town so their families can claim them."

"Of course." He studied me. "Are you all right?"

"No. But I will be."

He nodded and left the room. I stepped over Seth and began removing any hint of Maeve, Cecilia, and Porcia's presence in my home. It wasn't until sunup that the house once again looked like it had before my mother's death.

"Thank you," I said to the weary guards as they went downstairs.

"We will rest for two hours then must leave for the castle," Greydon said.

"Yes, Sire," the lead guard said with a bow before closing the front door.

Greydon turned to me and took my hand.

"Where are we going?"

"To bed."

I briefly considered pulling my hand from his as he led me to my mother's room, but I was too tired and didn't want to be alone. For all of my thoughts of accepting the past, the things that happened in this house still echoed in my mind. I couldn't stop seeing Maeve with Hugh in my mother's room.

Greydon seemed to know it too for he pulled me into his arms and tucked me close against his chest as we lay fully dressed on top of the covers.

"What was your mother like?"

I smiled slightly and shared my memories of her until I fell asleep.

"Can I interest you in a citrus tart, miss?" a server asked.

"I couldn't eat another bite if I wanted to," I said with a kind smile.

The dress I wore was impressive and well corseted. One of the many surprises that had greeted me since waking in an abundantly feathered bed at the castle. That I'd slept through leaving the estate, the carriage ride here, and being carried inside still amazed me.

The server took away my plate, and I looked at the table's three other occupants.

"I apologize for sleeping so late," I said to the King.

"Nonsense. Greydon told me all that you accomplished when you returned. And all that you had endured since your mother's death. I'm truly sorry, Eloise. For her death and for all that you suffered. We are forever in your debt as we were in hers."

"As I told Greydon, the past is passed."

"Almost. There are a few more things yet to attend to."

He stood and offered his arm.

"If you will allow me to walk with you," he said.

"Of course, Your Majesty."

"Ah, yes," he said, setting his hand over mine and leading me from the room. "Your Majesty seems too formal for a new daughter, don't you agree? We must decide on a new title."

"Shouldn't that wait until I agree to Greydon's proposal?"

"Do you love the boy?"

"The boy is right here," Greydon said dryly from behind us.

"Your Majesty, considering all that's happened because of Maeve with Sevil and my mother...doesn't it prove that love is not enough?"

"Just the opposite," he said. "If not for the love Sevil bore for her family and for the love your mother bore for you and Sevil, the kingdom would have fallen long ago." He stopped walking to look me in the eye. "Above all else, the future queen needs to feel a great deal of love for her future king and for her future people. I think you will do well in both."

Trumpets blasted outside the main doors, and the King heaved a sigh.

"Duty demands our attention, and I can see you need more time to consider Greydon's proposal. We will speak of this later."

As we started forward once more, I glanced back at Greydon. His deep blue gaze caught and held mine, and his promise that I would be his echoed in my mind.

CHAPTER 18

THE FOUR OF US, FOLLOWED BY THE KING'S ADVISORS, CONTINUED DOWN the steps toward the gate. Once there, we climbed the stairs to watch the proceedings from the top of the walls surrounding the castle.

"Good people of Drisdall," the King called. "This is a day for celebration. Before you stand the condemned. They are responsible for tormenting our kingdom with their evil magic. Their reign of terror is at an end, and Drisdall is once again the safe home you knew and loved."

The King nodded to a man below, who began listing Maeve's crimes as she was brought forward. The list of what she'd done was horrific, but so were her injuries. She could barely walk. Bruises covered her body, and blood covered her face. As I'd ordered, she'd been blinded and shaved.

As I watched, the hate I felt toward her bled out from the well in which I'd kept it imprisoned for so long.

"Maeve Grimmoire confessed to her crimes and has been sentenced to suffer as we have suffered," the King said. "Her life, what is left of it, is her own when she reaches the docks. Any who choose to take pity on her there, may."

The people jeered and threw rocks at her as she stumbled

forward. One hit her square in the hip and knocked her to the ground before she had gone very far. And, I felt pity as she lay there, struggling to get up, and wondered whether she would have been able to let go of her hate and anger for the King if she would have known her fate. I doubted it.

Once Maeve stopped moving, Cecilia was brought forward, and her crimes were listed as well. She sobbed and looked at the crowd before her as they reacted to her wrongdoings. She was no better than her mother, and she saw it as she looked for any mercy within the throng. Like Maeve, she was beaten and shaven but also branded.

"Cecilia Grimmoire confessed to her crimes and has been sentenced to endure the same suffering as those she tormented. Her life, what is left of it, is her own when she reaches the docks."

Being able to see, Cecilia ran forward, covering her head with her arms. She didn't pause when she reached Maeve's still form but continued down the road as rocks pelted her. I knew she would make it to the docks.

"Have I made a mistake?" I asked the King. "Will she, like Maverene, cause the kingdom grief in the years to come?"

"The old woman who was here yesterday did something so they can never use magic again without great pain and suffering."

"Her life will not be easy, then," I said, relieved that Rose had done such a thing.

"And that is why your punishment is just," the King answered.

Porcia was brought forward, and her crimes listed.

"Porcia, originally of the northern Devenire's, was taken from her family at a young age and forced to do Maeve's will or suffer Maeve's cruelty. She did not seek power; she sought only to survive. While we do not find her innocent, we also cannot condemn her to the extent we have condemned the first two women."

The crowd remained quiet as the King asked for a baker willing to employ her at a fair wage to step forward. Porcia looked at the people, her fear openly displayed on her face.

"I will take her on," a young man said, stepping forward.

"However, I cannot offer a fair wage. My business is new, and there is no profit for pay. I can offer a room and two meals a day, instead."

The King looked at Porcia.

"She will accept those conditions."

Porcia left with the man, disappearing into the crowd.

"To celebrate our freedom and the return of my youngest son, Prince Garreth, we will have another ball in one week's time. All will be invited."

With a wave, the King started down the steps, leaving Greydon to escort me.

"Would you walk with me in the private gardens?" he asked when we reached the main hall.

"Of course."

He led me through the court, which was already filling with people, and out to the private gardens. We walked in silence for several minutes.

"My full name is Greydon Perth Kaven Drisdall. The day Garreth was born will never leave me. I remember the terror of losing my mother and looking at the small baby who caused it. I held him to blame. Then, he was gone, too, and my father mourned deeply. I didn't fully understand the significance of what had happened that day until years later when my father told me I, too, needed to leave and gave me a task. Protect my brother. By then, I was old enough to understand that he wasn't to blame for our mother's death.

"While the kingdom thought I left often for diplomatic journeys, I was with my brother, teaching him about our family and how to be a prince."

"How old were you when you and your brother first met?"

"I was sixteen, and he was eleven. Elspeth raised him as her own and only told him of his true heritage the eve before I arrived."

"I can't imagine the shock of learning such a thing."

"He was angry the truth had been kept from him. That he'd been lied to for so long even if it was to keep him safe. In time, he forgave Elspeth and Father."

He stopped walking and faced me.

"And, in time, I hope you can forgive me."

"I understand why you said nothing about who you really were. And I am not angry. Not anymore. No matter what name you used, you never lied about your intentions, for here you stand, still determined to make me yours."

"And yet, you're still reluctant. Why?"

"I was content with the idea of wedding a servant. Of a simple life. Then, I was willing to sacrifice that dream to save the kingdom from whatever fate Maeve had planned for it. But I never planned to stay wed to the Prince. That's why I asked you to wait for me in the woods."

"You thought he would what? Set you aside after discovering you were no longer innocent?"

"That was my hope."

"So it isn't me you oppose but truly what I am?"

I didn't answer him.

He studied me for several long moments, his expression giving nothing away.

"When I met Idina, my first wife, she was everything my father told me a wife should be. Graceful, fair of face, soft spoken. I wed her because she was kind and compassionate. I knew she would become a queen who would never put her needs before the needs of the people of Drisdall. But she never made my heart race with a word or a look. Nor did she challenge my thoughts or choices. She didn't make me a better man like you do."

He gently touched my cheek.

"I never felt for her as I feel for you. You say you cannot accept what I am, and I say I cannot accept a life without you. Whatever it is you fear when you think of yourself as my wife, set it aside. I swear to you, if you agree to wed me, I will never give you cause to regret it."

I turned my head and kissed his palm.

"And I give you the same answer I gave your father. I need time. Reacting rashly to the choices life presents me has gotten me into more trouble than not. Whatever decision I make, I want to ensure it will be the best for everyone."

Frustration crept into his gaze.

"Please, Greydon. Is it not enough that I'm here? Can you not give me some time to let the events of these past months settle in my mind?"

He exhaled slowly.

"I apologize for pressing you. Would you like to sit and watch the water for a bit? I can fetch us something to drink."

"Thank you."

I settled on the stone bench as he left and listened to the burble of water as it ran over the rocks. Taking a slow, deep breath, I did as I said I would and let the reality of the current moment settle in my mind. Maeve was gone. Dead in the street by the people she sought to subjugate. I wondered if she had wanted to be queen before she met Aftan.

"Why do you hesitate to grab the future waiting for you?" Rose asked from beside me, startling me from my thoughts.

"How do you do that?"

"Magic, of course." She chuckled. "Are you going to tell me why you are refusing what so many would not hesitate to accept?"

"I never wanted to be queen. And certainly not someone's wife."

"And now?"

"I need to find my sister, Kellen. She ran into the Dark Forest."

"You know you cannot find her alone. Ask for Prince Greydon's help, and he will give it without condition. However, the need to find your sister isn't the reason you're not giving that man the answer he so desperately seeks. Is he cruel?"

"Not unless necessary."

"Do you find him unpleasant to look upon?"

"I very much like looking at him."

Rose harrumphed.

"Then it is a good thing that I asked for two small favors in return for helping you instead of one."

I'd forgotten about her stipulation and regarded her now with growing concern.

"And what two favors do you ask of me?"

"First is that you wed Prince Greydon."

"Why?"

"Because this kingdom is yet in need of you."

"But I have no desire to rule over anyone."

"Then don't. Serve the people. See to their welfare as only a queen can. Continue to protect them as you have."

Having been under Maeve's influence, my greatest fear in accepting Greydon's proposal had been that I would be expected to be cold and use the people to serve my needs, whatever they might be. But hearing Rose's words helped me start to see my error in how I thought of those with titles and wealth.

"And your second favor?"

"For some, magic is as natural as breathing. Is it fair or just for a queen to ask her subjects to cease breathing because one of the subjects might have wicked intentions?"

"I see." I looked out over the green lawn for a moment. "I will do as you ask."

"Good." She started to stand.

"You're leaving?"

"Indeed. If you recall, I was traveling to the Kingdom of Turre with my pig when I met you."

"Who is the pig?" I asked.

"That's a Beastly Tale better left for another time. But rest assured, I am not Maeve. I don't curse idly or for my own benefit."

I studied her for a moment, then nodded. Even if I doubted her word, which I didn't, there would have been little I could have done about it.

"I know I have no right to ask this, but on your way to Turre, would you be willing to stop at a cabin in the Dark Forest? Maeve used an apple to curse my sister, and I'm worried that even the King's guards might not be able to help her."

Rose patted my hand.

"I will check on her on my way to Adele."

"The place with the white towers?" I asked, remembering our very first conversation.

"That's right. Rule well, Eloise. Be a fair and just queen, and don't forget your promise."

When Greydon returned with our drinks, Rose had vanished into air.

"I have news," he said, sitting beside me.

"Oh?"

"I've told my father I have no wish to be King and asked that he name Garreth the first in line. He asked for some time to consider my request, but I know he will agree."

I stared at him in surprise. When I told Greydon I needed time and admitted why, I had never even considered he would abdicate. That he was willing to do so…

My throat tightened for what I felt for the man beside me.

"It won't change who I am," he continued, looking at me earnestly, "but perhaps it will—"

I grabbed the front of his jacket and pulled him down for a kiss. After a moment, I heard the glasses fall to the lawn and felt his arms encircle me. He deepened the kiss before breaking away.

"Does that mean you accept?"

"Yes, but only if you tell your father you're a fool for saying you'd give up your crown for a woman."

"Never. I would do anything to have you, Eloise. When are you going to understand that?"

I smiled up at the man who had stolen my heart.

"I think I'm beginning to understand that now. I'll wed you, Greydon. And, together we will serve and protect the people of this kingdom."

He swept me up into his arms and gave a whoop of joy as he spun me around.

I was pleading for mercy moments later. Instead of placing me on my feet, he continued to carry me as he strode toward the castle.

"I can walk."

"You can also run, and I'm not going to risk that. Not now that you've agreed."

He stopped moving to kiss me soundly. Garreth's raucous cheering echoed for a moment before I lost myself to the feel of Greydon.

CHAPTER 19

I WALKED THE FAMILIAR PATH TO MY MOTHER'S GRAVE AND LISTENED TO the bird song. As it always did when I was in the woods, the volume of the animals increased. I'd learned it wasn't only here they did that but in the castle gardens as well. In the days since agreeing to wed Greydon, he'd continued to use their clamor to find me.

Smiling softly at the thought of him, I entered the charred clearing and sat on the undamaged bench Hugh had made for us. It still hurt to think of him. I doubted that would ever stop.

"There's so much you probably already know," I began. "The necklace wasn't from Father but from the caster you tried to stop from hurting the queen and her unborn babe so long ago. Father didn't leave us willingly. He was cursed, like I was. Like Kellen is." I stopped for a moment, trying to control my fear for my twin. "I don't want you to worry about us, though. We're safe now. Maeve is gone. Dead by my sentencing. It was a harsh punishment. She was made to endure much of the suffering she'd brought to others."

I paused, recalling the scene and my pity for her.

"King Aftan said it wasn't jealousy that brought all of this about but her need for power. I think it was something more. I lived with her and saw her twisted form of love. What kind of family could create such a creature?"

Inhaling deeply, I set thoughts of Maeve aside as I'd promised myself I would do.

"I'm grateful that I had you and Kellen and Father and miss you all terribly. Judith and Anne are dead. Anne's Mother and cousin, too. As is Hugh." I brushed my hand against the wood, letting the grief out. Tears, long overdue, coursed down my cheeks. I didn't tell Mother how he'd tried to hurt me or how I'd needed to kill him in the end.

"So much loss," I managed through my tears. "No one person should have to bear so much loss in such a short time." I let out a shaky exhale.

"Greydon is doing everything he can to help me forget. But, he doesn't understand that some things will never be forgotten. At night, I relive much of what has happened. I wake shaking and cold. He's there to comfort me and redoubles his efforts to help me forget." I wiped at my warming cheeks as I recalled last night's efforts. "He's wonderful, Mother, and I know you would approve. Not for his position or title but for who he is as a man."

"We're to be wed in two weeks' time. The King wanted us to wed sooner, but I wanted to give enough time for the men he sent after Kellen to return with her." Worry ate at my mind once more. "She ran before the worst of it, but I don't think she was fully spared. I don't know what's befallen her. When Maeve returned from delivering the cursed apple, she said that Kellen was alive but that no prince would ever have her. But I will continue to love her no matter what's befallen her. The King's Guard will also search for Father, though the King warned me not to hold too much hope."

I sighed.

"There's a very likely chance that I will wed with no family in attendance. I will have a friend there, though. Well, of a sort. Remember the boy I hit in the head with the pan? The very one who I once spit a mouthful of ale at? He showed me kindness when I most needed it and paid for it with his eyes."

My tears started anew as I thought of Alfie's terror when I'd finally found him again. He was still shaken and startled easily at anyone's approach.

"I swore I would repay his kindness, and I have. There was a girl he fancied. I spoke to her on his behalf and explained what had happened. She's good for him and to him. With her, he's recovering and learning what it means to live with what's happened."

Much like me, I thought.

"They're to be wed soon. The celebration will happen just outside the castle gates. The King's generosity is vast. Something I wouldn't have guessed. I have a personal seamstress now. A young girl from a poor family. You would like her. She suggested I wear wool and cotton when all the others brought me silks and lace. Her reason was because I didn't look the pampered type. I looked like I was more likely to climb a tree." I laughed lightly. "She'll suit me well."

I sat for a while, feeling the sun on my face and listening to the bird song before I stood and gazed at the barren patch of earth that had once been covered by the pear tree, grass, and blooms.

"I snuck away from the castle and need to return before my absence is noted. But don't worry. I'll be back to plant another tree, and I'll visit often to watch it grow. Thank you for everything you did, Mother. I know you're still watching over me. Watch over Kellen, too. Bring her home to me if you can."

With an ache in my chest, I walked away from the grave. The animals continued to sing to me until the path opened to the yard. There, a semi-familiar face waited. Elspeth.

I crossed the quiet yard to join her by the front door.

"How did you know I would be here?"

She smiled and followed me toward the door.

"A location spell."

Horror filled me, and I set my hand on the door to steady myself. It took a moment for me to look back at Elspeth.

"Whatever you think I've done terrifies you," she said, pity filling her expression. "Will you tell me what it is before you set your mind against me?"

"Maeve did a location spell. It cost a child its life." The image of the small heart in a bowl flashed in my mind again. It was one of the many moments I relived at night.

Elspeth's expression turned to sorrow.

"That's because Maeve gained her power through blood magic, a perverted form of the magic casters are born with. Magic isn't in blood but in the manipulation of the life energies around us. It's meant to be natural. A balanced existence. As we stand here, I can feel the trees, the birds, and the grass around us. If I needed, I could draw some of that energy. However, just enough to manipulate but not enough to cause harm to that from which I drew."

"Can you feel my energy?"

"I can. Though I would never use the energy from a living creature, unless I had no choice. It can be dangerous."

"You're like Rose, then?"

Elspeth gave a half-laugh.

"Only in the most basic sense. Her abilities extend far beyond mine. Maybe even beyond the abilities of the casters who created the Dark Forest."

"Is she dangerous?"

Elspeth considered me for a moment.

"Anyone with power has the capacity to be dangerous. It's our actions that determine our character and intent. Do you believe Rose is dangerous?"

Instead of answering, I opened the door to my old home and gestured for Elspeth to enter. There was a chill in the air, and a slight mustiness had settled in from disuse. Moving to the sitting room, I set about building a small fire even though I didn't plan on staying long.

"Rose helped me in exchange for two promises," I said when I finished.

Elspeth was seated in Kellen's chair, which once again faced Mother's lounge.

"Oh? And what did she ask of you?"

"The first one was easy. She wanted me to wed Greydon." I sat in my chair and gazed out the window.

"You didn't want to marry him?"

"I wanted to marry Kaven, the man I knew, not the Crown Prince who will someday be King."

When I looked at Elspeth to see what she thought of that, humor lit her gaze.

"And the second promise?" she asked.

"She wants the ban against magic lifted."

The humor left Elspeth's expression.

"Why?"

"Because it's wrong. Magic is a part of our world. By forbidding those with the ability from using it, King Aftan is creating resentment and fear. As you said, anyone with power has the capacity to be dangerous. That applies to people who have magic and those who don't. It's not the magic that makes a person evil but how they use it."

"You are your mother's daughter," Elspeth said. "She often said the same thing to me about magic and about those with wealth. She didn't want to marry a titled man, either. Instead, she married your father, a merchant."

"You knew her well?" I asked, studying the old woman.

"Since she was as tall as my knee. Her mother would often come to me for potions to help with fertility. When they didn't work, Lady Thoning stopped coming but not Margaret." A smile lifted Elspeth's lips. "She was trouble in a good way. A restless spirit who wasn't content with the injustices in our world."

Elspeth sighed and reached out for my hand, which I reluctantly gave.

"I loved your mother as my own. Everything that befell her broke my heart. I'm so sorry she's gone." She gave my hand a light squeeze and released me.

"I read your letters to her," I said.

She shook her head.

"I warned her to burn them. It was dangerous to keep them."

"I'm glad she did. They serve as proof that you're telling the truth. Why did you leave?"

"To protect your mother, her new twins, and Queen Sevil's babe."

"Garreth?"

"Yes. Despite my warnings that it would weaken her further, your mother nursed that boy as her own along with you and your sister. A house full of babes was the safest place to hide him so I could track Maverene. But she was always just ahead of me."

"She had a mirror that showed her things."

Elspeth nodded.

"I thought as much, which is why I cloaked myself. Apparently, it wasn't enough."

"Greydon told me you raised Garreth."

"I did. I came for him when he was barely a year and old enough to be weaned. Yet, young enough never to remember anything."

"So Mother never planned to give Kellen or me away. It was Garreth you were coming for."

Elspeth laughed.

"Your mother would have never let you go. Not even to me. Is that why you're here? Did you believe she didn't love you?"

"No. I'm here for something I left behind. Something Mother gave me."

I led Elspeth to my attic space where I removed the rings gifted to me by the tree. The one Maeve had taken from me I'd found the night Seth died, and I'd taken care to hide it by the chimney with its partner.

"Mother knew long before I did that I was meant to be with Greydon," I said, holding out the rings.

Elspeth studied what I held then closed my fingers over the items, holding my fist.

"The Prince will be relieved to hear this," she said. "He thinks you're trying to run off."

I rolled my eyes.

"He still doesn't believe I will marry him."

"Have you given him cause to believe that?"

I grinned, recalling all that he'd suffered at my hand, some of it intentional, some of it not.

"At every turn," I said. "But I will spend the rest of my days assuring him that I am his and he is mine."

Elspeth surprised me with a hug.

"You and Greydon will do well together."

EPILOGUE

THE HIGHER PITCH OF DAVID'S VOICE WAS ANSWERED BY A LOW murmur. I smiled, thinking Greydon was already tucking our son in for the night. However, when I pushed open the door, I saw Aftan sitting on the boy's bed.

"I'm glad the bad woman was killed," my son said. "She shouldn't have hurt my mama."

"No, it was wrong for her to do so. And her punishment, though terrible and hard to behold, was just. Always remember to be fair in your rulings."

"Yes, Grandfather," David said. "But what of Auntie Kellen's story. I want to know what happened to her after she ran away."

I thought of my sister and felt a pang. It had been too long since I'd seen her.

Aftan chuckled and leaned down to kiss the boy's forehead.

"That will have to wait until another time. If your mama discovers I've kept you up this late with stories, she'll serve me stewed plums for breakfast."

"I like stewed plums," David said with a smile. "I'll eat yours for you."

Laughing, I pushed the door open further.

"Your grandfather is right about the time. You need to sleep, David."

He pouted a bit and sat up.

"I need to say goodnight to my brother in case another caster comes, and he needs to be hidden away like Uncle Garreth was hidden away."

I moved close to the bed, and David bestowed a sweet kiss to my enormous belly.

"You know that there are good casters, too. And besides, it might be a sister," I said.

"You're right. No caster will want to steal a girl."

The King and I shared a look, for Maeve had indeed done just that.

"To bed, little one," the King said. "And you too, Eloise. You should be sleeping, yourself."

"I was looking for my errant husband."

"Try the door next to your room."

I returned to our suite of rooms and tried the door to the adjoining room. For the first time in months, it was unlocked. I opened it and looked around the room with a growing smile.

"I can claim no part in the making of that," Greydon said when I ran my hand along the edge of a hand-carved cradle. "But I commissioned it."

I smiled at him.

"It's beautiful. As is everything else in here."

The soft green wall coverings, small wooden toys, and plush rugs were new to celebrate our second child's birth. Greydon's arms wrapped around my waist, and he gently rubbed my back. I leaned into him with a groan.

"That feels so good."

He chuckled.

"I can make you feel better."

I tipped my head back to look up at him.

"I'm sure you can. But your methods keep putting me in this state."

He picked me up and gave a fake stagger.

"How many children do you carry?"

"Don't even tease like that," I said. Barely halfway through my pregnancy, I'd begun to notice my enormity, as well. The thought of carrying twins didn't frighten me, but it reminded me of my sister and made me miss her dreadfully.

"Eloise, I'm sorry," Greydon said, noticing the fall in my expression and rushing to set me on our bed. "I love you without condition. One child or twenty. And we have the best midwife possible."

"It's not that," I said. "I miss Kellen."

"Ah," Greydon said.

"That's it? Ah?"

He gave me a sheepish smile.

"Of course not. However, the longing you feel for your sister is not something I can as easily remedy. She's a kingdom away. If you were hungry, I could quickly fetch you something to eat. If you were in pain, I could summon Elspeth. If you were lonely, I could read from your favorite book for hours until you would know I will never leave you."

"I want to see her again."

"And you will. But not until after this babe comes. It's not safe for us to travel with you in this condition."

I scowled at him.

"You're being stubborn. Why can't we just invite them here? Why must you condemn what happened to her? It's not her fault."

Greydon leaned forward and pressed a kiss to my belly.

"I never said it was. And I could never condemn her for what she's endured."

I hit his shoulder.

"Invite her."

He sighed.

"How will we explain her situation to our son?"

"With words. It was your father who told me it takes love and understanding to rule a kingdom. What better way to teach him than through telling him the full story of what happened to his Auntie Kellen?"

Greydon sighed, his hand sliding up my skirt along my leg. My pulse started to speed up.

"As you wish, my love. I will send out the invitation tomorrow."

I smiled and ran my fingers through his hair.

"Thank you."

"I will always do what I must to bring you joy," he said. "I will never again shirk my duties to you."

And he proved that thoroughly before I fell asleep.

THANK you for reading Tales of Cinder! Please consider leaving a review to let other readers know what you think of this series. It would mean the world to me!

Be sure to keep reading for more information about Kellen's story and other amazing books by MJ Haag.

AUTHOR'S NOTE

Thank you so much for reading *Tales of Cinder*! I have to be honest here...Cinderella's story was never one of my favorite fairy tales. I didn't like how the prince's only hardship was his need to marry (what a hardship!) while Cinderella had to endure all sorts of hell. And I especially didn't like that the prince never really did much to "save" her other than to remove her from a life of drudgery.

So, when I started to consider writing my own version, I knew I needed to do two things. The first was to stick closer to the original, darker version of her tale. The second was to ensure the suffering was a bit more equal *and* to provide a much better explanation as to why he didn't do more to help his "love." I also had Eloise kick him in the testicles a few times because I found their misunderstandings pretty funny.

While researching the original versions, I noticed the strong parallels between Snow White's story and Cinderella's story. It was almost like they could be sisters...so of course, that's what I did.

If Cinderella is one of your favorite retellings, I hope I wrote a retelling that gave you all the feelings. If so, stay tuned for Kellen's story. It won't be as dark (at least, I don't think it will be) and will probably be a lot heavier on the romance. I anticipate having that ready in summer 2024.

To ensure you never miss a release announcement, follow me on social media or sign up for my newsletter at mjhaag.melissahaag.com.

Until next time, happy reading!

Melissa

CHARACTER LIST

Eloise - *Cinderella* (Twin daughter of Margaret and Atwell).

Kellen - *Snow White* (Twin daughter of Margaret and Atwell).

Margaret Cartwright - Eloise and Kellen's mother.

Atwell Cartwright - Eloise and Kellen's father.

Hugh - A stablehand.

Judith - A housemaid.

Anne - A housemaid

Kaven - A royal servant.

Rose - Owner of the pig; a caster/enchanter.

Lady Maeve Grimmoire - Kellen and Eloise's new guardian.

Elspeth - A caster who Margaret knew.

Catherine - A housemaid.

Heather - A housemaid.

Aftan - The King of Drisdall

Sevil - The deceased Queen of Drisdall.

Greydon - Prince of Drisdall.

Grimm - A tracker/huntsman.

Cecilia - Maeve's daughter.

Porcia - Maeve's daughter.

Damnation is the final Tale of Cinder, which takes part in the Beastly Tales world. If you haven't yet read the Beastly Tales, you're missing out on a seductively dark Beauty and the Beast retelling. There are character crossovers between the two trilogies in Disowned, a Tales of Cinder prequel, that you're going to love.

THE BEASTLY TALES

Beauty and the Beast with seductively dark twists!

BOOK 1: DEPRAVITY

When impoverished, beautiful Benella is locked inside the dark and magical estate of the beast, she must bargain for her freedom if she wants to see her family again.

BOOK 2: DECEIT

Safely hidden within the estate's enchanted walls, Benella no longer has time to fear her tormentors. She's too preoccupied trying to determine what makes the beast so beastly. In order to gain her freedom, she must find a way to break the curse, but first, she must help him become a better man while protecting her heart.

BOOK 3: DEVASTATION

Abused and rejected, Benella strives to regain a purpose for her life, and finds herself returning to the last place she ever wanted to see. She must learn when it is right to forgive and when it is time to move on.

Tales of Cinder

Becareful what you wish for...

Prequel: Disowned

In a world where the measure of a person rarely goes beneath the surface, Margaret Thoning refuses to play by its rules. She walks away from everything she's ever known to risk her heart and her life for the people who matter most.

Book 1: Defiant

When the sudden death of Eloise's mother points to forbidden magic, Eloise's life quickly goes from fairy tale to nightmare. Kaven, the prince's manservant, is Eloise's prime suspect. However, when dark magic is used, nothing is as simple as it seems.

Book 2: Disdain

Cursed to silence, Eloise is locked in the tattered remains of her once charming life. The smoldering spark of her anger burns for answers and revenge. However, games of magic can have dire consequences.

Book 3: Damnation

With the reason behind her mother's death revealed, Eloise must prevent her stepsisters from marrying the prince and exact her revenge. However, a secret of the royal court strikes a blow to her plans. Betrayed, Eloise will question how far she's willing to go for revenge.

THE RESURRECTION CHRONICLES

Humor, romance, and sexy dark fey!

BOOK 1: DEMON EMBER
In a world going to hell, Mya accepts help from her new-found demon protector to find her family as a zombie-like plague spreads.

BOOK 2: DEMON FLAMES
Mya is taken to Ernisi, an underground Atlantis and Drav's home, where she learns that the shadowy demons are not what they seem.

BOOK 3: DEMON ASH
Returning to the bomb-ravaged surface, Mya seeks to stop everything that's trying to destroy what's left of the world.

BOOK 4: DEMON ESCAPE
While escpaing her captors and struggling to survive the zombie apocalypse, Eden encounters a new creature in her search for safety.

BOOK 5: DEMON DECEPTION
To gain protection and save her children, Cassie accepts the help of a certain dark fey and experiences the unexpected.

BOOK 6: DEMON NIGHT
Pregnant and trying to hide it, Angel agrees to coach Shax on how to win the girl of his dreams and loses her heart instead.

BOOK 7: DEMON DAWN
In a post-apocalyptic world, Benna is faced with trading her body and heart to the dark fey in order to survive the infected.

BOOK 8: DEMON DISGRACE
To gain protection and save her children, Cassie accepts the help of a certain dark fey and experiences the unexpected.

THE
RESURRECTION
CHRONICLES

The apocalyptic adventure continues!

BOOK 8.1: DEMON DESIGN
Driven by hunger, Brooke propositions the fey she's been sketching from afar for weeks and ends up with way more than a simple meal.

BOOK 8.2: DEMON DISCORD
After Terri's husband leaves her, she finds refuge with a fey who offers so much more than the familiar hate and bitterness she'd been clinging to for years.

BOOK 9: DEMON FALL
Struck by an unexpected loss, June turns her attention to making the Tenacity a better place with Tor's help.

BOOK 9.1: DEMON KEPT
A woman seeking to escape her past accepts refuge from two fey warriors determined to keep her safe and make her their own.

BOOK 9.2: DEMON BLIND
In a post-apocalyptic world, an optically impaired young woman makes the mistake of a lifetime and discovers glasses are just as hard to find as birth control.

BOOK 10: DEMON DEFEAT: PART 1
Andie is "sacrificed" for the betterment of humanity, only to discover risking her life isn't nearly as dangerous as risking her heart.

BOOK 11: DEMON DEFEAT: PART 2
In the epic conclusion, Andie and Molev work together to find a way to stop the hounds and evolving infected from destroying the community the survivors have built.

www.ingramcontent.com/pod-product-compliance
Lightning Source LLC
Chambersburg PA
CBHW060209030726
47499CB00004B/971